W9-CKL-909

DISCARD

PLACEBO

Center Point
Large Print

**This Large Print Book carries the
Seal of Approval of N.A.V.H.**

PLACEBO

A JEVIN BANKS NOVEL

STEVEN JAMES

CENTER POINT LARGE PRINT
THORNDIKE, MAINE

This Center Point Large Print edition
is published in the year 2014 by arrangement with
Revell, a division of Baker Publishing Group.

Copyright © 2012 by Steven James.

The text of this Large Print edition is unabridged.
In other aspects, this book may vary
from the original edition.
Printed in the United States of America
on permanent paper.
Set in 16-point Times New Roman type.

ISBN: 978-1-62899-339-4

Library of Congress Cataloging-in-Publication Data

James, Steven, 1969–
 Placebo : a Jevin Banks novel / Steven James. — Center Point Large
Print edition.
 pages ; cm
 Summary: "While covertly investigating a controversial neurological
research program, exposé filmmaker Jevin Banks is drawn into a far-
reaching conspiracy involving one of the world's largest pharmaceutical
firms"—Provided by publisher.
 ISBN 978-1-62899-339-4 (library binding : alk. paper)
 1. Large type books. I. Title.
 PS3610.A4545P53 2014
 813´.6—dc23
                                                      2014028576

To Pam Johnson,
For all of your help, all of your smiles,
all of your insights

Have you ever had a dream, Neo, that you were so sure was real? What if you were unable to wake from that dream? How would you know the difference between the dream world and the real world?

—Morpheus to Neo
in *The Matrix* (1999)

Is all that we see or seem
But a dream within a dream?

—Edgar Allan Poe
(1809–1849)

Who knows but that we all live out our lives in the maze of a dream?

—Weng Wei,
eighth-century Chinese poet

Part I
ENTANGLED

The Shore

September 24
Heron Bay, New Jersey
1:12 p.m.

You are there when they recover the bodies.

The day is gray with thick, somber clouds hanging heavily in the sky. Mist lurks above the bay, circling in a breeze that comes in damp and cold off the water.

You stand onshore watching the divers position their boat at the place where the witnesses say they saw the minivan go in. As you wait for them to reappear, your heart squirms like a thick, wet animal trapped inside your chest.

It was your wife's minivan.

And she had your two sons with her.

The silence is stark and chilled, disturbed only by the wet slap of waves against the shore.

For some reason, even though the van disappeared into the bay more than two hours ago, you still hold out hope that somehow Rachel and the twins have survived, that some inscrutable miracle has drifted down from heaven and stopped the water from pouring into the van.

You try to convince yourself that the vehicle has become a safe haven filled with air, a metal bubble of life—proof that a loving God exists and cares enough to step into time and save lives; you tell yourself that someday you'll all look back at this and stand in awe of the unimaginable possibilities of divine intervention.

You tell yourself that.

But then a pair of divers surface, tugging something with them.

And you see that it is one of your sons.

The body doesn't look real, more like a mannequin or a CPR dummy—frighteningly motionless, its skin pasty gray, its eyes open and staring unblinkingly at the blank, indifferent clouds.

It's only because of his clothes that you recognize which of your two boys it is—Andrew, the oldest by three minutes. You recall seeing him in that outfit earlier in the day, before you headed to the rehearsal for the show. Yes, it's Andrew.

Five years old and now he's dead.

As they lift him into the rowboat, his head lolls your way and water dribbles from his loose, gaping mouth. His eyes still refuse to blink.

For a moment you think it's some kind of mistake, a cruel joke the universe is playing on you.

No, no, that's not really him, that thing in the boat. Andrew is alive, of course he is. Any second now he's going to come running up the shore and yell, missing his r's like always, "Daddy! I'm okay! Don't wuwy, Daddy! I'm wight hewe!"

You catch yourself gazing along the shoreline. A few emergency medical personnel and police officers stand near the pier staring quietly at the divers, but that's all. No media. The cops have kept them professionally cordoned off on the road beyond the boat landing's parking lot. Besides the paramedics and police, the shoreline is empty: just a long line of lonely sand and jagged rocks curling toward the far shore now lost in the fog that wanders restlessly across the water.

Of course Andrew doesn't appear running up the shoreline. The body is real. Your oldest son lies dead on the rowboat, and now the divers are going back down to retrieve the rest of your family.

The pulsing beast in your chest writhes again and you find it getting harder to breathe. You want to leave, to turn away, to run and run and run forever until your heart is finally in a safe, emotionally dead and distant place and you get a phone call outside of time from the police explaining everything in objective, detached detail, but you know you have to see for yourself what happened to Anthony and Rachel.

You have to.

And so you stay.

And stare at the water rippling beside the boat, afraid to even blink. You wonder if this comes from what you do, the knowledge that so many things can be faked, that there are so many ways to make people's minds play tricks on them in that fraction of a second of misdirection, either through the gentle deception of sleight of hand or the almighty power of stage lights or camera angles. If you blink you miss everything. The old line, the clichéd standby: *Now you see it, now you don't!*

But nothing is faked here today.

It isn't long before the divers bring up Anthony. It takes longer with Rachel.

You hear some whispered words through a radio that one of the officers has and realize that it was her hair. It got tangled in some branches as they were removing her from the van. Then he turns down the volume, and the rest of the words squibble away and drop out into an uneven static.

For some reason as you watch the men bring the three corpses to shore in the boat, you don't cry. You know enough about how people react to tragedy to realize that this is shock, you're in shock. But naming the condition doesn't help; in fact, it almost seems disrespectful to label the numbness, like a subtle move toward objectivity, which is the last thing you want right now.

"Mr. Banks?" A voice, scratchy and soft beside you. You turn and see that it's one of the police officers, a sturdy woman, maybe forty, with dark eyes and a tight bun of sandy brown hair. "Is there anything I can do for you?"

"No."

"We'll have someone drive you to—"

"No. I want to see the bodies up close."

She takes a small breath as if she's about to dispute that and you brace yourself for an argument, but she replies simply, "I'll go with you."

You realize that letting you spend time with the bodies now, rather than at the morgue, might not be protocol, and you respect that this officer seems to care more about you than about policies and procedures. You hold back from telling her that you want to be alone with your family, and silently accept her offer.

The boat arrives at the pier and the two of you walk toward it.

None of the officers are joking around or using gallows humor like cops do on TV: "Looks like today's special is three for the price of one!" Maybe screenwriters stick those lines in the shows because treating death honestly would be too hard on viewers and ratings. Better to lighten the mood, tidy up reality, let us escape—at least for a few hours during prime time—into a more sterile kind of pain.

You arrive and look into the boat, then climb aboard and kneel beside the three corpses that used to be your family—the boys you ate breakfast with this morning, the woman you kissed goodbye just before you walked out the door.

You reach for her cheek and hesitantly touch its wet, claylike surface. You slide the snarled, wet hair from her eyes, and though you try to hold back your tears, you fail, and the rising squall of wind brushes wisps of fog across your face as if its ghostly, curling fingers are trying to wipe the tears away. Or maybe the mist is just trying to taste the pain and carry it farther ashore.

She did it on purpose. Rachel did.

Four people saw her veer off the road, drive through the parking lot beside the bay, and then accelerate as she hit the pier. Later, the investigators found nothing wrong with the van. Neither the steering wheel nor the gas pedal had jammed; the brakes were working fine. The trip off the pier was no accident.

Rachel had survived impact. There was water in her lungs, which meant she'd been breathing when the minivan filled with water. The air bag had inflated and there were no cracks spider-webbing across the windshield, no contusions on her head that would've indicated that she was knocked unconscious.

Still, I hope that somehow she was. I can hardly imagine her just sitting there conscious and aware, waiting for our two sons to drown, but by all indications that's exactly what she did.

The boys were strapped into their car seats and had never been good at getting them unbuckled on their own, so even if they'd known how to swim, they wouldn't have been able to get out of the van.

Though it chills me to think about it, I can't help but wonder what it was like for Drew and Tony in those final moments—feeling the minivan speed up, experiencing the momentary weightlessness as the vehicle left the pier, then the jarring impact as it hit the surface of the water.

And then.

Sinking. Slowly at first, but then more rapidly as water began to fill the van. And the questions a five-year-old might ask: *What's happening? When is Mommy gonna help me?* Or perhaps even a thrill of curiosity as the water passed the windows: *Is this what it's like for a fish?!*

But then, of course, the troubling realization that this was scary and bad. And, as the instinct for survival took over, struggling uselessly to get free, crying, then screaming as the water rose.

The boys' lungs were filled with water too.

They were breathing as the water rose to their lips, passed their mouths, swallowed their cries for help. I've done hundreds of underwater escapes over the years, and I know all too well how terrifying it can be when your breath is running out and you can't find a way to free yourself from your bonds. You try to remain calm, but there comes a moment when sheer terror eclipses everything. Six times I've passed out and had to be revived.

At least my sons only had to drown once.

And now.

Over and over I've searched through my conversation with Rachel earlier that day for any hint of what she was planning to do, any warning, however slight, of her dark intentions.

Everything had been so suburbally normal for a Saturday morning—I was slipping off to work for a few hours, then I'd be back to mow the lawn; Rachel was heading out with the boys to grab a few things at the grocery store for our dinner that night with the Andersons. Before I'd left, she'd seemed a little tired, but that was all.

I'd offered to ask her parents if they could watch the kids next weekend so we could sneak away— just the two of us—find a bed-and-breakfast in the country, somewhere outside of Atlantic City where we lived, take a little time to reconnect. To relax. Before the new season began.

"It'd be a good break for both of us before the new show opens," I told her.

"That would be nice," she said softly.

"That would be nice," not, *"Sorry, I'll be dead by then. And so will the boys. I'm going to drown them as soon as you leave the house."*

My friends, my family, the media, law enforcement—everyone who was touched by the case— searched for a reason why she did what she did: *Did she show any signs of depression? Was she noticeably upset that morning when you left? Were you having marital problems? Can you think of anything at all that would have caused her to do this?*

No, no, no.

No, I could not.

It was as if all of us were desperate to compartmentalize her actions under a specific heading—anger, loneliness, depression, despair—as if naming the motive, channeling all the terrible confusion and pain into one word, would have softened the blow, brought some sort of closure.

But we found no motive, no cause, no explanation.

A mother had inexplicably murdered her sons and committed suicide for reasons only she knew. Reasons that had drowned with her in Heron Bay.

I've tried to hate her for what she did, tried my hardest to despise her, to slice all the positive feelings I ever had for her out of my heart, but I can't make the love go away. Even after she killed my sons, even after that, I haven't been able to find a way to hate her. Part of me feels wretchedly guilty for still loving her, as if it's a failure on my part, as if it cheapens my love for the boys.

No reasons.

We found no reasons.

But something motivated Rachel to accelerate off that pier, and to make any sense of it I felt compelled to find a person to blame for not stopping her.

In the end I did. I found him. A man who'd missed a warning sign, some subtle indicator, some tiny clue as to her intentions—or possibly he'd said something, did something, without even knowing it, that'd pushed her over the edge.

He needed to be punished for his failure, and so I've reminded him of it every day for the last thirteen months.

And he has suffered acutely, just as he should, for letting his wife and his two sons die.

Sleight of Hand

Thirteen months after the drownings
Monday, October 26
1:53 p.m.

The highway snakes along the Oregon coastline like a great eel, twisting around the foothills that skirt the wild sea.

Surprisingly, the sky above us shines clear and bright and starkly blue. In the Pacific Northwest, this is a rare and welcome sight, and the Monday afternoon traffic is heavier than I would've expected. By the number of backpacks inside the cars and surfboards on top of them, I can tell that many of the drivers are outdoor enthusiasts heading home after a long weekend of enjoying the clear weather here on the coast or hiking in the nearby mountains.

I'm at the wheel of the van, and my friend

Xavier Wray sits beside me. At fifty-two, he's nineteen years older than I am, but he still has a closetful of tie-dyed clothes and still uses the word "groovy."

He shaved his head last year because he didn't think the ponytail went well with his receding hairline, and, as he said, he only had control over one of the two factors in the equation: "Start losing your hair and you look old; get rid of it all and you look timeless."

I can tell he's been watching me but trying not to be too obvious about it. Figuring he would say something soon enough, I wait him out, and just as I start thinking about the television exposé we're working on, he breaks the silence: "It reminds you of that day, doesn't it? The ocean? The shore over there?"

"Yes."

Silence.

"You want some advice, Jev?"

"Xavier, we've been through this before."

"Sure, but do you want some advice now?"

"No."

"You sure?"

"Yes."

"Okay, here it is." He brushes some lint from his faded season-one *X-Files* T-shirt imprinted with a picture of David Duchovny (looking quintessentially cool) and Gillian Anderson (looking urgently concerned), and the words "The truth is out there."

"Stop trying to move on."

I look at him quizzically. "That's your advice?"

"Yup."

"Stop trying to move on."

"You got it."

"That's what's going to help?"

"Yup."

"Well"—I give my attention back to the road—"thanks, Xav. I'll keep that in mind."

"Thinking about what's done, man, dwelling on it, trying to deal with it, I'm just saying, that creates a lot of emotional drag. Be where you are; let where you've been alone. Do that and the universe will lean in your direction."

"That's very Zen of you."

"There're always going to be holes in your heart in the shape of your wife, in the shape of your kids."

"And you're telling me, what? That I need to fill the holes with something else?"

"No. I'm telling you to stop staring into 'em and let 'em be there, a part of your story, a part that affects your future, sure, but not what defines it. Stop feeding your pain and it'll dissipate. Okay, that's it. That's what I wanted to say. I'm done."

"How long have you been waiting to tell me all that?"

"It just came to me. I'm in the zone."

"Uh-huh." I take a small breath. "Listen, I appreciate it, really, but let's talk about something else."

A long pause. "What do you want to talk about?" "Nothing really comes to mind."

"Okay." He sounds a little defeated. "Right."

Xavier and I have been close friends ever since we met three years ago in Las Vegas, when my new show "Escape: The Jevin Banks Experience" opened. That was before moving to Atlantic City. Before everything happened and I gave up performing.

He'd worked backstage on the strip for nearly thirty years before coming to work pyrotechnics for me. He lives in an RV, loves to blow stuff up, doesn't believe we landed on the moon, thinks Bush was responsible for 9/11, and still insists that Obama's birth certificate was a fake: "Why do you think it took him so long to produce it? And who surrounded him *every day? The Secret Service,* Jevin. And they're in charge of investigating counterfeit money. Right? *Counterfeit documents?* See? Just google it. It'll make you a believer."

Now I drive in silence and he quietly fiddles with the button camera I'll be wearing. Moving from stage pyrotechnics to cinematography has been an easier transition for him than I thought it would be. He has an eye for it. So much of it is about angles and staging and lighting, just like in a stage production. And since I'll be working incognito, he gets to use some of his favorite gadgets, like the button camera.

A Suburban passes us. A boy who looks about ten years old peers through the window at me as they go by. Even though my sons wouldn't be nearly that old by now, I wonder what they would have looked like if they'd have reached that age. It seems to happen all the time these days when I see kids.

They'd be taller, stockier, possibly into football or soccer or playing piano, but that would've been Drew, I'm guessing, rather than Tony. Probably video games for both of them. I would've taught them to ride their bikes, they'd have navigated through most of their years of elementary school and—

Stop it, Jevin. This isn't helping anything.

No, no it's not.

Emotional drag.

If nothing else, Xavier was right about that much.

I try to follow his advice and leave where I've been alone in order to get the universe to lean in my direction, but it's not as simple as he makes it sound. I've never been able to just tell myself to be happy—or sad, or angry, or anything. Something significant has to happen for my emotions to pendulum that far in another direction. It would be so much easier if I could just tell myself what to feel and then feel it, but that's not how things work for me. I only seem to learn the important stuff in life the hard way; I have to suffer before I change.

Setting the camera aside, Xavier finger-scrolls across the screen of my iPad to check my messages. "Looks like Charlene's gonna be a little late, but I think you two should still make it to the center by five thirty."

"It's what, about two hours from Salem?"

"Maybe a little less, but about that, yeah."

"Fionna send the files yet?"

He checks. "Not yet. Just another shot at a simile."

Fionna McClury, who works logistics and "information gathering" for us, is a single, stay-at-home mom who homeschools her four kids and works as a cybersecurity consultant to pay the bills. Fortune 500 companies hire her to try hacking into their companies in order to test their firewalls. Nine out of ten times she's successful.

Her kids help her sometimes for homework.

And sometimes she freelances.

For me.

She's a real pro at teaching her kids everything except English. Her Achilles' heel. Lately she's been trying to teach metaphors and similes and keeps sending us some of her own to critique before using them with her kids.

A little apprehensively, I glance at Xavier. "What is it this time?"

"'The plane was as fast as a metal tube flying through the air at six hundred miles an hour.'"

"Um . . . it's accurate."

"I'll tell her that." He types. Hunt and peck. It takes awhile. "Hey, I forgot to mention, I need this weekend off. There's a convention I'm going to."

"Bigfoot or UFOs?"

"Very funny. It's about tectonic weapons."

"Tectonic weapons."

"They're for real, I'm telling you. There's credible evidence that the Air Force has the U2, the HAARP antennae, microwave technology. Just blast another country's fault lines with electro-magnetic waves, take out their infrastructure without firing a shot. No boots on the ground. It's the weapon of the future. Intense stuff."

"Let me guess—Peru a few years ago? Haiti, Japan—test runs?"

"See, even *you* made the connection. Go to YouTube, search term *tectonic weapons*. It'll blow your mind."

"I'm sure it would, but why on earth would the US attack Haiti, Japan, or Peru?"

He taps his finger against the air as if to accentuate that my question was a way of agreeing with him. "Precisely, Jev. That is *exactly* the question we need to be asking."

Aha. "Okay."

"Okay?"

"You can have the weekend off. And you should text her, tell her we need those files tonight."

"Fionna."

"Right."

I guide the van along the highway and think about the TV series we're filming—another step in my transition from the stage to the screen.

For the last year, I've used my background as an illusionist to replicate the tricks and effects of dozens of fake psychics, televangelist con men, and fortune-telling scam artists.

I know all too well what it's like to search desperately for answers, and I can't imagine deceiving someone who's in that situation just to make a buck.

My stage shows did well; money's not the issue. I'm really not sure anymore what I want out of life, but I figure if I debunk hucksters who are taking advantage of vulnerable and hurting people, well, at least that's something positive. Something small but worthwhile.

The exposés have become a staple for cable's Entertainment Film Network, and while not paying nearly as much as my stage shows did, they've helped me keep my skills sharp.

Three episodes left under contract. Then I'm not sure what I'll do. It feels a bit like I'm in a sea with nothing on the horizon to sail toward. And nowhere I really want to sail.

Two shows ago, Entertainment Film Network's executive producer told me I needed to branch out in a new direction, merge my work with more of a bent toward investigative journalism—sort of an undercover illusionist. I'd studied journalism for a few years in college, so (at least to the producer) it seemed like a natural fit.

I don't have the name or face recognition of a Copperfield, Blaine, or Angel, and in this case anonymity would be to my advantage.

So, here I am.

But this trip is nothing like debunking a roadside psychic. The Lawson Research Center, or LRC, headed by theoretical physicist and Nobel laureate Dr. William Tanbyrn, has big dollars, big names, and a lot of credibility behind it.

It's true that since Dr. Tanbyrn started getting deeper into the study of the roots of consciousness, he'd fallen out of favor with some of the mainstream scientific community, but most of those scientists were discounting his findings without analyzing or carefully investigating them. It seems that for a lot of people, just the fact that he's now at the Lawson Research Center—a facility known for investigating the paranormal while also serving as a New Age conference center—is enough to undermine his credibility.

Needless to say, his most recent test results on mind-to-mind, nonlocal communication were controversial; the findings were widely disputed or simply disregarded, as were Dr. Dean Radin's in the books *The Conscious Universe* and *Entangled Minds*. However, Dr. Tanbyrn's research had made it into three peer-reviewed journals and, supposedly, had been replicated by two researchers in Sweden, although as far as Fionna and Charlene had been able to tell, that study hadn't appeared yet in any of the literature.

In essence, Dr. Tanbyrn and his team were claiming proof of unconscious psychic activity, or psi, saying they actually had hard data to back up the existence of some forms of telepathy. They claimed to have facts—scientific evidence, not just anecdotes of folks saying they could read other people's thoughts.

I find that all pretty hard to swallow.

Whenever someone claims psychic activity—whether it's a TV psychic, the gypsy at the fair doing cold readings, or a multimillion-dollar research center, my con-man radar goes up. As Xavier likes to say, "Wherever there's someone out to make a buck, there's someone about to lose his shirt."

I have some ideas on how Dr. Tanbyrn and his team are faking the findings, but I need to be sure. Get it all on film. That's what my three friends are going to help me do.

Charlene isn't at the rest stop when we arrive.

While Xavier heads to the vending machines for some Gatorade and Cheetos, I look over my notes about the center where Charlene and I will covertly spend the next three days.

But after a few moments I hear a girl in the

vehicle next to me crying and see the family with the ten-year-old boy that passed us earlier. The stressed-out-looking mom is urging her two kids out of the SUV.

"I don't care if it's a ten-hour drive." She's clearly exasperated. "Please, you have to get along with your sister." Her kids look as weary as she does. The girl, who's about seven or eight, wipes a tear from her eye.

Go on. It might help.

I slip out of the van, lean against the door, and pull out the 1895 Morgan Dollar I always carry with me. Rachel and I didn't wear wedding rings, but since I was a numismatist, she insisted we exchange coins. This is the one she'd given me at our wedding seven years ago. It was by no means my most valuable coin, but being worth $125,000, it wasn't one that I was about to use to buy a lottery ticket.

I accidentally-on-purpose let it drop. It rolls toward the boy.

After a glance at his mother for permission, he picks it up and hands it to me.

"Thanks." But as I accept it, I vanish it from my hand. "Hey, where did that go?" I act shocked that it's gone.

Both he and the girl search my hands, then the ground. I turn my pockets inside out to show them that they're empty, and that's when I palm the rest of the coins I'll need. Then I pretend to notice something beside the boy's arm. "Hang on. There it is."

I reach over and pull half a dozen, more commonplace silver dollars one at a time from his left armpit, letting them drop to the parking lot.

"Did you see that, Mommy!" the girl exclaims. She's definitely not crying now. Her brother searches both of his armpits for more coins. I gather up the ones that fell.

"Yes. I did." Their mother is eyeing me a little suspiciously, as if I'm the psychopathic magician she's heard about who lures kids away from their parents by doing coin tricks for them in rest stop parking lots.

Xavier is returning now, snacks in hand. He sees me entertaining the family and tries to hide a half-smile.

I do a couple more tricks—I'm in my element and it feels good—then I see Charlene pull into a parking spot a few cars away, and I tell the kids, "I didn't realize it before, but I can tell you two are good at magic too."

They look confused.

"Go on, reach into your jacket pockets." With the sight angle of the mother and the attention of the kids focused on my right hand, the two left-handed drops I did a few moments ago while I was finishing the second-to-last trick hadn't been easy, but after twenty-five years of doing this, I'd managed to pull it off.

The kids reach into their pockets and are each astonished to find a silver dollar.

"I told you. It's magic."

"That was really good," the woman tells me, finally sounding a little more at ease, then nudges her kids toward me. "Go on, give the nice man back his money. And thank him for the magic show."

Though visibly disappointed that they can't keep the coins, the children obediently offer them to me.

"Oh, those were in your pockets, not mine. I couldn't take those." I wink at their mother. "I hope you have a great trip."

At last, with a word of thanks, she allows the kids to accept the silver dollars, then corrals them toward the restrooms.

Charlene is getting out of the car, and Xavier, who has a mouthful of Cheetos, waves to her but speaks to me in between crunches. "You just can't stand it, can you?"

"Stand what?"

"Seeing kids cry when you know you can make 'em laugh."

"What can I say. It's my only redeeming quality."

"You're pretty good at blackjack."

"True."

Charlene rounds the van. "Hello, gentlemen."

We greet her and she watches me pocket my

30

remaining coins. Xavier, who's deep into his bag of Cheetos now, licks some cheese powder from his fingers.

Charlene sighs good-naturedly. "I see you're both up to your usual tricks."

"Old habits." I put the last coin away.

"How many silver dollars have you given away to kids over the years?"

"A couple, I suppose."

"Uh-huh."

She smiles and it looks nice. Brown-haired and congenial, Charlene Antioch has a girl-next-door innocence about her, but also a slyly sexy side that she keeps hidden except when onstage in my show—that is, when I still did stage work. I don't know how many times in the last six years I've made her vanish, sliced her into pieces, or let her chain me up and seal me in a water tank. But I haven't done an escape in over a year. The thought of Rachel and the boys in the van, trapped, drowning, has just been too much for me. I can't even stand being in small, cramped places anymore.

An escape artist who's claustrophobic.

So now he makes films exposing fake psychics. Pathetic.

Today Charlene, who's thirty-two but looks twenty-five and is a chameleon when it comes to outfits, has her hair in a ruffled, earthy hairdo that might've actually looked more natural on Xavier

31

than on her. Birkenstocks, a button-up shirt, and tan Gramicci climbing pants round out her neo-progressive nature-lover outfit. Undoubtably, she chose it because of the center we're heading to. I, on the other hand, wasn't so particular—black jeans, a faded T-shirt from one of the half-marathons I ran last year, a three-season leather jacket. Also black.

"How was your drive?" I ask her.

"Good."

Xavier crumples up the empty Cheetos bag, aims for a trash can ten feet away. Tosses. Misses. Goes to retrieve it, but rather than drop it in, he backs up for another ten-foot shot.

I glance at my watch. "We should probably get going. They're expecting us by five thirty and it's still almost an hour to the Three Sisters." The famous mountain range wasn't far at all from the Lawson Research Center and, coincidentally, was near the town where I grew up.

On his fourth try, Xavier finally hits his shot, and the three of us remove the cameras, the heart rate monitor, and the radio frequency (RF) jammer from the van. Even though Charlene and I have used them all before, Xavier insists on re-re-re-explaining how they work, how to keep them concealed, how Charlene would use the jammer and heart rate monitor tomorrow when she was in the chamber.

"Right." She takes the nearly invisible monitor

that'll record her heart rate and, in a gesture of modesty, turns to the side before unbuttoning her shirt to press it against her chest, just above her heart. Xavier confirms that it's recording her heart rate, prints out the results on the small portable printer we're going to take with us. Then, monitor removed and shirt rebuttoned, Charlene climbs into the rental car.

I turn to Xavier. "So you're going to get B-roll of the mountains?"

He pats his video camera. "I'll get footage of everything around here. By the time you're done with your little study, we'll be ready to edit this puppy. Get it to the network. Actually meet a production deadline for once."

"Great." I grab the gear we'll need and join Charlene in the car while Xavier closes up the van.

He takes off, and a moment after I start the engine, Charlene turns to me. "I saw you with that family in the parking lot. You really are good with kids, Jevin."

"Thank you."

"With everyone."

"Thanks."

A pause. "It's been a long time since you were onstage. Do you ever think you might—"

"No."

Another slight pause. "Okay." As I'm backing out of the parking spot, she reaches over and gently places her hand on my knee. Despite myself, I feel a tingle of intimacy at her touch.

I stop the car. Let it idle.

"We need to get used to this," she says softly.

"Yes."

On the video we sent to the LRC, we'd portrayed ourselves as being deeply in love, and from what I could tell, it was one of the main reasons we'd been chosen for the study. Consequently, I know that if we're going to pull this off, I can't let on that her touch makes me uncomfortable in any way.

But yet it does, because in the last few weeks my feelings for her have strayed beyond the kind a co-worker can comfortably have for someone if they're going to remain simply co-workers. Part of me knows that, yes, it's been long enough since Rachel's death that I should be able to move on and start dating again, but another part of me isn't so sure that I'm over the loss in the ways I should be before delving into another serious relationship.

Charlene removes her hand. "What are you thinking?"

"I'm thinking it's not going to be easy being a couple."

"I'm not trying to make you uncomfortable. If you're not up to—"

"I'll be fine."

A moment passes. The car is still idling. "We

were good on stage together." Her voice is gentle, like a brushstroke on canvas. It's an enigmatic statement and I do my best not to read too much into it.

She's just trying to tell you that you're a good actor, that together the two of you can pull this off.

"Yes."

"So then," she takes a small breath, "I'm not sure how to put this, but . . . you're going to be alright being my lover for the next three days?"

Pretending to be your lover. Pretending.

"Ready as I'll ever be." I have a sense that there's another layer of meaning beneath my words, a layer that I may not have intended, and a wash of slightly uncomfortable silence fills the car. Rachel's ghost seems to drift between us. Linger beside my shoulder.

Finally, I pull out of the parking lot and Charlene nods. "Good." But by then I've nearly forgotten what words of mine she's responding to.

I merge onto the highway and head toward the Lawson Research Center. Despite the meta-analysis Fionna ran on the test results, I'm still convinced that Dr. William Tanbyrn and his team are faking it somehow, because if they're not, if their findings are true, I don't have any idea how to wrap my mind around the implications.

Hollow Bones

From an early age Riah Colette knew that she was different.

She would go through the motion of hugs and good-night kisses with her mom and dad and little sister, Katie, but rather than enjoying the gestures, she would only notice how firm the hug was or how wet the kiss.

Her parents and sister spoke about love, said that they loved each other, that they loved her— but she couldn't understand what they meant, not in the sense of feeling something nice or meaningful toward someone else, which seemed to be the case with them.

Riah wasn't blind to the cues of affection that her dad gave her—the smiles and winks and the way he would position himself just so as he brushed against her when he passed her in the hallway.

He preferred her over Katie. That became especially clear by the way he began to treat her when she turned thirteen and started to look more like a young woman than a little girl.

And then there were the nighttime visits.

Katie wasn't old enough yet to earn that kind of special attention from their father, and at first Riah thought she should probably feel bad about it—that there was some sort of shame or injustice in her dad's favoritism toward her, but since he was her father, she had the sense that it was a good thing to please him. And so, the times in her bedroom late at night when he would knock on her door and she would tell him to come in, well, after a while they stopped feeling so awkward and became a way of making him happy.

Besides, he almost always gave her a present the next morning—a hairbrush, a pair of earrings, new underwear—as long as she promised not to tell her mother or Katie about the visits and as long as she kept the gifts a secret. And she had agreed.

One time when Riah was fourteen and she and Katie were in the woods near the stream on the edge of their property, Katie found a bird with a broken wing and brought it to her. Katie, who was nine at the time, was clearly troubled by the prospect of abandoning the bird in the forest. "We have to help it. If we leave it out here, it might die."

Of course it'll die, Riah thought. *All things die. So will you. Someday.*

But she didn't say any of that.

"Here," she said instead, "let me see it."

Riah had always been good at pretending that she cared about animals, and she could tell that her sister had no idea what was about to happen.

Katie handed Riah the bird, and she was struck by how light it was, as if its bones were made of air or the rest of its body was made entirely of feathers.

The lightness of the bird made it seem like what was about to happen would not be all that significant—after all, since the bird was so small, so tiny and young and helpless, not much would be different in the world after it was dead. Not really.

Riah didn't know what kind of bird it was, but it had blue feathers with streaks of gray and an orangish-yellowish beak. She could see the concern in Katie's face but felt only curiosity herself: *What will it be like to watch this bird die?*

It didn't struggle, didn't try to move its broken wing or attempt to squirm from her hand.

"What are you going to do?" Katie asked.

"I'm going to help it."

A few seconds passed, then Katie said quietly, "How?"

Cradling the bird in one hand, Riah placed her other hand gently on top of its head.

"Let's take it back to the house," Katie offered. "Then we can see if Mommy can help."

"It's okay." Riah closed her fingers around the bird's fragile head.

"What are you doing?" Now a sense of urgency. A nervousness—

Riah twisted her hand.

One quick and abrupt movement. The bird let out a tiny chirp that was cut off in the middle, but that was all. It didn't quiver, just became still.

"No!" Katie screamed.

That easy. That quick. Limp and still.

Riah lifted her hand to see what the bird looked like and saw that it didn't look very different at all. Just lay so, so amazingly still.

She knew that sometimes nerves cause animals to twitch after they're dead, that chickens will run around even after their heads had been chopped off. In fact, she'd seen something like that first-hand herself when she was about Katie's age. But that wasn't with a chicken. "I killed a snake," her dad had told her. "But it's not dead yet. Come on. I'll show you."

Riah couldn't understand how the snake could be killed but not yet dead, but her dad led her past the line of tomatoes in the garden behind their house, where she saw a shovel with a dirty red stain lying beside the body of a three-foot-long black snake. The head lay a couple feet away and was motionless, but the snake's body was curling and writhing furiously on the grass.

Killed, but not yet dead.

After a moment Riah had gone over and picked it up, then held it while it continued to squirm and spasm, held it while its severed neck leaked warm, sticky blood onto her hands, held it until it stopped moving for good.

And now, as she cradled the dead bird in her hand, she thought of that writhing, dead snake.

But the bird didn't squirm at all.

So still.

Katie, who was crying loudly, had almost made it back to the house. Riah wasn't surprised by her sister's reaction. Honestly, she wasn't surprised by her own, either. It'd been so easy to stop that bird's life, to quiet it into death, and now she realized that it didn't either bother her or please her, gave her no sense of accomplishment or of loss, no satisfaction or disappointment.

She knew that she should probably feel something, that normal girls would feel bad or guilty or sad in some way, or get upset and start crying like Katie had, who was now calling for their mother.

Katie, a normal girl.

Riah, the freak.

She laid the bird gently on the ground in a patch of dandelions near the stream, hoping that the gesture would somehow make her feel more reverent or more considerate of the bird's death, but all she really felt was a sense of curiosity at the angle of the bird's head and how it looked so odd twisted that way.

She tilted her own head and studied her reflection in the water, tried to see what it would've looked like if her head was bent in the same way as the dead bird's, but she couldn't quite get the angle right.

• • •

Back at the house, her mother had yelled at her, but her father had laughed it off. "Same as a racehorse," he said in his wet, thick-tongued way. "Those things break a leg, the owners put 'em down right there on the track. Doesn't matter who's in the stands—women, kids, makes no difference at all, they make everyone watch."

Riah's mother gave him a scolding look. "Hank, that's enough."

He gazed at his youngest daughter, who was still sniffling, and his tone became firm: "Day comes when you gotta learn that everything dies. Just a matter of time. Better to learn that now than later."

He went back to his corn bread and ham with a renewed passion.

"You don't need to upset Katie and you don't need to encourage the older one," Riah's mom said.

It'd been right around the time when Riah turned thirteen and her dad began visiting her bedroom that her mother had stopped referring to her by name and just started calling her "the older one."

Her dad grunted at the comment from his wife. "I'm just saying, killing a crippled bird isn't cruel. Put it out of its misery. It's the caring thing to do."

"Caring? Really?" There was unusual defiance in her mother's tone.

"Yeah." His eyes narrowed. "Really."

Riah watched Katie stifle back a tear. The girls had learned long ago not to argue with their father. He didn't take it very well—especially after he'd been drinking, as he had already this afternoon.

Her mother's leg got a little jittery beneath the table. "And is that what you'd want us to do to you? Snap your neck if you broke your leg? Would that be the caring thing to do?"

"Don't challenge me, woman." Each word had become a hammer blow. "Don't make me put you in your place."

Riah noticed a tiny tremor in her mother's hands and saw her throat tighten. She knew that on those nights when her father visited her bedroom, he often stopped by his own room first. She didn't know exactly what he did to her mother on those nights, but she knew enough. There was usually yelling and crashing and sometimes sobbing. Her mother typically wore more makeup than usual the next day. But even then, the bruises were still visible.

I wonder how long it takes her to put all that makeup on.

Now her mother seemed to compose herself and looked at her husband harshly, but she did not challenge him. Instead she rose stiffly, picked up her plate, and headed to the kitchen. "Come on, Katie," she said. "Help me with the dishes."

Katie quickly left the table and hurried to the kitchen, and then, when Riah and her father were alone, he gave her a wink and put his hand on hers.

Your mother yelled at you and he defended you. You should thank him. That's what you're supposed to do when someone helps you.

She smiled back at him, playing the role of a girl who cared about her father.

"Alright," she said, her voice soft, meant only for him. "After they're all asleep."

She knew he would understand.

"That's my girl." He stabbed his fork into his ham. "That's my good little girl."

Now, twenty years later, Riah headed across the Benjamin Franklin Bridge toward RixoTray Pharmaceuticals' corporate headquarters in central Philadelphia.

She knew that the CEO, Dr. Cyrus Arlington, was working late. It wasn't quite 8:30, and Riah hadn't told him she would be swinging by. He'd been in London, and she hadn't seen him since he'd left two days ago. Tonight she wanted to see how he would respond to the surprise.

That's what she did sometimes. Tested people to see how they would react to the unexpected.

To observe what normal people do.

To learn what it would be like to be normal.

It might have been her curiosity into human nature that was one of the reasons she'd become a doctor in neurophysiology: to understand how people think, communicate, feel—and maybe to begin to understand more of what it means to be human.

That was before joining Cyrus's neurophysiology research team to work on the neural decoding studies, before seducing him to try and discover more about the meaning of love.

Over the years she'd realized that if there was one thing she wanted, it was to find out what it would feel like to care about somebody or something the way other people did—where family members or friends mattered, where your heart might get warmed or anxious or broken. What would that be like, to feel more than just curiosity about someone else's joy or pain?

Riah paid the toll and guided her car toward the sixty-story mirrored-glass skyscraper that was rivaled only by the Comcast building for prominence in the Philadelphia skyline. Tonight she had a question to ask Cyrus, a proposal, as it were.

A way she had thought up over the last few weeks to find out more about the limits and depths of true love.

Serenity

5:28 p.m. Pacific Daylight Time

I'm anxious to get to the center, and it's not far, only ten minutes or so.

As we pass through Pine Lake, I realize it's exactly like I remember it: the Cascade Mountains rising majestically from the horizon with Mt. Hood dominating the range, creating a picturesque backdrop to the town that the demise of logging in the region had turned into a virtual ghost town.

I haven't been here in over fifteen years, but when I was a boy, I used to gaze at Mt. Hood every day on my way to school to see if it had snow on it. Usually there were a few days a year when the snow on the very top would disappear. One year, though, when I was in sixth grade, the snow stayed up there all summer.

Tapping the brakes, I slow down and guide the car off the highway and onto the winding mountain road that leads toward the Lawson Research Center's entrance.

I can still hear my dad talking about how the year-round snow cover was going to help the tourists stay longer. Good for the economy, the town. Good for the ski shop he ran.

That was two months before my mom left us and moved to Seattle, where I only saw her twice before she remarried and left for France with her new husband.

As a kid I thought that no matter how much the snow might've helped the local economy, it didn't help us, and in my childhood naïveté, I blamed the snow for what happened to my family, as if it were some sort of convoluted cause and effect. It's funny what you associate together when you're young, things that aren't related at all but that seem to be somehow interconnected.

I'd dabbled in magic before that, but that was the year I started taking it seriously. In the hope of somehow making my mother reappear.

"Jevin?" Charlene's voice draws me back to the moment. "Are you okay?"

"Sorry, I was . . . Yeah, I'm fine."

"I was saying, we're almost there. The turnoff is in a quarter mile."

"Right." A stillness passes between us. For some reason I feel the need to explain myself. "I was just remembering the last time I was here. As a kid."

"Good memories or bad ones?"

"A little of both."

I make the turn.

The newly paved access road winds through the towering pines of the old-growth forest. A large sign sits at the entrance, painted with both the name of the center and a symbol of a rather rotund woman in the lotus position with lines that make me think of electric sparks emanating from her head. I can't decide if it looks more like she's morphing into a porcupine or getting electrocuted while meditating.

We park and grab our bags from the back of the car.

Charlene closes the trunk. "I've been thinking a lot about this study, Jevin, wondering if it might be legit. I mean, this isn't the first research in mind-to-mind communication."

We haven't been on the same page with this project since I first proposed that we debunk the research. "True. But that's over the last seventy years, and with every year that passes, you have a more discernible decline effect: with more stringent testing procedures, the results are less and less conclus—"

"Conclusive, yes, I know, but this one was replicated nearly four dozen times with hundreds of subjects. I just don't see how they might have faked it."

"Nonrandom timing on the video-image generation, selective reporting, coached participants, confirmation bias, or something to do with the movement or focusing of the camera. It could be something as simple as switching the equipment or using a computer to mimic the sender's responses and create the atypical results before the external review of the findings. We'll find out."

Silence.

We head toward the main building. She looks at me. "Your dad still in the area?"

"My dad?"

"Yes . . . Is he still in the area?"

"He is."

"I was wondering . . . ?"

"He's still here."

"Okay."

"Yes."

"I was wondering if you might want to see him."

"You were wondering . . ."

"Go over to his place and—"

"Probably not a good idea. And I have to say, this conversation is starting to sound like a David Mamet script." As a fellow filmophile, I figured she would know what I was talking about.

"A script? You think? By Mamet?"

"Would you stop already."

She smiles.

Two elegant Japanese rock gardens with Native American symbols engraved in sandstone sculptures lie to our left. They look like they might've been more at home in New Mexico than here in Oregon.

I've never explained to Charlene why I ended up living with my grandmother the last four years I was in Pine Lake, and this doesn't feel like the right time to get into all of that.

"There should be time after the study," she offers.

A pause. "We'll see."

I imagine she must know this is a way of saying no without actually saying it.

"Right. Okay."

The path leads to a surprisingly modern building with solar panels, a garden to the south, and a fountain that's gurgling from the top of a three-dimensional sculpted peace sign. Beside the office door is another sign of the overweight, spiky-haired porcupine lady.

I open the door.

Gentle sitar music, along with the fragrant scent of a flowery incense, welcomes us as we enter the building.

The young woman at the counter has blonde dreadlocks dangling across her shoulders, a loose-fitting Indian shirt, an indiscernible number of bead necklaces, and a disarming smile. "Welcome to the Lawson Research Center. I'm Serenity."

I can't imagine that it's her real name, and despite myself, I end up trying to think of a cool New Age nickname for myself to help me fit in.

In lieu of a handshake, Serenity presses her palms together in front of her chest in a posture of prayer and gives me and Charlene a small, reverent bow from behind the check-in counter. I see that she has intricate tattoos on the back of her hands. Symbols from nearly every religion I'm aware of, and some that I am obviously not.

Charlene and I return the gesture.

"Is this your first visit to the LRC?" Serenity's voice is tiny and melodic. Birdlike.

I nod. "Yes. We're here for the study with Dr. Tanbyrn."

"Of course."

She glances at a sheet of paper taped to her desk, reminding me of a flight attendant referring to note cards on her first attempt at solo-announcing the preflight instructions. An open journal with a half-finished entry lies beside the cheat sheet. Scribbles fill the margin of the journal. "And you are?"

Charlene takes my hand and leans close to me as she tells Serenity the aliases we used when we sent in the video to apply for the study: "Brent Berlin and Jennie Reynolds."

"We prefer Wolverine and Petunia," I tell Serenity.

Charlene looks at me questioningly.

I shrug.

Our New Age nicknames.

"I'm Wolverine," Charlene explains.

"Actually, I—"

"He's Petunia."

"That's nice." Serenity nods understandingly. "Yes, of course."

Charlene winks at me. "Right, dear?" There's no

way I'm going to be Petunia for the rest of our stay, but arguing in front of Serenity doesn't seem like the loving thing to do, so I let it drop. I'll reaffirm my identity as Wolverine later.

"Sure," I mutter. "Dear."

Serenity consults her notes again. For walk-around and street magic, you need to be able to read other people's handwriting upside down and backward so that when you use mirrors you can decipher what they've written on cards you're not supposed to see. In time I got pretty good at it, and right now that skill was coming in handy.

"I think you'll find our campus inviting and restful. A place to quiet your thoughts, still your spirits, and bring a more harmonic centeredness to your inner being and to your relationship with each other." The words are obviously scripted, but she makes them sound authentic, like she genuinely means them, and I like that about her.

"Thank you, that sounds nice," I tell her honestly.

Charlene thanks her as well, then mentions something about how we'd been so looking forward to this, but I'm giving my attention to the lobby, taking in the simple, rustic setting that also carries an air of high-end architectural design. Outside the window lies a porch with elegant stonework and round porch tables with umbrellas spreading above them like protective canvas wings. I imagine the metal is recycled, that the canvas is organic and somehow both waterproof and biodegradable.

Charlene is still holding my hand, which is okay by me.

"They're serving in the dining hall until six, if you haven't eaten yet," Serenity tells us. I want to get settled, so I'm thankful Charlene and I grabbed a bite on the way here. "Breakfast is in the morning, six to eight. Dr. Tanbyrn will meet you at nine at the Prana building."

Charlene looks at her curiously. "I'm sorry—the piranha building?"

"Prana." Serenity seems surprised that Charlene doesn't know the word. "The life force. The life-sustaining force. Hindu."

"Right."

Charlene lets go of my hand.

Serenity holds out a map uncertainly. "I'm sorry, did you say you've been here before?"

"No." It's a dual-purpose answer—I hadn't said that, and we haven't been here. I accept the map from her.

Serenity settles back into her script: "There's a 7:00 yoga class tonight that you're welcome to attend, all at your discretion, of course. Here at the Lawson Research Center, we care more about your experience than your attendance at any of our quality scheduled events."

She hands Charlene a schedule. "We want this to be a place apart from the normal distractions of daily life. Too many people are tethered to technology, and it gives them a false sense of connection with other sojourners but splinters their attention from the most vital relationships, those with the people around them, and all too often it keeps them from being present in the moment."

Serenity makes it through all of that in one breath, which I find pretty impressive.

"So"—now she looks nervous—"Wolverine, Petunia, I will need to ask you not to use your mobile phones or other electronic computerized devices here on our campus. It's our policy." She sounds like she's apologizing.

Fionna and her kids had researched this place extensively, and Serenity's request comes as no surprise. We don't have any intention of forsaking our electronic devices during our stay, but Charlene fishes through her purse, produces her phone. Shuts it off. "Of course."

I turn off my cell as well. I wonder what the reception up here in the mountains will be like anyway.

Serenity directs us to our cabin, wishes us well, and prayer-gesture bows to us again. We reply in kind.

As we're walking down the path toward the cabin, Charlene shakes her head. "Wolverine and Petunia?"

"I was trying to fit in. And I'm supposed to be Wolverine."

"I kind of like you being Petunia."

"I'll bet you do."

We walk in silence until I make my suggestion for the evening's plans. "Tonight, instead of going to yoga, I think we should have a little look around the research center."

"Jevin Banks, you read my thoughts."

"Well, if I can actually do that, tomorrow's test is going to be a piece of cake."

I'm toting the bags, so when we reach the porch Charlene opens the cabin door and we step inside.

The Doll

The cabin is nothing special. No TV. No telephone. A kitchenette, a small living area, a bathroom. A bedroom with a king-sized bed lies at the end of a short hall.

Ah, that was something I hadn't thought through very well. One bed.

I consider going back to ask Serenity for a cabin with two beds, but I doubt that would help Charlene and me look like a couple who's deeply in love. I catch myself eyeing the couch to see if it'll be big enough for me.

The autumnal smell of wood smoke permeates the air, although it must be from somewhere else since there's no woodstove or fireplace in the cabin.

A sweep of the room with Xavier's latest

gadget—a pen-sized radio frequency detector—tells us there aren't any bugs and that Charlene and I will be able to talk freely while we're in the room. It's probably an unnecessary precaution, but in Xavier's mind you can never be too careful about these things.

It doesn't take us long to put our things away, and as Charlene is closing the dresser drawer, she turns to me. "So you're thinking wait till it gets dark? Go check out the Faraday cage?"

"Yes."

"And how do you propose we get into the building?"

I hold up a second hotel-style key card in addition to the one to our cabin.

"How did you get that?"

"At the front desk while you were talking with Serenity."

"You . . . how?"

"The key card coder. Serenity had a journal open and stopped writing in midsentence when we arrived. The slant, baseline, and connecting strokes of the passcode she'd written in the margins matched those on the sheet of paper containing her orientation notes."

"And you swiped the key without either of us noticing?"

"Yes."

She shakes her head. "You really are good, Petunia."

"Wolverine."

"Well, let's hope you're right about the code."

"We'll find out soon enough."

"As soon as it gets dark?"

"Exactly."

I pull out the two thick volumes that Dr. William Tanbyrn wrote—one before and one after his interest shifted from theoretical quantum physics to consciousness and its relationship to quantum entanglement. The words on the back of the second book touted:

> Dr. William Tanbyrn, who received a Nobel Prize in physics for his contribution in the development of mechanisms for studying the existence of loop quantum gravity, has embarked on a daring new field of study—the human mind and its interaction with the universe around us.

As I sit on the couch, Charlene leans close. "Didn't quite finish them yet, huh?" I can smell her perfume. I hadn't noticed it so much earlier in the car, but it's nice. A gentle touch of lavender.

"Barely got started." I'd been hoping to get through the books before our meeting this week with Dr. Tanbyrn, but he wasn't the most concise author I'd ever read, and I'd found the two five-hundred-page tomes a bit hard to decipher. "They're pretty dense."

"Well, tell me one thing you've learned so far."

"Not even quantum physicists understand quantum physics."

"Ah."

"Oh, and something else I found interesting: when electrons jump from one level in orbit around the nucleus to another, they don't travel through the space between the rings, they just appear at the next ring."

"What do you mean? Like teleporting? 'Beam me up, Scotty'? That sort of thing?"

"That's one way to put it."

"Where do they go?"

"No one knows."

"Sounds like science fiction to me."

"Me too. Except it's reality."

"Huh." She sounds more interested now. Peers over my shoulder as if she's going to stay for a while.

Her perfume really is nice.

I try to redirect my attention from her to the books.

"Let me read you a quote." I flip through the pages, but it takes me awhile to find the one I'm looking for. "Okay. Here: 'Nothing exists except atoms and empty space; everything else is opinion.'"

She considers that for a moment. "Sure. Even solid objects are mostly space, the electron orbiting the nucleus. Who wrote that? Dr. Tanbyrn?"

"Not quite. A little bit before his time."

"Einstein?"

"Democritus. He died in 370 BC."

"That's amazing."

I hand her one of the books. "Here. You can read this one if you want. I highlighted all the good stuff. Up to chapter 9."

But she straightens up. "Actually, I was thinking I'd take a quick shower, freshen up. It was a long day in the car."

"Ah, yes. Well, maybe later."

She pats my shoulder. "I'll let you do all the heavy lifting. You can fill me in when you're done."

Then she leaves me alone to my reading, and I settle in with my pen, highlighter, and the shorter, more recent of the two textbooks, and flip to the chapter on quantum entanglement and theories about the results of a meta-analysis of studies on identical twins. As I do, I can't help but think of Drew and Tony, who, just like so many identical twins, seemed to communicate with each other in unexplainable ways—finishing each other's sentences, making up words that the other boy seemed to instinctively know the meaning of, even, at times, giving the impression that they knew what each other was thinking.

As I begin to read, the memory of my two sons pinches my heart, and I can't help but wonder if this research will help me to understand them better or just make me miss them all the more.

• • •

Riah Colette showed her ID to the security guard in the RixoTray Pharmaceuticals corporate head-quarters' lobby, took the elevator to the top floor, and entered the suite where her paramour worked in his corner office.

Whenever Cyrus was in his office—no matter what time of day—his secretary, Caitlyn Vaughn, would be stationed at the reception desk out front. Riah nodded to her, and the young woman gave her a half-frown but waved her through.

Since Cyrus was a married man, he'd wanted to avoid his place from the beginning of their relationship, and Riah never let him come to her apartment, so that limited their choices. Some-times they would slip off to a hotel room, but more often than not they stayed here in his office.

Riah had the sense that the twenty-something redhead was jealous of her liaisons with her boss, and she wondered how many times Caitlyn had leaned close to the door to listen to the sounds coming from inside the office during her visits. It was something to think about. Perhaps she would ask her about it one of these days.

Quietly, Riah gave the door a light one-knuckle knock, just enough to let Cyrus know someone was there, but then entered before he had a chance to call her in.

He was on the phone, and she could tell he was taken aback by her arrival, but he quickly put on a smile and signaled to her that he would be with her in a moment, then gestured toward a chair: *Have a seat.*

She chose not to, but instead angled toward the window.

Impeccably dressed in a suit that cost more than most people's entire wardrobes, Cyrus looked sharp, powerful, confident. But also stern. Any gentleness he might've tried to portray was betrayed by his eyes, which were like two steel balls, blank and emotionless. Two miniature shot puts embedded in his head. Riah had seen him enjoy himself, oh yes, but had never seen him happy, not really. And that intrigued her. Because she couldn't remember a time when she'd been happy either.

He let his gaze drift from her face and slide down her body, along the curves of her dress, and she didn't discourage it. She felt no shame in using her looks and figure in her research into human nature, into attraction, into love. She kept in shape for this, and at thirty-four she'd been told that she was still striking, and she was used to eyes following her wherever she went.

Long ago, Riah had learned that sex was the way to please men. And when they're pleased they trust you, and when they trust you they share their secrets with you. As she'd overheard a female co-worker say one time, "If you can't tell some-one your secrets, you make intimacy off-limits."

So, it seems, sharing secrets leads to intimacy.

Riah wasn't sure yet if intimacy would lead to the one thing she wanted to feel most—love—but she held out hope that in time it would.

She knew Cyrus's office well: the wide windows overlooking central Philly, his framed degrees and awards hanging prominently on the walls, bookshelves that were neatly lined with medical textbooks and packed with paraphernalia from his travels around the world. In the center of the room sat his imposing mahogany desk that she and Cyrus would clear off sometimes when they decided not to use the leather couch in the corner.

And of course, at the far side of the room, the two aquariums: one filled with buzzing emerald jewel wasps, the other with inch-and-a-half-long cockroaches. It was a curious thing. Riah had asked him about that, but he'd never explained why he kept them.

She went to the shelf and picked up the voodoo—or, more accurately, *vodou*—doll that he'd brought back from his medical humanitarian visit to Haiti after the earthquake. In one sense, it was oddly appropriate that he'd brought it here to Philly. After all, there was a large Haitian population in the city, and some people said there were between five hundred and one thousand houses where people practiced voodoo in their basements. With estimates of twenty to fifty people participating in the services, that meant there might be as many as 50,000 serious voodoo worshipers in Philadelphia, putting it on par with Miami and even New Orleans.

The cloth doll had a painted-on face with pin marks through the eyes and in the groin area. Most of Cyrus's visitors found the doll disturbing, and he seemed to enjoy using it as a conversation piece and a chance to offhandedly mention his volunteer work in developing countries. Personally, Riah wasn't bothered by the doll, just wondered who, if anyone, the pins had been intended to harm.

Holding the doll, she stood beside the window and looked at central Philadelphia's streets spreading out before her like spokes from a wheel. She'd always thought that there were too many one-way streets in downtown Philly, probably caused by the disrupted traffic patterns around the monolithic city hall.

A proud city.

The city of the nation's birth.

And, historically, a good place to base a medical center or a pharmaceutical firm.

While studying medicine at Drexel, she'd learned that Philadelphia was the home of the first public hospital in 1751, the first school of pharmacy in 1812, the first private biomedical research institute in 1892.

In addition, the greater Philadelphia area was

the home of eleven other pharmaceutical firms' corporate headquarters. RixoTray, though the smallest of the twelve, actually had the second-highest profit margin. Due, in large part, to having Dr. Cyrus Arlington at the helm.

Riah stared out the window at Philadelphia's nighttime skyline while she waited for Cyrus to finish his call. Tonight she would ask him for the first time to come over to her place after work, and when they got there she would see how he responded to the surprises she had waiting for him.

Perhaps it would lead to love, she wasn't sure, but if nothing else, seeing his reaction would give her more information on how men respond to shared secrets.

Twilight

I hear the shower running in the bathroom.

Charlene had asked me to fill her in, so now I look over a two-sentence summary of quantum physics: "The observer's intentions and expectations about reality actually affect the outcome of reality. Without the observer the quantum wave function never collapses." Admittedly, the collapsing quantum wave was a concept I needed a little more time to really grasp.

As far as I could understand it, quantum

physicists claimed that since possibilities do not become reality without conscious observation, matter could not exist without consciousness. So, according to Dr. Tanbyrn, philosophers ask, "If a tree falls in the forest and there's no one to hear it, does it make any sound?" but physicists are forced to ask, "If there's no one there to observe the tree fall, does it even exist?"

As he writes:

> Our universe is both a puzzle and an answer, both a mystery and an adventure. From the earliest explorations of the human mind to probing the mysteries of existence, we as a species have always been question-askers. And now, with the advancement of quantum physics, the answers we find only produce more profound questions about what is happening on the subatomic level of the universe.

Remarkably, none of the explanations used to explain the activity of subatomic particles has been proven. Not M-theory, superstring theory, the multiverse. Basically, in understanding quantum physics, you need to remember that scientists still don't understand the nature of life, that although they can test how energy reacts under different circumstances, they still don't really understand what it is.

In some quarters it's even debated whether quantum physics should be considered science or a field of metaphysics.

My mind is spinning, not only because of the mystical-sounding quantum theories I'm reading, but also, admittedly, at the thought of Charlene showering in the next room over. I try to concentrate on the intricate concepts of the book, but the sound of the running water and the knowledge of who it's washing over is a little too distracting.

Hoping to divert my thoughts, I step outside.

Clouds have rolled in. The evening is cool. Jacket weather.

A light mist touches the air.

Almost dark.

I read for a few more minutes but can still hear the water running inside the cabin, so I take out my cell and go on a walk to check if I can get a signal and to see if the files Fionna was going to send me have arrived.

Two miles away

Glenn Banner did not think of himself as an assassin.

Yes, he had killed people, eleven so far, and always in the name of money, but still, when he thought of assassins, he pictured slick, highly paid professionals who hide on rooftops, snap ten-thousand-dollar rifles together, take out opposition-party political figures, and then, fake passport in hand, melt into the crowd on their way to another country to lie low for a couple weeks before their next hit.

When Glenn thought of an assassin, he didn't think of a guy who worked most days as a mechanic, a guy who was just trying to make ends meet, a divorced dad who was doing the best he knew to put food on the table and have enough cash left over to spend some time with his daughter on weekends. Mary Beth was six and lived with her mother and her stepfather two miles from Glenn's mobile home that lay on the outskirts of Seattle.

No, he didn't think of himself as an assassin.

But none of that changed what he was.

Lots of people had unsavory jobs they needed done, and that's where Glenn came in. Sometimes it meant getting compromising photos of someone, or scaring off an ex-spouse, or beating some sense into a young punk who wouldn't leave a guy's daughter alone. Small jobs really, but they were the sort of thing Glenn was good at, and they helped pay the bills.

But two years ago he'd moved up the food chain.

Toward more permanent solutions.

Yes, he looked more like the guy who lives down the block than he did a professional problem solver, but his low visibility was part of what made him so good at what he did. He was truly gifted at playing the role of a neighbor who enjoyed a few smokes with his friends, drank a few Buds on the weekends, and always bought his little six-year-old princess a toy from a truck stop on the way back from his assignments.

But truthfully, to him she wasn't a little princess. The kid was just a set piece in the life he was acting out. In the bigger game he was playing. But she served his purpose of creating sympathy among the people he knew, and that was reason enough to put up with spending time with her.

He parked the car at the edge of the county road that made a circuit around the center's sprawling campus.

He didn't want to drive onto the property, so he'd decided earlier to access it by hiking through the surrounding old-growth forest.

Tonight—collect the information that he could use against his employers. Tomorrow—solve the problem, pick up his paycheck, then blackmail the people who'd hired him.

No, he didn't think of himself as an assassin. He was just a guy heading off to work in a job that happened to be somewhat messy.

He made sure he had his knife—a 170 mm blade, Nieto Olivo series—with him just in case.

After all, as the saying goes, "Chance favors the prepared mind." Then Glenn began picking his way through the dying daylight that was filtering through the forest around him.

Sleepover

Though he was trying to keep his voice low, Riah heard Cyrus wrapping up his phone call: "Yes, we have a man in the area . . . He's good, he'll take care of everything . . . No, of course . . . Alright. I'il be there within the hour . . . Yes. By tomorrow afternoon it won't be a problem . . . And the video is on its way. You'll be impressed with the results."

An intriguing end to the conversation.

He said goodbye, hung up, and turned toward Riah. His eyes landed on the cloth doll she was still holding. "We've come a long way since then." He gestured toward it. "Shamanism, witch-craft, sorcery. Voodoo."

She turned it over in her hands. Studied the punctured eyes. "Some people still believe in those things. How was London?"

"Wet. Dreary. Tedious. And yes, I know."

"You know?"

"That some people still believe in those things. I saw a voodoo ceremony myself while I was in Haiti. A bit troubling, if you ask me. The whole goal is for the participants to get possessed."

"By a Loa."

He seemed surprised that she knew. "Yes."

"They call it being 'ridden,' as if the spirit was the rider and the person was the horse."

"You've done your homework."

Riah considered what type of response to give him, what a normal woman might say, then asked, "Why do you keep this thing around anyway? It's kind of creepy."

"To remember the trip, of course, but also to remind myself that superstition is erased by science. The more we advance in medicine, the less we need to believe in the supernatural. I didn't expect you tonight."

She strolled toward the bookshelf. "Is it a problem that I'm here?"

"No, I . . . No." But his body language told her that perhaps it was.

She placed the voodoo doll back on the shelf and considered how he thought, how she could play off that to get what she wanted. "I can leave. If that's what you'd like."

He seemed to consider that, then said, "No. Stay."

He came toward her, kissed her. She kept her eyes open while he did, studying his face as he pressed his lips against hers. Though she'd learned over the years to kiss in a way that turned men on, and did so now, she felt nothing—no attraction, no repulsion, no excitement. It was as if he were an object to her, a lab specimen. She knew that thinking about him in this way would not have been considered by most people to be healthy, but although she desperately wanted to, she didn't know how to think about her lovers in any other way.

At last, as he pulled away, she decided to try something that might convince him that he would want to spend the night with her. She lifted his right hand, kissed his index finger, then trailed it across her cheek down her neck, around the fringed neckline of her dress, and brought it back, touched it lightly to her tongue. She let her lips pucker to greet the moist tip of his finger. A light kiss, yes, but she had the feeling it would be terribly seductive and exciting to him.

She let go of his hand, and Cyrus let it linger beside her lips for a moment, then lowered it slowly to his side.

He took a deep breath to collect himself, then looked at his watch. "I do have a meeting in forty-five minutes."

"Forty-five minutes? That's plenty of time."

"Well, actually, I need to leave now to get there. It's at the R&D facility."

When she'd first applied for her job, she hadn't understood why RixoTray had built its research and development complex thirty minutes away, just outside of Bridgeport, but the more she'd thought about it, the more it made sense: keep the facility isolated, at least a little ways, from any terrorist threats to the country's fifth largest city, the one that held more symbols of freedom and independence than any other, the city that was known as the birthplace of modern democracy.

After all, if you were an Islamic terrorist group trying to strike at the heart of the Great Satan, you might choose New York City, the financial capital of the West, or Washington DC, the political capital of America, or LA, the home of the entertainment industry that spreads all those corrupt Western ideas around the world. Or you might choose Philly, the historical symbol of democracy. And since your people had already dramatically attacked NY and DC and targeted LAX, that left Philadelphia as a primary target. It was just a matter of time.

She looked at Cyrus, responded to his comment about the meeting by asking the natural question: "At this time of night?"

"It's with Daniel and Darren."

Well, that made sense. The twins didn't exactly keep normal office hours. "I thought they were in Oregon?"

"We flew them in earlier today."

Earlier today. She hadn't heard. "I'll come."

"No, that won't be necessary."

"I'm the principal investigator on the project. I'm the one who implanted the electrodes. I should have been told the two of them were back."

He was quiet.

She put a hand lovingly on the side of his neck. "I'll join you, then you can join me at my place. Actually, that's why I came here, to invite you to a sleepover."

He considered that. "A sleepover."

"Mm-hmm. It'll be fun." She sat on his desk and crossed her legs, making the most of the slit in her dress. "I have some new outfits to wear. A few sleepover games I thought we could play." She could tell he was definitely interested now.

Riah handed him the phone receiver from his desk. "Call your wife. Tell her you just got sent out of town on an urgent business trip. Something pressing that can't wait." In his position as CEO, it wasn't an unusual occurrence, and they'd used this excuse to their advantage before.

She waited for him to finish lying to his wife, then led him out of the building to the parking garage. She knew where his Jaguar would be and figured she could pick up her car tomorrow morning when they returned to his office.

They slipped into the Jag.

And took off to see the twins.

Undetermined States

No phone reception, not even one bar, not even enough of a signal to send a text.

Since the sun has dipped below the tree line, I click on the porch light and take a seat on the swing that overlooks the sweeping valley of tall, long-shadowed Douglas firs to wait for Charlene. The main research building lies somewhere across campus on the border of these trees.

After taking a little time to study the map Serenity had given us of the grounds, I scan the chapter on quantum entanglement that I read yesterday, jotting a few notes so I can summarize it for Charlene.

When I look up, I see that all the light has drained from the forest, and I can feel a growing twitch of excitement about our little foray into the research center. However, despite my anticipation, I can also feel myself getting uneasy about the thought of entering, even for a few moments, the Faraday cage.

When Charlene joins me on the porch, she has changed clothes but is still toweling off her hair.

She gestures toward the book I'm holding. "Learn anything new?"

"A couple things, yeah. I'll tell you on the way."

"I've been wondering . . . You don't think there'll be security?"

"It's possible. We'll use the back entrance on the lower level, the one by the woods. According to the info Fionna pulled up last week, it should be clear, but if we see any guards or security cameras, we'll bail."

I take the key card that I'd lifted from the front desk, a flashlight, and my friendly neighborhood lock-pick set just in case I'll need it, secretly hoping that I will. After all these years of practice, I can get through most locks in less than fifteen seconds. Most handcuffs in less than nine. It's a private game I play—always going for the record.

Charlene grabs the RF jammer and heart rate monitor and we leave for the research facility.

Glenn came to the edge of the property. He'd been prudent with the use of his flashlight and was confident no one had seen him moving through the forest.

There was no fence to scale, so after getting his bearings, he turned his flashlight off, quietly walked through a dark channel in the woods, and emerged on one of the walking trails that led down the mountain toward the main campus.

The night is cool and damp, a mountain night.

With the cloud cover, there's no moonlight, no stars to guide us. However, pools of hazy light escape from the windows of some of the buildings, and there are enough outdoor lamps mounted on the posts that parallel the walking paths for us to easily follow the meandering trail.

Charlene is close beside me, and I summarize the information I'd read at the cabin about the basics of quantum theory. "According to the Copenhagen interpretation, without measurement—that is, observation—a quantum system remains in an undetermined state of existence."

"An undetermined state of existence . . ." She mulls that over. "So, you're saying that reality isn't determined yet, so—what? Objective reality doesn't exist?"

"Quantum physicists would say that's right, at least not in the way we normally think of it. Unobserved reality exists, just in a fuzzy state of flux that they call a state of quantum uncertainty."

"A fuzzy state of flux?"

"Well, yes, but they say 'quantum uncertainty.' Sounds more scientific. Anyway, it doesn't stop there. The Copenhagen interpretation also states that upon observation, the quantum system collapses. In other words, it's forced into becoming one of its possible states—which basically refers to how it manifests itself. It's a little confusing."

"But how does it know which state to manifest into?"

"The intentions and expectations of the observer determine it."

While she chews on that, I mentally review the map of the grounds. There are more than two dozen buildings, including cabins, a retreat building, conference and dining facilities, a prayer garden, and a meditation chalet. It seems that whoever designed this place did his best to include everything a New Age devotee could want. One-stop shopping for spiritual seekers.

And of course, there was the research facility on the west side of the campus, the one founded by Thomas Lawson and now run by Dr. Tanbyrn.

The one we were heading to.

We pass the prayer garden and Charlene rubs her chin. "We're talking about subatomic particles, though, right? So how can a photon know the thoughts or intentions of the scientist observing it?"

"That's a good question. Physicists don't really have an answer to that."

"So, according to quantum physics, reality as we know it doesn't exist, and somehow subatomic particles can figure out when you're looking at them and form into what you anticipate you're going to see."

"Pretty much."

"And no one knows why or how any of this works."

"Exactly."

"Science sure has come a long way since Democritus."

Her hint of sarcasm isn't lost on me. Actually, I'm on the same page. "And here's something else: if you don't know where a particle is, you need to understand that it could be in any of its possible states or locations and treat it that way."

"Okay."

We come to a looming stand of trees, dark pillars on the fringe of light from one of the ornate streetlights sporadically positioned along the path.

"But," I go on, "you have to treat the particle as if it's in every one of those—at the same time."

"But it's not."

"It might be. Actually, it is."

"You're confusing me."

"Welcome to the club. And then you've got time and gravity and they basically muck everything up. With quantum states, there really is no past, present, or future. Physicists can't understand why we're not able to remember the future."

"Are you serious?"

"Yeah, and if you use quantum mechanics to do the calculations, gravity shouldn't exist in the weak state that it does."

"How's gravity weak?"

I pick up a stick. "See? Gravity should hold this down. I'm able to overcome the gravitational force of the entire planet."

"Huh. I never thought of it like that."

"Gravity is the least understood force in nature and seems to be incompatible with quantum measurement, which has really bugged scientists for the last eighty years. And that brings us to superstring theory and the search for the grand unified theory—"

"Okay, okay." She's beginning to sound exasperated. "But what does any of this have to do with the research they're doing here?"

"Well, from what I can tell, it's related to how particles act when you separate them. They're somehow connected, or entangled, in a way physicists can't really explain."

"Surprise, surprise."

"Right, well, if you split a particle and do something to one of the halves—say, change the orientation of an electron—the other half will instantaneously respond the same way."

A pause. "Go on."

"And they do this even if they're in different parts of the laboratory, or the planet, or the universe."

"That doesn't even make sense."

"Not when you think in terms of three or four dimensions, but the math of quantum mechanics leads physicists to postulate that there have to be at least nine or ten dimensions, probably eleven. As well as an infinite number of parallel universes."

"Of course. Parallel universes. Why not. And why stop at a few? An infinite number is so much more reasonable."

"My thoughts exactly."

We pass the dining hall. The research facility isn't far.

Rather than have the sterile, institutional appearance of a hospital or university research center, the building is constructed of beautiful pine logs and, in the trail's lights, has the look and feel of an Alaskan lodge.

Charlene looks at me. "So if I'm hearing you right, the particles might be separated by space—could be light-years apart—but somehow they're still interconnected?"

"Physicists typically call it nonlocality, or quantum entanglement."

"And that's what the study tomorrow is about. Only this time involving people."

"It looks like it. Yes."

"To see if people who are in love are somehow entangled?"

As we continue down the path, one confound I'd only briefly considered earlier comes to mind: in these studies, the results depend on the subjects being in love, or at least having a deep emotional connection with each other, but Charlene and I were only pretending to be lovers. If there really was anything to the test, that relational dynamic would inevitably affect the results.

I contemplate how the relationship of the participants to each other could possibly alter the outcome, and decide I'll try my best tomorrow to follow the test procedures in order to find out.

We leave the trail, skirt along the edge of the woods, and meet up with the path to the lower level of the research facility's exit door.

There are no visible video surveillance cameras, but to be prudent, as we approach the door we keep our heads down, faces hidden.

The key card reader has a number pad beside it. Serenity hadn't written down a password, and I'm not sure what I'll do if there is one.

I slip the card into the reader, and thankfully, the indicator light immediately switches from red to green. I hear a soft buzz and the door clicks open.

Nice.

"Here we go," I tell Charlene.

Then, snapping on my flashlight, I lead her into the building.

Third Floor

We find ourselves in a long, windowless hallway. Apart from the soft light emitted by the exit signs at each end, the only light comes from my flashlight.

In her research, Fionna had discovered that while some of the financial contributions to the LRC came from private donors, Dr. Tanbyrn's research had received a twenty-million-dollar grant from RixoTray Pharmaceuticals for a "cooperative research initiative."

Which seemed like an awful lot of money to me for research that might end up being bogus.

When we were first exploring this project, to make her poking around legal, Fionna had managed to land a consulting job with RixoTray to test their cybersecurity.

While she was doing her research, she'd stumbled onto some connections to research into the DNA segments called telomeres (which shorten as cells split, causing aging), and the enzyme telomerase, which seems to stop that process. In fact, in one 2010 Harvard study that appeared in the scientific journal *Nature*, telomerase was shown to actually reverse the aging process in rats.

Imagine being the pharmaceutical firm that developed a drug that stopped—or even reversed—the effects of aging in humans.

The financial rewards would be astronomical.

Fionna is still working on getting through the firewalls without being detected, and that was about all she'd come up with so far—no clear connection between the telomeres research and the Lawson Center. Last I heard, she had her seventeen-year-old son, Lonnie, working on an algebraic equation to hack the IPSec VPNs (whatever those are) for an extra-credit assignment.

I sweep the beam of light ahead of us, targeting the end of the hall.

"So, the Faraday cage?" Charlene whispers.

"Yeah, let's see if it really does block out all electromagnetic signals."

"You going to be okay with that?"

I'd made a decision earlier regarding the chamber. "I don't need to go inside. You can take care of that."

"Of course."

I see that she's eyeing the line of doors to our right. "So, do you know where it is?"

"Third floor. North wing, east side, end of the hall."

She stares at me. "How do you know that?"

With my flashlight I motion for her to follow me, and we head toward the stairwell. "In the LRC brochure, there was a photo of a researcher monitoring someone who appears to be resting on a reclining chair. Right?"

"Sure. That was the sender."

"Exactly. The person who's supposed to be transmitting loving thoughts—good energy, that sort of thing."

"Be nice, dear. That's going to be your job tomorrow. I don't want any negative vibes coming from you." She thinks for a moment. "But I don't understand the significance of that picture. The guy in the photo isn't in the chamber. So how can you tell where it is?"

We reach the stairs. Start to climb to the third floor. "Beyond him is a window. You can see trees outside the glass, but neither the tree trunks nor the canopy are visible. The forest is on this building's east side. Also, based on the relatively uniform height of the forest canopy behind us, I'm guessing that the floor the chamber is on—"

"Ah, I get it. The third story."

"Yes. And from the journal articles, we know that the distance between the sender and receiver is 120 feet. I'm anticipating that the easiest way to measure the distance would be if the chamber were on the same floor as the sender's room. Also, as we approached the building, I saw windows uniformly placed on the west side of the wing, but the room with the Faraday cage wouldn't have any. So, based on all those factors, including the length of the hall, the chamber will be located on the third floor, north wing, east side, at the far end of the hallway."

At the top of the stairs Charlene pauses. "There were blueprints in the material Fionna sent you, weren't there, Sherlock?"

I clear my throat slightly. "Come on. It's down here to the left."

Glenn arrived at the building, picked the lock of the first floor's exit door, and stepped inside.

Now to find the computer with the files.

Knife in one hand, flashlight in the other, he started down the hallway.

As Cyrus and Riah swung into a gas station on the way to Bridgeport, Riah couldn't help but wonder about this meeting with the twins. As the lead researcher on the team, she should have been notified that they were back in town.

After all, she was the one looking at ways of recording and electrically stimulating neural activity in the brain's language recognition center—in the Wernicke's area of the temporal lobe. Before a person speaks, neural signals command the body to produce those vocal sounds. She was the one searching for ways to decipher the signals and correlate them to specific linguistic patterns.

So. Questions.

Why hadn't she been told?

Why was Cyrus meeting with them after hours at the R&D complex?

And what was that phone conversation of his about: "We have a man in the area . . . He's good, he'll take care of everything . . . By tomorrow afternoon it won't be a problem"?

She had the sense that something dealing with the research had gone unexpectedly wrong.

Or maybe something has gone unexpectedly right.

Cyrus guided the Jag back onto the highway,

and she took note of her boss's demeanor. Over the last four months she'd grown good at reading him, and though he always looked focused, intense, now she thought he looked a bit ill at ease. Nervous? Possibly. But something else too.

Afraid?

Hard to say.

She would watch him closely, note his reaction when they met up with the twins at the R&D facility, and see what that might tell her about what was going on.

The Faraday Cage

The door to the room containing the Faraday cage, or anechoic chamber, is not locked, and the hinge gives a faint squeak as we enter.

The soundproof chamber sits in the middle of the room and looks like a giant walk-in freezer, but of course it wasn't designed to insulate food or regulate temperature. Rather, the metal walls were constructed to stop all electromagnetic signals from entering. There's no way of communicating with a person once he or she is sealed inside.

After all, if you were able to send radio signals into the chamber, faking a test like this would be easy. It was one of the oldest tricks in the book for televangelists or psychic healers who claimed to hear voices from "on high" or "the great beyond."

Simply have the "evangelist" wear a tiny earpiece radio receiver. A cohort reviews people's application forms and transmits to the guy the names and ailments of people in the audience. Then he "miraculously" calls folks out by name and announces that God has told him their disease or disability, and while everyone in attendance is in awe of his abilities, he "heals" the person.

True, those with enough faith might actually be helped simply because of the placebo effect, but most people wouldn't be healed at all. And then of course, the blame gets shifted back onto them: "God wanted to heal you, but you didn't have enough faith. I'm sorry. You just need to believe more."

Then comes the offering time for "gifts to the ministry."

A very slick racket.

Charlene opens the chamber door, and my thoughts cycle back to where I am now, here inside the research building.

I peer into the chamber. Someone has made an effort to try and make it look homey. Crammed inside are a reclining chair, a small end table with a stack of spirituality books, and a countertop with instruments to monitor the participant's heart rate, respiration, and galvanic skin response. A floor lamp sits nearby. But the feeble attempt at interior design doesn't do much to soften the impersonal atmosphere of the chamber's stark, copper interior.

During the test, only air will be fed into the chamber.

That's it.

A video camera hangs surreptitiously in the corner of the chamber.

Hmm . . . *That carries digital signals to the room with the sender. Is that how they do it? Somehow use the video cable?*

I notice a release mechanism on the inside of the door and realize that even if the door were latched shut, even if I were trapped inside, I would easily be able to escape—even without having to get out of cuffs or a straitjacket first.

Still, the idea of being in a closed space like this brings to mind my wife and sons drowning in our minivan, and I immediately feel my breathing tighten, my heart tense. I turn from the chamber and set up the equipment Xavier gave me at the rest stop.

I don't let Charlene see me trying to calm my breathing.

She closes herself inside the chamber, and we test the RF jammer to make sure that if Dr. Tanbyrn's team does try to send any signal other than the video feed into or out of the chamber, it'll be blocked.

Nothing gets through.

I take some time to check different frequencies and settings to make sure that Charlene will truly be isolated from all means of communication tomorrow during the test. There's no Wi-Fi in the building, perhaps for some sort of security reasons, and none of our mobile devices get through the walls of the chamber.

There are still lots of ways they might be faking the studies, but I feel confident that at least we won't be dealing with radio interference or frequency tampering.

In addition, the heart rate monitor Xavier gave us—the one Charlene will secretly wear to make sure that the center's findings actually match ours—is working and undetectable outside the chamber.

As we're finishing up the tests, she proposes that we place the RF jammer beneath the chair cushion so it'll be in place for tomorrow's test, but I don't want to take any chance it'll be discovered or removed before the test begins. "Palm it," I tell her, "and then place it when the research assistant turns her back." Over the years I've spent hundreds of hours rehearsing magic routines with Charlene, and although she isn't quite as good at sleight of hand as I am, she can certainly hold her own.

"Okay."

Thinking about the chair, I look for any ways of running low-voltage current through metallic threads to trigger the test subject's physiological responses, but find nothing. Charlene agrees to check it tomorrow again before the test.

We're gathering our things when I hear foot-steps in the hall.

Charlene and I freeze.

I click off my light.

A flashlight beam dances across the crack at the bottom of the doorway.

Okay, maybe they do have security guards here after all.

"Into the chamber," Charlene whispers, but I shake my head.

The intensity of the light skimming beneath the door is getting stronger. The person is definitely coming our way.

"We have to." Her voice is urgent. "Now."

She's right and I know it. There's nowhere else to hide. I take a deep breath and step into the Faraday cage with her. I try to tell myself that I'm really still simply in the room, not in an enclosed metal cube, but it doesn't work.

She swings the door nearly all the way closed so that no one would be able to see us—as long as they don't decide to open the door and have a peek inside.

Probably for my sake she leaves it open just a couple inches.

But already I can feel the walls pressing in on me. I shut my eyes and try to relax, yet imme-diately I feel like I'm no longer in the chamber but in the minivan with my family. It's filling with water and there's no way out. The doors won't open—I try them, the water is rising, the boys are begging me to—

The hallway door creaks open.

I open my eyes.

Through the crack in the chamber door, I see the flashlight beam cut through the thick blackness of the room. A person enters, and the abrupt heaviness of the footsteps leads me to think it's a man. Possibly quite large. He sweeps the beam through the room, and it slices momentarily into the crack of the chamber's slightly open door.

Charlene and I edge backward. Thankfully, the footsteps don't approach us but rather head toward the computer desk positioned against the south wall.

As the man passes by, it's hard to see what he's wearing, but it appears to be all black. No insignia, no uniform. So, not a security guard, not a custodian. I half-expect a ski mask, and though I catch only the briefest glimpse of his face, I can see that it's not covered. He's Caucasian. That's all I can tell.

My heart is racing; it feels like a meaty fist opening and closing inside my chest, but I realize that the nervousness is just as much from being in the chamber as it is from the presence of the intruder.

The office chair at the workstation by the wall turns, and a moment later the bluish light of the computer screen glows on, faintly illuminating the room.

Though I want to focus on this man and what he might be doing, my curiosity is overshadowed by my strangled breathing from being inside the chamber.

I lean closer, edge the door open slightly, then draw in a breath of air from the thin opening leading to the room. It seems to help.

From this angle I can't see what might be on the screen, but I do see that the man has placed a combat knife with a long, wicked blade beside the keyboard, and I find myself thinking of how I might defend Charlene if things turn ugly, if the man opens the chamber door. She's a tough and independent woman, in great shape from lap swimming and yoga, but she's slim and small-boned and she's not a fighter.

I've been taking TaeKwonDo for three years, but I'm only a brown belt. Besides, I'm weapon-less; he has a knife and a big size advantage. Still, I've spent a lot of time sparring and I can take care of myself pretty well in a fight.

However, I've never fought an armed assailant.

And I've never sparred in a space this small.

Though mostly shadowed, the look on Charlene's face tells me that she has noticed the knife as well. She is fingering the cross she wears around her neck.

I rest my hand on her shoulder to try to reassure

her, to tell her without words that things are going to be okay.

A tiny nod, then her hand goes on top of mine.

The intruder types for a few moments. The color of the monitor's glow changes, becomes brighter and white, and I guess that he has moved past the desktop to some specific program or file.

As the moments pass I'm caught up again thinking about the tight quarters, and I don't know how long I can stand being in here.

Based on what I've seen, people who've never experienced claustrophobia have no idea how desperate and frantic it makes you feel, when—

It's all about your breathing.

Calm. Stay calm.

I breathe, yes, I do, but it's not calm breathing at all.

Trying to distract myself, I think of the escapes I've done, all the closed-in spaces I've been in and how I've survived them—sealed tanks filled with icy water, the coffin I was buried alive in for two days, the controversial million-dollar bet I accepted from a TV psychic I'd debunked. He challenged me to an escape even I couldn't have come up with on my own: I was put in a strait-jacket, locked in a trunk with a parachute beside me, then dropped from a plane at 22,000 feet.

To give the chute enough time to open, I only had ninety-one seconds to get out of the strait-jacket, strapped into the chute, and out of the trunk. It hadn't seemed like such a bad idea at the time, but free-falling made it a lot harder to get out of the jacket than I expected, and then when I popped open the trunk, I didn't quite have the chute buckled and almost lost hold of it.

But I made it down safely and took home the million dollars.

And I had to admit that the adrenaline rush was something else.

You did that, you can at least stand being in here for a few more minutes.

But then the chair squeaks, alerting me again to where I am, and I see the saber of light from the flashlight swing around the room.

Toward the chamber.

The man's footsteps follow it.

My heart is beating.

Beating.

I grip my flashlight, which really is too small to serve as much of a weapon. "Get back," I tell Charlene softly. She steps backward.

The man aims his light at the crack.

And then the door to the Faraday cage flies open.

Blood

It happens all at once, in a swirl of light and shadow and movement, blurred and swift.

I flick on my flashlight and shine it into the eyes of whoever opened the door, hoping to momentarily blind him, perhaps give us a chance to push past him and escape, but he's quick and knocks it away. The flashlight goes spinning around the chamber, clattering to the floor.

Whipping, twisting shafts of light.

Dizzying in the darkness.

Directing his own flashlight into my eyes, he slashes the knife toward me, and as I avoid the blade he swipes it at Charlene.

She jerks backward but is too slow, and the knife slices through the sleeve of her shirt.

She gasps.

I see blood. The cut is deep. It's in her left forearm.

I go at the man, who's now in the chamber with us, and instinct and three years of TaeKwonDo sparring take over. I use an inner forearm block to knock his knife hand to the side. Then, despite the close quarters, I'm able to land a fierce front kick to his thigh. I aim a punch at his throat, but he's able to partially block it.

He feints at me, then swishes the blade in a figure-eight pattern in the air.

But he's holding the knife in his right hand, which is good for me because I'm on his right side. I avoid the blade, almost manage to trap his wrist. He expertly flips the knife around and raises it to bring it down toward my chest.

An ice-pick grip.

Bad idea.

I step forward, wrists crossed, and snap them up against his forearm to keep him from bringing the knife down, then I move toward him as I twist my right hand, grasp his wrist, and swing the knife he's still holding down, fast and hard, toward his leg.

The blade must be sharp, because it goes in smooth and quick and deep, not to the hilt, but far enough to do some serious damage.

Amazingly, he doesn't back off, only lets out a small grunt of pain. He holds his ground, levels his flashlight at me, and with the other hand grabs the hilt of the knife and pries the blade, dripping wet with his blood, out of his thigh. "Do not move." A coarse, low whisper.

This guy is either unbelievably tough or on drugs, or somehow the adrenaline was blocking the pain, because his voice remains slow and measured.

Still I cannot see his face.

My arm is hidden in shadows, and I pocket the item I took from him when I brushed my hand across his arm. Sleight of hand. I did it without even thinking. My heart is churning, my breathing fast. He didn't see. He didn't notice.

My TaeKwonDo instructor's words flash through my mind: "A tense muscle is a weak muscle."

I know that from my escapes as well.

Relax. Relax.

But I can't seem to. Charlene is here and this guy just cut her and I wasn't about to let him get close to her again. My fists are tight, my stance ready, my muscles tense and flexed. It's not ideal, but it's not an easy time for a tai chi state of mind.

I could make a move, but if something happened to me, I couldn't imagine what he would do to Charlene.

I edge in front of her.

Relax.

Relax and respond.

A wire-tight silence stretches through the air.

He backs up a little, but Charlene and I are still trapped in the chamber. She's pressing her right hand against the wound to stop the bleeding.

I'm about to ask if she's okay, but before I can the man speaks, keeping his voice in the gravelly whisper. "Who are you?" I say nothing. He swings his light toward my face. "Tell me who you are and who sent you."

I blink against the brightness. Don't reply.

"You tell me"—now his voice is ice—"or I will kill you both. Right where you stand. Do you understand me? Who sent you?"

He might have more weapons, a gun.

Based on the size and type of the knife he brought with him, I take the guy seriously. I search for what to say.

Think, Jevin, think—

"Who sent you?" He tightens his grip on the knife and tilts the blade first toward me, then toward Charlene.

I have an idea, go with my gut.

"RixoTray," I tell him. "To verify everything."

He keeps his flashlight directed at us. "RixoTray," he repeats softly, but it doesn't sound like a question and he doesn't ask me to elaborate.

Okay, don't let him ask a following question. Please don't let him ask a follow-up question.

All I can think of is helping Charlene. I don't want to fight this man, but in a rush of emotion I find myself wondering how far I would go to defend her if he came at us again. Would I die for her? Would I be able to kill for her?

Yes to the first. I wasn't sure about the second.

And thankfully, I don't have to answer it, because finally, without another word, our attacker backs slowly through the room and disappears out the door to the hallway.

I hurry to Charlene's side. "Are you alright?"

She's still holding her hand against her wounded arm. Her sleeve is soaked in blood.

"I'm fine."

"Let me see."

"No, Jevin. It's okay."

I lay my hand softly on her shoulder. "Charlene. Let me see."

Gingerly, she lifts her hand, revealing a dark, bleeding gash over four inches long, visible through the slit fabric.

Not good.

She quickly puts her hand back on her arm.

"Here." I take off my belt, wrap it around her arm, and carefully cinch it off, not as a tourniquet, but snug enough to serve as a pressure bandage, to slow the bleeding. "We need to get you to a hospital; you're going to need stitches."

"We have that test tomorrow."

"That doesn't matter."

"Jev, a man just tried to kill us. This is no longer just about some kind of ESP test. We need to find out what else is going on here, and we're not going to be able to do that from a hospital room. I'll be okay, we'll just bandage it up. I saw a first-aid kit in the bathroom at the cabin."

She knew first aid, had to, working as my assistant. CPR too. She was the one who'd brought me back after the water escapes I didn't quite succeed at. I figure she should be able to evaluate how serious the cut is.

But still—

Argue with her later. Just get her out of here.

"Okay, come on." I help her to her feet.

"You stepped in front of me, Jevin. I saw that. Thank you."

"Sure."

"Where did all that come from, by the way?"

"All what?"

"Those moves. How you swung the knife down into his leg? I've never seen you do anything like that before."

I've never had to.

"I guess those Bruce Lee movies are paying off."

"I guess they are."

Gently, I lead her out of the chamber and into the room. I'm not certain if she needs me to or not, but I support her with one hand under her armpit. She doesn't pull away.

Before we head to the hallway, she insists that we check the computer to see what the guy might've been accessing. "Go on. I'll be okay."

Though I want to keep moving, I tap the keyboard and wake up the screen, only to find that the computer is password protected. As Fionna had pointed out to me more than once, you *hack* a site, you *hash* a password. I had no doubt she could hash this one in seconds, but it might take me hours.

Obviously there was no time for that.

Did the guy hash it, or did he already know the password?

It was impossible to know.

"Let's get out of here, Charlene. Get back to the cabin and take care of that arm."

"Yeah. Okay."

A voice in my head: *That guy might not have been alone. Watch out in the hall.* Edging open the door, I tip the light quickly in both directions. After making sure the coast is clear, we head in the opposite direction from the spotty blood trail our assailant left behind.

Unfortunately, even though Charlene has her wound covered, we leave our own sporadic trail of blood as we go, and I wonder what kind of suspicions it might raise in the minds of whoever would be cleaning this floor tomorrow, but—

She whispers to me, "What made you think to say RixoTray when he asked you who sent us?"

"Follow the money." We reach the stairwell, cautiously start down the steps. "Where there's a twenty-million-dollar investment, there's a lot at stake. Behind every dollar sign there's an agenda. RixoTray has a dog in the hunt, and I took a stab that our guy would know that."

"A stab."

"Bad choice of words."

Obviously, Charlene knew that our shows in Las Vegas and Atlantic City were by no means financial failures and money wasn't a big concern for me. Over the years I've made some sizable investments, and I always keep an eye on them. After all, unless your income is in the stratosphere, you don't throw millions of dollars, or in this case, tens of millions, into a project and then fail to monitor its performance—even if that means doing so in unorthodox ways.

We reach the lower level, the other end of the hall from where we first entered.

"But Jev"—she's been thinking about what I said—"it's just as likely that he was sent by a competitor to find out what the research was about. In fact, that might even be more likely."

Hmm. "True. Come to think of it, all he did was repeat 'RixoTray' when I told him they'd sent us. He could've just been muttering that because it gave him information he didn't already have."

"Exactly."

Near the exit I see a small waiting area with six chairs and an end table just outside a door with Dr. Tanbyrn's name on it. We quietly leave the building and pick our way through the woods until we reconnect with the trail that leads toward our cabin.

I'm worried about her arm, about nerve damage, but I'm also thinking about our assailant, wondering who he might've been, what he was looking for.

And why he'd brought a knife like that along with him into the building.

Wound for Wound

Riah and Cyrus finished passing through the last of the three security checkpoints to RixoTray's R&D facility.

An ultramodern fortress of steel and glass, the building was surrounded by razor-wire fence, a myriad of electric sensors, even a fifteen-foot-deep moat that was made to look like an innocuous, landscaped stream.

This was where RixoTray researched the effects of its experimental drugs and developed new strategies for pushing out pharmaceutical products faster than their competitors. It was here where their biggest secrets were kept, here where they coordinated placebo tests for their drug trials, and here where they were close to a breakthrough in developing a commercially available telomerase enzyme to reverse the effects of aging.

In this building, tens of billions of dollars could be generated by a single discovery or lost by a single miscalculation.

Cyrus strode beside Riah through the main corridor on the east wing. The hallway was high-ceilinged and bright, with pictures of scientists and plaques of patents decorating the walls. The conference area they were heading toward was at the end of the hall, next to the renovated research rooms that served as a two-bedroom office apartment for the twins when they were in town.

It was just down the hall from Riah's lab. She was involved with electrical brain stimulation, specifically deep-brain stimulation (DBS), which had most often been used for treating people with Parkinson's disease, although it had also been used to help people manage obsessive-compulsive disorder, depression, and even the symptoms of epilepsy and Alzheimer's.

Primarily she used an EEG to scan specific areas of the brain involved in speech production, then, by identifying the sounds or syllables those brain waves represented, she was working toward translating those signals into actual audible messages.

A pair of guards stood sentry at the terminus of the hallway.

"We're here to see Daniel and Darren," Cyrus told them.

The broad-shouldered, shorter man nodded. He tapped his fingers subconsciously together, which Riah took to be a sign of nervousness. She wasn't surprised. When people close to the project found out what the twins had done, uneasiness was the natural reaction. Especially if you were going to be alone in a room with them. "Okay, sir. Yes. I'll get them."

He left, and as she and Cyrus waited for the twins to arrive, she found herself reviewing what she knew about them.

The best way to describe the two brothers was that they were practitioners of death—apparently two of the most effective ones the Army's Delta Force had ever trained.

As identical twins, Daniel and Darren shared something fundamental that so many twins share—the ability to communicate on a seemingly subconscious level in ways that defy typical categorizations. Of course, since she was the principal investigator on the team, part of Riah's job was to find out what those ways were.

According to the information she was privy to, the twins had been born to a teenage girl who'd been raped and decided to give her sons up for adoption rather than abort them.

Because of a clerical error, Daniel and Darren were separated at birth, adopted by different families, and raised separately in New Jersey and South Carolina, respectively. They never met until they were in their twenties, yet the similarities between their lives were striking.

They both lettered in soccer and wrestling in high school, both had girlfriends named Julie with whom they had their first sexual encounter, both tinkered with cars in their spare time, both worked in fast-food restaurants—not unusual for teenage guys, but both were fired for spitting on the hamburger bun of a female patron. Who was wearing a blue dress.

Yes, a blue dress.

The stories were astonishing, and when Riah first heard them, she'd thought they were manufactured to create a sense of awe or amazement at the two men. Or even that they were simply an honest mistake, an inadvertent misrepresentation of the facts, but after reading more identical twin studies—some dating back to the nineteenth century—she'd found herself believing the seeming inscrutable coincidences between Darren's and Daniel's lives. In truth, the similarities weren't nearly as incomprehensible as many of those found in the rest of the literature.

Both Daniel and Darren joined the Army.

Which is where they met.

A colonel visiting Fort Bragg saw Darren at the shooting range and mistook him for a soldier he'd seen the previous day at Fort Benning. After some inquiries and a bit of deciphering, Colonel Derek Byrne made the serendipitous connection. Some people might call it chance. Or fate. Or coincidence. Cyrus once told Riah it had to do with quantum entanglement, but whatever the reason, the colonel was able to reunite the two brothers.

They both made it onto the Delta Force and eventually moved into the United States Army Intelligence and Security Command.

Some people think that the CIA is responsible for the majority of the United States' political assassinations carried out abroad, but over the last few months, Riah had found out that those people are wrong.

After a little research of her own and some frank and astonishingly forthcoming conversations with the twins, she'd learned that the military's covert operatives were happy to work in the shadow of the CIA and let the spooks take the brunt of the media's scrutiny and Hollywood's ever-watchful eye.

Daniel once mentioned to Riah that he and his brother had "found their niche" in their new line of work. She could see that they were patriots through and through, and could only guess that they did as they were told by their supervisors without question, without reservation, without hesitation.

A month ago, out of curiosity, she'd asked Darren straight-out how many people he and his brother had killed. "None," he'd told her evenly. "But we have eliminated certain targets when necessary."

Riah knew this differentiation between "targets" and "people" was a psychological ploy used by the military to make it easier for soldiers to kill—depersonalize the enemy by calling them *combatants* or *targets* rather than allowing the soldiers to think of them as fellow human beings, as fathers and brothers and sons, as mothers and sisters and wives.

When Darren used the word *target,* however, it'd struck her that the difference in terminology wouldn't have affected her if she had their job.

Actually, as troubling as it might be, she realized that given the right circumstances, she would have found it relatively easy to kill, no matter what anyone called the victim.

Just like the bird when you were a kid. Grab the head. Twist.

And it goes still.

Limp and still.

She remembered that Darren had studied her face carefully as he waited for her to respond.

She didn't want the brothers to realize that she was like them in certain fundamental ways, so she hadn't pursued the matter any further. However, she'd gotten the sense that Darren saw something in her eyes that'd given away more than it should have.

Now in the conference area, Cyrus looked at his watch. "They're late."

"I'm sure there's a good reason," she told him softly. "They're very reliable men."

Back at the cabin, Charlene still refuses to let me take her to a hospital, so in the end I'm left to simply do what I can to cleanse and disinfect the wound with the rather ill-equipped first-aid kit in the bathroom.

Throughout the process, she gives me instructions, wincing at times but not crying, and I'm impressed by how well she's handling it. We're both rattled from the attack, of course, but surprisingly, still focused.

Finally, I butterfly the wound closed with alternating strips of tape and wrap her arm with the first-aid kit's Ace bandage.

She digs out some Advil, and after she's taken a couple capsules, she positions herself on the couch, then states the obvious: "Alright. Just so we're on the same page, we're no longer here just to debunk some research on mind-to-mind communication."

"Agreed."

"Should we go to the police?"

It was a good question, one we shouldn't take lightly. "Did you see his face?"

"No."

"Me either." I join her on the other end of the couch.

Honestly, I want to stay here at the center, keep looking into things, especially now that there seems to be another layer to everything that's going on. "So we wouldn't be able to identify him by anything other than his voice. Would you be able to do that?"

"Not the way he spoke, whispering like that."

"The same for me."

"So we could report it to the police, but they would, of course, ask what we were doing in the building."

I evaluate everything. "I think we should hold off contacting them until we know more."

"So you don't think we should back away from this?"

I have the feeling she already knows the answer to that.

I've never been one to back away from a challenge, and I can't see myself doing so now— even if it ends up being a little dangerous. It isn't about money or fame or anything like that. It's about the challenge. And about uncovering the truth. "No. I'm in."

"And you know me, Jevin."

"Petunia never backs down."

"Wolverine."

"Whatever."

To cover all my bases, I offer one last time to help her: "I still think we should take you to a clinic or something."

"Jev, think about the timing here: a thug with a combat knife shows up, sneaking around looking for some sort of computer files the night before this round of Tanbyrn's study begins. That has to be more than a coincidence."

"But it was a coincidence that we ended up in the same room as him in a locked building, wouldn't you say?"

"Maybe it was more than that."

"What do you mean?"

She sighs. "I don't know. I'm just saying we need to find out as much as we can about Tanbyrn's research and what that guy might've been looking for. Being part of the study tomorrow is our best shot at doing that."

Of course, I feel the same way. Fighting that guy had awakened something in me that imitating the tricks of psychics never had—a taste of danger that I used to know when I was doing my escapes. A surge of adrenaline, the paradoxical tightening of focus and widening of awareness that danger brings with it. There was a time when I wouldn't do an escape unless there was a chance I could die from it—something that I know was always hard on Rachel.

I contemplate what to say.

"Alright. So we keep an eye on your arm, but after the test tomorrow, I want to have someone who knows what he's doing take a look at that cut. Within the next twenty-four hours. Deal?"

She's a little reluctant but finally agrees. "Deal." Then she leans forward. "So, who do you think he was?"

"Honestly, I have no idea, but based on what I saw, I'd say he's not specifically trained in knife fighting, more of a street fighter."

"The grip he used?"

Nicely done.

I nod. "Yes, too easy for me to deflect. It wasn't one a pro would choose. So I'm guessing his background isn't in law enforcement or military. He learned to fight the hard way."

"By actually fighting."

Or killing.

"Probably. Yes." I stand. Pace. Take the 1895 Morgan Dollar from my pocket and flip it quickly through my fingers. Habit. Helps me think. "We really need to find a way to reach Fionna or Xavier. I want to know what files that guy might've wanted from that computer."

"Go outside. See if you can get a signal."

"It's no use. I tried earlier."

"Try down by the road, where we parked the car. It's more in the clear down there." I don't want to leave her alone, and I think she can sense my hesitation because she adds, "Go on. I'll be okay. Just lock the door behind you."

I glance at her forearm one last time, and when she folds her arms, apparently to show me that she's fine, I finally agree. "Okay. I'll be back in a few minutes. The light switch for the exterior porch lights is just inside the front doorway. I'll keep an eye on the cabin. If anything comes up, anything at all, flick the porch light on and off a couple times. I'll be watching; I'll get back here right away."

Taking both my phone and hers so I can try each of them, I leave the cabin, lock the door behind me, and head to the parking lot.

Glenn limped up to his car.

He was not happy.

If what the guy in the chamber had said was

true—that RixoTray had sent him and the woman—then there was an awful lot his contact was not telling him, and Glenn did not take well to having his employers keep things from him.

He opened the car door and tried to slide in without wrenching his leg but found it impossible. A flare of pain shot through him.

He cursed. Thought of what happened in that chamber.

In prison he'd learned to trust his instincts, and as it turned out, tonight they were right, because just before the fight he'd had a feeling, nothing more, that someone was watching him. That was what had caused him to turn from the computer and open the door to the chamber.

But then the guy inside had flashed his light in his eyes and Glenn was forced to defend himself.

Why would RixoTray have sent those two?

Unless they hadn't.

Unless the guy was lying.

With a great deal of pain, Glenn was able to position himself in the driver's seat. He started the engine.

Thankfully, the blade hadn't pierced an artery.

He knew enough about anatomy to know that if it had, he would already be dead.

Quietly, slowly, he guided the car onto the road.

He used his right hand to press down on the knee of his injured leg to keep from flexing the thigh muscles as he accelerated.

The trek back to the car had been brutal, pain rocketing up his leg with every step, no matter how hard he tried to keep pressure off it. But he'd dealt with it just like he'd dealt with things when he was locked up and took a shiv to the stomach and still managed to dig it out and slice out the eyes and cut off the ears of the block-mate who'd tried to kill him.

Glenn headed down the mountain road.

Whoever had been in that chamber had been quick. Strong. Had known how to fight.

But who was he? Who was the woman?

What were they doing there?

RixoTray Pharmaceuticals?

It could have been a lie, but it was a place to start.

Glenn prided himself on being self-controlled, on viewing things objectively, but as he drove back to the motel to take care of the leg, he felt fire rise inside of him.

He was a person who kept his word, so, yes, he would take care of the old man tomorrow afternoon at three like he'd been hired to do. But he wasn't going to stop there. He would find that guy from the chamber and return the favor, wound for wound, as the Bible put it in Exodus 21:25.

An eye for an eye.

Or in this case, a stab for a stab.

God's kind of justice.

Or at least Glenn's kind.

He found himself planning how things would go down: incapacitate the guy, cuff him, and then make him watch as he played with the woman for a while. At last, when he was done with her, stab him in the thigh—and if the blade just so happened to slice through his femoral artery, well, justice in real life didn't always have to stick to the letter of the law.

So, the plan for tonight: take enough OxyContin to kill the pain in his leg—God knows he had plenty of it on hand—then in the morning call his contact to identify the two people who'd been in that room. Tomorrow, after he'd completed his paying gig, he would deal with them.

He glanced at his wrist to check the time.

But noticed that his watch was missing.

He let out a round of curses. It must have fallen off during the fight in the chamber.

The Twins

I have the assailant's watch in my pocket.

I'd happened to lift it when I slid my hand across his wrist just before I shoved the blade of his knife into his thigh.

Truthfully, removing the watch was pure instinct from all my years of sleight of hand and street magic, not something I'd consciously planned. During the fight, the last thing I was thinking was how I might remove the guy's wristwatch, but in any case I have it now, and it might serve as some small clue that could lead us to identifying who our assailant was.

After trying unsuccessfully to reach Fionna or Xavier, I pause beneath one of the path's lights. Holding the watch in my shirt to keep from getting any more of my fingerprints on it, I carefully study it.

It's a Reactor Poseidon Limited Edition. Very nice. In my line of work you get to know watches, and even though Reactor is a small company, their watches are amazing. This one won't even get scratched if you shoot it with a bullet. I couldn't help but think that a regular street thug would have sold a watch like this for cash if he knew how much it was worth. So the guy we were dealing with might very well be better trained, more of a pro, than I'd earlier assumed.

The watch is relatively new. No engravings. No unique identifying marks, which isn't exactly surprising considering the craftsmanship and the durability of the materials.

Who knows, Xavier is into CSI kinds of things and would probably jump at the chance to dust the watch for prints. I could get it to him as soon as we meet up again, tomorrow sometime.

Inside the cabin I find Charlene at the table, flipping through the notes we'd used to prepare for this project. "Any luck?"

"No." I show her the watch, and we discuss it but can't come up with any other clues, and in the end I stow it in the bedroom and return to her.

I point to the RixoTray research documents that she'd spread out around her when I was outside. "What about you? Did you find anything?"

"Nothing related to quantum entanglement or mind-to-mind communication research. But they are doing research on the temporal lobe—the language-recognition capabilities of the Wernicke's area—by using an EEG to record brain images and identify thought patterns that relate to linguistic communication. It's similar in a way to helping paralyzed people communicate by identifying their neural responses to questions."

"Interesting."

"Once you know which parts of the brain control which parts of your physiology, you can send electrical currents to those areas to elicit a physical response. Scientists have been experimenting on helping paralyzed people move their limbs, blind people see variations in light, insomniacs sleep, obese people curb their hunger, and even doing work on reducing aggression in criminals. They can even cause hallucinations that patients can't tell from reality and reduce or eliminate intractable pain."

She goes on, "Researchers at a number of universities have implanted electrodes into monkeys' brains and then trained the primates to move robotic arms. At least four computer gaming companies are developing EEG-controlled games in which the games respond—"

"Let me guess—to the player's thoughts."

"Yes."

"Wow."

"Anyway, one division at RixoTray is focusing on direct brain-computer interfaces and communication. It's mentioned on a number of grant applications. A neuroscientist named Riah Colette, she's in charge of the study."

"Might be helpful to talk with her. See what the specific connection might be to what Tanbyrn's doing."

"Couldn't hurt."

We agree to follow up on that tomorrow. Then, after a little more discussion about who the attacker might've been, I can tell that Charlene's energy is fading and I realize I'm drained as well—both physically and emotionally. She goes into the bedroom to change and I grab a blanket from the bathroom closet.

When she emerges in the hallway, she's wearing a pair of sweatpants and a gray T-shirt. Nothing Victoria's Secret seductive, but it's easy enough to tell she's in good shape and I'm careful not to stare.

I hold up the blanket. "I'll take the couch."

"Really, you don't need to sleep on the couch, Jevin." Before I can respond, she catches herself and goes on quickly as if to avert any misunderstanding: "I mean, that is, there's plenty of room on the bed. I'm just saying it's okay if you want to sleep with me—next to me. Right? On the other side of the bed."

"Right."

"I'm not suggesting at all that we do anything other than sleep." She doesn't blush often, but she does now, and it's a little endearing.

"Of course."

This conversation could get awfully awkward awfully fast.

As if it hasn't already.

I have no doubt that if I climb into bed with her, even if she ends up sleeping like a baby, I'll be too distracted to sleep at all. And I know I'm definitely not ready for her to inadvertently snuggle up to me or accidentally drape her arm across my chest sometime during the night.

"The couch would be best," I tell her.

"Sure. Okay."

"Alright . . ." I search unsuccessfully to say the right thing. "So then. Good night. And . . . just be careful with that arm."

"I will."

"Don't roll on it or anything."

"I'll be careful. I promise."

I pass the blanket to my other hand. I really have no idea how to wrap up this conversation. "We'll see what it looks like in the morning. I still want to take you to the hospital."

"Noted." She smiles. "Good night, Petunia." Her tone is light, the blush is gone, the moment feels natural and familiar. She glances at the couch. "Seriously, if you can't sleep, you're welcome to the other side of the bed."

I nod. "Gotcha."

With that, she leaves for the bedroom and I drop onto the couch. It's a little short, but I usually sleep kind of scrunched up anyway and I figure I'll be alright.

As I lie down, I can't help but think of the attacker in the chamber, and I realize that what bothers me most is the fact that I wasn't able to stop him from hurting Charlene.

I promise myself that if we run into each other again, I won't make the same mistake, then I close my eyes, hoping to sleep, to clear my head, hoping that the dreams I've had so often over the course of the last year won't return.

But I'm anticipating, of course, that they will. After all, the nightmares of my children drowning while my wife sits just a few feet away and waits for them to die have been plaguing me for months.

It wouldn't be so bad if it was just a dream. But it's not. It's history.

For a while I'm caught in the time-between-times world of waking and sleeping where you wander into and out of awareness, then I'm vaguely aware of the fact that scientists don't really understand sleep, why we do it, what biological purpose it actually serves. We're never more vulnerable than when we're asleep, and if the most vulnerable members of a species die out, then natural selection should have weeded us out. From an evolutionary point of view, it makes no sense.

Never more vulnerable . . .

And then I drop away from where I am and tip into the world of my dreams.

The twins stepped into the conference room.

Gentle-looking, both of them, with an easy, measured confidence. No swagger. No posturing. Medium build. Wiry. Clean-cut. Soft-spoken.

If it wasn't for the scar snaking across Darren's left cheek, Riah wouldn't have been able to tell them apart.

She noticed that Cyrus was keeping his distance from them, and though it didn't entirely surprise her, she did find it informative.

She greeted each twin with a half-hug. Their friendship allowed for this, made it seem like the natural greeting. After all, when you've inserted nanowire electrodes up someone's artery and into his brain, it tends to engender a certain degree of trust.

Deep-brain stimulation used to be highly invasive and involved dozens or even hundreds of electrodes implanted in the brain through small burr holes drilled in the skull.

Not anymore.

Now, tiny polymer nanowire electrodes less than six hundred nanometers wide are used. Since their width is far less than that of a red blood cell, they can be inserted through an artery in the arm and guided through the vasculature up and into the brain, where they're used to deliver electric signals to stimulate the neurons in the hardest-to-reach parts of the brain.

The process had been around since 2006, but Riah had made advances that allowed for electric stimulation of the Wernicke's area, the temporal lobe's language-recognition center. She'd implanted the electrodes in the brains of the twins three weeks ago.

After a brief "How are you doing?" conversation back and forth, Cyrus cleared his throat slightly and offered Riah a smile that wasn't really a smile. "Riah, really. I think it would be best if you waited outside the room, gave us just a few minutes alone."

The words were condescending, but her feelings weren't hurt, though she had the sense that given the social context, they should have been.

Daniel and Darren watched Cyrus quietly. Before Riah could reply to him, Darren spoke up: "We trust Riah. She can stay. It's time we brought her in on the broader nature of the project."

"No." Cyrus shook his head. "I'm afraid that's—"

"Nonnegotiable," Daniel said firmly. He gestured toward his brother, who was still staring steadily at Cyrus. "We've been talking about it, my brother and I, and we were going to tell you tonight. That's one of the reasons we requested you come. She needs to know about Kabul or we don't move forward. It's time to integrate the findings from Oregon. It's the only way to make things work. As my brother said, we trust her."

Riah watched Cyrus. Having the twins contravene what you'd said like that would cause most people to squirm or backpedal or acquiesce immediately, but she could see a storm of resistance on Cyrus's face, a narrowing of his dark eyes. If he had been afraid before, he didn't appear to be so now.

It struck her that for all of his talk of trusting her, he hadn't been all that forthcoming but had been keeping things from her—that the twins were back in Pennsylvania, the nature of this visit tonight, why he wanted her to step into the hallway even though she was the head researcher on the electrical brain stimulation program.

Had he lied to her? Perhaps not lies, technically, but not the truth either.

As she thought about that, she realized that all the men she'd been with over the years, even her father when she was a little girl, had deceived her at some point, and eventually—some sooner than others—betrayed her in the most intimate ways possible.

A thought came to her, an epiphany about human nature that was both disquieting but also quite possibly the truth: *Betrayal is a facet of love.*

Could it be?

She waited for Cyrus to respond.

Could betrayal be as natural to our species as attraction is?

And another thought, almost poetic in its simplicity: *If familiarity breeds contempt, then what kind of dark children does intimacy breed?*

She was considering this when Cyrus replied to Daniel, "I'll have to clear it with Williamson."

"Yes."

"She'll be in bed by now. I'd be waking her up."

"Yes." Daniel reached into his pocket, produced his Droid. "Would you like to use my phone or yours?"

Testing Love

Tuesday, October 27

I wake up, tense, my heart clenched tight in my chest.

The residue of my dreams still circles through me. Dark and restless and unnerving.

I check my watch.

5:02 a.m.

An hour earlier than I'd planned on getting up,

but I know I won't be able to fall asleep again.

I stare at the ceiling, rub my eyes, try to forget the places my sleep took me, but the harder I try to put the images out of my mind, the clearer they become.

So I tell myself again that it was just a dream.

Only a dream.

I'm the one driving the minivan, Rachel sits beside me, and we're talking about something like the bills or getting the boys to their T-ball practice or something—it's not really clear, and of course that's the way dreams work—and then suddenly I'm not on the highway but veering off the road. Rachel gasps, "Where are you—"

I drive through the parking lot.

"Jev—"

Toward the pier.

"—Stop! You're going to—"

We fly off the pier, hit the water. The impact is jarring, and almost immediately Rachel is shouting and the boys are crying loudly, scared, terrified.

I'm the one at the wheel.

I'm the one killing my family.

We begin to sink rapidly, more rapidly than I would've thought.

It's a dream.

No it's not.

It's—

The twins are screaming and Rachel is climbing back to free them from their car seats, but I'm sitting motionless, watching the water rise inside the van. I realize that for some reason we're tilting backward and so the boys will drown first. I notice this in my dream—notice it, but do nothing.

The murky water outside the window swallows sunlight as we sink, but not enough to enshroud us completely in darkness. I can still see, I can still—

"Help me, Daddy!" It's Andrew, but I don't move, I just tell him it's going to be alright, that everything is going to be alright. Then Rachel is beside me again in the front—I don't know how, but she is; time and space have shifted and brought her here to my side because we are still in the dream.

The boys are strapped in the car seats, helpless and about to die.

Rachel doesn't threaten me or question me or accuse me but holds me close and tells me that she loves me. I say nothing, just turn around and watch the water rise over the terrified faces of our two sons.

Only then do I respond.

Only after it is too late do I scramble back, grab a breath, duck beneath the water that's pouring into the vehicle, and try to save them.

Only then.

When it is too late.

And that's when I awaken, at the same point I so often awaken when I have the dream—staring into the open, lifeless eyes of my sons with Rachel by my side. Sometimes, like tonight, she's holding my hand. Other times she's already dead, drifting motionless and bloated beside me.

Some days I wish I wouldn't wake up at all but would join my family in whatever realm of eternity they ended up in, good or bad, heaven or hell, as long as we could be together again.

But so far I haven't been that lucky.

I take a deep breath, sit up on the couch.

Exhale slowly.

The dream is fading away, but it leaves a dark thought-trail behind as it does, one that roots around inside of me and doesn't want to let me go.

Charlene, who'd studied religion in college, once told me that in Acts 14 Paul mentioned four things that serve as evidence of God's existence—rain, crops, food, and joy.

Joy as evidence of God. In a world as hurting and pain-filled as ours, where death always wins in the end . . . what else besides a divine gift of joy divvied out to the hurting could explain how people can laugh at all?

Unfortunately, God wasn't seeming all too real to me over the past thirteen months. Not if the evidence of his love was joy.

I hear something in the bedroom, the soft, comfortable sound of Charlene turning over in her sleep. I don't want to wake her, so as quietly as I can I find my shoes and jacket and slip out the door to the porch.

It's still dark, but in the porch light I can tell that the emerging day is drenched in early morning mist and a sad, drizzling rain.

From growing up in the area, I know it's a typical Pacific Northwest morning, the kind of weather people in the rest of the country might use as an excuse to stay indoors, settle down with a cup of tea and a good book. But in Oregon and Washington, rain is a way of life and mist is welcome, and being damp means feeling at home. The sayings I grew up with:

"Oregonians don't tan, they rust."

"Enjoy Oregon's favorite water sport. Running."

"I saw an unidentified flying object today— the sun."

In order to stretch my legs and clear my head, I start on a brisk walk along the three-mile trail that loops around the main part of the campus. The decorative streetlights beside the path glow languidly through the haze. It's as if I've stepped into a nineteenth-century London novel.

What happened last night in the Faraday cage seems to have occurred in its own distant dream-world somewhere. Time does that to memories— unfurls them at different speeds and in ways you wouldn't expect, putting more distance between events than the hours should allow.

Or sometimes it swallows the space between

experiences and time becomes compacted, seems not to have passed at all.

But now it's as if last night's altercation happened so far in the past that the Lawson Research Center should've changed dramatically since then.

However, after a few minutes I see its exterior lights through the trees and it looks like it should: rustic and rugged, sedately awaiting our visit for the test later this morning.

I think of the attacker, of the blade swiping through the air toward Charlene, meeting her arm, slicing into her. I hope she'll let me take her to the hospital later today, or at least to a clinic in Pine Lake, but based on her response when I tried to do that last night, I'm not optimistic. In the meantime, we seemed to be on the same page as far as going on with the test.

The reason we came to the center in the first place.

A test so simple it might actually be hard to debunk.

First, find a couple who are in love with each other. That's a prerequisite, at least for this specific line of research. Isolate one of the lovers in the Faraday cage, position the other in a room somewhere else on campus. Or, in this case, 120 feet down the hall.

The person in the chamber is the receiver, the other is the sender.

Next, set up equipment to record physiological changes in the receiver, and at random intervals show the sender the video of the person in the chamber, instructing him to think loving thoughts, give focused positive attention to her. If the receiver experiences physiological changes while he does that—and only while he does—it would be evidence of some type of nonlocal, unconscious psychic connection.

And that's exactly what Dr. Tanbyrn and his team claimed their tests showed.

According to them, in almost every instance, within seconds of the sender thinking focused, loving, positive thoughts, the receiver's heart rate, respiration rate, and galvanic skin response change—almost imperceptibly, yes, but enough to be measured. And when the sender stops focusing his thoughts and emotions on his partner, her physiological condition returns to a baseline state.

That was the claim.

But how was that even possible? How could that happen?

Entanglement on a quantum level? That seemed to be Tanbyrn's take on it. But even if that were the case, why would the person in the chamber be affected by only that one person's thoughts?

In other words, what about all the other people who care about her and might be thinking about her at the same time as the test's sender? After all, if the connection is truly nonlocal, it wouldn't matter where the other people were, how far away they might be.

So why would their positive (or maybe negative) thoughts fail to affect the person in the Faraday cage while just her lover's thoughts did? Couldn't other people love her just as much? What about a mother or a sister or a child? Couldn't their love be just as impactful? Just as resonant?

And how could you ever hope to design a test that would account for those other people's thoughts? Tell everyone who cares about the woman not to think about her at all during the test? But even if that were possible, how could you rule out the possibility that they hadn't done so anyway?

After all, one of the best ways to get someone to think about something is to tell him not to.

And of course, how much of a connection, how much love, was needed for any of this to work? What measurements could you ever come up with to test the depths of true love?

Really, as inexplicable as the results were, there were so many variables and confounds that at best it would only be possible to identify a relationship that was highly correlational, not one that was causal.

But still, even that much would be hard to explain naturally.

And so, as I walk the trail toward the river on the east side of the campus, that's what I try to think of a way to do.

Pathology

Philadelphia, Pennsylvania
8:16 a.m. Eastern Daylight Time

Riah lay awake, alone, in bed.

She had a lot to think about after her visit to the R&D facility last night.

When she and Cyrus left, he'd refused to come over to her apartment and had gone home instead to the arms of his wife.

Riah wondered what explanation he'd given Helen for his unexpected arrival—especially since there weren't any other flights that left for Atlanta last night after the one he'd told her he was going to take out of town—but Cyrus was an experienced liar and Riah was confident he'd found a way to be convincing.

Now as she repositioned her head on her pillow and stared at the wall, it occurred to her that she was disappointed—not that he hadn't come over to sleep with her, but because his absence hampered her study about secrets and intimacy and love.

Actually, it might tell you something about love after all.

She rose from bed, gathered the toys she'd purchased for her "sleepover" with him. Perhaps she would need them later, it was hard to tell. After all, their relationship had reached a cross-roads; she was aware of that, but she was still open to seeing what the future might bring, might teach her.

Carefully, she put everything away—the chocolate sauce in the cupboard, the handcuffs and other slightly more exotic, harder-to-obtain items in the closet.

She guessed that Cyrus had gone home rather than come to her place because the twins had pressed him to tell her about the research, and sleeping with his wife would've been his way of punishing his mistress for tagging along and putting him in that uncomfortable situation.

But fortunately—or unfortunately, depending on how you look at it—Riah didn't feel punished. As much as she wanted to, she didn't know how to feel heartbroken or thankful or excited or sad or any of those other emotions normal people have.

No.

No shame. No guilt. No anxiety about the consequences of her choices.

And of course all of this troubled her because she knew what it meant; what her lack of a conscience and lack of empathy and lack of concern for other people, in addition to her remorselessness for her actions—she knew what all of this was indicative of.

A condition that the Diagnostic and Statistical Manual of Mental Disorders described under the category "personality disorders."

Admittedly, by themselves those traits might not have been enough to convince Riah of her condition, but when you took into account high intelligence and charismatic charm, the diagnosis was pretty clear.

Riah Colette was a psychopath.

Not a murderer, no.

But a psychopath nonetheless.

True, many people with her disorder were violent, but not all of them were. Some were lawyers, others were used car salesmen, businessmen, politicians, athletes. Usually psychopaths took up professions in which narcissism, self-promotion, and deception served as assets. Often, of course, that meant careers with high levels of competition.

All competition requires putting aside a certain degree of empathy and understanding toward those you're trying to beat, so it made sense that people who lack a sense of moral accountability and compassion would be attracted to it. To compete is, essentially, to participate in an act of self-promotion. After all, how can you love, serve, and honor someone above yourself while you're wholeheartedly trying to defeat him?

Attempting to assure someone else's failure requires setting aside concern for his well-being, and to treat anyone that way requires a certain degree of psychopathology.

Once, Riah had been invited to a volleyball game between two Christian colleges. The fans on each side cheered when their team did well, but they also cheered when the girls on the other team made a mistake that put their own team ahead. Curious about this, Riah had asked the man who'd invited her, "Don't Christians believe in supporting each other?"

"Of course."

"So that doesn't apply when a girl is wearing a different color jersey?"

She'd meant no offense by the question, but he'd studied her in a subtly judgmental way. "It's just a game."

"Aren't you all part of God's family?"

"God is our Father, so all believers are brothers and sisters in Christ. Yes."

"Then why would you cheer when your sister misses the ball or fails to make a successful hit? Doesn't she feel bad enough already after making a mistake in front of hundreds of people? Why would you celebrate her failure or add to her embarrassment or shame under *any* circumstance at all?"

He glared at Riah and, perhaps as a way of showing he didn't buy into her reasoning, almost immediately joined the other fans around them in applauding when a girl from the other college missed a serve and put his team within one point of winning the game.

Riah had taken something away from that experience, something that might be an important insight into the way normal people think. Psychopathology is at least culturally pervasive enough to cause religious people to set aside some of their prophets' and leaders' most cherished values of selflessness, service, humility, and encouragement when they're watching or participating in a sporting event.

Even though it didn't make Riah sad exactly, it did confuse her. She could only imagine that if she were able to feel something as precious as compassion, she wouldn't be willing to give it up so readily over something as inconsequential as watching a group of girls hit a ball back and forth over a net.

Honestly, when Riah saw things like that, she wondered if she wanted to be "normal" at all.

But of course, for her, all of this was not just an academic question or a cultural milieu. It went much deeper, because she knew that she was a true psychopath in every sense of the term.

Over the years she'd tried telling herself that she wasn't like the psychopaths who kill, that she was different, that she could control her condition, master it even, and eventually learn to experience the emotional and experiential ups and downs that healthy, mentally well-adjusted people do.

She'd tried to convince herself that the difference between her and normal people was one merely of degree, not of kind, one that she could overcome with effort and understanding. But in the times when she was most honest with herself, she had to admit that the instinct to kill had burrowed inside her long ago.

The bird that she killed in front of her sister.

The other animals over the years when no one was looking.

The inexplicable curiosity she felt while watching things die.

And those nagging questions about what it would be like to take the life of another human being.

And so far all of her research into neuro-physiology had failed to show her how she might change, how she might learn to control the urges she had.

Notwithstanding all she knew about the brain, its pleasure centers, the way it processed reality, and even taking into account direct brain-computer interfaces and ways to elicit muscle responses by exciting certain parts of the brain, she had not managed to find the answers she was looking for.

Riah walked into the kitchen and looked at the clock on the microwave.

Almost 8:30.

She was mostly in charge of her own schedule at

RixoTray, as long as she checked in. Today she was supposed to be at work by ten and wasn't sure now if she would be going in at all.

She had a lot to think about after the meeting with the twins last night.

Finally, Riah decided she needed to process that discussion in light of her thoughts about who she was, what she was capable of, and what the two men whom she assumed shared her condition were working with Cyrus Arlington to do.

After a few minutes of reflection, she texted her supervisor and told him she was taking the day off for personal leave.

Dawn.

Returning to the cabin, I find Charlene awake and finishing a cup of coffee. The air smells of dark-roasted java.

She looks up, gives me a slightly concerned smile. "Hey, I was looking for you. Where were you?"

"Went for a walk." I decide not to tell her how long I've been up already.

I see that she has set out a mug for me by the coffeemaker in the kitchenette, and I angle across the room toward it. "How's your arm?"

She holds it up and stares at it as if she hadn't noticed before that it was injured. "Hurts some, but not as bad as I thought it would. I think it's going to be alright. How was the couch?"

"Not too bad."

She already knows that over the last year I've had trouble sleeping, and it probably goes without saying that my dreams had taken their toll on me last night as well. She doesn't ask and I don't elaborate.

"So then, dear"—she drains her coffee and goes for her purse, confirms that she has the RF jammer and the tiny, concealable heart rate monitor— "I believe we have breakfast and then a meeting with Dr. Tanbyrn."

I take a long draught of my coffee, finish most of it. Set down the mug. I can feel my stomach rumble. Truthfully, breakfast sounds like just what I need. "Yes, dear. I think we do."

On my walk I hadn't come up with any specific plan on how to debunk this research—or how I might replicate it through illusions or the tricks of mentalism. But getting video footage of this morning's test would be a good place to start.

I put on the small button camera that Xavier provided for me, and since I'll be needing the lap function on my stopwatch when Charlene is in the chamber, I make sure that it's working too.

It is.

Good.

To keep up the illusion that Charlene and I are in love, we walk to the dining hall hand in hand.

Riah stepped out of the shower.

Dressed.

And thought back to the events of last night.

In the end it was probably best that Cyrus hadn't come over because this way it gave her some time to sort through what the twins had told her.

Daniel had explained that the research being done in Oregon was meant to complement her own work here in Pennsylvania. "Dr. Tanbyrn and his team are mostly interested in studying the physiological changes in one person while another person who is emotionally or genetically close—"

"Or in our case, both," Darren cut in.

"Is attentively focused on him—"

"—in a positive, loving way."

"Mind-to-mind communication," she said dubiously.

"Yes," Darren answered.

Riah considered that. Even though she knew RixoTray was financially supporting the research, Cyrus had kept most of it under wraps and she knew surprisingly little about the nature of the research in Oregon.

She used diffusion tensor imaging, magneto-encephalography, fMRI, and EEG to measure the excitement patterns in the Wernicke's area of the temporal lobe. By better understanding how the two men processed communication, her team had been hoping to—

Aha.

"So, are you saying that if we could learn to excite the section of the brain related to mind-to-mind communication, you could heighten the—what? The connection? Intensify it somehow?" She was thinking aloud, and by the looks on the twins' faces, she was right on track. "Enhance the ability to . . . connect with each other?"

The twins exchanged glances and then nodded almost simultaneously. Cyrus's gaze crawled toward the clock on the wall as if he were perhaps expecting someone, or maybe he was just biding his time until he could maneuver the twins out of this uncomfortable meeting.

Riah knew that the Department of Defense was funding her research in the hopes of eventually developing a brain-computer interface to help troops communicate in the field by creating a device that could detect, decode, and then transmit neural linguistic information to other troops.

It could be used to help soldiers communicate in field conditions that wouldn't allow for normal speech, such as in the middle of a firefight when words couldn't be heard, or when any sound would alert the enemy, such as sneaking into a terrorist compound.

Communication of neural linguistic information.

Now she wasn't so sure that was all the study concerned.

Riah draped her necklace around her neck.

Began to brush her hair.

She might've felt used by Cyrus and the twins,

might've felt that her research was part of a big picture that she'd never been told about, and that was essentially true, but to a certain degree that was true about all the research at the R&D facility.

After all, the financial implications of an information leak were so devastating that just like in any sensitive government or private-sector medical research project, nearly all the researchers at RixoTray did their work strictly on a need-to-know basis. Progress was more often than not about one person piggybacking on the work of another to answer a question neither of them fully understood.

After the discussion about the center in Oregon, the conversation had shifted away from the Lawson Center's research, and Darren turned to Cyrus. "I was told you have the video."

"Not yet. But I will. Tomorrow. A courier will be delivering it."

Daniel addressed Riah: "When you see the video, you'll know what we mean. What the research concerns."

"Kabul?" she asked, referring back to what he'd mentioned earlier in the evening, when she and Cyrus first met up with them.

"Yes." Darren sounded pleased that she'd made the connection.

After that they discussed her findings at length, and it was almost as if she was the one who'd been brought in to do the briefing, even though she was the only person there who hadn't prepared for it at all.

Honestly, Riah didn't understand why the twins' conversation with Cyrus couldn't have all happened over the phone, but apparently they were the ones who'd called for the meeting, and their motives were not always easy to decipher.

At last when Cyrus stood to go, Darren had asked him, "So tomorrow, the video. What time will it arrive?"

"In the afternoon. Sometime between five and six."

"We'll see you at six then. In your office. And we would like Riah to be present as well."

A pause. "Alright."

"Williamson will be there?"

"She won't land in Philadelphia until six thirty. She's coming in at seven."

"Well, let's come at seven then too, so we can watch it together, make sure we're all on the same page. Everything happens when the president—"

"I know when it all happens." Cyrus was looking at Riah, and she understood that he was cutting off Darren to keep something from her.

"Alright," Daniel said. "So, seven?"

"Yes," Cyrus said coolly. "Seven."

So now, Riah decided to start an online search of journal articles concerning the findings of the center in Oregon. Even though she had until this evening to look into things, if the research was anywhere near as complex and detailed as hers, it might take at least that long to sift through it all.

She put on a pot of coffee, positioned herself in front of her computer. And began to type.

Dancing Pain

I'm anxious to get started with the study, anxious to get moving. But still, my early morning walk had left me famished, and I was glad there was a substantial breakfast laid out for us.

Now we're almost done. Charlene is finishing her plate of fruit, and I slide my empty bowl of oatmeal aside, then polish off the last of my cheese-smothered hash browns. "Too bad Xavier isn't here. I have to say, this food is amazing."

"By the way, what's the deal with him and cheese anyway?" She's looking at the smear of melted cheddar cheese left on my plate.

I shake my head. "I have no idea. About a month ago he just started eating it in some form every couple hours."

"That's so random."

"That's so Xavier."

"Good point."

The dining hall has nearly a hundred people in it, but since there'll only be ten or eleven couples in the study, the rest of the retreatants must be here for the yoga and centering conference that's going on at the same time on the other side of campus.

I gaze around, curious if the man who attacked us last night might be here. I hadn't seen his face well enough to identify him, so the only way I could hope to find him is by his limp, especially if he was limping *and* missing a watch.

From what I can see, there's no one here who fits the bill.

After dropping off our trays at the cafeteria's conveyor belt to the kitchen, Charlene and I cross the campus toward the Prana building.

The quiet fog hovers around us, and it reminds me again of my dreams, my family, of that day at the shore when I watched the divers bring up the bodies.

Fog.

And a chill.

And a cloud-covered sky.

And the terrible questions that have never gone away.

Why, Rachel? Why did you do it? Why did you kill my boys? Why did you kill yourself?

Perhaps the timing is coincidental, but Charlene reaches for my hand, and it seems like she's reading my mind and trying to reassure me, but in this case I don't hold on. It's almost like I want to dwell in my pain for a while alone.

Yesterday Xavier told me that there're always going to be holes in my heart in the shape of my wife, in the shape of my sons. Now his words come back to me: "Stop feeding your pain and it'll dissipate."

But maybe I don't want it to dissipate. Maybe I want it to cling to me, to remind me that if only I'd been more astute and attentive—if only I'd noticed what was going on in Rachel's heart or what was troubling her so much that death seemed like the only option, if only I'd been able to see her desperation—maybe I could've intervened and stopped things before they went as far as they did.

But I had not.

And it had happened.

And now she is dead and so are my sons.

Charlene doesn't say anything, and even though she isn't moving any farther away from me, I sense the distance between us grow slightly wider.

We enter the small retreat center that Serenity had told us was named after the Hindu word meaning "life-sustaining force." The reception desk is empty, but I tap a set of chimes hanging beside it and hear a male voice call from the back room that he'll be with us in just a moment.

As I think of a life-sustaining force, I have to admit that it sounds like something I could really use, but I also can't help but think of the *Star Wars* movies: "May the Force be with you." I'm not sure what I believe about unseen forces altering the universe, but gravity and magnetism seem to do alright, and even when you're in the debunking business, you have to keep an open mind.

However, disappointingly, George Lucas killed the whole Force idea in *Episode 1* when Qui-Gon Jinn referenced a connection with the Force depending on your midi-chlorian count. In the end even Lucas shied away from allowing the unexplainable to remain unexplained and came up with a scientific reason for why some people rather than others could live more in tune with the Force.

It was more scientific-sounding this way, of course, but from a storytelling perspective, a lot less satisfying.

Prana.

A life-sustaining force.

"Hope" would be a better name for it, for the force that really sustains us.

My thoughts cycle through my dreams and then land back in this moment.

The reception room is adorned with well-coordinated earth-tone furniture, a small conference table, and windows that offer a broad view of the fir and pine forest that stretches out of sight in the ethereal, otherworldly fog that has engulfed the campus.

When we were preparing for this assignment, I'd anticipated that Dr. Tanbyrn would do a general briefing this morning with all the couples who'd be taking the test today, but no one else is here. As I consider that, a man with thick 1970s sideburns emerges from the back and introduces himself as Philip, a grad student from Berkeley who was "honored to be one of the great Dr. Tanbyrn's research assistants."

"Brent Berlin," I tell him, using the name I'd registered under here at the center. "And this is Jennie Reynolds."

We shake hands, then he gestures toward three of the chairs.

"Have a seat. Let's get started."

Glenn Banner was high.

It helped with the pain, but it made his thoughts curl around each other in odd ways, as if they were made of elegant colors all dancing across the needles of discomfort that bristled up his leg.

That's what he thought of as he sat in his motel room and sharpened his knife: dancing pain.

Did he feel the stab wound in his quadriceps?

In the sense of pressure, of a tingling sensation, yes—but did he feel it as acutely as he should have for a deep-muscle puncture wound like that? Absolutely not.

Drugs can be wonderful things.

Still, he couldn't help but think that he should've gone after that man and woman last night. Should have killed them both and then gotten photos of their bodies to remember the night. Act on his impulses.

147

But what's done is done. You can't change the past.

But you didn't find what you were looking for either. You didn't find the files.

No, he hadn't.

Leaving right after he'd been stabbed had meant not having the opportunity to find the information he'd gone in there looking for, the data he'd planned to use against his employer to pick up a little extra cash.

The information he was interested in concerned the military's involvement in the study. The connections were still fuzzy, but while researching his employer before taking this job, he'd come across evidence of meetings between him and Undersecretary of Defense Oriana Williamson, as well as mentions of Project Alpha, which included amorphous references to two men, "L" and "N," whose existence—let alone identity—Glenn hadn't been able to confirm.

Since early this morning, he'd been trying to reach the man who'd hired him, but so far had been unsuccessful.

The guy just wouldn't answer his phone.

Glenn tried the number again.

Nothing.

It was supposed to've been an easy gig: take out an old man who didn't have long to live anyway, pick up the payment, buy some little gift for his daughter, Mary Beth, in order to keep up the appearance that he loved her, then get back to Seattle and blackmail the guy who'd hired him.

But now everything had gotten more complicated.

Glenn had been wounded, had failed to dig up the dirt he wanted to find on his employer, and had ended up with two special people he wanted to pay a visit to.

He tried to shift his focus to the task he needed to accomplish today.

Killing the doctor.

Honestly, he had no idea why the old man needed to die, but he doubted it was revenge, which left the most common reason you would hire someone like Glenn—the guy knew something he was not supposed to know.

Perhaps something to do with Akinsanya, the man who seemed to be behind everything? The one who'd connected his employer with him in the first place?

Glenn wasn't sure.

It was too much to think about.

He closed his eyes and disappeared into the swirl of euphoria and irritation and adrenaline that the wound and the OxyContin gave him.

Dancing pain.

After a long moment he drew in a breath that seemed to be made of liquid air, opened his eyes, collected himself, and pulled out the manila folder his employer had given him, then flipped through the sheaf of papers until he came to the doctor's schedule.

Personally, he would've preferred taking care of the old geezer this morning while he was asleep in his cabin, get the photo of the body, and get out, but for whatever reason the man who'd hired him wanted it done this afternoon at three, during the doctor's office hours.

Just another odd demand in a series of odd demands. This guy was obviously used to micromanaging his people, and Glenn did not like being micromanaged.

He was tempted to leave a message that he was going to take care of this assignment on his own time frame, in his own way. But admittedly that might not be the most prudent way to get paid, so although it was tempting, Glenn decided to stick to the original plan.

Three o'clock this afternoon.

Tanbyrn's schedule: the doc would begin the day at his cabin, get breakfast at the dining hall, head to the Prana building for a meeting with the people in his research study, then spend the rest of the morning and the early afternoon working with them before heading to his office from two to six.

Where he would die.

At three.

Yes, there might be other people in the building, but the place had a state-of-the-art design, and considering the method Glenn was leaning toward in regards to taking out the doctor, he was sure that collateral damage wouldn't be a problem.

Well, okay, not *sure,* but at least *reasonably* sure.

Glenn tried the guy's number again.

Still nothing.

Alright. Enough.

He'd gotten a pretty good look at the couple in the chamber, and he didn't figure it would be that hard to hack into the LRC's computer files, see if they showed up on any surveillance footage, see if—

So then why'd you even go there last night, Einstein? If you could've just hacked in? Why did—?

The anger he was feeling at himself was eclipsed by the subtle shift in the way he was experiencing his limbs, his legs, his hands, the stab wound in his thigh.

It felt like the drugs were beginning to wear off. He was tempted to take more OxyContin but was hesitant to do so. He needed to be on top of his game today.

Focus.

See if you can find the files, then find out who those two people are.

Start with the staff and current retreatants—that shouldn't take too long—then move out from there.

Focus.

He went to find his laptop to see if he could

hack into the Lawson Research Center's video surveillance archives. To find this couple he'd decided to kill for free.

A little pro bono work.

Two photos to add to his collection.

The Cane

The interview and pretest procedures take longer than I expect and end up chewing up most of the morning.

As time passes, three more couples come and meet with other research assistants, but Philip stays with us.

I'm getting frustrated that things aren't moving along more quickly, and by 11:30 I'm seriously annoyed and wondering why all of this couldn't have been taken care of before we came to the center.

A few minutes later, Serenity enters the room, pushing a cart containing our lunch—coffee, a platter of fresh fruit and veggies that I imagine were probably grown here at the center, and vegetarian subs on gluten-free bread.

I eat quickly.

Just as I'm finishing, Dr. Tanbyrn arrives.

He looks like he's in his early eighties and walks with an elaborately carved cane. He's bald with a grizzled beard, wears thick, out-of-style trifocals and thrift-store clothes, and has a dusty, professorial look about him.

At first I catch myself thinking that he doesn't dress anything like a Nobel laureate should dress, but then I'm struck with the thought that he's wearing exactly what I would expect an eighty-year-old physics genius to wear.

After a cordial greeting and some genteel small talk with all four couples, Tanbyrn spends some time reviewing the study's procedures, most of which Charlene and I are already familiar with. And, frustratingly, some of which Philip had already gone through earlier.

I want to ask Dr. Tanbyrn about the center's connection to RixoTray, who the assailant from last night might have been, or what he might've been looking for, but I know that if I bring up these issues with him at all, it'll need to wait until we're alone sometime after the test. After all, I'd have to admit that Charlene and I were sneaking around the Lawson building after hours, and after hearing something like that, it would be reasonable for him to demand that we leave the center.

When my wandering attention shifts back to him, he's in the middle of a sentence. ". . . so quantum waves are not elementally trapped in space and time as we are—or at least as we appear to be. Because of this, because of their entanglement with each other, even though they might be separated by time or distance . . ."

"They really aren't separated at all," one of the men interjects.

A nod. "Quite right. One thing is certain in quantum physics: the more we learn, the more we realize how little we know; and subsequently, the less sure we are of 'knowledge,' the blurrier the lines become between our understanding of animate and inanimate objects, our definition of life, our understanding of what it means to be alive. And the more mysterious the universe seems."

The woman next to me looks reverently at Dr. Tanbyrn. "It's so mystical, so spiritual."

"Beneath the veneer of the visible is an entirely different sphere, a fabric of dimensions and reality that holds this physical, observable one together. I am not by any means the first to explore this inexplicable quantum entanglement— this nonlocal connection between subatomic particles—but my research does lean in a slightly unique direction. Here at the Lawson Research Center, we are looking at the matter that those particles make up. In this case, organic matter."

"People." It's the woman beside me again. "To see if they're entangled." She giggles lightly, then corrects herself: "If *we* are."

"Yes," Tanbyrn replies. "Although I perhaps misstated myself. I'm not just looking at how people might be entangled or connected, but how their awareness of reality might be. In other words, how one person's individual consciousness might nonlocally affect another person's awareness, thoughts, or physiology."

There it is. The crux of the whole matter.

He announces that Charlene and I will be the first couple to do the test, then takes us to a side room and meets with us privately. "Have you decided who'll be the first sender and who'll be the first receiver?" His voice is aged and faltering but also kind, and he reminds me of my grandfather, who died when I was still in my teens.

"I'll be the sender," I tell him. "Jennie's better at deciphering my thoughts than I am at deciphering hers."

Charlene gives me a playful jab. "What? You can't read my mind?"

I shrug. "What can I say? I'm a guy."

"I knew you were going to say that."

"See what I mean?" But then, suddenly, the doctor's words sink in.

He'd said *first* sender. *First* receiver.

"But," I explain, "Jennie will be the only receiver. I'm not going to be in the chamber."

Dr. Tanbyrn taps a finger against his chin. "We like to repeat the procedure, reversing the roles so that we can test the receptivity of both participants."

"I think we'll just keep it to Jennie. The truth is . . . I don't do so well in small places."

"Aha, well. Yes, of course." There's no judgment in his voice, and I get the impression that he's dealt with claustrophobic participants before.

He rises unsteadily, leaning on his cane for support. "Well, come along then. It's not far. Just two buildings over."

But as he takes his first step, the cane slips on the pinewood floor. He flails his hands out to regain his balance and ends up grabbing Charlene's wounded arm. Despite herself, she cries out and pulls back, causing him to plummet toward the floor, and I'm barely able to drop down fast enough to catch him.

For a moment the air in the room seems to hold its breath.

Then eases.

Gently, I help him to his feet. "Are you alright, Doctor?"

"Yes, yes, quite." I'm still holding his shoulders, steadying him. "Oh my." He's shaken, breathing hard, gazing at Charlene. "But are *you* alright, my dear?"

She's grimacing, and I can't imagine how much it must've hurt to have him squeeze her arm like that. "Yes, I'm okay."

"I am so sorry." He sounds deeply distressed. "I just lost my balance. I—that's never happened to me before."

Once he's standing on his own, I hand him back his cane.

He gestures toward Charlene's arm. "Are you sure you're alright?"

Only then do I notice the blood that's seeping through her sleeve.

He has a curious, perceptive look in his eyes, and I wonder if perhaps earlier this morning he might've seen the blood on the third floor of the Lawson building and is now somehow piecing things together.

Charlene presses her hand tenderly over the wound to quell the bleeding, and when she replies to Tanbyrn, she avoids explaining how the blood got there. "I better go get this cleaned up."

I offer to go with her but she declines.

"No. I'll meet you two there." Then she excuses herself to return to the cabin, leaving Dr. Tanbyrn and me alone.

He waits for me to speak, as if it's my responsibility to absolve him of the guilt of harming her. "Don't worry, it wasn't you. She hurt her arm last night. The scab must've just broken open. It's not serious." The only thing I'm not really sure about is that last part. Because the cut might be serious. "Are you sure you're okay?"

"Yes, Brent. I am. Thank you for arresting my fall."

"Glad I was close enough to help." I gesture toward his cane. "Do you need a hand?"

"I believe I'll be fine. Thank you."

After a slight pause, he leads me to the lobby. I

slow my pace to remain next to him just in case he loses his balance again. His cane taps heavily on the floor beside me as we walk past the reception desk, out the door, and into the gray morning mist.

Kindling

Pine Lake, Oregon
12:31 p.m.

Glenn Banner was able to connect the dots.

On his hacking attempts, even though he hadn't uncovered the incriminating information he'd been searching for last night, he had found his way into the Lawson Research Center's video surveillance archives and had been able to pull up the footage of the two people he'd seen in the chamber as they registered at the front desk late yesterday afternoon.

He paused the video.

Zoomed in on the screen of the computer on the registration desk.

Saw the names: Brent Berlin and Jennie Reynolds.

And the name of the cabin they'd reserved.

Hmm.

So, whether it was RixoTray who'd sent them or another firm altogether, by staying on campus the pair would be close enough to poke around in the evenings. Perhaps trying to dig up information on the military's involvement—that is, if they were aware of it.

Of course, it was always possible they were looking for something else.

Additionally, if they were participating in the study rather than attending the yoga retreat, they would have the chance to speak with the doctor, perhaps squeeze information from him.

Glenn googled their names, but they were both so common it was like looking for a needle in a haystack. He couldn't help but think they were quite possibly aliases anyway.

It was possible that the couple would've left the center last night after the altercation, but the cut on the woman's arm hadn't been life-threatening, and if the secrets buried in the computer files at the center were as important as Glenn thought they might be, he wasn't convinced that the two intruders would've left the center yet.

He really needed to talk to the man who'd hired him.

Glenn tried the phone number once again.

And this time, at last, the guy picked up. "What is it?" The voice was as blunt and impatient as always.

Glenn filled him in on what'd happened last night at the research facility, leaving out the part about being too slow to stop the guy from swinging the knife down and plunging it into his thigh. And of course, leaving out the fact that he himself had been there trying to find information that he could use in his blackmail attempts.

"What were you looking for?"

"I was doing research on Tanbyrn."

"I provided you with all the information you need. I even gave you the passcode for—"

"Listen to me, there are things you're not telling me, and I don't like being kept in the dark."

Rather than respond directly to that, his employer returned to the topic of what had happened in the chamber. "You say there were two of them there? A man and a woman?"

"Yes." Glenn gave him a description of the couple. "Who are they?"

"I don't know."

"The guy said you sent them."

"I did not send them."

Glenn considered that, didn't reply.

Only two possibilities: either this guy was lying or the man in the chamber had been.

Glenn had the sense that a man whose life was being threatened would be a bit more likely to tell the truth than someone who'd hired an assassin to kill an old man.

"I want some answers here," Glenn said. "This whole thing is—"

"The way it is." A tense, hard tone. "I tell you what you need to know. Don't get demanding with me. You wouldn't want me to start considering you a liability."

Glenn felt his grip on the phone tightening. "I'm not the only one in this conversation who's at risk of becoming a liability."

For a moment neither man spoke. Both held their ground, both retained their status, until Glenn decided he was ready to move past his threat and get on with business. "I'm set to take care of Tanbyrn at three."

"I'll have your money waiting."

"What about the couple from the research facility?"

"Forget 'em. I didn't send them. Just take care of your job, the one you were hired to do."

He didn't send them? Did someone else from RixoTray? Another firm?

Glenn was surprised that his contact didn't seem concerned that a competitor may have sent the couple. Was he faking it? Or maybe the guy didn't have anything to hide after all. Maybe the whole blackmail idea had been a mistake.

"I'm going to take care of them."

"No you're not. You're—"

"They might've seen my face."

"I don't care about that. I just want you to do the job you were hired to do and then get out of there without leaving any evidence behind."

Glenn responded by hanging up.

Abruptly.

He shut off his phone.

Pissed off now.

Not happy.

No.

No, he was not.

He placed his hands palms-down on the table. Took a breath.

Alright. He would do what he'd been hired to do. The transaction with the doctor was a done deal. That was professional. That was business. The matter of the couple from the chamber was personal. A loose end he could not risk leaving unattended.

He thought about how to kill Dr. Tanbyrn.

Though he'd obviously deliberated on it earlier, he preferred not rushing into a decision as important as how to murder someone without thinking through all the options. It was better to make your decision closer to the actual event and adapt as necessary.

For the most part, Glenn avoided guns. Because of that, he'd used wire in the past, plastic bags (twice), and once—on a unique and rather memorable assignment—a blowtorch. But all in all, he preferred his knives, and they'd served him well the six times he'd used them for their intended purpose.

When you use a knife, almost always, even if someone knows what he's doing when he's fighting you, he will get cut. A Kevlar vest will stop a bullet, but because of the amount of force generated at the tip of a blade when you thrust it forward, even a vest won't stop a knife.

Yeah, well, what about the guy last night? He didn't get cut. He did pretty—

Irritation.

Anger at himself.

Save the knife for the couple.

Wound for wound.

Something else for the old man; what you were thinking of before.

So after a short internal debate, Glenn decided to go ahead with his original idea.

Fire.

Tanbyrn's office was located at the end of the hallway on the lower level. There was a reception area just outside his office that would serve Glenn's purposes well. More accurately, it was a waiting room. There was no receptionist there. No secretary. All of which made it ideal.

The building was constructed of logs, and with its central air system, it would circulate the smoke even as the wooden structure burned. The smoke and the alarms would clear the building of other people.

But Glenn would seal Tanbyrn in the office so he couldn't escape—easily enough done.

Elevator—no problem.

Stairwells and exit doors—chain them shut.

Glenn would light the fire just outside Tanbyrn's door. The campus was isolated enough so that the county's volunteer fire department would never be able to arrive in time to save the building, and the center had only rudimentary fire suppression resources on-site.

Either the flames would get Tanbyrn or the smoke billowing up the vent just outside his door would do the trick.

Glenn could use the furniture in the waiting area along with a petroleum-based accelerant to create the thick smoke he was looking for. Yes. And since fire destroys most, if not all, forensic evidence, and fire investigations usually take weeks to complete, Glenn would have plenty of time to disappear.

Admittedly, he wasn't an expert at arson, but he had torched two buildings: a warehouse and a duplex. Both assignments had gone well, both resulted in the intended insurance payouts— although he did have one small regret. He hadn't meant to kill that little girl in the apartment. He'd been told it was empty.

Well, you know what? Live and learn.

In this case, fire would be a good choice.

But it'll destroy the computer files you were looking for.

Screw it.

Let that be.

Just get this done, get the money. Find the couple from last night. Take care of them. Close this thing up.

And then move on.

He reviewed his plan for the next couple hours:

check out of the motel, grab a copy of *USA Today*, stop by the hardware store in Pine Lake and pick up the items he would be needing, then get back to the center by two to make sure he had enough time to get everything ready for the big show at three o'clock.

Flocking

12:43 p.m.
2 hours 17 minutes until the fire

Dr. Tanbyrn, Charlene, and I walk down the hallway of the research center. Philip trails behind us as if Tanbyrn is royalty and he's giving him the wide berth he deserves.

Charlene has changed shirts, and the sleeve puffs over the fresh bandage on her arm.

No one comments on it.

I notice that the drops of blood that were on the floor in here last night have been washed off.

Again, I think of how Tanbyrn studied Charlene when he saw the blood on her arm earlier. I can't imagine that he'd helped mop the floor or clean up the blood, but regardless of who did—or even whether or not Tanbyrn knew about it—somebody had seen the blood, so someone was aware that there'd been at least one wounded, bleeding person in here last night.

• • •

Entering the room where we encountered the assailant is a bit surreal.

I look around, searching for any sign of blood or of a struggle in here—or in the chamber whose door is now wide-open—but I don't see any.

Illuminated by the overhead fluorescents, the room has an entirely different feel than it did when I was directing my flashlight around here last night. A slightly built but stately African American woman stands near the desk, introduces herself as Abina; she's apparently another research assistant. She gives us the same reverent prayer-gesture bow that Serenity offered us when we checked in last night. Charlene and I respond in kind.

"That's a pretty name," Charlene tells her. "Abina. What does it mean?"

"It's Ghanaian. It means 'born on Tuesday.' I was born on a Wednesday, though. Wishful thinking on the part of my mother. She was in labor, actually, longer than she expected."

Charlene smiles. "Ah."

Abina is wearing a flowing, colorful African dress that swirls around her resplendently as she moves through the room. A myriad collection of metal bracelets jangles from her delicate wrists.

A photograph of a shimmering mountain vista sunset glimmers on the screen of the computer that our assailant was using last night. From the

166

view, it looks like the picture might've been taken from one of the LRC's scenic overlooks.

I wish I could get alone with the computer, look up any recently accessed files.

Specifically those opened last evening.

"Well." Dr. Tanbyrn smiles. "It looks like we're all set."

I decide to say goodbye to Charlene before she enters the Faraday cage, and I offer her a hug. "See you in an hour, dear."

She holds me. "Goodbye, honey."

I whisper to her as softly as I can, "If you get a chance, check the computer."

She nods. Kisses me on the cheek.

Though simply for show, the terms of endearment and the show of affection impact me, and I gaze into her eyes a moment longer than I probably should.

As I step back, Abina smiles at us.

Well, at least we were being convincing.

Dr. Tanbyrn still doesn't seem sure of himself with his cane as he leads me and his impressively sideburned graduate research assistant 120 feet down the hall, to the room where I'll be watching for Charlene's face to appear on a video screen.

I don't want him to lose his balance again, so I stay close as we travel down the hall.

We enter the room and I look for transmitting devices, video cameras, anything the researchers

167

might be using to alter or fake their findings. While I do, I make sure that I surreptitiously turn in a full circle so that the button camera gets a 360-degree view of the room.

Obviously, Dr. Tanbyrn could simply have programmed his computer to print out fake results—that was something we would need to check on before we went on air with our show, but for now I wanted to eliminate as many other factors as I could.

I see the window, the reclining chair, a desk, a few office chairs, the same view as the photo in the center's brochure.

Nothing out of the ordinary.

Positioned in front of the reclining chair is a widescreen, hi-def television, blank now, but I anticipate that it's where the video of Charlene sitting in the chamber will appear once we get started.

Dr. Tanbyrn picks up a tablet computer from the desk and finger-scrolls across the face of it. The TV in front of me flickers on and a video starts, but it's not Charlene in the chamber; it's a nature special about how birds fly in flocks, simultaneously changing direction as if they have a collective consciousness.

A collective consciousness.

Well, that made sense, considering the doctor's area of interest.

Philip stands quietly by the door. "We've found

that leaving people alone helps them to not be distracted or nervous." He smiles, but for some reason it makes him seem less trustworthy. His teeth are just too straight, too white. A televangelist's grin.

I decide I'd rather keep an eye on the two of them during the test to make sure they don't alter any of the test conditions. "Thank you, Philip. But feel free to stay. You won't be distracting me. I assure you." I indicate toward the two chairs near the window. "There's plenty of room."

His momentary hesitation is a red flag to me, and I begin to not trust the graduate student from Berkeley.

Dr. Tanbyrn gives Philip a glance, then tells me, "Of course, Mr. Berlin. Whatever will help you relax."

"Wonderful."

Somewhat reluctantly, Philip takes a seat, and Dr. Tanbyrn dials the Venetian blinds down so they shut out the meager light that's seeping in from the fog-drenched day outside.

So now, relax.

When you're doing water escapes, especially cold-water escapes, if you don't learn to lower your heart rate at least a little, you end up using your oxygen too quickly, and it dramatically decreases your chances of escaping in time, so all escape artists learn to control their heart rate, at least to some degree.

In the days when I was performing my stage show, I not only had to learn to hold my breath for up to three and a half minutes, but I had to learn to relax enough to lower my heart rate to fewer than thirty beats per minute. Now that I haven't done it in over a year, it seems pretty impressive. Back then it was just me going to work, doing my job.

Right now I figure I'll relax as much as I can, try to stick as closely as possible to the test procedures. After all, we were making our own recordings of Charlene's physiological state, so we would know if their test results were faked or in some way falsified.

I lean back in the reclining chair and lay my hands across my stomach, not just so that I can relax, but so I'll be able to tap the lap timer button on my stopwatch every time Charlene's image appears. This way we'll have an accurate record of the instances when her image was being transmitted onto the screen, and we'll be able to compare it to changes that might appear in the printed record of her physiological states.

Dr. Tanbyrn dims the lights and takes a seat while I watch the birds flock across the screen in unison and wait for the video of Charlene to appear.

The Placebo Effect

It was the middle of the afternoon, and Riah had spent most of the day so far reviewing the journal articles written by Dr. Tanbyrn and his team at the Lawson Research Center in Pine Lake, Oregon.

Some of the material, particularly the unconscious communication between two lovers, she found unbelievable, but yet surprisingly well-supported by the center's detailed documentation.

And she did agree with a few things.

She knew that the mind is a powerful thing, that it's possible to alter your own physiology through your thoughts, a puzzling fact that physicians and scientific researchers have known since the 1780s.

The placebo effect.

Just give people a harmless pill, a sugar pill, an aspirin, whatever, tell them it's the latest pain medication or a drug to treat a severe medical condition they have, and depending on the ailment, 30 to 95 percent of them will be helped, at least to some degree—more than those in a control group that isn't receiving any treatment.

Of course, the effectiveness of the placebo isn't the same with every illness or injury or with every patient, but in some cases the placebo group actually experiences more of a positive effect than the people taking the drug that's being researched.

Yes, at times the brain can heal the body even better than medicine can.

And astonishingly, according to a 2011 study, patients even benefited if they took a placebo *and were told it was a placebo*.

Honestly, no one really had a clue how that worked.

And the placebo effect was far-reaching.

Placebos hadn't been used just to control pain, but people taking them had been healed of cancer, had controlled their schizophrenia, and even, in a few isolated cases, had been cured of Parkinson's disease. Body builders who thought they were taking the newest anabolic steroids gained muscle mass as fast as those who were taking steroids—and even suffered the negative side effects they would've if they were actually taking the steroids.

How is it possible that our thoughts alone can cause us to feel less pain—even allow patients to feel no pain during amputations? How can our thoughts cure us of cancer, or manage the symptoms of schizophrenia or Parkinson's, or help us build muscle mass?

All of that? Just by our thoughts?

It was a medical mystery.

Riah also knew that thoughts can do more than heal, they can have a negative effect as well—sometimes called the *nocebo effect*.

In her research into humanity, she'd read the aptly titled book *Man's Search for Meaning* by

Viktor Frankl, a Jewish psychiatrist who was a survivor of the Nazi death camps in World War II.

In the book he tells the story of another prisoner who'd had a dream that the war would end on March 30, 1945. But as the day approached and the men heard reports of the battles, it seemed less and less likely that the fighting would end on that date. On March 29 the man became ill. On March 30, when the war didn't end, he became delirious. On March 31 he died.

In his case, he hadn't died from any diagnosable medical condition, he had died from lack of hope.

His thoughts had ended up being fatal.

Undeniably, thoughts can heal and they can kill.

And as far as affecting another person's physiology, we do that all the time. All you have to do is kiss someone or aim a gun at his head or slap him in the face. He may get aroused or afraid or angry, but in every case his heart rate, breathing, and galvanic skin response will change. In fact, when two people are alone and in close proximity, their heart rate and respiration begin to emulate each other's and they begin to breathe in sync with each other.

But the issue here wasn't the physical effects of thoughts on your own body, or the effect of your presence with or actions toward someone else. The question was: could your loving thoughts affect another person's physiology when you're not present, when you're not communicating with him in any tangible way?

Medical science, of course, said no.

But the quantum physics that Dr. Tanbyrn was researching seemed to say yes.

All of this made Riah increasingly interested in what would be on the video that Cyrus was going to show her at seven o'clock tonight.

With traffic in central Philly, she would need to leave her apartment by six.

That gave her just over two hours.

And there was one thing left that she needed to do.

Someone named Williamson would be at the meeting as well.

Riah was going to find out who that person was.

I see Charlene's picture appear on the screen.

Without letting Philip or Dr. Tanbyrn notice, I gently tap the button to start the lap function of my watch.

"Okay, Mr. Berlin." It's Dr. Tanbyrn from behind me, speaking softly. "I'd like you to concentrate on the image of the woman you love. Imagine what it's like being with her, holding her hand, kissing her, having intimate relations with her."

Admittedly, I'm a bit surprised by the bluntness of his request. Not only would it be a little distracting to take things as far as he's suggesting, but the idea of sexually fantasizing about Charlene while watching her on the screen has a sleazy, voyeuristic feel to it. Doing so would've made me feel more like a Peeping Tom than a co-worker and friend who respects her as a woman. So instead of following his request to the letter, I focus on my affection for her rather than my physical attraction to her.

Think loving thoughts.

Loving thoughts.

Concentrate on the image of the woman you love.

The woman . . .

She looks relaxed and comfortable sitting in that metal chamber, and I can tell she has no idea that I'm watching her.

. . . you love.

Despite my efforts to keep my thoughts on a purely platonic level, I can't help but notice how attractive she is—not runway-model beautiful, but naturally pretty—the kind of woman who doesn't need makeup to turn heads but can really dial up the volume and be striking when she wants to be.

What really is love? At its essence? Action? Emotion? Attraction? All three?

Think about the woman you love . . .

When I first started looking into this research, I'd thought I might end up inadvertently thinking about Rachel during the test, might return to the feelings I had for her while she was still alive. But although those feelings are present to some degree, they're bookended by time—we met, we fell in love, we married, had kids, and she died. I'll never stop caring for her, loving her, but I'll also—

No, Jevin, she didn't just die, she killed herself and she murdered your sons.

Grief marked with a sting of caustic anger grips me, making it harder to be present in this moment, and while I'm trying to focus on Charlene again, her image disappears and the bird documentary comes back on.

I tap the watch's lap function button again to record the end of the video segment of Charlene.

I'm not sure how well I did in sending my positive thoughts through the building to her, but at least I couldn't be accused of not putting forth my best effort. Dr. Tanbyrn encourages me to try to stop thinking about Charlene now and let my attention drift toward other things.

I've already started to do that, but it's not easy to put her out of my mind, or to obviate my thoughts of Rachel and the boys.

The birds flock across the screen, moving together just as fish do, as if guided by an unseen hand, and watching them, I can't help but be struck with a sense of wonder at the natural world.

An admiration, an awe, a sense of marvel I've always had.

Ants build intricate tunnel systems. Bees build

hives. But how does each member of the hive know what his job should be? How does each ant know where to dig? Ask a biologist and she'll typically answer "instinct," but that's like explaining how you saw a woman in half by saying it's "magic." It's an explanation that doesn't explain anything; just more smoke and mirrors, misdirection, to keep you from asking the questions that really get to the heart of the matter.

Instinct.

Really?

That's the explanation for every adaptation, trait, and inborn desire of every species? Even of behavior that could not possibly be taught to offspring, or of environmentally cued responses that could not be passed on in the genetic code? There's a gap in logic there that most people simply overlook or aren't willing to acknowledge.

Charlene's picture appears again, and I turn my attention to her, start the timer on my watch.

Over the next half hour or so, her image appears twenty-six times—I keep track as I tap the button on my watch to record the exact timing of the appearances.

And although I'll need to analyze it later, the timing of the image generation certainly does seem to be random.

Sometimes the segments come on only a few seconds apart, other times several minutes pass between them, so unless I'm missing something, I can't imagine how Charlene could ever guess when her image is being played for me—and even if she could, there's no believable way she could alter her heart rate and respiration within a handful of seconds in ways that would coincide with each of the video segments.

Every time her image disappears, I do my best to lend my attention to the bird video, but with each passing minute I become more and more curious about what the tests will show, about whether or not Charlene's physiology will have been altered, even in the slightest degree, by my thoughts.

Finally, Dr. Tanbyrn announces that we're done. He graciously thanks me for being part of the study, and then consults the tablet computer again. "Give us just a few minutes, and then we'll go down the hall and see how Jennie is doing."

The DVD

1:38 p.m.
1 hour 22 minutes until the fire

Glenn arrived at the center.

With his fake beard and wig, he knew he would never be positively identified, even after the surveillance video was analyzed later, after the fire.

Rather than hike through the woods on his injured leg, he drove straight to the registration building, pulled into the parking lot, and went inside to get a visitor's pass for the day.

RixoTray Corporate Headquarters
Philadelphia, Pennsylvania

Caitlyn Vaughn, Dr. Cyrus Arlington's faithful receptionist, ushered the courier into his office.

An earlier arrival than Cyrus expected.

The courier handed him a package stamped "Official business. Requested material."

Cyrus knew, of course, that it was the DVD containing the video footage of what had happened in Kabul thirty-one hours earlier.

He also knew that he needed to watch the footage privately before allowing the twins, Riah, or Undersecretary of Defense Oriana Williamson to see it. And definitely before passing it on to Akinsanya. He was not someone Cyrus was prepared to disappoint.

He paid the courier, closed the door, and locked it so that even his nicely endowed and seductive young secretary, the one he'd slept with when she was in accounting and then transferred up here before starting his relationship with Riah, wouldn't interrupt him.

It was vital that Williamson was on board with this—the funding depended on it, and it was important that the twins were reassured about the efficacy of the program, since it would affect how things went with the president's policy speech tomorrow morning here in Philly in front of the Liberty Bell.

The Liberty Bell.

How very patriotic of him.

Cyrus carefully opened the package.

According to the administration's press releases, the speech was going to "contain broad and far-reaching initiatives aimed at strengthening the economy and regaining the confidence of the American people in Washington's ability to make a positive and lasting impact in their lives and throughout the free world."

The speech would include policy proposals for reinvigorating the economy, decreasing unemployment, broadening health care coverage, enhancing the development of alternative energy to reduce dependence on foreign oil, and making "judicious" cuts to the military—pretty much the same topics the president had tried to tackle during his last three years in office but had made almost no headway on.

But if Cyrus's sources were right, this time the announcement he was going to make regarding health care was going to change everything in the pharmaceutical industry for years to come.

Cyrus flipped open his laptop, inserted the DVD.

Waited for the password prompt to come up.

Really, the footage was the fulcrum upon which everything balanced. That, and the work of—

What about Riah? What will she think when she sees it?

Well, yes, what about Riah?

Truthfully, she'd become more of a distraction lately than she was probably worth. It might be necessary to get her out of his hair in a way that she would not bother him again. If the video showed what he thought it would, she wouldn't be needed anymore.

Maybe when this was over, that thug Glenn Banner would be interested in making another twenty-five thousand dollars.

A possibility.

Either that or Atabei.

Yes, the woman from Haiti, the one he'd met on one of his trips down there to help out after the earthquake. She might actually be a better choice.

In either case, Cyrus decided he could deal with Riah later, when everything was completed; for now the main issue was the video. He couldn't take any chances that the footage would be unconvincing to Williamson and the twins.

The prompt came up, he typed in the password to unlock the video and pressed Play.

181

Loving Thoughts

1:43 p.m. Pacific Daylight Time
1 hour 17 minutes until the fire

I return to the room that contains the Faraday cage.

Dr. Tanbyrn and Philip walk quietly beside me.

We find Charlene standing in the corner near the computer workstation, chatting lightheartedly with Abina. I'm struck again by the contrast between how innocuous things in here seem now compared to how menacing they'd become last night. Charlene smiles at me. "So, how do you think it went?"

Although I'm glad to see her, I'm a little upset at myself for not discovering anything so far about how—or if—the staff here might be faking the tests. "I'm sure it went as well as it could," I tell her vaguely.

She turns to Dr. Tanbyrn. "When will you have the results?"

"In about an hour. There are some numbers I still need to run, and I have to check in with another couple. If you could kindly meet me in my office at, say, a quarter to three?"

I would've expected that he could use his tablet computer to analyze the data within seconds, but when I think about it, actually, this would give Charlene and me a chance to see if our tests, the ones taken from the heart rate monitor that Xavier had given her, showed anything close to the findings that the doctor and his crew typically found. Charlene and I might even have enough time to look over the footage I took with the button camera I'd worn during the test.

"Alright," I tell him. "We'll see you at 2:45."

We leave the building and find that the day is still foggy, still devoid of wind. The smokelike tendrils of mountain mist seem to drain sound from the air, creating an almost eerie stillness that not even birdsongs are able to taper into. Even the squish of our steps on the soggy trail seems dampened by the heavy air.

"Seriously, Jevin, how did it go?" Charlene asks. "Did you do your best to think of me in a positive light?"

"I did."

"And to think loving thoughts?"

"And to think loving thoughts. Yes."

I wait for her to ask a follow-up question or crack a joke about how difficult that must've been—sending loving thoughts to her—but she's quiet, and I'm not sure if that's an invitation for me to speak or a way of letting the conversation drift in another direction entirely.

"Hopefully, it'll be enough," I add.

"Yes." She takes a few steps. "Considering."

"Considering?"

"That we're not in love."

"Of course. Exactly . . . So what were you thinking about while you were in the cage that whole time?"

Her answer comes without any hesitation. "I was thinking about you."

"About me."

"Yes."

Her words both surprise and do not surprise me, assure me and unsettle me. "Well . . ." I'm really not sure how to proceed here. "It'll be interesting to download the data. Print it out."

"Yes, it will."

And we wouldn't have long to wait.

The outline of our cabin lies fifty yards ahead of us in the fog.

Dr. Cyrus Arlington ejected the DVD from his computer.

The video was convincing.

Very convincing.

After watching it, he didn't foresee any problem in assuring Williamson and Akinsanya of what was possible. And the twins would certainly be heartened by the footage.

He looked at the clock.

4:51 p.m.

So, 1:51 in Oregon.

In just over an hour the doctor would be dead and there wouldn't be any chance of him going public with his findings regarding Project Alpha. With what he knew, there was just too much of a possibility that he could piece things together, and now that things were this close, it wasn't the time to take any chances that Tanbyrn would be able to do that.

Cyrus's eyes landed on the two aquariums in the corner of his office.

Last week Riah had asked him about them, but he'd never explained why he kept the *Ampulex compressa* wasps or the *Periplaneta americana* roaches. So now, perhaps the best way to explain would be through a little demonstration.

And besides, letting one of the wasps do her work would lend a certain irony to the occasion of the four people watching the DVD in the next room. Considering what the footage contained.

Predator.

Prey.

Submission and helplessness.

Two hours might be cutting it a little close for the wasp to finish her burrow, but at least it would be enough time for her to get started with the roach.

Cyrus walked toward the aquariums,

It was time to let his little parasitoid play.

Parasitoids

1:53 p.m. Pacific Daylight Time
1 hour 7 minutes until the fire

Back at the cabin, Charlene and I connect her heart rate monitor to the small printer we'd brought along and print out the results of her EKG. Then I compare the results with the times recorded on the lap timer of my watch, which denoted specifically when her image appeared on the screen.

Strangely, even though it would be evidence of something I didn't believe in, I find myself hoping that the test results will match, as if that would be some sort of sign that Charlene and I were meant to be together.

But you don't believe in signs.

You don't believe—

I stare at the two sets of data.

And the results are bewildering.

In almost every case, the fluctuations of her heart rate correspond directly to the times when I was focusing my thoughts and emotions on her.

I literally scratch my head. "Honestly, I have no idea how to explain this, Charlene. You put the RF jammer beneath the cushion on the chair like we talked about last night?"

"Yes."

Everyone's heart rate, respiration rate, blood pressure, and other physiological processes are constantly changing as we move, as we respond to our surroundings and other people, as we feel apprehension or guilt or fear or pleasure or excitement. Still, there's a baseline that our bodies will return to when we're in a relaxed state, as Charlene was in while she was in the chamber.

However, what I'm looking at here are not random fluctuations; rather, they match, with startling uniformity, the instances when I was focusing my thoughts on Charlene.

But when, of course, she had no idea I was doing so.

These are our results, not the center's. This was with our equipment, not theirs. There was no way they could be faking this. And I could think of no explanation as to why her physiological signs should have fluctuated as they did, when they did.

I try to keep an open mind, but it's hard to know what to think.

This morning I started out trying to debunk this research, not confirm it, so despite my reservations, I have to rule out the variable of confirmation bias, however unlikely that would be.

Keep an open mind.

Charlene stands beside me, studies the printouts I'm holding. "So, Jevin, it looks like you and I are entangled."

"So it would seem."

"I wonder how long this has been going on."

"Our entanglement?"

"Yes."

"I, um . . . I couldn't say."

I feel like a junior high–age boy standing next to the girl who's just given him a note with the question, "Wanna be more than friends?" And two boxes, "Yes" and "No." And then the words, "Check one." And I know which one I would check, I know how entangled my heart is, but I'm afraid to tell her. Something holds me back. Maybe it's the fact that I haven't been with a woman since my wife died. And how to act now, in this moment with Charlene—the right thing to say eludes me.

We look into each other's eyes and she doesn't look away, and I almost get drawn beyond myself, almost let the shock of seeing the data we were just reviewing drift away. Almost, but not quite. Because the impact is still there—the results have snagged my thoughts and I just can't shake them, can't ignore the implications.

I think she can tell I'm distracted because a flicker of disappointment crosses her face and she looks away, toward the window. Toward the fog. "It's almost two. I know Xavier will be anxious to hear about the test. Let's see if we can find a way to reach him or Fionna, tell them what we found. We might be able to reach them if we drove a little ways down the road."

Go on, Jevin, say something.
Wanna be more than friends? Yes or no?
Yes.

Now she looks at me. "What do you think?"

I start to reply, to answer her previous question about how long this entanglement has been going on, but all that comes out is, "Sure. We can head straight to Tanbyrn's office from the parking lot. Save some time. That should be fine."

A pause. "Yes."

"Okay."

"Okay."

Tell her how you feel. Tell her!

My hands feel awkward and unsure of themselves as I fold the printouts, put them in my pocket.

Yes or no?

I just can't find the right words to say.

Then Charlene steps out of the cabin and I follow her, thinking back through the conversation, replaying it, rehashing what I should have said but didn't.

I wonder how long this has been going on.

I have evidence that there really is something to Dr. Tanbyrn's tests. That there really is something tangible to my feelings for Charlene.

What measurements could you ever come up with to test the depths of true love?

Maybe I had them on that sheet of paper in my pocket.

• • •

For a few moments Cyrus admired the beautiful, sleek jewel wasps. Perfectly evolved predators. Beautiful *Ampulex compressa* specimens.

A parasitoid is an animal or organism that takes control of another organism, killing it so that it can implant its offspring inside the host.

But in this case, Cyrus's female jewel wasp wasn't actually going to kill the cockroach herself—her offspring would do that when it hatched and then consumed the cockroach from the inside out while it was still alive.

He leaned over the aquarium that contained the inch-and-a-half-long, squirming *Periplaneta americana*. There were twenty roaches in there, but he would just be needing one today.

He eased the cover to one side.

Fast little creatures. Able to move up to four feet per second, which was comparable to a human running over two hundred miles per hour. It took him a few tries, but in the confines of the aquarium, it wasn't too difficult for him to corner one. He picked it up, pinching it firmly to keep it from twisting free from his grasp.

With his other hand he closed the aquarium, carefully edged the cover to the wasps' aquarium slightly to the side and dropped the cockroach in, then quickly closed the opening again before any of the fifteen wasps could escape.

The roach immediately skittered across the dirt

floor, instinctively looking for a place to escape its wide-open, exposed position, especially with so many predators buzzing around it.

The roach hit the aquarium's glass wall, began scurrying along the edge of it, desperate to find cover in the small leaves scattered across the floor. Millions of years of evolution willing it to run, to hide, to survive.

The cockroach was five times the size of a wasp, but that made no difference to the wasps.

One of them took the lead and flew in a tight, circling pattern, undoubtably working out the best way to approach the future host for her child.

Glenn pinned the visitor tag to his shirt, left the registration lobby, and returned to his car to retrieve the pack of supplies for the job at hand.

With the wound in his leg, he couldn't help but limp, and that bothered him, made him irritable, but he would spend time recovering when all this was over. After he'd been paid.

In the distance, near the registration building, he noticed two people—a man and a woman—round the corner and head toward the parking lot.

2:07 p.m. Pacific Daylight Time
53 minutes until the fire

We're not yet to the car, but I pause, try my cell.
  Nothing.

"Let's drive down the road toward the valley," Charlene suggests. "The gorge might be wide-open enough for you to get a bar or two."

As we walk toward the car, she hands me her cell. "You know how much I like talking on these things. I'll drive; you try to reach Fionna. We have different carriers. Who knows? It's worth a shot."

"You're the only woman I know who can't stand talking on the phone."

"Careful now, dear."

"I'm just saying."

I hand her the keys and we cross the parking lot.

Glenn could hardly believe it.

The two people angling toward him were the ones who'd been in the chamber last night.

Don't let them see you!

He slipped into his car and tilted the rearview mirror. Watched them climb into a sedan not fifty feet away.

No indication they'd noticed him.

Good.

He didn't know if they'd gotten a glimpse of him last night in the Lawson building. He'd kept his light in their eyes nearly the whole time, so it was unlikely they could identify him, but still, it was a possibility. So now as he observed them, he was careful to keep his head turned slightly so they wouldn't be able to see him if they looked in his direction.

The woman was behind the wheel. She backed the car out of the parking spot, aimed it toward the road that led from the center to Pine Lake.

Glenn took note of their license plate number.

So.

It looked like he had a decision to make.

Yes, he wanted to follow them, of course he did. See where they were going, then corner them, do some work on them. But that would put the time frame with the doctor in jeopardy.

They'll be back. They weren't carrying their luggage, the bags they had on the video when they were checking in.

Yes.

True.

You know their plate number now, what kind of car they have. You'll be able to find them again. Just get to the Lawson Center, check out the reception area, make sure the chairs will work. Take care of the doctor, then deal with them. You'll have plenty of time.

Okay.

Glenn waited for the sedan to disappear, then left his car. Carrying his backpack with the supplies in it and walking as quickly as his injured leg would allow him, he headed toward the Lawson research building.

First things first.

Visit the maintenance closet on the first floor and disable the building's sprinkler system.

• • •

Two miles from the center, I'm able to reach Fionna.

"Jevin, I've been trying to get ahold of you since yesterday. What happened?"

"No cell reception up here in the mountains."

"So you didn't get the files I sent you?" She sounds exasperated.

"No. What did you find?"

Her tone changes. I can tell she's calling to someone across the room. "Maddie, put down those scissors and let go of your brother's pony-tail!"

I hear a faint, disgruntled "Yes, ma'am."

The joys of being a mom.

I motion for Charlene to pull the car to the shoulder so we can make sure we don't lose the connection.

"Here's what I found." Fionna is back on the line with me. "RixoTray isn't just working with the Lawson Research Center. They're working with the Pentagon. DoD."

"Really."

"Yes, it has something to do with the president's speech tomorrow and with Kabul, the suicide bombing attempt earlier this week. The guy who was going to blow up the mosque."

I hadn't heard anything about that. "What happened?"

"There's not much to tell, just that a suicide

bombing attempt was unsuccessful. The media isn't saying much. A couple al-Qaeda cell members were killed. There are differing accounts of how many."

I couldn't see how that would have anything to do with what was going on here at the center, but if there was a connection, the timing of the bombing attempt in Kabul and the confrontation with the thug here last night might be more than coincidental.

"You should hear Xavier," she tells me. "He's all over this. Conspiracy stuff, you know him."

"I can only imagine. What else?"

"A few things. That's the big—" Here she stops again, calls away from the phone to her kids: "I'll be there in a minute. Just stick the noodles in the pot and cover it." Then she's back on the line with me. "Late lunch. We had a field trip this morning."

She's in Chicago, where it really would be a late lunch. I would've called it an early supper. "No problem."

"Anyway, I was about to say, the files might be too large for you to download to your phone. You'll need to use my FTP server." She gives me the info I'll need to log in, but it looks like I'll have to wait to get the files until I can use my laptop after the meeting with Dr. Tanbyrn.

Charlene taps the clock on the front console of the car: *We need to hurry.*

2:18 p.m.

I give Fionna the quick rundown of what happened last night: sneaking into the center, meeting the assailant, Charlene getting injured. Before I can tell Fionna about today's tests, she asks concernedly about Charlene, "Is she alright?"

"Yes. Do you want to talk to her?"

"Yes."

Charlene unequivocally shakes her head no.

I hand her the phone.

She glowers at me, then speaks to Fionna. "Hey . . . Good." I try to fill in the blanks, guess what Fionna might be saying: "How's your arm? Are you sure it's not serious?"

"Yes . . . Fine . . . Okay," then Charlene hands the phone back to me.

Five words. That's it. Less than ten seconds.

This woman really does not like talking on the phone.

I accept the cell, tell Fionna, "It's me again."

"Xavier's done getting the B-roll for you. He offered to slip up there, meet with you two tonight, catch up."

"I'll call him. Set something up."

Now it really is time to go.

"So you mentioned the guy looking through the computer files . . ." Fionna seems to be anticipating what I'm about to ask her. "Let me guess, you want me to dig around, find out what he might've been searching for." It was more of a conclusion than a question.

"Searching for or deleting, yes."

"I had a look at their files before you went there, Jev. You know that. I didn't see anything suspicious."

"Take another look. Go deeper. Explore the military connection."

A pause. "Alright. Lonnie's looking for a little extra credit. I'll get him on it." Lonnie is her seventeen-year-old son. Not even out of high school yet, and already he's presented twice at DEFCON.

We end the call, and only after I'm lowering the phone do I realize that I didn't get a chance to tell Fionna about the test results, about my entanglement with Charlene. It doesn't look like there's enough time to call Xavier right now, but I text him, tell him I'll call him later this afternoon after our meeting with Tanbyrn. I leave out the news about the watch for the time being. Later I'll drive down here again, download the files from Fionna, and fill Xavier in.

Charlene pulls onto the road, does a U-turn, and takes us back toward the center for our appointment with Dr. Tanbyrn.

5:27 p.m. Eastern Daylight Time
33 minutes until the fire

Riah locked her apartment and left for her meeting with Cyrus, the twins, and the person named Williamson, whom she had not yet been able to identify. Yes, it was a little early, but if she got there before the twins did, she could spend a little time talking with Cyrus, find out more about the connection with the Lawson Research Center.

As she climbed into the car, she was thinking about all she'd learned over the course of the day concerning Dr. Tanbyrn's research in Oregon, and she was becoming more and more curious about exactly what the video Cyrus was going to show them would contain.

Cyrus watched as the beautiful *Ampulex compressa* made her move.

She flew toward the cockroach and they seemed to battle for a moment, curling and twisting and tussling with each other, the cockroach trying to escape, the wasp trying to make her first sting.

And then she did—with a quick flick she inserted her stinger into the roach's spine, into its central nervous system. In only seconds the cockroach lost control of its front legs and collapsed.

That was the first sting, the one that paralyzed the roach just enough to set it up for the second sting.

The one into its brain.

The venom of this second sting was a dopamine inhibitor. It wouldn't stop the roach from moving, but it would stop it from moving under its own volition. Once this venom was injected, even after the venom from the first sting wore off and the roach had control of its legs again, it would not try to run away. It would be completely under the wasp's control.

Now she wrapped herself carefully and tightly around her prey's head so that she would be able to slide her stinger into the precise spot she was looking for. Just a millimeter to either side and she would kill the roach. She had to get it right the first time, but evolution had taught her what to do.

Truly remarkable.

Of course Cyrus was aware that this was an act, not a genetic trait; neither was it a behavior that she was able to pass on to her offspring. Inexplicable, yes.

So be it.

She knew how to do it, so instinct must have taught her.

But now, as he watched her position that stinger, he thought again of the astonishing precision of this act. How could any wasp ever develop these two separate venoms, know to look for this type of a roach in the first place, then know exactly where to make each of the stings? She wouldn't be able to reproduce unless she could do all of this, so how could this knowledge ever be passed on genetically? It was almost enough to make a person believe that there was a designer behind the process of natural selection.

But would the benevolent deity that religious people believe in really design something like this? A wasp that could create, for lack of a better term, a zombified cockroach to use as a living host for her offspring?

A god with a streak of sadism, sure, but a loving one? That seemed incomprehensible.

The wasp pressed her stinger against the roach's head.

Inserted the stinger into its brain.

Injected the venom.

And waited for it to take effect.

Charlene guides the car into a parking space.

It only takes us a few minutes to walk across campus to the Lawson Center.

We enter through the front door and decide to take the elevator instead of the stairs down to Dr. Tanbyrn's office on the lower level.

And as we wait for the doors to open, she asks me about my father.

Old Wounds

2:34 p.m. Pacific Daylight Time
26 minutes until the fire

"So now that we know you can get cell reception," Charlene begins, "maybe later—after we meet with Tanbyrn—you can get in touch with your dad."

"I'm not sure that'd be the best thing to do."

The elevator doors slide open and we step inside.

"What happened between you two, anyway? You never told me."

I press the "L" button. "We didn't do so well together after my mom left. He changed, he . . ." Is there a good way to say this? Not really. Just the simple way, the blunt truth: "He became angry."

There's so much more to explain, but it would be opening up a can of worms that I didn't think this was the right time or place for.

The doors close and we descend.

On the lower level, Charlene is quiet as the doors whisk open again. She remains quiet as we exit and head down the hallway toward Tanbyrn's office. Any blood that she or the assailant might've left behind last night on this level has been cleaned up, just as it was on the third floor.

"So, you're saying he wasn't just angry at her for leaving?" We're halfway down the hall. "Not just at her?"

"I suppose that's a good way to put it."

As we approach the small reception area in front of Dr. Tanbyrn's office, I see a man sitting on one of the chairs reading a magazine. A daypack rests on the floor beside him.

He looks up as we join him.

"Do you know if Dr. Tanbyrn is in?" I ask him.

He shifts his gaze from me to Charlene before answering, and when he does he clears his throat slightly. "No. Not yet."

A sweet feeling came over Glenn. A secret rush of quiet power.

He could tell that they didn't recognize his voice. Last night he'd tried to mask it, and apparently, it had worked. However, when he went on, he was somewhat tentative, testing the waters: "Do you know where he is?"

"I know he had a few things to take care of. We're scheduled to meet with him at 2:45."

"2:45?" Yes. This was working. It really was. Still no glimmer of recognition on their faces.

"Yes."

"Well"—Glenn nodded knowingly—"I'm in no hurry. I can wait until you're done."

Charlene and I give him some space and sit on the other side of the room, a small footstool between us. I expect that now that we're no longer alone, she'll drop the subject of my father.

But she does not.

Instead she lowers her voice. "It's not your fault that your mother left."

"I know."

"It's . . ." She hesitates. "It would be good if you could try to fix things between the two of you. Between you and your dad."

"I'm with you on that."

Although the man across the room is still staring at his magazine, I can only imagine that he's also doing what anyone would be doing in his situation if they heard two people nearby talking in hushed tones—eavesdropping.

Just in case he is, I go with Charlene's assumed name. "Jennie, we've never been close." I'm doing my best to not let the stranger hear me. "I don't want to call him because it would be uncomfortable for both of us, it wouldn't solve anything, it would just open up old wounds, and I think in the end one of us would probably say something he would regret."

"How do you know it wouldn't solve anything?"

"Experience."

A moment passes.

Where is Tanbyrn?

"You know my dad died, right?" Her voice is low but has an intensity to it. "When I was twenty-five, I told you about that? Right after my divorce?"

Charlene had been married for only a short time before her husband decided he preferred the eighteen-year-old girls taking his high school lit class to her. She rarely spoke about it, and now I'm a bit surprised she's even mentioned it.

"The car accident."

She nods and it takes her awhile to respond. "I never had the chance to say goodbye to him. There were things between us that, well . . . should have been said. Things . . ." Her sentence trails off, and it's clear that she's deeply moved by the thoughts of the father she lost and the things she never told him. "Well, I think you understand what I mean."

I'm not sure what to say. I do understand, and for her sake, as a way of showing that I empathize with her, I want to tell her that yes, I'll call my dad and talk with him about all those things that accumulate over the years, but I already know he won't want to see me or talk to me.

"Let me think about it. I'm not brushing you off. I need to figure out what I might say."

She accepts that and agrees that it's a good idea.

Then we're both quiet.

I check my watch.

Ten minutes to three. Dr. Tanbyrn is running late.

Charlene picks up a magazine that she is almost certainly not interested in.

I do the same.

Honestly, Glenn could not believe his luck.

Here they were, delivered straight to him, and if they were going to meet with the good doctor in his office, that meant that he could deal with all three of them at once.

But what about what you had in mind for the woman? About making the guy watch?

As tempting as all of that was, Glenn had to

admit that it would be smarter to let them burn alive with the physicist. Simpler. Easier.

Wound for wound for wound.

A tidy, happy ending after all.

Then move on.

He kept his eyes trained on the magazine he was holding.

Despite himself, he felt his heart beginning to hammer.

Don't give anything away. Don't let them guess who you are.

He turned the page of the magazine he was not reading.

Eavesdropping is nice, listening in on people's secrets, peeking into their lives, but as Glenn had learned over the last couple years, there's an even deeper thrill you get from eavesdropping on the people you're about to kill.

There's something special when they have no clue, when they think that life is just going to keep going on the way it always has. Status quo. Time in a bottle; nothing to worry about.

But when you know that's not the case, when you know that the person's death is imminent, only minutes away, the secret knowledge is like a drug. The feeling is rich and sweet and intoxicating, and there's nothing else like it. That's probably what drives serial killers to act out their urges so often. The sense of ultimate, godlike power over your helpless little prey.

Even though he wasn't able to concentrate at all on the words, Glenn dutifully kept pretending to read the magazine.

As soon as the doctor showed up.

As soon as all three of them were in the office.

Then he would act.

He realized that deep in his heart, he really did feel an obligation to something greater than just a paycheck—a calling to do this sort of thing. A duty, so to speak, to death.

His heart raced, his anticipation sharpened.

Yes, there really were moments of pleasure and satisfaction in this job.

Most days it wasn't like this, but today he had to admit that he could lose himself in this work if he wasn't careful, could become more than just a guy doing a job, could start to view himself as something he'd never before been able to admit to himself that he was.

An assassin.

The venom took effect.

The roach made no further effort to squirm or get away.

And it would make no further effort to escape. Not ever. Even when it was being burrowed into or eaten from the inside out by the wasp's young larva.

Sometimes the wasp that has stung the roach will break off one of the roach's antennae and drink some of its blood, which was what the wasp in Cyrus's office now chose to do.

Afterward, she waited until the roach had the use of its front legs again, then led it into the corner of the aquarium. She guided it by grabbing its one remaining antenna and directed it to the place where she was about to entomb it with bits of leaves and mud.

The process could take hours, but she would seal the helpless roach in her tomb and then lay her egg on its abdomen.

The roach would remain there, still alive but without trying to escape. After three days, the wasp larva would hatch and, a few days later, burrow into the roach and devour some of its internal organs to make enough room to form a cocoon.

Still it wouldn't try to crawl away, even as this was happening.

Six weeks after that, the young jewel wasp would emerge from the hollowed-out cockroach carcass, make her way out of the nest, and fly away.

Dr. Cyrus Arlington considered all of this and its symbolic connection with all that he was trying to accomplish with the twins, with how the predator controls the prey. More than simply a matter of national security, as Williamson believed, this project would help usher in the next step in human evolution.

A string of facts, of connections, only he was aware of.

As long as the twins did their job.

Adaptation.

Survival.

Adding twenty healthy years to the average life span of *Homo sapiens*.

Twenty years or more.

And he would be at the forefront, leading his species' foray into a bold and uncharted future.

Dr. Tanbyrn arrives, greets Charlene and me, as well as the man who was waiting for him when we came in. "May I help you?" Dr. Tanbyrn asks him.

He stands, shakes Tanbyrn's hand. "Dr. John Draw. I contacted the center and they told me I'd be able to meet with you at three. I'm doing some research in superstring theory and its connection to the emerging research in M-theory. I've been a fan of your work for a long time. I was in the Northwest and hoped that perhaps we could sit down and chat for a few minutes."

A question mark crosses the doctor's face. "With whom did you speak? To set up the appointment?"

"Honestly, my office manager made the arrangements. I can come back another time—if that's better?"

"No, no." Dr. Tanbyrn taps the screen of his

tablet computer, checks the time. "I'll be glad to meet with you. Can you give us half an hour?"

"That would be perfect."

Then Tanbyrn addresses me and Charlene and gestures toward his office door. "Let's take a look at these results."

Yes, Glenn had been somewhat arrogant, talking so freely in front of them, trusting implicitly that they would not recognize his voice. But it was just another part of the thrill he was tapping into.

He waited until the three of them entered the office before limping to the far end of the hallway to take care of the exit door.

Entombed

Dr. Tanbyrn's office is a small, paneled cubicle. Overstuffed bookshelves line the walls, and a computer monitor that must be at least ten years old sits on his desk next to a dusty ink-jet printer, all a stark contrast to the cutting-edge technology of the research room.

The office isn't as small as the Faraday cage, but it's certainly not one I would want to spend much time in. Windowless, cramped, dominated mostly by the behemoth gray industrial desk. A calendar and a variety of papers with dozens of scribbled equations lie pressed beneath the thick sheet of glass covering the desk.

An overwhelmed inbox sits beside the computer.

Tanbyrn ambles around the desk to have a seat in the chair on the other side. "Forgive the clutter. I'm afraid my cleaning lady is off this week." I'm not sure if he meant that as a joke or not, but I smile. Two folding chairs are propped against the bookcase, and I set them out for Charlene and myself.

Despite the fact that I want to talk to the doctor, the tiny office distracts me, reminds me of a time when I performed a show in Rome three years ago. A Vatican official who'd attended the performance and had been impressed by my escapes took me and Charlene on a tour—albeit an abbreviated one—of the tunnels and crypts that lie beneath the Vatican.

The guide told us that in medieval times, some monks would use bricks and mortar to seal themselves into small alcoves, leaving out only one brick—just a small opening through which the other monks would deliver food and water, and out of which the entombed monk would pass his waste.

For years that cell would serve as the monk's home as he prayed and reflected on God in solitude—until he died, and the other monks would slide the final brick into place, making the cell their brother monk's tomb.

Our tour guide praised the monks for their "sacrifice of holiness," but I wondered how anyone who purposely cut himself off from the opportunity of ever serving someone else could be considered holy. Charlene, calling on her university classes in religion, had asked our guide how the actions of these monks squared with Basil's words in his *Rule*, the guidebook for monks since the fourth century: "Whose feet therefore will you wash if you live alone?" Our guide had simply told us somewhat cryptically that there were different kinds of service and different levels of sacrifice.

It'd struck me then, and in the doctor's office now, it strikes me again that in medieval times the holiest men chose to live in solitary confinement, but today we consider that to be one of the worst punishments imaginable and reserve it for only the most heinous of our criminals. We sentence our greatest sinners to the life the Church's saints used to freely choose.

Dr. Tanbyrn spreads a sheaf of papers across his already cluttered desk and looks up at us. "Let's just be honest with each other, now. You're not here for the program, are you?"

I feel a stone sink into my gut. "Excuse me?"

His gaze shifts from me to Charlene, then back to me. "Kindly tell me what you're really here at the center for."

Glenn finished chaining the far exit door shut.

Strode toward the door to the stairwell to take care of that as well.

I stare at Tanbyrn, taken aback, unsure how to respond.

Option one: try to keep up the charade that Charlene and I are lovers and simply entered this project to be a part of the study in the emerging field of consciousness research and the entanglement of love.

Option two: be honest with him, lay my cards on the table, and see where that might lead.

Obviously he knows you're here under false pretenses. He knows or he wouldn't have said anything.

I wonder if it's possible that the test results he ran have something to do with his conclusion about why we're here. Could they have given something away? As extraordinary as that seems, it's possible.

Tell him the truth.

Get some answers.

"Truthfully, Dr. Tanbyrn, you're right. When we applied for the program, we did have a different agenda in mind than simply participating in your research."

Charlene gives me a look of surprise.

"And that was?"

"Debunking it."

A pause. "I see."

"But how did you know? How did you—"

"Philip told me about the blood he cleaned up from the floor. When I accidentally grabbed Jennie's arm—is that even your real name? Jennie Reynolds?"

"Charlene Antioch," she tells him.

"And I'm Jevin Banks," I add.

"I see." He takes a long breath. Intertwines his fingers. "Yes, well, after I grabbed your arm, Charlene—and I am quite sorry about that—I noted the amount of bleeding, and since no one had checked in with our staff nurse last night or this morning, it got me to thinking. I looked up the address you provided on your application forms and found that it doesn't exist. It did not require a great deal of deduction to conclude that you were likely the one in the Faraday cage last night, the one bleeding on the floor."

This is it. This is where he asks us to leave, tells us that we shouldn't be here. I'm about to speak, to try to finesse whatever information I can from him, but he leans forward. "However, two questions remain: why were you bleeding on the way out of the building and not on the way in, and who left the blood going in the other direction?"

"We weren't the only ones here," Charlene tells him. "A man attacked us with a knife; Jevin was able to wound him before he left."

The doctor looks more than a little concerned. "Attacked you with a knife?"

She nods.

I cut in, "We think he was trying to find something on the computer in the room with the Faraday cage. Is there anything in your files or on that particular computer that's sensitive? Something an intruder might be interested in?" I think back to last night, add one more question. "Perhaps someone from a pharmaceutical company?"

"RixoTray?"

"Or a competitor. Yes."

Tanbyrn is quiet.

Charlene gestures toward her injured arm. "The man might have hurt me much worse if my arm hadn't been in the way when he swiped that blade at my abdomen. Thankfully, Jevin knew what he was doing and stopped him. The man threatened to kill us both if we didn't tell him who'd sent us."

"And who did send you?"

"EFN," I tell him. "Entertainment Film Network."

"Entertainment Film Network."

"I have a television show."

"Oh. I see."

Guessing that the information Fionna found out for us earlier is the key here, I go on quickly: "The computer files the man in the room last night was looking for, I think they have something to do with the military, a suicide bombing attempt earlier this week in Kabul."

He stares at me. "Who did you say you are again?"

I decide to go with the truth and launch into telling him everything he needs to know.

Interruption

Glenn chained the stairwell door shut, snapped the lock closed.

Walked to the elevator.

Disabling one is remarkably easy.

You simply insert something into the base while the doors are open in order to keep them from closing. As long as they don't close, the elevator won't leave that floor.

Glenn reached into his pack and pulled out a hammer, pressed the up button, and waited for the doors to open.

When they did, he jammed the handle of the hammer into the opening between the floor and the shaft, then pounded it down with his heel, making sure it was so tightly forced in that it wouldn't come out without something like a crowbar to pry it loose.

He took care of the remaining stairwell but left the exterior exit door closest to the doctor's office alone for the time being so that after he'd started the fire he would have a way out of the building.

The other rooms on this level were small meeting rooms. No other offices. No other people.

The floor was sealed off.

Glenn returned to the reception area, removed the magazines from the end table, then carefully and quietly tilted it beneath the doorknob to the doctor's office. He wedged it securely in place so that there would be no opening that door from the inside.

When you're lighting a fire in a building that you're trying to bring down, you need to direct the flames to where they'll spread the quickest. Typically, that means starting the fire on the building's lowest level in a corner where there's plenty of combustible material, where the walls and ceiling reflect both the heat and the movement of the combustible gases even while channeling the flames upward.

Which was precisely what he was about to do.

There were six chairs in the lobby outside the doctor's office. The plastic coating along with the latex foam and the gasoline would form a fast-growing fire with plenty of smoke. By using two piles of chairs, Glenn was confident the reception area would be fully involved within minutes.

He began to stack the chairs, making sure that one pile was directly beneath the vent that fed air into the doctor's office.

The more I tell Dr. Tanbyrn about my history of researching psychic claims, the less pleased he looks that Charlene and I are here. I finish by admitting that our test results matched the ones he'd been finding, the ones he'd published in the literature. "I'm no longer trying to debunk anything you're doing. I'm just trying to get to the bottom of what's going on here."

As he evaluates what I've said, he slowly and gently rubs two fingers together.

Charlene leans forward. "Dr. Tanbyrn, do you have any idea who that man last night might have been?"

He takes a small breath. "Your life was in danger last night, Miss Antioch, Mr. Banks—both of you. That troubles me deeply. I think there are a few things you should know." He nods toward Charlene, then gestures toward a manila folder on the bookshelf near her. "My dear, do you mind getting that folder?"

She rises.

Retrieves the folder.

Dr. Tanbyrn lays it out on the desk in front of him and begins flipping through it, carefully scrutinizing each page of equations as he does.

Glenn finished with the chairs and was reaching into his bag to get out one of the two-liter bottles of gasoline he'd brought with him when the nearest exit door opened and a slim black lady wearing a gaudy African dress walked in.

She looked at him, then at the stacks of chairs. "What are you doing?"

He set down the bag. Folded it shut. "Oh, I'm sorry, didn't they tell you?"

"Tell me what?"

"We're cleaning the floors."

She lowered her head slightly, one eyebrow raised. "Cleaning the floors?"

"I'm from the agency." Glenn smiled innocently.

"What agency?"

He smiled. "Here, let me show you my ID." As he approached her, he made like he was reaching for his wallet, but instead, with his side turned to hide his hand, he was sliding it along the back of his belt toward his knife's sheath.

Her gaze went past him to the end table he'd propped against the door to trap the doctor and his two visitors in the office.

"Why is that table leaning against the door?" Caution bordering on suspicion. She took a small step backward toward the exit.

He found the sheath, snapped it open. "I just needed to slide it out of the way."

She was about ten feet away, but he knew he could be quick when he needed to be, even with his wounded leg.

The woman leaned to the side and called, "Doctor Tan—" but that was as far as she got. It was all she could say, all she would ever say, because then he was on her. He clamped one hand over her mouth and whipped out his knife with the other. She tried to call for help and was certainly a squirmy one, but he managed to hold on to her long enough to tuck the blade up into her tight little belly.

Even though he still had his hand over her mouth, he could hear her gasp.

"Shh, now. Don't fight it."

She was still trying to pull free, but the strength was beginning to seep out of her, allowing him to firm up his grip.

He slid the blade out, raised it to her throat. Drew it to the side in one swift, firm motion and let go of her body.

She fell clumsily to the floor. The only sounds she made now were the wet, sputtering ones from the base of her throat, and she didn't make those for long. Her body twitched a little before lying still at last, a dark gaping wound across her neck, a spreading stain of blood across her belly.

Quiet now.

No more trouble.

That's a good girl.

Glenn wiped off the blade on his jeans.

Alright.

It was time to finish this up.

He dragged her toward the chairs.

Pulled out the gasoline bottles.

And set to work.

"There it is." Dr. Tanbyrn points to a page, spins the papers around so we can see what he's pointing at. "Project Alpha. I work with two men. They fly in, do some tests, fly out. I don't even know their real names. We call them 'L' and 'N.' It's funded through the Department of Defense."

The Pentagon. Yes. The same thing Fionna had uncovered about the research at RixoTray.

The page is covered with detailed algebraic and scientific equations that I have no idea how to decipher. "What kind of tests?"

Dr. Tanbyrn has been surprisingly open with us, but now seems to second-guess himself. "I'm not sure how much more I should . . ." His eyes come to rest on Charlene's arm and he hesitates.

The chapters I've read of his books flash through my mind: quantum entanglement, non-local communication, the interconnection of life on the subatomic level, relationships—

That's it. That has to be it.

"They're twins, aren't they? 'L' and 'N'?"

He looks at me long and hard. "Yes, Mr. Banks. They are twins. Quite special twins indeed."

Glenn soaked the chairs with gasoline, then splashed some on the dead woman, just because he thought it might be interesting to watch that dress stick to her skin, and then take her with it as it went up in flames.

"How are they special?" I ask him.

For a moment I think I smell gasoline.

Gasoline? But that's—

"Well, you see—" Dr. Tanbyrn begins.

Charlene grabs my arm to stop me. "That's gas, Jevin."

"Yes."

I stand. Start for the door.

Glenn backed up.

Lit a match.

Tossed it onto the stack of chairs beneath the air vent and watched the flames lick up the fabric. They were hungry and immediately fell in love with the wood.

No, this fire would not take long at all to devour the building.

I smell smoke and tell myself it's from outside the building, just like when I smelled wood smoke last night when Charlene and I first entered our cabin.

But I know that's not the case.

I try the doorknob. It turns, but the door won't open.

Oh, not good.

221

Not good at all.

"What's going on?" Dr. Tanbyrn asks.

"Grab your things. We're getting out of here."

Glenn lit the other stack of chairs.

Lit the dead black woman.

Then he splashed the rest of the gasoline on the floor as he backed toward the exit door.

I slam my shoulder against the door, but it stays firmly in place. Smoke is beginning to curl beneath the door and billow down through the vent above my head. It's acrid and black and it's coming in fast.

"It's the project." Dr. Tanbyrn coughs. " 'L' and 'N.' "

"What's it about?" Charlene urges him. "What makes the twins so special?"

I go at the door again, harder, hoping to jar loose whatever is jammed up against it.

Glenn lit the pool of gasoline on the floor. Stepped out the exit door. Pulled out his remaining chain, lock, and key, threaded the chain through the door handle, wound it through the metal post of the fence beside the walkway, and snapped the lock shut.

There was no way out of the building's lower level.

· · ·

Nothing.

The fire alarm goes off, the sprinklers on the ceiling do not.

I search for something to smash against the door.

The desk is too large to move, or at least too large for me to push with enough momentum to take out the door.

"Communication. Physiology—" Dr. Tanbyrn's explanation is chopped up by hoarse coughing. "Identical twins are much more effective than individuals. I was providing feedback to help them direct and focus their alpha waves, studying the negative . . . the effects . . . if they were . . ."

Charlene has snatched up Tanbyrn's desk phone, but the line must be dead because she drops the receiver again. Pulls out her cell.

Smoke is quickly filling the room. "Get the papers," I tell them. "On the desk. Project Alpha. And the iPad."

"Eleven o'clock." His voice is harsh. "When the eagle falls at the park . . . The twins said—I don't know what it . . ."

I back up and try a front kick against the door, directly beside the doorknob.

A tremor runs up the door, but that's all.

No reception. Charlene pockets her phone.

Tanbyrn is coughing. He's stopped trying to explain the research and is just trying to breathe.

Go. You have to get out now!

With the thick smoke filling the cramped quarters, it isn't going to take long at all for the air to become too toxic to sustain life. I pull my shirt up over my mouth, shout for Charlene and Tanbyrn to do the same.

The vent above us is far too small to climb through.

Back to the door. I try a side kick, but whatever's holding the door shut doesn't budge.

Flames snake down through the vent on the ceiling.

Charlene is supporting the doctor. "Hurry, Jev!"

No windows. No other doors. This is it.

You need to get this door open.

Now.

I try to think of what might be holding it shut.

If this fire was started by a professional, it might be an angled door jammer, a rod with suction cups on its two ends, one that attaches to the door, the other to the floor, so the harder you press on the door, the more firmly the other end suctions to the floor. I did an escape from a room sealed shut with one in a show in Denver a decade ago—

A chair? The end table, a doorstop of some kind?

Impossible to know.

Whatever was there, I can think of only two ways to get out: pop the hinges off the door or slide something through the space beneath the door and push it hard enough to break the seal and knock the jammer—or chair legs, or whatever—out of the way.

The door's hinges are on the other side, so that's not an option. Instead I'd need something thin enough, long enough, strong enough to push under the door and shove whatever was there out of the way.

And I know exactly what that is.

I turn away from the door.

Toward the thick sheet of glass covering Dr. Tanbyrn's desk.

The Glass

I sweep my arm across the desk, knocking everything to the floor.

Glass is fragile when dropped on end or when pressure is applied to the middle of it, but lengthwise, a sheet as thick as this might just do the trick.

As long as it's not too wide to fit under the door.

Dr. Tanbyrn is coughing harshly and leaning awkwardly against the bookshelf.

"Help me get this glass," I shout to Charlene. "We need it over by the door!"

As Glenn limped away from the building, he could see a dozen or so people stream down the front steps. None of the three people he'd sealed in the office were among them.

He ducked out of sight behind a tree to watch the place go up in flames.

And fingered the folded-up copy of the front page of the current issue of *USA Today* he had stuffed in his jacket pocket.

Charlene and I have to slide the desk aside to make enough room to get the glass onto the floor.

We position it in front of the doorway, I push it forward, and—thank God—it fits beneath the door. It's at least five feet long, surely long enough to reach the bottom of whatever is lodged against the doorknob. I guide the glass forward a few feet until it meets with resistance.

Dr. Tanbyrn slumps to the floor. Charlene hurries to his side.

Okay, this is where things either went right or very, very wrong. There's nothing else in this room we could use to get out of here.

If the glass cracks or shatters, you're going to die in here.

You're going—

Stop it.

I pull the glass toward me, then press it forward again, nudging the far edge firmly against whatever's holding the door in place. I don't have a great grip, but it seems like it should be sufficient enough to give me the force I need. I push harder, but the glass goes nowhere, the object it's touching doesn't move.

I try again. Nothing.

"Slam it," Charlene calls urgently. "Jar it loose!"

No choice. I have to try.

Praying the glass won't crack, I grip the end firmly, draw it toward me, and then as swiftly and solidly as I can, I shove it forward.

This time I feel a brief bump of resistance, then the glass keeps moving. Whatever was propped up on the other side of the door clatters to the floor.

Yes!

By now the doorknob will undoubtedly be too hot to touch. I leap to my feet and bunch up the front of my shirt around my hand, but as I'm about to open the door, Charlene yells to me, her voice coming from the floor beside the desk. "Jevin, get over here! It's Tanbyrn! He passed out!"

Oxygen

I kneel beside the doctor.

He's lying still. Breathing but unconscious. Charlene tries to shake him awake, but he doesn't respond.

I shake him myself, call his name. Nothing.

The room is nearly filled with smoke.

You need to carry him, get him out of here.

Yes, but how would we—

The glass will be too hot to hold.

Maybe not, maybe you can get past the fire.

Quickly, I tug off my leather jacket.

"What are you doing?" Charlene is gasping for air herself.

I hand her the jacket, then hurriedly guide the glass back into the room and prop it upright against the desk.

"Jevin, what's the jacket for?"

"Hold the glass in front of you." I can barely see her through the smoke. Both of us have to yell now to be heard. "I'll carry Tanbyrn, follow you out the door. Tilt it, slide it across the floor, use it like a shield to protect you from the flames." I help her pull the jacket sleeves over her hands to protect them from getting burned. "Keep your head low and move fast!"

I lift Dr. Tanbyrn, drape him over the back of my shoulders, fireman's carry. Charlene holds the edges of the glass, her hands protected by the leather sleeves of my jacket. The glass plate is heavy, but she should be able to lean into it, move it in front of her along the floorboards, even with her injured arm. At least I hope she can.

With my shirt bunched up around my right hand, I reach for the doorknob.

"Will the flames rush in?" Sharp concern in her voice.

All fires are hungry for oxygen and it's possible

the flames would pour in, but we don't have a choice. I needed to open this door.

They might, yes—

"I don't know."

I grasp the knob.

Turn it.

And open the door.

Flames

A rush of smoke swirls around us, but thankfully, only a few flames lick into the room. The door gets hung up for a moment on what'd been holding it shut—which I now see is the end table from the lobby—but with enough pressure I'm able to slide it aside and open the door all the way.

Heat rages everywhere.

Flames are already consuming the walls. Much of the floor is also on fire, but there are enough spots that look free of the blaze that we should be able to get to the nearest exit door.

"Go on!" I holler to Charlene, and she leads the way, holding the glass in front of her. I follow closely behind. I'm not sure how effective the glass shield is, but it does seem to be keeping some of the flames away from her face.

Even though in my shows I've been set on fire, escaped from burning buildings, and been blown up innumerable times by Xavier, those were all controlled situations. None of that compared to the heat singeing my face and arms, burning my throat with every breath right now.

After only a few steps, I notice a body lying nearby. It's scalded, and I can't identify who it is until I see the metal bracelets encircling one of the charred wrists.

Abina.

A thick knot of anger forms inside me.

Whoever did this can't be far. Find him. Stop him.

Charlene doesn't pause, and I take that to mean she hasn't seen the research assistant's body. It's a small thing, but at least it's one thing to be thankful for.

We shuffle forward.

The air is rigid and fiery in my lungs.

We're about ten feet from the exit door, but by now I can tell that the glass idea doesn't seem to be working as well as I'd hoped. It's awkward for Charlene to maneuver and seems to be slowing us down. In front of us, blocking the way to the exit door, is a pool of flames.

"Tip it forward!" I yell. She does so immediately, and the glass hits the floor and shatters across the floorboards, sending a whoosh of smoke and displaced flames to every side. But the place where the glass fell is momentarily clear of the blaze, so we rush across the glass shards, make it to the exit door.

"You okay?"

"Yes!" Her reply is muffled by the popping, crackling fire.

I lean my hip against the push bar and the door pops open, but only about six inches, then catches on a stout chain.

No!

A rush of desperation.

I shift Dr. Tanbyrn's weight to keep him balanced on my shoulders, then smash my side against the door, but it's useless. I study the chain and see that it has a keyed lock, not a combination lock, holding the two ends together.

Oh yes.

"Charlene, my belt!"

She's worked with me on hundreds of escapes and knows about the belt buckle, the narrower-than-normal prong. I have no idea how many locks I've picked with it while sealed in trunks, coffins, airtight tubes—

She tugs the jacket off her arms, unbuckles the belt, snakes it out of my belt loops, and hands it to me, buckle first.

Holding it carefully, I slide my hand outside.

A one-handed pick, not easy, and it's been months since I've picked this brand of lock . . .

But I haven't lost my touch. It takes less than ten seconds, the lock clicks open, the ends of the chain dangle free. I grab one of them and yank the chain loose even as I throw my hip against the door.

It bangs open.

Charlene and I emerge from the building and run toward the clearing to escape the smoke and the raging flames.

You're okay. You made it!

Hopefully, Dr. Tanbyrn did as well.

Assault

As gently as I can, I lower him to the ground.

Charlene leans close. "Let me." She's more experienced at first aid than I am. I clear out of the way.

She tilts Dr. Tanbyrn's head to open his airway. Checks to see if he's still breathing.

I stand, look around.

The day is still damp, still gray, smudged darker now by the heavy black smoke from the blaze.

The guy who set that fire is probably still on the campus, probably—

I see someone standing just off the trail that leads along the edge of the forest behind the building and recognize him as the man who was waiting in the reception area when Charlene and I arrived.

"He's still alive." Relief in her voice.

The man is half-hidden by a tree, and he must have seen me watching him because he turns and heads into the woods, limping.

From last night's knife wound.

That's it.

You're mine.

"Take care of Tanbyrn," I shout to Charlene. I'm already sprinting toward the woods, wrapping my belt around my left hand. "I'll be right back."

Glenn glanced behind him.

The guy was pursuing him.

Alright. Let him follow.

The fog would help.

Find a spot out of sight from the rest of the campus.

Take care of this guy for good.

Then get to the parking lot and clear out before the fire trucks and the cops show up.

I throw a branch aside, jump over a root, and race toward Abina's killer, eighty yards ahead of me, barely visible on the edge of the fog.

You're a runner. He's injured.

You can catch him.

Catch him, yes. But then what?

Stop him. Do whatever it takes to stop him.

Whatever it takes.

Seventy yards, maybe sixty-five.

He killed Abina. Tanbyrn might die. He tried to kill Charlene.

Yeah, I would stop him.

With my lungs still feeling like they're filled

233

with smoke, I'm short of breath and I can sense that it's slowing me down, and despite the wound in this man's leg, he's amazingly fast. Last night he had a knife sticking out of his thigh, now he's racing through the forest like he was never hurt at all. It was quite possible the knife hadn't gone in as deeply as I thought it had.

But still, I'm gaining.

Sixty yards.

He reaches a ravine and disappears into a patch of thick fog that has settled into the valley. Logs covered with moss. Dense ferns on the ground. The trees here are ancient. Primeval. Fog lurks between them like threads of living smoke.

The mist brushes against my face and arms and it feels good, cooling the reddened skin. I can only hear the sound of my choked breathing, my muted footsteps on the forest floor. Other than that, all is still and quiet in the fog.

I'm jacked on adrenaline from the fire, the chase, the thought of fighting this guy, and my heart is slamming against the inside of my chest. I arrive at the edge of the ravine and then descend into it, trying to find the path through the underbrush where he might've gone. At last I come to a small clearing in the trees.

Fog all around.

No sign of him.

I slow to a jog.

Stop.

No sound of him running. The ground has leveled off and the fog is thicker here. I can only see fifteen or twenty feet in any direction. Towering trees surround me. He could be anywhere.

Puffs of breath circle from my mouth in the cool air as if they were bursts of steam evaporating before me. I listen but hear nothing apart from my ragged breathing.

I was in a fire only minutes ago, now I'm in the chilled forest and a shiver runs through me.

Backtrack? Did he backtrack?

No, he's here.

Fists raised, I crouch. Ready stance.

If he were still running, I would hear him, at least be able to tell what direction he was heading in.

But I hear nothing.

He's close.

He's here. Behind one of the trees.

I inch toward a large tree to my left, one wide enough to conceal a person.

"They're following me," I shout, I lie. "You won't get away. I've seen your face. I can identify you."

That much was true.

I move closer to the looming tree and hear a crunch of leaves ten feet to my right. Instinctively I whip around toward the sound, but no one is there.

A trick.

Misdirection.

Tossing something away from yourself—it's what you would have done!

I snap my head in the other direction and see a branch as thick as a baseball bat swinging toward me. I try to duck, drop to the side, but I'm too slow.

The branch collides with the left side of my head and sends me reeling to the side. I fall hard, face-first onto the forest floor. A rock that's jutting up between the roots smacks into my right side, and I hear a muffled crack.

A burst of pain shoots through me.

My rib.

My head throbs, feels like it's filled with its own heavy, thunderous heartbeat. The world becomes a splinter of dots, stars splintering apart in my vision. I try to push myself to my feet, but the world is turning in a wide, dizzy circle and I can't seem to make my limbs obey me. My side screams at me, and I don't make it past my hands and knees.

Focus. Focus!

Out of the corner of my eye, I see the man approaching me.

I don't make it to my feet. He kicks me hard in my injured side and the ground rushes up at me again. I barely hold back a gasp of pain when I land. If the rib wasn't fractured before, it's almost certainly broken now.

Everything around me seems to be edging outside of time, but in my blurred vision I see him raise the branch, step closer. I roll away from him and feel the whoosh of air beside me as he brings the branch thwacking down right where my head had been only a moment earlier. A spray of mud splatters across my face.

My injured side squeezes out a jet of pain that courses through my chest every time I take a breath.

Get up, you have to get up to fight this guy.

Forcing myself to stand, I feel another swoop of dizziness, but I hide it from him. Face him.

He discards the branch, flips out a knife.

So he has a weapon.

But so do I.

Carefully, I wrap one end of the belt around each hand. It's one of the simplest ways to defend yourself when someone comes at you with a knife. If you know what you're doing, you can trap the wrist of your opponent's knife hand, control the arm, and take him down.

And I know what I'm doing.

As long as you can stay on your feet.

The pain coursing up my side and pounding through my head makes it hard to focus.

He's stationary, less than ten feet away, studying me, no doubt planning how best to attack me.

He holds the blade straight out to slice at me like he did last night when he went after Charlene.

No ice-pick grip this time. He's learned his lesson.

As I breathe, breathe, breathe, try to relax, somehow, even though I'm distracted by the pain, my senses seem to become sharper, more focused. I catch the sound of a stream nearby that I hadn't noticed. I smell the pine needles and the moist decay of the soil, feel the droplets of sweat trailing down my forehead and the warm blood oozing from the side of my head where he hit me with the branch.

He watches me.

Don't black out. Do not black out.

But I'm unsteady and feel like I might.

I blink, rub the back of my fist across my eyes, and my vision clears enough for me to see the streak of blood splayed across his sleeve. I can only guess what he did to Abina before setting her on fire.

A shot of anger tightens my focus again.

"Her name was Abina," I tell him.

"What?"

"The woman you killed in there. Before you started the fire."

"Ah." He taps the edge of his lip with his tongue. "Stuck her in the belly like a squirmy little pig. She would have squealed and squealed. Died quick, though. When I did her throat." He demonstrates how he killed her, miming the action with the knife. "Burned kinda nice in that outfit too. Almost like she was dressed for the occasion."

Rage, white and hot and like nothing I've ever experienced, overwhelms me and I like it. Feel fueled by it. I snap the belt taut between my hands and realize I'm no longer thinking in terms of stopping this man. That's not exactly the right word.

Everything becomes clear: only one of us is going to walk out of this forest alive.

"How's your leg? How about we do the other one too?"

His grin flattens. He flips the knife into his other hand. "Wound for wound."

Stall, Jevin. Stall long enough and help will arrive.

But no, I don't want to stall.

I want to take care of this right now.

Besides, I know help isn't on its way. We're hidden in the fog more than a quarter mile off the trail and down a ravine. Even if I called for help, the dense forest and the drizzling rain would devour the sound. No one knows where we are, no one is looking for us. Besides, there aren't any cops around, so even if someone from the center did come, that would only mean one more unarmed person for this guy to attack.

Glenn eyed the man who'd bested him last night in the chamber.

A line from a movie came to mind: "You are the

pus in a boil I am about to pop." Glenn thought that, thought it, but did not say it.

But yes, popping a boil was a good way to describe what he was about to do to this man.

I move toward him.

He's passing the knife back and forth from hand to hand, trying to intimidate me. Not wise—it leaves you unprotected for a fraction of a second each time you do it.

"I like it better this way." His voice is all acid and filled with disdain. "I can make it last longer than the fire would have."

"So can I."

He feints left, lunges right, sweeping the knife toward me. I stop the attack with an inside block and let my momentum carry me through and land a left leg round kick to his side, then I twist away, sweeping my leg backward to take him down, but he's quick and plants himself, blocks with his left shin.

Kick his leg. His thigh. It's injured.

I go for it as he maneuvers toward me, but he evades the kick. He jabs right, then slashes the blade toward my stomach, catching my shirt, grazing my skin. He quickly goes for me again, but I block his hand, get in close, and smash his jaw with the back of my fist. It's a solid punch and it hurts my hand, but I know it must have hurt his face even worse.

He has the knife in his right hand, and I go for that wrist with the belt, try to wrap it so I can disarm him, but he savagely slashes the blade against the belt, severing it. I drop the two ends as he punches me hard in my injured side, and I can't help but crumple backward in pain.

My head is pounding fiercely and my balance is still off. I'm queasy, dizzy. It feels like everything around me is slipping off the rim of reality into a widening gray blur.

I straighten up. Face him. Give him no indication of how weak I feel. "Why set the fire? To kill Tanbyrn or destroy his files?"

Spittle hangs from his lip and he sneers, blood covering his teeth from where I punched him. He doesn't speak, but there's a stony hardness in his eyes, a look that seems to say, "I'm willing to do anything it takes to see this through. Are you willing to do as much to stop me?"

That's the look in his eyes.

And I know it's the look in mine.

The fog swirls aside as he rushes at me. His blade flashes toward my cheek and I deflect his arm, land another punch to his jaw. He spins, but I step to the side, heel-kick his injured leg, then his knee, buckling it, and as I do I strike the back of his neck as hard as I can with the straightened edge of my right hand.

He goes down quick, with a heavy, wet thud. I expect him to be on his feet in a second, and I wait, ready, my heart jackhammering in my chest.

The man does not rise.

Two thoughts flash through my mind—*he's hurt and he can't get up; he's faking it and he's going to stab you as soon as you move closer.*

There's no way my knife-hand strike disabled him. I'm strong, but I'm not that strong.

He's faking it.

Only then do I see that his right arm is buckled beneath him. That was the hand that held the knife.

Still he does not stand.

I call to him. He doesn't answer.

Check, you have to see.

Sparring didn't prepare me for this, didn't teach me what to do next. When you're in the gym, you help your partner up when he goes down. But not here, not in a real fight. There's no way I'm going to flee, but I'm not sure I want to get closer to him either.

He doesn't move.

I edge toward him.

If I go in any closer and he rolls toward me with the knife, I'm not sure I'd be able to jump out of the way in time. He might manage to stab my leg, even my stomach.

I take a breath, try to calm myself, but it's not exactly happening.

Something I'm going to have to work on.

If there was a way to roll him over without getting close enough for him to cut me, then I would—

The branch he hit me with.

Yes.

I retrieve it and approach him.

His back is rising and falling slightly with each breath, and that makes me think he really is hurt. Someone who was faking it would probably hold his breath to make it look like he was dead.

Only a couple feet away now.

I call to him again, but still he doesn't reply.

Using the end of the branch, I press against his shoulder to roll him onto his back. He's a big man and it takes some effort, but then he does roll over and I see the blood soaking his shirt and the handle of the knife protruding from his abdomen.

The blade is buried almost to the hilt, angled up just beneath his sternum. I can only guess that the knife tip either punctured his heart or is close to it. Either way, it went through his lung, and the frothy blood he's spitting out tells me how serious the wound is.

His eyes are open. He's still breathing, but his teeth are clenched and he's obviously in a lot of pain. He coughs up a mouthful of blood and it splatters across his chin. If I turned him onto his side, it would keep the blood from pooling in his throat, help clear his airway, and keep him from aspirating on his own blood, and if he hadn't killed Abina, I might have done that right away. But because of what he did to her, I'm not sure I want to help him at all.

But then I have another thought.

You need to find out what he was looking for before it's too late.

Alright.

I kneel beside him.

Last night I saw him yank a knife out of his leg without flinching. To make sure he won't pull out the blade now and kill me with it, I remove the knife. Toss it to the side.

He winces, then sneers.

I turn his head to the side to help clear his mouth of blood, and it does seem to help him breathe.

"What were you looking for in the center last night?"

He spits, coughs a little, doesn't respond.

"Who are you? Who sent you here?"

"Akinsanya will find you." His voice is sputtering and wet with blood.

"Akinsanya? Who's Akinsanya?"

No response. Just a smug grin.

"Who's Akinsanya?"

Nothing.

A compassionate person might've reassured him, told him that he was going to be okay, that help was coming. But that would have been a lie, and besides, right here, right now, more than compassion was at stake. There's justice too, and after what he did to Abina, what he tried to do to Charlene, what he might've succeeded in doing to Dr. Tanbyrn, I don't try to comfort him. Instead I lean close. "You're dying. But it might take some time. I'll help it along if you tell me what you were looking for."

Something in his eyes changes.

"Go on," I tell him. "I'm listening."

"Screw"—his word is stained with hatred and a pathetic kind of defiance—"you."

Alright then.

I stand up.

Watch him.

I don't hurry things along, but let him die at his own speed.

It takes awhile.

And I'm not at all sorry that it does.

The last thought Glenn Banner had was not regret for what he had done, not remorse, not sorrow, just anger that he hadn't killed this man, that he hadn't gotten to spend some time with that woman from last night.

Well, at least you got to watch that skinny little whore burn.

Then the darkness descended.

And the silent, writhing journey toward forever began.

The Photos

I wait a minute or two after his breathing stops just to make sure that he's gone, then I check his pockets.

A set of car keys, a cell phone, a lighter, a crumpled-up copy of the front page of today's issue of *USA Today*. A wallet.

Opening up his wallet, I find out that his name was Glenn Banner. He lived in Seattle. A felon. I'm surprised to see that noted on his license, but it's there, probably some helpful little law that I wasn't even aware of.

I figure I have a right to know as much as I can about the man who tried to kill me, so I don't feel any guilt searching him like this. I'm not going to take anything with me, I'll leave everything here for the cops; I just want some information.

There's twenty-nine dollars cash in his wallet, four credit cards, no family photographs. But there are photos—eleven of them.

A dark chill slides through me when I realize what they're pictures of.

Corpses.

Eight men, two women, plus one body that's mangled so badly I can't tell the gender of the victim. Some corpses had been stabbed, two have plastic bags over their heads, others were strangled with wire. The first page of a *USA Today* newspaper lies beside each body.

To prove they died on that day.

Eleven horrible crimes that will finally be solved when the police follow up on this. Eleven families who'll find out the truth. Terrible, brutal, yes, but at least they would get some sense of closure to their pain, and surely there's some degree of justice to that, to knowing the truth?

Hard to say.

I've never been able to find the reason lurking behind why Rachel killed herself and our sons. I tell myself that knowing the truth would make a difference, would help me move on. But there's no way to tell if it would really help anything at all.

I put the photos back in the wallet, slide it into his pocket.

On his phone, I check the last ten numbers called and received. Since I have nothing to write with, I record them on my own phone, typing them into the notepad. When I'm done, I return Banner's phone to his pocket as well.

The last thing I find is a crumpled sheet of paper with a seemingly random series of sixteen numbers, upper- and lowercase letters, and punctuation marks: G8&p{40X9!qx5%8Y

All I can think of is that it's a password or some kind of access code. I record it in my phone's notepad as well, then stuff the scrap of paper back into his jeans pocket again.

The rain is picking up now, and I'm anxious to see if Dr. Tanbyrn has awakened—and to find out if anyone else might've been trapped in that fire.

All around me the forest looks the same, so as I navigate through the mist, I snap off twigs at regular intervals to mark the way so I'll be able to lead the police back to Banner's body.

I know I was acting in self-defense when he died; in fact, when he fell on the knife, I was just trying to keep him from killing me. I hadn't planned that, it was an accident, but still, I hope there won't be any kind of trouble with the police when I show them his corpse.

After I find the trail, it's not far to the research building, which, despite the rain, I can see is already mostly consumed by the blaze.

Rain and smoke smudge the day.

Charlene isn't in the place where I left her and Tanbyrn, and I'm not sure if that's a good sign or a bad one.

I study the area, searching for her.

Emergency vehicle sirens scream at me from the access road to the center, but it's too late for the firefighters to save much of the structure, and unless Banner had a partner we don't know about, there is no arsonist for the cops to track down. All I can think of is that hopefully no one else in addition to Dr. Tanbyrn and Abina was hurt or killed in the fire.

A group of about twenty people has gathered

beneath the roof of a deck built along the back of a nearby cabin, presumably to escape the rain. A few people are silently watching the blaze, others have formed a semicircle and are staring down at a body.

Tanbyrn.

I quicken my pace.

Two people lean over him, Charlene and a woman I don't recognize. Two of the women in the semicircle are holding their hands over their mouths, and I can't imagine that's a good sign.

The attention of the crowd turns to me as I approach, and the people part to let me through. Someone asks if I'm alright, perhaps noticing the blood smeared across the side of my head or the hitch in my step from the pain in my side.

"I'm fine. Thanks."

I make it to Tanbyrn's side and Charlene looks up at me. "He still hasn't woken up."

But at least he's alive.

At least—

"Did you . . . ?" she begins, then seems to catch herself and stands. The woman who's kneeling beside Tanbyrn apparently knows what she's doing—perhaps she's a doctor or a nurse—and Charlene must feel comfortable leaving him alone with her because she leads me away from the group of bystanders to the corner of the porch, where we can talk privately.

"What happened? Did you catch him?" Then

she sees the wound on the side of my head. "Jevin!" Out of concern she reaches for it, but instead of touching it, just ends up pointing at it instead. "Are you okay?"

"Yes. Was anyone else hurt?"

"No. It doesn't look like it."

"Good." I lower my voice. "The arsonist, he's dead."

"What?" She stares at me. "You killed him?"

The first fire truck appears, lumbers toward the flaming building with one set of wheels on the trail, the other on the wet, uneven ground beside it.

"It was an accident. He came at me with the knife. I blocked his arm, kicked out his leg, and when I hit him again, he went down. He landed on the blade."

She lets that sink in.

I gesture toward Tanbyrn. "How is he?"

"Hard to say. He needs to get to a hospital. You killed the guy? Honestly?"

I'm not quite comfortable phrasing it like that, but technically I have to admit that it's correct. "Yeah, I guess I did."

Her eyes have returned to the gash on my head. "Are you sure you're okay?"

A few police cars and an ambulance emerge from the fog, following the fire truck. One of the men who was on the porch leaves and signals to the ambulance to come this way. The driver veers away from the path and aims the vehicle toward us.

Gingerly, I touch the wound. It's already swollen pretty badly and is quite tender. I'd been so distracted thinking about Tanbyrn that I hadn't been as aware of the pain pumping through my side, but now that I pause and breathe and think about where I am, what happened, it seems to become more pervasive again. The knuckles of my right hand are sore from when I punched Banner's jaw. The skin on my hands is still red and tender from the fire.

"A little beat-up," I admit. "But yeah. I'm okay."

She's quiet, and I imagine she's mentally running through the fight, trying to picture me—or maybe trying not to picture me—killing a man.

"He was the guy from last night," I tell her. "The same guy who was outside Tanbyrn's office when we arrived."

"Did he . . . Did you find out anything?"

"His name was Glenn Banner. From Seattle." The ambulance pulls to a stop. Two paramedics leap out, and the crowd parts to give them access to Tanbyrn. "I found a note with a code on it, and I've got some cell numbers for Fionna to follow up on." I'm not sure how to tell her the rest, so in the end I decide to just go ahead and say it. "Charlene, he killed Abina."

"What? Abina?"

I nod.

"How?" Shock and disbelief in her voice.

"Charlene, it's not really—"

"What did he do to her!"

I hesitate, realize she will settle for nothing less than the truth, and give her the whole story. "He stabbed her, then he slit her throat. He burned her body in the fire."

Charlene's face hardens into a mixture of revulsion and rage.

For a moment I debate whether or not to tell her about the photographs in his wallet, but it's pretty clear this isn't the time for that. Unsure what to say, I finally just mumble an honest but inadequate acknowledgment that I understand how devastating this news is. "I'm sorry."

The paramedics are giving Dr. Tanbyrn oxygen and transferring him onto a gurney that they've lowered beside him.

"Did he suffer?" Charlene's words are soft, but there's fire beneath them. "Did he suffer before he died?"

"Yes. He did. It wasn't quick."

"Good."

She stares past me for a moment, then notices the slice in my shirt where Banner's blade made its mark when he came at me. She reaches out and tenderly slides her finger along the edge of the frayed fabric, the light cut underneath it. The pain and anger on her face fade, and a look of deep concern takes its place. "Thank God you're alright."

"Yes."

"But that poor woman." Her voice breaks. "I can't believe she's dead."

I see a tear form in the corner of Charlene's eye, and I draw her close. She wraps her arms around me and leans against me, and despite the pain that crunches up my side as she does, I don't flinch. I just let her try to draw strength from me, even though at the moment I don't really feel like I have a whole lot of extra strength to offer anyone.

The words from a few moments ago echo through my head:

"Did he suffer before he died?"

"Yes. He did. It wasn't quick."

"Good."

Yeah, maybe there is a degree of justice to that after all.

Bloody Soil

The sheriff's department deputies question me about the assailant, and I walk three of them to the place where Glenn Banner's body lies sprawled on a bed of soggy, bloody pine needles. They ask me to explain what happened, talk them through the fight, and I do. Blow by blow.

Two of them jot notes while the third, a man with a snarled brown mustache whose name tag reads Jacobs, slowly circles the body, taking photographs with his mobile phone. I figure I don't need to tell them about the pictures in Banner's wallet. They'll find them soon enough.

I'm finishing recounting what happened when Deputy Jacobs begins to go through Banner's pockets.

He locates the phone, the note, the keys, the newspaper page, the wallet. He flips it open and after a moment pulls out the photographs.

Pauses.

He quietly calls the other men over, and the three of them go through the photographs of the dead and mutilated bodies one at a time. A dark, uncertain storm of shock and fury seems to settle all around us in the small clearing.

I wait for them to finish.

Honestly, I'm unsure how much they'll want to question me, or even if they might take me to the station or arrest me. After all, a man is dead, and I was the one fighting him when he died. I have no idea what the legal ramifications might be, but the longer I stand here, the more I begin to wonder.

Finally, one of the officers, a looming, sloping-shouldered man with a stern face, turns to me. "Looks like you're lucky to be alive."

"Yes."

I wait to see what will happen next. He folds his notebook shut, turns to Jacobs. "Walk Mr. Banks back to the center. He needs to have those EMTs take a look at that contusion on his head." Then he addresses me again. "And Mr. Banks . . ."

Okay. Here we go.

"Yes?"

"Looks like you saved us some trouble here, saved the taxpayers a lot of money. I'm sure as questions arise, we'll be in touch." Without another word, he puts away the notepad, turns back to the body, and Deputy Jacobs motions for me to return with him up the hill.

It takes a moment for the facts of the situation to settle in, but then it strikes me that although there'll undoubtedly be more questions to answer and probably sheaves of paperwork to fill out, for now it looks like the officers aren't going to give me a hard time about Banner's death.

Instead the tall officer had essentially thanked me for getting Banner off their hands.

I'm a bit surprised by my initial thought, but in the end I agree with it: *Actually, you know what, Deputy? It was my pleasure.*

Jacobs trudges beside me as we ascend the muddy hill. "They'll probably want to take you to the hospital. Check you over."

Actually, that wouldn't be bad. It would give me a chance to see how Tanbyrn is doing.

And get your ribs X-rayed. A fractured one could puncture your lung.

Yeah, that would ruin my day.

You can't do the kind of stunts I've done over

the years and not come away with your share of broken bones, and I've cracked ribs before but never seriously broken one. Either way, deep breathing or coughing was not going to be fun for the next couple weeks, but it would be good to find out the severity of the damage.

"Also," I tell him, "there's a woman who needs to come along. That guy cut her last night. Sliced her arm. She's back at the center."

"Alright." He pulls out his walkie-talkie. "Let's get you two an ambulance."

Riah presented herself at Cyrus's office, and the receptionist, Caitlyn Vaughn, led her grudgingly through the door.

She entered and found Cyrus alone, studying the aquariums containing the wasps. Without even mentioning their meeting with the twins last night, he invited her to join him. "Come here, Riah. There's something I want you to see. She's building her nest around the roach. I think you'll like this part."

On the way to the hospital, I call Xavier and tell him to meet us there, then I contact Fionna and give her the phone numbers I'd pulled from Banner's cell and the alphanumeric code I'd gotten from the sheet of paper in his pocket. I also mention Project Alpha, the name of the research program Dr. Tanbyrn had started to tell us about just before the fire. "Look into it. See what you can find out. And see if you can find any reference to someone named Akinsanya."

When we were in his office, right after we smelled the gasoline, Charlene had taken Tanbyrn's folder of notes and his iPad and stuffed them into her shirt to save them from the fire. Now, in the ambulance, she has the iPad on her lap, but we find that it's password protected and we can't access the files. The algorithms on the sheets of paper are still as unintelligible to me as they were earlier when I was sitting at Tanbyrn's desk.

I ask Charlene how she's holding up.

"I don't know . . . I mean, what happened to Abina . . ." A deep sadness pervades her words. "It's so senseless. She seemed really nice and I can't believe that guy just . . ." She shudders. "I'm worried about Tanbyrn too. And about you— about your head." I'm a little glad I hadn't told her about my ribs.

The paramedic had given me an ice pack and I'm holding it tenderly against my swollen temple. I take a shot at trying to lighten the mood: "You didn't see that branch. It got the worse end of the deal."

She smiles faintly at that.

I reach over and take her hand.

For a moment she's quiet, then speaks softly: "The test is over, Jevin. We don't need to pretend anymore."

I don't always know the right thing to say to her, but this time I do. "I'm not pretending."

And instead of pulling away, she repositions her hand to hold more tightly onto mine.

Savants

Things at the hospital proceed quickly.

Xavier is waiting for us and, despite the objections of the nurses, hovers while they fret over the contusion on my head and while a doctor takes a careful look at Charlene's arm. I overhear the doc tell her that she's still in the window to get stitches, but that it was good she came in now.

Tanbyrn is still unconscious, and because of the amount of smoke inhalation, his age, and his apparently frail health, he's listed in critical condition. The doctors say it's possible he may slip into a coma.

I take some Advil for my mild concussion, the nurses leave me alone while they order an X-ray for my ribs, Charlene heads down the hall to get her stitches, and I start bringing Xavier up to speed, but I'm distracted by the furry-looking bologna and cheese sandwich he's eating. "Where did you get that thing, anyway?"

"A vending machine."

"A vending machine."

"Yup."

"Looks like it's been there a month."

"Tastes like it too." But that doesn't stop him from taking another bite. "But I've had worse."

"I'm not sure I needed to know that."

He listens carefully as I go on with my summary of what happened at the center, and in between bites of his sandwich, he interrupts to make observations about the heat flux of the fire, the likelihood of full-room involvement—flash-over—in the doctor's office. "The paneled walls lined with books—man, you wouldn't have had much time."

"Let's just hope we got out soon enough for Tanbyrn."

"Yeah." A pause. "You did good back there, bro."

"Thanks."

"I bet it felt good too." Talking with his mouth full.

"You mean helping Tanbyrn?"

He polishes off the sandwich, licks the grease off his fingers. "Yeah, that and escaping—getting out of the office, through the fire, picking that lock to get out of the building. I bet it felt good to be back in the zone again."

"The zone?"

"Who you are, Jev. What you do. You're an escape artist."

"I'm a filmmaker."

"No. You're an escape artist."

No, you're not. Not anymore.

I leave the topic alone. "Hopefully, Tanbyrn will pull through."

"Yeah." A moment passes. "So you got the footage with the button camera?"

"It's at the cabin back at the center."

"And the test didn't appear to be faked?"

"Not that I could tell, no."

"So that means if the entanglement stuff is for real—that means you and Charlene are—"

"Friends."

"Friends."

"Right."

He winks at me knowingly. "Gotcha."

"No, no. Don't do that, Xav."

"What?"

"That whole innocent 'gotcha' routine. We're just friends."

"Who are entangled."

I open my mouth to respond, change my mind. "Never mind."

He produces a pen from his pocket and flips open his leather-bound journal. Actual paper. Very old-school. "You mentioned that Tanbyrn told you about something called Project Alpha."

"He said it involved two men, twins. He just called them 'L' and 'N.' Said they'd fly in . . ." Something else the doctor mentioned comes to mind, distracts me.

Right before you smelled the gasoline, what did he say?

Negative?

Negative what?

Xavier waits. "You alright?"

"Yeah, I'm just . . ." My thoughts scurry off in a hundred directions.

"So they'd fly the twins in . . . and . . . ?"

"Sorry. Right. He mentioned that the studies involved communication and physiology, alpha brain waves, that identical twins are more capable of . . . well, he didn't clarify. I assume that he was studying the negative effects of something concerning the mind-to-mind communication. He never had the chance to explain."

Xavier writes in his journal while I verbally try to sort through what we know: "RixoTray is funding research on mind-to-mind communication. According to Fionna's research—wait . . ." This was high-stakes conspiracy stuff, right up his alley. "Dr. Tanbyrn was studying the phenomenon of one person's loving thoughts nonlocally affecting the physiology of the person he or she loved."

"Uh-huh. And your results with Charlene bore that out."

Not this again. "I told you we're—"

"Friends."

"Right."

"Gotcha."

"Stop that. And don't say 'gotcha.'"

"See, you really can read minds." He crumples

261

up the wrapper from his sandwich. Sets it aside.

"Xav, my point is, it's two people who genuinely care about each other. I'm not certain they would need to be lovers exactly."

He sees where I'm going with this. "So, you're thinking family members in this case? These two twins?"

I stand. Pace. Weave the 1895 Morgan Dollar through my fingers to help clear my head. "Right. Tanbyrn mentioned they were special. Well, what if they have a really close emotional connection like my boys did? Drew and Tony. You remember that. At times they seemed to almost read each other's minds."

Even though Xavier wasn't related to the boys, he'd fulfilled the role of the cool uncle every kid wishes to have, and I know he misses them acutely.

"Yeah, I do remember. There were times when they would finish each other's sentences. Like they were connected in a way no one else is."

For a moment I'm quiet. "I don't think I ever told you about what happened one day with Drew. When his side started hurting."

"What was it?"

"I was playing with him outside. T-ball. I was behind him holding his arms, helping him with his swing, when suddenly he dropped the bat and turned and clung to me, hugged me. 'What's wrong?' I asked him. And he started crying. I knelt and held him. 'What is it?' And he said, 'It hurts, Daddy!' He was holding his right side. That's when I heard Rachel calling for us from inside the house. It was Tony. His appendix had burst."

"You're kidding."

"No. Drew's pain went away while we were driving to the hospital, but still, I wracked my brain trying to figure out how it had happened. It couldn't have been a coincidence—but if it wasn't, then what was it? What caused Drew to feel Tony's pain?"

Xavier taps his pen against the page. "You hear stories like that sometimes. People waking up in the middle of the night with chest pains and finding out later that their mom or dad had a heart attack at that very moment, or having a gut feeling not to walk down a certain street and then finding out there was a mugger who was caught down there. Once when my sister and I were in high school, she had the sense one night that she was being watched, and when she turned off the light to her bedroom, she saw a face of one of the boys from her class outside her window."

"That's disturbing."

"You should have seen what I did to him when I caught up with him the next day. Anyway, all this stuff, these gut feelings, déjà vu, premonitions, UFO sightings, stigmata appearing on people—I know you don't like to hear this, but there's a lot that happens out there that just can't be easily explained."

Discounting his reference to UFO sightings, he's right that there are a lot of things out there that can't be explained, at least not in the typical ways, and since I've spent the last year trying to prove that those things can be explained, the fact that he's right annoys me.

He goes on, "Do you think there might be senses that some people have that others don't?"

"You mean a sixth sense?" I don't even try to hide my skepticism at that. "No. I don't buy that."

"Step away from the idea of psychic powers for a minute."

"And aliens."

"Okay, and aliens. Think about it, what if there are senses that we're supposed to have, that aren't breaking any physical laws or depending on any divine or malevolent forces—only gifts, skills, talents that aren't any more supernatural than twins sharing behavioral traits that genetics can't explain. Nobody calls autistic savants who can perform complex quadratic equations in seconds 'psychics.' "

"You mean even though they haven't studied math."

"Yes. Or Down syndrome children who can hear a tune once on the piano and can perform it flawlessly—"

"Okay, I see what you're saying."

"In the past those people, or maybe child prodigies, might've been considered psychic or witches or demon-possessed, but modern science—although it can't always explain the behavior—has, for some reason, grown to accept them as unusual, outside of the realm of normal experience, but not paranormal."

He pauses, then out of nowhere he waves his hand through the air as if to erase our conversation, and I'm not sure why; he seemed to make a good point. "Anyway, I don't want to lose my train of thought. You were telling me that these twins, 'L' and 'N,' they flew in, Tanbyrn did some sort of tests, they'd fly out. We don't know what the tests are about, but we do know that RixoTray has been funding them."

I'm more than happy to leave the topics of psychics and UFOs behind as well. "Last night Charlene was reading over the notes that Fionna drew up on RixoTray, and she came across the name of a doctor in Philadelphia. Riah something."

Negative.

The doctor said he was studying the negative effects—

Oh.

Flipping the coin faster. "Xav, what if it's not just loving thoughts that affect people?"

"You mean negative thoughts? That's what Tanbyrn was looking into with these two guys?"

"I don't know, but—"

Negative.

Why would the Pentagon be involved with this?

Xavier waits. "But?"

"But what about this." I stop finger-flipping the coin. Stare at him. "If one person can affect the heart rate of another person—even slightly—just by his thoughts, could he learn to do more than that?"

He straightens up. "Are you saying what I think you're saying?"

"Yes, affect his heart rate to a greater degree—possibly give it an uneven rhythm, cause it to beat faster, or—"

"Stop it."

"Yes, exactly. Or stop it."

Project Alpha

For a long time neither of us speaks. It all seems unbelievable to me that the research might have gone in this direction, but whether this was all conjecture or not, the facts we have so far do seem to fit this line of reasoning. "Project Alpha is a cooperative program with the Department of Defense."

"The government." Xavier nods as if that explains everything. "Just like Star Gate."

"What, you mean the TV show?"

He waves his hand dismissively. "No. It has nothing to do with that or the movie. Star Gate was a CIA program back in the nineties. They were studying psychics to try and use remote viewing—basically, observing something without being physically present."

"Clairvoyance."

"Right. They were hoping it would help with intelligence gathering."

"Which, obviously, it would have." Normally I'm doubtful about Xavier's government conspiracy theories, but in this case, considering everything that's happened over the last twenty-four hours, I'm a lot more willing to listen. "Go on."

"They also tried to use psychics to manipulate objects—telekinesis—so you could conceivably cause a Russian nuclear reactor to overheat, or a torpedo to explode while it was still in the firing tube of a sub. That sort of thing."

Telekinesis is one of the most common tricks of television "psychics," and one of the easiest ones to replicate—bending spoons, making objects float or vanish, affecting the performance of machines—I'd been doing this stuff since I was a teenager. But those were all illusions, and what Xavier was talking about here was on a whole different level. "So did the CIA have any success?"

"The short answer is no." He seems to balance that mentally, reevaluate it. "There were mixed results in the remote viewing arena, but that's about it. Anyway, they dropped the program. The Air Force and DoD dabbled in similar research over the years, but nothing really came of it."

Knowing Xavier and his predilection for conspiracy theories, if there was anything at all to this research, he would've been all over it.

I reflect on what he said. "Okay, but that was a couple decades ago. Now, with Tanbyrn's research, with recent discoveries in neurophysiology and neurobiology, the nature of consciousness, this deeper understanding of quantum entanglement—"

"The Pentagon has picked it up again—that's what you're thinking?"

"That's what I'm wondering."

Everything I've done exposing fake psychics seems to argue against what we're talking about here. Telekinesis, clairvoyance, altering someone's heart rate by your thoughts. The idea of directing negative energy toward someone to harm him in some way, or even kill him—it was just too much. Reminded me of River Tam in *Firefly*: "I can kill you with my brain." This couldn't possibly be the right track.

"No, Xav. To kill someone by your thoughts? That's crazy."

If it were possible, why not just do that with Tanbyrn? Why hire an assassin to take him out?

"But," Xavier replies, "there are stories of shamans, witch doctors, voodoo priestesses doing that—cursing people—stories that've been around for centuries."

"That's just folklore. Like the legends about the fakirs in India levitating or being buried alive for years on end, and so on. You know as well as I do that every trick in the book can be replicated without any supernatural explanation. You helped design half the effects in my last stage show."

Xavier taps his lip, deep in thought. " 'But to emulate is not to disprove.' A wise person once told me that."

"I appreciate the compliment but—"

"He also told me that replication is not refutation, that just because you can find the counterfeit of something doesn't mean there isn't the real thing. Just because there's counterfeit currency doesn't mean there isn't actual currency out there somewhere."

"Xavier, I—"

"It could be that science is just now discovering what people of faith have always known—that our thoughts and expectations about reality affect its outcome in real, tangible ways. That's what quantum physics is all about, right? The role of consciousness in collapsing quantum wave functions, that without an observer, reality never manifests itself?"

"You read Tanbyrn's books too?"

"Skimmed a few chapters while you were at the center. Think about it: nearly every religion believes in the power of thoughts and prayers, curses and blessings. They're a huge deal in the Judeo-Christian tradition, especially the Old Testament. And then of course you have the New Testament where Jesus was clairvoyant, telepathic, and telekinetic."

I stare at him. "What are you talking about?"

Xavier ticks the reasons off on his fingers as he lists them: "Clairvoyance—he saw Nathanael under a fig tree when he wasn't present. Telepathy—he read the thoughts of the Pharisees. Telekinesis—turning water into wine, having Peter catch a fish to pay the temple tax and the fish has a coin in its mouth . . ."

"Oh, so you're saying that Jesus either made the coin appear there or somehow made the fish swallow it and then swim into Peter's net."

"Right." Next finger. "And as far as prayers and curses—his prayers drove demons out of people, healed them, even raised people from the dead."

"He didn't curse anybody."

"He cursed a fig tree and made it wither."

I'm not sure if Xavier just made that up or not.

He looks triumphant at his list, however, it's easy enough to rebut what he said. "Okay, suppose for a moment that those stories are true, not just folklore. If Jesus was who he claimed to be, if he was God, then those were just miracles."

"Just miracles? What do you mean *just* miracles?"

"I mean, he was God. He could do anything."

"No, he couldn't."

I look at him skeptically. "Jesus couldn't do anything."

"The Bible says he couldn't do any great miracles in his hometown because of the people's lack of faith. It doesn't say he wouldn't do them, it says he couldn't."

I shake my head. "No. I can't imagine that's in the Bible."

"Look it up. The power of God himself was strangled by the lack of belief."

"That's a little extreme, I'd say."

"Besides, he told his followers that nothing is impossible if you have enough faith, that they would do even greater things than he did if they believed: that if they had enough faith, they could tell a mountain to stand up and move across the street."

"How—how do you know all this, anyway?"

"Sunday school. I was a very attentive child. And I've done a little research over the years. Some people think Jesus was from another planet. Or another dimension. Could have been a time traveler. It's not really clear."

"Aha." Now that sounds more like Xavier.

I'm not exactly sure where all of this leaves us. The inexplicable test results from the study earlier today come to mind—my thoughts actually causing Charlene's heart rate to change.

Maybe there is something to this idea that thoughts alter reality, but I still feel really uncomfortable going there. "Xav, regardless of the power of curses or blessings or prayers or faith or miracles or focused thoughts or chi or any of those things to alter reality, there's one tangible step we can take to verify if any of this relates to Project Alpha."

"What's that?"

"Find out what Dr. Tanbyrn's diagrams and algorithms mean. And figure out a way to access his iPad." I stand, open the door. "Come on. Let's find Charlene. Last I heard she was down the hall getting stitches."

Stitches

Riah was watching the wasp build a nest around the helpless cockroach when the twins entered the office.

"Oriana called us," Daniel told her and Cyrus. "She's running a little late but should be here in the next twenty minutes or so."

So, Williamson's first name is Oriana. But who is she?

"We'll wait for her before starting the video," Daniel said to Cyrus, then: "But more importantly, did you hear about Dr. Tanbyrn?"

Riah immediately recognized the name; after

all, she'd spent the day studying his research findings.

"No. What happened?"

"There was a fire at the center. He's in the hospital."

Cyrus looked puzzled. "In the hospital?"

"He was almost killed in the fire. Apparently, the arsonist who started the fire is dead."

"Really?"

Darren answered for his brother, "The news report wasn't really clear if he died in the fire or if he died when he was fleeing and the authorities tried to apprehend him."

Cyrus was quiet for a long moment. "Well, let's hope Dr. Tanbyrn pulls through."

Darren set a tablet computer on the edge of the desk. Scrolled to an online news feed. "I'll keep an eye on the story. Dr. Tanbyrn's condition will no doubt be of concern to Oriana."

"No doubt." Cyrus reached for the intercom button on his desk phone next to his open laptop. "I'll have Caitlyn bring us some coffee. While we wait."

It takes a few minutes, but finally Xavier and I find Charlene in an exam room two doors down an adjacent hallway. There's a fresh bandage on her arm.

"How many stitches did you need?" I ask her.

"Sixteen."

"Sixteen." Xavier nods. "Nice. We're talking some quality scar material there."

"I don't want a scar, Xav."

"Hey, they make great conversation starters. I've got one here on my knee from—"

"How's it feeling?" I cut in, directing my question at Charlene. It's really not a good idea to get Xavier started on scar stories.

"Local anesthetic. I can't really feel it at all."

"Glad to hear that."

We move on to the reason we came, and she listens reflectively as I tell her what Xavier and I have been debating. When I finish, she gets right to the point: "If your thoughts could be fatal to someone else, it would be almost like having the ability to spread a thought-borne virus. How on earth could anyone fight against that?"

"Magneto," Xavier mutters. "His helmet blocks Professor X's telepathy from working. We could use a couple of those."

The irony that Xavier's first name is Professor X's last name isn't lost on me.

"Too bad they're not real," Charlene responds.

"You never know."

Actually, knowing Xavier's friends, I wouldn't have been surprised if some of them were working on something like that as we speak.

A thought-borne virus.

An apt way to describe what we're talking about. Frightening. I tell Charlene, "We came in here so we could take another look at the pages from Tanbyrn's files. See if we can find a way into that iPad."

As she's pulling out Tanbyrn's notes and iPad, the door beside me opens and a severe-looking nurse emerges, straddling the door frame. "There you are." She levels her gaze at me as if she's sighting down the barrel of a gun. "They're waiting for you in the X-ray room."

Charlene looks at me concernedly. "X-ray?"

"Just to check on something." I'd kept the rib injury to myself, but now I gently tap my side. "Might be a cracked rib."

"You broke a rib?" she gasps.

"Cracked it, maybe. Just a little. I'm not sure if it's—"

"Jevin, why didn't you say anything!"

A guy's gotta at least try to be heroic.

"Um, no reason. Exactly."

She looks at me reprovingly. "That rib better not be broken or I'm going to have to hurt you."

"I'm not sure that's really going to—"

The nurse clears her throat.

I signal to her that I'll be with her in a moment, but say to Charlene, "I'll be back as soon as I can. See if Fionna can help you get into that iPad. And Xavier, this guy Banner killed at least one person today. I want to find out what's at the bottom of all this. Call your friends and have them pull up everything they can on Star Gate and Project

Alpha. Any other telepathic research the military might be doing. I want the best conspiracy theorist minds out there on this thing."

He smiles. "Groovy."

As I leave, I notice I have six text messages from my producer at Entertainment Film Network telling me to call her.

Well, I guess someone's been watching the news.

But this doesn't feel like the right time to talk with her. I need to sort through some things first, decide exactly where we are on this project. Pocketing the phone, I follow the rather stout nurse to the X-ray room.

Cyrus Arlington knew that if that idiot Banner had been careless, there was the possibility that the police would be able to tie him to the fire. To the attempt on Tanbyrn's life.

He'd never given Banner his name, had used only a prepaid cell phone that no one would be able to trace, had paid him the down payment of $12,500 in unmarked, nonsequential bills. But still . . .

As he waited for Oriana to arrive and drank the coffee that Caitlyn had brought in, Cyrus thought of what he would tell the police if they ever came knocking at his door.

While his jewel wasp finished encasing her roach.

Oriana

I'm lying on my side on the X-ray table finishing the second of four X-rays of my ribs when my phone rings. The technicians had asked me to leave it on a counter inside the protected area where they were working, but even from here I recognize the ringtone.

Fionna.

Well, that was quick.

I excuse myself, and the frizzy-haired woman working the X-ray machine declares in no uncertain terms that she needs two more slides before I can go anywhere.

"No problem." I slip past her into the hall and answer my phone. A bit chilly without my shirt on.

"Nothing yet on Akinsanya or Tanbyrn's iPad," Fionna tells me. "It would be a lot easier if I had it in hand. But I do have something for you. Guess who your arsonist has been calling?"

"Who?"

"The CEO of RixoTray Pharmaceuticals."

"What?"

"It was with an unregistered prepaid cell, but I was able to backtrace the call and follow the GPS location to—"

"Wait a minute. If it was unregistered, how did you backtrace it?"

"Through AT&T's tech center."

"You hacked into their—"

"Not exactly. They hired me to do that last quarter. I kept my notes. Anyway, the GPS location for a previous call matches his residential address, and the most recent call just happens to line up with his office at RixoTray's corporate headquarters."

"Nice work."

"That's why you pay me the big bucks."

Actually, it was.

"Also, that passcode, the one you found in Banner's pocket, well, it's not just a password to the Lawson Center's RixoTray files, it's the one to a certain person's computer."

"You're not saying it's the same guy? The CEO?"

"Yup. Dr. Cyrus Arlington."

Okay, now that's interesting.

How would Banner have gotten Arlington's personal password?

"So, Fionna, this is all illegal, of course? Everything you just did?"

"Well, RixoTray did hire me to try getting past their firewalls and hacking into their system. I guess I'm just good at my job."

That works for me.

"Anyway, I pulled up Arlington's computer screen. There's an image, the beginning of a video. It's paused. It has something to do with—"

"Let me guess." I think of our earlier conversation, anticipate what she's going to say: "Kabul. The bombing that was averted."

"Right." Fionna sounds disappointed. "Of course, I can't be positive, but it looks like it, yes. How did you guess that, by the way?"

"What you told me earlier; I'm starting to think like you. Listen, can you send me a copy of that image?"

"Better than that. I'm going to send you a link to the screen. If he starts the video, you'll be able to watch it right along with him."

"You deserve a raise, Fionna."

"I could use one. Donnie needs braces."

We hang up, and against the firm objections of the X-ray technician, I grab my shirt and leave to find Xavier and Charlene.

The X-rays can wait. Right now it's movie time.

Riah heard the door open.

A woman entered, brisk and businesslike. Hair short, an Ellen DeGeneres boy cut. She was slightly built, just over five feet tall, but carried a commanding presence that drew the immediate attention of everyone in the room.

She nodded toward the twins, greeted Cyrus, then directed her gaze at Riah. "You must be Colette."

Riah was a keen enough observer of human behavior to realize that there were certain societal protocols on how to address people, how to treat them. It didn't mean that she necessarily understood why those conventions were in place, but it was immediately obvious that this woman did not follow them.

"Dr. Riah Colette, yes," she told her. "I'm the head researcher on this project." She decided to try something. "You don't have to call me Dr. Colette, though. I'm fine with Riah."

A small fire appeared in the woman's eyes, and Riah could tell she was not used to being spoken to so directly. The response intrigued her. Oriana might be an interesting person to observe. To test.

"I am Undersecretary of Defense Oriana Williamson. And that's what you will call me."

Undersecretary of Defense? Riah wasn't sure how high exactly that went up in the Pentagon's command chain, but she knew it had to be close to the top.

Fascinating.

Undersecretary Williamson, who was currently dressed in civilian clothes, looked away from Riah toward Cyrus. "I don't care if she's been vetted. I told you it was too late to bring anyone else in on this. I do not like—"

"I'm not just being brought in on this," Riah corrected her. "I mentioned a moment ago that I'm the head of the project at the R&D facility. I'm the one developing the neural decoding—"

"Synthetic telepathy."

Riah had never liked that term. It made what she was doing sound somehow paranormal when it was simply the development of a brain-computer interface. "What's your connection with it? Again?" She purposely posed the question in a challenging way to gauge how Oriana would respond. Riah was struck by the fact that Cyrus had at some point vetted her, gotten her military clearance to be here tonight.

Or did the twins do it?

The undersecretary scoffed at her. "You have no idea what this project is about."

"Ma'am." Daniel stepped forward, interrupting them. "Dr. Colette knows more about deep-brain stimulation of the Wernicke's area than anyone. If we're ever going to make this work with individuals, rather than just twins, she'll be the one to figure out how."

Darren nodded. "My brother and I need her in on this project if we're going to be able to move forward with it on the time frame we've discussed."

Williamson let out a small sigh of resignation. "Dr. Colette—"

"Riah really is fine."

A set jaw. "Dr. Colette, you realize that the material on this video is absolutely confidential and you may not share what you see with anyone. It concerns matters of national security."

National security?

She really had been vetted.

"Well?"

Riah had no idea who she might even be tempted to share the contents of the video with. "Of course."

The Undersecretary of Defense pulled out a sheaf of papers. "Before we move forward, I need you to sign these release forms."

"She's been cleared," Cyrus reiterated. "She wouldn't be part of the project if she weren't."

"It's alright," Riah told him, then quickly scanned the papers and signed them.

The undersecretary collected the papers, filed them in her briefcase. "Alright. Let's watch this video."

Cyrus gestured toward the hall and picked up his laptop. "It'll be easier for everyone to see if we use the screen in the conference room."

The Footage

Charlene, Xavier, and I find an empty exam room. Slip inside. Xavier closes the door behind us. "I made some calls. I have some of the best people out there working on Project Alpha and Star Gate."

"Good."

As he's locking the door, my phone vibrates. A text.

The link from Fionna.

I click it.

An image comes up: a room with plaster-covered walls, a ceiling fan, and a window overlooking a Middle Eastern city.

The twins sat across the table from Riah and Undersecretary of Defense Williamson. Even though Riah knew that all the other people in the room were previously acquainted, she didn't feel out of place. A lack of social anxiety was actually one of the perks for people with her condition.

The sprawling oval conference table lay centered in the room. Cyrus tapped a button on a console on the table, and the lights dimmed to a preset for watching videos. Then he depressed another button, and a large screen lowered from the ceiling and covered the front wall.

Williamson steepled her hands, leaned forward, asked Cyrus, "So have you seen it yet?"

"Not yet. No." He connected his laptop to the projector system.

She faced the twins. "And you?"

"No."

Riah didn't wait for the question. "I haven't seen it yet either. But I'm looking forward to it."

"Well. So am I."

The image from the laptop appeared on the projector screen. A room in Kabul.

Cyrus tapped the space bar and the video began.

• • •

The video begins.

We watch as the camera pans across the room, revealing two bearded men in Middle Eastern clothes standing beside a table. They're speaking rapidly in a language I don't immediately recognize.

"It's Arabic," Xavier announces.

"How do you—" Charlene begins.

"Shh."

One of the men steps aside, and I can see a table littered with wires, cell phones, detonators, a pile of nails, and several boxes of ball bearings. The audio on the recording is remarkably good, and I can hear the rush of traffic and the intermittent blaring of horns outside the window.

The taller of the two men walks toward the window and tugs at the threadbare curtains. They don't close all the way, however, and leave a gap nearly a foot wide, allowing for a narrow view of the building across the street.

"The guy who's filming this . . ." Xavier points to my phone's screen. "He's gotta be wearing a button camera like the one I gave you. Doesn't look like his buddies know they're being recorded." He studies the video carefully, mumbles something about the grade of the C-4 on the table. "Oh yeah. That's gonna leave a mark."

There are three suicide vests beside the explosives.

A few more words in Arabic.

I'm pretty sure I know how this is going to end, and I can feel a palpable rush of apprehension.

You're about to watch these people die.

The man beside the table faces the person filming the scene and speaks to him. I have no idea what he's saying, but I do make out the words "Allahu Akbar." The person with the camera repeats the words, and the tenor of his voice confirms that he's male. Then all three men echo the phrase again.

The man closest to the table takes off his long-sleeved shirt and picks up the suicide vest.

I think again of what Fionna told me earlier: there was a thwarted attack on a Kabul mosque, an unconfirmed number of terrorists were killed.

The research Dr. Tanbyrn was working on before the fire was a joint project between the Pentagon and RixoTray Pharmaceuticals.

RixoTray's CEO, Dr. Cyrus Arlington, was in communication with Glenn Banner hours before the fire.

Mind-to-mind research . . .

Telepathy . . .

The twins . . .

If you can affect someone's physiology, can you consciously change it?

If you can alter someone's heart rate, could you stop it?

All the facts circle elusively around each other, and I try to find a way to fit them together.

"Oh," I whisper. "They're going to kill him."

"What?" Charlene breathes.

"Watch. The guy with the vest, they're going to kill him."

The man slips the vest on, tightens some straps to secure it in place, then puts his loose-fitting long-sleeved shirt back on over the vest. It's not noticeable beneath his shirt, and if I didn't know he was wearing it, I never would have guessed that he was an armed suicide bomber.

I can feel my chest tensing up.

The taller man, the one nearest the window, peers past the ratty curtains for a moment, then joins his two cohorts in the middle of the room.

I hear the words "Allahu Akbar" repeated again by the three men in the group.

The man wearing the vest turns toward the window.

And then.

Explodes.

For a fraction of a second you can see the blast, a blur of color and fabric flaring toward the camera lens overwhelmed by a deafening roar.

And then there's nothing but a blank, silent screen.

Neither Charlene nor Xavier speaks.

So I was wrong.

They didn't stop the guy's heart.

Manipulating matter? Telekinesis? They made the bomb explode?

That seemed even more implausible.

At last Charlene speaks: "Wow."

Xavier shakes his head. "How did they get this footage? The camera was destroyed, so this footage was obviously being transmitted to someone—and then that person sends it to the CEO of one of the world's largest pharmaceutical firms? Are you kidding me?"

"I don't think he intended to do that," I tell them.

"Who?"

"The suicide bomber. It's hard to tell, but it didn't look like he reached for the vest. Neither of the other guys touched the cell phones to detonate it. Also, he put his shirt back on right after putting on the vest. Why would he do that if he was just going to blow up his buddies right there in the room?"

"You think it malfunctioned?"

"No. And I don't think he detonated it. I think somehow the twins did it for him."

Cyrus shut off the video and Riah waited for him to comment, for any of the four people she was with to speak.

Finally, Williamson did. "So it works."

"Yes," Daniel said quietly. "Apparently it does."

I expect Xavier to be on the same page with what I just said, to agree with me about the evil schemes of the federal government's secret psychic research and black-ops assassination programs, but both he and Charlene seem skeptical. "Tanbyrn's study concerned mind-to-mind communication," he reminds me, "not telekinesis."

"As far as we know. But it could have something to do with quantum entanglement. Manipulating matter nonlocally. Remember? Like the nuclear reactor or the torpedo?" But even as I try to convince them, I begin to doubt it myself, and the more implausible the whole telekinesis angle seems. I sigh. "You're right. I don't know. We'd need more information to tell."

The link on my phone expires, and when I try to refresh it, I'm unsuccessful.

I doubt Fionna would have severed the connection. Maybe someone at RixoTray did.

Just in case the video comes back on, I leave the browser open, set down my phone, and ask to borrow Charlene's. She's more than happy to give it to me.

I really have no idea how deep all this goes or who we can trust, but Abina is dead, Dr. Tanbyrn might die, the three people in the video are dead. RixoTray's CEO is involved with this and has ties to the Pentagon as well as to the guy who carried those eleven photographs of corpses in his wallet. There's no way all of this was simply a local law enforcement matter, and with the DoD's involvement I don't trust going to the federal government with what we know either.

For a moment I consider contacting the media, but then the obvious fact hits me in the face—*You film documentaries, Jevin. You are the media.*

I'm not about to just sit on the sidelines until more people start showing up dead.

"Charlene, last night you told me about a researcher at RixoTray who was in charge of this program. What was her name again?"

"Dr. Riah Colette."

I navigate to the internet browser on her phone.

"Are you going to call her?"

"No, I think we need to talk to her face-to-face."

I find what I'm looking for. Dial the number.

"Then who are you calling?" Xavier asks.

"I'm getting us a plane. We're going to Philadelphia."

Family Ties

Charlene looks at me curiously. "Philadelphia?"

"Arlington is there. He's connected with Banner, with the attempt on Tanbyrn's—and our—lives. Colette is there. RixoTray's headquarters is there. If we're going to crack this open, we need to be there too."

"What about the police?" she asks me. "Or the FBI? Shouldn't we just go to them?"

Xavier shakes his head. He must've been thinking the same thing I was a minute ago. "And when they ask why we suspect that the CEO of one of the largest pharmaceutical firms in the world is involved in conspiracy to commit murder, I suppose we'll just tell them that we hacked into his computer and phone records after getting the information off the body of the man Jevin killed."

That was an interesting way to put it.

I'm still on hold, waiting for someone from the charter plane company to speak to me. "Right now we have ties between all these things but no proof. Until we know more, we'd be accused of making unfounded accusations."

"Which would be true," Xavier points out.

She considers that.

"We do exposés, right?" I think of Abina again, of justice, of uncovering the truth. "Well, let's expose something that really matters."

The charter service's rep picks up, apologizes for the wait, and asks how she may be of assistance to me.

So far no one had offered Riah an explanation.

At last Cyrus typed on his keyboard and a photo appeared on the projector screen.

Three people: a Middle Eastern woman in her late thirties standing beside a dark-skinned, attractive girl in her teens, and the bearded man who'd strapped on the suicide vest in the video.

Riah was surprised that a fundamentalist Muslim suicide bomber would allow his wife and daughter to be photographed without their burkas' veils covering their faces.

Is it a fake?

"Malik was married," Cyrus explained. "He had a wife and a fourteen-year-old daughter. If he'd backed out, not gone through with it, they would have been punished."

Riah had heard enough about the culture and beliefs of Islamic fundamentalist society to know that "punished" in this case probably meant publicly shamed, or quite possibly raped or even killed.

"What do you mean if he'd backed out?"

"This way," Undersecretary of Defense Williamson said, not answering her question, "by all accounts it looks to the other members of his group that it was an accident."

"What does that mean: this way it looks like it was an accident?"

"We let him do it."

Still no direct answers. "You let him do what? Detonate the vest?"

Cyrus said, "Riah, your research, your work with the twins, helped save innocent lives, protected Malik's wife and daughter from retribution had he failed to go through with his mission, and it helped eliminate a terrorist threat and take care of three members of an al-Qaeda cell."

"I research ways to decipher neural activity related to linguistic patterns. How did my research do any of that?"

"Dr. Colette," Daniel offered, "this man was planning to kill himself and possibly hundreds of innocent people at a mosque. People who had assembled to worship God."

"But you're saying this wasn't an accident? That somehow you let him do it. Does that mean you influenced him to do it?"

"He was planning to do it already."

Riah wasn't rattled by the fact that no one was giving her a straight answer, but she was becoming more and more curious about why that was the case. "You're telling me that you somehow convinced this man to kill himself?" She looked at the twins. "But how?"

It took Darren a long time to answer.

"The circumstances concerning his death are one of the reasons we wanted you here. We need you to help us put them into context."

Okay, so that was finally an answer, but it was certainly not the one she'd expected.

"How can I do that?"

The twins rose almost in unison. Daniel said, "We'll meet you tomorrow morning at 9:15 in the R&D facility, room 27B. We'll explain everything then."

Based on the concern Cyrus and the twins had shown earlier for Dr. Tanbyrn's condition, Riah had expected that the topic of the fire at the center in Oregon would come up again, but now it appeared that everyone was ready to leave. All of this was fascinating and intriguing to her. She agreed to meet with the twins in the morning, if only to find out what they were using her research for: "I'll be there. I'll see you at 9:15."

And that was that.

They headed toward the door, Oriana mentioned to Cyrus that she would tell her oversight committee to extend the funding, and then she excused herself as well.

The meeting had ended in the same shroud of questions that had pervaded it.

Cyrus escorted Riah past Caitlyn Vaughn at the reception desk and down the elevator. "About last night, coming over to your apartment . . . the sleepover. Does the offer still stand?"

Riah understood that his question was a test, a way of feeling out how needy she was, how dependent on him, and she decided to show him that she was not the dependent one in their relationship. "I'll have to think about that."

She paused, then turned to him, looked deep into his eyes, and trailed her finger across his cheek. "Say hi to Helen tonight for me, will you? Tell that thoughtful wife of yours that coffee tomorrow afternoon sounds like a wonderful idea."

"She invited you out for coffee?"

"Good night, Cyrus."

Then Riah left for her car.

Let him chew on that for a while.

If she'd been a person capable of feeling pleasure, she would have smiled. As it was, she tried one on to see how it felt, but it didn't make her feel anything at all.

I'm not really a fan of commercial airlines, and thankfully, my stage shows over the last decade have done well enough to give me the freedom to be able to bypass those long security lines and groping TSA employees.

It didn't take me long to book the charter plane.

Both Xavier and Charlene know that money isn't really an issue for me, so neither of them bats an eye when I tell them the price tag—just under six thousand dollars per hour. Plus landing fees, fuel, and overnight expenses. "It's really not that bad, actually."

"What does that work out to per peanut?" Xavier asks.

"Hors d'oeuvres," I correct him. "And lobster bisque. Only the best for my friends."

Excusing myself from them for a minute, I find the restroom, then on my way back down the hall, I call Fionna to see if she recorded the video. "I did. I'll get you a copy. Sorry I lost the connection to the laptop after it was finished. Someone on their cybersecurity team must have stumbled onto the breach. But don't worry, I got out before anyone would've been able to find out who was there."

I tell her about our plans to go to Philadelphia.

"How can you be sure that Dr. Colette will even be there?"

Good point. "Um . . ."

"Hang on a second."

Momentarily she gets back into their system and confirms that Dr. Colette's schedule includes some meetings in the morning there in Philly.

"So," Fionna says, "have the charter plane swing by and pick me up."

"What do you mean?"

"Pick me up. Here in Chicago."

"Are you serious?"

"Sure. I'm already up to my neck in this with you, Jevin, and it'll be easier if I can work things from the inside."

"From the inside of what?"

"With RixoTray. It looks like I have some rather troubling news to give them—their cyber-security isn't nearly as good as it needs to be. In fact, the CEO's personal computer is at high risk of a security breach."

There was no arguing with that.

She goes on, "That's something I should discuss with him in person. If I'm with you, I can guarantee you a meeting with Arlington. Besides, you're flying from Oregon to Pennsylvania. You'll practically go right over my house. I'm not sure, but I'd guess a charter plane will need to refuel on a flight across the country."

"Actually, these planes are equipped to—"

"You know as well as I do"—she refuses to give up—"that you'll make more progress if I'm there. I can do a few things from here to try and access that iPad, but from what I've seen, the security on it is reasonably good. It might take me awhile remotely, but I guarantee that if I had it in front of me, I could hash that password in two minutes or less."

Even though I have complete confidence in her ability to work something like this from an off-site location, I have to admit that it would be good to have her there with us in Philadelphia, especially when it came to getting us an audience with Dr. Arlington.

Stopping by Chicago won't really add that much time to the trip. You could still make it to Philadelphia by morning.

"Okay, you've convinced me. I'll set it up and let you know the details about when and where to meet us."

"And my kids come too."

"What? No, that's not—"

"This might take a couple days. I can't leave them alone that long, and it's too late to find someone who'd be able to take in four children."

Lonnie is seventeen and very responsible, but I couldn't help but agree with Fionna that it wouldn't be a good idea to leave him alone to watch his three younger siblings. Fionna doesn't have family in the area, and while she could farm the kids out to their friends' houses, that might be awkward. She was also right that this would likely involve a couple days of work. Still, even taking all that into account, I'm hesitant to say yes.

"I don't know, I'm—"

"They'll be safe in the hotel rooms you're going to get us, if that's what you're worried about. They'll have plenty of security. After all, we're staying at a nice hotel, right? Because it'll really be a lot easier if there's room service."

"This isn't exactly—"

"My kids like to swim, so let's make sure there's an indoor pool."

I wish I could tell her that there wouldn't be enough room on the plane for her and her kids, but the Gulfstream 550 that's on its way to Portland would actually have just enough seats.

I rub my head. "Really? You want me to fly your kids to Philly?"

"You're already paying for the flight, why not get your money's worth? Besides, they're due for a field trip, and they've never been to the City of Brotherly Love."

"You told me earlier today that you took them on a field trip this morning?"

"That doesn't really count. It was in the same state."

Oh. Is that how it works.

"I see."

"You won't regret having them along. Trust me. They can help me out, and from what I've seen, you could use it. I mean, this project is about as confusing as when you have two dozen gerbils running around a pet store and you're trying to catch the one with the little white tuft on his left ear, and you can't seem to find him because all the other ones are just too dang frisky."

I knew a simile would sneak in here eventually. Or an analogy. Or metaphor. I'm not really sure what that one was.

"Where do you get these from, Fionna?"

"Sometimes they just come to me. So?"

I hold back a sigh. "Okay, they can come. But I'm not guaranteeing you a pool."

"Hot tubs in the suites will be fine." She turns from the phone and I hear her calling to her family, "Kids, pack up your things. We're going to Pennsylvania!"

Part II

MEANS of DISPOSAL

Critical Condition

Cyrus slipped into his Jag and took a deep breath.

Had Helen really invited Riah out for coffee? Or was that a lie? If Helen had asked her to meet, did she know about the affair?

He felt his temperature rising.

Who was the wasp here and who was the cockroach? Who was the helpless one? Riah was not the one calling the shots in this, he was. And he was not about to have her try to control him, try to seal him in a corner.

Her mention of Helen annoyed him, really annoyed him. And then, of course, there was this whole botched job with Tanbyrn.

The assassin was dead and the doctor was not.

Cyrus pounded the steering wheel.

How could you have been so stupid to hire an inept goon like him!

Frustrated, he drove toward the drop-off point at First Central Bank, the place Akinsanya had told him to leave the DVD of the footage in Kabul.

Earlier, while they were waiting for Oriana to show up, Cyrus had decided that if the police came knocking, he would tell them the truth: yes, he had been in touch with Banner, had spoken with him on several occasions.

And he would also tell them a lie—Banner had been blackmailing him from the beginning, threatening to expose his affair with Riah.

The conversation played out in his head:

"How did he find out about you and Dr. Colette?" the cops would ask him.

A lie: "He told me he had a tip. That's all he said. He had photographs. Compromising ones."

"What did you pay him?"

The truth: "So far, $12,500. He wanted more. Another twelve five."

"Then why would he burn down the building where they were doing research related to RixoTray?"

A lie: "I have no idea. Dr. Colette is in charge of the research project. She might be able to help you with that."

The blackmail angle worked. It explained the money, the fact that Banner had been in touch with him, and the reason Cyrus had kept it all a secret. Admitting to the affair might not help his marriage, but he could work through all that, play the repentant husband, reconcile, move on. Or maybe go back to Caitlyn. She really was a fine little office helper.

But for now there was still the issue of Tanbyrn.

Put quite simply, he knew too much.

You never know—he might already be dead.

Cyrus put the DVD in the mail slot of First Central Bank. The bank was, of course, closed. He had no idea who Akinsanya was, had never met him, only spoken with him on the phone.

He didn't know why Akinsanya had chosen this location, but he was not going to question him, not after the photos Akinsanya had sent him of what he'd done to the people who'd betrayed him or failed him in the past. All using a needle and thick, black thread.

Back in the car, before starting the engine, Cyrus considered his course of action.

He had a meeting tomorrow morning at nine with the vice president at the White House. Papers to verify, a myriad of details to arrange.

Cyrus took out his cell phone, surfed to a dozen news sites, one after another, to see what details had emerged about the fire at the Lawson Research Center.

He found out that the famous Nobel laureate Dr. Tanbyrn wasn't dead yet. Some guy had gotten him out of the building just in time. But the doctor was in critical condition with carbon monoxide poisoning and had slipped into a coma within the last twenty minutes or so.

Well, that was a bit of good news.

The circumstances surrounding Banner's death were still sketchy, but apparently he was killed while fighting one of the people at the center.

Some professional he turned out to be.

Tanbyrn's in a coma. Nonresponsive. If he ever does recover, he'll probably have brain damage.

Just get through until tomorrow night. There'll be time to deal with Tanbyrn later, once things have settled down.

After thinking things through, Cyrus decided to go home, get everything ready for tomorrow, and keep an eye on the situation with Tanbyrn. Yesterday he'd briefly considered contacting Atabei. Maybe, with Tanbyrn in a weakened condition like this, that would be the best route to take after all.

Yes, keep tabs on his condition and make a decision in the next couple hours regarding Tanbyrn.

After contacting the charter flight service again and making arrangements for us to stop by to pick up Fionna and her children in Chicago, I put in a call to make our hotel reservations. With people streaming to central Philly to hear the president's speech in the morning, there aren't many vacancies, so it takes a little time to find some rooms, but finally I do.

Because of our early morning arrival, I book the rooms for both tonight and tomorrow so we'll be able to check in immediately when we get there and not have to wait for the normal check-in time later in the day. It's only a couple thousand dollars more for an extra night for the four rooms, and it would save us the hassle of stowing our luggage until the afternoon. I figure it's worth it.

I return to Charlene and Xavier and ask him if he can give us a ride back to the Lawson Center so we can get our car and our things from the cabin.

"What about your X-rays?" he asks.

"Only if they can get me in quickly. Our flight leaves from Portland in less than four hours, and with the drive back to the center, it's going to be cutting it close." I watch Xavier carefully to see how he responds to the next bit of information. "We'll be meeting up with Fionna and her kids in Chicago on the way. They're coming with us."

"Fionna?"

"That's right."

"And her kids?"

"Uh-huh."

He's quiet for a moment. Despite his unwavering support for people living off the grid and his suspicion of the federal government's role in just about every evil of modern society, he's surprisingly never been a big fan of homeschooling and has made the mistake of mentioning to Fionna that he thought she should've sent her kids to a charter school or a private academy of some type.

Families who homeschool usually have pretty strong convictions for why they do it, and Fionna was no exception. I'd seen her and Xavier really get into it a few times.

All good-naturedly, of course.

I think.

I pat him on the shoulder. "Just don't bring up

the homeschooling thing and you guys will do fine."

"Uh-huh," he mutters. "As long as she doesn't try out any of her similes on me, we'll do even better."

I'm tempted to tell him about the gerbils-on-the-floor analogy but hold back. "Let me get those X-rays, and then I want to check on Dr. Tanbyrn again before we leave."

Malik's Daughter

Two cracked ribs. Neither serious.

The ER doctor and the radiologist both interpret the X-rays the same way. It's a welcome piece of good news in the sea of an otherwise dark and turbulent day.

Rest and time would help me heal. And that sounded a lot better to me than dealing with a pierced lung.

We proceed quickly to Tanbyrn's room.

Even though Pine Lake is a small town, with the news of a Nobel laureate nearly dying in a purposely set fire, it's no surprise that the national media is already camped outside the hospital doing live feeds. Thankfully, the sheriff's department has kept them from getting through the doors.

At the room, Deputy Jacobs, the mustached cop who'd gone through Banner's pockets when I led him and two of his fellow officers to Banner's body, is standing sentry outside the door.

At first I'm a little surprised to see him stationed here, but considering the fact that this crime spree involved arson, at least one homicide, and possibly eleven others by the same person or team of people, the extra security made perfect sense.

Deputy Jacobs gives us a nod as we approach and anticipates what we came for. "He slipped into a coma."

What? Charlene mouths.

A silent nod.

"Is it possible we could see him?" she asks.

"I'm afraid not. They don't want him disturbed."

"How would we disturb him if he's in a coma?"

Jacobs has no answer for that.

"It's possible that he's aware of what's going on, that he needs to have someone reassure him—"

"I'm sorry, that's—"

Charlene folds her arms. "Can you imagine what it would be like if you were lying there and part of your brain was aware of how alone you were, how hopeless your situation was, and no one was there to comfort you? How do we know for sure that's not the case?"

Deputy Jacobs isn't up for a fight tonight. "I suppose it can't hurt. I'll go in with you. But just for a couple minutes; I don't want the docs walking in on us."

"I'll stay here in the hall," Xavier offers, "and knock if I see any doctors coming."

Inside the room, we find Tanbyrn lying motionless on the bed, the blankets tucked neatly around him, leaving the outline of his slight frame sketched beneath the covers. Only his head and arms are visible. He's on a ventilator and has tubes running into his arms, and all of this makes him look vulnerable, frail, and smaller than he really is. The subtle hum of hospital machinery and the lemony scent of antiseptic fill the air.

The room has only dimmed lights and the generic, nondescript feel of hospital rooms everywhere.

I think of how many people die in these generic rooms and how tragic that is. A whole life of uniqueness and individuality funneled down into a room that's interchangeable with a hundred thousand others just like it all around the country.

Feel-good movies will tell you, "Pursue your dreams," or "Follow your heart and everything will work out in the end," or "Love conquers all," or some other cliché that sounds good at first but doesn't stand up to reality, to the way things really are.

Because dreams don't always come true.

And following your heart sometimes only leads you deeper into despair.

And love doesn't conquer all. Death does. Like

it did with Rachel and the boys. Death won. Death always wins in the end.

We approach the bed.

I have no idea if Dr. Tanbyrn can hear me or not, but I tell him, "We got the man who started the fire." I doubt that talking about anyone dying is the best thing to do at the moment, so I leave out the news about Banner's death and Abina's murder.

Charlene sits beside the bed and takes Dr. Tanbyrn's hand. "You're going to be okay."

Considering his condition, I'm not sure she should be telling him that, but truthfully, when she does the words sound so heartfelt and confident that I almost believe they'll come true.

Positive thoughts. Remember, they make a difference.

And prayers.

Thoughts and prayers.

Even though I wish we could ask him about Project Alpha, I'm at least reassured that we have a plan, that we're on our way to—

A series of knuckle raps on the door from Xavier tells us that there's a doctor on his way to the room.

"We should go," Deputy Jacobs tells us quietly.

I assure Tanbyrn that we're going to find out who was behind everything. Charlene gives him a light kiss on the forehead and tells him she'll be praying for him, then we slip out of the room, meet up with Xavier, and leave to retrieve our things from the center so we can make it to Portland by the time our plane lands to pick us up.

Riah did not find herself sad that the three men in the video had been killed in the explosion, but she did find their deaths to be unfortunate and untimely in the sense that the men probably had more things they would've liked to accomplish before they died.

Possibly, but they were planning a suicide attack, after all.

In either case, other than acknowledging that a premature death might not have been on their agenda for the day, Riah felt no sorrow or pity or grief.

It was her condition, her curse.

Her reality.

However, she couldn't help but remain curious about Malik's wife, the woman who would now be forced to fend for herself in a male-dominated, patriarchal society, and Malik's daughter, the fourteen-year-old girl who would now have to grow up without her father. Riah guessed that the girl had loved him and wondered what she was going through.

What would that be like? To grieve the death of a loved one?

Would the Afghan girl see her father as a hero

who'd died for his beliefs, or as a coward who chose to escape a harsh life and slip into paradise, leaving his wife and daughter living on the hellish outskirts of a war zone?

Riah thought back to when she was that girl's age, to the days when her father first started tying her to the bed and having his way with her. What if she'd loved him and then he had died? How would that've felt? Or what if she'd hated him instead? Would she have celebrated?

But he had not died.

Instead he was living in a decrepit farmhouse in the middle of Louisiana. Riah's little sister, Katie, was still alive too, was on her third marriage, rented a squalid little apartment in San Diego, had three kids, and hadn't spoken with her since their mother's funeral.

Their mother had fallen down the basement stairs six months ago and broken her neck when her head hit the concrete floor.

The coroner labeled her death "accidental." Riah's father had been home at the time, and Riah thought that it was at least as likely that after decades of physically abusing his wife, he'd pushed her down the stairs or smashed her head in and then shoved her body down the steps to make it look like an accident, but there was no way to prove his involvement one way or the other.

But regardless of the circumstances regarding her mother's death, Riah knew that her father was a guilty man, guilty for what he had done to his daughter.

Or daughters.

She had her suspicions, but never could get Katie to tell her if their father had done the same things to her.

Riah knew that someday she would visit him and discuss the fact that he had not treated his children in an honorable manner, discuss it in a way that he would understand.

She was confident she could come up with something unforgettable.

But now, tonight, she went to bed thinking about Malik's daughter, about watching that fourteen-year-old girl's father explode.

Tomorrow morning she would be meeting with the twins to find out what role her research had played in that man's death, in that fourteen-year-old girl's loss.

And, presumably, based on what Darren had said to her in the conference room, what her role might be in killing even more fathers just like him.

Heading East

The drive to Portland goes surprisingly quickly, and Xavier, Charlene, and I find the Gulfstream 550 waiting for us on the tarmac.

The pilot, a fortyish woman with golden retriever

eyes and an enigmatic pair of pigtails, introduces herself as Captain Amy Fontaine. The copilot is a quiet, slightly overweight man named Jason Sherill.

Our flight attendant, a young Indian gentleman who speaks with only a faint Indian accent, tells us he is Amil and is at our service.

We shake hands, give them our names, and take our seats in the jet's cabin.

Though the price tag for this flight isn't cheap, I've used this company before, and as I look around the jet, I'm reminded that I'm getting my money's worth. The cabin is ultra high-end, elegant—swiveling, reclining captain's chair seats, four flat-screen televisions, not to mention the individual monitors for each seat. A couch sits at the back of the plane near the galley and restroom.

Xavier stows a duffle bag full of his toys. He winks at me. "You never know what tricks you're going to need up your sleeve."

"No, you don't."

"I have a few things here I've been working on."

"What are those?"

"Oh, well, you see, that's a surprise, Petunia."

I stare at him.

"Charlene filled me in."

"Great."

As Captain Fontaine pulls the plane onto the runway, Amil informally gives us the required preflight information—apart from the senseless instructions about powering down your phones and electronic devices. "If it were even remotely possible that your electronic devices could affect the navigation of an airplane during takeoff or landing, do you really think the FAA would allow you to bring the items on board?" He almost slips into a stand-up routine. "Can you imagine a jet crashing and they find out that the cause was someone forgetting to turn off his noise-canceling headphones? My friends, you could run a cell phone kiosk next to the cockpit and have an MRI machine stationed in the back of this cabin, and it wouldn't affect the navigation of a plane one bit."

I liked Amil already.

We take off, and as we break through the clouds, I see the final glimpse of sunlight fading along the edge of the sky. I can't help but think of all that has happened since the sun went down yesterday evening: the fight in the chamber, the test this morning, escaping the fire, seeing Abina's body, watching Glenn Banner die at my feet.

It feels like a lifetime has passed since the last sunset.

Like a dream.

But it's real.

The pain and death and questions, all real.

My thoughts float back to my nightmare last night about seeing my wife and sons drown. How I felt. How helpless. How terrified.

Needless to say, I'm not too excited about going to sleep now, on the plane.

In the waking world, when you're haunted by the past or troubled by the present or nervous about the future, you can distract yourself—go for a run, watch a movie, check your email—but when you're asleep and you're facing something terrifying, you can't turn away, can't even close your eyes and pretend it's not happening.

In a sense, I guess, we're powerless to escape our dreams. We're forced to live them out, forced to watch whatever our haunted past wants to throw in front of us. Even though we may know it's not real.

Cyrus made his decision.

He slipped quietly to the garage, careful not to wake his faithful, innocent, and rather oblivious wife.

The more he'd thought about it, the more he'd realized it would be best not to wait until morning to deal with the situation with Tanbyrn.

He backed the Jag out of the driveway, pulled onto the silent, deserted street.

Over the last nine months, Cyrus had explored every avenue available to him for clearing the way for his research concerning the release of the new telomere cap. During that time he'd considered the broad-reaching implications of Dr. Tanbyrn's research on quantum entanglement and its connection to human relationships, its connection both in positive ways and in negative ones.

Cyrus was a man of science, but if there was one thing quantum physics was teaching us, it was this: there is not always a scientific explanation for what happens in the world. Logic evaporates when you reach the subatomic level. Reality is much more malleable than it seems.

He wasn't sure he believed in Mambo Atabei's practices, but he had seen some things in her ceremonies that he couldn't reasonably explain. Based on Tanbyrn's research, there were scientific reasons, matters of quantum entanglement, that might have been able to explain some of the effects, but that seemed to Cyrus to be a bit of a stretch.

Admittedly, he was somewhat embarrassed by his forays into this field, but when tens of billions of dollars were at stake, it was worth a little unorthodox dabbling.

He had a relatively good relationship with the Haitian woman, and he speculated that she might just be able to help if he gave her a big enough donation.

Guiding the Jag down the street, he aimed it toward South Philly. Toward the high priestess's house.

After we level off, Amil offers us caviar hors d'oeuvres and wine in tall, fluted glasses.

Xavier takes out his button camera and puts it on. When he sees me looking at him curiously, he explains, "We were supposed to be filming a documentary. You never know what kind of footage we're going to need. We may end up with a film yet. Don't worry, I'll be unobtrusive." Then he asks Amil if he has any cheese, crescenza if possible, and Amil looks at him blankly.

"We have some cheddar in the back, sir."

"That'll do."

Amil passes us to get to the refrigerator in the back of the cabin.

I suggest to Xavier and Charlene that we review what we know, make a game plan for the rest of the night, and they swivel their chairs toward me.

Charlene flips open her computer, positions it on her tray table. I ready my iPad. Xavier produces his pen and journal.

"So," I begin, "here's what we know. Fact: RixoTray Pharmaceuticals funded a research program that focused on the quantum entanglement of people's consciousness and its effect on the physiology of partners who have a deep emotional relationship."

Xavier summarizes the research of Tanbyrn in one simple, succinct phrase: "The entanglement of love." He looks at me slyly. Then at Charlene.

Uh-uh. We are not even going to go there.

"Fact," I go on, "a pair of men, twins known only to us as 'L' and 'N' who are special in some way, would fly in, meet with Tanbyrn, and fly out. We still don't know what the tests consisted of, only that they had to do with the negative effects of something."

"And with alpha waves," Xavier adds, then graciously accepts an elegant platter of sliced cheddar from Amil. "Directing them. Focusing them."

"Yes."

"Fact"—he takes a bite of his cheese—"Glenn Banner killed the young woman at the center and started the place on fire. Motive still unclear."

Charlene is typing as she tracks along.

"Fact," he continues, "Banner's cell phone was used to contact Cyrus Arlington, the CEO of RixoTray Pharmaceuticals. Also, Banner had a passcode with him that led Fionna to get past the firewall and into Arlington's personal computer."

At that, Charlene pauses, lets her fingers hover over the keyboard. "Which brings us to the video. One of the people from a terrorist cell was recording and transmitting footage of another cell member putting on a suicide vest. The vest—by the way, Xavier, you knew what language they were speaking. Do you know Arabic?"

"I can identify it, can't speak it. I once worked for a Middle Eastern singer in Las Vegas."

"Well, the vest detonates . . . where does that leave us?"

I sigh. "Square one."

She glances at me. "Square one?"

"We have a collection of facts and inter-relationships but no *why* behind them. No motive. Why was RixoTray funding Tanbyrn's research? Why have Banner burn down the Lawson research building? Why was one of the terrorists filming and transmitting the video? Why was Banner in touch with Arlington? Why was Arlington watching the video? Why is the Pentagon interested in any of this?"

Xavier adds, "And how does Dr. Riah Colette fit into the mix?"

"And who is Akinsanya?" Charlene chimes in.

"Right. A pile of whys, one big how, and one big who."

A moment passes. Xavier takes another bite of cheese. Chews. Swallows. "By the way," he asks me, "did you ever review the footage you got when you were taking the test at the center?"

"No. Do you think that still matters?"

"Probably wouldn't hurt to have a look at it. Stick it on a jump drive and I'll glance it over."

I'm reminded of Banner's watch and I retrieve it from my carry-on bag, explain to Xavier how I got it.

"I don't think we need prints anymore. Looks like you got yourself a new watch, bro."

"Looks like I do." I slip it on. It looks good.

"So . . ." I type in a few notes myself. "I know we all need some sleep, but let's see if we can make a little progress before we reach Chicago. Xavier, could you follow up with your friends about Project Alpha and Star Gate?"

"Sure."

"Banner warned me about someone named Akinsanya, that he would find me. Let's see if anything about Akinsanya or this video has been leaked to the internet or to any of the conspiracy theorist circles."

"Gotcha."

I glance at Charlene. "You still have the notes that Fionna dug up earlier, right?"

"Sure."

"Why don't you go through them and see if you can find out more about the telomerase research or the EEG research. If you have time, go online and pull up what you can on Drs. Riah Colette and Cyrus Arlington."

"Check."

"I'm going to study Tanbyrn's books and look for anything related to the negative effects of mind-to-mind communication."

Then we turn our chairs from each other and get started with our work as we head east, toward a new day.

The Needs of the Many

Dr. Cyrus Arlington had never killed anyone.

Per se.

Yes, people had died because of his actions, or, more accurately, because of his lack of action, but that's the way the system was set up, the only real means of scientific advancement when you're doing medical research on human subjects.

After all, you need a control group, a baseline. So if you're testing a new drug, you give your experimental medication to one set of patients, a placebo to another, and you need a third group, a control group, that receives no treatment at all. It's the only way to measure the true efficacy of a drug.

Of course, as the test progresses, even if the drug appears to be working, you don't stop the trials in the middle to administer it to the dying people in your control group. It's not just a matter of protocol, it's a matter of science. Even with a double-blind study, there are too many factors that can affect the research, so you need a large enough sample to really verify your findings. If you assume too much too early, it could be detrimental to the lives of millions of people in the long term.

So, yes, some people will inevitably die during

the process, but it's the only way to collect the data that you need to determine whether or not a drug is effective.

The needs of the many outweigh the needs of the few.

And of course, the more people you have in your control group, and the more time they go without getting their potentially life-saving drugs, the more of them that will die.

But they would, of course, die anyway. Eventually.

Ultimately, health care is a numbers game, and there are only two rules, two guiding principles that are taught at every school of medicine in the country:

Rule #1: Everyone dies.

Rule #2: There's nothing you can do to change Rule #1.

"We prolong life; we do not save it," one of Cyrus's professors at Harvard Medical School had told him. "Don't try to be the savior of the world. Just do your best to help ease the greatest number of people's pain as much as you can, for as long as you can. At its heart, that's what medicine is all about."

The Hippocratic Oath: *Primum non nocere.*

First, do no harm.

Not quite as in vogue today as it used to be, not with physician-assisted suicide and third-trimester abortions, but the point was well-taken.

And so, during his twenty years of overseeing research before taking over as RixoTray's CEO, Cyrus had been part of hundreds of studies and seen thousands of people die. It wasn't his fault that cancer or AIDS or congestive heart failure took those people from the world. But paradoxically, even though he had not killed them, if you wanted to be technical about it, he could have stopped the tests. It was, in one sense, his fault that the people didn't live.

They might've been saved if compassion for them trumped the scientific advancement that their deaths advanced.

But it had not.

It could not.

The needs of the many outweigh the needs of the few.

For a while, watching others die, even though he knew he could stop the process, had been like a thorn in his thoughts, an uncomfortable irritation that made his daily work less enjoyable, but you have to move on, have to come to terms with your role in life. And Dr. Cyrus Arlington had done just that.

He'd begun to look at the big picture and had initiated the most expensive research program in the history of his company to find the cure for aging, which would, in many ways, be the cure for everything.

Telomeres, protective caps on the ends of

chromosomes, erode as cells reproduce, and so the cells eventually degrade and enter a state referred to as "senescence" when they no longer reproduce. This causes the effects we associate with aging—dementia, increased risk of stroke, muscle atrophy, and decreased organ function, sight, hearing, and so on. Put simply, the enzyme telomerase protects the telomeres from degrading and thus slows aging.

If it were possible to use telomerase on humans to stop telomeres from shortening when cells reproduce, there would be no reason for those cells to begin breaking down. Would it add years to your life? Yes. And undoubtably, it would also dramatically increase your quality of life during the decades up until then.

Stopping senescence halts the negative effects of aging and, at least in the 2010 Harvard studies on rats, *reverses* those effects by increasing neural function, regenerating nerves, and rebuilding muscle tissue.

But there was a problem. Cancer cells initiate telomerase, which is one reason cancer cells don't degrade with time, so increasing telomerase in the body of a person who has no cancer would cause him to become more immune to it, but someone with cancer would become more riddled with it.

All of this means that if you could create a drug that releases telomerase, you would either need to administer the drug to people who don't have any cancer cells growing in them, or give the enzyme to people in short doses so that it decreases the risk that the cancer cells they already have would spread.

Unless the drug increased the level of telomerase only in cells that were not cancerous.

And that's exactly what RixoTray was on the verge of producing.

It would be the one drug that everyone on the planet would want to take, and it would make thousands of other drugs obsolete.

The pharmaceutical company that could create the first-generation telomeres protector would be positioned to become one of the most financially lucrative firms on the planet. Perhaps one of the most profitable companies of all time.

And that company was going to be RixoTray Pharmaceuticals.

They needed a little more funding, yes, and a little more time. The funding would come from the Pentagon, and the time would come from— well, it certainly wouldn't come from the added restrictions the president was going to propose in his speech tomorrow at eleven at Independence Park just outside of the Liberty Bell building.

Cyrus threaded his Jaguar down the narrow streets of South Philly. Groups of gangbangers huddled on the street corners; abandoned buildings littered the block. The row houses in this primarily African

325

American neighborhood were all in disrepair. And it was not the kind of place someone of Cyrus's stature would normally venture.

He was heading to the house with the dumpster in the cramped alley behind it. The dumpster that accepted the remains of what happened in the basement of that building during the night.

Despite the low-income demographic of the neighborhood, Cyrus wasn't afraid to leave the Jag on the street. He was known as a friend of Mambo Atabei, and no one around here would dare cause any trouble for one of her friends.

He parked in one of the four spots in front of her house left vacant for her visitors. Walked to the porch, knocked on the door.

Waited for her to answer.

There were generations of African Santería practitioners in Philadelphia who have been around since colonial times. And although Mambo Atabei was not from Africa, the ceremonies she performed had been originally exported from there to Haiti, adapted, and then imported from Haiti to North America.

The cloth doll in Cyrus's office was, of course, a gimmick. No one who was a serious voodoo worshiper would use a doll like that. It was for the tourists in places like New Orleans and some of the neighborhoods in Miami. Real voodoo has much deeper roots and much different methods.

When the door opened, Cyrus could smell

incense. It was meant to mask the other smells that emanated from the house, or peristyle, as it was known in Mambo Atabei's religion.

She stood in front of him, fiftyish, slim, black—she hated being called African American because, as she said proudly, she was Haitian, not from Africa, not from America. "You don't hear Caucasians preface their identity by naming their ancestors' continent of birth: 'European-American' or 'North American–American.' All of this political correctness is only thinly veiled bigotry used to create divisions between people groups that need to be drawn closer together, not separated by hyphenating their identities."

"Dr. Arlington." Her voice was soft and congenial but had a raspy edge to it. The result of a throat injury sometime in her past.

"Mambo Atabei."

"It's been, what? Two months? Three?"

"Something like that."

Without another word she invited him into the living room.

The brown and white doves that she would use in the basement were caged in the corner of the room, out of reach of the gray cat that stalked across the footstool in front of her couch. The doves squabbled with each other, oblivious to what awaited them. The cat eyed them with calculated interest.

Cyrus wondered about the cat. He hadn't known

Mambo Atabei to use cats, but he wasn't really sure what all went on in her basement. He'd only witnessed her using doves and chickens—although he did know that larger animals were part of some of the ceremonies she performed.

A wide variety of liqueurs and rums were collected on an end table in the corner of the room. An HDTV, two chairs, a lamp, a crucifix on the wall, a shelf of DVDs, and knickknacks rounded out the room. A typical living room.

At the far end of the room, a curtain was drawn across an open doorway. He knew that the curtain concealed the steps that led to the basement.

A basement that was not quite so typical.

He'd been down there on numerous occasions, just as an observer. But he'd seen what went on around the pole, the *poteau-mitan*, in the middle of the main room, had seen what caused the dark stains on the dirt floor beneath it.

There is, of course, a dark side to voodoo, a strand that's not about dancing and drinking or trying to find out some insights about life from a Loa. There's a side that has nothing to do with blessings or celebration.

It was the side Mambo Atabei counted herself a part of, the highly secretive Bizango Society.

Cyrus was not easily rattled, but Atabei had a certain unnerving quality about her and studied him with a quiet intensity that made him slightly nervous. "And what exactly can I offer you tonight, Dr. Arlington?"

"I'd like to put something into play."

"Regarding?"

"A man who is in a coma."

"A coma."

"Yes."

He knew that in Atabei's tradition, a donation for services was expected. The nature of the request determined the size of the donation. "I'm willing to make a donation to the peristyle." For now he held back from telling Mambo Atabei exactly what he wanted from her. "A sizable one."

She tapped the thumb of her right hand against her forefinger, evaluated what he'd said.

He heard bleating from the stairwell to the basement. A goat.

He pretended not to notice it.

"What is it exactly that you want me to do?" she asked.

And Dr. Cyrus Arlington told her, in depth, the nature of his request.

Production Value

The jet's engines purr, but other than that the plane is quiet as Xavier and Charlene do their research beside me.

It's been half an hour and I've been scanning Dr.

Tanbyrn's book. He actually does make reference to potential negative effects of quantum entanglement when it comes to thoughts, mentioning some of the same examples as Xavier used with me earlier today—shamans and witch doctors. Curses.

After all, if placebos can be used to help people heal themselves merely by their thoughts, could their thoughts also be used, conversely, to destroy them? Certainly, the debilitating effects of psychosomatic illnesses and depression were just two examples. And if a person really can affect another person's physiology by his thoughts, as Tanbyrn had demonstrated, there was no reason to believe that the effects would necessarily always have to be positive.

His conclusion: if either blessings or curses affected reality, the other would imperatively do so as well.

As Dr. Tanbyrn wrote:

> Most religions believe in the power of blessings and curses. In medicine we have placebos that eliminate pain or, in some cases, treat diseases. In psychology we find that the power of positive thinking affects behavior, and there is ample evidence that those thoughts can actually rebuild neural pathways that have been damaged by severe depression. From

quantum physics we know that an observer's thoughts and intentions determine the outcome of reality. So we have religion, medicine, psychology, and physics all saying essentially the same thing—our thoughts and intentions have the ability to affect reality in inexplicable, but very real, ways. To shape the outcome of the universe.

The last statement seemed like hyperbole to me, but it was a similar point to the one Xavier had made when we were talking earlier in the hospital.

A couple of observations that I find significant: according to Dr. Tanbyrn, it's more effective if the person who is cursed knows it and believes in the power of the curse. Research on curses that were spoken over people who were unaware of it or didn't believe in them had mixed results. The deeper the personal connection, the more pronounced the effect, just like in his love entanglement studies at the Lawson Research Center.

Tanbyrn didn't mention Jesus cursing the fig tree, but he did mention Balaam being hired to curse the Israelites in the Old Testament.

After a lifetime of studying the secrets behind illusions and mentalism, I can't help but be skeptical about all of these claims. However, the test results from when Charlene was in the Faraday cage showed that my thoughts had somehow affected her physiology, and the dozens of research studies mentioned by Dr. Tanbyrn in his books add validity to the theories. Needless to say, the findings at least piqued my curiosity.

Whatever the actual relevance of all this, one thing is clear: Xav was right; for thousands of years people of faith have believed in the power of words, thoughts, and intentions to both heal and to harm. And recent breakthroughs in the study of quantum entanglement and human consciousness support those claims.

My phone vibrates, and I see another text message from my producer at Entertainment Film Network.

Oops. Forgot all about that.

Now that I'm on my way to Philly, it's definitely time to give her a call.

I speed-dial Michelle Boyd's number and she picks up almost immediately. "Jevin! What happened? I've been texting you all night."

"It's been a crazy day. I assume you heard about—"

"Of course I heard. Are you kidding me?" She's excited, sounds almost exuberant. "Fill me in. I need to hear it. Your take on everything."

It takes me a few minutes to relay the story of the fire at the center and Abina's death and the fight with Banner and Dr. Tanbyrn's hospitalization. For now I leave out the detail that I'm in the air on my way to Philadelphia.

"What about the study? Were you able to debunk it?"

"No, but at this point I don't think that's really the primary issue."

"Of course it's not the issue. This Tanbyrn deal, this fire, that's the story. This whole thing with the doctor is great."

I feel myself bristle at her words. "Great? How is it great that a man is in a coma?"

"No, no, no, not that. That he survived! I'm talking production value. What a great story—human tragedy, heroism, a life-and-death struggle. Viewers will love it. If we can just pull some footage together before tomorrow's—"

"Production value? That's what this is to you? Viewers will love the fact that a man—"

"You're missing the point here, Jev. This is a Nobel laureate who was the target of an arsonist's flames. Viewers will love that you saved him, that he's valiantly fighting for his life. Don't you see? It's the perfect way to take your series in a new direction. We were aiming for more of an investigative approach this time around anyway. And I mean, let's be frank, debunking psychics and sideshow acts? Come on, Jev, even you have to admit that that gets old after a while. Viewers want something unique, something fresh, something different."

"So, a dying man is fresh and different."

"Listen to me, Jev, every news station in the

country is following this story, but you have the inside scoop. You were there. You saved a man's life, for God's sake. This isn't just Tanbyrn's story, it's yours."

On one level, I know that what she's saying is true—other networks will cover this, and I had been there; I'd experienced it all firsthand. It was certainly a tragic and gripping story that viewers probably would love, and it made sense that Charlene and I would be the ones to tell it. I can't put my finger on precisely why I'm not excited about pulling what we have together into an episode, apart from the fact that it seems to be leveraging a man's suffering to promote ratings.

Which, of course, it is.

"Dr. Tanbyrn might die," I tell Michelle. An obvious fact, yes, but I feel like it needs to be said.

A pause. "Yes, well, that would be tragic, but viewers would be forced to think about their own mortality in light of his death and would be inspired to live better lives themselves. They'd be moved to tears, would remember him and his work in a positive light. If he makes it through, he's a fighter; if he succumbs, he's a martyr in the name of scientific advancement. Either way, we come out ahead."

That's it.

No one comes out ahead when an innocent man suffers. And no one comes out ahead when an innocent person dies.

"I'm out."

"What do you mean, you're out?"

"I mean I'm out. I'm not going to be involved with this."

"You have to be. You drop this and I'll drop your show, I swear to God—"

"Do it. You just said that debunking psychics and sideshow acts gets old after a while. And yeah, you're probably right. I don't need the money and you don't want the show. Find something you're excited about and we both win. There's plenty of extra footage left over from previous shows. I'll give it all to you. It should be enough for you to round out the season."

"I don't want that, I want *this*. I want Tanbyrn."

"Get used to disappointment."

I hang up and notice Charlene eyeing me. "Breaking out lines from *The Princess Bride* now, are we?"

"In this case it seemed appropriate."

"So, I couldn't help but overhear that—your side of the conversation, at least. We're officially freelancers now, I take it."

"Yes. I suppose we are."

"It actually might be better this way."

"Yes." I feel an unexpected spark of excitement at the thought. "It just might."

Daymares

I find myself dozing on and off as we fly east. Eventually I wake to Amil's voice telling us that we're approaching Chicago's Midway International Airport. The lights in the cabin, which have been low for the last few hours, are still dimmed, but he turns them up slightly.

Xavier is in the back of the plane snoring contentedly, but Charlene is across the aisle from me resting, her eyes closed. I'm not sure if she's asleep.

She has a blanket pulled up to her chin, and I watch her for a moment, thinking about when I observed her in the Faraday cage earlier today. She's as unaware now that I'm watching her as she was when I was viewing her on the video screen.

I feel like I'm intruding on her somewhat, admiring her like this, and just as I'm looking away she opens her eyes. "Hey."

"Hey."

She yawns. "So we're almost to Chicago?"

"It looks like it, yes."

She rubs her eyes and repositions herself in her seat so it's easier for her to talk with me. "I guess we didn't get a chance to connect with your father."

The comment takes me back a bit. I hadn't even thought of my dad since my conversation with her earlier in the day.

"When this is over, I'll be in touch with him. I promise."

"It might not be over for a while."

I wasn't exactly sure why it was so important to her that I talk with my dad, especially since she'd never brought it up before this week, but I figure she has her reasons, and right now I decide I'm not going to probe. "Give me a couple days. I'll call him on Friday afternoon, okay? Even if we're still caught up in the middle of all this."

Another small yawn. "Fair enough."

She closes her eyes again, snuggles up in the seat, and I wonder how awake she really was, if she'll even remember our brief conversation later.

Far below us, the steady flow of cars accelerating, decelerating, pumping through the city streets looks like glowing blood cells passing through dark veins. The cars look so small, but obviously, their size and speed are distorted by distance and by the plane's velocity.

It's all about perspective.

Only by taking into consideration our current elevation and airspeed could a person calculate the actual size and speed of the cars. As my mentor in magic, Grayson DeVos, used to tell me, "Only perspective brings truth into focus. Where you stand when you look at the facts will determinc how they appear. Never forget that when you design your show. The audience's perspective is even more important than how well you execute the effect."

Maybe that's what we needed here.

Perspective.

Maybe you're looking at all of this from the wrong angle entirely.

When you study illusions, you have to study the limits of memory to better understand short-term and long-term memory and how to use them to your advantage in a performance. Long ago I read about memories people have in which they see events not through their own eyes but as if they were hovering in a corner of the room watching the events take place.

Most people have them, often from traumatic incidents. In fact, they're so common that neurological researchers have a name for them: observer memories.

I have one of them myself, from when I was nine and a group of half a dozen junior high–aged boys surrounded me. They began to drag me toward an old quarry that people had turned into a junkyard before it was filled with water to create a small lake for fishing and ice-skating on that otherwise neglected side of town.

No one dared swim in the lake because the bottom was still strewn with junk—bedsprings and broken glass and rusted car parts that were visible beneath the surface on the rare days when the lake was clear enough for you to see down more than a few inches.

It was a lake we all feared. But they dragged me toward it, and when I recall it now, it's not from the point of view of a boy being pulled toward the water by the other boys, but from a distance, as if I'm watching it unfold from a perch in a nearby tree.

I can see the older boys laughing and I can see myself struggling to be free, crying out for them to let me go. Finally, at the water's edge they shoved me to the side, into a stand of tall grass. Then they smiled at each other and patted me on the shoulder: *It was just a joke. We were never gonna hurt you; we were just kidding around.*

I ran home but never told my parents for fear that they would think I'd overreacted or, worse yet, been a coward.

And since then, when I remember that day, I don't see the events through my own eyes, but as if I were watching it all happen from somewhere beyond myself.

Observer memories.

But how could they even be called memories when my mind was filling in the blanks, making up the details, viewing things from another, imaginary person's point of view?

Observer memories are fictions that our minds tell us are true.

The same as optical illusions.

In magic we play people's expectations against them. The observer's mind fills in what he or she would *expect to see* rather than what's *actually being seen.*

I notice that Charlene has her eyes open again. She's watching me quietly. "You look deep in thought."

"Just thinking about how our minds can do strange things, can convince us of things that aren't real. Sometimes we see things that aren't really there, sometimes we don't see things that are. We're all experts at fictionalizing the truth."

For a moment she's quiet. "There's a legend that when Columbus was sailing toward the New World, none of the natives saw the boats, that the idea of the giant boats approaching was so foreign to their way of thinking that even though their eyes sent the signal to their brains, it didn't register."

"Not until they landed onshore, you mean?"

"Well, actually, while they were still out in the water, a shaman saw the ripples and was curious what was forming them. He stared at them, studied them, until eventually he saw the boats. When he told the villagers, they were shocked and at first didn't see anything. But they all believed in him and eventually came to see for themselves that the ships were there. So the story goes."

"So, it was their belief in him that helped them see the boats."

"Yes."

We begin our initial descent to the airport.

"Jevin, you've told me you have nightmares. About your boys. About Rachel in the van."

"Yes."

"Have you ever had one when you were awake?"

"You mean a hallucination?"

"A nightmare, but only you have it during the day."

"No." But there's something in her tone, something beneath the words. Then I catch on. "But you have? Is that what you're saying?"

"When I was a girl, a man killed three people in my neighborhood. Stabbed them. His wife, his daughter, then the woman who lived next door."

I'd never heard this before. "That's terrible."

"I was eight at the time and I heard the sirens outside—you know, from the police. Someone from the neighborhood had called them. I was standing at our front window; I saw the man walking toward our house, right down the middle of the street, holding that knife in his left hand. It was still dripping blood."

The plane banks and we slope down into the final descent.

"My parents had gone over to a neighbor's house just down the block when it happened. I don't remember exactly what they were doing or why they'd left me alone, but they didn't make it

341

home until it was over. The first police car came racing around the corner, but the man, Mr. Dailey, didn't stop. He just kept walking directly up the driveway to my house. He must have seen me inside the window because he smiled and tipped the knife in my direction. I should have run, I suppose, or hidden in the closet or something, but I didn't. I was just too terrified to move."

I hear a palpable chill in her words from the dark memories that haunt her.

The ground draws closer. My ears pop from the pressure, refuse to equalize.

"Right as he was walking up our steps, they shot him. The police did. He wouldn't put down the knife. I was watching through the window, just a few feet away. He died right there on our porch, his blood splattered across the glass right in front of me. That's when I ran to hide. I've never told anyone I saw him die. Not even my parents or the police knew I was there when he was shot. They thought I was downstairs watching TV."

When she pauses, I sense that it's just to regroup, not to give me a chance to respond, so I wait and at last she goes on, "Since that day, I sometimes see Mr. Dailey. I'll look up from reading and he'll come around the corner in my bedroom and hold that knife up and smile and just stare at me. I've seen him in restaurants and at bus stops. Sometimes I'll be sitting talking with my friends and he'll walk into the room, just like you or me, and I can't tell if he's real or not. And then he pulls out a knife. Sometimes he'll walk up to me and swipe it toward me, toward my stomach."

I'm reminded of what happened in the chamber last night when Banner tried to kill her by swiping the blade toward her abdomen.

Apparently she's thinking the same thing because I notice her gazing at the arm where she got her stitches. "I guess it's a hallucination, but I've always thought of it as a nightmare that I have while I'm awake. A daymare. I know it's not real, but everything inside of me tells me that it is. That's how powerful our thoughts can be. They really do change things, Jev, our thoughts do."

There's not a whole lot of difference between her daymares and my observer memories. In both cases our minds were filling in details, forcing us to see what wasn't real.

Why don't we just call observer memories what they are: retrograde hallucinations?

The saying about our eyes playing tricks on us comes to mind. But the saying isn't true, I've known that since my early days of magic. Our eyes don't play tricks on us, our minds do. Our eyes only gather information; our minds interpret it. We perceive the world not so much by what we actually see but by how our minds expect it to look, by what construct we use to make sense of the data.

Observer memories.

Fictionalized truth.

Hallucinations.

Perspective.

Our wheels touch down. The landing is a little rocky, as if the plane is unsure of itself as it settles onto the runway.

Clearly, Charlene is deeply moved and upset from sharing the story about Mr. Dailey. I reach across the aisle, put my hand gently on her shoulder. "You okay?"

"Yeah."

It's not true what they say about things being "only in your head." If it's in your head, it's in you, and you can't escape your thoughts, can't flee their effect on you. Call it psychosomatic if you want, but when thoughts affect your physiology, the problem is never just in your head.

Misdirection.

Seeing what you expect to see.

Why did the suicide bomber put the shirt on over his vest? If the video was simply of a malfunction in the vest, what did it have to do with RixoTray? With Dr. Cyrus Arlington?

I consider that for a moment. The implications for what we're trying to do here.

Eyes playing tricks on you.

A different perspective.

Captain Fontaine stops our taxiing beside the charter jet terminal.

Charlene folds up the blanket. "I hope Dr. Tanbyrn will be alright."

"So do I." But my thoughts are still on the video, on the behavior of the suicide bomber, the ways perspective and expectations affect what our minds tell us is real.

I'm not sure what any of it means and I make a decision to look into it later, but it'll have to wait. For now Fionna McClury and her four children are already waiting for us just outside the nearest hangar.

Socialization

I put a call through to the hospital in Oregon and find that there's been no change in Dr. Tanbyrn's condition, and by the time I'm done the door is open and Fionna and her kids are lining up to board the plane.

Fionna has a shock of red hair that she always seems to have a hard time taming and endearing green eyes that beg you to look deeply into them, but it's not easy to. One of her eyes wanders, and when we first met, I found it difficult to guess which of her eyes to look into when I spoke to her. For a while I kept switching my focus from one eye to the other until she abruptly told me to just choose one because going back and forth like that was making her dizzy.

She has two girls and two boys, all four years apart, almost like clockwork. Mandie is five, Maddie nine, Donnie thirteen, and Lonnie is seventeen. I'm not sure why she gave her boys and girls names that sounded so much alike, and I have no idea how she keeps the names apart, but from the first time I'd met her, I've never heard her call any of the children by the wrong name.

After two marriages that didn't work out, she's sworn off men, but she's also mentioned to me how important it is for her kids to have a good male role model, and I could tell she was conflicted about the whole issue.

Amil stows the McClurys' luggage in the back of the plane, and Fionna lets the kids troop aboard first, their eyes wide, mouths gaping.

"Sweet." It's Donnie, the ponytailed thirteen-year-old who has looked up from his cell phone just long enough to take a quick glance around before texting someone again. Last year he'd somehow convinced his mom that he needed an earring, and in his tattered jeans and long hair, he looks more like an aspiring rock star than your typical Midwestern homeschooled kid.

Lonnie strolls aboard, confident, perceptive, lean, and already handsome at seventeen. Mandie, the youngest, has both arms wrapped around a stuffed dog that's nearly as big as she is. Nine-year-old Maddie wears stylish glasses and is toting a well-worn copy of *The Count of Monte Cristo*.

Fionna ascends the plane's steps just behind them. She's wearing two buttons on her jacket: "Moms against Guns" and "NRA Member."

She is not an easy woman to figure out.

She offers me a nod and a smile. "Jevin."

"Hey, Fionna."

Because of how often we use videoconferencing, it's been a few months since we've all been together face-to-face. She leans in for a peck-on-the-cheek greeting.

As the kids pass by Xavier, they all greet him as "Uncle Xav." Then they settle into their seats.

"It's great to see you, Fionna," Charlene tells her.

"You too."

Xavier shakes her hand. "Hello, Ms. McClury." He lends a degree of respect to her name.

She regards him lightly. "Hello, Mr. Wray."

"And how is the homeschooling going these days?"

"Quite well, thank you. How's the search for the Loch Ness Monster?"

"It's coming along."

It doesn't take long before we're in the air again. Fionna asks for an update and I quickly brief her on what's going on, what we've found out.

When she hears about the documented negative effects of mind-to-mind communication and the idea of using a thought-borne virus to stop some-one's heart, she shakes her head. "That's about as unnerving as a warm toilet seat at a highway rest stop."

"Ooh . . ." Charlene cringes. "That one's just troubling."

"And memorable," Xav mutters. "I don't think I'll ever look at rest areas the same way again."

Fionna smiles. "Thanks." Then she turns to me. "So, you have Tanbyrn's iPad?"

Charlene retrieves it and hands it to her.

Earlier, Fionna had said that she could hash the password in two minutes or less. I decide to time her. A password prompt appears on the tablet's screen. She begins to tap at the virtual keyboard. I start my watch.

From behind us I hear Xavier talking with Maddie, the nine-year-old, who's staring out the window at the receding lights of Chicago.

"So, a field trip, huh?" he remarks offhandedly.

"Yes."

"Should be fun."

"Yes."

"A chance to get out of the house."

Oh, don't do this, Xavier. You're going to regret it if you—

"Uh-huh."

My watch tells me Fionna has one minute fifty seconds left. Without looking up, she calls back, "What makes the biggest difference in a child's education, Mr. Wray? According to the latest research, what's more important than the teacher's educational background, the school district, technology available in the classroom, socio-economic and racial demographics, even parental involvement?"

She's still working on the iPad.

One minute thirty-five seconds left.

"Let's see . . . the culture of the school? At some inner-city schools, no one even takes books home because of peer pressure. Because it's not considered cool."

"Yes, that's a factor," Fionna admits—her fingers are flying across the virtual keys—"but I'm talking about the most important factor: class size. The smaller the class, the better kids learn. Until you get down to twelve students, where it levels off. And what educational alternative offers that the most readily?"

"But what about socialization?" he counters.

Oh, bad move, Xav.

This was going to be brutal.

I look his way and notice Maddie staring at him questioningly. "Socialization?"

One minute left.

"Yes," he tells her. "It's how you make friends." He directs the next part of his answer toward Fionna. "Some people call it preparing for the real world." It's not sarcasm, not even criticism in his voice, but there's definitely a challenge there.

Fionna stops typing. Gazes at him.

Forty-five seconds left.

Here we go.

"Yes, that's right," she agrees, "socialization. It means preparing for life beyond school and learning to get along with people of all ages in a healthy manner. Maddie, why don't you go ahead and answer Uncle Xavier. Does homeschooling do that?"

Back to the iPad's keyboard.

Thirty seconds.

The socialization objection is such a typical one leveled against homeschooling that I wonder if Fionna has coached her children on how to respond to it. But Maddie doesn't look like she's trying to recall what her mother might've told her, she looks like she's really thinking about it.

Xavier waits.

We all watch Maddie to see what she'll say.

After a bit she replies, "So do you think the best way to prepare kids for the real world is to bus them to a government institution where they're forced to spend all day isolated with children of their own age and adults who are paid to be with them, placed in classes that are too big to allow for more than a few minutes of personal interaction with the teacher—"

Twelve seconds left.

"—then spend probably an hour or more every day waiting in lunch lines, car lines, bathroom lines, recess lines, classroom lines, and are forced to progress at the speed of the slowest child in class?"

Two seco—

Fionna punches one final key. "Done," she announces, looking up from the iPad.

Man, she really was worth her pay.

It's quiet in the back of the jet for a moment, and Charlene whispers to me, "Not too many times you find Xavier speechless."

"I heard that," he calls to her, then clears his throat slightly, addresses Maddie. "Your mom taught you to say all that, didn't she?"

"No." She pauses, thinks about that. "But if she had, wouldn't it show that she prepared me for the real world?"

Silence. Then Xavier's voice. "Amil, do you have any more of that cheese?"

Fionna smiles faintly: *Gotcha.*

The password prompt clears away, revealing the desktop screen. "Now, let's see what Project Alpha is all about."

Fionna is fast, but most of the files require her to type in another unique password. I have no idea how Tanbyrn could have kept them all straight, but it's taking Fionna awhile to work through them.

Finally she gets discouraged and sighs. "I think I need a break from this."

"You probably need some sleep," Charlene tells her. "Rest. Get back at it when we reach Philadelphia."

The truth is, we probably all need some sleep.

So that's what we do until the sun begins to glow on the eastern horizon and the City of Brotherly Love lies beneath us, its bridges straddling the Delaware and Schuylkill rivers, its skyscrapers rising into the cobalt-blue, unfolding day. Strands of high and lonely clouds stretch across the lower part of the sky.

And we land at the Philadelphia International Airport.

Philly

Wednesday, October 28
7:21 a.m.

I've been to Philadelphia at this time of year before, and the temperature is usually in the midfifties. Today the temps are lower, the day is clear, and the wind bites fiercely at my face as I step onto the tarmac.

Everyone is quiet as we head to the terminal; no doubt they, like me, are still half-asleep, still transitioning back to the waking world.

Memories of the path that led us here, the events of the last thirty-six hours, pass through my mind, bringing with them a hailstorm of harsh emotions.

Fury.

Grief.

Curiosity.

Confusion.

Abruptly, my thoughts are interrupted by Fionna. "Did you get the hotel rooms all figured out?"

"Should be all set. Sorry, no pool, but the suites do have whirlpools."

"How many rooms did you get?"

"Four. I figured I could share with Xavier and you and Charlene could stay in the same room, as could your boys and your girls—don't worry, the girls' room adjoins yours so you can leave the door between them open."

"Actually, I'm more concerned about my boys. It might be best if you could room with Lonnie and Xavier could room with Donnie. Keep an eye on them."

"Um . . ."

She smiles. "Just kidding. I appreciate everything."

"No problem. Anyway, their room is beside ours. We'll make sure they don't party too late."

"Much appreciated."

We're almost to the terminal. Amil has his cell phone out and asks me how many taxis we'll be needing.

I'm about to tell him two when Xavier leans close to me and whispers, "Get a limo for Fionna's kids. They'll love it."

Nice.

Good thought, Uncle Xav.

"One taxi," I tell Amil. "And one limousine."

353

On the helipad on top of RixoTray's corporate headquarters, Dr. Cyrus Arlington boarded one of his company's three Sikorsky S76A executive helicopters.

The drive to DC would have taken nearly three hours—more if traffic was bad—and he didn't have that kind of time today. Too much to do before this afternoon.

As the pilot completed the last-minute safety checks, Cyrus wondered what Mambo Atabei had accomplished for him last night and how it might affect his agenda for the day. Already he found himself thinking of her as a loose end. One that might need to be tied off permanently, just like Tanbyrn.

As the largest individual shareholder in the company, Cyrus stood to lose tens of millions of dollars if the legislation went through. He knew that name-brand drugs are safer and more effective than their generic counterparts. But also, yes, of course, more expensive.

For good reason.

If you were a novelist and spent a decade writing a book, and then someone came along and copied 95 percent of your words, packaged the book similarly to yours, and sold it at a fifth of the price, that person would be guilty of copyright infringement. It's the same as the Chinese and Russians producing designer handbags or watch knockoffs that sell for a fraction of the price of the original products.

Yet generic pharmaceuticals are enthusiastically welcomed by the general public.

Because they're cheap, not because they're ethical.

But still, incomprehensibly, they are legal.

There were two factors at play in the pharmaceutical industry regarding protection from generic drug infringement: data protection and patents.

According to the 1984 Hatch-Waxman Act, generic drug companies can release drugs to the marketplace without clinical trials as long as the companies can prove that their drug is equivalent to the name-brand drug. This allows them to earn income off the millions or billions of dollars of research and development that they don't have to pay for. There's only a five-year span of time after the release of data related to the drug's research before the equivalent generic drug can be released to the public.

Thankfully, however, for RixoTray and other pharmaceutical firms, their biopharmaceutical products also have patents that run not for five years but for twenty. However, considering that the only way to protect intellectual property on a research-based project like this is to file for the patents early, and research and development of the drug might take eight or ten years, the twenty-year protection shrinks to ten or perhaps twelve at the most.

Since the five-year data protection and twenty-year patent protection time frames run concurrently and generic drug companies will often sue to have patents overturned, the actual length of time between the release of the name-brand drug and its generic equivalent can drop to five or six years. Not a lot of time at all to recoup your R&D investment.

And that was about to change.

Cyrus's man had told him that if the president got his way, the time frames were going to be cut in half.

The helicopter took off.

He sent a text to the vice president's people that he was on his way, then reviewed what he was going to say to Vice President Pinder about the legislation initiative that the leader of the free world was going to propose in just under four hours.

We step into the Franklin Grand Hotel down the street from Independence Park.

Xavier was right. The kids went crazy over the limo ride.

I figure that neither Dr. Colette nor Dr. Arlington will be at work yet and we have some things to get together before meeting with either of them anyway, so after stopping by the front desk to check in, I suggest that we get settled and then the grown-ups meet in Xavier's and my suite to figure out our plan for the morning.

In the elevator, Mandie gets the honor of pressing the button to the twenty-second floor.

One wall is glass, and as we ascend we see the Comcast building nearby. Fionna mentions that it was built to look like a giant flash drive, and everyone agrees that it really does. For a homeschooling mom, school is always in session, and she explains to the kids that Philadelphia is sometimes known as the "City of the Nation's Birth" and that it has the largest number per capita of Victorian-style homes in the US. "The city hall is also the largest city hall building in the world. No steel reinforcement; it's all concrete, brick, and marble. It was built in 1901 and has more than two hundred statues surrounding it. The statue of William Penn on the top of the tower is thirty-seven feet high, and the circumference of his hat is more than twenty feet."

The elevator pauses at our floor and the doors open.

"Who can give me a definition of circumference?" she asks her kids.

As Maddie does so, we all troop off to our respective rooms, and Xavier mentions quietly to me, "She's quite a woman, isn't she?"

"She sure is."

The Question Behind All Questions

7:55 a.m.
3 hours left

After dropping off my bags in the room, I decide that before our meeting begins I'll grab some coffee and bagels for our crew from the coffee shop across the street.

As I pass through the crosswalk, a young mother pushing a stroller ferrying a warmly bundled-up baby boy joins me. She greets me and I wish her good morning back. "That's a cute baby you have," I tell her honestly.

She beams. "Thank you. His name is Frankie."

A moment later she and Frankie walk out of my life, but they send my thoughts cycling back to the days when my sons were that age.

And I think of Rachel too—the young mother who loved them and then took their lives.

In the months following their deaths, lots of people gave me advice, and almost none of it helped. Especially not the line about the ones who've passed away "living on in our hearts."

My family lives on in my heart as much as the memory of the night I got drunk in college and totaled my car, as much as the recollections of food poisoning sending me to the hospital for a whole weekend last year.

A memory is a memory is a memory. And that's all it is, so if that's all we can claim for our loved ones when they die—that they live on in our hearts—then that's a pretty puerile and insulting thing to say to a grieving person.

Memories. The fictions we tell ourselves are true.

But perhaps wishful thinking is less painful than the brutal truth: "Don't worry, you'll remember Rachel and the boys for a while, then life will go on and they'll slowly get crowded out of your heart by other, more trivial things. And then, of course, before too long you'll die too, and eventually all of you will be forgotten in the sands of time."

Unless eternity is real, unless heaven is more than a fairy tale, death always wins in the end.

The air inside the coffee shop is interlaced with the sweet smell of freshly baked cinnamon rolls and aromatic coffee. I load up on half a dozen giant cinnamon rolls drenched in icing, some bagels and breakfast sandwiches, as well as coffee and lattes for the adults, and head back to my room.

One piece of advice that did seem to help, though, at least a little bit, was something one of my ultramarathoner friends told me: "Hang in there. It'll never always get worse." It's a saying ultrarunners have to remind themselves at eighty or ninety miles into their hundred-mile races that eventually the trail will get easier. At least for a little while.

Obviously, life for everyone has its ups and downs, and I've had lots of good times over the last year, but a pervasive heaviness has settled into my heart, as if the default setting of my life has changed from joy to disappointment. Grief might actually be a better term.

Life might get worse, but it'll never always get worse.

According to my friend.

But maybe it should. Maybe if you're the guy who fails to notice the warning signs in the actions of the woman who would eventually become your sons' murderer, maybe then it should get worse for you until you die and are forgotten in those sands of time too, along with them.

All these thoughts are stirred up simply from seeing that ebullient young mother's joy over her child. Charlene's words from last month come back to me, when she told me that joy is evidence of God.

Well then, if that's true, what is grief evidence of?

On my way through the lobby, I contact the hospital again and find out that Dr. Tanbyrn is still in a coma. I ask the nurse in charge to text me or call me if his condition changes. Since I'm not family, it takes me awhile to convince her, but in the end she agrees.

As I approach my room, Charlene meets up with me in the hallway. "So how are your ribs this morning?"

"Still tender. Your arm?"

"The stitches are tugging a little, but not too bad. Your head?"

"Manageable. Burns from the fire?"

She shrugs. "Nothing serious. You?"

"I'm good."

"Good."

Remarkably, I do feel better. Not 100 percent recovered, but at least on the way, and that's one thing to be thankful for. I'm glad she's doing alright too.

Inside the room, we find Xavier has showered and changed. His eyes widen when he sees the food, especially the box of cinnamon rolls. "I'll take some of those to the kids."

I hand him the bag and he leaves to deliver breakfast to the McClury children.

"He really likes those kids," Charlene observes.

"I'm thinking it might be more than just the kids."

"I'm thinking you might be right."

We pull out our notes and for a few moments we're quiet, and I realize I'm slipping back into my retrospection about the loss of my family.

At last when Charlene speaks, I hear gentle caution in her words. "Jevin, you need to be careful."

"About?"

"The times you disappear."

"The times I disappear?"

"Into the past." A pause. "Into your pain."

Her words hit me hard and ring as true as Xavier's did on Monday, when he talked about my past being a part of my story but not what defines it. "Stop feeding your pain and it'll dissipate," he'd told me. "Be where you are; let where you've been alone. Do that and the universe will lean in your direction."

But how? How do you get to that place?

I take a long time before responding. "What are we supposed to do when life makes no sense, Charlene? And don't just say we need to make the best of it. There's no best to make of it when your sons are murdered by your spouse."

"I know."

"So?"

A moment passes. "I don't know, Jev."

I let my thoughts crawl over everything again. "I guess it all comes back to the question behind all questions."

"I don't know what you mean."

"The question 'Why?' Why do bad things happen? There are never enough 'becauses' to answer that final 'why.'"

"I have to believe that there is, that there's a reason why God would—"

"Would what?" The words come out before I can stop them, taut and cutting and fueled by my brokenness: "Would allow two little boys who're strapped in their car seats to drown? Would allow their mother to sit by and let it happen?"

"It makes no sense to me either. I don't know why we hurt so badly and hope so much for something better. But I do believe that somewhere there's a reason behind it all."

"God works in mysterious ways? Is that it?" Even as I'm saying the words, I feel bad about the tone I'm using with her, but it's as if these feelings have been churning around inside of me and now they're geysering out all on their own.

Charlene seems to be at a loss for words. Finally she stands and walks to the window. Gazes at the day. "Jevin, when Jesus was dying he cried out to God, asked him why he'd abandoned him."

"And what did God say?"

Her eyes are on the skyline. "Nothing."

I'm quiet. So not even Jesus could unriddle the mystery of suffering, the feeling of being abandoned by God. I'm not sure if that's supposed to reassure me or not. Honestly, it only serves to make the answers I'm seeking seem more elusive than ever.

Charlene faces me, says softly, "There's a

teaching in the Bible that all things work together for the good of those who love God."

"And how did being tortured to death work out for Jesus's good?"

Oh, that was just great, Jev. Just great. Keep attacking what she's saying when she's just trying to help.

"Charlene, I'm sorry. I shouldn't have—"

"It wasn't the end when he died."

"He rose."

"That's what Christians believe. Yes, St. Paul said death has been swallowed up in victory."

The idea that death could be conquered, that life would win in the end, strikes me as too good to be true, but also as the most necessary truth of all.

"Do you believe that?" I ask her.

"If I didn't, I'm not sure how I'd find enough hope to make it through the day."

I have no idea how to respond to that. I haven't felt hopeful in a very long time. And I haven't felt very prepared to make it through my days either.

She approaches me. Her voice is tender. "Jevin, who are you angry at, yourself or God?"

"I'm not angry."

"No, don't do that. Not with me."

"Do what?"

"Brush me off. Hide. I know it's there. I can see it. How you've changed."

I find I can't look her in the eye, but then she puts her hand gently on my chin, turns my head so

I'm facing her again. "Rachel had problems, Jevin. She was ill—"

"Okay, let's just—"

"Something broke inside of her and she didn't have the chance to get it fixed."

"Charlene, stop."

"There's no way you could have known, no way you could have—"

I pull away. "That's enough!" I've never spoken to her like this before, and I'm sorry, so sorry, for snapping at her. "Charlene, I'm—"

"It's okay." She pauses and I can tell there's more she wants to say. "I loved her too, Jevin. We all did. But her choice wasn't your fault. She's the one who did that terrible thing, not you."

"Ever since it happened, ever since that day, I've been trying to hate her for what she did to my boys."

"I know."

"I can't seem to."

"I know."

All the questions and anger and desperation that has been piling up for the last thirteen months overwhelms me. It's like a weight too heavy to bear, one that's smothering me and isn't ever going to let me go. "I don't forgive her, Charlene. I'll never forgive her. And don't tell me I need to forgive myself, because I don't even know what that means."

"No, I wasn't going to, Jev. You don't need to

forgive yourself. You need to stop hating your-self."

I'm standing there, reeling from the impact of her words, when the hallway door opens and Xavier and Fionna step into the room for our meeting.

Dilemma

8:10 a.m.
2 hours 45 minutes left

"Hey, kids," Xavier calls. "You two behaving yourselves?" He's halfway through one of the mammoth cinnamon rolls. Fionna has Dr. Tanbyrn's iPad in hand.

I turn to the side so no one can see my face. I'm afraid a tear will escape, but I make sure it doesn't.

The question behind all questions.

The one not even Jesus knew the answer to: *Why?*

And Charlene's words: *"You don't need to forgive yourself. You need to stop hating yourself."*

Yes, yes, I do.

But how?

She assures Xavier that, yes, we were behaving. It takes me a few seconds to collect myself, then we all gather around the suite's executive conference table beside the window that overlooks Independence Park.

I try to refocus my thoughts, dial us back to the task at hand. It's not easy. Shutting away your pain never is. "Okay, I know we were all working on different things on the plane. Let's take a sec, summarize what we have, then move forward, see if we can figure out what Arlington's connection with Glenn Banner might be." From the looks on Xavier's and Fionna's faces, it doesn't appear that they can tell I was so close to losing it.

Charlene offers to go first. "I found Colette's and Arlington's vitas online, as well as some references to the research and patents they've been involved in, mainly in the area of recording brain waves and electrically stimulating parts of the temporal lobe. Also, the further you delve into Arlington's background, the more you find the telomerase studies coming up again and again. There's proposed legislation that could affect its release date. RixoTray has started clinical trials. I'll email everyone what I have."

"I think we should contact Dr. Colette first," Fionna suggests, "before we do anything else, see if she can help us."

It seems reasonable. Fionna goes online, locates Colette's home phone number, and I try it. No answer. I'm about to leave a message when Xavier stops me. Taps my phone's screen to end the call for me.

"What?"

"Really, what are you going to tell her, Jev? That you're a magician who thinks her boss might be connected to a homicide and arson in Oregon, a top-secret military thought-borne virus psychic research program, and a conspiracy to stop suicide bombers in the Middle East?"

"Hmm. Yeah. Maybe better to talk in person."

"And what if she's involved? Did you think about that?"

I set down the phone. "Okay. Let's table that for the time being."

My emotions are still wrenched from my conversation with Charlene. They feel raw and exposed. Concentrating on this meeting isn't going to be easy.

How do you stop hating yourself? Where do you even begin?

I have no idea.

Xavier takes a final bite of his cinnamon roll and out of habit begins his explanation with his mouth full. "I didn't find out—"

But the mom in Fionna immediately kicks in: "Let's not talk with food in our mouth, Mr. Wray."

"Oh. Right." Some people might have taken offense, but the way she said it was friendly enough, and Xavier swallows, apologizes. "Sorry. I was saying I heard from one of my buddies who's . . . well . . . connected. He said he did a little checking, and Project Alpha was started just over a year ago."

Fionna is typing on her virtual keyboard. "Which would correspond to when Dr. Tanbyrn's studies were first published."

"Exactly. It was named Project Alpha after the first published article detailing a researcher's ability to translate brain waves of linguistic information. Back in 1967."

"1967? This line of research has been around that long?"

"Yup. That was the year Edmond M. Dewan taught himself to turn on and off the alpha rhythms in his brain—they're brain waves that are associated with mental states and relaxation. So, by relaxing himself at conscious intervals while recording those alpha wave changes with EEG, he was able to communicate Morse code messages. Through his thoughts."

Charlene leans back. "Whoa."

"Of course, scientists have come a long way since then in recording brain waves through functional magnetic resonance imaging, diffusion tensor imaging, and magnetoencephalography. Lots of people think the government is already monitoring their thoughts." He pauses and looks at us ominously. "I know people who know people who've already had it happen to them, and pretty soon it's going to be as widespread as—"

"And the military connection?" I direct him

back to the topic at hand before he can launch into a tirade on how the government is controlling and policing our thoughts.

"Yeah. Project Alpha goes high up in the Pentagon; in fact, the second in command in the DoD, Undersecretary of Defense Oriana Williamson, is on the oversight committee. There's no sign of the Kabul video on YouTube or WikiLeaks, so whoever received it has kept it under tight wraps. Nothing on Akinsanya either, except that the name is Nigerian. It means 'the hero avenges.'"

He takes a breath. "Jev, I watched the footage you managed to get while you were taking Tanbyrn's test and didn't see anything unusual. As far as I can tell, you and Charlene really are entangled."

"Really?" Fionna raises an eyebrow. "Entangled?"

A clarification is in order here. "I'm not sure that's really the best word. Charlene and I have been working together for a long time. It's natural that we would have a close interpersonal relationship."

"A close interpersonal relationship." Xavier nods. "That's a good way to put it."

"Yes," Fionna agrees. "That sounds accurate."

Charlene is watching me expectantly.

After a fumbling silence I say, "Um . . . let's figure out the right terms to use later." I indicate to Fionna. "So? Anything?"

She holds up Tanbyrn's iPad. "Well, I wish I had some good news, but so far I haven't been able to find anything more specific about Project Alpha on this thing. If there was some secret data floating around out there somewhere, it must have been on another computer."

"The one Banner was checking just before he attacked us in the chamber?" Charlene muses.

"Possibly. And it looks like Tanbyrn had some doubts about the future of the program. Funding. President Hoult apparently wants to nix it. Oh, and Lonnie isn't bad at math, so I left the sheets from Tanbyrn's folder for him to look over, see if he can decipher them." Most seventeen-year-old guys wouldn't exactly be excited about deciphering a Nobel laureate's scientific quantum mechanics equations, but Lonnie was not your typical teenage guy. "What about you, Jev? Dig up anything?"

"Tanbyrn touched on studies about both prayers and curses. It seems there's more than just anecdotal evidence supporting the effectiveness of both of them—the one to heal, the other to harm. A . . . well . . . close interpersonal relationship seems to be vital to both."

We all take a minute to process what everyone has said.

I draw things to a close: "I think the first order of business is setting up that meeting with Arlington."

Fionna types on the iPad, then announces that he'll be out of the office this morning. She consults the screen. "According to his personal calendar, he'll be back at noon. He has a meeting in DC this morning." She sounds disappointed, and for good reason. We'd all been hoping that by announcing that she'd hacked into his personal laptop, she could get us an audience with him this morning.

"What about the people from RixoTray's cybersecurity department?" I suggest. "Certainly there'll be someone there interested in speaking with you before you report your findings to the company's CEO?"

"That makes sense. But that doesn't help you get to Arlington. And what exactly would you want me to find out from them?"

"When we first watched the video of the suicide bombers yesterday, it was after office hours here in Philly. See if you can get a look at the footage of the surveillance cameras in the lobby or, ideally, the reception area in Arlington's office suite. Find out if anyone else entered. It'd be helpful to know if Arlington watched the video alone or had company with him."

"Nice." Xavier holds his fist out toward me until I bump it with my own, then he offers to go with Fionna. "It might be good to have two of us there to deal with anything that might come up."

"What might come up?" she asks.

"Stuff." He looks around awkwardly. "You know. That might need handling."

"Handling."

"Hey, you never know what you might run into."

"Well . . . I suppose I could use a minion."

"Let's go with 'assistant.'"

"I can work with that."

I collect some of my notes. "Good, and Charlene and I can try to set up a meeting with Dr. Colette. Fionna, see if you can find out where she'll be."

It takes a few minutes, but finally she finds what she's looking for. "According to her calendar, Dr. Colette will be at RixoTray's R&D facility up near Bridgeport this morning. I'm guessing it's about half an hour drive from here."

It strikes me that somewhere along the line I forgot to get us all cars. It's less than a mile to RixoTray's headquarters, but I figure Fionna and Xavier should at least have a car at their disposal. I make a quick call, get two executive cars and drivers for the day, and we get back to business.

"But how'll we get through security?" There's skepticism in Charlene's voice. "Surely they won't let us just walk into their R&D facility, not without an appointment."

I find myself palming my 1895 Morgan Dollar, finger-flipping it. "True. Security is sure to be hypertight."

"Go in as custodians?" Fionna suggests. "Or service workers?"

Xavier shakes his head. "Not enough time to put something like that into play. Besides, those people would almost certainly be vetted. Possibly even fingerprint ID'd."

"New employees?" Charlene suggests. "We just got a job? We show up for the first day of work?"

"Too easy to check."

"How about we're there for a business meeting? Or what about the truth: we're working on a documentary and have some questions we need to talk with Dr. Colette about concerning her research?"

That's actually a tempting thought, but I doubt it would work. "It'd be too easy for them to just deny us access; we need something they can't say no to."

Fionna has been typing and now sighs. "There are three security checkpoints to go through. And Xavier's right. They have fingerprint identification at the front gate."

"Okay . . ." Xavier is thinking aloud. "So we need a way of getting two people who've never been there before, who the guards aren't expecting and won't be able to verify the identity of, into an ultra-high-level security pharmaceutical R&D complex in a way that won't arouse suspicion."

And that's when it hits me. Misdirection. The thing I do best. "Well put, Xav. And I think I know just how we can pull it off."

Complaint Procedures

They all eye me curiously.

"Government inspectors from the Food and Drug Administration following up on a complaint about the treatment of human subjects in their telomerase research."

Everyone mulls that over for a moment.

Xavier gives a slow nod. "Government agencies are always reshuffling staff, renaming divisions, reworking their logos. Bureaucracy at its best. Shouldn't be that hard to fake the paperwork, and it would make sense that they wouldn't know you. But what if they decide to follow up? Call the FDA?"

"We'll put your phone number on our cards."

"We'd need IDs." Charlene taps her chin thoughtfully. "Official ones."

"There's a FedEx Office store down the street. I saw it when I was getting the coffee. It's amazing what you can pull off with a color printer, some card stock, and a laminator."

Oh yeah. I was liking this. I could get used to being a freelancer.

"Fionna, we'll need official-looking documents. Can you come up with those in an hour?"

She screws up her face. "No. Not ones that could fool the guards. But . . . maybe my kids can help me—do a little research on FDA complaint procedures. Extra credit." After a moment of reflection, she nods. "I'd say we should be able to come up with something."

"I'll give you a hand," Charlene offers.

"Great." I stand. "I'll help Xavier with the IDs and business cards. Charlene, you and Fionna tackle the paperwork; there's a business center on the second floor. You can print what you need down there, or join us at the FedEx Office."

We use my phone to take Charlene's and my pictures for the IDs, then the two women head out to convene with the kids and Xavier grabs his computer. "Come on," he tells me. "Let's go do something illegal."

Dr. Cyrus Arlington landed in DC.

Strode off the helicopter pad.

There was already a car there waiting to take him to the White House.

Mambo Atabei carried the goat's headless carcass into the alley behind her home and tipped it into the dumpster.

She'd been ridden by her Loa for more than six hours last night, so long that the other members of her peristyle who were involved in the ceremony had begun to worry about her.

But she was thankful. Being possessed for long stretches of time was the most rewarding part of what she did, the reason she'd gotten into all of this in the first place.

Some people claimed that Loa possession was a hallucination brought about by cultural expectations, wishful thinking, and a little too much rum. That was an easy way to explain away what happens. Let them think what they wanted.

After turning from the dumpster, she brushed some of the goat's hair off her shirt. The blood was still there. That wasn't going to come out nearly as easily.

Then she went to check the news to see how everything had panned out concerning the doctor in Oregon.

Darren took a deep breath, said to his brother, "Ready?"

"Ready. Lancerton, Maine, huh?"

"Let's see how well this works."

Then the twins closed their eyes, relaxed, and focused their thoughts on the same thing. Just as they'd been training for so long to do.

Oil and Blood

8:39 a.m.
Lancerton, Maine

Adrian Goss had slept in a little and was still a bit groggy as he walked toward the woodshed.

Behind him, smoke curled from the cabin's chimney, wisped into the crisp Maine day, and wandered toward the steel-blue sky like a slowly uncurling snake.

He trudged through the mud and thought of the wood stacked by the side of the shed, of splitting it, and he thought of his wife, who would be home anytime from working the graveyard shift at the hospital.

And he thought of his son.

It would be his birthday next week, turning eleven, and Adrian had decided to buy him a football—real pigskin. Official NFL size and weight.

Eleven next week.

A fifty-year-old guy with an eleven-year-old kid to raise. Not ideal in some regards, but not that unusual. Besides, love can overcome something as trivial as the age span between a father and his boy.

Adrian passed the 1972 Chevy Impala chassis in

his yard and the thick stump he used to balance the wood on when he chopped it, pressed open the shed door, heard the harsh squeal of the hinge.

Oil it.

He'd been meaning to.

Yes.

Later.

He stepped into the woodshed. Light filtered through the cracks between the boards that made up the walls. The shafts of light seemed like giant slivers that he should avoid but would never be able to if he was really going to cross over to the other side of the shed.

Yes. Oil the hinge.

His thoughts seemed to blur together. Strangely, as if they were sliding over each other. Layers of ideas. A mesh that was impossible to sort through.

Shadow and light. Just like the shed.

A birthday present for his son. Eleven.

For a moment Adrian stared at the dust filtering through the slanting light and tried to remember why he'd come into the shed in the first place. He blinked and looked around.

It was something to do with his wife. Something to do with her and the argument they'd had last night.

His eyes landed on the shelf. A chain saw, tools, grease for the lawn mower. Spark plugs. A small metal oil can.

Adrian felt light-headed, like he had in high

school after that tackle against Woodland in the state semifinals, when he'd had to sit out the rest of the game because he was seeing two of everything. That running back—what was his name? Terry something. Or Tommy. Something like that. Number eleven.

No, wait. His son was Terry. Yes. His son.

Adrian walked toward the shelf, braving the slivers of light, but they passed across him like they didn't care, like they weren't interested in eviscerating him, in slicing through his flesh and meat and bone.

At the shelf with the chain saw. Paused—

No, the game wasn't in the semifinals. They didn't make it that year.

Reached for the oil can.

No.

He came in here to get something for his son.

No, it was somehow about that argument with his wife.

Yes. About the house. The wood, the stove, and outside there wasn't enough wood around, so why couldn't he have split more of it, because when she got home from work in the morning, what was she supposed to do, chop their wood too?

No, he'd told her, of course not. He would do that. He would take care of it.

He passed the oil, the chain saw, went to the southwest corner of the shed, toward the axe.

Southwest corner? Why would he even think of

it like that? He'd never called it the southwest corner before.

The shed's angled sunlight brushed against his face in between the flutters of velvety black shadows. It didn't hurt at all. Not one little bit.

He blinked and tried to collect his thoughts again. Something wasn't right. Something wasn't clicking. There was the high school football game and his son's birthday and the wood to be chopped and the number eleven, the number of the player.

No, that's what Terry was turning on his birthday, and Adrian still didn't have a gift for him.

Light and shadow and light.

Toward the axe.

His son's birthday, yes.

He lifted the axe, swung it gently. He was a man used to hard work, and the axe felt comfortable in his hand. At ease, as if it were an extension of himself. Another limb with a sturdy-bladed end.

Something for his son.

Adrian was aware of the sunlight becoming alive, crawling against his skin. Every particle of dust, friction, friction, flowing sandpaper coursing through the air! Rubbing. Troubling!

Split the wood.

Split.

Adrian left the shed, shut the door behind him. Heard it creak.

Fix that. Oil it.

After Terry's birthday.

The azure sky above him seemed to stretch forever. Beyond forever.

He went to the woodpile, axe in hand, sunlight falling all around him.

Azure? Where did that word come from?

After he turned eleven.

Trish had argued with him last night and accused him of being lazy.

Lazy.

He wasn't lazy.

He positioned the wood upright on the stump. He would show her. Prove it.

She was always doing this. Always nagging him, getting on his—

He would show her.

He raised the axe; yes, yes, he would prove it to her.

Adrian felt the muscles in his shoulders and back flex, his forearms tighten as he gripped the axe handle with a stranglehold, raised the blade above his head, and then, slicing through the sunlight, shredding it and leaving it hanging in tatters around him, he swung the blade down. It struck the log but did not cleave it in two.

Swing through the log. Don't aim at the top of it, aim at the stump. Swing through it.

Through it.

Focus not on connecting with the top of the log, but rather the stump on which—

On which.

The log rests.

He tugged the blade free, repositioned the wood, heaved the axe backward over his head, then brought it forward again, harder than before.

Vaguely, he heard the axe connect with the stump. The two split logs dropped to the sides, but for some reason they did not bleed. For some strange reason he thought of this, of how nice it would be to see them bleed.

In the sunlight.

But they did not.

Blood could be used to oil that hinge on the shed.

He tossed the split logs aside and grabbed another log off the pile.

His wife accused him of being lazy.

He would need blood to fix the woodshed.

Behind him, from the end of the long driveway that wound along the edge of the woods, he heard the sound of a car's engine and the crunch of gravel. Trish. Coming home from work.

The graveyard shift.

She mocked you last night. Accused you of being lazy. But you're not lazy. You're a hard worker. You're—

Anger fueled the force of his next swing.

The two split logs flew to each side of the axe head as it hewed the log and sank into the stump beneath it.

But once again the split logs did not bleed.

The car stopped beside the house.

He wrenched the blade free.

Your son doesn't turn eleven until next week. You can pick him up at school today when you're done here. Pick him up early. Bring him back home.

He would need that blood to fix the woodshed door.

A car door slammed.

Eleven years old. Next week.

"Hey," Trish called. "How's it coming?"

Adrian turned toward her and realized that she was mocking him even now. It was her tone of voice. It was all there in her tone of voice.

You need to oil that hinge.

"It's coming," he heard himself say, but it wasn't really like he was saying it, instead it was more like he was somewhere else nearby hearing another person talk to his wife.

The axe felt comfortable in his hand.

An extension of himself. Another limb. With a bladed end.

Blood in the sunlight.

He walked toward her.

Oil and blood.

And then the door to that troubling woodshed would never bother him again.

"Hello, honey," he said. "Welcome home."

Preemptive Justice

8:51 a.m.
2 hours 4 minutes left

"Well?" Daniel asked his brother. "Do you think it worked?"

They were both easing from their trancelike states in the dimly lit research room at the RixoTray R&D facility. No one else was there with them. This was one experiment they'd been careful to conduct on their own.

After what happened in Kabul, they'd decided they needed one more test. After all, it was essential that they see this through, finish their mission successfully, and neither of them felt quite ready to do that yet. What they were attempting was unprecedented in their field and would change the landscape of espionage and covert warfare forever. It wasn't something they could fail at, not when so much was at stake.

"We should check the news," Darren said. They both rose, he went to the computer on the desk. Daniel made a few phone calls, including one to their contact, the one who'd salvaged things in Kabul. The one who'd told them about the man in Lancerton.

Riah was the kind of person they were confident

could help them. Not only because of her expertise in deep-brain stimulation but because of who she was inside—how much like them she was. Even though she might not've been aware of what she was really capable of, they could tell. It'd become more and more clear to them over the last few months.

She would be here soon and they wanted to tell her everything.

True, they would have to kill her when this was over, just to be safe. But she could be of use to them in the meantime in completing their assignment.

The two brothers hadn't yet decided which of them would eliminate Dr. Colette. That little detail was still up in the air.

At the FedEx Office, I buy two clipboards, one for me, one for Charlene. No government inspector impersonation kit would be complete without them.

"You do know," Xavier tells me, "we'll probably get in big trouble with this."

"I'd say almost certainly."

"Too bad there isn't any fine print somewhere, a way to skirt around possible prosecution."

I kick that around for a minute. "You know what, let me get in touch with my lawyers. They might be able to come up with something that Fionna can add to the forms, noting that we're there for entertainment or educational purposes only, or that by allowing us to access the facility, the guards release all liability. Something like that."

Xavier looks at me skeptically. "You really think your lawyers can come up with something that'll cover our butts?"

"Hard to say, but that's what lawyers do best. And my lawyers are very, very good at what they do."

"Well, you pay them enough."

"True. And it's not like the guards would take the time to try to translate the legalese double-talk."

"No one reads fine print on forms like that anyway."

"That's true too. They don't even read iTunes updates."

"I do."

I pause. "I know. But honestly, regarding a waiver, when you know what you're doing, you can create a disclaimer big enough to cover your butt even if you were to steal the moon."

"Steal the moon?"

"I don't know. I was trying to think of something big."

"You keep using analogies like that and you're going to start giving Fionna a run for her money."

Now he was just being mean.

I gesture toward the cards he's holding. "The

lamination machine's over there in the corner."
Then I fish out my phone and make the call to the
law firm.

Riah arrived at the R&D facility and passed
through security.

She was still uncertain what all this was about,
but she sensed that helping the twins was a good
thing, the right thing, to do.

If that was indeed the case, it looked like she
would get a chance to help the government stop
terrorist threats by working with Daniel and
Darren to do whatever it was they actually did
when they thwarted that potential suicide attack in
Kabul.

"We let him do it," they'd told her last night.
How did they "let" the suicide bomber do it?

She wasn't sure, but obviously it had something
to do with her research and Dr. Tanbyrn's
findings.

Hundreds of people might've been killed at that
mosque, and if she could assist in stopping things
like that, help to remove terrorist threats, that
was probably an honorable, perhaps even, in one
sense, a noble thing to do.

Preemptive justice?

One way to look at it.

She was obviously no expert on morality, but
even she could anticipate that if the man in
the video had been shot or arrested, insurgents

would've claimed that he was an innocent civilian who'd been unjustly killed or imprisoned by imperialist Americans. After all, news is all about spin, almost never about truth. Scratch away at the surface of what people say and you'll always find an agenda lurking beneath the words.

That was one thing she'd learned about human nature. One thing she knew for sure: you can't take what people say at face value.

And spin like that would put more American soldiers at risk.

Yes, if there really was a way for her to help the twins eliminate threats without endangering the military's intelligence assets or personnel, it would certainly help the war efforts, probably save lives, and—

It would be the right thing to do. A way to serve the greater good.

So, yes, the greater good.

As she walked down the R&D facility's east corridor toward research room 27B for her meeting with the twins, she became more and more curious about what exactly she could do to help them kill.

Or eliminate targets.

Whichever term you preferred to use.

The Recruit

9:13 a.m.
1 hour 42 minutes left

Dr. Tanbyrn died.

We receive the news while we're gathered in Xavier's and my room getting ready to head out.

It shakes us, all four of us.

Personally, I hadn't been seriously considering the possibility that he would pass away but rather had settled on the expectation that he would recover.

The tragic announcement lends a renewed sense of focus and intensity to what we're doing. Now Dr. Cyrus Arlington is not only somehow connected to the death of Abina but also to that of Dr. Tanbyrn, the researcher he and his company had spent millions of dollars funding.

And Arlington was somehow connected to the video of the three men in Kabul, although how he might be tied to their deaths was still unclear.

We quietly take the elevator to the lobby, step outside, and find our two executive cars waiting for us out front.

Charlene and I climb into one of them, Fionna and Xavier disappear into the other, and the four of us leave the hotel to find out how RixoTray

Pharmaceuticals was entangled in arson, terrorism, conspiracy, and murder.

Cyrus was waiting outside the vice president's office when he saw on his phone's news feed that Dr. Tanbyrn had died.

So.

Atabei had come through for him.

Or the fire did, that coma did. Tanbyrn could've simply died from complications brought about by smoke inhalation.

Possibly, but—

"Dr. Arlington?" It was the receptionist, jarring him out of his thoughts. She wore a telephone headset and was tapping the receiver by her ear to end a call.

"Yes?"

"The vice president has been held up talking with Congresswoman Greene. He told me he'll be here within the hour. He apologizes for any inconvenience."

"Not a problem." Buoyed by the news of Tanbyrn's death, Cyrus didn't mind waiting another hour for the vice president of the United States. "Not a problem at all."

"Please, Riah, have a seat," Daniel told her.

She positioned herself across the table from the two brothers. The mammoth MEG machine took up the far end of the room. Countertops covered with medical instruments lined the walls. A sink, two computer desks, and a small conference area rounded out the room. All familiar to her. All part of her everyday world.

"Last night," she began, "you told me that you would explain how I could help you do . . . well, whatever it was that happened in Kabul."

"What do you think happened?" Darren asked.

"Somehow you made that man detonate his vest. I don't understand how—except that it must involve my neurophysiology research and Dr. Tanbyrn's psi studies."

"Yes, of course." Daniel stood. "Riah, if we could identify a threat, a terrorist, and without putting any soldiers in harm's way—"

"Get him to blow himself up."

"That's one option, yes. Or kill him quietly, in a way that was untraceable. Think about it. If it were possible."

She did think about it.

Identify a terrorist and somehow convince the person to blow himself up—like the man in the video. Let the terrorists take themselves out.

Or kill him quietly?

In an untraceable manner?

What did that even mean?

Tanbyrn's research: altering galvanic skin response, respiration rate—

Heart rate.

She took a shot at it: "Cardiac arrhythmia."

Daniel nodded. "Or a cerebrovascular accident."

In other words, a stroke.

But how?

She didn't know, but she did realize that what they were saying didn't quite fit with what she'd seen on the video of the suicide bombers. "Is that what you're telling me happened in Kabul?"

"At this point we're not quite ready to cover all that happened," Daniel said apologetically. "I wish we could, but we're awaiting word on an incident in Maine, then we can explain everything. But for now, we promised to tell you how you can help us."

Darren continued for him, "My brother and I were engaged in a study with Dr. Tanbyrn regarding the effects of mind-to-mind entanglement. Ways to nonlocally affect another person's physiology. Daniel and I share a certain connection with each other, you know that. Even more so than most identical twins."

"Yes."

"In the studies, by working cooperatively, we were able to cause a person a great deal of—"

"Discomfort," Daniel cut in.

"Discomfort?"

"Pain," Darren specified. "Fluctuations in cardiac activity and synapses in neural activity in the centers of the brain that register pain."

"And you're saying you did this nonlocally?"

They nodded.

She reflected on what she knew of Tanbyrn's research. Did it really involve the possibility of negatively influencing another person? If it were possible, as he claimed, that your thoughts could affect another person's physiology, then—

Especially if you know which areas of the brain to alter. Especially if you had an identical twin with whom you shared the ability to communicate in unexplainable ways . . .

Especially if—

Ah.

So that's where she came into the picture.

Stimulating the Wernicke's area.

Exciting that specific area of the temporal lobe.

"You're actually talking about—"

But before she could finish, Darren got a text message, looked at his phone, then interrupted her: "Goss's wife and son were found dead at the house. The sheriff has Adrian in custody."

"His son and his wife?" Daniel said.

"Yes."

Riah had no idea who Adrian was or who the Goss family was, but she was intrigued that more people connected with the twins had died.

Discomfort.

Pain.

Death.

She waited; Darren took a breath. "Well, it looks like we can tell you exactly how you can help us after all."

No Wind

9:20 a.m.
1 hour 35 minutes left

Charlene and I sit quietly in the back of the executive car as our driver maneuvers through traffic, taking us to Bridgeport.

The silence accentuates how affected we both are by the news of Dr. Tanbyrn's death.

I think of what Michelle Boyd, my producer at EFN, told me last night about viewers being forced to think about their own mortality if Tanbyrn died, and then being inspired to live better lives themselves.

But that's not exactly how I feel.

Not inspired to live a better life for myself—inspired to bring down the people who took his life from him. That was more like it.

In a way, I feel like I did yesterday afternoon when I was facing down Abina's murderer in the forest in Oregon—a sharpening of my senses, a dialing in of my attention.

And it felt good.

It's like the higher the stakes are being raised, the clearer my focus is becoming. It reminds me of the times when I was performing my stage show and I would do stunts other people referred to as death-defying.

I always liked those.

Kinda miss them.

Knowing that I'm all in, that there's no turning back and no backing down, it's what I'm made to do. And it's good to have that feeling back. I just wish it wasn't coming today on the heels of someone's death.

I couldn't shake the thought that the footage of the suicide bomber and his two associates blowing up was one of the keys to unlocking what was going on here.

On the plane, I'd made a mental note to take a closer look at the footage, and I figure now's probably a good time to do so.

To give Charlene and me privacy, I close the sliding glass shield between the front and back seats. Then, on my laptop, I pull up the video Fionna had sent me. We watch it several times, study it carefully, looking for anything we might have missed earlier.

But find nothing.

Just when I'm about to abandon the idea, Charlene motions to me. "Hang on." She reaches over, taps the space bar, pauses the video. "I think I saw something. Back it up a little bit."

I finger-scroll backward, to the moments imme- diately preceding the explosion.

She points to the screen. "There. Outside the

window, across the street. You can see it between the gap in the shades. A glint."

I enlarge that part of the video, study it closely. "On the third-floor window of that building."

"Yes."

I zoom in on the image even more, but the footage isn't the highest resolution and the image becomes blurry. I back it up a bit, and Charlene reads my mind: "Could that be a scope? From a sniper's rifle?"

The picture isn't clear enough for me to tell for sure. "I don't know. It's possible."

"Play it again. From the start."

We cue the video at the beginning: the men in the room, the table with the vest and explosives, the man tugging the curtains partway closed, the glint, the explosion—

"Why doesn't it billow outward?" I whisper.

"What?"

In the sharp sunlight I really can't tell for sure. "Let me play it through again."

I start at the beginning again, pause the video just before the explosion, then play the footage forward as slowly as the computer will let me.

"The curtain. It looks like it billows into the room as the explosion happens."

Once more we study that crucial moment in the video, and it certainly does appear that a fraction of a second before the explosion occurs, the curtain on the left side swirls inward.

"The wind?" she suggests. "Or a breeze from the ceiling fan?"

"There wasn't any wind, there weren't any ripples in the curtain earlier, and the ceiling fan wasn't on. So that leaves us with . . ."

It's all about sight lines, misdirection, and—

"A bullet passing through it." She leans back in her seat. "It's a fake. A sniper shot the vest, blew it up."

Expectation. The audience sees what they expect to see.

I think through what we know, balance it against what we don't. "Let me ask Xav if that type of C-4 would detonate from the impact of a sniper's bullet."

I speed-dial him while Charlene slides the computer onto her lap to watch the footage again. Xavier picks up, speaking quietly; apparently they'd just been escorted into RixoTray's corporate headquarters and I've caught him in the hallway leading to the cybersecurity office. After quickly recounting what Charlene and I noticed, I ask him about the possibility of detonating C-4 by firing a round into it.

There's a pause as he considers my question.

"No. C-4 is a secondary explosive, needs a primer . . . but if the sniper aimed for the primer or the electronic control, it might. Depends on the configuration and design of the vest, where the bullet struck. The point of impact might also explain the brief delay, why there was actually time to see the curtains flutter. But a sniper wouldn't aim for the vest. He'd aim for the head."

"Unless the whole intention was to make the video look like something other than a sniper attack."

"So you're thinking a sniper was stationed in that other building, knew what room these men would be in, sighted through the window, waited until one of them put on the vest, then shot it in the exact place to detonate it?"

"When you put it that way, it doesn't sound quite so plausible," I admit.

"I'm not saying it isn't plausible, just thinking aloud. Let's suppose it actually went down like that. It would mean that all of our postulating about the entanglement research—"

"Was completely off base."

"Yeah."

Perspective.

You only find the truth when you look at the facts from the right perspective.

I try to evaluate things. "The sight line would've allowed the sniper to hit each of the men. Maybe the vest just played into the narrative better."

"Like one of your tricks."

"Like one of my tricks."

"Is it definitive? Can you tell for sure if there's a sniper over there?"

"No. But the curtains, the glint across the street,

the fact that the guy didn't reach up to detonate the vest himself—they all make it a legitimate possibility."

"I'll have a look at it as soon as I can with Fionna. She might be able to do something about the resolution. But it might be a little while. We're almost to the cybersecurity office."

"Good. As soon as you can."

We end the call.

Reviewing the footage had only brought more questions—if there was a sniper, did that mean someone was faking the effects of this research? Could everything we'd been hypothesizing be on the wrong track entirely?

Hopefully, meeting with Dr. Colette would bring us some answers.

Because for the moment it felt like, as Fionna might say, someone had just knocked over another cage and there were even more gerbils than before underfoot.

The Need to Kill

The twins asked Riah to help them kill someone.

It was that simple. That's why they'd called her in.

Given all that she knew, all that'd happened in the last couple days, the request wasn't by any means out of the blue, but hearing Darren actually say the words, actually ask her to help eliminate a threat to national security, was instructive.

And inviting?

Yes, admittedly, it was.

Before letting them go on with their explanation, she returned to the topic of Goss and his family. "So you did that?"

"Yes," Darren said.

"But how?"

"Something went wrong. We were trying to influence him to take his own life, but he did not. He slaughtered his family instead. With an axe. We weren't able to—"

"Who did he kill first? The mother or the son?"

They stared at her. "I don't know," Daniel said.

I wonder what their wounds look like. How much blood there was.

"Why him? Why Adrian Goss?"

"He was the man who raped our mother." Darren's words were matter-of-fact. "The man who impregnated her."

"Adrian Goss was your father."

"Yes."

A close personal connection.

The prerequisite for Tanbyrn's research.

"Did you love him?"

Another quizzical look, but then both twins avowed that no, they had not loved him. Had not even known his identity until recently.

"We failed," Daniel began. "We need you to—"

"Use the electrodes to stimulate the Wernicke's area of your brains."

"Yes."

"To enhance your ability to cause discomfort in others."

"Yes."

Pain.

Death.

Exactly how all of this was possible was still unclear to her, but if Dr. Tanbyrn was right, the answer lay somewhere in the realm of quantum entanglement, an answer she would have to investigate more in-depth later when she had time.

"How did it feel?" she asked them. "To find out that a boy and a woman whom you had not targeted died in such a violent manner?"

"Disappointing," Darren admitted. "It meant that on our own we weren't as effective as we'd hoped."

There was no remorse in his voice, not even a hint of sorrow over the loss of the two innocent lives.

She trusted the twins implicitly, knew that they were patriots, knew that they had only the best intentions in mind. And she trusted that they truly did need her help, that the next target truly was, as they said, a well-funded terrorist, an enemy of the state.

But could she help them kill?

She thought again of the fourteen-year-old girl

in Afghanistan whose father had blown up, she thought of the son and wife of Adrian Goss, and she remembered being a teenager herself, holding that fragile-boned bird in her hands. Most of all, she remembered snapping its neck simply to see what it would be like to kill it. She knew that just like everyone, she had the capacity to kill. And to do so for no other reason than curiosity.

But could she kill a human being?

Yes.

Yes.

She absolutely could.

In an illuminating rush of insight, she realized that in a certain sense it was something she'd always wanted to do. Just like with the bird—to find out what it would be like. To find out if it would make her feel anything at all.

But there was one thing she needed to know before she would agree to help the twins. "People say that love lies at the core of human nature. To love and be loved. Do you believe that?"

"No," Daniel told her.

"Then what do you think people want?"

"People don't want to *be* loved; they want to *feel* loved."

"To feel loved."

"Yes. Would you rather be secretly despised by a partner, a lover, a spouse, but live your whole life believing that he deeply loves you, or would you rather be deeply loved by someone and yet never find out about it? Would you prefer a lifetime of feeling loved or a lifetime never finding out that you were?"

Riah wasn't sure how most people would answer that question. She'd been told she was loved many times but had never known what it was like to feel it. Not for one minute of her life.

She took a moment before responding. "Don't people want more than to simply believe they're loved? Don't they want the real thing—without any deception, without any betrayal? Don't people fundamentally want both love and truth?"

"It's very rare to have both," Daniel said, not quite answering her question. "Wouldn't you agree?"

"Yes. I would imagine that it is."

Rare. Too rare in this world of so many people who were so soon going to die.

She realized that the feeling really must be what mattered most, and that given her nature, it was not something she would ever experience.

Not ever.

Given her nature.

She made her decision.

"I'll help you," she told them.

Darren looked satisfied at her response. "We'll call you within the hour to tell you where to meet us. Bring the equipment."

With the nanowire electrodes already in place in the twins' brains, the instruments she would need to send the electrical impulses to their Wernicke's areas were minimal. She could carry them in a small day pack.

Darren pulled out three cell phones. "There's a time frame here. We need to move on it this morning. There are two numbers preprogrammed into each phone, one for each of the other two. After each number has been connected to, the phone's chip will erase itself, so if anything goes wrong, just hit number one and number two to speed-dial the other phones. It will erase the chip in yours."

Everyone took a phone.

The twins left.

And Riah went to her computer to verify what they'd told her regarding the man who lived in Maine slaughtering his family with an axe earlier that morning. She hoped she could find some photos.

After all, she really was curious about the details, about what fatal axe wounds in the body of a woman and a young boy would look like, if they would bear any semblance to the wounds in the snake her father had beheaded when she was just a girl, the one whose body she held until the wriggling stopped.

Killed but not yet dead.

Then finally, after a few minutes, both.

GPS

"It's as hot as a monkey's armpit in here."

The three computer technicians from RixoTray's cybersecurity team stared at Fionna.

"Um . . ." The youngest of the three techs nodded toward the only woman on the team. "Can you take care of that?" She headed off to fiddle with the thermostat.

A few minutes ago Fionna had introduced Xavier to the RixoTray cybersecurity team as her associate, promoting him from minion and assistant to associate. It seemed like the right thing to do. Now he stood by her side.

"So, you were able to get into Dr. Arlington's laptop?" The guy asking her the question looked like someone you'd picture appearing on Wikipedia's "computer geek" entry. Young. Skinny. Black-framed glasses. Messed-up hair. Holding a Dr Pepper in one hand and a bag of Doritos that Xavier was eyeing in the other. He seemed to be the one in charge, but from what Fionna had seen so far, her son Lonnie would've been more than a match for this guy at a keyboard.

"Yes," she said. "I was able to get in."

"We identified the attempt. Blocked it." Nacho Chip Boy was defending himself, but Fionna wasn't impressed.

"Only after I was in for five minutes and forty-two seconds. I could have erased data, altered research findings, transferred funds, anything I wanted to, long before you identified the breach." She didn't tell him about getting in again earlier that morning to access Dr. Colette's and Arlington's personal calendars.

The young man opened his mouth as if he were going to respond, then closed it. Said nothing.

She gestured toward the computer desk. "May I?"

He stepped aside and she sat down.

Xavier moved next to her, asked the guy if he was planning on finishing his Doritos.

"Yes."

"Right."

Fionna tapped at the keyboard.

First she went to the company's mail server to show the tech team how she got in. She fudged on that just a little, didn't give away all her tricks, but it offered her a chance to note any emails to Dr. Arlington's account. The latest was encrypted. She typed. Not encrypted anymore. "Oops." She acted like that'd been a mistake.

The message was from someone named Brennan Sacco concerning the president's speech.

Interesting. She flew past it. "Video surveillance? Last night? In Arlington's suite?"

A pause. "Why do you need that?"

"When I was in the system yesterday, I found evidence that someone else had been there, had compromised his computer from inside his office." Yes, it was a lie, and since telling lies was not something she would ever want her children to do, she felt a little bad about it. But in this case it seemed necessary, and sometimes grown-ups have to make grown-up decisions.

After a small hesitation, he showed her which directory to use to access the footage.

Fionna pulled up the cameras and the screen split into four sections, one for each of the security cameras in the lobby and in Arlington's executive suite. She cued them to thirty minutes before the video had started and pressed play, then fast-forward.

"The system is set up so that when people check in at the security station," the guy with the Doritos said proudly, "one camera is directed at their face. Then, after the guard types in their driver's license number or RixoTray security code clearance number, their name appears on the screen."

Xavier grunted. "Is that the best you can come up with for a multibillion-dollar international pharmaceutical company? A security code number? You never heard of facial recognition? Unbelievable."

My sentiments exactly, Fionna thought.

On the screen, a woman entered. Her name appeared: Dr. Riah Colette.

Fionna took note of it, then fast-forwarded the footage again.

Soon two men came in. Twins. No identification came up on the screen, but yet they were allowed to pass through both the main entrance and Arlington's office suite, just like Colette had done.

"There aren't any names for them," Xavier said. "That a glitch?"

"They've been here before," one of the techs answered. "They have clearance."

"Of course they do," Xavier replied somewhat rebukingly. "They're walking right through your checkpoint."

And then, as the footage rolled, one more person came through the door and one more name appeared on the screen.

Undersecretary of Defense Oriana Williamson.

While Fionna continued working on the keyboard and schooling the pharmaceutical firm's cybersecurity team, Xavier slipped into the hallway to call Jevin and Charlene to share the information about the Sacco email, the names of Dr. Colette and Undersecretary of Defense Williamson, and the fact that a pair of identical twins had entered Arlington's office just minutes before the video began.

• • •

So now there were gerbils everywhere.

I end the call with Xavier so he can get back to Fionna and the cybersecurity team.

Mentally, I review what I know about the research, the video, the Pentagon connection, the thwarted terrorist attack.

The twins, Undersecretary of Defense Williamson, Arlington, and Colette all saw the video.

A thought-borne virus.

What had Fionna said yesterday when she first mentioned the bombing attempt earlier this week? A reference to the president's speech . . .

Now this email from Brennan Sacco about the speech.

"Charlene, see if you can find out who Brennan Sacco is."

She thumb-types on her phone. Goes online. Surfing she doesn't mind—just talking on the phone.

I close my eyes, try to process everything.

Tanbyrn was worried about funding.

The president wants to end Project Alpha.

"He's the president's speechwriter," she explains.

All the facts merge, pass each other, then lock into place again.

We had the connection between Cyrus Arlington and Glenn Banner . . . brain imaging . . . Charlene's mention of the legislation that could affect the telomerase drug release date . . . the clinical trials—

I have no idea if the sniper was real or not or how the video related to any of this, but it obviously concerned killing those—

Affecting someone nonlocally. A top-secret research program on the negative effects of nonlocal psi activity . . .

Oh.

Eleven o'clock at the park.

"Charlene. The president's speech. That's it."

"What?"

"Track with me here. Tanbyrn told us 'when the eagle falls at the park'—something he overheard the twins say. The timing isn't a coincidence—remember what you told me Monday night? Banner and now the Kabul video. The legislation, the speech. Everything is converging."

When the eagle falls at the park—she's mouthing the words. "Independence Park?"

I tap at the phone to bring up the image I'm thinking of, the one she needs to see. "Yes." I spin the phone toward her, showing her the image of the Great Seal of the United States. "And the eagle is—"

"You're not thinking that the twins are going after the president!"

"That's what I'm thinking."

"No, that's crazy." But it doesn't sound like she's convinced of her words. "I mean . . ."

We had threads weaving everything together, but for the moment they were still tenuous, more

411

like strands of a spiderweb—the design was only visible when you moved back and looked at the whole thing at once.

Perspective.

But did we have all the strands yet? I backpedal a little. "No, it's not enough. Not with what we have."

"It doesn't matter if it's not enough to prove it, Jev, there's enough there to make it feasible. We need to warn the Secret Service."

But with each passing moment, I'm feeling less confident of my conclusion. "What would we tell them? That a pair of identical twin telepathic assassins might try to send a thought-borne virus to the president? We don't have proof, a time frame, an established motive, anything. We don't even know who the twins are." I sigh as I realize the truth. "Really, all we have is a collection of circumstantial evidence. If that."

But she doesn't budge. "Jev, if there's even a slim chance that his life might be in danger, we have to report it. We at least have to tell them what we know."

"They'll probably take us in for questioning."

"Yeah. Probably."

That's the last thing I want right now, but I do sense that she's right about contacting the authorities. However, I'm not exactly thrilled at the prospect of convincing them to take a threat like this seriously.

If you call the Secret Service, they'll be able to track the phone's GPS.

Staring out the window, I assess our situation. How to give the Secret Service everything they need without being brought in as accessories or suspects?

"Charlene, let me use your phone."

She hands it over. "Why my phone?"

"You'll see."

It takes me a few minutes to get through to someone who'll actually talk to me. I thought there'd be some sort of hotline to report threats against the president, but I have to go through almost as many prompts as you do when you call for computer tech support. Finally a real woman's voice comes on. Boredom and annoyance in her first two words: "Name, please."

Using an alias right now would probably not be a good idea.

But neither would giving her your real name.

"I have information about a possible threat against the president's life."

"What is your name?"

"I just said I have information about a threat against—"

"Name."

"You're not listening to—"

"Who am I talking with?" She's losing what little patience she might have had.

"Jevin, and this is important."

With an audible sigh, she decides not to push me for a last name: "What information?"

"It involves a pair of twins. Who, well . . . they might attack President Hoult at any time."

"Who are they?"

"I don't know. But they go by the initials 'L' and 'N.' "

" 'L' and 'N.' "

"That's right."

"And how are they going to attack the president?"

I'm aware that the answer to her question is going to sound ridiculous. I could spend time trying to explain the quantum physics of it all, but I didn't even understand most of that myself. I just go ahead and say it: "By their thoughts."

A stretch of silence.

"Sir, you do know that it is a federal offense to threaten the life of the president of the United States. Even to joke about it."

"No, I'm not threatening his life, and I'm not joking. I'm telling you that I think there's a plot against him. It has to do with a top-secret Pentagon program called Project Alpha. The twins work for the Pentagon. Sort of." With every word, I can tell I'm losing more and more ground.

"So this assassination plot was hatched at the Pentagon."

"Well, that or a pharmaceutical company."

"I see."

I rub my forehead.

"And how did you come about this information?"

It would take way too long to explain everything. "That doesn't matter, this is—"

"Sir, how exactly are these twins going to kill the president by their thoughts?"

"Maybe stop his heart. I'm not sure."

"With the use of their psychic powers?"

"You have to believe me—"

"Excuse me for just one moment." When she puts me on hold, I know it's over. This is never going to work. I imagine she's calling for a car to pick us up right now, or possibly checking to make sure she has a lock on our GPS.

I hang up.

"Well," Charlene acknowledges, "maybe that wasn't the best idea after all."

"Maybe you should have made the call."

"Are they going to follow up on anything you said?"

"I doubt it. We need to find the twins ourselves. Lead the Secret Service to them."

"Then we can't let them find us first."

We come to a bottleneck in traffic. "That's why I chose your phone. I thought I'd give you the honors." I hand her cell to her.

She catches on. "Are you saying . . . ?"

"Yup. Something we both know you've wanted to do for a long time."

With a gleam in her eye, she rolls down her window and pelts her cell phone onto the road. It shatters in a lovely little explosion of technology.

"That felt really good."

"I'll bet it did."

Of course, it was certainly possible that NSA or the Secret Service had already tracked our location, even traced the phone number back to Charlene. In fact, they might've already dispatched agents to find us, but I was counting on the fact that in the congested traffic they wouldn't be able to figure out which car the phone had been thrown from and, as we drove on, wouldn't be able to find us.

Yet.

The plan: find Dr. Colette.

Then the twins.

And then let the Secret Service find us.

The First Baby

Riah found no photos of the axe murder victims.

Which was a bit disappointing.

But the search for the pictures of the dead family made her think of her own family once again. Her dead mother. Her father. Her sister. And the question of what people really want: feeling loved or being loved.

She loved you when you were a child.

Yes. She did.

But you never loved her.

Riah drew out her phone, tapped in a number that she hadn't called in six months but had committed to memory long before that.

A woman answered. "Hello?"

"Katie Burleson?"

Immediate suspicion. "Who is this?"

"This is Riah."

Silence.

"Your sister."

"How many Riahs do you think I know?" Katie's words scorched the air.

"It's been a long time since we spoke and—"

"If I wanted to talk to you, I would have called you. It's not like you're hard to find. I'm hanging up now and I don't want you to call this number again."

"Katie—"

"Goodbye—"

"He did things to me."

Riah waited for the line to go dead but it didn't.

"Our father," she went on, "he did things to me. Things a father should never do to his children."

"Of course he did."

A pause. "You knew?"

"Is that why you called? To try and make me feel sorry for you? What do you think happened when you went off to college? Do you think he just got interested in Mom again? Really? Are you kidding me?"

Riah found her sister's words informative and sensed that she should feel a deep sense of rage against their father for violating Katie too.

In the background, Riah could hear Katie's youngest child crying, and a thought struck her: Katie had her first pregnancy, her first abortion, shortly after moving out of the house. She'd always said her boyfriend Jose was the father.

"It wasn't Jose's baby," Riah said softly.

"Don't call this number again." And then, without saying goodbye, Katie hung up.

This bitter woman, this hurting woman, had known innocence, known love as a child, but both had died over the years because of their father.

Or perhaps because Riah had never done anything to stop him.

She was left wondering what to do.

She could never help her sister feel loved, it wasn't in her nature, but could she do something else, not out of love exactly, but in the service of justice? An act on her sister's behalf?

Yes.

A very specific act.

Yes.

To right a tragic wrong.

The greater good.

Riah made a firm and certain decision to pay a visit to their father as soon as her duties with the twins were completed.

Credentials

9:48 a.m.
1 hour 7 minutes left

RixoTray's R&D facility lies on the outskirts of Bridgeport, surrounded by a dense wooded area that I suspect also belongs to the firm to create a buffer between their facility and any corporate or residential encroachment.

Our driver slows, gets in line behind the four cars in front of us. They all pass through the checkpoint without a hitch, and only moments later we pull to a stop beside the guard station.

The driver and I roll down our windows. The guard looks at me with a practiced air of suspicion but ignores our driver as if he doesn't even exist. Apparently, Charlene and I are the ones he's most interested in.

"Driver's licenses, please."

We produce them, as does our driver. We all hand them over. Charlene and I also give him our fake FDA credentials. "J. Franklin Banks," I tell him, avoiding drawing attention to my real name, my stage name, the one I used on TV. "Food and Drug Administration." I briefly hold up my clipboard and its attached documents to show him that I mean business.

He gazes at the driver's licenses, then studies the creds carefully. Fionna had told us they would check our fingerprints, but that didn't concern me much, since, unless you've been printed by law enforcement or as part of a corporate security program, your prints won't show up on any kind of watch list.

As expected, the guard holds out a small electronic pad about the size of a smartphone. "Fingerprints, please."

All three of us, in turn, place our forefingers on the pad and no red flags come up. He goes on, "What is the purpose of your visit?"

"We're here because of complaints involving a research project," I tell him. "We need to speak directly to Dr. Riah Colette."

He hands the creds to his partner to study as well. Then looks over a clipboard of his own.

"I don't see your name on our appointment list."

"No, of course not."

He looks at me questioningly.

Charlene scootches toward me, leans toward the window, addresses him. "The FDA no longer announces spot inspections or visits of this nature before they occur. In the past, people have shredded documents and destroyed evidence when they've received prior knowledge of our visits. Arriving unannounced is the only way to assure that none of that happens."

Before he can reply, she goes on, "This complaint

involves ethical violations involving the use of human test subjects in experimental drug trials. It is a highly sensitive matter and these are serious allegations. I'm afraid that's all we're authorized to tell you."

Oh, she was good.

I've saved the clipboards and their paperwork as the pièce de résistance. Now I hand them to him.

The line of cars behind us is growing longer.

The guard flips through the official-looking documents that Fionna and Charlene drew up based on the information Fionna's children had gathered on actual FDA complaint report forms.

I can tell he isn't reading any of the fine print.

They never read the fine print.

Except Xavier on iTunes updates.

At last the guard looks at his partner, who shrugs and passes the IDs back to him. He returns the clipboard, driver's licenses, and FDA credentials to us and waves us through.

Charlene whispers to me, "One down, two to go."

Air Force One touched down at the Philadelphia International Airport.

Originally, before delivering his eleven o'clock speech, the president had been scheduled to visit a charter high school to encourage the students to be good citizens and strive toward academic excellence, but he'd changed his plans earlier in

421

the morning to give himself more time to review what he was going to say.

The Secret Service, of course, mentioned nothing about the reported psychic assassination plot as they escorted him from the plane.

Not only was this latest threat ludicrous, but the Secret Service has a policy: never notify the president of any threats against his life unless there is immediate and imminent danger. Considering the fact that he receives more than twelve thousand death threats a year, keeping him up to speed would mean updating him hourly about all the people who wanted to kill him.

And the Secret Service never cancels presidential events just because of uncorroborated death threats.

The speech at the Liberty Bell would go on.

Still, as absurd as this threat was, they had to follow up on it, just as they have to follow up on every threat to his life—all twelve thousand. Two agents had been sent to bring in the person who'd called it in, and whose GPS location had been pinpointed and verified by NSA.

In the lobby of the research facility, Charlene and I again produce our credentials and paperwork.

We place our things on the conveyor belt, step through the full-body scanner, and the security guard working the X-ray machine tells us we'll need to leave our cell phones with him. "I'm sorry. There are no pictures allowed, no recording devices of any kind inside the building." He sounds tired. Looks tired. I wonder how long he's been working already today. Or last night.

I hadn't thought through this part of the plan. I'm not sure if government inspectors would need to keep their phones with them. While I'm debating what to say, Charlene speaks up. "Only one of us carries a phone and it's illegal for us to leave it behind. Look at page fourteen of the complaint form."

"I'm sorry, it's our policy to—"

"I'll give you a phone number. Call it and explain your policy to the federal agents who will—"

He cuts her off by holding up a hand in surrender.

Yeah, she really was good.

He exhaustedly motions for us to move along. At the final checkpoint we're handed visitors' passes, and one of the sentries, a mountain of a man who must weigh at least three hundred pounds, tells us he will escort us to Dr. Colette's office.

I jot something on the clipboard. A shopping list, actually, but taking notes is a way to mess with him, to show that Charlene and I will be the ones calling the shots and not him. "Yes. Please"—I gesture toward the hallway, indicating for him to lead us—"take us to Dr. Colette."

Brandy

9:57 a.m.
58 minutes left

"Thank you for seeing me, Mr. Vice President."

"Of course."

Cyrus had been at the White House to meet with other high-level administration employees a dozen times, the vice president half a dozen. He wasn't a lobbyist, but he'd been consulted about the ongoing health care legislation debate and the issue of counterfeit pharmaceuticals—a growing problem, especially the ones being smuggled in from southeast Asia.

And of course, anyone who'd donated as much to a presidential campaign as Cyrus had personally done, and as RixoTray had corporately done, was welcome at the White House. It was the way the system was set up, the way institutes of power have always operated. Money speaks. And the more of it there is, the more loudly it's heard.

"Have a seat, Cyrus," the vice president invited. "Would you like a drink?"

Of course, it was too early to begin drinking socially, but the vice president was not a coffee kind of guy. Not many people knew how early he typically got started on his brandy each day, but he had not kept it from Cyrus.

"Cognac. Thank you."

"Good choice."

Over the last couple years, they'd occasionally discussed the fact that the vice president hadn't gotten his party's nomination last time around, but it wasn't a topic he liked to address, so Cyrus typically refrained from bringing it up. But with the election next year, and considering the nature of his visit here today, he decided to address it, at least tangentially.

As the vice president produced an elegant bottle of cognac from his desk and poured each of them a drink, Cyrus said, "So, Hoult is already in election mode?"

Vice President Pinder brought Cyrus his drink. "You know how these things go," he said evasively. "Now, before we get down to business, how is Helen?"

"She's good. Luci Ann?"

"As beautiful, supportive, and as much of a shopaholic as ever."

Cyrus raised his glass. "To our wives."

"To our wives."

They clinked glasses. Drank.

The cognac was extraordinary, and Cyrus complimented the vice president on it.

"Camus Cognac Cuvee 3.128, rated by many connoisseurs as the best cognac in the world. We have only so many heartbeats, my friend. It'd bc a shame to waste any of them on cheap brandy."

They both drank for a moment. Cyrus knew they didn't have a lot of time to talk, especially since this meeting had gotten started late, but he also knew that etiquette required that he not jump immediately into discussing business.

"So"—Pinder was the one to break the silence —"how is the telomerase research going? Have you come up with a cure for aging yet? A way to offer me a few more of those heartbeats?"

"Working on it. We've started clinical trials. Another year or so and we're hoping to have FDA approval."

"Well, I'd ask to be one of your human guinea pigs, but I think I'll wait until you get the kinks out."

"Probably a good idea."

A small smile. "Hopefully, I'll still be around to benefit from it."

"Hopefully, we both will."

They sipped their drinks, then the vice president moved things forward: "I'm guessing you're here about the speech."

Cyrus set down his glass. "You know the president's new initiatives will not serve the American people: the proposals regarding the expedited release of generic pharmaceuticals."

The vice president scratched at the back of his neck, then stood. "Let me play devil's advocate here for a moment, Cyrus. Pharmaceutical companies are some of the most profitable companies in the world. Every year they post billions of dollars of profits while millions of working-class Americans struggle under the exorbitant price of prescription drugs. Making generics more readily available could save thousands of lives each year."

Prolong, not save.

Rule #1: Everyone dies.

Rule #2: There's nothing you can do to change Rule #1.

Cyrus had heard all this before. "Actually, pharmaceutical firms aren't as profitable as most people think. Oil companies, tech firms, insurance companies, banks all have higher profit margins. Big business has always been an easy target for liberals to take potshots at. You know that."

The vice president rolled his shot glass back and forth in his fingers reflectively.

Cyrus continued, "Also, the Food and Drug Administration has made it harder than ever to get new, life-saving drugs onto the market. Out of a thousand compounds studied in prediscovery and then put through a decade of preclinical and clinical trials, only one will ever become an FDA-approved drug. The R&D costs are—"

"Yes, yes, I know. Astronomical."

"The FDA allows generics to be up to twenty times less effective in crossing the blood-brain barrier than trade-name pharmaceuticals. So when you're talking about anticonvulsants, mood stabilizers, and antidepressants, the public ends up suffering the consequences. Not to mention that 10 percent of generics are inert."

Vice President Pinder sighed. "Cyrus, I am on your side on all this, always have been. But the president isn't going to change his mind. At this point there's really nothing I can do."

"But if you could?"

"If I could?"

"If you could make it easier for us to get our pharmaceutical products to the public without the added restrictions the president wants to put on the industry, would you? If you could keep producers of generic pharmaceuticals from taking advantage of our research and then undercutting us on the price, would you do it?"

"I've always done all I can to support scientific innovation and the advancement of pharmaceuticals for the betterment of the American people."

"Yes."

"So are you asking that I speak with the president about this? Because I assure you that he's not going to back down. He is quite firm on what he intends to do."

Cyrus knew the president wouldn't back down. That wasn't what he'd come here to talk about. "We could really use someone at the top who sees things more clearly than Hoult does. Who realizes that without our R&D, the life-saving drugs would never exist in the first place, that we need time to recoup our investment before we're undercut by generics."

"Once again we are on the same page."

The vice president laid his hand on the desk and gently massaged the elegant wood as if it were the skin of his lover, who Cyrus knew was not Luci Ann, his beautiful, supportive, shopaholic wife.

Varied love interests.

Something else the two of them had in common.

"If I were able to effect change," the vice president said, "if I were ever to become president, I would never unfairly target pharmaceutical firms or the important work they do in improving the life and health of the American people."

So.

Yes.

Cyrus had what he'd come here for. The reassurance that the VP would promote legislation that was in line with RixoTray's goals.

"If you were ever to become president."

Vice President Pinder looked at him knowingly, said in his eyes much more than he said with his words: "If that were ever to happen. Yes."

Cyrus rose, warmly thanked the vice president for his time and his cognac.

"Have a safe flight back to Philadelphia," Vice President Pinder said as they were walking toward the door. "I hope we'll be able to speak again soon."

"I'm confident that we will."

Riah got the call from Daniel sooner than she thought she would. He asked her to meet him and his brother at 10:45 just off the I-76 Belmont Avenue/Green Lane exit. "Darren will call you with the exact location as soon as possible. Bring everything you'll need."

"I will."

And then she began to gather her things.

Departure

10:04 a.m.
51 minutes left

Our hulking escort leads us to Dr. Riah Colette's office and announces that we're from the FDA and would like to speak to her. She appraises us, notices the official-looking documents attached to our clipboards, invites us into her office, and closes the door.

Gotta love those clipboards.

Her purse is on the desk. Her car keys and folded-up laptop beside it. Either she's just arriving or she's on her way out. But if she was following the schedule Fionna had pulled up earlier, I knew that Dr. Colette was not just coming in to work.

"My name is Jevin Banks." Time for the truth all the way around. "This is Charlene Antioch."

"Dr. Riah Colette." She's an attractive woman, dressed respectively but not pretentiously. She doesn't look the least bit intimidated to see us or to have heard from the guard that we're inspectors from the FDA. I have the sense that most people in her position would, at least to some degree, be nervous or defensive. Not her. She doesn't ask why we're here or how she might help us.

How to do this.

Don't jump into talking about an assassination conspiracy. Find out what you can first. Find out if she's involved.

"We have a few questions," I tell her, "and we think you're the right person to answer them."

"I'm afraid I'm in a bit of a hurry. I have an appointment I need to be preparing for. Perhaps you could talk with one of my assistants?"

Charlene speaks up. "It really needs to be you, I'm afraid."

"What is it concerning? Exactly?"

I take a breath. "The twins."

She gazes at Charlene, then at me.

"You're not from the FDA." It's a statement, not a question.

"No, we're not. Yesterday at the Lawson Research Center in Oregon, we were investigating

431

Dr. Tanbyrn's research for a television documentary. A man named Glenn Banner started the building on fire. We barely escaped. Dr. Tanbyrn got out with us, but died this morning from complications caused by smoke inhalation."

She takes a seat on the edge of her desk.

"I had not heard that."

I don't detect any sense of loss in her words, but there's no coldness either. It's as if the news is informative to her, that she's acknowledging how tragic it is but isn't in the place right now where she's ready to mourn for the dead doctor.

Charlene lowers her voice. "A woman was also killed in the fire. One of Tanbyrn's research assistants."

Dr. Colette is quiet. "I'm not exactly sure how I can help you."

From doing cold readings while emulating the tricks of professed psychics, I'd gotten good at reading people and I catch no sign that Dr. Colette isn't being straight with us.

She isn't involved. Trust her.

I go with my gut. "The man who started the fire, Glenn Banner, had been in touch with Dr. Arlington."

"And how do you know this?"

"Banner's cell phone. We know you're in charge of the division that has a connection to Dr. Tanbyrn's research. The Pentagon is involved as well."

She studies me carefully. "You're doing a documentary?"

"Right now we're just concerned with stopping more people from being killed."

A moment passes. "Is there anything else?"

Get to the assassination plot.

The twins.

"There's a connection to the video that you, Dr. Arlington, Undersecretary of Defense Oriana Williamson, and the twins watched last night."

"Well." She seems more impressed than taken aback. "You have done your homework."

Charlene steps forward. "Dr. Tanbyrn told us he was studying the negative aspects of the twins' special abilities. His research points to using avenues of quantum entanglement to affect another person's physiology in a negative manner."

Dr. Colette doesn't seem surprised by that. "Nonlocally."

Man, she's not hiding anything.

I nod. "Yes."

"Anything else?"

The plot. Tell her what you suspect.

"The suicide bomber didn't kill himself. He was shot by a sniper." I take a stab at this, go for it: "We think the president of the United States might be the next target."

"The president?"

"That's right."

"And why do you think that?"

I tell her about our line of reasoning about the telomerase research, Tanbyrn's murder, the press release, the proposed legislation, the phrase the twins used about the eagle falling at the park, the Brennan Sacco email. The more I explained it, the more everything seems to fit together in a pattern of gossamer threads.

When I finish, rather than sticking to the topic of the potential assassination plot, surprisingly, Dr. Colette focuses instead on the footage in Kabul. "How do you know it was a sniper?"

I pull out my laptop. "I'll show you."

Dr. Cyrus Arlington was in the helicopter on his way to Philadelphia when he got the text from Caitlyn telling him that the police were waiting for him at the landing pad. "It has something to do with a man named Glenn Banner."

Not a surprise.

He texted her back a word of thanks.

Then rehearsed what he would tell the officers about his relationship with the dead arsonist.

Riah carefully evaluated what the two people who'd been imitating FDA inspectors told her. They had all their facts straight, that much was true, but how could the enemy of the state mentioned by the twins be the president of the United States?

It wasn't possible to tell for certain whether or

not a sniper had been involved in detonating the suicide bomber's vest in Kabul, but after reviewing the footage she had to admit that it was certainly possible.

The sniper might explain why the twins were so adamant that you help them.

But sniper or not, they had affected Adrian Goss's neural processing abilities on their own, so the president could still be in danger. After all, what if they were able to do the same thing to one of the Secret Service agents guarding the president?

But some things just didn't compute. Did the twins know that they'd been unsuccessful in Kabul? If there was a sniper, who hired him? The twins? Oriana? Cyrus?

What if they all did? What if they've just been playing you ever since the beginning?

Less than forty-five minutes ago, she'd agreed to help the twins eliminate a national security threat, but there was a lot more going on here than met the eye, a lot of currents flowing beneath the surface, and she wasn't sure she was in the right position at the moment to trace where they all came from or in which direction they were flowing.

The man who'd introduced himself as Jevin Banks was watching her closely, waiting for her response.

Honestly, she had no reason to doubt anything

he or Ms. Antioch had said, especially considering the risk they'd taken getting this information to her, the effort of creating fake IDs and documentation, of working their way past three security check—

"Who are the twins, Dr. Colette?" I ask her.

She hesitates only slightly before answering. "Darren and Daniel are military-trained assassins."

Oh.

Well, that made sense.

Darren, ending with an N; Daniel, ending with an L. Is that it? The reason for the initials?

I couldn't be sure, and right now it didn't matter.

But why would they target the commander-in-chief? Why, if they worked for the military? What possible motive could they have?

I realize that at the moment that doesn't matter either. Their plan, whatever it consisted of, did.

"We need to stop them," I tell her. "Do you know where they are?"

"No. But I'm supposed to meet them at 10:45. They told me we needed to move on it this morning."

"Before the president's speech," Charlene notes.

"It would seem so. It won't take long to send the electrical impulses to the electrodes once I get there. I'm not sure how long it would take for them to focus their thoughts, but I'm guessing not too long. Are you certain that it's the president they're trying to kill?"

"No," I admit, "but—"

Her desk phone rings, startling all of us.

"Excuse me." She picks up the receiver, listens to someone on the other end, acknowledges that she understands, then hangs up.

"There are two Secret Service agents at the front gate. They're asking about you."

Oh, not good.

Somehow they'd tracked us after all.

And now they were here, and undoubtedly, they were going to bring us in for questioning.

For a moment Dr. Colette stares out her office window at the trees surrounding the property, then picks up the phone again, taps in a number, and speaks into the mouthpiece. "Yes. Those two agents? Send them in."

She hangs up.

So.

That's how it's going to go.

"If the Secret Service goes after the twins," she explains, "there are going to be a lot of dead Secret Service agents out there. Daniel and Darren are that good. But they'll listen to me, and they're going to wait for me. I think I can stop them, stall them at least. And you know more about this than I do. I want you to come along." She snatches up her purse and a small daypack. "We'll take my car. By the time those agents get here to my office, we'll be off the property. Let's go stop the twins."

Oh yeah.

That's what I'm talking about.

"I could really grow to like this woman," Charlene whispers to me as we hurry out the door behind her.

"Me too."

The Embalming Room

10:27 a.m.
28 minutes left

Darren snapped the man's neck as his brother took care of the woman just a few feet away.

Both of the targets died quickly and with very little struggle.

Darren let go and the man's body thudded to the carpet. Daniel was more considerate, lowering the woman's corpse gently to the floor.

Both the male funeral home director and his female embalmer lay staring unblinkingly at the ceiling.

They had, appropriately enough, died in the building where they'd prepared and then displayed so many other bodies. Dying in this place dedicated to the dead.

Darren closed the shades of the funeral home's west-facing window.

The Schuylkill River flowed swiftly past the edge of the property, providing a panoramic view of the late autumn trees lining the other bank. A prayer garden and flower bed lay in the funeral home's yard, but the lawn stretched fifty feet beyond them to the six-foot drop-off to the river.

The Faulkner-Kernel Funeral Home was located on River Road, less than twenty minutes from central Philly. The tranquil setting provided "a picturesque, restful setting that no other funeral homes in the city can offer," according to the brochure the twins had picked up earlier while they were scouting out sites they might use.

A picturesque, restful setting for families to come and view the embalmed corpses of their loved ones.

A place far enough from the city center to allow for on-site cremation.

The brothers had wanted that option available to them for disposing of Dr. Colette's corpse.

Out front, the hearse sat in the curving driveway leading to the front doors. Parking was limited, so Darren imagined that during an actual funeral, the people attending would have to park on the side of the narrow road winding along the riverbank. He'd parked their sedan behind the hearse.

He and his brother had needed a place where they would be isolated and would have equipment that Dr. Colette could use for any medical procedures she might have to do if things didn't go as planned. So, a place that would have at least a rudimentary operating room.

The embalming room would work.

After all, that wasn't the kind of place someone would be tempted to suddenly walk into, even if for some reason a visitor were to show up at the home. The room offered them everything they needed. Seclusion. Isolation. A private setting where they would be able to relax and focus their thoughts enough to kill the leader of the free world.

For a moment Darren studied the two bodies on the carpet. Then, for the time being at least, he and his brother laid them to rest in two of the caskets in the funeral home's small but well-stocked showroom.

A pair of unfortunate but necessary civilian casualties.

He checked his watch.

10:29.

Twenty-six minutes before they were scheduled to begin with Riah.

"She'll be at the exit at 10:45," he told his brother. "I'll call her a few minutes beforehand with the address. That should give us just enough time."

Last-Minute Revisions

10:33 a.m.
22 minutes left

"Read me what we have."

"Mr. President, I would rather—"

"I want to hear it while there's still time to change it."

Brennan Sacco had only been brought in as one of the president's speechwriters six months ago, but he'd discovered right away that it was always this way with President Jeremiah Hoult—last-minute changes. Some of which never even made it to the teleprompter.

Now the presidential limousine caravan turned onto Market Street and passed Declaration House. Five limos so that no one would know which one actually carried the president. Today Brennan was in the fourth, along with the president and two Secret Service agents.

Yes, it was unusual for a speechwriter to work this closely with the president, but Hoult had always insisted that the most important part of his job was sharing his vision for the future with the American people, and the way to do that was through communication.

Obviously, he didn't know that Brennan was

being bribed by Dr. Cyrus Arlington to share his own communication with him, leaking the contents of the speeches concerning health care issues.

President Hoult had a copy of this morning's speech on his lap, but rather than read along, he studied his reflection in his ornate handheld mirror. Tweaked his hair a bit. "Go on. Read it to me."

"Yes, sir," Brennan said reluctantly. "We'll pick it up in the middle. 'The American people are tired of the status quo, tired of politics as usual, tired of Washington insiders and Wall Street millionaires controlling their lives and finances when they're barely able to make ends meet. And they're tired of oil conglomerates and giant pharmaceutical firms making record profits while they can barely make their monthly mortgage payments.' "

"That's nice. I like the contrast between profits and payments. Nice alliteration there, and also with 'make, monthly, and mortgage.' "

"Thank you, sir."

President Hoult noticed a few hairs out of place, took a small spot of hair putty, rubbed it between his fingers to warm it, and worked it into his hair. "Plays off class envy too. That works well with my constituents."

"Yes, sir, Mr. President."

"Go on."

Brennan cleared his throat. " 'They want change,

and one of the ways we're going to give that to them is through health care reform. Today I'm pledging to sign an executive order to cut the waiting period in half between the time when drugs are released to the public and when the generic equivalents of those drugs can be made available. That's the kind of change Americans want. That's the kind of change they deserve.'"

Normally it would be Congress's job to pass new legislation, but a president can bypass all sorts of laws by issuing an executive order, as both Bush and Obama had made eminently clear.

The limos entered the cordoned-off underground parking garage below the Independence National Historical Park's visitor center.

No other cars had been allowed inside it today.

With the Secret Service's presence, for the time being at least, this was the most secure parking garage on the planet.

"Go on. What's next?"

"This is the part I'm still not quite happy with. It has a little too much spin, seems to make those who disagree with you sound heartless and cruel."

"Let's hear it."

"Yes, sir. 'This isn't just a matter of politics, it's a matter of deep humanitarian concern to all Americans. It's a matter of the basic human right of every individual to have affordable health care. It's unconscionable for millionaires and billionaires to keep lining their pockets while letting millions of hardworking middle-class Americans suffer or even die when the drugs that could save them are already available but are prohibitively expensive. This profiteering at the expense of the welfare of fellow Americans in need cannot go on any longer.' "

"Perfect." President Hoult folded his hands in his lap, looked reflectively out the window at the concrete walls passing by. "Yes. Very nice. Now, the rest. The part about cutting frivolous military spending on dead-end programs to reinvest in our country's treasured public school system: construction paper for kindergartners instead of ESP programs that'll never produce results—but don't put it quite like that."

"Of course not, sir."

Their driver parked the limo.

"Come on. I want you to help me make sure we have that last section nailed down."

"Yes, sir, Mr. President."

Then Brennan Sacco, the president, and his entourage went to the preparation room in the Independence Visitor Center to finalize the speech.

A Distraction

10:38 a.m.
17 minutes left

Lonnie deciphered Dr. Tanbyrn's equations.

Fionna and Xavier were back at the Franklin Grand Hotel in Xavier's room, reviewing the footage of the suicide bombers, when he knocked on the door. Fionna had been able to enhance the image enough for Xavier to verify that it really was a rifle's scope in the window across the street. They were about to contact Jevin when Lonnie appeared.

"What did you find?" Fionna asked him.

Lonnie explained that the notations had to do with differences in quantum entanglement related to the amount of alpha wave activity in the brain during various mental states. "Apparently, a relaxed state of mind is necessary for both the sender and receiver during mind-to-mind communication."

"Both?" Xavier said. "Both the sender and the receiver?"

"Yes. Mom, I was wondering, these algorithms, are they for real or was it just an assignment?"

Both.

"It was an assignment."

The truth, but not quite the whole truth.

445

Grown-ups making grown-up decisions.

"Nice work, Lonnie. It's possible that Mr. Wray and I will have to step out for a bit, so I may need you to watch your siblings again."

"We'll be fine. The girls are reading, Donnie's playing video games."

As soon as he'd exited the room, Fionna speed-dialed Jevin, put the call on speakerphone, but before she could tell her friend anything about what they'd found, Jevin detailed his and Charlene's deductions regarding the possible attempt on President Hoult's life. "Dr. Colette told us that the twins are military assassins."

"Of course." Xavier nodded soberly. "I knew black ops would fit in here somewhere. It all makes perfect sense."

Fionna relayed to Jevin what Lonnie had found regarding the necessity of both the sender and receiver being relaxed at the time of the connection.

"I don't know for certain the kind of time frame we're looking at here," Jevin said. "The reference to the eagle at the park, the eleven o'clock time mentioned by Tanbyrn—"

Xavier cut in, "Means it's going down this morning."

"Yes. I think we need to assume that. Dr. Colette thinks the twins will wait for her, but they'll want to move on it as soon as we get there. We're on our way to find them now."

"What can we do to help?" Xavier asked. "Do you want us to meet you there?"

"No. If Lonnie is right and the relaxed state of mind is vital for both the sender and the receiver, we need to make sure the president isn't going to be able to relax until the twins are stopped."

"You're thinking a distraction."

"Yeah. A big one."

He looked at his duffle bag and Fionna saw his eyes light up. "I have just the thing."

They ended the call.

Fionna asked him, "You're not thinking of blowing something up, are you?"

"Oh, something even better than that."

"Hmm . . . would it be safe for the kids to see?"

"Oh yeah. This'll be a great educational experience. In fact, I think I'm gonna need their help."

Dr. Cyrus Arlington met Detective Rothstein and Sergeant Adams as he departed the helicopter at the landing pad on top of RixoTray's corporate headquarters.

He told the two Philadelphia Police Department officers the story about Banner blackmailing him, and he was surprised at how readily they seemed to believe him. They informed him they would be contacting him later to follow up on a few things, then left him alone. Just like that.

Problem solved.

Or at least postponed.

It was time to contact the twins. Make sure everything was in place.

And then let Akinsanya know things were a go.

10:43
12 minutes left

Just as we reach exit 338, Dr. Colette gets the call from Darren with the address—the Faulkner-Kernel Funeral Home on River Road, beside the Schuylkill River.

A funeral home? Why a funeral home?

"It's not far," Riah tells us. "Should be less than ten minutes."

Charlene suggests we try the Secret Service again, but Riah is against the idea. "Believe me, if law enforcement shows up, the twins will think nothing of slaughtering everyone there. These two are specialists, but they won't move on the president without me."

But in the end I decide there's too much at stake.

I call the Secret Service and tell them the address on River Road, however, just like before, it doesn't sound like they're taking me seriously. They insist that I not hang up, but I do. They know as much as we do now and it's up to them to take action.

I keep the cell on.

Let them track my GPS. We'll take them right to the twins.

For the president's visit, the Secret Service had stationed agents throughout the greater Philadelphia area and had two on the north side of the city near the Schuylkill River.

Policy dictated that they follow up on every threat, no matter how preposterous, so the district command center immediately dispatched agents to the funeral home.

President Hoult straightened his suit coat, checked his tie, then looked over the final notes and revisions he'd made to the speech.

His press secretary leaned into the room. "They're almost ready for you outside, Mr. President."

"Fine."

"Is there anything you need?"

"No. How does my hair look?"

"It looks perfect, sir."

Then she left and President Hoult took a moment to calm himself, as was his custom, before addressing the nation.

Collateral Damage

Special Agents Wendy McAuley and Tyron Harris approached the funeral home's front door.

It was a routine check, one of dozens they'd been assigned to do in the last two weeks. Yes, you try to take every call seriously, but after a while it's hard. Especially when 99.99 percent of them turn out to be crank calls.

Just like a paramedic who's no longer affected by seeing severe trauma, or a homicide detective who gets numb after viewing corpses day after day, Secret Service agents eventually get so used to investigating death threats against the president that it becomes run-of-the-mill.

Agent McAuley gave the door a knock. "Unbelievable," she muttered. "Psychic assassins."

"What are you going to do?" Agent Harris yawned. "So, remember the last time we were in Philly?"

"Cheesesteaks."

"Get this call over with, go grab some lunch?"

"Geno's or Pat's?" McAuley asked him.

"You know I'm a Pat's fan."

"No, it's gotta be Geno's all the way—with the onions well-done. They're so much—"

A nondescript man in his late twenties opened the door and greeted them cordially. "Yes?" He wore a name badge that told them he was the funeral director. "May I help you?"

They showed him their Secret Service creds. "We have a few questions for you," Harris said. "May we come inside?"

"Of course." The man stepped back, ushered them in. And swung the door shut behind them.

Three Cars

Dr. Colette draws her car to a stop along the side of the road leading past the Faulkner-Kernel Funeral Home.

A hearse, a sedan, and an SUV with shaded windows and government tags are in the cramped parking area. Charlene gestures toward the SUV. "What do you know, the Secret Service beat us here."

Riah identifies the sedan as that of the twins.

The morning is quiet, just the sound of the river flowing by and a few geese honking as they settle onto a small boat landing just north of us. The sunlight is warm, but the wind funneling down the river valley feels crisp and wintry.

There's no sign of the twins or the agents.

"So?" Charlene asks. "Plan of attack?"

Riah retrieves the bag of medical instruments she'd brought with her from the research facility. I'm not certain why she brought them along, unless it was somehow to convince the twins she was going to help them after all, to buy time. She turns toward the front door. "I need to talk with them."

But something's not right. It's too quiet. "Hang on."

"What?"

"If the agents have the twins in custody, why haven't they brought them back to their car?"

She stops.

The twins got to them already.

"Wait here," I tell the women. "I'll go."

"They'll be expecting me," Dr. Colette reiterates. "Even if they've done something to the agents, they won't harm you if you're with me."

"She has a good point," Charlene agrees.

A quick internal debate. "Alright. But I go first."

I lead the way to the door. When I knock, no one responds. I try the doorknob and find it locked.

"If the twins are expecting you, Riah," I'm thinking aloud, "why don't they open the door, and if the agents are safe, they'd answer the door too, wouldn't they? To see if we might be coconspirators?"

"I'm not sure."

I stare at the keyed lock. It looks manageable. I don't have my lock-pick set with me or the belt buckle prong of the belt Banner severed yesterday, but I can use something else.

"Charlene, can I borrow one of your earrings." She hands it to me and I kneel to work at the lock. "This'll only take a second."

The Empty Holster

"Dr. Arlington."

Cyrus immediately recognized the voice. Akinsanya. His heart almost stopped.

He turned and saw a dark-haired, stocky man close the office door behind him.

"How did you get in here?"

"Your receptionist was kind enough to grant me entrance. I convinced her that I was an old friend. Cyrus, you've been compromised."

"No, I—"

"Those who've been compromised"—Akinsanya approached him—"have become liabilities. And you know what I do with those who've become liabilities."

"No." Cyrus was backing toward the window. "You have to listen to me, there's nothing to—"

But then Akinsanya was on him, a choke hold to knock him out so the young redheaded receptionist in the next room wouldn't hear what was going on.

Then Akinsanya began to do to him what he did best, working quickly and proficiently with the needle and thick thread he had brought along. Today he tried something unique, something he'd never done to anyone else before, but he was a creative man and always ready to expand his horizons. Especially when it came to utilizing the items that his immediate environment provided him.

In this case, the contents of two aquariums.

A crowd of more than a thousand people had gathered in Independence Park. At first they were focused on the stage and the much-anticipated arrival of the president, but then a woman and her four children pointed to the top of the Franklin Grand Hotel. "There's a man!" they cried. "He's gonna jump!"

The attention of the crowd immediately shifted to the man standing on the edge of the hotel's roof.

I ease the door open. I think about calling out for the agents or the twins but then think better of it.

The lights in the foyer are off, but a shaft of light escapes from the cracked-open chapel doors on our left and from a hallway twenty feet beyond them. Before us, elegant cushioned chairs sit next to a guest book on a lectern. Thick carpet. Heavy shades keep out the sunlight. A quiet, reverent mood.

No movement.

No sounds.

I hand Charlene her earring, and she edges closer to me as she puts it back in. "Jevin, I don't think—"

I hold up my hand: "Wait." I hear footsteps, then a voice somewhere in the hallway or just beyond. It's indistinct and I can't make out the words.

Riah hears it too. "It's the twins." Her voice is low. "I can't tell which one."

So, not the Secret Service agents, and even though I can't discern the muffled words from the other room, there doesn't seem to be any fear in them, no urgency, no intimidation.

I don't take that as a good sign.

They're assassins. This is stupid. Get out of—

"I don't like this, Jevin," Charlene whispers.

Riah hasn't moved. "I should go ahead. Talk to them."

"Just a sec." If the twins had done something to the Secret Service agents, I doubted they were going to take kindly to Riah's arrival. They would surmise that someone had leaked their location, and I doubted they would have shared it with too many other people besides her.

I don't like the idea of putting either of the women in danger, but I don't like the idea of backing away either, not when we're this close. Even without Riah's help, the twins still pose a threat to the president.

Glancing around, I look for a weapon. A hall tree for hats and jackets and a small coat area with empty hangers sit to my right. A decorative bin holding half a dozen umbrellas rests beside it.

No, not an umbrella. That won't do anything.

Not if a couple Secret Service agents had been overpowered by these assassins.

All in. Remember? No turning back, no backing down. Just like your escapes. It's what you were made to do.

I indicate for the women to stay where they are. "I'll be right back." I sense that they're about to protest but move forward before they can.

Edging closer to the chapel, I press the door open a little more.

Two rows of wooden pews, ten in each row. A closed coffin sits in the gentle light at the front of the room. Paintings of serene meadows on the walls. Other than that the room is empty.

I take a few more steps to get a better view of what lies down the hallway—

That's when I see the legs of someone on the floor in a room partway down the hall. Trousers. Men's loafers. The person isn't moving.

From where Charlene and Riah are waiting by the front door, I can't imagine they can see the body and I don't want them to.

He might still be alive.

Quietly returning to Riah and Charlene, I hush my voice. "Get to the car. Drive away. And call 911. I think someone's hurt. I have to check; don't argue with me. Go. Call 911. Get out of here." I eye Riah. "Both of you." I make it clear by my tone that there's no room for debate. I'm not sure how she's going to respond, but after a small moment she nods. I hand them my phone.

A voice inside of me tells me that I really should go with them.

No, Jevin.

That person might be alive.

Stop the twins.

All in.

No, I wasn't about to leave the building and wait for who knows how long for cops or more agents to show up, only to find out later that I'd left someone dying on the floor when I could've saved him.

Besides, I really doubted that the Secret Service would've sent only one agent here. That meant there might be another victim.

Or someone else to help you. Someone's who's armed.

Finally, the women step silently toward the door.

I decide that an umbrella's better than nothing and go for one after all. The end is tipped with metal, and I figure I can use it like a bayonet if I need to. It might not be lethal, but it would sure slow someone down.

Cautiously, I creep past the chapel again and make my way toward the hallway. As I get closer, I see more of the man's legs. For the moment, no other sounds.

I tighten my grip on the shaft of the umbrella and realize I haven't heard the front door opening. I glance back, see the women still in the foyer. Charlene is talking softly, urgently, on the phone. Dr. Colette is standing stoically beside her, watching me. I gesture again for them to go, and Charlene holds up a finger to indicate that they will in just a moment.

At last they ease out the door.

Good.

Okay.

Heart hammering, I round the corner.

The man on the floor has an earpiece attached to a white coiling cord that disappears into his suit coat. His head is twisted gruesomely to the side at an angle a head was never meant to turn. Eyes open. Staring.

Quickly, I scan the room. More elegant furniture. A prayer stool in the corner. A cross hanging from the wall. Heavy floor-length drapes pulled across unseen windows. No one else is present.

No sounds.

Two other doors are propped open. One leads to the crematorium. Through the other doorway, I can see a tiled floor. Old metal gurneys and countertops of chemicals and medical instruments.

The embalming room.

I make a decision: *See if this guy is alive, then go. Get out of here.*

Silently, I crouch and press two fingers against the agent's neck. No pulse. Nothing.

But then I hear movement in the embalming room, someone walking across the tiled floor.

See if he has a gun. Move!

I'm no marksman, but I am a practiced shot. Mostly I've fired guns at Charlene while I'm blindfolded. That was for part of our show.

This was for real.

I feel for a shoulder holster on the dead man, find his gun, and as I'm removing it, I hear indistinct voices in the embalming room, and a man in jeans and a black sweater crosses the doorway, walking backward, dragging a woman across the floor. She's not moving.

The other agent.

Then the person dragging her speaks. This time I hear him clearly: "Go get the man."

I scurry to the wall, duck behind one of the chairs.

Stillness. Perception. Expectation. There's no reason for him to suspect that anyone else is in the room.

He'll focus on the task, why would he look your way?

Still, I hold the gun ready, umbrella tucked behind the curtain beside me.

The man enters the room. He's athletic, walks with poise, confidence. Doesn't look my way. Identical to the other man except he wears a green sweater.

This twin grabs the wrists of the dead Secret Service agent, tugs him toward the door to the embalming room, but as he turns the corner, the flap of the dead man's jacket flips open, revealing the empty shoulder holster.

Countdown

In a beat while I still have the advantage, I respond.

Ditching the umbrella and swinging the handgun in front of me, I dash across the room, through the doorway, and shout, "Do not move!"

But only one man is here now, and it's not the one who pulled the male agent's corpse into the room. A wicked scar scribbles down this twin's left cheek. He looks at me calmly, holds out his hands, palms up, to show that he's unarmed. The dead woman whom I saw him dragging a moment ago lies at his feet.

"Who are you?" he asks.

There's one other door leading out of this room. His brother must have fled the second he realized the agent's gun was missing.

"Don't move." Then I call out the door, "I have the gun! I'm aiming it at your brother. Step out with your hands up."

No response. No sound. The man in front of me appears unfazed. "Who told you to come here? Dr. Colette?"

I'm trying to keep an eye on both him and the doorway. "I said I have your brother!"

No reply.

How to do this?

How to do this?

Make sure this guy's not a threat.

"Get on your knees."

He doesn't move.

"Now."

But that's when I hear the front door bang open and Charlene cry out, "Jevin, he's got—ouch!"

"Don't!" Anger flares up inside me. "Touch her!"

He got outside, got to the women!

"Give my brother the gun," the man down the hallway demands. He's still out of sight, as are Charlene and Riah.

The twin I'm aiming the pistol at speaks to me calmly. "My brother will kill her, I assure you. He has the other agent's gun. Now set down your weapon. Kick it to me."

From the foyer: "I'll give you five seconds."

No!

"Five—"

Thoughts whip through my head: *If you shoot this guy, his brother will kill Charlene, Riah too—*

"Four—"

But if you stall long enough—

"Three—"

The police or more Secret Service agents can get—

Charlene: "Jevin, he—!"

"Two—"

461

"Okay!" I lower the gun. "I am. Let her be!"

The man with the scar indicates toward the floor. "Slowly."

I bend down and place the gun on the floor, then slide it toward him. While he retrieves it, I stand, brushing my hand across my pocket. He doesn't notice but gestures toward the wall to my left. "Stand over there."

I cross the room.

"Okay, Daniel," he calls to the foyer. "Bring her in."

I survey my surroundings. The surgical tools on the counter across the room could serve as weapons. There's a scalpel, a small saw, and a trocar—a hollow, spear-like probe about a foot and a half long. One end is attached to a rubber tube that leads to a pressure pump and plastic tub of yellowish liquid, the other end is sharpened, with a hole in it. It doesn't take a genius to figure out that the trocar is used for filling body cavities with embalming fluid.

The plastic tub has a warning on it: FORMALDE-HYDE.

Yes. If I could get to that—

Riah and Charlene enter through the doorway, followed by Daniel, who holds a gun identical to the one I'd found.

The crowd gasped as the man stepped off the roof of the Franklin Grand Hotel.

Then exploded.
And disappeared in midair.

I berate myself for leaving the women alone, for not getting them out of here. "Are you two okay?"

They both nod.

"Riah." Darren's voice is flat. "Who are these people?"

She doesn't respond to his question but asks one of her own: "Why the president, Darren? How is he a threat to national security? Why are you doing this?"

He motions for her and Charlene to stand beside me and they do. All of us have our hands up. Daniel joins his brother, who replies to Dr. Colette, "He wants to shut down Project Alpha, but what we're doing here, Riah, this will save the lives of thousands of American soldiers."

Daniel goes on, continuing as if he's thinking the exact same thoughts as his brother: "It'll give us the upper hand around the globe in fighting terrorism. You must know that too. We can't just abandon it."

"More people like Malik?"

"Yes"—it's Darren now—"his death saved hundreds of lives. That's just one example. We can save tens of thousands more." He looks at Daniel, who says, "The cuffs."

"Yes."

Daniel stows his gun on the counter next to the

trocar and embalming fluid. He leans over the dead woman's body and removes the pair of steel handcuffs she was carrying, slips them into the back pocket of his jeans, then visits the man's corpse and retrieves the cuffs from him as well.

I'd given Charlene back her earring a few minutes ago. If I were cuffed right now, I wasn't sure how I would pick the lock.

I opt for stalling and think back to what Glenn Banner said when he was dying—the threat, the man who would find me, the hero who avenges. "It was Akinsanya, right? He was the sniper in Kabul, wasn't he?"

The men look at me with interest but say nothing.

"Okay, Riah," Darren begins. "It looks like we're going to have to move to a new location. We'll take care of things from there. You're still going to help us, aren't you—or have you changed your mind?"

She points to Charlene and me. "I'll help you if you let these two live." I'm not sure if she's bluffing. I sense no deception in her words. She brought the medical instruments, and I wasn't sure if maybe she'd been planning to help them all along.

It was definitely possible.

The brothers exchange glances, then Darren nods. "Come over here, Riah. Daniel, cuff them."

Riah obeys while Daniel strides toward us.

Charlene lifts her hands so that they're behind her head.

I want to keep them talking. "You had the sniper shoot the guy's vest because you can't do it, can you? That's why you need Riah. You can't do it without her. But Arlington thinks you can, so—"

Darren cocks his head. "Who are you?"

"Jevin Banks, the magician."

"Magician?"

My thoughts are racing. "What about Williamson? Is she involved, or were you just using her to help secure funding for Project Alpha?" Honestly, I'm not certain about any of these conclusions, but I'm not really trying to get them to admit anything. It's all misdirection.

What I do best.

Daniel tells Charlene to turn around, put her hands behind her back. She does. When she lowers her hands from behind her head, I see that one of her earrings is missing.

I hold up my hands to show him that they're empty.

But the right one is not.

When I stood up a few moments ago, I palmed something from my pocket.

The 1895 Morgan Dollar.

Sight lines. Darren hadn't seen me do it.

It's the only advantage I have.

And I'm going to use it.

The Trocar

Daniel handcuffs Charlene's wrists behind her, then she turns her back to the wall and I know what she's doing: using the earring she just palmed. I'd give her just under thirty seconds to get free. She's not quite as fast as I am, but she definitely has skills.

He approaches me, and I turn and feel him click the cuff around my left wrist, but that's when I make my move. I whip around and, in one motion, swipe the Morgan Dollar violently toward his right eye.

Based on how deeply it gouges in, I'm guessing there'll be no using that eye again. I don't care how tough you are, that was going to hurt.

He cries out and throws his hand to his face, and while he's disoriented I grab his shoulders and tug him toward Charlene, positioning him in front of her to use as a human shield, but Darren is leveling the gun at us, and even with Daniel in the way, I have a feeling he might be able to pick off me or Charlene. He eyes down the barrel, but Riah throws herself against his arm, and when he fires, the bullet ricochets off the floor.

The other gun is on the counter.
Get it. Go!

I shove Daniel to the floor and rush at Darren, who tugs free from Riah. I have enough speed and connect with a front jump kick to his brachial plexus on the inside of his upper arm, whip my hand out, and manage to knock the gun away— sleight of hand, instinct—but he's so quick he snags my leg in midair before I can retract it and whips me around, sending me crashing against one of the metal gurneys.

As I leap to my feet, I hear Charlene cry out from behind me, and I glance back only to see Daniel grab her arm and hustle her out of the room toward the hallway that leads to the funeral home's entrance.

No! Stop him, he—

But Darren comes at me. He's better than I am, and every move I make he's one step ahead of me. He deftly blocks my uppercut, does a spinning side kick that connects with my fractured ribs. I gasp and stumble backward, almost toppling over the dead female Secret Service agent.

A crippling throb of pain overwhelms me when I try to draw in a breath, and as I struggle to regain my balance, Riah valiantly tries to help and goes for Darren's arm again, but he backhands her brutally in the face, sending her reeling into the wall. She smacks it hard with her forehead and sinks limply to the floor.

As he's bending down to retrieve the gun, I grab him with both hands and drive him backward. He crashes into one of the metal gurneys, the momentum sends it spinning toward the counter, and that's when I see that Riah has risen and flipped on the switch to the motor attached to the trocar. Embalming fluid immediately floods the tube.

On his feet again, Darren reaches for my head.

He broke the necks of the Secret Service agents. He's going to—

I spin, rotating him toward Riah.

And she plunges the trocar into his side. And depresses the trigger.

He draws in a strangled, horrid-sounding breath and looks down, stunned, at the hollow metal rod that's augered in between his ribs, that's filling his lungs with embalming fluid. He grips it with both hands to pull it out, but Riah rams it in farther and he gasps, then crumples to the floor, making sounds I never want to hear again.

Charlene.

Go!

As Riah watches Darren die, I bolt across the room, down the hallway, through the foyer, and out the front door.

Daniel is sliding into the driver's seat of the Secret Service agents' SUV. Charlene lies on the driveway next to the hearse, her hands still cuffed behind her. She isn't moving.

No!

I rush to her.

No, no, no!

When I turn her head toward me, she groans.

Oh, thank God you're alive. Thank—

"Stop him." She coughs slightly. "He's still going to kill . . ."

"Are you—"

"Yeah." She still seems dazed, and I don't know why Daniel didn't kill her, but I'm thankful—

"I'm fine. He's going after Hoult." There's no hesitation in her voice. "Stop him!"

"Alright." I jump to my feet. "I will."

And how exactly are you going to do that?

Improvise.

Daniel is backing up to pull around the sedan. The SUV rides high, has runner boards beneath the passenger's and driver's side doors.

That'll work.

I sprint alongside the vehicle and reach for the passenger-side door handle but can't quite catch it. Daniel aims the SUV toward the road and I try for it again.

Can't hold on.

Do this!

Now!

He accelerates.

On the third try I snag the door handle, yank the door open, and, striding off the runner board beneath it, leap inside. Either it surprises him or he's trying to throw me from the vehicle because he swerves wildly, but I'm already in with him. The door bangs shut and I reach for the wheel to crank it to the right. Toward the yard. Toward the Schuylkill River.

Where I'll have the advantage.

Yeah, improvise.

He elbows me savagely in the face, but I hold on, wrench the wheel again, and we bounce across the lawn toward the drop-off to the water.

And as we launch off the edge, I hit the button to roll my window down.

Cuffed

The impact is even more jarring than I expect.

The air bag smacks me in the chest and knocks the wind out of me, causing a whole new flood of pain to rupture up my side from my cracked ribs. The current grabs the vehicle, tilting it forward and redirecting us downstream. We're low enough for water to pour in through the open window, and the SUV tips in my direction.

After all the cold-water escapes I've done, I'd figured I'd be more able to withstand the shock of the river water than Daniel would, but I'm out of practice, and with the fractured ribs I'm having a hard time breathing at all.

Both of the air bags are deflating, giving us more room to move. Daniel, who's handling the chilly water better than I thought he would, wrestles to get his door open, but I clutch his arm and hold him back.

"Your brother's dead," I tell him. "It's over."

Pain wracks my side with every breath. With the open window, the SUV is sinking fast and the water is almost to my chest.

"I know. His left side."

But how? He left before—

Oh, just like your boys. He feels the pain his brother felt.

He punches my jaw, stunning me, then wraps his hands around my throat and shoves my head down. I struggle to get free, but his grip is fierce and he manages to get my face beneath the water that's cascading into the SUV.

I wish I could smack the handcuff dangling from my wrist into his face, but the angle's not right for that arm.

But it is right for the other arm. I'm still wearing the watch from Banner, the one built to withstand a bullet, so I use that instead. I swing my wrist backward, smash it into Daniel's face. His grip weakens just enough for me to fight free, sit up, grab a breath.

Water is rising fast. He goes for his door again, then sees the handcuff still hanging from my wrist, seizes my arm, and drags it toward the steering wheel.

Oh—

No.

I try to pull free, but he hits me hard in the jaw again, causing me to see stars.

"I'll kill her," he says evenly. Looks at me with

eyes fierce and cold. "The woman back there. Her life for his."

Don't let him get out. Do not let—

He angles my wrist to snap the cuff to the steering wheel—

Now.

You've done it before in your stage shows. It's not that hard of a move.

In an instant, I twist my hand around, slap the open side of the handcuffs to his wrist, and smack the lock mechanism against his chest to ratchet it shut, cuffing his wrist to mine.

Descent

For a moment it's as if he doesn't realize what just happened, then he yanks powerfully at his arm, but there's no getting free. The water is almost up to our necks. I don't know how deep the river is—we haven't hit bottom yet, and it looks like water's going to fill the vehicle before we do.

Water splashes into my mouth. We won't have air for more than a few more seconds.

Daniel wrenches at the cuffs again but it does no good.

"Never threaten a guy's girl, Daniel. It's not a good idea."

The force of the current swirls the SUV and

takes us farther down, and the water roils higher. I snatch one final, deep and painful breath, then the water is over my head.

As his mouth goes under, I hear a fierce, enraged scream that uses up a lot of air, and that's bad for him. It's seriously going to shorten his life.

I used to be able to hold my breath for three and a half minutes, but not in water this cold, and that was back when I was practicing every day. I figure the temperature will cut into that time; I might have a minute, maybe less.

You can still get out of this.

Pick the lock. You need to pick the lock.

How?

Beside me, Daniel is struggling to get away, but that's a mistake because he's using up the precious oxygen in his blood. You want to stop moving. That's the secret.

Hang on, Jev.

His hand goes for my throat. I try to pull it away, but he's stronger than I am.

Not like this, Jev.

Don't let it end like this.

Again I try to pry off his hand but can't.

The water is too cloudy for me to see him anymore, but I can feel him squeezing harder. He jerks again at the cuffs, but then his grip on my throat begins to weaken. A moment later his arm goes slack and he begins to shake uncontrollably. I know what's happening, what he's going through.

I've been there myself. It'll go on for a few more seconds.

And then it will stop.

Which it does.

They died like this. Your boys did. And Rachel did too. Drowning in that minivan.

How much time?

Thirty seconds.

Maybe.

Maybe not.

Cuffed to him like this, I can't think of a way to get out. My first thought is to try to get his body out of the vehicle and swim it to the surface, but I have very little air left in my lungs, the current is strong, and I'm exhausted. I'd never make it.

This is your punishment for not stopping Rachel. Dying like your family did.

Drowning.

All is dark and cold as the SUV comes to rest on the river bottom.

My strength is fading.

I'm sorry, Rachel. I'm sorry, Tony. Drew. I loved you.

I do love you—

Relax.

Maybe I deserve to die.

I hear Charlene's words: *Stop hating yourself . . . Rachel had problems . . . She was ill . . . Something broke inside of her and she didn't have the chance to get it fixed.*

Death always wins in the end.
It was her choice, Jevin, not yours.
Death always wins.
Yes.
In the end.
I did love you, Rachel. I do. I can't help it.
But I couldn't save her.
No one could.
I think of the two women. Rachel, Charlene. One gone. The other waiting for me. Three lives wound around each other. Destinies intermingled.
Entangled.
I think of how much the death of those I loved affected me, wonder how much my death will affect Charlene.
You can postpone death, but you cannot conquer it. Only one person, the one who rose, ever has.
One day death will have its way with me.
But that doesn't need to be today.
You're an escape artist, Jevin Banks. So escape.
Yeah, I think I will.
Pick the lock. You have to pick the lock.
I don't have anything with me to—
Well—
Except for one thing.
The car key.
But not the key exactly.
What it's attached to.

Convergence

With my free hand I feel for the key, find the looped wire ring that connects it to the keyless entry fob. I try to twist it from the ignition, but the car is still in drive. I pop it into neutral, remove the key.

My air is giving out fast. I don't have long.

Stay calm, Jevin.

Lower your heart rate.

Just like you used to. In your show.

But a torrent of air bursts up from my mouth.

No! Come on, focus!

The wire resists at first, but when I jam my fingernail in and twist, it uncurls a little bit. I don't need to unloop it all the way, just enough to get it into the handcuff's lock.

It takes a few seconds, a few precious seconds, but I manage, and once it's in the lock mechanism, my fingers know what to do. Instinct.

The cuff snaps open, I pull my hand free from the assassin's corpse and snake my way out the open window, then push off the side of the SUV with my feet to propel myself toward the surface. I stroke as best I can with my broken ribs, and as soon as my head breaks through, I sputter and gasp for breath.

The current has pulled me toward the middle of

the river, and the bank is more than fifty feet away.

With the water moving this fast and as weak as I am, it won't be easy to make it that far.

I hear my name and see Charlene, cuffs gone, sprinting along the shoreline. I'm too out of breath to reply, but pivot in the current and start to swim toward her.

Fighting the current is tough. I wish I'd done laps with her this last year, kept in shape for swimming. I manage a few strokes but that's it. I'm too weak, it hurts too much, strains the muscles around my fractured ribs.

I begin to sink again, and the last thing I see before the dark water swallows me is Charlene throwing off her jacket and rushing toward the water.

Riah stared at Darren's body, the trocar still embedded in his side, still pumping embalming fluid into his corpse.

She'd always wondered what it would be like to kill a human being. And now she knew.

It felt like nothing. No more impactful or moving than tying her shoes or putting on makeup.

Watching him while it happened had only made her wonder how long he would twitch before he stopped quivering for good, just like that snake's body that she held when she was a girl.

Killed but not yet dead.

But now Darren was both.

Finally, she turned off the pump.

Leaving the funeral home, she saw that the SUV was gone. Tire tracks led to the river, but none of the three people—Daniel, Mr. Banks, or Ms. Antioch—were anywhere to be seen. Perhaps they all drowned. That would be unfortunate if they had other things they were hoping to accomplish today.

She had killed one person and could kill again. She could kill her father. Yes, she could do it and feel no remorse whatsoever.

Now you know. Do it for Katie.

At her apartment she already had the items she would need to restrain him while she did her work—the things she'd acquired for her sleepover with Cyrus.

He raped Katie, the incestuous pedophile sexually abused and raped both of his daughters.

Both of them. So many times. He impregnated his youngest daughter and caused her to stop believing in love.

Perhaps killing him was the closest Riah would come, could ever come, to loving her sister and even her dead mother.

It wasn't much, but it was something. Yes, human beings do want to love and be loved. To experience the real thing. Riah had wanted that for herself but had been unable to ever attain it or express it. But even if she couldn't, she could at least act on behalf of justice, on behalf of those she wished she could have cared about.

Planning how she would take care of her father, Riah Colette, the psychopath, left the funeral home to get the items she would be needing from her apartment.

The president's speech was postponed. The police disbanded the crowd and thoroughly searched the rooftop as well as the pavement below, but they found no sign of the man who'd leaned off the edge of the Franklin Grand Hotel, exploded, and apparently disintegrated in midair.

The dark-haired man who'd introduced himself as Cyrus's friend had left a few minutes before, and when her boss didn't answer his phone, Caitlyn Vaughn decided to check on him.

She found him tied to his office chair, slowly regaining consciousness.

His lips were stitched shut with thick black thread. His shirt was off; the skin of his stomach had been sliced open and then sewn back up. Beneath the skin something squirmed, then something else, until the whole surface of his belly began to quiver and bulge unevenly, and when she glanced at the aquariums in the corner, she saw that the one containing the roaches was empty.

There were only a few wasps remaining in the other.

Looking back at Cyrus, she saw a wasp squeeze out from between his lips, tug itself free, crawl across his cheek, and then lift into the air.

Caitlyn had never seen anything so disturbing and she felt repulsed. Turned away.

But then hesitated.

This was the man who'd slept with her and promised to leave his wife to be with her, but had not. This was the man who'd flaunted his affair with Riah Colette right in front of her, and then had sex with her right here in his office while she was just outside the door, forced to listen to everything.

This was the man.

He'd lied to her. Used her. Only. For. Sex. Betrayed her.

And so, as Caitlyn Vaughn went to the desk phone to call 911, just perhaps she did not dial the number as quickly as she might have if Cyrus had treated her more like a woman deserves.

I hear sounds wrestling for my attention. The river. A roar in my head. Sirens. A voice: "Jevin." It's Rachel, coming from somewhere beyond space and time, calling to me. "I love you, Jevin."

Rachel—

No.

She's gone, Jevin.

She's dead.

She's—

"Jevin—"

My head begins to clear.

No, it's Charlene. Not Rachel.

Rachel drowned when she killed your boys.

It's hard to open my eyes, and when I manage to at last, it makes me dizzy, but I see Charlene leaning over me. "Jevin! Thank God you're okay!"

I cough harshly and my side roars with pain. I turn my head, spit out a mouthful of water.

Charlene eases her hand beneath my neck to support me.

Yes, those are sirens in the background. Around me light is swimming with sound. I close my eyes and cough, draw in as deep a breath as I can, try to lean up on my elbow, but my side screams at me again and I end up dropping to my back. Gazing at Charlene, I see that she's soaking wet. "You pulled me out."

"Yes."

"Mouth to mouth?"

"Yes."

Okay.

"That's the seventh time I've drowned and you've saved me."

"Who's counting."

"I'm glad you got out of those cuffs."

"I'm glad I was wearing those earrings."

I gesture toward the water. "Did he come up?"

She shakes her head.

A moment passes. I don't know how to say this. "Charlene, did you, a moment ago . . . I thought I

481

heard someone say 'I love you.' I thought it was Rachel."

"Yes."

"Was it . . . ?"

"Yes."

I can't tell if she means that it was my imagination or if she means that it was her. For some reason it doesn't feel right to ask her to clarify.

There are so many things I want to say to her. So many things I need to say. Her hand is still under my neck. "In the hotel," I tell her, "you said that without hope you wouldn't be able to make it through the day."

Our thoughts can heal us or destroy us. Placebos. Curses.

"I remember."

Blessings. A love that conquers death . . .

The idea that death could be conquered, that life would win in the end . . . an idea too good to be true, but also the most necessary truth of all.

"Prana." The word barely comes out. I'm feeling weaker than I thought.

She leans close. "What?"

"The life-sustaining force. I finally know what it is. It's hope."

The placebo for grief, for hating yourself. The only way to move on.

"Yes." Her eyes smile at me. And I can't remember ever seeing her look so beautiful before. The longer we look into each other's eyes, the more right it feels, and finally she says softly, "We're entangled, aren't we?"

I draw her close, and by the way I kiss her, I doubt she'll need to read my mind to know the answer.

Another Goat

52 hours later
Friday, October 30
3:04 p.m.

"That's really nice," I tell Xavier. We're watching CNN. They're re-airing the footage that a woman at Independence Park took on her cell phone of the guy stepping off the Franklin Grand Hotel on Wednesday. "You can't even see the cables retract, not even on film."

"And the explosion covers everything."

"Misdirection."

"Yup." He dips a cracker into his cheese spread, swipes out a sizable dollop. "People see what they expect to see. Not what's really there."

I shake my head. "And you just rode down the elevator afterward?"

He shrugs. "I had a couple minutes to myself before anyone got up there." He glances at the bag in the corner. "I always wanted to do that stunt. Something I came up with for your next stage show."

"I don't have a next stage show, Xavier."

"Not yet, dude. But I know you, and you won't be able to stay away from it forever."

"Well, you made that look better than I ever could." He looks pleased.

The women and kids should be here any minute. He goes for another cracker full of cheese spread.

"I gotta ask you, Xav. What's the deal with you and cheese anyway?"

"You want some?"

"No, actually, I have a policy: I never eat anything that smells like my feet."

"I wouldn't eat anything that smells like your feet either."

"What I'm saying is, why are you eating cheese all the time?"

"You've heard of quirks, of course."

"Sure."

"Well, I felt like I needed one to be a more well-rounded individual."

"You needed a quirk? What, are you serious?"

"Sure. It took me awhile to come up with something a little different. Subtle, a little idiosyncratic, but understated. I like cheese; it was a good fit. I'm much more interesting now. Don't you think?"

"Um. Yeah." The news program switches to early polling numbers for next year's election. I flick it off. "Are you still planning to go to that tectonic weapons conference this weekend? You never told me."

"I fly out early tomorrow. Donnie's coming with me. He seems to have an interest in alternative news. Fionna gave him permission. She's really keen on field trips."

"I've noticed."

As if on cue, there's a knock at the door. "Are you guys ready?" It's Charlene.

We join the women and four kids in the hallway and head for the elevators.

We'd decided to stay in Philadelphia for a few more days.

Some of our time had been spent, of course, in interviews with the police, the Secret Service, and the media, but surprisingly, the law enforcement officers hadn't hassled us as much as I'd thought they would. Perhaps because of what we'd been through, or what we'd stopped from happening— the events the government was denying ever occurred.

Which didn't surprise Xavier one bit.

We'd tried to find Dr. Colette to corroborate our story, but she hasn't been seen since the funeral home incident. At first I wondered if she had perhaps been planning on helping the twins after all, but then I remembered that she'd killed Darren and I decided that was unlikely. I figured she would show up soon enough.

And so.

The president was fine. Undersecretary of

Defense Williamson was facing a congressional hearing, and Dr. Arlington was in the hospital with some sort of serious infection, although details concerning what'd happened to him hadn't been released to the public. Still no idea on who Akinsanya was.

Earlier today I'd tried calling my dad as I'd promised Charlene I would do, but as I suspected, he hadn't answered or returned my call. For now, the things we all put off saying would have to wait.

As a result of the news coverage, Michelle Boyd begged me to come back to Entertainment Film Network. In addition, I received offers from four other networks to launch a new series, but I declined all the invitations.

Freelancing seemed like a good idea for the time being.

Fionna has offered to act as our tour guide, and as we emerge from the elevator she announces that we're going to visit the Pennsylvania Hospital this afternoon. "It was cofounded by Benjamin Franklin in 1751 and was the first hospital in the western hemisphere. At first they had a difficult time paying for costs, so they charged spectators an admission fee to watch operations."

Five-year-old Mandie wrinkles up her nose. "That's gross."

"Cool." Donnie smiles. "That'd be awesome."

Maddie gives him a sigh and a head shake. "You are such a boy."

"And you're such a girl."

"Thank you."

We leave the hotel. No limos or executive cars today. My side still aches, but walking doesn't hurt too badly. It feels good to get some fresh air, and the Pennsylvania autumn trees are stunning.

Fionna goes on with her explanation. "There was no anesthesia, of course, so people got to choose between opium, whiskey, or getting smacked on the head with a mallet wrapped in leather to be knocked unconscious for the operation."

"What's opium, Mommy?" Mandie asks.

"Something that's very bad for you, dear." Fionna pauses, looks reflectively at the horizon. "Here's one: when the man thought about getting smacked on the head with a mallet wrapped in leather to be knocked unconscious for his operation, he looked about as excited as the second-place kid in the Scripps National Spelling Bee after misspelling the word *idiot*."

"Hmm," Xavier acknowledges. "That one I actually like."

"Thank you, Mr. Wray. I think I'm finally getting the hang of this."

Yesterday Fionna took us to the Eastern State Penitentiary, which is now a tourist site. When I saw the thirty-foot-high walls that were also ten

487

feet thick, I started thinking of ways I could walk through them.

Occupational hazard.

I'd come up with two ideas at the time. Now, on the way to the Pennsylvania Hospital, I think of one more, a good one that'll work even with live audiences watching from both sides of the wall. And the top of it.

Might be a good publicity stunt to launch a new live stage show.

Charlene is by my side and says quietly, "Penny for your thoughts."

"I think I'm going to walk through a wall."

"Sounds fun. Will you be needing a lovely assistant?"

"I could probably come up with a way to work someone in."

"Glad to hear that." She takes my arm in hers. "As long as it's me."

"There's no one else even in the running, Petunia."

"I'm glad to hear that, Wolverine."

The man who had shot the vest of the suicide bomber, the man who went by the name Akinsanya, had, of course, lied to Darren and Daniel about Adrian Goss. Adrian was not their father; he had known their mother, yes, but he was just a person Akinsanya had come up with to serve as another test.

He boarded the plane for Dubai, a place to hide out until he could regroup. Figure out his next step.

In the last two days, RixoTray stock had plummeted and he'd lost over four million dollars. Yes, his investment portfolio had taken a major hit, but in Akinsanya's business, money was easy to make. More significantly, because of Arlington's reckless and illegal actions, the whole telomerase research project was being brought into question.

And that really was the problem.

He took his seat in the first-class cabin.

Yes, lay low until the dust settled, then pursue the second option—the singularity. If he couldn't use the experimental telomerase drug to extend his life indefinitely, downloading his consciousness onto a computer would.

Akinsanya looked out the window.

He was going by an alias today, of course.

After all, he'd served in the US military for thirty years, had just recently left. He was the man who had first found Darren at Fort Bragg and Daniel at Fort Benning. Akinsanya was Colonel Derek Byrne. And he was not at all done with his mission.

Cyrus opened his eyes and saw Mambo Atabei sitting beside his hospital bed.

He would have cried out for help, but the damage to his throat from the wasps was too severe. It wasn't clear if he'd ever be able to speak again. In fact, the doctors were saying it was a miracle that the swelling hadn't completely closed off his airway.

A miracle?

Well, Cyrus didn't exactly believe in miracles, or, conversely, in curses, or in any of the spiritual forces of good or evil that religious and superstitious people acknowledged.

But honestly, he didn't like considering the possibility that there was something to Atabei's practices—or the role they might've played in Tanbyrn's death. And right now, seeing her here, he realized he most certainly did not want to find out.

Atabei assessed him. "The kind officer at the door let me through when I told him I was your spiritual advisor. I wish I could apprise you that my Loa ordered me not to perform a ceremony regarding your well-being tonight, but that would be untrue. She informed me that you had intended to kill me."

Cyrus's eyes grew large. He tried to speak, made only unintelligible sounds. His wrists were strapped to the sides of the bed, so he couldn't press the call button beside him for help.

How?

You never told anyone!

"I just came by to tell you that so you'd know what's coming. Expectation always helps in the equation, belief plays a very important role in shaping the future." Atabei patted his arm and stood. "Well . . . I should probably be going. It looks like I need to be buying a goat on the way home."

Fire and Ice

Two months later

My publicity guys are truly geniuses.

The timing of walking through the Eastern State Penitentiary wall in Philly had been really brilliant. We'd finished the documentary on the events in Oregon and Philadelphia, and it aired the same night as the penitentiary special, coinciding with the week my new stage show opened in Las Vegas. We sold out the first month of the run in the first twenty-two minutes after tickets went on sale online.

We dedicated the documentary to Dr. Tanbyrn and Abina, donated the proceeds from the television special and the run of the show to the Lawson Research Center. All Charlene's idea.

I hear a knock on the greenroom door three minutes before I need to be on stage.

"Yes?"

Xavier leans in. "Jev, there's someone here to see you." I'm about to tell him that I don't have time to see anyone right now, that he should know that, but he goes on before I can say anything. "It's your dad."

"What?"

"He's waiting just down the hall."

My father and I still hadn't spoken. I could hardly believe he was here. Regardless, this was not the time to talk.

At least see him, at least make plans to meet up after the show.

"Okay, tell him I'll be there in a sec."

Two minutes.

As I leave the dressing room, I can hear music pounding through the auditorium and my blood begins to rush. This is it. What I was made to do. What I truly enjoy. Joy as evidence of God, of victory over the pain of this broken world? A place so touched with despair? Charlene believes that. I'm not quite there yet, but maybe I—

I see my father waiting for me. Slim. Salt-and-pepper hair. My features. What I'll look like in twenty-five years.

"Dad."

"Jevin."

He clasps my hand. Our handshake is stiff and unfamiliar.

Charlene stands near the edge of the stage. She looks at me urgently, points to the lift that will take me to the platform hidden high above the audience. I hold up one finger: *I'll be right there.*

"Dad, I'm glad to see you, but could we talk later? I need to go." My eyes are on the lift.

"I'll ride with you."

"Um . . . okay."

We step onto the platform. Begin to ascend. Neither of us speaks. Smoke from the smoke machine hovers in the air and curls past us in ghostlike wisps as we ride through it. Finally I break the silence. "So you got the ticket."

"Yes. Thank you." We ride in silence again. "So you gonna do any escapes tonight?"

"Yeah. It's a good one. I call it 'Fire and Ice.' I'll explode above the audience"—that idea came from Xavier, but I keep that to myself—"then appear in a block of ice onstage."

"Kinda like Blaine, when he was sealed in the ice for sixty-three hours? Or Dayan for sixty-six?"

"Well, I figured instead of standing around in there for three days, I'd just escape from it."

I check my watch.

One minute.

We reach the platform.

"No more claustrophobia, then?"

"You heard about that."

"Charlene might've mentioned it."

"Oh." I didn't know they'd been talking. "Well, I'm not sure I'll ever be over it completely," I tell him honestly. "But you find a way to—"

"Move on."

"Yes. To move on. Listen, after the show we can—"

"Yeah." He puts his hand on my shoulder, looks at me. "Hey, listen. I'm proud of you, okay? You know that, don't you?"

He'd never told me that before. Not once.

"Yeah, Dad," I tell him, because it's what he needs to hear. "Of course I do."

Things'll never always get worse.

He smiles. "So, go do your escape. I'll be watching."

"Okay."

My watch tells me thirty seconds.

My father takes the lift back down as I walk onto the girder. We don't wave to each other, but he offers me a small nod. I nod back.

So, Charlene's been talking with him.

And now it's going to be your turn.

A doorway between us was opening. One worth stepping through.

Below me, the spotlights cut through the vast auditorium, swishing above the crowd, bright sabers welcoming me back home.

I clip into the system Xavier designed. The wire is invisible, as are so many of the things that support us when we fall.

The lights change and the music rolls forward, deep and ominous.

My cue.

I take a breath.

And close my eyes.

And tip into the empty air.

To make an entrance these people will never forget.

Acknowledgments

A special thanks to David Lehman, Pam Johnson, Dr. Todd Huhn, Trinity Huhn, Jennifer Leep, Jessica English, Heather Knudtsen, Shawn Scullin, Ariel Huhn, and Tom Vick, who all offered me invaluable editorial insights.

Thanks also to Howie and Tom for handing me the trocar, to Noah Tysick for leading me to the peristyle, to Steve Glaze for helping me take flight, to Eric Wilson for showing me the waterfalls, to Kate Connors for your research on pharmaceuticals and patent protection, and to the Mind Science Foundation for expanding my horizons.

Steven James is the author of many books, including the bestselling Patrick Bowers thrillers. He is a contributing editor to *Writer's Digest*, has a master's degree in storytelling, and has taught writing and creative communication on three continents. Currently he lives, writes, drinks coffee, and plays disc golf near the Blue Ridge Mountains of Tennessee.

Center Point Large Print
600 Brooks Road / PO Box 1
Thorndike, ME 04986-0001 USA

(207) 568-3717

US & Canada:
1 800 929-9108
www.centerpointlargeprint.com

LESBIA BRANDON

LESBIA
BRANDON

by

ALGERNON CHARLES
SWINBURNE

*An historical and critical commentary
being largely
a study (and elevation) of Swinburne
as a novelist*

by

R A N D O L P H   H U G H E S

London

THE FALCON PRESS

*First published in 1952
by the Falcon Press (London) Limited
6 & 7 Crown Passage, Pall Mall,
London, S.W.1*

*Printed in Great Britain
by the Peregrine Press Limited
Widnes, Lancs.*

. . . là-bas une pourpre s'apprête . . .

Mallarmé

CONTENTS

Editor's Note

Only eight of the chapters have titles in the manuscript; the title of Chapter XV is on the back of one of the galley-proofs; some chapters are unfinished, or the completing pages are missing; in the case of one (ii) the preliminary part is missing; in that of others both completing and preliminary parts are wanting; it is as good as certain that except in the case of (i) and (ii) these missing portions are no longer extant.

FOREWORD

FOREWORD

IT IS PERHAPS WELL TO BEGIN BY SAYING THAT LESBIA BRANDON is not the real nor an acceptable title of this work, by far the most important of the very large number of Swinburne's writings which have not yet been published. It is not Swinburne's, who never gave a name to the novel; it was most inappropriately (as I show in my Commentary) applied to the book by the grossly incompetent Wise or the almost as grossly incompetent Gosse,[1] who impudently constituted themselves the absolutist guardians of Swinburne's literary remains and also of his reputation according to their standards. But as this false title has acquired a standing through its presence in Wise's Catalogues, and has been used of the work whenever the latter has been mentioned in all publications relating to Swinburne printed in the last forty years or so, it has seemed best not to seek to alter it. In spite of the scruples of competent scholarship, it is too late to do so: the world has heard, with a certain curiosity, of 'Lesbia Brandon', has known that it must and will one day be printed, and it is the expectation of a work

---

[1] It is more probable that Gosse was the inventor of this inapt if not inept title of the book. In the *Life*, he says that 'Swinburne carried out this scheme in a . . . romance called, from the name of its heroine, *Lesbia Brandon*', unwarrantably implying that the book was thus called by Swinburne. He is equally wrong when, in the same passage, he says that 'Swinburne thought he had [whatever that means] completely dropped this work' [presumably once he had had it sent to the printer]. These are not the only errors in this short paragraph of seven lines. This is typical of Gosse's misnamed *Life*, which is crowded with errors of fact as well as with much worse things.

of that name (rumoured 'immoral' or 'shocking') that the present publication comes at long last to satisfy.[1] At long last: the work was written some eighty years ago, and about seventy years ago Swinburne had the greater part of the manuscript set up in type; it was then, and for some time after, his firm intention to complete the book and have it published. But Watts-Dunton, as I have related in the historical part of my Commentary, with low and persistent cunning thwarted this design, and finally discouraged Swinburne from going on with this or any other novelistic work. The greater part of the manuscript[2] was sold, an indecently short time after Swinburne's, death, along with the manuscripts of most[3] of the rest

[1] It is likely that existence of the work under this title was put into circulation by Gosse from at least as early at 1877. See the extract from his journal cited in the historical section of my Commentary.

[2] Other portions were acquired by Wise at later dates; and apparently a few pages never came into his possession. Detailed information and discussion regarding this matter will be found in Chapters I and III of the Commentary.

[3] Wise, in his Introduction to *A Swinburne Library*, 1925, says 'A number of manuscripts of *published* pieces was sold by Watts-Dunton to a London dealer, but nothing *unpublished* failed to become my property' (Wise's italics). This is categorical enough, but it is not true. For one thing, the manuscript of *Lucretia Borgia* ('The Chronicle of Tebaldeo Tebaldei') did not go to Wise; and it is at least possible that he did not secure the chapter of *Lesbia Brandon* entitled 'Another Portrait' (for the mysterious fortunes of which see the section of my Commentary dealing with *The Text*). And so on: for the matter does not end here. W. T. Spencer, in *Forty Years in My Bookshop* (1923) says he purchased from Watts-Dunton 'after Swinburne's death' the manuscripts of 'about twelve unpublished poems', as well as of a considerable number of other works. Mr. W. Partington (who reproduces as true Wise's mendacious assertion that everything unpublished was bought by him) records in *Thomas J. Wise in the Original Cloth* (1946) that 'a London Bookseller ******* ******* managed to get a foot in, and secured as many as one hundred and two MS. pieces—greatly to the surprise and chagrin of Wise'. If the number of the cryptic asterisks (of which there is a surprising and tantalizing abundance in Mr. Partington's book) stands here for the letters of the 'London Bookseller's' name, he was in all likelihood Walter T. Spencer; if he was not Spencer, it is very probable that another batch of unpublished

IV

of Swinburne's unpublished work, by Watts-Dunton to Wise
for some £3,000, a low figure for such treasures, but doubtless
a tidy sum in the eyes of the man who had thus committed an
act of vile treachery against his friend. For it was a betrayal;
nearly all Swinburne's unpublished work and full rights[1] over
it were thereby transferred to about the last person in the
world who should have charge of it; it was delivered into the
hands and caprice of a completely uneducated pedlar who not
only had no literature but was prodigiously incompetent in

(*Note* [3] *continued*)—

works, besides the some twelve poems acquired by the latter, must be
added to the tale of those which did not become Wise's property. Wise
ignored completely the statement in Spencer's book, which appeared
some two years before *A Swinburne Library*; he must have been
acquainted with this book (and more than probably received a presentation copy of it), as he knew Spencer very well, and is mentioned in the
book in terms of undeserved laudation sure to flatter his vanity and—
like so many other glowing testimonials to his abilities and virtues—
give a feeling of security to the impostor and criminal that was his
central self. Spencer had the reputation of being a very shrewd expert
in the science of books in which Wise passed as a master.

[1] Or virtually full rights. The copyright was not his, and so he could
not publish without permission of the owner of it (which, however,
Gosse's influence could be counted on to obtain in the extremely unlikely event of any reluctance being displayed). But apart from that
he could do just as he liked with the work. He could sell and disperse
it with no record of whither it had gone (and he did so in the case of
a very large amount of it—to the despair of anyone engaged on Swinburne scholarship). He could even break up units and—again with no
record of the facts, of course—scatter—gainfully, it goes without saying
—the constituent parts in various directions (and he did so in a large
number of cases: Mr. Partington records that the MS. of the book on
Blake was thus 'broken up, and leaves inserted in some twenty-five
Swinburne first editions (genuine and spurious) sold to Wrenn "to add a
bit to their value" '; I could supplement this instance of shocking
vandalism with others that have come under my observation). Worse
still, he could destroy it (and he actually did so—doubtless under
pressure from Gosse—in at least two cases, as he himself confesses: one
apprehensively wonders how many other cases there were which, much
more characteristically, he kept dark—beyond the reach of the most
subtle processes of detection).

the lowly business of bibliography in which he managed to palm himself off as someone who enjoyed supereminence. (See the marvellous tributes to him from reputed experts in the Prefaces to the volumes of the Ashley catalogue: as it is impossible to believe these gentlemen were knaves, they must have been the other thing in the well-known brace of alternatives. 'A fixèd figures for the time of scorn': thus each of them is for ever in virtue of the testimonial he gave to the biggest dunce in the whole history of their profession.) He was also an indelicate criminal, a forger, and Watts-Dunton was not without some inkling of this;[1] which renders still heavier the charge he incurred by thus disposing of his friend's property.

To make things worse, Gosse was immediately and henceforth conjoined in an unholy partnership with Wise in all that concerned Swinburne. The full history of that partnership I shall give in an excursus in my next book on Swinburne, and I shall say very little about it here. Some simpletons believe that the adjunction of Gosse made things better; that he was a scholar of fine parts who kept a controlling hand over the blundering ignorance of Wise and corrected his many terrible errors. All this is a myth; Gosse was little better than Wise, in spite of a tenacious legend to

---

[2] At least Watts-Dunton (before the sale) spotted that certain items in Wise's *Swinburne Bibliography* were 'forgeries and piracies' (his words) and he told Wise so, and threatened to denounce these 'damned things' (his words again) in one of the principal literary reviews. He had some idea, then, that Wise was a shady character. But Wise succeeded in bamboozling him (or perhaps—a much graver matter—in winning his adhesion in spite of abiding knowledge or suspicion) to such an extent that a few years after Swinburne's death Swinburne's 'best friend' was signing himself 'Yours affectionately', 'Your affectionate friend' in letters to the forger which can now be seen in the British Museum. Watts-Dunton of course had what he no doubt thought a good reason for cherishing Wise, for had not the latter by his purchases increased Watts-Dunton's already ample means, derived partly from his inheritance of all Swinburne's worldly possessions, including a sum of money large enough to be called a fortune?

the contrary. He was not really educated, he was no true scholar, and, what is worse, he had a malignant animus against Swinburne, and was the chief agent of the misrepresentation from which Swinburne still suffers. All this I shall show, with dynamitic proof at need, in my next book. (I chivalrously warn anyone who thinks of entering the lists against me on behalf of Gosse—or any other persons I attack in this book—that this will be a perilous piece of charity.) It is enough to say now that the editing by him and Wise in conjunction of Swinburne's posthumous publications is one of the most scandalous things in the history of letters. I have, except in a minority of cases where I have not been able to see the original holographs, collated these publications with the manuscripts; it is putting it with safe leniency to say that on the average there is one serious error, and several lesser ones, in every ten lines of verse, and one serious and several lesser ones in every twenty lines of prose; what is even more disgraceful, in dialogic pieces lines are sometimes assigned to the wrong speaker; the letters too suffer from the conscienceless incompetence of these two malefactors: not only are there serious errors in what they do publish, but, *without any sort of indication to the reader,* whole passages are sometimes omitted, presumably because there is something in them offensive, not to civilised taste, but to an old-maidish squeamishness which was one of the qualities that gave distinction to Gosse. (It must always be kept in mind that not only was Gosse a co-editor with Wise in all these cases, but that he did the work of final revision (I have proof of this). His responsibility for the disgraceful errors and omissions is therefore greater than that of Wise: no antics of special pleading can ever secure him from damnation.[1]) The result is

---

[1] Mr. Partington, referring (in connexion with Swinburne's literary remains) to Gosse's association with Wise, calls him 'the confidential friend'. Is there something of cryptic irony here? One would like to think so. He also says that 'the collaboration between the two friends

in reading any of the considerable quantity of Swinburne's posthumous work brought out by this pair one can
never be sure that one is reading what Swinburne actually

(Note ¹ *continued)*—

was of the happiest and most genuine character'. Is there behind this
entirely veracious statement a reserve of meaning which Mr. Partington
prefers to leave in abeyance? Again, one would like to think so. But
Mr. Partington nowhere gives any express indication of Gosse's mal-
feasance in the matter under discussion. On the contrary, he represents
him as a providential coadjutor who corrected Wise's errors in the
editions of Swinburne's unpublished works and brought these editions
to a state of scholarly perfection. (Gosse, it is true, did correct some
errors, but he allowed the worst howlers to pass.) In his effort to excul-
pate Gosse Mr. Partington resorts in certain cases to special pleading
which collapses when it is competently examined. I must limit myself
to giving only one example of this here. Gosse and Wise had taken
as being Swinburne's certain pieces of drivelling and twaddling doggerel
by 'A.C.S.' which had appeared in *Fraser's Magazine* for April 1848
(when Swinburne was barely more than ten) and in later numbers over
the next few years. The bright pair of confederates thought them
'immeasurably superior to the incoherent vapourings of Shelley's early
muse', and Gosse was so confident that 'A.C.S.' could be no other than
Swinburne that he unreservedly ascribed them to the latter in the
abominably travestying article on him which he contributed to the
Dictionary of National Biography (and which still scandalously keeps
its place in that highly reputed and quasi-official publication as if it
were definitively true and quite adequate within its limits). Wise had
many years before attributed some of them to Swinburne in one of his
characteristically incompetent bibliographical ventures, and he now
(1912) issued all of them in a couple of pamphlets. But unfortunately
it transpired that the 'A.C.S.' in question could not be Swinburne (as
rudimentary mother wit would have been sufficient to show at he outset); and meddlesome outsiders, inconveniently more competent than
the asinine pair, proved that these were the initials of Sir Anthony
Coningham Sterling. Never was so ignominiously discrediting a
showing-up: Gosse, as well as his associate, was revealed as pitifully
wanting in a sense of literary values and even in sense *tout court*: he
stood forth as a dolt whose place was not in the world of letters. But
Mr. Partington tries to whitewash Gosse; he puts all the blame on
Wise, would have us believe that Gosse was misled by Wise, and
couldn't have known any better. But this won't do. Apart from the
failure of elementary sense in face of the simple facts of the case, Gosse
was not acting in the dark: he had received notice from 'The Pines' in

wrote.[1] When I conveyed this information to a distinguished friend at Oxford whose main business as a professor and author is with literature he wrote back that he was 'appalled': and all those who have to do with Swinburne will share this sentiment of dismay.

I have not even yet indicated the worst with regard to Gosse: he did his best to secure the destruction of work of the poet in at least two cases (and therefore possibly or rather probably in other cases of which there is no sort of record). First, there were certain sonnets which he implored Wise to destroy completely.[2] Were they so Rabelaisian or bawdy or

---

(Note [1] continued)—

1902 (*à propos* of Wise's bibliographical attribution) that Swinburne 'repudiated' the verses in question. This repudiation he had then with high-handed and impudent disdain dismissed as nonsense: of course he knew better than Swinburne himself whether Swinburne had or had not written verses which he, Gosse, had taken it into his head to ascribe to Swinburne. Mr. Partington, it need hardly be said, gives no inkling of this devastating fact, which is easily accessible (nor has it been recorded by anybody else)—I suggest nothing more of course than that Mr. Partington's scholarship is less extensive than is required for the handling of *le cas Gosse*, especially by anyone rash enough to appear as counsel for the defence.

[1] It is a matter of urgent importance that all these works should be reissued in their integrity, purged of the distorting errors introduced into them by this couple of miscreants. I have, in the intervals of other tasks, re-established the text of many of them (including not a few of the letters), and I shall bring them out on future occasions, and also the *inédits* which, because of prudishness or critical debility, Gosse and Wise thought should be withheld from publication. (Even those of them which are not of superlative value intrinsically are at least interesting as materials for the intellectual and aesthetic biography of the poet in various stages of his career.) These partial publications will be contributory to a larger design: that of issuing a corpus of all the writings of Swinburne (including the letters) that were not printed during his lifetime.

[2] Whether Wise complied there is no decisive evidence to show; there are extant unpublished sonnets which *may* be those in question; but they equally may not be; an uncomfortable uncertainty will always remain on this point. Wise, sometimes at least in the matter of cataloguing, did not give way to Gosse's suppressive or destructive

risqué or blasphemous or otherwise shocking that they were
calculated to bring a deep blush to the cheeks of maidens and
curates and people such as Gosse? Was their subject-matter
certain unmentionable relations (quite fictitious of course) in
a coach or elsewhere between Queen Victoria and Wordsworth or Lord John Russell? (Swinburne in his *Sturm und
Drang* years did write a drama in French on this topic which
Rossetti and other of his highly gifted friends found vastly
amusing.[1]) No, there was nothing in the least naughty about

(*Note* [3] *continued*)—

demands: there are cases in which he persisted in making mention of
work which the latter was anxious should not come to the knowledge
of the world. It was a quality of his felonious defects that he was less
strait-laced than his partner in disastrous wardenship over Swinburne's
affairs. Here, Wise really helped to protect the poet against Gosse's
subversive designs.

[1] W. M. Rossetti, writing to Watts-Dunton a few months after the
poet's death, asked if he had 'found any trace of a very amusing performance by Swinburne, earlier than the Cheyne Walk days; a drama
in French called *La Sœur de la Reine*. It is a rollicking skit, over some
detached pages of which we used to laugh hugely, purporting to deal
with the early life of Queen Victoria. Lord John Russell, of all men
in the world, figures as her ardent and I fear overmuch favoured
lover.' Wise, in one of his bibliographical passages, affirms that 'no
trace remains' of this piece. 'Watts-Dunton', he says, 'informed me that
it was "shockingly improper", and had long since been destroyed.' But
Wise, as so almost incredibly often elsewhere, is wrong here: some
trace, and more than a trace, does remain of this drama (originally
conceived as a 'tale', as is recorded in an unpublished letter in the
course of which Swinburne gives an outline of the plot). There is
extant a dialogue in French between Queen Victoria and Lord John
Russell which is evidently a part of it. (Here the sovereign defends
herself against the complaint of Lord John Russell, her *amant en pied*,
that the position he now occupies in this capacity was once held by the
poet Wordsworth.) This is a typescript copy acquired by the owner
from Wise: and so Wise apparently knew more than he indicated of
the piece, and it is even more than probable that he lied when—as
late as 1925—he declared that no trace of it remained; he presumably
had once possessed the manuscript of the copy he sold—in accordance
with a dodge of his for further increasing his revenue by the sale of

them; nothing that could offend a churchwarden or the most fanatical devotee of the royal house. They were purely and simply political verses; verses on Continental politics in the late eighties; and Gosse did not happen to like the political opinions conveyed in them. So he begged Wise to destroy them completely . . . Gosse was guilty of many high-handed actions, many enormities, with regard to Swinburne, but this would take a lot of beating. Of course it is—or should be— elementary, axiomatic, that *no* work left by a writer, and especially a great writer, should be destroyed by anybody, and least of all by a person who is infinitely below him·

In the second case also there was no question of offence against taste or morals. Gosse urged Wise to destroy a piece of fiction by the poet. He found it flat, dull, feeble, childish,

---

(*Note* ⁴ *continued*)—
transcripts of manuscripts he had sold to other buyers. (And all of these typescript copies which I have seen are—like the verses and prose posthumously published by him and Gosse—very unreliable: the number of errors in them is remarkable—and disturbing, when one thinks that they will probably be reproduced, propagated and perpetuated in theses and books where these texts are cited as if they were genuine.) These latter details of hitherto unrecognised procedures (Messrs. Carter and Pollard and Mr. Partington have revealed only a part of the seamy side of Wise's history) I give here as a further indication of the quality of the grasping rascal who (conjoined with Gosse) had for all too long practically absolute power over Swinburne's unpublished writings.

La Sœur de la Reine, by the way, is not to be confused with *La Fille du Policeman*, a prose story in which Queen Victoria also figures with attributes and propensities and in rôles that have no place in strict history. The manscript of this story or novel (of which, as Swinburne himself said in an unpublished letter, the 'mildest ingredients' are 'rape, perjury, murder, opium, suicide, treason, Jesuitry') is extant, or at least most of it is (one whole chapter of it is among the Swinburne manuscripts which are in my possession). Swinburne of course wrote these two pieces in a spirit of ribald (but never obscene) fun. Obscenity—in the sense of mere smuttiness or sniggering indecency— is not to be found anywhere in his works, published or unpublished: which is not to say that they are not in them things which by the standards of prim and proper orthodoxy are most horribly shocking.

and even unintelligible; it ended even before it had got going; it was not representative of Swinburne; it was a tentative in a line for which the poet had no aptitude; he must have just been reading Poe for the first time: this story was a direct imitation of *The Mystery of Marie Roget*; altogether, it was without any value whatsoever, and therefore Wise should consign it to the flames. Even if all these arguments were right, the plea for destruction is nothing less than monstrous. But all the arguments are wrong, and so the monstrousness has a comic quality. So far from being flat, dull, etc., the narrative is to a large degree the reverse; it is a competently constructed opening of a story of detection, or rather of a story in which detection will follow; with skilful adequacy it introduces the main characters and presents a series of facts which form a crescendo of mystery; and it successfully does its main business in arousing the curiosity of the reader. But it is unfinished, and the curiosity receives no satisfaction. In short it might with no great impropriety be called a sort of *Edwin Drood* on the scale of the *nouvelle*. That Gosse should make the absurd charge that it ends before it begins and should even find it unintelligible as it stands is not surprising: he did not have enough wit to see that it is a mere first part of a mystery-story of which the resolving sequence is missing (whether it is lost or was never written is a matter on which I have no information). As for its being non-Swinburnian, here again the contrary is true; in felicity and telling economy of phrase particularly, and in highly effective strokes of portraiture (very summary here of course) it is as characteristic of Swinburne as anything in his more realistic fiction; in these qualities he holds of himself alone; if there is any influence in other respects, it is almost exclusively that of Balzac —the Balzac of *La Maison Nucingen* and other works treating the sordid and fierce 'combat compliqué' of interests pursuing money; certainly there is no sign of imitation of Poe (whom Swinburne more than probably had read for the first time long before): there is nothing here of the cheap meretriciousness and the tawdry romanticism of the American, nor of any of the other qualities by which he scored facile success. So much for Gosse's critical faculty and his intellectual capacity in general: his pronouncements on this unfinished story are typical and serve to give his true measure. His attempt to secure destruction here is perhaps even more serious, more outrageous, than in the case of the sonnets. For here he wished to do away with work, not because of anything (even political) in its contents, but solely for aesthetic reasons: his impercipience (and insipience) impudently declared valueless competent work by a man immeasurably his superior as an artist (he himself wasn't one at all), and simply on that ground he sought to have it annihilated.[1]

All these things I call criminal. I am indifferent to the thesis of an American lady that Gosse was to some extent implicated in Wise's activities as a forger: for me he is criminal enough independently of that charge (which at first sight I am not inclined to take seriously).[2]

[1] Wise had enough sense to resist the dullard's brutish demand, and fortunately the piece may still be seen.

[2] The lady in question—Miss F. Ratchford—has recently had communicated to me through a common friend in America the latest stage of her indagations into these very entertaining mysteries. Those acquainted with previous chapters of this tale of detection may be interested in the following extract from the communiqué with which I have been favoured:

'. . . I have definite documentary proof that Forman had a part in manufacturing the forged Tennyson's *Last Tournament*, 1871, . . . and that Gosse certainly had criminal knowledge of *Sonnets*, 1847, both before and after he sponsored it. It is more than probable that he knew or guessed the whole scheme, and again it is certain that he occasionally lent his aid in authenticating the forgeries. A.W. Pollard by his own statement, knew in 1910 the nature of more than a dozen of the forgeries in the British Museum, and yet he had them catalogued as honest books, a recommendation Wise made good use of . . . None of Gosse's defenders has faced the evidence fairly—very few of them have even seen it. I wish I might talk the question through with someone who in full knowledge believes him innocent, but who yet is open-minded enough to consider and analyse the evidence fully. I do not want to convince him, but I do want to know how he interprets facts which to my mind are conclusive.'

In view of these and other facts I make no apology for the acerb terms in which I refer to him and Wise in the course of my Commentary. My language will doubtless give offence in certain quarters, but I claim that it is never in excess of the occasion.

These remarks about Gosse and Wise are somewhat parenthetical within the section beginning 'At long last', but they are not irrelevant: such were the two persons in whose sole keeping *Lesbia Brandon* and its fate lay for many years.

They decided that it should not be given to the world; nay more, as late as the Bonchurch edition of the *Life* (1927), Gosse announced that 'it ought *never* to be published' (my italics), in the opinion of himself and the distinguished felon with whom for a long time past he had been on terms that were almost fraternal. (They were as thick as two thieves, as Miss Ratchford might say, giving a more than figurative sense to that homely expression. I of course intend here no more than the figurative sense as far as Gosse is concerned.) One can be pretty certain that Gosse was the main if not the sole author of this very impertinent decision, contrary to the express wish and intention of Swinburne while he was engaged upon the work.[1]

---

[1] Wise, as I have indicated, had not Gosse's old-maidish scruples. There is a comical wobbling in his opinion as to the worth of *Lesbia Brandon* (reflecting no doubt a certain ill-ease on his part under pressure of Gosse's insistence that the work was too immoral to be published in any sort of edition). Thus, in *A Bibliography of the writings in prose and verse of Algernon Charles Swinburne*, 1919, he speaks of it in the following terms:

'The story is unquestionably autobiographical, and the hero is a distorted image of the youthful Algernon'. ['Distorted' may be tersely described as bosh. For the opposite true view see, in my Commentary, the account of Herbert Seyton as a very faithful portrait of Swinburne.] 'As such it is of interest. But the whole thing is morbid and unwholesome, and no regret need be felt that Swinburne failed to continue and complete the work.'

This judgment is omitted altogether in *A Swinburne Library* (1925). In the *Bonchurch Bibliography* (1927), however, it is reproduced with-

Readers of to-day will wonder at this decision; will be surprised that Gosse should have sought to prevent from coming into its own a work of much great beauty and of interest otherwise, by interdicting it to, among others, those qualified to appreciate it and therefore entitled to have knowledge of it. (One shudders to think what, had the Gosses of the world had their way, would have happened to a good deal not only of Aristophanes, Catullus, Juvenal, Martial and Rabelais, but even of Plato and Shakespeare and many other writers of classic rank studied by the young of both sexes at the most respectable seats of learning and not kept by ecclesiastics of an enquiring turn of mind in secret nooks of their libraries.) It is true that Swinburne himself spoke of it (in a letter to Sir Richard Burton) as being 'more offensive and objectionable to Britannia than anything I have yet done', and thereby indicated that there was much in it to shock respectability. But the sensational effect he anticipated is hardly possible to-day: it is too late: after D. H. Lawrence's *Lady Chatterley's Lover,* Joyce's *Ulysses,* and other freely circulated and well-nigh universally tolerated ventures in parrhesiastic pornography, *Lesbia Brandon* must seem harmless to Britannia.

But, in this matter of subject and handling, Swinburne did, in *Lesbia Brandon,* make a considerable advance for the time (and, indeed, so far as English literature is concerned, for the whole of the rest of the nineteenth century and the first three lustra of the twentieth. Thomas Hardy, for

(*Note* [1] *continued*)—
out change up to the words 'of interest'; but in the last sentence we find piquant modifications. The work has now become only 'to a certain degree' 'unwholesome', and '*no* regret *need* be felt that' etc. gives way to '*some* regret *must* be felt that' etc.! Such self-stultification makes Wise a competitor for the prize which Latourcade holds for achievement in this field. He no doubt slipped in these alterations without saying anything about them to Gosse, who was very slack in supervision or any of the primary obligations of scholarship that is better than bogus.

example, who is regarded as a rebel against orthodoxy, is spinsterish compared with Swinburne in his treatment of anything in the sexual line). The attitude of the Victorian Britannia in this connextion is well indicated by Thackeray's protest against it in the preface of *Pendennis*:

'Even the gentlemen of our age . . . , even these we cannot show as they are. Since the author of *Tom Jones* was buried, no writer of fiction among us has been permitted to depict to his utmost power a MAN. We must drape him, and give him a certain conventional simper. Society will not tolerate the Natural in our Art. Many ladies have remonstrated and subscribers left me, because, in the course of the story, I described a young man resisting and affected by temptation.'

That Thackeray, who adapted himself easily to conventions, and was indeed a very conventional person (he found 'an impure presence' in every page of Sterne), should have written these almost despairing words may be regarded as significant. He spoke thus some fourteen years before Swinburne began *Lesbia Brandon*. But the monstrous thing he denounced was still sovereign after this interval, and it continued to be for long years to come. In 1864, the probable date of the earliest part of Swinburne's novel, Thackeray's melancholy observation was repeated by Meredith in *Sandra Belloni*: hitting at what he called 'the Tribunal of the Nice Feelings', he asked 'Is sentimentalism in our modern days taking the place of monasticism to mortify our poor humanity?'; and, passing from the general to the particular, 'In another age, the scenes between Mrs. Lupin and Mrs. Chump, greatly significant for humanity as they are, will be given without offence on one side or martyrdom on the other. At present . . . it would be profitless to depict them.' (It was the prospect of the 'martyrdom' spoken of by Meredith that led Swinburne to take up the challenging attitude expressed in his letter to Burton.) But Meredith's protest had no more effect than Thackeray's. Seven years later an arch-fool called

William Forsyth, a barrister who had taken silk, perpetrated a book on *Novels and Novelists of the Nineteenth Century* (which is worth reading because its absurdity is really funny) and in it he drivelled as follows on the subject of *Tom Jones*:

> 'The truth is, that it would be impossible to give an analysis of the novel, or even describe the plot except in the most meagre terms, without offending against the respect due to female delicacy now.'

Later still, R. L. Stevenson, who in his inner moral nature was a barbarically rigid Pict, as prudish as Gosse himself (with whom he got on famously), wrote that the same masterpiece was not only 'dull and false', but also 'dirty', a pronouncement which the asinine Forsyth would have signed with pleasure. Things aren't any better by 1890; in that year Hardy put forth once again, in terms more cogent because more reasoned, the demur made by Thackeray in the middle of the century:

> 'Life being a physiological fact, its honest portrayal must be largely concerned with, for one thing, the relations of the sexes, and the substitution for such catastrophes as favour the false colouring best expressed by the regulation finish that "they married and were happy every after", of catastrophes based upon sexual relationship as it is. To this expansion English society opposes a well-nigh insuperable bar.'

But there was still no lifting of the bar, and no notable superation of it, for a good while yet. Some twenty years after Hardy's plea for sense as against muddled obscurantism, H. G. Wells found it necessary to make a strenuous declaration of revolt and independence and brave enterprise over the whole of human life:

> 'If I may presume to speak for other novelists, I would say it is not so much a demand we make as an intention we proclaim. We are going to write, subject only to our limita-

tions, about the whole of human life . . . We cannot present people unless we have this free hand, this unrestricted field. What is the good of telling stories about people's lives if one may not deal freely with the religious beliefs and organisations that have controlled or failed to control them? What is the good of pretending to write about love, and the loyalties and treacheries and quarrels of men and women, if one must not glance at those varieties of physical temperament and organic quality, those deeply passionate needs and distresses from which half the storms of human life are brewed? We mean to deal with all these things, and it will need very much more than the disapproval of provincial librarians, the hostility of a few influential people in London, the scurrility of one paper, and the deep and obstinate silences of another, to stop the incoming tide of aggressive novel-writing. We are going to write about it all.'

All that is excellent, and so are all the other protests, which, like the counter-samples of stupidity, are typical, and sufficiently indicate the power of the suppressive curse which affected English letters for well over a century. But Swinburne, in *Lesbia Brandon*, some fifty years before Wells made his Grand Remonstrance, had already kicked over the traces and assumed the liberties demanded by the author of *Ann Veronica*. He had well initiated 'aggressive novel-writing'; he had done more than 'glance at' 'those varieties of physical temperament and organic quality, those deeply passionate needs and distresses from which half the storms of human life are brewed'. Precisely because he had done so Gosse, at a date later than all these protests, decided that *Lesbia Brandon* should *never* be allowed to reach the printer.

The work is not complete (chiefly owing to the machinations of Watts-Dunton, as I have explained in my Commentary). But Swinburne finished the greater part of it, and enough for the main lines of the story to be apparent. Because, however, of its incompleteness, there are certain knotty problems connected with the story or plot (discussed in my Commentary) of which I can offer no more than very tentative solutions. Some of them, indeed, I would call insoluble. Those who like working at such things will find them as fascinating as the mystery of *Edwin Drood*. And thus a defect will turn out to be an attraction.

But even if the work were less complete and (viewed as a whole) less incomposite than it is, and offered no adventitious interest in the way of mystery, it would still demand publication. For its parts—or most of them—are of high excellence and importance independently of their function in the general structure of the story.[1] It contains a number of passages of poetic beauty unequalled in the English novel and unsurpassed in works of any kind. It contains scenes and even whole chapters remarkable for power or delicacy of a novelistic as distinct from a purely poetic sort. It is rich in psychological insight and subtlety, and it deals successfully with types of character or temperament that had never been handled in the novel before. And in the case of one of the personages, who is very largely autobiographical, it provides much information on Swinburne himself, new matter for the veridic *Life* which is so sadly needed.

On several counts, then, whatever its shortcomings as an unfinished whole, it is imperative that it should appear. If

---

[1] What Saintsbury says of Flaubert's novels applies equally to *Lesbia Brandon* (with deduction necessitated by the incomplete state of the latter): 'One takes up Flaubert and reads a chapter, or two or three, with hardly any reference to the already familiar story. His separate tableaux are . . . admirably and irreproachably combined. But their individual merit is so great that they possess interest independently of the combination. He is a writer upon whom one can try experiments with one's different moods, very much as one can try experiments with different lights upon a picture . . . His cabinets have secret drawers in them which are only discoverable after long familiarity . . . All this is so rarely characteristic of a novelist that it has, perhaps, seemed to some people incompatible with the novelist's qualities—a paralogism excusable enough in the mere subscriber to the circulating library, but certainly not excusable in the critic.'

Gosse had any percipience of these facts, all the greater was his crime in seeking to have the book suppressed; if, as is much more probable, he was impervious to them, he stands out all the more as a dullard who ought to have kept away from literature. The dilemma is ineluctable, and nothing that Gosse's dupes or fellow-fools can do will make it otherwise.

It may not be over-egoistic of me to say that the preparation of *Lesbia Brandon* for publication, and in especial the primary business of establishing the text, has been an immense labour. I don't suppose any editor of a Latin or Greek work has had a more formidable task. This is chiefly due to the almost incredible incompetence of Wise. With the exception of one chapter, and a few (still untraced) pages of another, he acquired the whole of the extant manuscript, arranged it in what he thought was the due order, and then had it indiscerptibly bound in a sumptuous cover as though it were definitive beyond any question. But his order is very largely a chaos. Not only are several chapters wrongly placed, but a large number of the pages of one chapter are intermixed with a large number of another, so that the resulting compost is a wild confusion that gives an impression of something like lunacy. The restoration of order here was not always helped by Swinburne's handwriting, which frequently comes very near to being indecipherable. Then Wise included two chapters which raised insoluble problems, and which I always felt could not belong to the work; it was only towards the end of my labours that the fortunate discovery of a series of jottings on an uncatalogued scrap of paper in the British Museum confirmed that my suspicions here were right. And so on: I have given a full account of these matters in the last section of my Commentary.

Apart from certain chapters obstinately withheld by Watts-Dunton, Swinburne had the whole of the unfinished work set up in type, in the form of galley-proofs, towards the end of 1877. More than one set was printed; a number of these are extant, in varying degrees of completeness, and I have seen most of them.[1] But inspection of them has not been of great help in clearing up the mess left by Wise. For they too are to a large extent chaotic. (Swinburne himself complained that 'the whole' was 'most carelessly arranged'.) For instance, one chapter is split up into three parts, and these, separated from one another, are printed among others chapters in the order 2nd, 3rd and 1st. (To make things worse, this is one of the two afore-mentioned chapters of which Wise with characteristic hebetude, intermixed sheets in his arrangement of the manuscript—acclaimed as a masterly achievement, a monument of 'infinite patience' by Lafourcade, for whom the bungling forger was a man of very superior parts.) There are also in the galleys verbal and punctuative errors, but this is a very small affair compared with the muddled state of the chapters.

In spite of all difficulties, however, I think I can guarantee the text here published as correct from every point of view.

I have referred to a few extant sheets which I have not been able to trace. They contain the end of the first and the beginning of the second chapter, and are probably not more than the 'one or two' sheets mentioned by Lafourcade in his *La Jeunesse de Swinburne* (1928) as being in the possession of Mr. de V. Payen-Payne (who died a few years ago). I call them 'extant' because, if they existed as late as 1928, it is practically certain that they do so to-day. But in spite of a great deal of trouble—investigations in numerous quarters, and advertising here and in America—I have so far not been able to locate them, and unfortunately the work has to go to press to this small extent more incomplete than it is owing to circumstances in the past which are altogether beyond remedy. For it is more than probable that nothing else is missing except what was not written by Swinburne; there is no reason at all to believe that of what he did write of

---

[1] And concerning the few of them I have not been able to see I have secured all the information I want.

the work anything is lacking save these very few pages.[1]

The failure to trace them is an illustration of one of the most serious difficulties with which scholars occupied with English (not to mention other modern) authors have to contend: in many cases it is impossible to know what has become of manuscripts. A properly enlightened government (a desideratum not likely to be realised in the present age or aeon) would forbid the passage from the country of any manuscript of at least authors of a certain degree of importance; and would make compulsory the registration of the whereabouts of any such document into whose-ever hands it passed.

In the search for these sheets, however, I unexpectedly learned of the existence of a whole chapter which I thought had been lost for good; for there is no record of its survival in any of the catalogues of Wise, who would have been anxious to secure it had he known of its availability, and Lafourcade thought it had passed out of existence. This is 'Another Portrait' (ch. X); an enquiry I addressed to the Huntington Library, San Marino, California, as to whether

---

[1] A few other parts of the manuscript are still missing; but the contents of these are provided by the galley-proofs; this is the only matter in which the latter have been of any substantial use. It should be mentioned, however, that several of them contain, in Swinburne's handwriting, not only corrections of printers' errors, but also modifications of the text of the manuscript. I have regarded these as superseding the parts of the manuscript concerned, and they are all incorporated in the text as given here. That text, therefore, is derived from a variety of sources:

I. The British Museum manuscript redeemed from the chaos in which it was left (in a bound volume) by Wise (which chaos was found not only acceptable and unquestionable by the servilely uncritical Lafourcade, but also admirable—a masterpiece of reconstruction achieved by the patience, sagacity and finesse of the almost angelic Wise);

II. a portion of the manuscript in Amercia;

III. revisions of the original MS. text contained in a number of galleys now in different hands. (For information on all these points see the last section of my Commentary.) As thus established, the text is my own property.

it possessed the missing sheets in question, elicited a reply in the negative, but that this chapter was in its possession. I am much obliged to the authorities of this library, who kindly sent me a photostatic copy of it, and also permission to reproduce it.[1]

I must also here record my great obligation to Mr. J. S. Mayfield of Washington, D.C., who has gone to considerable trouble to assist me in my search for missing parts of the manuscript. He circularised all American University and public libraries which I had not approached myself; and also private libraries, and even private collectors of whose existence I could not have known. That the quest has been in vain does not lessen my very lively gratitude. Mr. Mayfield also sent me a complete photostatic copy of his set of the galley-proofs, and also of letters which in various ways were useful to me. I am also much obliged to Mr. A. Whitworth, sub-Librarian of the Brotherton Library, University of Leeds, who was very helpful in sending me much detailed information concerning the galley-proofs in that library, thus supplementing the knowledge of them I acquired on a visit to Leeds not long before the War. I also have to thank Mr. C. A. Elliott, Provost of Eton College, and Mr. C. A. Gladstone, late housemaster of that school, for giving me (for my Notes) explanations of various Etonian terms (some of them now obsolete) which Swinburne employs in *Lesbia Brandon*. I can no longer thank the late Mr. L. S. R. Byrne, for many years a master at the school, and an authority on bygone Eton, for useful information in the same connexion.

Lesbia Brandon is really part, and the largest part, of a novelistic cycle; one of several moves, under pressure of a long-continued obsessive urge, towards a grand work of fiction (or 'creative history', as he preferred to call it) which the

---

[1] There is no doubt as to its being genuine; I say this because forgery of Swinburne manuscripts is a new addition to the industrial life of America. I have seen two samples of this enterprise (one of which had taken in an American University): both were palpable forgeries to anyone who was really competent in Swinburne.

author, for various reasons—the chief of which I have indicated in my Commentary—never achieved in what may be called its potential fulness. The earlier *Love's Cross Currents* is another stage in this enterprise; and yet another is the much later tragedy *The Sisters*, which is a novel in verse. Besides these, there are two unpublished fragments, one anterior to *Love's Cross Currents*, and the other to *Lesbia Brandon*, which are tentatives towards these latter works; I have therefore given them in an appendix immediately following the text of *Lesbia Brandon*. Thus this volume contains all Swinburne's hitherto unpublished work that belongs to the cycle in question, and it is principally by what he accomplished in this cycle that his position as a novelist will be determined.

I have frequently referred to my Commentary in what precedes, and I now pass by way of conclusion to a brief apologia of it.

Wise's outrageous bungling of the text and my re-ordering of it, and the sources of it—(that is, the manuscript in its different lots, and the galley-proofs)—all these matters require discussion. Moreover, the only available 'history of *Lesbia Brandon*', as Wise calls it, is that given by Wise himself in his bibliographies, supplemented by Lafourcade (in his huge thesis *La Jeunesse de Swinburne*), who for the most part does no more than follow Wise. But practically every item of this 'history' as given by Wise (and Lafourcade) is altogether wrong.[1] It was necessary therefore to provide the true history. Then the only critical study of the book is Lafourcade's, which, apart from a few inept remarks by Wise, is the sole source of any idea of *Lesbia Brandon* which may be possessed by the world.[2]

---

[1] And when I have had occasion to test Wise elsewhere I have generally found that he is very largely wrong. It is such things as this, and not undetected forgeries, which furnish the gravest charge against the eminent gentlemen who, in the form of prefaces to the volumes of the Ashley Catalogue, gave fulsome testimonials to his competence in the province where they are supposed to be experts.

[2] Scrappy references to the work by other writers may be ignored in this connexion.

But Lafourcade's study is very incomplete, and there is a large amount of error in it, mostly of the Boetian type of which throughout his thesis (and elsewhere) there is a plenitude to what must be a record extent. (*Le grand chancelier de la bêtise*—this is how one thinks of him in his own language as one meets blunder after absurd blunder in his gargantuan tome, which still wins obeisant esteem from critics who have not the equipment to judge it.) A redressive examination and appraisal of the work was therefore necessary. Finally, there is no adequate study—one may say that there is none at all—of Swinburne as a novelist in general; as such he is simply ignored by Saintsbury, Baker, and other so-called historians of the novel. Hence the necessity for still further redressive work.

In other words, for several reasons, *Lesbia Brandon* must be accompanied by a commentary.

I have written one in three sections according to the following plan:

1. A history of what may be called the external facts of *Lesbia Brandon*; and in particular of the tactics of Watts-Dunton which thwarted its progress and completion and finally diverted Swinburne from his career as a novelist.

2. The story. An account of the cycle: the two fragments, *Love's Cross Currents* and *Lesbia Brandon* itself. I have not hesitated to examine *Love's Cross Currents* at some length, although it is not an unpublished work; for it may be regarded as practically unknown (it is not so much as mentioned in any standard history of the novel); Lafourcade, it is true, gives an account of it, but it is far from satisfactory; (and in any case, Lafourcade's main and only really important work on Swinburne is in French, and is not easy to obtain, so that the general run of readers will have no acquaintance with it). Moreover, *Love's Cross Currents* is Swinburne's only complete novel in prose, and therefore may fairly be taken as a measure of his capacity in this line when he was subject to no frustration; furthermore, in its structure it is regular or canonical, is successful as such, and thus disposes of any fancy

C   XXV

that the author of *Lesbia Brandon* was incapable of writing a novel in the proper or strictest sense of the word: presentation of it is therefore indispensable as a preliminary to anything one has to say about *Lesbia Brandon*. It will be gathered that I rate *Love's Cross Currents* high; I regard it as a *chef-d'œuvre méconnu*; moreover, taking *Lesbia Brandon* into account as well, I place Swinburne very high as a novelist. Much of this section of the Commentary is devoted to the substantiation of this estimate, which will doubtless (at first if not at final sight) evoke surprise and even worse things. But I do not anticipate any really serious refutation.

In the course of this section I have had to examine the criteria by which novelistic work is generally judged, and this has involved going somewhat into the philosophy of the subject—and philosophy here as elsewhere means no more than an endeavour to get down to what is really fundamental. (A thoroughgoing work on the aesthetic of the novel is very much needed; English histories of or treatises on the novel are far from fulfilling this need; at the best, they are concerned mostly with comparatively external questions of technique, and rarely if ever touch on matters that lie at the heart of the subject. There is, of course, in English, especially in essays by philosophically-minded practitioners of the novel, some approach to these matters, but it is tantalizingly sporadic, and always leaves one with a feeling that the promised and interglimpsed land still remains in the distance. German attempts are usually too much within the limits of an *a priori* system, which often is not primarily aesthetic in its scope. Things are better in France, but here too the desideratum will be looked for in vain.[1] Until there is some such work, in

---

[1] Take for instance the, on the whole, very interesting *Problèmes du Roman* (*Confluences*, 1943), a collection of over sixty essays by over fifty writers. It is not often that there is even an approach here to problems that are fundamental. Again, Léon Bopp's *Equisse d'un Traité du Roman* (N.R.F., 1935) looks imposing, but it is schoolmasterly, external, superficial and naïve, being little more than a series of labels, a repertory of classifications, so dreary that one cannot get

which there will be disengaged certain *principia* in such a way that they will be pretty sure of being accepted by open-minded intelligence, criticism of novelistic fiction will hardly ever be firmly based, will always tend to be capricious and aleatory, and a book like *Lesbia Brandon* will be in danger of being dismissed as faulty by the test of criteria which are not properly applicable to it.²) I venture to claim that I have at least shown that the most generally accepted canon of the novel, that formulated by Stevenson, Hardy and Arnold Bennett, for instance, and by the most influenital French critics, and regarded by them as the one and only ideal, a supreme form after which all good novelistic work must aspire, has not universal validity, and is not the only nor necessarily the highest norm for the evalution of success. I have even suggested that there is something of error in it; that in large part it arises from conditions peculiar to another art, and has been illegitimately (in so far as necessity and primacy

(*Note* ¹ *continued*)—
through them. M. Mauriac's *Le Romancier et ses personnages* is much nearer the real thing; and various essays and longer studies by Thibaudet are nearer still : they are perhaps—and more than perhaps— the best work in this line that has been produced in France and even in the modern world as a whole. It is a great pity that Thibaudet never wrote the *Métaphysique du Roman* towards which his genius moved at times. It would have supplied the desideratum to a very satisfying degree : but 'tout cela est si facile en rêve!' he exclaimed when he gave up the project for ever.

² A typical illustration of erroneous appraisal consequent on a wrong or at least very highly questionable assumption of what a novel should be is Bourget's rating of Flaubert's *L'Education sentimentale* as inferior in rank to *La Princesse de Clèves, François le Champi,* and *Eugénie Grandet*; because, in respect of structure, it does not satisfy the quasi-official canon as do these last three novels. But *L'Education,* viewed apart from any preconceived theory, is immensely greater than *La Princesse de Clèves* and *François do Champi,* and has vastly more beauty, and certainly no less power, than the other member of the trio. Bourget was one of the acutest and subtlest critics of modern times : which makes this example all the more telling and monitory. He would assuredly have shaken his head over *Lesbia Brandon,* and given it a place well below such supreme things as *La Princesse de Clèves.*

are claimed for it) transferred to the novel, which of its specific nature is not subject to those conditions.

Swinburne had the originality of genius, and in the ultimate, whatever his obligations to influences, his work was the projection of his unique personality, a creation resulting from powers which were in himself alone. But there were obligations to influences ('Le grand homme n'est jamais aérolithe', as Baudelaire observed); and in this section I have sought to get at the sources of certain of the themes of *Lesbia Brandon* and also of certain elements of technique. Most of these sources are French; and here I introduce English readers to work—such as that of Latouche—which is practically unknown in this country; and even in the case of Balzac it is to be feared that the writings to which I call attention are not very well known.

And in this section I deal (but only briefly, for reasons which I shall explain presently) with a side of Swinburne's nature and life which would come under the rubric of *Abnormal psychology*; but I have shown that it is not nearly so abnormal as is commonly supposed; and here I have advanced considerations, points of view, facts for which novelty may be claimed.

If there is any part of the Commentary by which I am inclined to set particular store myself it is this second section.

3. The text. An account of the manuscript and the attendant problems; an account of the galley-proofs; the sequence of chapters as determined by me.

The general reader will no doubt not bother about this last section; but scholars will expect it in the case of a new book of this sort of which the sources of the text present a large number of problems; and it is essential in order to justify my own arrangement of the text, which differs considerably from that of Wise, and also from that of the galley-proofs, which are the only ones that have been in existence so far.

It was my intention originally to include a section on what some would call the pathological side of the work; but, if this were to be done at all adequately, there was so much to be said that I finally decided to reserve it for treatment in a separate book that will appear at no distant date. This supplementary volume, entitled *Swinburne: the Arcane Side*, will be mainly occupied in a general way (but also with a good deal of particularity) with the poet's sentimental and erotic life, will bring forward much new matter, and will incidentally explode various legends that have long had currency as unquestionable gospel, and do execution upon certain numskulls or cads, not all of whom have yet passed to Hades. But I have touched very summarily on these 'pathological' matters in parts of the second section of my Commentary and also here and there in the Notes. My views on these questions differ pretty well totally from any that have hitherto been advanced; and in particular from those of Lafourcade, which are almost official at present. I have restated, again very briefly, the definition of Swinburne's masochism I gave in a passage of *Lucretia Borgia*; it has remained unique, and I make bold to think that it is the only one that is really consonant with the facts. I repudiate (with supporting evidence) the theory that Swinburne was in any true sense of the word a sadist, and that he was sterile in any way at all.

In addition to the Commentary, I have added a further section of explanatory notes, which may be welcome to the general reader. There are many things in the text which call for elucidation, some of which even literary and other specialists would find it hard to explicate. Take, for instance, the first page: who is the 'greatest analyst' not only 'of flesh' but also 'of spirit' 'that ever lived'? Swinburne does not name him; he gives a clue in the mention of 'his Georgian girl', but who is this personage?

Certain of the Notes are not so much elucidations as excursuses conveying on matters in the text information which would not conveniently go into the Commentary. Such are those on Swinburne's French, on his masochism, and on his remarkable anticipations of the erotic dream-symbolism of

Freud and Jung. These excursuses contain a good deal of new material that may be viewed as strays or fragments of an intellectual and other biography of him which as yet is for the most part potential.

Furthermore, I have given in the Notes parallel or other illustrative passages, sometimes from Swinburne's published works, but mostly from unpublished ones (and chiefly those which Gosse would have suppressed or destroyed if he could have had his own way). Thus in the Notes, as well as in have had his own way). Thus in the Notes, as well as in *Lesbia Brandon* and the appendices, there is a fair amount of Swinburne that the world has never seen. Finally, I have decided to give in the course of the Notes the more interesting of the cancelled passages of the text of *Lesbia Brandon* and the two fragments. Some of these are passages that Swinburne would have liked to publish, but which even he thought too bold for the time; others throw light on the text; others are interesting as showing his approach to certain aesthetic effects.

I would say a little more in justification of the tone of various passages in the Commentary and Notes.[1] This is a

---

[1] I have, after completing my work, and while it is in the press, made this tone still sharper in certain places after reading Mr. Hare's *Swinburne, a Biographical Approach*, which appeared too late for me to notice it while my work was in progress. But I have added a p.s. rapid criticism of it in an excursus that follows the first section of my Commentary. In this excursus I have not only taken stock of what Mr. Hare has to say about *Lesbia Brandon*, but, at the risk of being unduly digressive, have gone on to examine the more inportant of his charges against Swinburne. In doing so I have (in terms that will no doubt upset the literary genteel) done on a small scale what I shall do at much greater length and more decisively in the *Life* towards which I am working: I have smashed the most serious items of the idious legend, the creation of malice, ignorance and stupidity, of which Swinburne has been a victim for a very long time, and is so more than ever to-day owing to the undisturbed credit enjoyed well-nigh universally by this work of Mr. Hare's. This extension of the excursus is not so very digressive, seeing that my own work in the present volume is largely devoted to clearing away misconceptions regarding Swinburne and to establishing him as he really was.

fighting book, a book of challenge, as any effective work on Swinburne would have had to be for a long time past, and must be more than ever in an age that takes the American Mr. Ezra Pound and the American Mr. T. S. Eliot seriously— and how seriously!—as literary artists, and hails them as masters of the Word.[1] (The bigger values for which Swin-

[1]As possible readers of a future generation may be hazy on the subject of Mr. Pound, it may be well to give the following information, which sums him up *in parvo*. He joined the enemies of his country in World War II, and, with his usual vulgar cacophony, busily exercised on their behalf what we may politely call his abilities. Duly captured after the collapse of Italy, he was not duly tried and condemned to death. Instead, he allowed (if a word signifying mere acquiescence is the right one) himself to be tried by another jury, and to be found insane. This verdict, in the words of *The Times*, saved him 'from standing his trial on charges of treason'. Either, then, the fellow is an imbecile or (ignoring the 'or/and' possibility) the most craven of cowards. In this latter case Dr. Johnson's dictum that patriotism is 'the last refuge of' a certain class of individuals stands in need of revision. (I would not condemn or in any other way blame a man for renouncing his nationality and giving his services to another country—that would be a perfectly reasonable act if he found the other country more congenial—, provided he acquired new citizenship with its obligations as well as its advantages by getting himself naturalised, or, if he did not, were ready to meet any consequences of courses that all the world would judge traitorous.) The next part of the story is one of the most delectable enormities in the whole of human history. (Flaubert would have gloated over it for his *Bouvard et Pécuchet*.) Mr. Pound, duly certified and incarcerated as a lunatic, sent out from his asylum a rigmarole of rubbish called *The Pisan Cantos*. The following are a few lines (of a barbaric something that is neither verse nor prose) from this mass or mess of garbage (they are honestly representative of its qualities as a whole, and even of its unity—which is quite non-existent):

but a snotty barbarian ignorant of T'ang history need not
deceive one
nor Charlie Sung's money on loan from anonimo
that is, we suppose Charlie had some
and in India the rate down to 18 per hundred
but the local loan lice provided from imported bankers
so the total interest sweated out of the Indian farmers
rose in Churchillian grandeur

XXXI

burne stood—grace, harmony, sure and exquisite form, real architectonic, real music, never any failure of these, always a constancy of them, and every now and again that magical thing which is 'not a fourth sound, but a star'—true and high art, in short—the art of power as opposed to the art (or rather want of art) of fumbling impotence, genuine creation as opposed to the mere representational attempt to convey contemporary chaos—these values, which are not the fads and

(Note ¹ continued)—

as when, and plus when, he returned to the putrid gold standard
as was about 1925 . . .
and they have bitched the Adelphi
niggers scaling the obstacle fence
     in the middle distance
and Mr. Edwards superb green and brown
     in ward No. 4 a jacent benignity,
of the Baluba mask: "doan you tell no one
   I made you that table"
        methenamine eases the urine
and greatest is charity
to be found among those who have not observed
     regulations . . .

tempora, tempora and as to mores
by Babylonian wall (memorat Cheever)
   out of his bas relief, for that line
we recall him
   and who's dead, and who isn't
   and will the world ever take up its course again?
very confidentially I ask you: Will it?

with a mind like that he is one of us
   Favonus, vento benigno
   Je suis au bout de mes forces/
That from the gates of death,
   that from the gates of death: Whitman or Lovelace
   found on the jo-house seat at that . . .

Arachne che mi porta fortuna;
   Athene, who wrongs thee?
     τίςἀδικεῖ
That butterfly has gone out thru my smoke hole

fashions of this or that generation, which are not transient, and have always reasserted themselves in the greatest periods of history (and will surely come into their own again), have little chance of winning acceptance in an age by which Mr. Pound is accepted as a master.) I have dealt drastically and with no attempt at amenity with several previous workers on Swinburne: Wise, Gosse, Lafourcade, and others. 'Do you take all your predecessors in this line to be fools?' I shall no doubt be asked. The answer is that at least most of them—and especially the traducers of Swinburne—have their place in this class. The answer is hubristic, risky, and will cause the hornets to stir. But it is the only honest answer, and in every case it is supported by facts that cannot be conjured away. The great majority of these people are grossly incompetent, shockingly ignorant, and, judged by their literary opinions and mode of expression (most of them write like Poor Poll), have no sense of letters.

(*Note* [1] *continued*)—

[This sciolistic smatterer, a *primaire* if ever there were, chucks in scraps of foreign speech here and there, a piece of charlatanry that impresses the poor admiring boobs, even more incult than himself, who make up the school of Pound. Charlatanry? Yes; there is absolutely no need, rational or artistic, for these bits of non-American lingo; they do not arise from the context or assist it in any way; they belong to no artistic process; they are just orts out of the void. They are part of the exhibitionism of a literary scarecrow making himself more grotesque by this additional frippery. Properly considered, these chunks of French, Italian, Greek, etc., are an epitome of Mr. Pound and all his rubbish: *tout est en tout* certainly in this case. There are of course neophytes—and more mature energumens—of Pound who will tell you that all this is part of the esoteric mystery and glory of the Master—esoteric beyond art as even the greatest of the Elect have known it so far; and if you deny this you are a philistine insensitive to new forms of beauty. Etc., etc.: but this is simply balderdash from dupes taken in by the effrontery of the charlatan. Any fake can be palmed off on the uninstructed or the timid with this sort of story; a vast amount of contemporary fake-work depends on it for its acceptance as art. It is high time someone took his courage in both feet as well as in both hands and kicked this trash to the odure-heap which is its due place.[

XXXIII

(Aeschylus); this may be, but these creatures obviously never saw it; in a Platonic state they would be sent to labour camps or put into the retail trade.[2]

I would ask that my work in this volume—the Commentary and also parts of the Notes—be taken as a new book on Swinburne, and not merely as a series of scholia. It and the companion *Swinburne: the Arcane Side* (and also *Lucretia*

(Note [1] *continued)—*

<pre>
        and Awoi's hennia   plays hob in the tent flaps
              k-lakk . . . . . thuuuuuu
                  making rain
                      uuuh
  2, 7, hooo
          der im Baluba
        Faasa!   4 times was the city remade,
    now in the heart indestructible . . .
</pre>

Tripe is too good a word for such stuff, for tripe is not altogether without worth. (The most apt description of the Cantos is in the first line of the poem of Catullus which is numbered xxxvi. Its honest English equivalent can't be given here.) These incoherent splutterings might be thought to bear out the verdict of the panel of alienists—but they are no worse than other stuff he has been throwing off for years past: if they be taken as proof of imbecility he has been imbecile for most of his literary life. Now (and here we come to the pearl, the *clou*, the cream of the whole thing), this madman's slop, this Calibanic twaddle, was awarded the Bollingen prize for 'the highest achievement of American poetry for 1948'. The awarding committee (The Fellows of the Library of Congress in American Letters) included Mr. W. H. Auden and Mr. T. S. Eliot (who in many ways burgeons from Pound). This to a considerable extent gives the measure of these two coryphaei among the 'moderns'. It also gives the measure of the present age taken as a whole (one of the most degenerate in history, and particularly in literary history), and thus comes within the course of our argument. (According to a London newspaper, 'there is an enthusiastic Pound Circle in London. It meets every month . . . to read his poems and discuss his life and philosophy'. To comment on this would be to paint a lily which has its own peculiar perfection.

[2] And so would the Pound & Co. crew and all others who are congenitally akin to them. If it be objected that true as well as pseudo-poets would find no favour in Plato's Republic, I would point out that

Borgia) will be groundwork for the veridic *Life* (and also *Study*) which I hope to be able to do before the next war comes upon us.

DECEMBER 1949

(Note ² continued)—

I have said not Plato's but a Platonic state, meaning an organisation of the type advocated by the great anti-democrat, and not his system with all its details. For in the ideal authoritarian polity true poets would be part of the *élite* holding lordship over the banausic and menial rest of the population ('banausic' here applies not only to mechanics in the literal sense, but also to most if not all magnates and other top-dogs in all systems that have been in force so far. And of course 'menial' is used only of those who are—or should be—of that class by nature, and not by accident of birth or fortune: the sentiment expressed can give offence to no sensible man.) The ideal of course is more than probably unrealisable or even unapproachable, at least in any state of history than can be foreseen at present.

XXXV

LESBIA BRANDON

CHAPTER I

HER EYES HAD AN OUTER RING OF SEEMING BLACK, BUT IN
effect of deep blue and dark grey mixed; this soft and
broad circle of colour sharply divided the subtle and tender
white, pale as pure milk, from an iris which should have been
hazel or grey, blue or green, but was instead a more delicate
and significant shade of the colour more common with beast
or bird;[1] pure[2] gold, without alloy or allay, like the yellowest
part of a clear flame; such eyes as the greatest analyst of spirit
and flesh that ever lived[3] and spoke has noticed as proper to
certain rare women, and has given for a perpetual and terrible
memory to his Georgian girl.[4] In a dark face, southern or
eastern, the colour should be yet rarer, and may perhaps be
more singularly beautiful than even here, where it gave to
the fair and floral[5] beauty of northern features a fire and
rapture of life. These eyes were not hard or shadowless; their
colour was full of small soft intricacies of shade and varieties
of tone; they could darken with delicate alteration and
lighten with splendid change.[6] The iris had fine fibres of light
and tender notes of colour that gave the effect of shadow; as
if the painter's touch when about to darken the clear fierce
beauty of their vital and sensitive gold had paused in time
and left them perfect. The pupil was not over large, and
seemed as the light touched it of molten purple or of black
velvet. They had infinite significance, infinite fervour and
purity. The eyelashes and eyebrows were of a golden brown,[7]
long and full; their really soft shade of colour seemed dark
on a skin of white rose-leaves, between a double golden flame
of eyes and hair. Her nose was straight and fine, somewhat

1

long, and the division of the nostrils below a thought too curved and deep,[8] but their shell exquisite in cutting and colour;[9] the point where it rose from the forehead was hardly hollow at all, and a dimmer golden down was perceptible between the brows; which took a deep and rich curve toward the temples. The cheeks were perfect in form, pale but capable of soft heat and the flush of a growing flower; the face reddened rarely and faintly and all at once, never with a vivid partial blush, but as if the skin were suddenly inlaid with the petals of a young rose from the lowest ripples of the springing hair to the fresh firm chin,[10] round and clear as a fruit, planted as with tender care[11] above a long large throat, deeply white and delicately full. The ears like the nostrils were models of fine grace, carved and curved to perfection; the temples rather flat than rounded, soft like fresh snow, threaded through with visible veins; the lips small and shapely not scarlet but a shade brighter than purple or crimson leaves; a mouth that could suffer and allure, capable beyond others of languor and laughter.[12] An age averse to sculpture would refuse to read the inventory of her bodily beauties; and paper is a less competent material than marble to perpetuate[13] such things for the delight of a casual artist here and there. Nature and religion alike have made the art impossible and comdemnable to all races of modern men. From the waist to the feet she was not unlike the Venus of the Tribune;[14] but her arms were no more like than was her head to the hybrid head and patchwork arms[15] of that state. They were full and frank, exquisitely attached;[16] the shoulders fruitful and round as the breast, the hands narrow and long, palms and fingers coloured with rose and pearl.

While yet a boy her brother was so like her that the description may serve for him with a difference. They had the same complexion and skin so thin and fair that it glittered against the light as white silk does, taking sharper and fainter tones of white that shone and melted into each other. His hair had much more of brown and red mixed into it than hers, but like hers was yellower underneath and rippled from the roots, and not less elastic in the rebellious undulation of the curls. The shape of face and set of head was the same[17] in either, but the iris of his eyes,[18] which might have been classed as hazel more fairly than hers, was rather the colour of bronze than of gold, and the shades and tones of its colour were more variable, having an admixture of green like the eyes of pure northern races, and touched with yellow and brown; except for the green in them, best definable as citrine eyes, but not easy to define; soft and shifting like brilliant sea-water[19] with golden lights in it; the pupils purple and the rings violet. Either face would have lost could they have changed eyes; the boy's even when his face was most feminine were always the eyes of a male bird. Looked well into and through, they showed tints of blue and grey like those of sea-mosses seen under a soft vague surface[20] of clear water which blends and brightens their sudden phases of colour: they were sharp at once and reflective, rapid and timid, full of daring or of dreams: with darker lashes, longer and wavier than his sister's: his browner eyebrows had the exact arch of hers, and the forehead was higher, of a thicker and harder white: his lips were cut out after the model of hers, but fuller and with less of purple; the cheeks and neck were not less clear and pale, but had gathered freckles and sunburns in the hard high[21] air; his chin and throat were also copies from her on the due scale of difference, and his hands, though thinner and less rounded, were what hers would have been with a little more exposure to sun and wind:[22] under any pleasant excitement the sudden blood began to throb visibly at his finger-tips, threading the flushed skin with purple or blue.[23] The face and hands of both were perceptibly nervous and sensitive, his perhaps more perceptibly than hers. As the least contact of anything sharp would graze the skin unawares and draw blood before they knew it, so the lightest touch of pain or pleasure would strike and sting their nerves to the quick. In bright perfect health they were as susceptible in secret[24] of harsh sounds, of painful sights and odours, as any one born born weaklier;[25] whatever they had to suffer and enjoy came to them hot and strong, untempered and unallayed.[26] Both had the courage of their kind, nervous and fearless;[27] inherited . . . . .

[*Portion of manuscript missing*]

CHAPTER II

[Portion of manuscript missing]

. . . . . the senses and the flesh. Having cried for a time, he slept; and at his waking felt first the bitterness of mere cold. The old servant came and took him back, knowing that he knew his father was dead. The corpse lay with lips still apart, and brows that seemed unquiet. He had said little[1] during the last hours of his life; asked for his wife twice, and would not hear that she was dead; bade someone keep Herbert from the water and send for him if the boy disobeyed. Then, moving with his hands, 'My father wouldn't hear of it,' he said; 'his own was lost at sea. I should have done better. Ay, but lost on land for all that,—cast away and broken: not your fault, sir, not yours. She thrives, though; but I should have taken the little thing and kept it for all that.[2] I said her children would never thrive if she married: she'll die a barren stock—barren.' After which he fell into a vacuous mumbling state of speech and mind, and gave no more clue to the old story of his weary life, ended and emptied now of interest for anyone alive.

They buried him three days after; his daughter and her husband arrived the day after his death, and took charge of the boy. These three and the old woman alone attended the funeral; he was buried by his wife, in the barest part of the grey slope which lay between the church and the water: a naked unquiet descent of land whose lean pale growth of grass was shaken and vexed by every wind that rose: for on all sides the bleak churchyard fell away sharply and steeply from around the small church at top; on two sides the thin stormy stream went about it, and the shallow noise of its

5

rapid windy flow was heard all round the hills. The grass was all flowerless, and full of low[3] stained gravestones.

After the burial Kirklowes was left in charge of the old servant and a neighbour, and Herbert went to Ensdon with his sister. A shrill wind shook the trees and bushes about the old house as they started; the day was sharp and the light hard and fitful. No rain fell, but the flooded burn had not yet gone down; the long reeds sang sharp in the wind, the flowerless heather heaved and quivered under it by fits. Following the watercourse they passed out of the line of moorland and under the grey and yellow crags that faced the low barren fields beyond; dividing these and twice recrossing the broader stream, their road rose again over green hills and between small wayside rocks, formless and weather-scored. After miles of high lonely land it went down among sudden trees and out into a land of old woods and swift streams, backing and doubling, crossing and mixing; and over copse and down from the right hand came a sound and a smell of the sea. At the next turn they were in sight of it; a spring-weather sea, grey and green as leaves faded or flowering, swelling and quivering under clouds and sunbeams.[4] The wind played upon it wilfully, lashing it with soft strokes, kissing it with rapid kisses, as one amorous and vexatious of the immense beautiful body defiant even of divine embraces and lovers flown from heaven: far out among shafts and straits of fugitive sunshine, near in under cloud-shadows, waking with light blows and sharp caresses infinite and variable smiles[5] of weary beauty on its immortal face, soft sighs and heavy murmurs under the laughter and dance-music of its endless stream. The water moved like tired tossing limbs of a goddess, troubled with strength and vexed with love.[6] Northward and southward the grey glitter of remote foam flickered along the extreme sea-line, marking off the low sky so that water and cloud were distinct. Nearer inshore, the sea was as an April field of sweet and pale colour, filled with white and windy flowers.

To this, the only sight of divine and durable beauty on

which any eyes can rest in the world, the boy's eyes first
turned, and his heart opened and ached with pleasure. His
face trembled and changed, his eyelids tingled, his limbs
yearned all over: the colours and savours of the sea seemed
to pass in at his eyes and mouth; all his nerves desired the
divine touch of it, all his soul' saluted it through the senses.[8]

'What on earth is the matter with him?' said Lord
Wariston.

'Nothing on earth,' said his sister; 'it's the sea.'

'Oh, he'll soon make friends with that; I'll teach him to
swim.'

Ensdon[9] lay about two miles inland; a large inconsistent[10]
house of yellow sandstone, defiant of architecture, with deep
windows, long thin wings, and high front. Rains and sea-
winds had worn it and the crumbling sandstone here and
there had fallen away in flakes, being soft and unmanageable
stuff. The whole place had a stately recluse beauty; fields and
woods divided the park from the sea-downs; behind it were
terraces, old elaborate flowerbeds and the necessary fish-ponds
devised by Catholic artifice for pious purposes in Lent and
retained by Protestant conservatism for picturesque purposes
all the year round: framed in low flowering bushes and ranged
at equal lengths with turfed walks passing into the underwood and dropping down the terraces. A green moist place,
lying wide and low, divided from the inland moors by a windy
wall of bare broken crag, and with all its lower fields facing
the sea and the sun: sparing rather than lavish of natural
fruit and flower, but with well-grown trees and deep-walled
gardens to the back of it.

Here for the first few months Herbert lived at large and
strayed at will, being somewhat spoilt by his friends. Lord
Wariston carried his wife to town for a month or two, leaving
him under the nominal care of the parish clergyman, a man
meeker than Moses, who taught him riding on the meekest
of steeds. As to work, he put him through none; and the boy
fell upon the Ensdon library[11] shelves with miscellaneous
voracity, reading various books desirable and otherwise,

7

swallowing a nameless quantity of English and French verse and fiction.[12] Being by nature idle and excitable he made himself infinite small diversions out of the day's work, and was by no means oppressed by the sense of compelled inaction. Well broken in to solitude and sensitive of all outward things, he found life and pleasure enough in the gardens and woods, the downs and the beach. Small sights and sounds excited and satisfied him; his mind was as yet more impressible[13] than capacious, his senses more retentive than his thoughts. Water and wind and darkness and light made friends with him; he went among beautiful things without wonder or fear. For months he lived and grew on like an animal or a fruit: and things seemed to deal with him as with one of these; earth set herself to caress and amuse him; air blew and rain fell and leaves changed to his great delight. Reading and riding and wandering, he felt no want in life; three men only kept him company now and then, the clergyman, the land-steward, and the head groom; and all these made much of him in a quiet way. The housekeeper, under whose wing he mainly lived and fed, was a not ignoble sort of woman, well-trained and well-read, beyond the run of women above her or beneath. For all these but chiefly for her he had all due regard; but for places rather than persons he had a violent and blind affection. Small pools in the pouring stream[14] roofed with noiseless leaves out of the wind's way; hot hollows of short grass in the slanting down, shaped like cups for the sun to fill[15]; higher places where the hill-streams began among patches of reeds, extorting from the moist moorland a little life; dry corners of crag whence light trees had sprung out of the lean soil, shadowing narrow brown nooks and ledges of burnt-up turf slippery with the warm dust of arid lands; all these attracted and retained him; but less than the lower parts about the sea. In a few months' time he could have gone blindfold over miles of beach. All the hollows of the cliffs and all the curves of the sand-hills were friendly to his feet.[16] The long reefs that rang with returning waves and flashed with ebbing ripples; the smooth slopes of coloured rock full of small brilliant lakes

8

that fed and saved from sunburning their anchored fleets of
flowers, yellower lilies and redder roses of the sea; the sharp
and fine sea-mosses, fruitful of grey blossom, fervent with
blue and golden bloom, with soft spear-heads and blades
brighter than fire; the lovely heavy motion of the stronger
rock-rooted weeds, with all their weight afloat in languid
water, splendid and supine; the broad bands of metallic light
girdling the greyer flats and swaying levels of sea without a
wave; all the enormous graces and immeasurable beauties[17]
that go with its sacred strength;[18] the sharp delicate air about
it, like breath from the nostrils and lips of its especial and
gracious god;[19] the hard sand inlaid with dry and luminous
brine; the shuddering shades of sudden colour woven by the
light with the water for some remote golden mile or two
reaching from dusk to dusk under the sun; shot through with
faint and fierce lustres that shiver and shift; and over all a
fresher and sweeter heaven than is seen inland by any
weather; drew his heart back day after day and satisfied it.
Here among the reefs he ran riot, skirting with light quick
feet the edge of the running ripple, laughing with love when
the fleeter foam caught them up, skimming the mobile fringe
that murmured and fluttered and fell, gathering up with
gladdened ears all the fervent sighs and whispers of the tender
water, all delicate sounds of washing and wandering waves,
all sweet and suppressed semitones of light music struck out of
shingle or sand by the faint extended[20] fingers of foam[21] and
tired eager lips of yielding sea that touch the soft mutable
limit of their life, to recede in extremity and exhaustion. At
other times he would set his face seaward and feed his eyes
for hours on the fruitless floating fields of wan green water,
fairer than all spring meadows or summer gardens, till the
soul of the sea entered him and filled him with fleshly
pleasure and the pride of life; he felt the fierce gladness and
glory of living stroke and sting him all over as with soft hands
and sharp lips: and under their impulse he went as before a
steady gale[22] over sands and rocks, blown and driven by the
wind of his own delight, crying out to the sea between whiles

9

as to a mother[23] that talked with him, throwing at it all the scraps of song[24] that came upon his lips by chance, laughing and leaping, envious only of sea-birds who might stay longer between two waves. The winter dangers of the coast were as yet mere rumours to him; but the knowledge how many lives went yearly to feed[25] with blood the lovely lips of the sea-furies who had such songs and smiles for summer, and for winter the teeth and throats of ravening wolves or snakes untameable, the hard heavy hands that beat out their bruised life from sinking bodies of men, gave point to his pleasure and a sheathed edge of cruel sympathy to his love. All cruelties and treacheries, all subtle appetites and violent secrets of the sea, were part of her divine nature, adorable and acceptable to her lovers. Why should the gods spare men? or she, a sure and visible goddess, be merciful to meaner things? why should any pity befall their unlovely children and ephemeral victims at the hands of the beautiful and eternal gods? These things he felt without thinking of them, like a child; conscious all over of the beauty and the law of things about him, the manner and condition of their life. The sharp broken speculation of children feels much and holds little, touches many truths and handles none; but their large and open[26] sense or perception of things certain[27] is malleable and colourable by infinite influences and effects.[28] Sensitive by nature, and solitary by accident, a child will taste as keenly and judge as justly as few men do. Without the talent of thought, or any disease of precocity, neither sick nor weak of brain or body, he may be[29] capable of deep and acute delight drawn from casual or indefinable sources. Not incompetent to think, he is incompetent to use his thoughts; fancies may fill him as perverse and subtle[30] and ambitious as a grown man's dreams or creeds. His relish of things, again, will probably be just and right, his faith and his taste wholesome, if not twisted round and disfigured by the manipulation of fools, preached out of heart and moralized out of shape. This present boy, whose training on the whole was duly secular, had made himself, apart and not averse from the daily religion taken and taught on trust,[31] a new and credible mythology. He was no sample of infant faith or infant thought; he was very generally and admirably ignorant, neither saint nor genius, but a small satisfied pagan. The nature of things had room to work in him, for the chief places in his mind were not preoccupied by intrusive and unhealthy guests wheeled in and kept up by machinery of teaching and preaching. There was matter in him fit to mould into form and impregnate with colours:[32] and upon this life and nature were at work, having leisure and liberty to take their time.

His sister on her return found him well and wild, and was pleased; but her own coming child was just then the main thing with her. It was born a little before time in August; hardly born and hardly reared. She herself was ill for long after, though not long in danger : and her beauty threatened to go off. The child was unlovely and unhealthy, not attractive at first nor afterwards; and the mother was not by nature a specially maternal woman. Her boy was named after his father, and grew in time into a likeness of him; a parched and stunted resemblance, such as may exist between sickness and health. To Herbert this first intimacy with a baby was a matter of some interest: its helpless and hopeless defects of size and weight, its curious piteous mask of features, its look of vegetable rather than animal life, its quaint motions and soft red overflow of irregular outlines[33] touched and melted him in a singular way: he grew visibly fond of the red and ridiculous lump,[34] and it put out impossible arms and fatuous fingers when he came in sight. Towards all beasts and babies he had always a physical tenderness; a quality purely of the nerves, not incompatible with cruelty nor grounded on any moral emotion or conviction. It was pleasant to him to press the warm senseless flesh with lips or fingers, and bring into the wide monotonous eyes and upon the loose dull mouth a look and a light of recognition and liking. The poor small wretch would writhe and wag itself at him, and lay harder hold on his finger than another's[35] with creasing cheek and triumphant lips. Neither father nor mother could see why;

but when a year and two months later Lady Wariston bore
twins, a boy and girl, strong and fat and well-liking, the first-
born was eclipsed in all their eyes alike. These younger and
quainter morsels of man and woman were delicious beyond
dispute. They had curls, and good colour, and brilliant ways
of all kinds; they were sharp and healthy, well shaped and
well tempered. Towards the end of 1848 another boy was
born, small but sounder and more like the mother than any
of the rest. By that time Herbert was ripening for Eton, and
more reticent altogether than he had been. For the first two
years he had been allowed to drift and dream at random; his
brother[36] had taught him little but swimming and riding, and
thus had won his heart twice by what he did and by what he
did not. Herbert was rising twelve when first taken in hand
by a tutor to any serious purpose: and though not a bad
fellow had become evidently afflictive to his friends, wilful
and idle and exigent in a noticeable degree. Lord Wariston
applied for help to a maternal uncle who had not visited
Ensdon since the marriage; as indeed few friends had; partly
through disputes consequent on that alliance, partly through
the year or two of weak health which followed on Lady
Wariston's first confinement. The answer was prompt and
amicable; Mr. Linley knew of a sufficient scholar about his
nephew's age, thirty or so it might be, a colleger at Eton in
Lord Wariston's time, he might recollect; who had since
graduated with fit honours, and having thrown up any chances
which the church might have held out was afloat in an
honourable way on the world of scholarship, and open to any
engagement of the present kind. Himself a man of graceful
and accomplished learning, Linley was a counsellor whose
words carried weight with them: and the person commended
to notice was his tried and intimate friend. For some years
after leaving college young Denham had lived with him as
librarian and secretary. It was understood, Mr. Linley added
in a duly delicate way, that if his friend entered on this new
office of licking a cub into schoolboy shape, and breaking a
colt into Eton harness he must have single and imperial con-

trol over the subject of this experiment; the vile body must lie at his mercy who should undertake to train the crude mind to any good purpose:[37] and he would not work by sufferance under correction of alien authority. Give him the boy to work on, and he would do his best, using what means he found hopefullest: would teach him, govern him, fit him for school and study if man could do it: and would take his stand on the result. The chance was thankfully caught at, and Mr. Denham arrived a month later, in 1848.[38] Herbert knew that his troubles were now to begin; he had wept and kicked now and then over sums and grammar, and had usually succeeded in shaking himself free for a time of the burden. Few children had ever enjoyed eleven years of such idleness and such freedom: and no seagull likes to have his wings clipt. The scissors must cut close that were to fit this bird for a perch in the school pen. Herbert had passed through his two first stages and was ripe for a third; first the heather age, then the seaside age, and now the birchen[39] age: this last began later with him than it does with most boys, but was to prove a warm and fruitful period. The moors had done their best for the boy, and after these the sea-rocks; enough work was left for the schoolroom to do.[40] A certain defiant fear and daring curiousity rose up and went out to meet the new life and its new law: and all these small changes and fancies left marks upon his mind. His first friends in the household had given him jocose and serious hints as to the sort of rule he was now to live under.

"Ye know what ye'll get when the tutor comes, Master Herbert? My word but ye'll catch it! There'll be no shirking allowed; if ye come late down, sir, he'll just say, 'Take him up', and once he's got ye horsed[41] he'll whip ye till the rod wears out, and ye'll be let down crying and roaring, and your skin all bloody and smarting;—eh, my word won't you cry, too! and he'll say, 'No crying here,'[42] or—'[43] and ye'll just have to grin and gulp it down, sir."

This vivid and sanguine prediction had been so often hurled at him in the same swift words and eager[44] accent that

the housekeeper's fervid eloquence[45] and elaborate narratives
of punishment inflicted on boys of her acquaintance, and
specially on her present lord in his earlier days, had become
matter of interest at once and laughter to a boy as yet
innocent of birch. Lord Wariston too had often threatened
him with the flagellation to come, but the menaces were
always mere chaff and bran.[46] It was a quite unbroken and
virgin ground which was now to be ploughed and harrowed
in the approved fashion by the scholastic instrument of husbandry. He had made no friend of his own age, and wanted
none; the only acquaintance he had was a boy two years older,
son of a Mr. Lunsford whose estate abutted on Lord Wariston's to the north, and whose boy Walter was the one male
among a flock of smaller children. He had been some four
years at Eton; a long-limbed, dark-skinned boy,[47] as yet without any too prominent quality; ambitious of effect and fond
of ease; good at many games, and not dull at any sort of work.
From him Herbert received patronage and instruction, and
returned him a modified reverence and a qualified affection.
They were thrown together a good deal in holiday time; the
two houses were within a morning's walk of each other, but
Mrs. Lunsford being invalided many years since never went
out and kept her husband close to her side. Their boy was
popular with the Wariston household, and fond of his friends
there: a comparison of the boys had brought clear before
Lord Wariston the necessity that Herbert's training should
be at once and sharply seen to.

For the last month or two of his free childish life Herbert
clung daily to the sea, diving in and out among cliffs and
coves, and tracking with small rapid feet miles of the blown
sand and stormy seabanks. Under the March winds the sea
gained strength and splendour, and its incessant beauty
maddened him with pleasure. His blood kept time with its
music, his breath and pulse felt and answered the sweet sharp
breath that lifted and the long profound pulse that shook the
stormy body of the sea. The reefs clashed and the banks
chafed with violent and variable waves; the low[48] rocks

thundered and throbbed underfoot as the water rang round them, and wave by wave[49] roared out its heavy heart and lost its fierce fleet life[50] in lavish foam. Beyond the yellow labouring space of sea that heaved and wallowed close inshore,[51] the breakers crashed one upon another, white and loud beyond the sudden green line of purer sea.[52] In thunder that drowned his voice, wind that blew over his balance, and snowstorms of the flying or falling foam that blinded his eyes and salted his face, the boy took his pleasure to the full; this travail and triumph of the married wind and sea filled him with a furious luxury of the senses that kindled all his nerves and exalted all his life. From these haunts he came back wet and rough, blown out of shape and beaten into colour, his ears full of music and his eyes of dreams:[53] all the sounds of the sea rang through him, all its airs and lights breathed and shone upon him:[54] he felt land-sick when out of the sea's sight, and twice alive when hard by it. It was in this guise that he first met the man who was to rule and form his life for years to come.[55] Drenched and hot and laughing, salt and blown and tumbled, he was confronted with a tall dark man, pale and strong, with grey hard features and hair already thinned. Mr. Denham had noticeable eyes, clear brown in colour, cold and rapid in their glance; his chest and arms were splendid, the whole build of him pliant and massive, the limbs fleshless and muscular. But for the cold forehead and profound eyes he seemed rather a training athlete than trained student.[56] The forehead was large in all ways, and the strong prominent bones made the outlines coarse. Nothing in his face seemed mobile but the nostrils; and these were its weakest feature. The nose and mouth had a certain Irish air, corrected by the strong compression of the lips which if relaxed would have changed the whole face; but they never did relax, whether in talking or laughing, drinking or sleeping; they should have been full and soft, and were thin it seemed not because they had grown thin through natural change but by dint of purpose and compulsion. Life repressed and suppressed strength[57] were not indiscernible after sharp

15

scrutiny of his face. The skin looked blasted and whitened, as if it had once been brilliant and smooth: it was now colourless and dry, lined and flaked with dull tints of diseased colour. As his eyes fell on Herbert, the boy felt a sudden tingling in his flesh;[58] his skin was aware of danger, and his nerves winced.[59] He blushed again at his blushes, and gave his small wet hand shyly into the wide hard grasp of the strong and supple fingers that closed on it. Denham had broad hands on which the veins and muscles stood in hard relief; well-shaped and strong, good at handling oar and bat, the nails wide and flat and pale, the joints large and the knuckles wrinkled; hands as significant as the face. The soft sunburnt hand with feminine fingers lay in his almost like a roseleaf taken up and crushed; his grasp was close and retentive by instinct; he kept hold of the boy and read his face sharply over, watching it redden and flinch. Lord Wariston who was by recollected the look, and remembered how quiet and tough a hold the man had as a boy, and how when young and fresh he had made an excellent tyrant, notable as scholar and bully alike. 'I hope you won't begin by giving Herbert such a licking as you gave me once,' he said for a fragment of a laugh. 'I wouldn't have been your fag then for something.'

'Don't remember the licking myself,' said Mr. Denham. 'However, if your brother is to fag for me I shall keep him up to his work. Twelve next month, is he? Ever been flogged yet, my boy?'

'I can answer that if he won't', said his sister; 'Herbert has that pleasure still to come.'

'High time,' said Lord Wariston. 'You have but a dunce to begin upon, Denham; but I daresay you have not forgotten how to take him in hand.'

Mr. Denham soon made his own way. Lord Wariston retained among other qualities of the boyish period a certain awe of this senior, tyrannous and brilliant in former days, which soon grew into a regard flavoured with admiration and dashed with aversion. This last ingredient melted gradually as they grew intimate. Wariston was a man rather idle than dull, and Denham a clever not unworldly scholar who had seen beyond his reading, and could talk well. The household was so quiet and the circle so narrow that it would have been hard to hold off or exclude even a less acceptable man. Lady Wariston, who had lost hair and flesh after her children were born, had now repaired the loss and her beauty was more large and vigorous than in her girlhood. Denham was barely past thirty, and his boyhood and youth had visibly been abstinent; he soon suffered more from the sister than the brother at his hands; and Herbert had not a good time of it at first, fresh as he was to punishment.[60] Two days after his arrival Denham saw good to open fire upon his pupil, and it was[61] time indeed to apply whip and spur, bit and bridle, to the flanks and mouth of such a colt; the household authorities supported and approved the method of the breaker, under whose rigorous hand and eye he began to learn his paces bit by bit; a breaker who was hardly over-strict, and out of school hours amiable enough,[62] and idle as the boy often was, he soon began to move on except in the mournful matter of sums. As Friday was consecrated[63] to the worship of that numerical Moloch at whose altar more boys have bled than ever at that of Artemis, Herbert was horsed afresh every Friday for some time.[64] He was soon taught not to appeal to his sister; once assured that he was in good training and not overworked, she gave him all condolence but no intercession. Nothing excessive was in effect expected of the boy;[65] Denham had always a fair pretext for punishment and was not unjust or unkind; and in time Herbert had learnt[66] to be quiet and perverse; it had grown into a point of honour with him to take what fate sent him at his tutor's hands with a rebellious reticence, and bear anything[67] in reason rather than expose himself to an intercession which he could not but imagine contemptuous; and thus every flogging[68] became a duel without seconds between the man and the boy.[69] These encounters did both of them some good; Herbert, fearless enough of risk, had a natural fear of pain, which lessened as he grew familiar with it, and a natural weight of indolence which it helped to

17

quicken and lighten; Denham eased himself of much superfluous discomfort and fretful energy by the simple exercise of
power upon the mind and body of his pupil: and if the boy
suffered from this, he gained by it often; the talk and teaching
of his tutor, the constant contact of a clear trained intellect,
served to excite and expand his own, he grew readier and
sharper, capable of new enjoyment and advance. And Denham, a practised athlete whose strength of arm Herbert knew
to his cost, encouraged him to swim and ride and won his
esteem by feats which his slighter limbs were never to emulate. In summer they went daily into the sea together, and
the rougher it was the readier they were for it; Herbert
wanted no teaching to make him face a heavy sea; he panted
and shouted with pleasure among breakers where he could
not stand two minutes; the blow of a roller that beat him off
his feet made him laugh and cry out in ecstasy: [70] he rioted in
the roaring water like a young sea-beast, sprang at the throat
of waves that threw him flat, pressed up against their soft
fierce bosoms and fought for their sharp embraces; grappled
with them as lover with lover, flung himself upon them with
limbs that laboured and yielded deliciously, till the scourging
of the surf made him red from the shoulders to the knees,
and sent him on shore whipped by the sea into a single blush
of the whole skin, breathless and untried. Denham had to
drive him out of the water once or twice; he was insatiable
and would have revelled by the hour among waves that lashed
and caressed him with all their might and all their foam.
Standing where it was so shallow in the interval from wave to
wave that the seething water in its recoil only touched the
boy's knees, they waited for a breaker that rose to the whole
height of the man; Herbert would creep out to it quivering
with delight, get under the curve of it and spring right into
the blind high wall of water, then turn and drive straight with
it as it broke and get his feet again on dry ground, sand or
shingle as it pleased the water to throw him; and return, a
little cut or beaten as it might be, with fresh laughter and
appetite, into the sweet white trouble of the waters. Denham,

though not such a seagull, had a taste for all work of this kind, and perhaps gave the boy something more than his fair credit; for the magnetism of the sea drew all fear out of him, and even had there been any discomfort or peril to face, it was rather desire than courage that attracted and attached him to the rough water. Once in among green and white seas, Herbert forgot that affliction was possible on land,[71] and in his rapture of perfect satisfaction was glad to make friends with the man he feared and hated in school hours. The bright and vigorous delight[72] that broke out at such times nothing could repress or resist; he appealed to his companion as to a schoolfellow and was answered accordingly. 'He was a brick in the water,' Herbert told young Lunsford; 'like another fellow you know, and chaffs one about getting swished,[73] and I tell him it's a beastly chouse[74] and he only grins.' This intimacy was broken by one tragic interlude; bathing had been forbidden on all hands one stormy day before the sea had gone down, and Herbert, drawn by the delicious intolerable sound of the waves, had stolen down to them and slipped in; having had about enough in three or four minutes, he came out well buffeted and salted, with sea-water in his throat and nostrils and eyes; and saw his tutor[75] waiting just above watermark between him and his clothes. Finding him gone, Denham had quietly taken a tough and sufficient rod[76] and followed without a superfluous word of alarm. He took well hold of Bertie, still dripping and blinded; grasped him round the waist and shoulders, wet and naked, with the left arm and laid on[77] with the right as long and as hard as he could. Herbert said afterwards that a wet swishing hurt most awfully, a dry swishing was a comparative luxury.[78] He did not care to face again the sharp superfluous torture of these stripes on the still moist flesh;[79] and from that day he was shy of facetious talk in the water or out: thus the second stage of his apprenticeship began.

Lady Wariston's notice[80] might have given some excuse for hope to a man less clear-headed than Denham: who was too reasonable ever to mistake the delicate intimacy and familiar courtesy of her tone for anything even as warm or deep as friendship. She had affections, though less excitable and fervent than her brother's; of any possible passion she seemed to give but slight promise. Father and brother she had loved warmly and well; her husband also, and chiefly since marriage; but with a dutiful and temperate love half made up of kindness and half of habit: a love of durable homespun quality, good as a working or a walking dress. It had held out now some years, and was likely to hold out twenty more; after which one may hope a woman's consistency may be assumed as a thing indubitable, duly warranted, and stamped with the domestic trademark. She had never made friends of her own sex, and never did to any purpose. Denham was the first stranger she had ever met on constant and intimate terms. That after some months had gone he could not meet or pass her without passion and pain she knew no more than Herbert or Wariston. The man's active power of reticence was in exact and admirable balance with his passive power of emotion. His manner was in faultless keeping with circumstances; keen eyes, if such had been there, would have seen no more than did the unsuspicious eyes about him. But the hidden disease in spirit and heart struck inwards, and daily deeper: it pierced him through the flesh to the mind. Silent desire curdled and hardened into poisonous forms; love became acrid[81] in him, and crusted with a bitter stagnant scum of fancies ranker than weeds. Under the mask or under the rose he was passing through quiet stages of perversion.[82] He could not act out[83] his sin and be rid of it; he held it as though in his hand night and day till it burnt his palm to the bone. He had strength enough to keep his fingers closed and clenched over the bad handful; to open them and cast it out he had not strength enough. Duty doubtless or religion might have helped him; but the man, self-reliant and continent by nature, was much of a heathen. Will all his desire to be near her he was not sure of his love: the intense attraction had some features not unlike intense antipathy. Fever and tremor came over him because of her; but when these subsided and

made way for thought 'he was angry, and passed from scorn of
the effect[84] to abhorrence of the cause. Her he did not hate,
but he hated his love for her. As he could not embrace her,
he would fain have wounded her; this was at first; gradually
the wound rather than the embrace came to seem desirable.
He had grown used to a sense of despair; to give and take
pleasure was so far beyond hope that it soon passed beyond
desire; his dreams were other than these. Devotion was still
mixed with his passion; but a deadly devotion that if need
were could kill as well as die.

The moods of his unchangeable desire were changeable
and many; he spoke now gently and now harshly; talked much
one day and another not at all. Being excellent at his proper
work, he did not vary much towards Herbert, always keeping
him well in hand; but at times too he was readier to help and
amuse,[85] more accessible and amiable. He could talk of things
worth hearing, whether serious or light; his talk was full of
salt and savour grateful to many with whom he mixed.
Towards Wariston he felt real friendship, and in time became
to him at once pleasant and necessary. As librarian, manager,
friend of the house, Lord Wariston was resolved he should
stay when Herbert's pupilage was over. Meantime his chief
diversion was to play upon the boy's mind as on an instrument; to feed it with various food and watch what might
prove most palatable. Idle as he was, Bertie was not dull to
such impression; and in effect preferred stories to sports, and
was excitable rather in head than in limb. It did not improve
his chance of learning; he made verses on Helen and Clytemnestra before he could well construe. Except on Fridays he
began even to take delight in hearing his tutor; and early
in the week felt sometimes as if strong liking for him were
not impossible. Sitting over his work opposite, he let his fancy
fill with dreams about the man; how he lived, what he knew,
why he was thus and not otherwise. To be for five minutes
as he was would have been revelation enough of real life. To
retain his own eyes and see also with another man's—to retain
his own sense and acquire another man's—this would have

been satisfaction. That there was more in this man than for example in Wariston, he felt and knew. 'Maggie, do you like Denham?' he wanted to ask her, and could not. Once he had taken the words upon his lips, and suppressed them again. Another time he stopped midway in the division of a sum, goaded by a desire to ask Denham if he liked her: they were the two chief figures in his world, for unless at exceptional times he now saw little of Wariston and thought less. He sat bending gravely to his work, and thinking nothing about it.

Suddenly he lifted his eyes not less gravely, without any impudent intention, and said: 'Mr. Denham. What was Electra like, do you think?'

'Is that question in Colenso?[86] Let me look at the key.'

'No, but what do you?'

'I think Herbert Seyton will be flogged[87] before long at this rate. Stick to your sum and don't be a young ass.'

'I want to know, please.' Bertie said this in a subdued tone of imperious complaint, and the voice was very like his sister's when put out of her way: a soft, clear, musically resolute voice, pretty in women and boys.

'Look here, Herbert, if I have to whip you again as I did last week, you won't like it; you won't half like it.' He lifted his hand and let it fall heavily and sharply, with a switching motion sideways. 'Anyhow,[88] I will not have you idle and impertinent while in my charge. What do you mean by such questions?'

'I didn't mean to cheek you, sir, really. I thought about it till I couldn't help.'

He had not spoken willingly; but the heat of the day, the deep vibration of the outer summer air, the murmur of unseen motion in the long quiet of profound noon, the low remote chime of the regular sea, absorbed him as in a dream and filled him with fancies that made the figures swim and spin in his head when he looked at them, and fretted him out of dreamy thought into sudden speech.

'What put it into your head?' said Denham amused.

22

'Because I wonder if she was like her aunt—Helen you know, sir.'

Denham laughed at the grave interest in his lifted face: he had a kind of liking for the boy's quaint frank manner. 'I never thought about it, Bertie, at all. I don't suppose she was.'

'She was much older than her brother you know. Perhaps she saw Helen. Then she could have told him. I should have liked to be Orestes: not when he grew up you know. I think she was like. Because if she had been like her own mother instead, he couldn't have killed her. Clytemnestra I mean.'

'That's a lucid and coherent view, no doubt. Perhaps she was like neither of the sisters.'

Herbert meditated on this new point, but would not allow the likelihood.

'I think she was like Helen. I pretend she was. Don't you think—'

'Well, what more? out with it and get to work again.'

'My sister would have stuck to me like that?'

'As Electra to Orestes? perhaps; I dare say.'

He spoke in a dry slow tone, hardening his voice, which had been rather soft, and half humorous.

'I know she would. And nobody could be more beautiful.'

With which the boy glanced up at Denham through his eyelashes. The shy sly light in his eyes seemed to irritate the other as he caught he look.

'Finish that sum in five minutes or I'll flog you.'

Herbert did not finish it, and had a flogging which[89] left him incapable of any sense but wonder why Denham should hit so hard this time, and give him two sharp cuts extra which took[90] his breath away, making him gasp and sob.[91] He rose from his knees wincing and quivering, with fiery cheeks blotted by tears;[92] and made no more allusions to Electra for a day or two. But he forgot the affair before his tutor did. It pleased Denham to lead him into fresh suggestions as to such heroines of legend. Intrigue of an usual kind was hardly in the man's line; he had not the capacity for such work: but in

23

a dumb sombre fashion he liked to play about the dull and steady flame of his desire. He would never directly talk to Herbert of his sister; but would indulge himself by turning the boy's mind that way, that he might talk of her under a veil. He did not want sense and dignity: there was nothing in him of bad taste to ridicule, nothing of cowardice to contemn. Only, in a sad scornful humour not unworthy of pity and respect, he would return now and then to flicker heavily about the light, to flutter angrily about the fire, which allured him but could not scorch.

One day[93] they went out, bathed, and walked some way along the sands, past windy weeds and dry blown flowers, between fuming pools and trembling reaches. They were on good terms; Bertie had done well for a week or so,[94] and his tutor was in the mood to encourage[95] his idle eager talk. 'I punished you for chattering' he exclaimed 'at the wrong time, but you may fire away now: I rather like to hear you.' Some boys would have collapsed at this; Bertie expanded. He was still voluble and impulsive, not afraid of remark or ashamed of excitement. It appeared he had been thinking much 'about things' and had educed a fact of some value from the floating mass of evidence; namely that in every story and in every row ever heard of there was a woman somewhere. 'Yes,' said the other, 'from Troy to Actium downwards; why, there was a woman at the bottom of your last trouble, Bertie: Electra was it?'

The boy flushed and flinched as Denham patted him. 'I think they were right to put a lot of women in the sea: it's like a woman itself: the right place for sirens to come out of, and sing and kill people. Look there, what a jolly wave for one to come riding in upon.'

'They stay on shore now mostly' said Denham: 'but I don't know that they do the less harm for that. There are worse things than drowning I should think.'

'I shouldn't like to drown, either,' said Bertie. 'It's beastly to feel the water at one's throat when one can hardly swim a stroke further. I suppose it's their fingers that choke you.'

'I can't say; but I've no doubt their hands are strong enough; no doubt.'

'Do you think they were really beautiful, or only looked?'

'I think they were. Ulysses would have gone after them if he could; and he was a hard man to take in: he had experience.'

'Circe, and Calypso, and Penelope,' said Herbert in a reflective way: 'I'd rather have seen Circe, I think.'

'If they had been all three made into one—'

'Oh,' said the boy, 'that would have been jolly for him.'

'Yes. He would have been happier than other men; or unhappier.'

This perplexed Bertie, who could not follow the drift of the dialogue further, having throughout missed the meaning of the other speaker. He lay down with his cheek to the shingle, and his fingers played with it sleepily, while Denham sat silent. Before long they went home.

CHAPTER III

A DAY'S WORK

A MONTH LATER THE SEA WAS AGAIN TOO COLD AND ROUGH FOR bathing to be permissible; but as it was early in September, and Walter Lunsford was still at home and had come over one morning to Ensdon, the two boys went down together to the beach with a furtive intention to bathe. But when at the water's edge, Walter, like a rational landsman, thought better of it. 'Look at that boat a little off shore with a small boy in it, how it pitches. And besides, you're safe to be nailed if you go in, you'll never get all that hair dry in time.' But Herbert was stripped already, and went into the water defiant of possible suffering at sea and probable suffering on shore. His elder stood on the ridge of pebbles and watched him; he could hardly swim two strokes on end; he shouted and laughed as the waves beat and drove him. After some twenty minutes, during which he had wallowed and plunged among the steep hillsides of water,[1] his elder hailed him and he struggled inshore, having never got out of his depth; each breaker knocked him down and flung him up, pitched him high and sucked him back. By this time the boat was too near the shore for safety, and small as it was the rower could not manage it; he was clearly beaten, but might yet make way if he had luck.

Herbert had come out and was dressing, when the boat vanished for a minute and rose with the next wave empty. The boy had torn his clothes off again when Lunsford caught him. 'Don't be an infernal young ass, Seyton. It can't be done.'

'Let me go, I say; damn you,' said Herbert. 'Will you let me go?' and being naked and wet, his lithe body twisted and slipped out of Walter's hands. He went straight at the next

wave, laughing; sprang into it with shut eyes and was hurled
back with thunder in his ears, with limbs and face lashed by
lighter shingle driven straight through the yellow water. The
sea was thick and solid with sand and flying pebbles, and
waifs of weed fastened round the boy's throat and hampered
his legs. Feeling the shingle under him, he rose reeling on
his feet in the sudden shallow, breathed deep, and made for
the next breaker. A few short sharp strokes brought him close
and the recoiling water sucked him into the curve of the sea.
Loose foam fluttered along the edge of it, but he got over
before the crash, swimming lightly across the heaving half-
broken ridge of wrinkled water. Then, half in half upon the
following wave, he saw something struggle and labour. The
groundswell[2] had forced him some yards to the left already.
In the instant after the last breaker fell through and hurled
itself inshore with all its foam and weed, the sharp side of the
reef showed naked, baring its black shark-toothed edge. The
boy had time to think what a bore it would be to drive upon
that edge and there break up: also that it was a chance more
in the game, and either would happen or not.[3] He could not
swim further in the heavy refluent sea that shifted and
seethed; keeping half afloat in front of the breaker, he was
drawn out again towards it by the fierce rapid reflux, lifted
into it and with it as it came in gathering up all the strength
and stream of the sea and repelling the reluctant ebb of the
spent wave. To swim with it was easy, and for a breath of
time he kept high on the broad grey back of the wave about
to break;[4] then with one furious stroke which seemed to drain
his breast of breath he reached and caught at the head of the
figure. At the same minute he felt a hand clutch at his side
and slip off,[5] and the wave as it went over and flew into foam[6]
with the thunder and hiss and impulse of a cataract hurled
both at once, blind and deaf and breathless and fearless, far
up the shingle. The violence of the stroke had driven them
well apart; the wide wave, ruined into mere waste of weltering
froth and wallowing water, drew down with it as it sank only
a mass of hurtling pebbles. Herbert, who had been thrown up

within three yards of the reef, rose on his feet again, gasped, and laughed. The other a boy about a year younger, lay still grasping the shingle with clenched instinctive hands.

'Well, you are a muff, Bertie,' said Lunsford. 'The poor devil would have been all right if you hadn't laid hold of him.'

'He's all right now; he's shamming. Here, you fellow, get up, will you? By jove, won't you catch it for smashing your governor's boat? I say, Lunsford, just pull him higher up and punch his head: I can't, I'm so awfully pumped. Psht! the sea's gone in at my nose and got into my throat.'

'Serve you right for being such a damned young fool: you look as if you'd been swished all over. I suppose you're not hurt?'

'Not a bit,' said Herbert, using his shirt as a towel; 'but I say, do pitch into that chap, he makes me funky: he *is* all right, isn't he?'

He gave proof of that by sitting up and snorting: he was not heavily bruised, and had only lain still for a minute or so, stunned by the hard wet blows and blind with returning fright.[7] When the boat capsized he was barely twenty strokes out of his depth, and by good luck the sea had pitched him straight on shore, sound in limb if not in wind.

'Told you he was shamming, little cad,' said Herbert. 'Now, young fellow, you just hook it, will you?'

'You're a nice lot, you are', Walter struck in. 'You've half killed that fellow[8] there and if he hadn't gone in after you, you'd have been drowned.'

'What a jolly lie!' said Herbert. 'I didn't pull him out. If he says I saved his beastly life I'll punch his head.'

But the boy had begun to mutter in a strangled wheezy fashion some kind of thanks, staring with his drenched eyes at the naked figure salted and sodden with sea from hair to heel. This Herbert naturally resented. 'All right, don't be a fool, there's a good chap, and don't talk rot. Oh, damn it, I say, will you cut? or shall I shy this boot at your head? you just wait till I've got my breeches on and I'll give you no end of a licking. I say, Walter, kick him;' specifying the manner of kick required, in a tone of despair and wrath, as the boy grew more demonstrative in a dull stuttering way.

'What a young brute you are, Bertie,' said his friend when the 'little cad' had moved off, spotting and salting the sand with waterdrops from his soaked clothes.[9] 'I'll bet you've made that poor chap miserable.'

'I say,' said Bertie, ignoring that question. 'I've cut my legs like fun.'

He was upon the whole a curious pictorial study: his skin beaten by the waves which ahd thrashed him to a bright pink like the inside of a shell, incrusted in other places with flakes of white brine and inlaid with shreds of black weed, perversely adhesive and difficult to detach from some parts. There were a few scratches about his body from the sharper stones, not graver in appearance than certain other[10] cuts which[11] he had forgotten; but on Walter's suggesting that he must have shown the marks when he turned his back on the young cad, his face grew hot and he stamped on the shingle with a foot already cut. This recalled his attention to the leg, which was a good deal scratched below the knee; and while he sat drying himself Lunsford kept up a sharp fire of chaff which made his cheeks tingle up to the underlid. Dressed at last and shod, though with hair still matted and dripping under the cap, he broke in upon his comrade's fluent speech, thus:

'Look here, Walter, I want you to promise you won't tell about that chap being in the water. Don't, please, there's a good fellow, really. I don't mind chaff, but there'd be a row made perhaps, and no end of jaw, and I couldn't stand it.'

He was enough in earnest to wince and flush at the thought.

'Well, if you don't like; but I think that's rot, you know. After all it was a tremendously plucky thing to do: you might have come a most howling cropper.'

'Oh, I say, please don't,' Bertie cried out sharply, as if he had just had a stinging lash over the cheek. 'It makes one feel such a beastly humbug and sneak; and I didn't come any cropper: and if any fool were to begin jawing now it would

29

make me sick, and I should like to break his neck. Promise you won't tell; do, there's a trump.'

'The kid will though,' said Lunsford.

'Oh, by God, so he will,' said Herbert, driven desperate. 'I wish there were no kids in the world, they are so jolly stupid, they will blab: little beasts, I hate them. I wish he was dead.'

'He'll come up to the house with his governor to return thanks, and bring half the fishwives in the village, and they'll want to kiss you.'

'Cut after him and tell him he'll be licked into pulp and peelings if he can't hold his jaw.'

'He's at home by this time, I know whose kid he is; old Mathison's.'

'I hope he'll give him a most infernal licking.'

'I say, hadn't you better cut home?'

'All right; and shan't I catch it just! I wish old Denham was that fellow's tutor.'

Lunsford looked after him with rather surprised eyes, in which there was a certain scornful admiration. The boy's childish and sensitive follies were absurd at his age; younger only by two years than his critic. There was a strong feminine element in Bertie Seyton; he ought to have been a pretty and rather boyish girl. The contrast would have been greater then: now he looked at times too like a small *replica*[12] of his sister, breeched and cropped.

Faithful history, desirous that the character and training of one actor on her stage should be duly understood, may be allowed to look after the boy a little and record the result of his small adventure. Entering the house before dressing-time he encountered his tutor. The wet hair, the face still salted from the sea and breathing at every pore of sea-water, the stained tie and dishevelled collar, gave damnatory proof[13] against him. Passing over any form of question, Mr. Denham simply let one sentence drop from pale and close lips: 'To-morrow after breakfast, my boy, before we begin work.' Herbert passed him without appeal. The evening wore through much as usual; but some inflexion in the boy's voice[14] as he said good-night irritated the restless nerves of his tutor, who fell asleep upon a resolution to pay him off thoroughly. At breakfast Lady Wariston noticed in her brother's manner a certain shyness that was neither insolence nor timidity but very like both.

'Is Bertie in trouble again, Mr. Denham?' she said when they rose.

He smiled. 'The face speaks for itself, Lady Wariston.'

It was pale and visibly hot, with tightened lips and tremulous eyelids.

'This won't do at Eton, you know, Herbert,' said Lord Wariston as he passed.

'Poor old Bertie,' said his sister. 'Come and tell me about it when it's all over. And don't flog him within quite an inch of his life, Mr. Denham, please.'

There was a singular light in the man's eyes as they followed her passing out after this speech; a sharp hard look with a cruel edge to it, but full of hidden heat; the light and heat of dumb desire, of desperate admiration, of bitter and painful hatred. Something too of wayward and hopeless pleasure was in their dark grey globes, latent and tacit.[15] Suffering, self-contempt, envy, and the rage of inverted love and passion poisoned in the springs, all were absorbed by the keen delight of a minute while her skirt brushed him and her eyes touched him. A pungent sense of tears pricked his eyelids and a bitter taste was in his tongue when she went out. Her god-like beauty was as blind and unmerciful as a god. Hating her with all his heart as he loved her with all his senses, he could but punish her through her brother, hurt her through his skin; but at least to do this was to make her own flesh and blood suffer for the pain inflicted on himself. His feet were cold; his head was full of hot and sickly fancies; his heart beat as hard as Herbert's when they entered the library, though[16] his will controlled and quenched the agitation of his nerves.[17] The likeness infuriated him; but he subdued the fury; eyes of cold anger and judicial displeasure followed the boy's

31

movements. Bertie winced under them, but saw nothing singular in their expression; there was no fierceness in its gravity, no variation in its rebuk.e

He made a last appeal, looking up in Denham's face.

'Please, sir, I wasn't in the water long. And it wasn't rough —not very. I promise I won't[18] bathe again this year by myself.'

'I don't think you will, Herbert. I mean to make sure of that:[19] and I advise you as a friend not to keep me waiting, or I shall have you hoisted; and then you must take the consequences. Go down'—and poor Bertie 'went down' after the manner of schoolboys at the block.[20]

'Now mind, I mean to punish you severely; after an offence like this you can hardly expect to come off as easily as usual.'

He spoke in a clear harsh note, with brightening eyes and tightening lips, as he watched the boy wince; his words had edges and cut like a harsh look.

'Must I tie your hands? or will you promise not to resist?'

'I won't move; or put my hands back: I won't, on my honour', said the boy:[21] but the first stroke made him leap and writhe, catching his breath with a sharp sob:[22] Denham knew better than to flog too fast; he paused after each cut[23] and gave the boy time to smart.

'Will you tie my hands please—or I'm sure I can't—keep my word?' quoth Bertie in a sharp small shaking voice, turning half round and holding his wrists out. Denham was rather moved for the minute; but the cold fit of cruelty was upon him. He tied the small wrists tight and laid on the lithe tough twigs with all the strength of his arm. There was a rage in him now more bitter than anger. The boy sobbed and flinched at each cut, feeling his eyes fill and blushing at his tears; but the cuts stung like fire, and burning[24] with shame and pain alike, he pressed his hot wet face down on his hands, bit his sleeve, his fingers,[25] anything; his teeth drew blood as well as the birch;[26] he chewed the flesh of his hands rather than cry out, till Denham glittered with passion.[27] A fresh rod[28] was applied and[29] he sang out sharply: then drew himself tight as it were

32

all over, trying to brace his muscles and harden his flesh into rigid resistance; but the pain beat him; as he turned and raised his face, tears streamed over the inflamed cheeks and imploring lips.[30] It was not the mere habit of sharp discipline, sense of official duty or flash of transient anger,[31] that impelled his tormentor; had it been any of these he might have been more easily let off. As it was, Denham laid on every stripe with a cold fury that grew slowly to white heat;[32] and when at length he made an end, he was seized with a fierce dumb sense of inner laughter; it was such an absurd relief this, and so slight. When these fits were on him he could have taken life to ease his bitter and wrathful despair of delight.

'Here,' he said, contemptuous of the boy's brief bodily pain, and half relieved by the sight of it;[33] 'give me your hands to untie. You've felt the last of this rod, my boy. Come, stop crying. I hope you'll never have anything worse to cry for; you'll be the luckiest fellow I know.'

But Herbert, after a double dose of flogging, was not in a condition to see this: he did readjust himself,[34] with sundry sobs and pauses and then stood tingling and crying, with hidden face and heaving shoulders: only looking up when he felt his tutor's eyes on him. His own as he raised them were as full of light as of tears; the light that comes into the eyes of one still fighting against pain, hot with fever and brilliant with rebellion, shot out under the heavy eyelashes fringed thickly with tears. Denham flinched in his turn; his eyes fell, and he smiled. He had never seen the two faces so like before; the eyes were hers now that pain had brightened and tears softened them: and the boy seemed to his fancy conscious of the electric effect somehow produced. He was tempted to whip him again. Herbert's mouth, still trembling with pain, was already defiant; the red curve of the lips and the dimple below quivered like his sister's when excited or pleased, and the nervous sullen beauty of outline[35] was hers when irritated or fatigued. Pain had brought out in sharper relief the lineaments of that likeness which had in part impelled him to inflict pain: he had punished the boy for being so like her,

33

and after punishment he was more like than ever: as he stood opposite, his face had the very look most hateful and most beautiful on his sister's face. Denham could have beaten the fair clear features out of shape with his clenched hand: he began to hate this boy too, with a hatred not the less keen that there was no mixture of love in it; though such mixed passions, the product of emotions inverted and perverted,[36] were in him more durable as well as more vehement than any simple affection.

'Sit down, sir, and get to work', he said before Herbert had well readjusted his braces.

'Please, sir, mayn't I stand?' said Herbert with a pathetic impudence.

'No, sir; sit down this instant,'—and the boy did, with infinite precaution;[37] Denham plied him with alternate sums and syntax till there was a very fair list of blunders registered against his name.

'You'll be very sorry for this on Friday, Herbert: very sorry; and with good reason.'

'I can't get them right this morning, sir,' said the boy, pushing his hair up with a dolorous gesture. 'And things won't stay in my head.'

'They must be well whipped into you, then, and I dare say they will,' said his tutor. 'Come to me at—'

Here the door opened, and a servant announced that her ladyship must see Master Seyton at once. As he came wincing and shuffling into her room, she ran up to him and caught his shoulders with her hands.

'My dear Bertie, what is all this? it seems you have been doing the most splendid things, and nobody was to be told. Did you really save that boy's life? because if you did you are a live hero and we shall have to make much of you.'

'I'm sure I didn't,' said Herbert in a tone indignantly plaintive.[38] 'Why do fellows tell such beastly lies?'

'Didn't you go in after him?' said Lady Wariston, pressing the boy against her.

'Aie!' said he with a squeak of pain; 'Please don't! you

34

hurt most awfully. No, I didn't. I was in the water, that is I was just out, and I went in again for a lark. There.'

'Did you see the boat upset?'

'Well, of course I did,' said Bertie in the manner of a tamed savage. 'I couldn't help that, could I! It's rather strong to pitch into me because a fool of a kid who can't swim capsizes his governor's fishing boat.'

'Did you swim out to the boy and bring him in?' said his sister, laughing and shaking him softly by the arms.

'I say, please, if you don't mind—'

'Oh, poor boy, I daresay your arms are strained and cut—just sit down and talk English if you can.'

'But I can't, you see,' said Herbert, laughing against the grain. 'I don't mean about talking: only I'd rather stand please.'

'My dear boy, why didn't you say at once? and you wouldn't have been flogged. It's your own fault, and a great shame: but I hope it wasn't much this time?'

'Oh dear no,' said the boy, who was shy of the subject in her presence and voluble among males. 'That is, he hit rather hard, but[39] I shall be all right presently.'[40]

'You poor child, if we had only known![41] I'm sure you bore it well; and I dare say he has half killed you.'

'I didn't then,' said Herbert, reddening to the very eye-lashes; 'I blubbed like a girl. Don't talk about it, please. I know I'm a beastly coward. Some fellows can stand no end of cuts, and never sing out; wish I could.'

'Admitting that, how did you manage in the water?'

'I told you, didn't I? I was in the way, and there was this fellow sinking (I suppose he could swim a stroke or two when he was pitched out), and he tried to get hold of me, and I funked rather for I thought he'd lug me down, and a stunning big wave broke right over both of us and chucked us on shore out of reach; and he wasn't hurt and I wasn't hurt, and I went home and got jolly well swished and I hope he did: and that's all about all. I've got no end of sums to do and I don't want to catch it again.'

'I shan't let you off like that, however: you must see the boy's father, who has brought him up to thank you: come along and don't make faces, you're not going to be swished as you call it.'

'I say, I can't, really: it is such rot. Oh, I wish they were both'—(he swallowed the last word or so). 'Fellows are such awful fools,' he added in a reflective and decisive manner, as of one laying down the law with regard to a vexed question of natural philosophy.

Lady Wariston collared the boy and marched him out. He went with a sufficiently bad grace, smarting and sulking; his flesh still tender from punishment, his temper chafed and his pulses feverish, ready to cry with angry shyness and shame. Once confronted with Mathison he was courteous enough;[42] the man's keen and grave old face, fresh with the savour and bright from the breath of the sea—his hair yellowish grey as the paler foam passed over by the sun—his fixed imperious mouth and athlete's neck—his clear, wary, untameable eyes which had seen many dangers through, had overlived and overcome much trouble, and had never been abased in man's sight or altered[43] in sight of death—kindled and filled the boy's fancy; his small repugnant modesties and puerilities[44] were knocked out of him and put to shame[45] in a presence that seemed to him old and pure and strong and simple as the sea. Mathison said nothing coarsely; he gave thanks in clear clean words, without any fulsome incrustation of praise. Lady Wariston said afterwards that her brother seemed to catch the man's manner, and replied in words as courteous and un-embarrassed. Mathison nodded gravely with a graver smile, when he disclaimed in a clear earnest way the groundless charge of having run any risk or made himself of any use. Then came the explanations; Herbert forgot his stripes on hearing how the younger boy had put out alone to carry a message across the bay which had he gone by land could not have been delivered in less than six hours; how he had got too near shore off Wansdale Point, had lost his head and pulled wrong, and how once among the breakers he had given up, letting the boat pitch and drive till it lurched over; then, thinking he might likely be thrown on shore if he could but keep afloat and follow without fear the impulse of the waves, had been beaten out of breath by their violent shifting surges, buffetted and throttled and plucked hither and thither for a minute or so, but still on the whole borne inshore; had seen faintly with beaten and blinded eyes a white form afloat hard by, and caught and lost hold of it, and felt the whole weight of the breaker upon him; had been hurled straight through the noise of the sea and shot up on shore as from a sling, several feet from the other figure. ('There,' said Bertie in a triumphant parenthesis, 'you see I didn't pull him out.') Waiving that point as immaterial Mathison wound up: 'Ye wouldn't have done like that now, sir.'

'I couldn't have managed at all,' said Herbert, 'and I think that little chap was very plucky; I don't know anything about handling a boat.'

'It's like ye'll not,' said Mathison. 'Ye tâke to the wâter, though.'

Herbert caught at this. 'Oh, I say, will you take me out sometimes when there's a jolly sea.'

'You musn't drown him for me, Mr. Mathison, that's all,' said his sister. 'We couldn't spare this piece of good just now.'[16]

'Better ask the kid to look after me,' Herbert muttered audibly.

'I shall make Wariston speak to Mr. Denham, Bertie, and get you a holiday,' she said on their way back.

'I'd rather have it on Friday if you don't mind,' said the boy, moved to prudence by painfully private considerations:[47] and mindful, for one thing, that the benches of a fishing-boat were somewhat hard seats. 'And then I'll go out with those fellows.'[48]

'I don't know that. Well, you shall have the rest of the day clear, however.'

She took him back into the library, where Mr. Denham was reading[49] with a fitful relish impaired by straying thoughts.

'For once,' she said apologetically, 'Mr. Denham, will you lend me this boy for the remainder of his lesson time? it will be punishment enough for my intrusion to be saddled with his company all day.'

'Lady Wariston, I must say Herbert deserves no sort of indulgence.'

'I'm not quite sure,' she said, caressing the boy's neck and hair with her right hand softly and proudly. 'He has been punished already.'

Herbert's eyes turned towards the place of execution, and hers following them noticed what lay at hand.[50]

'I can't leave Bertie in such a dangerous neighbourhood,' said his sister. 'I must carry him off by force then?'

Denham looked her in the face, shaken inwardly and throughout by a sense of inevitable pain. Curiously he seemed to contemplate himself with a quiet scientific wonder; to feel the pulses of his fever, to examine and approve or condemn the play played out on the inner stage of his mind, to count up the acts and scenes of the tragic agony underlying for him all these infinitely little incidents, childish and comical chances of the day. Standing with her hand over Bertie's shoulder, the woman waited half smiling.[51] The glory and the terror of her beauty held down desire and absorbed despair. Rage rose in him again like a returning sea. Furious fancies woke up and fought inside him, crying out one upon the other. He would have given his life for leave to touch her, his soul for a chance of dying crushed down under her feet:[52] an emotion of extreme tenderness, lashed to fierce insanity by the circumstances, frothed over into a passion of vehement cruelty. Deeply he desired to die by her, if that could be; and more deeply, if this could be, to destroy her: scourge her into swooning and absorb the blood with kisses; caress and lacerate her loveliness, alleviate and heighten her pains; to feel her foot upon his throat, and wound her own with his teeth; submit his body and soul for a little to her lightest will, and satiate upon hers the desperate caprice of his immeasureable desire; to inflict careful torture[53] on limbs too tender to

38

embrace, suck the tears off her laden eyelids, bite through her sweet and shuddering lips. During the momentary pause which gave time for these and other visions not more wholesome of things not more feasible to swarm and subside, his face told no tales; the eyes alone let out perhaps some look of admiration. For two creatures more beautiful never stood together; either face had a look of resolute petition and defiant appeal: either smiled with the same lips and looked straight with the same clear eyes. If mere infliction of pain had so subdued the boy's face to perfect beauty that it was now identical with hers in expression also, what final transformation to some delicious excess of excellence would suffering not work upon hers? what tender and passionate pain would it not awake in those faultless features, touching them with an intolerable charm and a grace of life too beautiful to bear? Even thus, they were a strange sample of perfect repeated work: but to have seen her eyes also overflow, her lips tremble and her limbs heave with exquisite and hopeless pain, would alone have quenched the violent thirst of his mingling passions.

He was not really silent half a minute, though it seemed to him long since she had spoken when he answered her with smile for smile.

'I cannot resist force. If you take it upon yourself to ruin my pupil, I am not responsible, you see.'

'Well, I will take my chance,' she answered; 'thank you. I dare say you are as glad to be relieved as poor Herbert.'

She made herself pleasant beyond words to the boy all the rest of that day. His little piece of daring, his perfectly honest dislike of notice and candid dread of praise, had taken her fancy: she played and sang to him as he stood by her, to his infinite enjoyment. Voice and memory were alike faultless; she gave him out of her store of ballads and sea-songs enough to haunt and excite him for days. She talked and made him talk freely; many hours passed and found and left them in perfect pleasure. He expanded towards her and she inclined towards him more and more: he grew up to her as she bent down to him. Old words passed and old things revived; there was nothing yet of bitter or black in the memory of either. In the past time towards which they had turned back, their thoughts and lives had not been more clean and frank and sweet.

'Do you remember those stepping stones in the lower burn?'

'Yes, and when the flood came and we were forbidden to try them.'

'And who tried to cross when my father was up at the Frashets, you bad child!'

'I was cheeky enough before I tried, and then I lost my pluck at the third, and you came and lugged me out.'

'I can see your legs plunging and sliding about: You did deserve flogging that time, Bertie. Nine and a half, you were; four years ago.'

'You were in a jolly rage with me.'

'Rather; it ruined my things, you know, fishing for boys in the rapids. I hadn't much to ruin.'

'That was a stunning thing to do, if you like: what a plucky boy you would have been.'

'One's enough in a house, to say the least: I don't think you wanted a big brother to show you the way, Bertie. Come, do you remember this?

> O weary fa' the east wind[54]
>   And weary fa' the west:
> And gin I were under the wan waves wide
>   I wot weel wad I rest.
>
> O weary fa' the north wind
>   And weary fa' the south;
> The sea went ower my good lord's head
>   Or ever he kissed my mouth.

Weary fa' the windward ricks,
  And weary fa' the lee;
They might hae broken an hundred ships
  And let my love's gang free.

And weary fa' ye, mariners a',
  And weary fa' the sea;
It might hae sunken[55] a seven score men
  And let my ae love be.[56]

'Don't I remember!' said Herbert: 'you used to sing it when my father was out, before candles came.'

'Ah!' said Lady Wariston, sighing as though for idleness.

'It was a very jolly place, poor old Kirklowes was. The burn here is nothing to the Frashets burn. There was no sea, though; and fancy no sea!'

'Sometimes I wish I never dreamt of it now. I don't like hearing the rapids when I'm asleep or near waking, and the wind about the house, and all the burn roaring after the rain: then I know that must be the sea and I'm somewhere else, and wake up—I could cry very often.'

'I dream that way, too, and I don't like it either; it makes one feel sick after the old place, as if one was awfully hungry and too seedy to eat.'

'I know. All sorts of things come back and taste bitter in one's mouth, literally. How splendid it was in the spring; and quite trees enough.'

'Quite,' said Bertie emphatically.

'Between the moors about the water-heads; prettier than these; perfect little places, with firs and rowans and birches; but we won't talk about that sort to-day.'

'Well, don't then,' said Herbert, much aggrieved.

'Poor Bertie! I must sing something again to put it out of your head, I suppose. This used to frighten you a little once, do you recollect?'

41

Quo' the bracken-bush to the wan well-head,
'O whatten a man is this man dead?'

'O this is the king's ae son,' quo' she,
'That lies here dead upon my knee.'

'What will ye do wi' the king's ae son?'
'The little fishes shall feed him on.'

'What will ye strew for his body's bed?'
'Green stanes aneath his head.'

'What will ye gie for his body's grace?'
'Green leaves abune his face.'

'What will ye do wi' the rings on his hand?'
'Hide them ower wi' stane and sand.'

'What will ye do wi' the gowd in his hair?'
'Hide it ower wi' rushes fair.'

'What shall he have[59] when the hill-winds blow?'
'Cauld rain and routh o' snow.'

'What shall he get when the birds fly in?'
'Death for life and sorrow for sin.'

'What shall come to his father the king?'
'Long life and a heavy[59] thing.'

'What shall come to his mother the queen?'
'Grey hairs and a bitter teen.'

'What to his leman, that garr'd him be slain?'[60]
'Hell's pit and hell's pain.'

'I like that,' said Herbert. 'It's so jolly vicious: and I like the water being a woman.'

'Do you think that's what makes her answers so spiteful? What a bleak little piece of verse it is; you can feel the wind in the ferns blowing down the burn-tide to where the body lies, bending the fern-leaves and making them talk: and the water lapping and curling and twisting about it. I fancy it a sort of heugh, wet and low down and well hidden away, very cold and green; where the slayers[61] had left him thrown down and struck through; like that field with a well-head in it beyond the Birkenshaw—I beg your pardon,[62] Herbert—where we used to go after the cotton-grass: I can't help it if it was there, you know. I can see the body lying there with its rings in the burn.'

'I wonder what he had done to the woman.'

'All those stories are best half-told; they frighten more and stick closer: but they're always much the same, and a very good story.'

'Oh, I say, here are those fools coming. I suppose I'd better cut.'

'Two sets at once; that's an infliction. Come down in good time, Bertie.'

'I wish there was no dinner: why do people come here, I wonder?'

'Go to bed then, or dine in the steward's room. Perhaps Mrs. Bulmer would let you into the nursery. Don't be stupid, and I'll look after you. Besides, I don't know who's likely to oppress you, but I am always in fear of my life with Lady Midhurst.'

'I shall hook it, that's all. I'm sure Mathison would let me sleep at his crib. I say, what a tremendous old swell he is.'

'Yes, but never mind. Lord Charles Brandon will talk horses to you.'

'I don't care about horses; and I hate old Brandon: he's a cad.'

'His daughter writes splendid verses, people say, and is to be a beauty.'

'I think she must be rather a fool to write: women ought to sing. How old is she? dark or fair?'

'Seventeen: and very dark, I believe.'

'That is rather what I like, though.'

'You had better get engaged now, and marry when you leave school: she is evidently the right age and style, and as Lady Midhurst would say, will have money in time; all her mother's; tied up so that the horrid horse-jockey of a father can't touch it.' (This she said in facsimile of the elder lady's manner.) 'I foresee that Lesbia Brandon is your fate.'

'Oh, but that settles it. Where did she get such a beast of a name? Lesbia! sounds like a sick poodle.'

'Irish; the mother was Irish. Now I must go and prepare for them.'

Lady Midhurst and Mr. Linley were just of an age, and coeval with the century. Many others besides her present hostess were afraid of the venomous old beauty, who had gone all to brain and tongue, her former friends said. She was still handsome in a keen birdlike fashion; voluble and virulent with a savour of secret experience. Outside her own family she regarded any man or woman as a *fera naturae*,[63] and followed the game simple with an eye to sport. Certain optimists believed her capable in private of good-nature and affection. She visited at few houses, and rarely; but was excellent in a small dull company by way of salt or spice. She was fond of art and voracious of literature; and knowing somewhat of each had never tried her hand at either. A completer heathen had not existed in the pre-Christian era. When in good humour, she was a woman of good counsel; and her humour was seldom bad. She had done many good turns, and many evil; and was ready, as the case might be, to help or to hinder, to set up or to upset. Fluent elaborate scandal was an offence to her and she could at need suppress it swiftly and finally; but quick brief words of comment, citations or nick-names sure to bite and burn, she could coin, stamp, and pass, almost in a breath; and would afterwards drop the victim as

44

a sheep with its owner's mark well singed into the fleece: [64] she never slew the slain twice. Her husband had been dead many years; her one daughter, twice married and once divorced, did not visit: and the wise woman, as Lord Wariston called her, stood by herself as a little lonely power.

Mr. Linley was a slight smooth-faced man, with thin hair and good features; though somewhat too like a shaven satyr with the ears rounded; fair-skinned, with large reverted lips and repellent eyes. They were grey and bright, mobile and significant;[65] their gravity and mockery were alike impressive and repulsive. Sometimes too the whole face bore the seal of heavy sorrow and a fatal fatigue; as though restrained self-contempt and habitual weariness of habit were too strong for the endurance of a tough and supple nature. His nephew, who as a child had found him amiable, liked him still: and some younger men and older women tolerated or enjoyed his company; many others abhorred him as a thing foul and dangerous,[66] who had no reason assignable. No special scandal clove to his name; he had married early in life a handsome heiress who brought him one son and died seventeen years after. To her and to their son, now also dead, he was said to have behaved ill, even cruelly: but such rumours were loose and light as dust or down. His worst social fault was a propensity to rambling cynical declamation; he had tried political life in his youth and dropped it as a barren nuisance. 'His notion of talk,' said Lady Midhurst, who had ranged herself against him of late years only,[67] 'was monologue *plus* a listener; and his monologues were dithyrambics of the dog-kennel[68] school of philosophy. His idea of satire was an ounce of decaying salt in a pail of fresh water: the froth of a snake without the sting. A beautiful speaker, if you wanted plentiful words, unsavoury meanings, and no purport; a master-marksman, who let fly his shot nowither, and drew the bow with unwashed hands.' And so forth. He was a scholar and collector, fond of books, coins, prints, and bric-a-brac of a secret kind, kept under locks and behind curtains; he had lived much in Paris, and when decrying the English would hint at close

45

relations with French public men. Some two years after this, in 1852, he used to assert that he had watched the birth, baptism, vaccination, schooling, and adolescence of the second empire: giving the dates. 'If you like to believe him,' said Lady Midhurst, who professed a faith in the house of Orleans, 'it was he who suggested the massacre to M. Beauharnais,[69] and he was on the boulevards by the side of Leroy.' (Worlds, Lady Midhurst averred, should not induce her to call the man Saint-Arnaud.[70] She retained this habit of severe accuracy during the Crimean War,[71] to the infinite perplexity of her acquaintance.) ' "Oui, messieurs, rien que cela; c'est moi qui fis le Deux Décembre. Le prince président avait perdu la tête; il verdissait à vue d'oeil: je vis qu'il fallait en finir".' (Her burlesque was better, if broader, than Lady Wariston's; she had always been excellent at theatricals.) ' "Vous avez la bonté de croire que c'est un homme fort? Du tout; il ne sut jamais improviser, et il manque d'aplomb. Au fond ce n'est qu'un doctrinaire; du reste, le meilleur homme du monde." For my part,' Lady Midhurst wound up, 'I believe him (not the emperor) capable of half he says; that is, he has the heart for it, but not the head. As for the correspondence with MM. Fialin[72] et Cie.,[73] I should like well to see his autographs.' She called him among friends Talleyrand-Bridoison;[74] he called her in private Madame de Faublas.[75]

Lord Charles Brandon was a man endurable but indescribable. His one feat when off the turf had been his marriage;[76] and for this it is said he was indebted to other exertions than his own. The venerable Marquis of Burleigh, twenty years his senior, having married at sixty-five a low-born maiden who brought him by way of dowry good looks, copious ridicule, and a brace of boys within the year, could not but recommend to a younger brother, thus twice cut off from one chance, a prompt and profitable union with some equally ineligible female in the bonds of unholy matrimony. (These epithets and their application, it may be noted, appertain of right to Lady Midhurst.) One was happily at hand, against whose fortune, at least, scandal had never thrown a word of suspicion. Her dearest enemy could not call her poor; her friends had called her worse. Otherwise her lord might scarcely have wooed and won her as he did. His unimpeachable heiress died in giving birth to the one child on whom her only desirable possessions were settled: and his daughter's birth, compassionate friendship had to remark, fully counterbalanced the advantage of her mother's death. Especially as the lord of Burleigh, noteworthy as gentlest of consorts and hopefullest of parents, considered that his double duties, to the sex and to the family, had been duly and dexterously discharged by the union of an old friend and a younger brother. How he throve so well none could accurately say; an authority before cited asserts that he was paid by his grooms to break in his own horses; which seems an insufficient and inconclusive explanation. He took a perplexed pride in the daughter who stood between him and wealth; and was altogether a good sort of fool, and in spite of a noisy life rather innocent than not, the same authority informs me. She must be a judge of innocence, Mr. Linley said.

These two contemporaries had met by the way, and a third passenger in the same compartment might have assisted at such a battue[77] of reputations, such a holocaust of character, as few are invited to enjoy. Having tacitly taken truce till the train should arrive, they began their murderous work with the bitter relish[78] of grey gladiators. With sudden net and short pike-thrust they entrapped and despatched victim upon victim. Feeling the taste of blood on their tongues, they grew fiercer, and mangled the martyrs with superfluous and luxurious cruelty. In due time they naturally fell upon the family they were about to bless with their benign presences; and lacerated its members in a fashion worthy of Nero with his claws on for practice at the circus.

'Splendid,' said Lady Midhurst; 'I never saw pure beauty before. You must go into heaven or hovels to find it, I perceive. The father was a labouring man, people tell one.'

'Farmer; lived on his own land, that is. You know that Wariston married the other children as well?'

'Daughters?'

'I think not; two or three boys I seem to have heard of, fresh from the paternal plough. It must be a household of the most incredible: [79] I have never been there since. In his father's time it was very fairly oppressive. My poor sister you remember; and her husband was a mere ox.'

'Quelle horreur!' said Lady Midhurst; 'cela dut être pour elle un supplice épouvantable:' (She embarked upon French here to draw him on and out, with a faint copy in her voice of his own inflexions. Also there was now a third passenger, who sat peering meek and mute over his paper, an apparent curate.)

'Epouvantable, c'est le mot. The black ox[80] had trodden, not on his foot, but on his tongue: he talked beef, and should have eaten hay.'

'I suppose the son inherited his taste for farm produce.'

'It seems so,' said Mr. Linley, glittering with venom so as to look swollen and burnished like a chafing snake.

'It is beyond words,' said Lady Midhurst in a tone of deliberate enthusiasm. 'Her eyes! de l'or fondu, de l'or bruni; one must go to Balzac to see such eyes.'[81]

'It's a pity her hair will take no sort of dye; for of course she has given it the chance, poor girl.'

'I admire it, and don't see that dark hair would improve her. Elle est toute confite en fleurs, et cette chevelure-là sent le printemps.'

'You are very good. It is not Scotch hair, I admit, but the golden age is over for top-knots.'

'Her cheeks white roses and her mouth a red. Decidedly, your nephew is a wise man. She must have had followers as the servants say, in her own class.'

'She had no class,' said Mr. Linley. 'They were by way of noble too, rather than otherwise, I believe.'

'Par example!'

'As to birth, you know: ruined: I suppose they could call three potatoes in the world their own.'

'Three cranberries, you mean,'[82] said Lady Midhurst, looking out at the moor country as they passed. 'I perceive we are near.'

It was a long drive from the station, and by the time they were at Ensdon either gladiator, to speak by figures, was tired out and recumbent on a heap of slain. They drove up in the moist low twilight, not unseen from upper windows: and Lady Wariston, having dismissed her brother and her ballads, came down to meet them. They had never seen her in London so royally beautiful: their epigrams curled up at sight of her and stung themselves to death. Her actions had the vivid grace and splendour of fire: her slowest gesture or most gradual smile had a light and a sense in it. Music moved with her motion, a colour and an odour of beauty seemed to pass out of her as she stirred and spoke. There was more than a tune in the passage of her feet, better than a song in the gracious and equal harmonies of her talk.[83]

She told Lord Wariston before dinner of Herbert's experiences. He had been shooting for most part of the day, and was still out when Mathison came. The recital pleased him and he engaged that Herbert should get off better next time. The boy must come down to dinner of course, and the ladies must take charge of him when they left. He was aware that his uncle's talk across the wine did not pay to the possible innocence of boys that delicate respect enjoined by the Roman[84] moralist.

At dinner there were Fieldfares and Chalfords in abundance, mainly feminine. The grey brilliance of Lady Midhurst's rapid mobile eyes flashed once at each and passed on to another, hopeless of sport. She had a well-trained and perfect power to look without staring and see without looking. Before they went in Lord Wariston, standing next her, said so suddenly that her eyes were startled into a smile as visible as lurked under her lips, 'Margaret, where's the boy?' and as he appeared shy and reluctant brought him up to Mr. Linley who was speaking to the tutor, 'This is my little brother.'

'Pardieu!' said his uncle inaudibly. 'Where are the wings?'

Lady Midhurst raised her glasses at this query with scarcely

49

the shadow of an approving laugh. They had both started at sight of the boy, remembering rumours[85] talked over by the way. His fresh, graceful, complete beauty was unspoilt by any grave fault of manner: the critics could find no taint on him of effeminate or vulgar bearing.

'He might have been years at Eton,' Lady Midhurst said. 'I never saw such a beautiful young male. Something like a grandson of mine, but looks handsomer to-night, at least. Spoilt a good deal, I suspect.'

'Ask his tutor,' said Lady Wariston; 'he is responsible.'

'Hm; and looks as if he knew it,' said her elder. 'No, I recant; a boy is not likely to get spoilt in such hands; or under them. What's his name? Herbert? not my idea of the name at all.'

'Well, sir, do they call you a good boy?' said Mr. Linley with a Napoleonic pinch of the chin.

'I don't know,' said Herbert. 'Not to my face.'

'I don't imagine your character is written on your face. Do you suppose they have reason to speak ill of you behind your back?'

'It's a chouse if they do, that's all.'

'A Cupid only to be birched by the hands of Venus,' said Mr. Linley to his nephew with a glance from Denham to Lady Wariston as the boy moved off, getting near a male Fieldfare of eighteen who patronized him through awkwardness and fear of the female race. 'What a beautiful woman the mother must have been.'

'Never saw her,' said Lord Wariston; 'died when he was born.'

'The little brother looks as if he could kick now and then; I daresay he wants a brushing pretty often: a moderate brushing, about enough to tickle[86] the flies off—they will settle on milk, and he is quite as fair as his sister, for all one sees: a little gentle irritation. I shall catechize him this evening, Denham; the boy must be well worth flogging.'

'A very hopeless case if he isn't,' said Lord Wariston; 'I don't think he is in such a desperate way as that.'

'I mean he looks promising; clever enough, you can see by the eyes and mouth, if he were properly brought out; but idle, I would wager. A boy not worth his birch must be a block-head or a blackguard.'

'He is quick enough,' said his tutor; 'but infamous at sums, and his verses are good once in two years; fair in metre, I can't say he is liable to false quantities, but flat and poor through mere laziness. I hope for nothing above the middle fourth at best, this year; and he'll never be sent up[87] at this rate.'

'Except in the bill,'[88] said Lord Wariston; 'but they tell me swishing is likely to fall off.'

'Décidément, cela vaut la peine de vexer,'[89] said Mr. Linley in the tone of one who makes an original remark.

Herbert has never guessed for which of his sins he was placed between Lord Charles Brandon and a Miss Chalford, whose other neighbour was a Fieldfare of twenty-seven, much enamoured of her; Sir John's second son, and a noticeable fool. Upon him she turned a cold and tawny shoulder, paying loud and obtrusive attentions to the boy, who felt as if sitting naked on live coals and compressed his lips and eyebrows at each necessary movement.[90] She wished he would ride with her; had no brothers of his age; Tom and Charley shot; did he? so glad he did not, and was sure he rode well: heard he liked the water; horridly unsafe, and her brothers didn't. Did he like school? ah, perhaps would when he went; Tom was taken away after one half, there was such bullying; and he was flogged once, and Mr. Chalford made a row about it; and the masters never even apologized; it was most horrid altogether; she hoped Herbert would never never be flogged at school; was sure he was too clever to deserve it, and too good; but how much nicer to work at home with a tutor who really understood one; was he at all afraid of Mr. Denham? Herbert unblushingly denied any such fear; meantime the mute Field-fare almost wept upon his plate. Miss Chalford was certain Herbert had no cause, but she was afraid of men who looked clever:[91] she wished so much she had been born clever. Here the Fieldfare of eighteen, who had not left school six months, and had lately assured Herbert that he still tingled at the word 'block',⁹² burst into blushing and bubbling laughter as he noticed in his junior opposite a certain shuffle of body and flush of face unmistakeable to any eye trained in a public school. Herbert felt the laughter like a swift lash round the loins, and his cheeks caught fire; his fingers turned to thawing ice, the roots of his hair pricked and burnt the skin; he smarted and sickened with helpless shame and horrible fear of the next word or look. He did not even see how the transgressor for his part turned white and black with horror at himself and made apparently endeavours to get bodily into his napkin. He did not hear Lord Charles ask when he was to be at Eton and whether he liked the prospect of being young Lunsford's fag: also whether he knew what he had to expect at school in case of delinquency. 'On voit qu'il a froid dans le dos, cet enfant,' said Mr. Linley to Mrs. Chalford, who replied, 'Ah, yes, quite, of course,' with a laugh that would have consigned her at once to a private asylum for incurables, had she been under scrutiny of any qualified couple of examiners; the dialect of Balzac in the accent of Paris was to her a new fashion of French. To his surprise Lady Wariston answered for her on his other side; 'Avouez qu'il y a de quoi.'

'He is delicious, your brother; I grudge him to Eton.'

Chalfords and Fieldfares, fathers and sons, overheard and struck in upon this. Lady Midhurst, hopeless of better game, fell upon the nearest Chalford and worried him with dexterous feline mouth; Lord Charles told a school story which Herbert could follow, and promised him a mount if ever he came far enough south-east; there were no other fellows to meet, but his daughter was a good horsewoman. By this time the boy's head had cooled and cleared again, and he asked in what he took for the manner of an adult; 'But Miss Brandon writes, doesn't she—verses?'

'Ah, you know that? It doesn't spoil her riding: do you care for verse?'

'Awfully,' said Herbert; adding with a judicious reserve, 'when it's good.'

'Lesbia could do your verses for you when you go to Eton; she can manage elegiacs; never could myself and was always getting swished for mine some fifty years ago; I remember in 1800 or thereabouts I and another fellow,[94] poor Tom Midhurst, (this in the due murmur),[95] were so used to our flogging every after twelve,[96] the praepostor[97] of our division wouldn't have dared show up[98] a bill without our two names in it; would have been as much as his skin was worth. Tom and I would toss up at the last which should take his turn first, and have it over;[99] plucky fellow he was too.'

'I should this he was,' said Bertie, looking at his widow.

'Yes, but we got quite used to it. No chance of your coming in for that sort of fare at school; they spoil all you boys now. We were rather fast boys I'm afraid; Midhurst ran wild enough till they married him to Miss Cheyne; perhaps afterwards, I don't say. She was magnificent in 1820 I can tell you; there was a famous portrait of her with their baby, poor thing: hm, well, there are stories[100] about us all, my boy; most of us that is.'

'Was she really a stunner?' said the boy.

'She and Miss Garth were rivals, and the Cheyne won by long odds,' said Lord Charles, finally forgetting his auditor's age. 'Linley remembers her coming out, and he's thirteen years my junior. The daughter was a beauty you know, and they say her daughter[101] will be: shouldn't like to marry into the race though. About your age I suppose or younger,' (he said this as his eyes met the boy's, expanding and intent.) 'Should you like the grandmother-in-law? I should think not. Time enough to settle when you get through school, eh? If my daughter had been a boy she'd have been still at Eton, and I'd have told her to look after you; she's half male as it is I think sometimes; don't know where she got all her brains; she turns out verses you see in English, admirably; and she can do Sapphics fit for a sixth-form.'

'Latin?' said Herbert; 'I hate them; beastly metre, I tried

53

it once and came to grief. I can manage elegiacs though. What does she write about in English?'

Her father was somewhat thrown out. 'Well, I suppose she writes about the natural sort of thing for verses; lovers; she always takes the man's part; not the old rubbish about girls dying for love of men. She's not in that line: and women are such fools mostly who write about men. Lady Midhurst said a little thing of hers about a fellow looking at a nun and thinking you know by Jove what an infernal shame it was one couldn't get at her through the grate—said it was splendid, and she would be the real modern Sappho: it set her up tremendously, for our friend over there at the top of the table has known all the great lights[402] in that line of business—Mrs. Lemons[103] you know and Miss Handon and all that set I suppose: corresponds with some of them now, I've no doubt.'

'I should like awfully to read that; but why does she do things in Latin, like a boy? isn't it rather rot, Latin verse? I wouldn't.'

'I should think not, my poor boy, and you'll have had some score of good reasons to like it less by the time you begin your third or fourth half; and you'll hardly prefer second editions corrected and illustrated with cuts, engraved and taken on the block, by an eminent hand; plenty of cuts to every school-book, you know. But a girl who doesn't know what flogging means naturally doesn't hate things that remind a fellow of birch and make him writhe; ah, I thought you were big boy enough to understand that, Master Herbert; you've found out what the twigs mean, have you? it's as well to be prepared, and not go to Eton as I did, with a clear skin; to be sure I was but eight or nine, but I can remember how I cried at my first flogging, and suffered for it. So as Lesbia never was in the bill in her life and couldn't be switched for her false quantities she rather likes the work; always had a hand for languages and says it's good metrical practice; I believe the truth is she wanted all her life to be a boy, as everybody thought she would till she was born, and must

54

needs have a boy's training and do a boy's lessons; minus the rod afterwards, you know. Curious woman her governess was, and encouraged it; they were wonderfully fond of each other. I had nothing to do with them: never tried to manage: they did very well, and got through all manner of things by themselves. Lesbia talked of suicide when the woman talked of marriage; nothing came of it either way. I'll let you see some of the verses if you like: wasn't much in that line myself at thirteen.'

The loose-flowing talk, often broken and resumed, here lapsed into a lull on all sides, over the dawning dessert. Lady Midhurst had absolutely blown her bird to pieces; riddled through and through, it gasped and fluttered horribly, dripping by fits a moribund beak in wine. Lord Charles had chattered enough for himself and his small neighbour, and had no more to reveal of puerile recollections of paternal previsions. Mr. Linley lay on his guns, fully charged with talk fit for masculine ears alone, and angrily expectant of the last departing petticoat. On a sudden Herbert was stung by the sound of his own name; and felt as though a hot iron were clapped to his skin and a sharp hook were twitching his back, when he awoke to the horrible knowledge that his brother-in-law was narrating, with laudatory note and comment which made him tingle with blushes from scalp to sole, his supposed rescue of little Mathison.

'So my brother seeing him in the water went in after him and swam till he laid hold of the fellow by the hair; and though he couldn't well pull him on shore unassisted, he held on till the sea threw both boys up together. A man could have done no more, and you can think what a heavy sea there was yesterday: and I hope you agree it was gallantly done by the boy.'

Herbert sat quivering and wincing as though again under the birch: his throat swelled and contracted by turns, his cheeks and eyelids smarted as if touched and pricked by flame. It was the worst minute of that day to him; and as Lord Wariston ended he broke out like a younger child, for-

getful of adult airs;—'Please don't, you know I didn't really:
if you don't mind:'—the last words sharp and shuddering
with a repressed sob. Under the torture of shame and violated
reserve, which he felt as a thing dishonourable and unfair—
with the proud quiet delicacy of some children, too innocent
and ignorant to deserve the name of modesty, laid waste and
insulted in him, overhauled and abused, bared and branded
by the gross hands of public praise—conscious too that there
had been in his own eyes nothing really noticeable or creditable in a defiant freak undertaken without real aim to pursue
or real fear to overcome—he tasted his unshed tears and
tightened his face to subdue them. His intense and bitter
desire to do something worth praise doubled the pain he felt
at being praised for a thing not worth it.

After their host's speech a male or two applauded with
soft ironical hands, and sundry women with rustling tongues:
but nothing was to be got from the boy but a sight of twitching cheeks and long low eyelashes, till his excellent old
neighbour stung him afresh—'Well done, my boy, and your
schoolfellows ought to hear of it.'

'Oh, please look here,' said Herbert, facing him with wide
eyes under their quick vibrating eyelids. 'I didn't, upon my
word; and when I was in I funked. I didn't mean, and I
didn't like, and it's a great chouse to say I did and make a
fellow feel a sneak. Because I haven't the pluck. And it's
beastly to have to say so. I-I can't even take a swishing
properly—not like what you said, you know.' (This was
uttered in a very low quaver of the voice.) 'Please don't think
that, or let people say it; it's not true; and it's a shame.'

'Tears of the young Achilles,' said Lady Midhurst.

'Cupid and the bee, rather,' said her rival at the lower end
to Lady Wariston as she rose smiling, and swept off her
brother with the women.

'I believe just now you could make that boy head a forlorn
hope,' said Lord Charles when the men were settled.

'You could make any boy,' said Mr. Linley. 'The difficulty
is to distinguish those who would if they were not made;

and when you find them, to put them under confinement.'

'The little chap will go no end of howlers by and by, he's so handsome; fancy the rows he'll have with women,' said the Fieldfare whom Miss Chalford had ignored while talking to Herbert. He was willing to regain in the eyes of her nearest brother the dignity proper to a man of his years, not ignorant of London or life.

'Allow me to differ,' said Mr. Linley, who had a horrible delicacy of ear and could listen with ease and profit to remote whispers. 'That is not the beauty which lasts; it might perhaps hold out in a woman'

'I must say then,' said the venturous Fieldfare, 'it's a pity he wasn't born a girl.'

'That, again, I confess I do not see. Any sort of beauty is good at all times and pleasant while it lasts. No doubt it is not the kind from which the possessor gets most pleasure; the broad-blown beauty and pink perfection[104] that goes with a shapely bulk and an efflux of hair over cheek and mouth is valuable—to an immoral person; there are, as you observe (doubtless on good grounds), women whom such rather common and cheap honey-pots allure and refresh. I doubt this boy's growing up so handsome; he may retain some good points.'

'What can be the use of good looks then if a fellow can't keep them when they might help him to some fun?'

'To give pleasure while they last to others; as a singing-bird does, or a flower. You don't ask a rosebud to turn into an apple; and a deer doesn't enjoy venison.'

Here the philosopher, who had an innocent relish for sweet scraps worthy of notice as his one harmless taste, absorbed certain prepared fruits with amorous suction.

The bewildered Fieldfare looked at his neighbouring Chalford with eyes dilated and swimming aghast under aspiring eyebrows. 'What the devil does that mean?' he asked dumbly; and the Chalford answered in like wise, 'Mad.'

Lord Wariston talked of birds to Mr. Chalford the father; Sir John Fieldfare, in mild despair of the due babble, assailed

Mr. Denham, who proved unmalleable. The youths drank and twittered. Lord Charles said suddenly to his neighbour; —'Your friend wears well, I think.'

'Not so badly,' said the sage; 'but yellow, I must say, yellow. Always had an inclination to the sunflower. And so very vicious that she must have overgrown her age.'

'But she has been admirable; not white and red of course; but for a pale woman perfect: and she keeps the features.'

'A qui le dites-vous? I never cared much for white and red. Art's above nature in that respect,[105] with King Lear's leave;[106] if you know how to lay it on, and where, and when. Certainly she was rather noble once in her way; my way it was for a time.' (His face looked older than his senior's as their heads neared.) 'But longevity isn't in the nature of the beast. She is nothing now but husk and fangs.'

'Come,' said his nephew, 'let her alone, will you? She's a clever woman all through, not like a fool with a sharp wit; she can be delicious; and I've been in love with her ever since I was fourteen[107] and she tipped me at school.'

'She likes innocence, I know,' said Mr. Linley; 'does the philoprogenitive most creditably and naturally. Very likely she is now playing Dione (wasn't that Cupid's grandmother's name, Denham?) and choking the small god with verbal comfits.'

'Well, I like a woman to be fond of boys and girls,' said Sir John.

'A singular taste,' said Mr. Linley, 'if you cut it in half; it is agreeable to reflect how frequently a part at least of your liking must be gratified. But we know why Wariston defends the Midhurst; she tried her daughter on him some fourteen years ago, and though he drew the line there you observe he retains a sort of benevolence towards the whole race. I never thought that girl's marriage[108] would hold water for long. Epouser les deux générations as Balzac has it may be very well for a woman; a man may not marry his mother-in-law. Why, good heaven, he was absolutely one may say the girl's step-father.'[109]

'I won't have it,' said Lord Wariston; 'choose another family, please.'

'Except that your poor friend Midhurst was alive at the time, I think?'

'Time of the marriage? no,' said Lord Charles; 'he died some time before; years. Not so very long after old Sir Francis. Quite used up you know; never was a strong fellow.'

'I was right then; but I won't press the point, Wariston. Do you remember the girl her brother[110] married on a broad principle of philanthropy? died of that portentous ass their son.[111] There was a model, and too early lost to her sex. Her lord was the one man in London—'[112]

'Mr. Chalford, the wine stands with you,' said Lord Wariston to the youngest of that race, who was devouring the narrative with open ears, earnest lips, and kindling eyes unconscious of horror and wrath in his father's.

'It wasn't the face,' proceeded Mr. Linley, his own more suggestive than ever of a niche or corner in some improper bas-relief; 'and the shoulders were bad. You know what Savigny said of her? a very good summary, but that fellow always would talk as if every woman that came in his way were professional—an operatic habit. "Peu de taille, pas de maintien; mais des tours d'œil, des jeux de visage—et puis des jambes! des jambes à faire—à faire crever un octogénaire:[113] le plus joli cou-de-pied, fin, délié; les genoux blancs, lisses, ronds[114] et gras—de satanés genoux! ne pas lire satinés."'

'Lord Wariston, what are we to think of the crops?' cried out Sir John Fieldfare in an exquisite agony of virtue, looking birch-rods at his late school-boy, the lout of eighteen, not too loutish to follow the last rapid and chuckling speech with an evident and ominous relish, which in a boating-boy and incipent athlete gave small promise of that muscular morality and sinewy sanctity preached and extolled by performers in the writing-school of Christian gymnastics.

But the man never sat as host or guest who by any mild means could silence or divert Mr. Linley. 'That was poor

Savigny's account: I spare you the greater part. "Elle avait une saveur plus *femme* que les autres femmes," he said; "personne ne jetait comme elle cette odeur d'amour[115] qu'on aspire avec ses nerfs, et qui même au loin fait frémir les narines de plaisir." I never saw such an entente cordiale between the two races.[116] Mind, I'm not responsible for the legs; he may have borrowed them from the ballet and jumbled two women together in the confusion of his memory; besides you never could tell how much guess-work went to make up that dear good Savigny's little rhapsodies. Died of his tongue at last you know, poor fellow; shot himself if ever a man did, when he provoked[117] Chantocé. I daresay he was thinking of someone else; a dancer no doubt "Que diable, il y a d'autres jambes au monde," I told him once. "Il raffolait des chevilles," as he said: a graceful taste.'[118]

Lord Charles Brandon joined in here, dragging with him the chaste heir of many Chalfords, who being given to sport would not drop the chance now seized of conversing with the old ex-jockey, even at the risk of his verbal virtue. Mr. Linley, who as he said really could not talk English after a certain point had been reached in debate, plunged into a French anecdote, illustrative of legs; beyond which no story-teller could pass.

'Pardon, mon cher oncle, mais il me paraît que nous nageons en pleine régence,' said Lord Wariston at length, softly.

'Entre deux vins,' added Mr. Denham in an undertone.

It cannot be said that Lady Midhurst had done herself equal justice in the drawing-room. Towards children she was undeniably soft-hearted; and the sight of beauty, which she had sense enough keenly to enjoy, softened instead of sharpening her. Here was the main difference between her and Linley; she was not a bad woman for a cynic. Cruel she certainly was on occasion; cruelty amused her and she liked to make her cuts tell; but she was not, like some, impregnated with cruelty as a sponge with water. She had often pure impulses and kindly passions: and could even be simply tender

when the fit was on her. Many children were drawn to her
by something in her face when turned towards them which
no adult enamoured or not had ever found there; something
too slight and too settled for a smile, too gracious and sincere
for a salute; a tacit play of meaning under every feature that
seemed to receive and return a caress. She appeared to thank
them with all her changing[119] face for having clear fresh faces
of their own: her eyes found out theirs and dwelt on them
as tired lips that drink pure water dwell on the draught to
prolong it. When rare beauty or new pleasure came in her
way, despite all the humorous violence and sharp-edged paradox in her talk, she was impelled to touch it tenderly; not to
strike and hurt it with a furious amorous admiration and rage
of angry delight. She had not run all to nerves, nor plunged
quite overhead into the fertile and tenacious mire of physical
philosophy.[120] Just now she had withdrawn the boy from the
neighbourhood and persecution of younger women, leaving
them to murmur small things to each other. Some were eques-
trian, some clerical, some critical; and they talked each after
their kind.

'What is the truth about this, will you tell me?' she asked
him with a serious courtesy pure of patronage or persiflage,
for which he was thankful. He told her in a few and frank
words.

'Well,' she said, 'I am sorry for you having it brought up in
that way; some boys would have liked the tribute; I understand that you don't. But don't show it again as you did, if I
may advise you. You will never get through a crowd of fellows
if you carry such a weight of nervousness. Don't be sensitive:
leave it to dowagers and old cats.'

'I like cats,' said he.

'So do I: but if you belong to the race, and shed sparks
when your fur is rubbed backwards, there will always be
hands to do it. Without a little sense you can't have manli-
ness though you may have all the daring in the world, do you
see? Now it's quite clear you don't want what they call
pluck; and if you hadn't been rather a nice sort of honest child

you would have swallowed the praise without salt or sauce.'

'I couldn't do that you know,' said Bertie, quieted. 'I should have been such an inf—such a most beastly sneak and liar.'

'I should like you to know a fellow about your age[121] who calls me his grandmother; he won't die of precocious modesty. Doesn't get much petting or praise, poor child, and has to do the business for himself. He calls me a trump however I am told, which is of course flattering: hein?'

'I don't think he can be far wrong,' said the other boy looking at her.

'Child, what odd eyes you have! like sea-water with sparkles of sunshine about it.[122] Never mind; I can't help studying faces and talking them over: I wish I could paint instead. There is a portrait of your sister, I see; very bad.'

'Isn't it a beast?' said Herbert frowning and glaring at it. 'I hate it: the fellow who did it was the awfullest little snob.'

'Poor Mr. Fairfax! I know the hand.[123] He can do a slight[124] face and the sort of mouth that goes with ringlets well enough: but as for painting from that model—'

'Ah,' said her brother, 'look at her!'

'It is worth while no doubt. I must catch a live artist and bring him here instead of a stuffed man out of the Academy. Let me see your eyes again to compare. So you have been crying to-day, I see: I hope not without cause: I won't inquire. How do you get on with that tutor?'

'I hate him,' said Herbert, pricked into candour by the pain of his blushes.

'I suppose it's proper,' said Lady Midhurst. 'Having seen you look at him, I needn't ask if he flogs you. Don't colour and shuffle in that way. He is probably right; flogging never did a boy of thirteen any harm, they tell me.'

'I shall be fourteen in the spring, early.'

'As it's now early in autumn, I don't see your point, my dear boy. I won't torment you; don't stay by me if you hate old women.'

She said this so prettily that he drew close against her, and

saw revived and reformed the traditional beauty of her
younger face. The caress in her accent had still between whiles
something of magnetic attraction. She drew his hands into her
own and held them.

'It is good of you to stay. I remember your brother Wariston
at the same age. I think he took to me rather; he was always
a good fellow.'

'He is a stunning good fellow,' his minor said; 'only—'

'You wish he would observe time and place? the intention
was most kind. I have known many sorts of men, and never
found anywhere such a trustworthy kind of good nature as
Lord Wariston's. I found him out at first sight when I went
down once to Eton with my brother to see his son there—
rather what you call a little sneak[125] then, but a very excellent
young man now' (she said this with an inexpressible expression of face and voice)—'and my nephew Cheyne told me a
fellow in his division had just been whipped for doing a
young one's verses[126] instead of his own, and showing up about
six lines to his aggrieved tutor: "put off till it was just time
for pupil-room, you know, like a jolly fool," his friend said:
"wanted me to do this. Fancy a fellow being such an ass who
was never in any row before." What do you say?'

'He was a brick; but what did they do to the fellow?'

'I believe he was sent up for good;[127] so there's the moral
for you.'

'But what a sneaking young brute he must have been; I
hope the fellows gave him a licking.'

'Don't get any notion of providential justice into your head;
it doesn't pay except in Carlyle—and the Bible of course,'
said Lady Midhurst, reverently. 'You can read both by and
by; meantime I advise you to adapt yourself to the nature of
things. No, I believe the youth never told, and I know your
major never did. It was fair enough so far; he shirked his
work, and got his flogging. He was a quiet fellow, not very
clever at that sort of thing, I imagine; the verses were most
likely an excuse for sending up the smaller boy, by way of
reward for general merit. By the by I rather think it was his

cousin, young Linley. They can't have been very good as Wariston—Arden[128] he was then—never was sent up himself. One must face the misfortunes of virtue in this universe, my dear child, and put up with the prosperities of vice.[129] I have no doubt our friend Mr. Linley would tell you so;[130] and that was rather vicious of his boy.'

'I should think it was, beastly.'

'Well, you see Wariston just now meant to do you such another good turn, and put both feet in it this time—as I suppose you would say. He thought you had got shy and sulky under the complimentary chaff about your looks; very bad taste, but if you had been a browner burlier style of boy, or less unluckily like your sister, he might not have cared to air his pride in you or vindicate your claim to pluck. I saw him look at you once or twice and he said to me the second time it was clear you were getting bullied and sat upon, but he would set things right in good time. They thought you would be what I call marmosetted and made into a Prince Pretty-man, and he meant to come to the rescue. One can see he likes you better than anything but your sister; it was real pride in your pluck.'

'Ah, but there was no real pluck,' said Bertie. 'He is a trump though all the same.'

Lady Wariston talked to the mothers Fieldfare and Chalford; from other parts came the continuous chirping and cheeping of the maidens, thin and perpetual as the simultaneous flood of far other talk from the lips of Mr. Linley in the dining room. 'Consecration to be that week; the bishop quite indifferent about full service; detestable, and such a perfect choir.' 'I call it the very worst style, and the mother is like a shopwoman.' 'If the bay did, it was a fluke; I'm sure he never meant to put her at it; never saw a man in the field who looked less like business.' And so forth till a keen and daring voice struck across the soft reedlike notes. 'Lady Midhurst, you are monopolising our small hero.'

'Yours?' said Lady Midhurst; 'I assure you not.'

Miss Chalford, though not susceptible or sensitive, felt the iron edge of her voice pierce to the bone. Lady Wariston simply said, 'Pray don't make a hero of Herbert,' and let the matter lie; but the elder, having once been incited to sting, was ready to flesh her fangs again. Her eyes were so hard and brilliant that in pure fear of her tongue Lady Wariston proposed music, and a duet was the grievous result.

'I am sure those people are coming out of the dining-room,' Lady Midhurst said to Herbert, 'I feel so vicious.'

She looked so as they entered and her eyes met Linley's; the boy slipped away from her. The sage distributed a few delicacies of speech and attention among the younger women and fell into private talk with Mr. Denham. Lord Wariston stood near his old friends and his wife was beset by Sir John and Mr. Chalford, as before by their females. This group was so near the next that Lady Midhurst began to murmur in French; it grew evident that her desire was to encounter Mr. Linley and exchange a pass or two.

'Voyez donc ce scélérat qui ricane,'[131] she said; 'je parie qu'il s'agit de quelque horreur.' In effect Mr. Linley's face flashed with mute laughter at intervals. Lord Wariston thanked her for his uncle. She had forgotten the relationship and remembered only that he had talked to her that day for six hours: ignoring her own share in the talk. 'Il a causé politique,' she complained, 'de sorte que j'ai la cervelle bourrée de faits-Paris.'

'Je ne dis pas qu'il ne soit point un peu gobemouche, le cher oncle,' Lord Wariston said by way of following suit, as he always did with her.

'Gobemouchard,'[132] said Lady Midhurst, so much elated by her extraordinary compound as to utter the queer sound audibly. It was but a one-legged pun, or broken-backed rather, but the word pleased her: for indeed the political flies swallowed by Mr. Linley were mainly hatched in such air as she hinted at, caught and administered by such hands.

'Entendez-vous la Faublas qui vise au calembourg?'[133] said Mr. Linley to Denham in his lowest note.

'Why are you talking French at both ends of the room?'

said Lord Charles. Mr. Denham by way of answer looked towards his pupil who was close at hand and safe from female notice.

'Ah, come here, boy,' said Mr. Linley, laying hold of him by the arm. 'I want to ask you another question or two.'

Herbert came sulkily enough, and stood up as if waiting for immediate chastisement. The torturer had a little pack of questions ready which he used to apply to every boy who came in his way, secure that one or two must always hurt: it was the sole notice he ever took of children. The minutest form of trivial tyranny, the poisonous pin-pricks and wasp-stings of puerile cruelty, gave him some pleasure, in default of a graver infliction. His method was vexatious and stupid, like a dull woman's spite, and therefore always told upon the young intellect.

'Being as we are informed a hero in full bud, of course you speak truth. Do so now.' He enforced this injunction with a spitefully sportive blow which happened to be more or less than a pleasantry to poor Herbert on this occasion.[134]

'I want to know when you were flogged last?[135] or are we to understand that you never came too near a birch in your life? Come: you can't look me in the face[136] and say it. You do get a good taste of the twigs now and then, don't you—with all the nice fresh hard buds[137] on, you know? and they sting, don't they?'[138]

Herbert's eyes appealed in vain to his sister; she was some way off and they were in a quiet corner out of the world's way. So he looked straight into the grey shining face of his captor and said 'Sometimes.'

'I thought so. And now, Mr. Herbert, will you inform me when the habitual rites of marriage were last solemnised between your person and the birch?'[139]

The boy's cheeks contracted and his whole body quivered with the sharp sense of shame, as he muttered two words with dry and sullen lips, looking down with a hot pale face.

'I could have sworn it. Good heavens, Denham, what a tremendous flogging this boy has had!'[140]

'You may be sure he deserved what he got. How can you see?'

'I can tell he has been soundly whipped as easily as if I saw him bathing, or as if you had applied the birch to his hands and face. It would be a shame to cane him on the hands though. They are the smallest[141] for a boy I ever saw; and caning would spoil them,[142] eh, boy? Don't cry now, though.'

'I'm not going,' said Herbert.

'I hope you don't spare him, Denham. It would be a sin to spare a boy like this. Flog him well when you do flog him, pray; he will live to be thankful to you.[143] You'd be very soon spoilt else, my good boy, I can see;[144] I only hope your school-masters will do their duty. I know boys; some of them ought to lose a little blood every day they live.' His eyes devoured the boy's drawn face and twisted hands; he seemed to inhale his pain and shame like a fine and pungent essence; he laughed with pleasure as he saw how the words burnt and stung.

'Mr. Linley,' said Lady Midhurst in her clearest key, 'when you have tormented the boy enough will you come to my rescue?'

Linley, who in his agreeable humour was about to wind up with a touch or two of the old school[145] so given as to make the boy feel each word like a cut, and taste twice over the bitterness of birch,[146] was compelled to let his victim slip[147] having tortured him to the extreme verge of tears; and Herbert, flushed and cowed and choking, turned towards his sister. Her eyes met his and pitied them, adding a promise well understood.[148] At each screw of the rack he had reddened and writhed; now he breathed hard, with an equine shake of his head, and stood back well out of the way till his friendly senior by some five years found him out. 'Was he chaffing you about getting swished? what a damned shame,' said this Field-fare, now amicable and vinous. 'Old chaps will, they like to see a small boy wriggle. I say, how he made you smoke; I thought you were going to blub, twice. Those sort of fellows know nothing else about boys, you see, and they think it's the sort of

thing to say; my older governor used to chaff *me* once. Don't
know what else to say to a fellow: and know he won't like *that*;
old bucks. But I say, young one, you should have heard this old
chap over his wine: by Jove, what lark he was; he made the
others look no end blue: there was one most jolly story—'

'I don't want to hear his rotten old stories,' said Bertie;
'old beast, I should like to see his neck wrung.'—But he was
held fast in a remote corner out of general earshot, and
listened between loathing and laughing; meantime Lady
Midhurst had entangled uncle and nephew in the mazes of a
discussion on art and literature, suggestive of Teutonic tea.
Mrs. Chalford and one or two elder virgins, not absorbed by
the male youth, followed afar off and trembling; the mother
of Fieldfares adhered to her hostess.

'You can impeach the man at any bar you please,' Lady
Midhurst said, 'and as to his tendency, I'll defend the thing
when you define the word. But I know this, that all daylight
has gone out of the world with him.[149] We have stars and
candles in plenty, at home and abroad; but the nature of
things can afford us no more suns.'

'Joli bout de feuilleton,' said Linley.

'I suppose the journals went into white mourning and
chuckled under thin whines—Blondet, Lousteau et Cie?'[150]

'There were the due notices: was not Hugo's oration[151]
enough?'

'Excellent, so far: but a great man who is in a fair
way to be philanthrope malgré Dieu[152] et poète malgré lui,[153]
must hate in his heart that hard bland philosophy which
takes and turns over revolutions and rumours, demigods and
democrats, with the composed contempt of a god astray among
the giants.'

'I don't see it at all,' said Lord Wariston, 'and I have read
Eugénie Grandet.'

'That is perfect,' said Lady Midhurst. 'Enough to make
him turn in his grave.'[154]

'Women overrate the books,' said Linley, 'but the man was
a statesman spoilt.'

'And this man fell in love last year with Madame Marneffe,[155] just as I lost my heart to M. Crevel,' said Lady
Midhurst.

'I deny it, and I think better of you: Valérie is a copy in
water-colours of Madame de Merteuil[156] en bourgeoise, with
half the lines effaced.'

'Not in the least: no more like the Merteuil than I am.'
(Not so very unlike then, said the other with his eyes.) 'She
is a Titaness, and fights heaven; the enemy is obliged to take
her in flank at last; and that smallpox[157] always seemed to me
to spoil the face of the book itself. She is epical, the marquise,
enormous; only you don't see it for the red heels and powder.
Shepherds and satyrs troop after Balzac's little nymph, Hulots
and Crevels and Steinbocks; the other has gods against her
and men beneath; she is a Prometheus in petticoats, and
might be put into Milton as mother of sin and death. It takes
all the weight of heaven to crush her; and I don't believe she
was beaten at last.'

'You are miles beyond us all,' said Lord Wariston. 'Who
is the heroine?'

'As you allow Mr. Linley to entrap me into admissions,
you must allow me to come out like the Boston ladies in
Dickens. I feel the soul of a Hominy within me; permit me
the tongue of Toppit and the licence of a Codger.[158] We might
get up the scene with Mr. Linley for Pogram and the boy
there for Jefferson Brick.'

'But who was Madame de—chose—Merteuil is it?'

'I didn't begin, if you please,' said Lady Midhurst: 'ask
the others if you like. We are old enough to read most things,
after all. It is the greatest and the gravest book of a century,[159]
if you will but look into it, and not over it or under. And
did not some German of heavy and eminent virtue—Schiller
I think—say it was excellent reading for women, and as
wholesome as admirable? Mrs. Chalford, did you ever read
Laclos?'

'I once read Paul et Virginie,'[160] said the matron; 'as a girl.
I never read French novels now.'

'I never could think it equal to his Télémaque,'[161] said Lady Midhurst.

'Télémaque,'[162]—ah'—said Mr. Linley, 'an admirable work, but painful. I could never overlook all that was implied by the idea of leaving any one qui ne pouvait se consoler.'[163]

Lady Midhurst bit her lip hard and applauded him with her eyes; whenever he became cynically insolent in company, or towards women, her heart relaxed and warmed to him.

'Painful, as you say, but a noble moral. Let us return to Balzac. Nothing could console *me* for his death; except these Latter-day Pamphlets.'[164]

'Do you take Scotch ale[165] with Laffitte?' said Linley.

'They are superb,' said Lady Midhurst, 'and affect the nerves as deliciously as thunder.[166] There is no such fun in the world; not in Rabelais I should imagine; by the little I can gather up about the great unreadable, he seems to have more of human wisdom and less of divine perversity.'

'A Puritan on a hippogriff,' said Mr. Linley: 'nothing more.'

'You say the sun set with Balzac,' said Lord Wariston; 'what do you find here?'

'Lightning, and a noise of water and wind,' she said with a faint inflexion of the mock-heroic sort: 'sounds and sights worth attention in their way. Reading this man's prose is all but seeing a battle. Reading Balzac is all but eating the fruit of knowledge and seeing men with the eyes and the sense of gods. Naturally Adam goes northward and Eve southward. Not but what I like the tune of trumpets too.'

'Wariston prefers the prophetic art to the dramatic, I have no doubt,' said his uncle: 'but I am with you and France.'

'What delights me,' said Lady Midhurst, 'is that tone about art. It is so admirably right on the wrong side; il a raison à force d'avoir tort.'

'Begotten Scotch and bred German, born preacher and reared philosopher, surely he has a double, a quadruple right to be wrong on matters of art,' said Linley.

'I maintain he is not so wrong. For, honestly, if art is not worth more than virtue, it must be worth less; and in that case may as well go overboard. But if it is?'

'Vous allez effaroucher votre monde,' her ally said in his rident and strident undertone.

'Du tout; nous devons être trop assommants; voyez, comme on nous laisse en paix.'

'Well, I am for plastic art, against drastic morals myself: but, Lady Midhurst, if an easel is the altar, do you call Balzac a fit high-priest? he flounders violently in details,[167] and mixes his colours now and then with a perverse or a shaking hand.'

'I don't know. I do know that he always works with the dignity of an artist. All your men here want self-respect. His chief imitator,[168] whom in ten years some of you will be placing at his side or higher, cannot as yet make a book: has never tried but once; and then it was the autobiography of a blackleg; excellent, admirable; but not wrought out under reasonable conditions. He may do it some day: he will never do it but once, and will then spend his time and strength in accumulating about and under it masses of brilliant incoherent material, mixed with pure crude rubbish and overlaid with the coarse gilding of lachrymose or ironical vulgarity.'

'It is charming to hear him called cynical,' said Linley; 'a man sentimental all over and all through, eaten to the very bone with corrosive sentiment. We shall never see his better though, nor his like.'

'Another thing you forget, that he is really what a Frenchman of genius (with leave of a moral public) never is, unsavoury. The corners of his books are unswept; he has a tendency to the rancid: you smell grease on him. People will call the *Parents pauvres* unclean and swallow this Engish uncleanness with an appetite. Balzac is always great and radically right; he has a right to his materials; he will never choose them wrongly and will always use them greatly. The other will always choose by preference things absolutely unfit for choice; dirty trifles, trivial dirt; or if one must use the terms, snobbishness and shabby gentility, and even these he handles on the wrong side. The great man finds if necessary

71

for all such little things their proper holes and niches in his work, and stows them away with due scientific equanimity. His imitator thrusts them to the front of his work, holds them up, howls, whimpers, points, shakes his fists, roars and weeps over them: stands aghast in public, and bursts into tears on a platform. Bah! look at the great man and say which side he favours when you find out; let the world know when you catch Shakespeare condemning the moral state of Iago, or Balzac deploring[169] the perversity[170] of Madame de San-Réal.[171] Those who can stand anything may do anything; they have only to give proof that they can. If they try and do badly, they stand, or rather they fall, self-condemned. Meantime at all events, don't let us be told that people could if they would; that give them Balzac's licence and opportunity they could do Balzac's work: an intellect of that size and weight makes its own opportunities and enforces its own licences: and works, to revert to our prophet, "if not with leave given, then with leave taken".'

'The recent loss and the nascent rivalry have made you eloquent; but are not other lights left after sunset, and as good in your eyes? Tennyson, Hugo, Carlyle?'

'The planets Venus, Jupiter and Mars—or Saturn if you prefer. Poets may stand higher, but they are not so visible and useful—in my working-day heaven, at least. The sun is less lovely, but all the world feels it. And now that we have cleared the field will you make them give us some music?'

Talk had subsided round them on all hands, and the evening was ripe for a diversion; one or two of the guests played and sang after the most usual fashion; then Lady Wariston rose by request and took their place. What she sang was new to the company: a song made, according to tradition, by a Jacobite ancestor in 1715, the night before execution. She sang it with a clear brilliant melancholy in her voice and face; in her deep fixed eyes looking out straight and far under the lifted level of quiet eyelids; in the delicate distinct cadence of the brief and brave words. Her singing was impaired by no cheap obtrusion of facile pathos, and no flourish of flamboyant notes; she seemed to see into the prison and beyond, to speak without fear and with no ignoble regret: as though the spirit of that lost life and ruined cause had passed into her and issued again at her lips.

> There's nae mair lands to tyne, my dear,[172]
>   And nae mair lives to gie;
> Though a man think sair to live nae mair,
>   There's but one time to die.
>
> For a' things come and a' days gone,
>   What needs ye rive your hair?
> But kiss me till the morn's morrow,
>   Then I'll kiss ye nae mair.
>
> O lands are lost and life's losing,
>   And what were they to gie?
> Fu' mony a man gives all he can,
>   But nae man else gives ye.
>
> Our king wons ower the sea's water,
>   And I in prison sair;
> But I'll win out the morn's morrow,
>   And ye'll see me nae mair.

Her eyes as she ended met Herbert's, glittering and grown great; either beautiful face was expanded by passion and pleasure as a flower by heat and light. The verses had bitten and stung them sharply; they felt through all the nerves of body and soul the delight of mad and violent devotion, and their blood beat with the senseless and splendid rapture of martyrs conscious of a losing cause. Linley, cool towards their emotion and moved only by their physical beauty, watched both faces curiously, with his mouth and cheek quivering; Denham's fingers compressed the cushion of the couch he sat on and the hand trembled like that of one in a palsy; Lady Midhurst, sensitive still of music and metre, felt upon her hard clear eyes a dimness without tears: the old sorrow and the valour shown long ago struck upon her senses, and she submitted herself to their touch and attraction, and the guests smiled or sighed their thanks according to their kind.

Lady Wariston came and sat down by Lady Midhurst, her brother following; the elder received her eagerly, and without thanks.

'And that is true, Lord Wariston tells me?'

'Yes: there were men in those days; and madmen.'

'I wish madness were more catching; the worse the cause, the better they who hold to it, I sometimes think. So your people lost all in the '15?'

'And a little remainder in the '45.'[173]

'I daresay my ancestors fattened upon yours; we were on the Dutch side of things. Now that boy will never speak to me again.'

'Oh! you couldn't help,' said Herbert.

'Merci,' said Lady Midhurst. 'One is not comfortable on the wrong side, but at times it must be pleasant to feel heaven against you and right with you. I suppose your mad Jacobites had divine minutes of despair, when all was done in vain and all but faith gone for good. People always in the end come round to have a weakness for martyrs. The world will make as good men yet, if none more honourable; and duly kill them off. If I had been a man and able I should like to have had a hand in the defence of Rome against these French.[174] Being an old woman, I prefer not to go in for heroes by word of mouth. Would you have liked to take a turn in the rebellion, Herbert?'

'Shouldn't I? and it wasn't one you know,' said the boy whose hand she had taken again and was pressing the fresh warm fingers against her soft dry palm.

'Tiens, what a state you have sung this boy into! feel his wrist; and there's a pulse beating in these finger-ends. Wouldn't you like to stand up and be shot at, now? suppose you were taken in arms?'

'I don't think I should mind, anyhow, if it was all right.'

'There, go and get quiet; talk to Miss Chalford—what is

it? Fieldfare—she's help you to cool down. What a face the child had just then! don't excite him too often.'

'He's not the sentimental unwholesome sort of boy,' said his sister; 'it won't hurt him, and he was always rather hot upon that song.'

'I don't wonder, having the blood in him. There is always something attractive in failure after a certain time, as strong as there is for the minute in success. If those men had succeeded, and entailed upon us a third inevitable revolution, no mortal would have stood up for them now; but considering that their cause was doomed and desperate throughout we have all a weak side for the worst of them. Yes, it must be a great unique delight to reflect when one is finally stranded: 'the Gods are very strong and can take most things and ruin them at their pleasure; but no God in heaven can take a man's honour except with his own leave, by his own act.' One understands then that they should set no great store by land or life.'

'People do nowadays, it seems.'

'Not all of them; only the causes are inverted, and heroism has changed sides: but Mazzini is worth many a Derwentwater.[175] You will see something come of that if I do not. I don't believe in revolutions or what they call peoples et tout ce fatras; they will explode to a certainty, and much will be burnt up and burnt out; progress won't hold water and philanthropy won't keep afloat. As for democracy and illuminated masses, I hate the very smell of such cant; but I can see where the men are, and why; there are not too many of them about in the world. We have none; France will have none much longer; Italy is the great mother of men after all. Mind, I don't say the men are not mad, or not fools; but it's something to be men. They won't do what they expect, I fancy: but something they will do.'

A little after this they broke up; the male guests, all but Linley, branching off to the smoking-room, whence Herbert was excluded in spite of his Fieldfare's intercession. He was tired enough with various small excitements to fall asleep while undressing; and when his sister according to her tacit promise entered his room she found him lying back on one side in a long arm-chair, with eyes shut fast and cheeks warm with sleep, his hair crushed against the cushion into a tangle of tortuous gold and flickering with fiery colours in the reflected firelight which lit up his face from below, brightening round the throat and chin, leaving shadows about the mouth and glittering against the close eyelashes and rough curls that caught its gleam and reflex. The head was curiously beautiful, with the pure animal grace of Ampelus rather than of Cupid: a head to be caressed by Bacchus and carved by Polycles. Something of pain still hung about the eyelids, swelled slightly and veined with more visible blue from the morning's tears: but for this, it might have been the face of Ampelus indeed, could the sculptured head have taken English colour. Lying there tired and hurt and quiet, he touched her with a new love; she bent down and pressed her lips into his; they answered the kiss before he woke, and clung close and hung eagerly upon hers; and as the eyes opened the arms went round her with a hard embrace.

'You lazy boy, you don't want me to sing you to sleep after all.'

'Yes I do, and it's very jolly of you to come. Oh, I say, what a beastly time it has been.'

'You got on very well with Lady Midhurst; so did I for once.'

'She's a brick; but isn't old Linley a brute, just!'

'I thought he was teasing you at one time.'

'I say, don't talk about it, please, it makes me so hot.'

'I'm not going to talk at all. Put something on over that shirt and listen if you want to be sung to again, and then get to bed.'

'You sit there and let me alone,' said Herbert, pushing her into the chair and kneeling down with one of her hands between his. She beat time on his hair with the other hand, and sang low; the ballad was an older and more battered fragment of verse than her others, but a favourite with him;

the dropped syllables and rough edges of ruined metre, worn
half away in the passage of the poem downward into modern
lips and changed accents, did not impair its charm to ears
familiar with the wind on moorside and sea; and the fierce
crude expressions of sorrow and anger shocked neither boy
nor woman, bred up as their minds had been in border air
on the fresh and strong meat of ballads,[176] in which the lyrical
tradition is not soft of speech nor demure of step. Her hand
never moved in his as she sang; he hardly breathed till her
voice fell, and his face seemed to absorb hers with all its
features. She looked across his head into the low fallen fire,
with a set face, singing.

> *God send the sea sorrow,*[177]
> *And all men that sail thorough.*
>
> *God give the wild sea woe,*
> *And all ships that therein go.*
>
> *My love went out with dawn's light;*
> *He went down ere it was night.*
>
> *God give no live man good*
> *That sails over the sea's flood.*
>
> *God give all live men teen*
> *That sail over the waves green.*
>
> *God send for my love's sake*
> *All their lovers' hearts break.*
>
> *Many sails went over sea;*
> *One took my heart from me.*
>
> *All they saving one*
> *Came in landward under the sun.*

Many sails stood in from sea;
One twined my heart and me.[173]

Waves white and waves black,
One sail they sent not back.

Many maidens laughed that tide;
I fell down and sore sighed.

Many months I saw kiss;
No man kissed there mine, I wis.

Many gat there brooch and glove;
I gat but loss of love.

I rose up and sighed sore;
I set my face from the shore.

On my fingers fair gold rings,
In my heart bitter things.

In mine hair combs of pride,
I stood up and sore sighed.

I looked out over sea;
Never a man's eye looked to me.

I cried out over the tide;
Never a man's mouth on me cried.

I came there a goodly thing;
I was full wan ere evening.

I came there fresh and red;
I came thence like one dead.

I came there glad and lief;
I came thence with heart's grief.

God give all men grief, I say,
That sail over the seas grey.

I laid my head to the sea-stone;
I made my bed there alone.

I made my bed into the sand,
Betwixen sea and green land.

Betwixen land and green sea
Swevens and sorrows fell on me.

In yellow sea-sand washen well
Weary watches on me fell.

There all a night I lay:
I would I had died or day.

There in the young light
I looked over the waves white.

There all a day I stood,
Looking over the sea's flood.

I saw waves black and green,
But no man's sail between.[179]

I saw waves blue and white,
But no sails under the light.

There was no wind came by me
But it was salt, and full of the sea.

There was no wind passed me by
But I was like to die.

I sought long and I sought sore,
And aye my tears fell more.

I found sorrow and much pain,
But not my love again.

God give me a green bed
And no pillow to my head.

God give me brief life's breath,
And a good sleep after death.

The fire had sunk suddenly a little before she ceased, and its last long jets of light shot up sharp at short intervals. Her voice held the boy silent after had done singing; the faint profound light in her eyes, fixed and withdrawn, touched him like music; her hair, reluctant against combs and braids, seemed to hang and vibrate like a curled cloud after sunset in a clear sky, impelled and moulded by the wind, filled and coloured by fiery light: its curling labouring mass of fervent gold made small unequal shadows on her neck and temples, as the rough and waved outline struggled and rippled outwards. Kneeling with his face lifted to hers, he inhaled the hot fragrance[180] of her face and neck, and trembled with intense and tender delight. Her perfume thrilled and stung him; he bent down and kissed her feet, reached up and kissed her throat.

'You smell of flowers in a hot sun,' he said, kissing her feet again with violent lips that felt the sweet-scented flesh pressing them back through its soft covering.[181] She laughed and winced under the heat of his hard kiss, drawing one foot back and striking lightly with the other, which he took and pressed down upon his neck.

'Oh! I should like you to tread me to death![182] darling!'

She took him by the hair[183] and shook his head to and fro, laughing as the close elastic curls rebelled against her fingers.

'I say, let your hair go,' said Herbert, pressing his arms under hers: she loosened the fastenings, and it rushed downwards, a tempest and torrent of sudden tresses, heavy and tawny and riotous and radiant,[184] over shoulders and arms and bosom; and under cover of the massive and luminous locks she drew up his face against her own and kissed him time after time with all her strength.

'Now go to bed, and sleep well,' she said, putting him back. His whole spirit was moved with the passionate motion of his senses; he clung to her for a minute, and rose up throbbing from head to foot with violent love. All the day's pleasure and pain came suddenly to flower and bore fruit in him at the moment.

'I wish you would kill me some day; it would be jolly to feel you killing me. Not like it? Shouldn't I! You just hurt me, and see.'

She pinched him so sharply that he laughed and panted with pleasure.

'You are the most insane child I know, and will be quite mad at this rate before you are marriageable; and Miss Brandon will have to dispense with you. Good-night and let me go, or you will be late to-morrow, and get punished again.'

'I should like being swished even I think, if you were to complain of me or if I knew you liked.'

'Poor old child, I'm afraid you had enough of that this morning; don't get into more trouble, for I don't happen to like it at all. Good-night, dear: I know; I love you too' (as he caressed her with signs and speechless kisses, flattering her with hands and eyes significant of love). 'I know you do: and I you, and more than I can say. There, that's often enough and plain enough. Now, my dear old minor, as Wariston calls you, please let me go once for all.'

'I'm glad you're not a boy though,' said Herbert.

He fell asleep with her kisses burnt into his mind, and the ineffaceable brand of love upon his thoughts: and dreamed passionately of his passion[185] till he woke; seeing her mixed with all things, seeming to lose[186] life for her sake, suffering in dreams under her eyes or saving her from death. How far his sudden sharp delight in her beauty and her gracious habits served to change and colour his natural affection, to stimulate his devotion, and make passionate his gratitude, he never thought or felt. But the one keen and hard impression left on him by the whole day's work was this of desperate tenderness and violent submission of soul and body to her love; the day but for her would have been mere torture and trouble throughout; she had made it in part too pleasant to forget; and this he never forgot: the memory of it, and the strong fervour and spirit[187] of love which was the fruit of it, gave in the end a new tone and colour to his life.

CHAPTER IV

AFTER THAT DAY'S WORK HERBERT BECAME (IN LORD
Wariston's words) his sister's lapdog and lackey. He fell to
work at her bidding, and worked well: Denham thought and
spoke better of his chances of scholarship. Margaret was
pleased, and made less of him than before; this was her instinct, as it was his to become more loving and submissive,
when she grew less tender. She told him he was not half a
boy, and was more than kind or gracious to young Lunsford;
who on his part waxed more superb[1] and scornful in his deal-
ings with her brother. All this Herbert accepted with the most
loyal affection and good faith: he never thought himself fit
for any higher office than an acolyte's, and he had a warm
belief in his one sister and one friend. After Christmas his
schooltime began; he left Ensdon in a blind passion of pain,
full of the sense of his sister's last touches and words, and like
one torn alive out of life or all that was sweet in it. It was
rather a physical than a sentimental pain; he felt the sharp
division and expulsion, the bitter blank of change, like a bad
taste or smell. Away from home and the sea and all common
comfortable things, stripped of the lifelong clothing of his life,
he felt as one beaten and bare. For some short time back he
had seen enough of the boating people to miss their converse;
and it was worth missing. Mathieson, his first friend, was 'a
man plainly noble and nobly plain'; in his speech as curt as a
squall of wind and as salt as a puff of foam; in his nature as
sweet as the even breath of the sea, loveable and loving to the
boy in whom he at least found no fault. Next to Margaret
and the children, Herbert missed nothing so much. It was
very bitter and dull to him, to be taken up and dropped

I   83

down into the heart of a strange populous place, beautiful and
kindly as he like others should have found it. But he found
at first only the sharp stupid sense of perplexity and exile. His
world felt very empty of pleasant light and fire, very full of
strange fog and inclement air. He was late in school and out;
it was no life for him.[2] Other elders besides Lunsford were
kind to him, and his tutor more than they, seeing there was
no vice or stupor in the case, but mere bewilderment. Hardly
once or twice he girt himself up and did a decent stroke of
work in pupil-room or playing-fields, and relapsed into the
fog. He soon found he could not fight his fate, and took it as
it came, with a sad and passionate abandonment. No possible
training for a schoolboy could have been worse than his had
been: and it now bore him painful and unprofitable fruit.
He had a dear and close friend or two, with whom he rambled
and read verse and broke bounds beyond Datchet or
Windsor,[3] dreaming and talking out the miles of green and
measured land they tramped and shirked over. It was a new
country to his eyes, veiled with light pendulous leaves and
inlaid with sleepy reaches of soft water; pleasant and close,
and sweet and wearisome. The seagull[4] grew sick in an aviary,
though (it may be) of better birds. Instead of tender hanging
tendrils of woodland he desired the bright straight back-
blown copses of the north; and instead of noble gradual
rivers, the turbid inlets and wintry wilderness of the sea.
Child as he was, and foolish, the desire of old things was
upon him like a curse. So his first half came to its end sadly
enough; and the next somewhat worse. Meantime his sister,
living month by month a lonelier life, grew troubled as a
water grows without perceptible wind. She could find nowhere much comfort or interest in her life; the great world
wearied and vexed her, and her husband, a countryman born
(after the order of many such another good English noble as
Lord Althorp),[5] was willing enough to live in quite a dull life
full of petty circumstances. Occupation sufficed him; but
emotion was wanting to her. Before marriage he had cantered
easily round the enclosure of habitual pleasures and amuse-

ments trained to hand; a few years of youth had sufficed him, and he had turned off into the the matrimonial stable with an honest appetite for the rack and the collar of legitimate attachment. It was already enough for him to ride and read and legislate. But for her, in town or country, the life she lived was by no means enough. And unluckily she had no love for London. She was not brilliant in society, and her beauty shone there through a cloud. Her husband did not embitter⁰ and did not enliven her life. She would have done him no wrong; but he did her no good. He had for her a little love, and she had much liking for him. He could fill up his life with little satisfactions, but she could find no single and sufficient expression of her wants and powers. In those years, a maiden at heart, she had a vague and violent thirst after action and passion. She did not rebel against what was, but she desired what might be. Of one thing only she never thought; of love. This emotion had never yet even grazed her in passing. She dreamed of chances and changes, of deeds impossible and improbable results; but being wife and mother from her girlhood, these dreams were neither tinged nor shaped by any virgin fancies of affection given and taken. They came and went indeed from nothingness to nothing. For her children even had no hold on her; a certain tenderness towards the youngest was her main maternal quality. On the whole she preferred Herbert, 'her first baby', as she said, 'the old child' to whom she had played the part of mother and sister in one for some years: and to him she was not too tender. At times it struck her that she would live out her time without colour in her life.

CHAPTER V

THE HOUSE HAD BY THIS TIME WON A CERTAIN REPUTE OF AN uncertain sort. It amused some; by no means all. It was people during the country season by a fair number of passengers. In the September of 1854 it was full of picked guests; very few names of note among them, but a company pleasant and graceful enough within reasonable limits. Charades and proverbs[1] were acted and other small enjoyments found out and gone through. Lady Wariston had grown out of the quiet intolerance of people in general which at first kept her passive and averse to fresh faces. She was seemingly warmer and really brighter. A delicate rapid grace, soft and keen as the play of light flame, moved now with all her emotions. She spoke more and trod quicker than in past years. Her children were now old enough to please her: and her health had been strong and sound ever since the youngest was born.

Herbert was still at home when the house began to fill, and did not enjoy the change.[2] He had fallen into unsocial indolence and the turbid delight of dreams. Quiet usually and excitable always, he grew brilliant all over with pleasure when once in reach of it. He had swum and ridden and lounged through the last month with full content: the new faces and fixed hours that now came into fashion were vexatious. One visitor only he was curious to see. Miss Brandon was of the party this time, as well as her father. The worthy jockey[3] had grown in old age to like a quiet house and old friends. His daughter had published, if not wholly under the rose yet duly under the roseleaf, a volume of verse. Her name had of course taken a veil of disguise, and of course the veil was translucent. This book, among much other worse and

86

better poetry, Bertie had caught up and greedily fed upon. There was a certain fire and music in the verse at its best which had stung and soothed him alternately with gentle and violent delight. Where the writer was weakest, she was weak in a way of her own, rather from the relaxation of nerves overstrung than from the debility of nerves incompetent of passion. She could articulate and attune emotion, and her verse had in its a pulse and play of blood,[4] a sensible if not a durable life. Her first fruits had fervour and fragrance enough to attract the appetite of a boy.

Her arrival was delayed by chance and came by surprise. The afternoon had been wholly absorbed by the elaborate rehearsal of actors in the evening's show-proverb.[5] The whole crew was in full masquerade; Lady Midhurst, a perfect actress at fifty-four as at fifteen, was in rococo costume; which naturally whetted the tongues and lifted the eyes of her coeval friends with deprecation and disgust; Lord Wariston and Mr. Linley in the due powder and red heels, lace and silk; Lady Wariston, who acted in another part of the entertainment, was dressed after a Venetian picture, with Lunsford major as a cavalier[6] and his two brothers[7] as pages; Herbert, who much against his own will had been ousted from a share in this division of the work and voted into a leading female part, was chafing under compliments and chaff from old and young. 'Quem si puellarum insereres choro',[8] Mr. Linley had said twice already; and the boy's look was certainly deceptive. His full and curled hair had been eked out with false locks to the due length, and his skin touched up with feminine colours: so that 'solutis crinibus ambiguoque vultu'[9] he was passable as a girl. Between loyalty to his sister, who abused it by her entreaty and command that he would submit, and a muffled reluctant sense of some comic faculty, he had yielded, and began to catch the infection of amusement.

'How on earth am I to receive these people?' said Lady Wariston. 'I can't go down as Lucrezia.'[10]

'I don't see why we shouldn't all go as we are,' said Lady Midhurst. 'It won't help them to guess the word, seeing us all at once. And I will *not* dress more than four times a day: so I for one remain en marquise till the dressing-bell. And you might introduce your sister; he is perfect.'

'So is the suggestion', said Mr. Linley; 'perfect.'

'Not if I know it,' said the young lady: 'it's nuisance enough to wear this beastliness at all: and they'd see at dinner.'

Lady Wariston caught at his hands which were raised to pull out the false hair. 'It can't be done again,' she said; 'you shall wear things of mine at dinner, and put on these again afterwards, but your head must stay as it is, it takes hours to do. You won't ruin the whole thing and miss the best fun?' She was singularly animated all that week, and acted Lucrezia Borgia to young Lunsford's Gennaro[11] with exquisite power and grace. At this minute especially she looked younger than her years, luminous with laughter and excitement.[12] Mme. de Rochelaurier[13] recognized in her a 'grâce fauve', and would 'hardly have given her twenty-four'.

'Now do, Bertie, like a good boy: be a good dog, sir', tapping his nose which was not yet on a level with her own. 'I'll present you as a rising poetess. You'll be able to sit at her feet and learn her secret: it's a chance for a boy going in for poetry.'

'I'm not,' said Bertie, who went in but moderately for grammar.

'Introduce him with that blush on,' said Mr. Linley, 'and the thing's done.'

'If Lord Charles were to fall in love with your sister? he always admired you profoundly,' said Lady Midhurst.

'A susceptible race,' said Linley; 'it's in the blood. And meantime they are cooling down I should say for want of a reception.'

Not all the boy's rage and scorn after these last remarks could give him nerve or will to resist his sister's. She marched him out before her a slave as of old, amid the due applause. A few of the rest went with them to receive the visitors, who were found expectant. Father and daughter rose to meet them, surprised and smiling.

88

Miss Brandon was dark and delicately shaped; not tall, but erect and supple; she had thick and heavy hair growing low on the forehead, so brown that it seemed black in the shadow; her eyes were sombre and mobile, full of fervour and of dreams, answering in colour to the hair, as did also the brows and eyelashes.[14] Her cheeks had the profound pallor of complexions at once dark and colourless; but the skin was pure and tender, the outline clear and soft: she was warm and wan as a hot day without a sun. She had a fine and close mouth, with small bright lips, not variable in expression; her throat and shoulders[15] were fresh and round. A certain power and a certain trouble were perceptible in the face, but traceable to no single feature: apart from whatever it might have of beauty, the face was one to attract rather than satisfy.

After the due explanations, Lady Wariston, laughing only with the eyes, did as agreed on present her sister. Lord Charles, who had not seen Bertie for years, and whose memory was known to be loosening, accepted the introduction without a rising eyebrow or questioning lip: it was possible enough that there should be a younger sister now first producible.

'Very like her sister, the young lady is,' he discreetly observed. 'By the by, where's my old friend—Robert—or Hubert was it?'

'Staying with a schoolfellow,' Lady Midhurst thought. 'Helen, what have you done with that boy?'

'He's at old Lunsford's,' quoth Helen: 'hope he likes it.'

'The girl talks like a schoolboy while her brother's holidays last,' said Lady Midhurst to Miss Brandon. 'As her godmother, I ought to look after her language. However, you have a true believer in her for all that; she is verse-mad.'

Lesbia looked curiously into the false girl's eyes, and took her hand; it was hard in the palm for a girl's, and specked with sunburns.

'I should have guessed not,' she said. 'You look fonder of riding, now.'

'I like riding, too,' said Bertie in a small voice; he began to taste the fun and dread detection.

'Does you brother get on well as school now?' said Lord Charles: 'is he in the boat? or only in the bill, eh?'

'Oh, no,' Miss Seyton said scornfully; 'too much of a muff; they'd have let him steer I daresay if he could, but he shirked it; lazy young brute he is, and doesn't get swished half often enough, I think.'

'Par example!' said Lady Midhurst; 'he seems to keep you well up to your slang, my dear child, at any rate.'

'You are rather hard on him,' said Lesbia; 'is he older or younger than you?'

'Twin,' said Herbert: regaining his lost ground by the happy touch.

'I should like to see him.'

'When you've seen her you've seen him,' said Lady Wariston.

'He must be a handsome fellow then by this time,' said Lord Charles.

'Not enough of him for that,' said Linley: 'he might be with more inches.'

'I think he must be as it is,' said Miss Brandon; 'I should like to see him; he must be very fond of you.'

'Well, I don't think he hates me,' said Herbert, suppressing a puerile grin into a feminine smile.

Lesbia took his cheeks between her hollowed hands and pressed them rather hard, till he looked at her with wide shining eyes from which the light of laughter had vanished and melted into eager and dubious passion.

'You have not really read any verse of mine?' she said.[16]

The query almost throttled Herbert for the minute; then he said: 'I thought I had.'

'Then you shall tell me later what you like best.' Her voice was like a kiss as she said this, the boy thought: remembering the only kisses he knew, his sister's.

At dinner that evening Herbert in his masquerading dress happened to sit by Miss Brandon; he had been taken down, to complete and compose the jest, by Walter Lunsford, who pinched his arm on the way so that it showed more black than blue and more blue than white next morning; but he neither laughed nor flinched. It was enough that Miss Brandon should neglect her male neighbour for his or for her sake. During the tedious courses they interchanged many little forms of speech and fragments, pleasant and gracious from her to him.

'What part was he to act?' He told her; in the fragment of a scene cut out of the great play for the uses of their charade,[17] he was the princess Negroni.[18] 'And you know French enough?' said Lesbia; 'you are clever.' This was a new light let in upon Bertie.[19] He thrilled and flushed through all his pores at the thought that this first praise should come from this quarter.[20]

'I wish you had taken another piece to cut up and mince down,' said Miss Brandon. This remark, it may be observed, upset Herbert so much that his presentation of the Negroni that night fell short even of his own hopes. 'If it had been "Les Burgraves"—(the boy's eyes took fire)—I should like to act Guanhumara to your Régina. Could you get up the part? could we rehearse in private? Ah—but Otbert?[21] who could rehearse with us?'

'Oh, I'd be Otbert too,' said Bertie seriously. 'You know, Guanhumara and Régina never meet.'

'Yes; but Otbert and Régina always do. Still—I see what you mean—you would play Régina to anyone—au premier Otbert venu—and Otbert to my Guanhumara. I may call you Helen—my dear Helen, that is truly a boy's notion. But I am glad you know the play so thoroughly; and surprised.'

'But you—Guanhumara!' said Herbert. 'I think I see you.' She laughed and said one line low in his ear:

Oui, mon nom est charmant en Corse, Ginevra!

He answered, with eyes neither moist nor bright, looking down, overpowered by the weight and splendour of the verse.

Ces durs pays du nord en font Guanhumara.

CHAPTER VI

(FRAGMENT)

'HE WOKE HIS FATHER AND BROUGHT HIM OUT. THE SEA WAS running so high that old Mathison thought it was just madness to try it but he went for all that. They got to the ship somehow, and took six of the women there on board. This lot they managed to land, and put out again. It seems they had a frightful pull of it this time, and were caught in some current before they well knew. There's a groundswell alongside the reef there, and they couldn't make head against it.'

'But they got to the ship this time, didn't they?'

'Well, they did it, Lord Wariston, but in this way. They had to row out of the straight line, and strike in again as they could, avoiding the current. When they were under the ship's side again they got some of the crew off, but there was one girl¹ left, who had fallen fainting, and this young fellow got sight of her, and gave his oar to a sailor and went on board again and let her down and wouldn't take his place as the boat was over full already, and waited with the rest of the crew; and before his boat could put out a third time they had all gone down together.'

'Well, that's about as good as Balaklava, Bertie, I think.'

'Rather,' said Herbert, quivering from hair to heel; his eyes were wet and fiery, and his hands clutched the cloth.

92

CHAPTER VII

Dis-moi donc, la blonde,
Si tu veux mon coeur,
Ou bien une fleur,
Ou bien tout le monde?'[1]

'I do like those jolly spoony songs; they are such rot; and so good.'

'I wish you wouldn't sing out of tune and push your horse against mine. You can't ride[2] that hard-mouthed beast; you sit like a schoolboy.'

'I hope so; I could ride fairly when I was one, you know.'

'You've forgotten the dodge then, for you flounder along like a sack, howling in French, with your elbows out: don't be such a tailor. And above all don't foul me—as if you were steering for the first time.'

'Oh, well! I can't ride and I can't sing and I can't steer or pull; and I don't mind. Pitch into me. I'm a muff, and I like it. Doesn't the wind smell sweet rather? But I wouldn't go in for blondes if I could write songs. I say, would this do?

Dis-moi donc, la brune
Au sourire amer,
Veux-tu de la mer,
Froide et sombre lune?

Si tu veux—ma foi!
Cette mer profonde
Qui tremble et qui gronde
Là-bas, c'est à toi.

'I say, it scans, doesn't it? I meant it to be rot.'

93

'In that case, Seyton, it's a brilliant success. But I suppose it scans.'

'That's the use of being an attaché,[3] you get to know these things. I say, if I deserve it—as I shall in five minutes—I wish you'd horsewhip me; I'm so awfully happy[4] I know I must be coming to grief.'

'I will if you don't ride straighter and talk better sense. Do look out there.'

'Well, that was a shy. These horses of Wariston's are no end nervous: it's the trainer's fault.'

> *La vie est une onde;*
> *Mais si j'étais Dieu,*
> *Ton plus petit voeu*
> *Referait le monde.*

'No, that won't do; it's cribbed. Damn the great men, they use the world itself up, and we other poor little kids have all our best words taken out of our mouths. There you are again. I shall call this mare Infelice.'

'Felice, if she takes you safe. But cribbed or not, your song beats me. What do you mean?'

'Oh, things come and go, but they wouldn't if she wished otherwise and I were God and could grant her wish, don't you see? You can't expect one to sing sense extempore: not better sense than that. Just look down there at the sea now. There's no sense in that noise, and by Jove, is there anything like it? I only ask you. That song's in tune, anyhow. Let's gallop, there's lots of light.'

Both made forward in silence, riding hard, swallowing at every bound of the horsehoofs the delight of the wind as a wine: drinking the cold sweet night with nostril and lip. Overhead the grey ghost of a moon, with sharp edges and hollow cheeks through which you saw the blue horror of remote darkness—the broken glass of the sun—seemed as if hung to move along the torrent of the blowing wind. Rare stars sprang into sight and went out between the bright wan bays of cloven cloud. All the sky seemed mobile, a rapid

masque of faint colours and mutable forms. Below and beyond
the dim windy world of earth, past the blown moors and swept
cliffs, the pale sea flashed and swelled and sounded.

The riders pulled up on the rim of a sudden slope, dipping
down towards a cleft in the cliffs through which a thin loud
stream struggled into the sea. Herbert drew breath as he drew
rein, and laughed with pleasure.

'Isn't it a jolly time? the sweetest morsel of the night; but
you're not up in Falstaff.[5] I suppose we must walk them down
this bit. Why they don't make the roads passable just where
one want a good footing I can't think. You go first, please, she
funks it. Isn't the sea there like silver? and not a bit of moonlight: it went out just over Cauldhope. These waves break
into blossom like flowers. You don't know what the sea is by
daylight—I mean, till you see it by night. Look, you can't see
the bushes there, and you see the foam.'

They were again on a level track, rough and green: and
began to push onward at a pace delightful even by day. The
turf rang softly under the muffled hoofs, broken now and then
by a jarring interlude of stonier ground: but in the main
they went over clear uneven spaces of forsaken road. This
forlorn green track ran in a vague and fitful line between
the moors bending inland and the cliffs breaking seaward; it
had never been more than a bridle-road, and was now hardly
that. As they went, Herbert began again to sing or shout fragments of rhyme recalled by the place and the hour.

> *O whatten a thing had ye there to drink,*[6]
> *Or whatten a thing to eat?*
> *Either the wine that is sae red,*
> *Or honey that is sae sweet?*

> *Honey was never sae sweet, mother,*
> *And wine was never sae red;*
> *But it's my lady's bonny mouth*
> *I kissed intill her bed.*

'I wish I knew the rest; you don't of course.'

They were at a rough part of the road, and Lunsford rode on, cautious and silent; if his eyebrows or shoulders rose in contempt, Herbert did not see: and struck up again, as they came on softer ground.

> *There's nae man by yon wan burn-side,'*
> *Nor is there by yon sheugh;*
> *But there is a dead man in thae brackens*
> *That loved me well eneugh.*

> *There's nae bairn in my father's house*
> *Nor in my father's ha';*
> *But there is a bairn between my sides*
> *That's worth his landis a'.*

'I believe you're possessed,' said Lunsford; 'you've got a howling devil. What a fool you are. If you're not drunk, shut up.'

'Or you'll lick me?⁸ we're not at Eton. I'm possessed—with the wind; impregnated, like the mares in Thessaly:⁹ smell it. I like this beast's pace after all. When did Lord Charles die, I forget?'

'Why, last year of course; what's that to you?'

'Oh, a good deal less than nothing. Poor old devil, he was a good-natured old ass. I wonder what it's like dying? I feel as if one need never die if one chose not; I've no doubt people do choose some time or other, and it's remembered against them; you want to get off dying, and the destinies remind you there was a time when you could have prayed for death; if one could only keep one's will strung so as always to wish for the same thing—then—I say!'

They were in sight of the bay under Wansdale Point in full windy moonlight; the waves went racing under the blue night like a concourse of flying flowers, matched for speed, and playing at white horses, but their breaking and blossoming beauty betrayed their floral kind; the edge of sand they kissed, leaving the banks of shingle still dry and hard against the muffled yellow light, was one long wavering wreath of visible sighs and kisses, radiant and weary and passionate;

they saw the thin white line of loving foam flicker and fluc-
tuate up and down with tender motion as mutable as fire.
Above, the sky was by this time, as Bertie said, a leopard's
skin of stars: and the grass of the downs was full of running
wind and falling light.

'Well, five minutes more,' said Walter; 'thank God. I'm
sick of this.'

Herbert and he rode on quietly enough now and were
received at the stables in five minutes' time; whence they
passed in peace to supper and bed. That night Lunsford slept
well enough; but Seyton had a strange dream. Foam and
moonlight in his eyes, wind and sea in his ears, brought about
this irrational vision; aided, a cynical critic might have
thought, by unusual wine in his brain. He saw the star of
Venus, white and flower-like as he had always seen it, turn
into a white rose and come down out of heaven, with a reddening centre that grew as it descended liker and liker a living
mouth;[10] but instead of desire he felt horror and sickness at
the sight of it, and averted his lips with an effort to utter
some prayer or exorcism; vainly, for the dreadful mouth only
laughed, and came closer. And cheek or chin, eyebrow or eye,
there was none; only this mouth; and about it the starry or
flowery beams or petals, that smelt sweet and shone clear as
ever; which was the worst. Then, with a violent revulsion of
spirit, he seemed to get quit of it; but then his ears instead
were vexed with sound. The noise of the sea hardened and
deepened and grew untunable; soon it sharpened into a shrill
threatening note without sense or pity, but full of vicious
design. He woke as the salt froth[11] seemed coming round lips
and nostrils and ears, with a sense of sterility and perplexity
which outwent all other pain. The torture of the dream was
the fancy that these fairest things, sea and sky, star and flower,
light and music, were all unfruitful and barren; absorbed in
their own beauty; consummate in their own life. After an
hour's beating of the brain against and about such fancies
and the fears engendered from them, he slept again and
soundly till long past dawn.

CHAPTER VIII

ON THE DOWNS

HERBERT SAT UP AT HER FEET, AND FIXED HIS EYES UPON THE fiery beauty of her face

'You used to care for my verses as a boy?' she said in a soft vague voice.

'I can't tell you how much, honestly.'

'I wonder what you could have seen in them. People don't like them, as a rule; nor do I much. They are part of myself; only a dead part; cut off.'

'Not dead; you don't think they won't live?'

'You must be very young,' said Lesbia. 'But I wish I knew as much as you; and as little.'

'I don't understand,' said Herbert. 'I only know I wish I were likely to be—' here he stopped and his eyes fell.

'Like me? you would like to be such a man as I am a woman, was that the compliment coming?' she asked with a strange irony in her look, with a mixed accent of pity and scorn, of wonder and regret.

'Of course you can chaff me. Only look here, I don't know how to say it, but please let me try. I can't ask—I mean I can't say how I should like to be—to be that or something like it; because if I were I could tell you what I can't now. I don't know that I want even. Only I must after all.' (He went on with his eyes on the ground, grasping the heather violently with both hands.) 'Because I think you know. I would—I don't like trying to say. Only upon my honour I think, I do quite believe, as far as a fellow can know about himself at all, if you liked, if you thought it would amuse you, I would go right over the cliff[1] there and thank God. I should like to have a chance of pleasing you, making a minute's

98

difference to you. And I don't care about other things as I did.'

His voice never shook and paused but little during this speech, but it had a depth of quiet heat unmistakeable, a steady and even pulse of passionate sound. The sound was stranger to Lesbia Brandon than a new language to ignorant ears; sweet and singular and senseless.

'I shan't put you to the test. But will you look at me? Well, I see you would.'

It was easy to see; for the face turned to her, neither red nor pale, was all thro' like a still fire, intense and hopeful, wholly ready for death or life.

'Poor boy. You would really, now.'

'Yes. But not because I'm a boy at all. I'm not so young. I'm twenty-four. Oh, I know—if you don't think I would I can't help. Only if you told me. I don't want to die for nothing like a fool in a book. But if you did! Oh, by God I can't think about it. If you said you should sleep better to-night for thinking of it, would I not? I believe I should die thinking it would make you² smile to yourself when you thought of it. I'm not worth anything else but I don't believe another man in the world loves you quite like this. I don't ask for anything, mind. I only hope you're not vexed or troubled. I didn't mean you should be.'

'No,' said she; 'but I am sorry, and glad in a way. I wish I could be you for five minutes, and understand it. As it is I can't. But you have spoken to me as no one ever did. I never thought people could look at me in this way. I'm not modest, I know they might want to marry me, money or no money: some at least of the men who have tried. But you are quite right and they were not what you are. I feel it to the heart. And now you must take me as I am. If I could love or marry, I am sure I could love and marry you, absurd as people would call it. But I can't. I don't know why, at least I don't wholly know. I am made as I am, and God knows why—I suppose. You quite deserve that I should be fair to you, and truthful. I never felt for anyone what I feel for you now, and shall while I live. I do really in a way, so to speak, love you. And you can see by my way of telling you this that I can never by any chance love you otherwise or love you more. Make up your mind to that once for all. And I shall be—as I am—grateful to you. But you must understand there may be love between us, but must be no more lovemaking. I am not marriageable. Neither you nor I will ever revert to this. I hope and think you know I am speaking the plainest truth as kindly as I can.'

'Yes,' said Herbert quietly; 'I was sure of it; quite. I didn't mean.'

Something in his still and sincere voice made her eyes grow dim for once. But the woman was all but incapable of tears.

'I only ask for one thing,' he said again. 'No, it must be for two: first to forgive me for this; and then to believe that if ever you could want or wish for any service or action of mine I would come from anywhere and give up anything to do it. If you would promise to give me the chance in case it ever should come it would be very good of you. I won't talk about dying or devotion or any rubbish if I can help. But I would do that. I don't say how gratefully or gladly. If it were to be your husband's bridesman;[3] there. I would if you wanted me. I couldn't help, I know. Or to do any wrong, I'm afraid.'

'I shall never ask you to do either of those things,' said Miss Brandon, with a smile deeply sad and ironical, but not untender. 'For the rest, I promise what you like.'

'Thank you,' said Herbert looking her in the face. 'I did think you would.'

'I wish this did not make you unhappy.'

'It will not now; not too much.'

'I don't know if you would like it or not, but I should like to feel thoroughly that we were not less than brother and sister.[4] It would not make the gulf between us wider than it is.'

'I suppose not,' said Herbert. 'Yes, in a certain way I should like to know I might call you—anything but Miss Brandon.'

Lesbia was so wholly ignorant of man's love as not to feel

herself cruel; and he loved her too much to show that he
did: but his heart was wrung and stung meantime by strange
small tortures.

'Then we are to be friends, Herbert, always? But I see:
you won't answer me in kind.'

And in fact he was silent for a little, and did not answer
her in any kind: he sat and felt a breakage inside him of all
that made up the hopefullest part of his life. But being too
old a male to express suffering by any puerile suffusion of
tears or blood, he did before long make some courteous and
vacuous reply: evidently insufficient; for Miss Brandon re-
joined: 'I cannot see why we shouldn't be friends: I might
be your elder brother. But—if necessary, I'll disown you.'

'You needn't do that,' said Herbert, in a voice clear and
fresh enough. 'I'll do my best as a—cadet; if I must.'

'You won't say junior; I see: and you won't call me—by my
name.' (She was a little struck for the moment by his readi-
ness of recovered sense and speech.) 'I have called you—by
yours; and you won't say—'

'Lesbia,' said her lover, trembling with inward love, burning with outward defiance. 'Is that right?'

'I don't know. I am three years older than you; at least.'

At this Herbert sprang to his feet and spoke.—'I don't know
or care—or (of course) believe; but you shouldn't say that to
me—now. I thought it was all right—or wrong—before;
wrong for me of course I knew it was. But you talk of this and
that, and ages and Christian names; and you know what a
sort of thing it is to me.' (Here he checked himself, feeling
in private the resurgence of a profitless and passionate desire
to beat his face upon the ground at her feet; which would
have been no less ludicrous than unfruitful.) 'It's all my life,
really: I beg your pardon; it's your fault you see if I say that
sort of thing. Though it's true. You make me: but I don't
mind; though I meant to hold my tongue, and thought I
could.'

At first Lesbia had watched him with wide eyes; they were
narrowed now, and wearied: drawn together as it were by

gradual somnolence.—'You mean—well—you don't care for age or name—on either side?' she said heavily.

'You know what I mean, I suppose,' said Herbert, angered.

'I wish you knew,' she replied, brightening for a moment: 'and yet—no. It is good for you to be in trouble.'

'That's in the Psalms,' he observed: being by this time naturally brilliant and original.

'Yes; that you may learn—! have you learnt?'

'No: not why you—chaff me now—like this.' (He did not make his pauses to sob, or breathe hard, or bow; but merely to look at her, and wonder: having still perfect command of himself; a poor possession.)

'Because you don't like my name, and I rather like yours. I dare say we are both right.'

'I'm only waiting for the word of command,' said Herbert, with a false light smile.

'And I can't give it,' said Lesbia, with an equable amiable face. 'I've no doubt if I could you would organize a forlorn hope. Don't let your mind dwell upon the chance; it doesn't exist.'

'Well, I shan't serve under other flags; for some time.'

'*C'est selon,*' said Miss Brandon; 'and here we are at home.' For they had been on foot and homeward again, without thinking of it, longer than they knew.

CHAPTER IX

TURRIS EBURNEA

THERE WAS AFLOAT IN LONDON ABOUT THIS TIME A LADY OF aspiring build, handsome beyond the average and stupid below the elect of her profession. She had a superb and seductive beauty, some kindness of nature, and no mind whatever. Tall, white-faced, long-limbed, with melancholy eyes that meant nothing and suggested anything, she had made her way in good time. Her trick of mournful and thoughtful manner, assumed where other women let fall their grave or gay assumptions, was an implement which stood her in good stead: her sad eyes and drawn lips forged money in mints where swifter fingers and brighter faces had failed. She was a shining light in what her patron Mr. Linley called the demi-semi-monde. 'Above the street, below the boudoir,' said the sage. She was not 'idealless'; her ideal was marriage; apparently inaccessible for years. Nevertheless she clung to it with a fervent faith, a soaring hope, which revealed to astonished and admiring friends the vitality of a dubious intellect within her. Had an honest woman been half so stupid, all men would have fled from her with shuddering. Coarse or fine, she never in her life said a good thing. She had not even the harlot's talent of discernment. A preacher might have yawned under the infliction of her talk.

In spite or in consequence of these natural gifts, Miss Leonora Harley held a certain outpost and commanded a certain respect in the world of her own choice. Her father's name was Farmer; a name to him miserably satirical; he was a labourer, and had christened his daughter Susan. Mr. Linley was always happy to insinuate that he first had taught her a new name and a new trade: quoting, as he waved before her (in presence of friends) an old white hand—

Illa rudem cursu prima imbuit Amphitriten:[1]

but the woman always laughed a long dumb laugh when his pretension was brought before her. 'He taught me—French,' she would say, with a long pause and a short smile. In effect, seduction was not the sage's favourite sin: he was exuberant in riper quarters; to bite green fruit, as he said, was a pleasure for truant schoolboys.

He now floated between cynicism that was almost grotesque and goodwill that was almost noble. He liked his nephew and his nephew's wife; they pleased him in sense and spirit, being neither ugly nor foolish. It would be a good thing for their brother to launch him imperceptibly into life; and his old friend Miss Harley might here be of use. She must needs make her game; and having made it, she could not but purge the young fellow's head of puerile fumes and fancies. And then, being in fact of no unkindly nature he thought of young Seyton's prospects not without pleasure. A certain recrudescence of personal ambition rose, subsided, and revived within him. 'By God! I who can't start now on my own hook—who have given it up—if I start this boy, I may follow, catch him up, distance him—' here even his vaguer fancies paused, and melted into a dim vision of concordant abnegation and success.

Three things at least were clear, as necessary to be done; to lay hold on the right man; to push him on to the right place; and to supplant him at the right time. It was rare to find a boy of his age and rank so passionate on political matters as young Seyton: who, besides, was not exactly a fool, and therefore might be worth laying hold of. The means of influence were in his hand. Besides, a genuine kindness, a contemptuous sincerity of compassion, impelled or at least induced him to lend a hand and labour to lift the young fool out of the slough of sentiment and despondency, in which he believed young Seyton to be still weltering in vain.

The plan was laudable and kindly; but the instrument, he

knew, might turn restive. 'Flesh and blood do not make dead metal,'[2] he remarked one evening to his wine; 'but—!' He ran over her beauties in his mind.

She had the darkest brown eyes, pale yellow hair susceptible of curls, and colourless features. Her throat would have done credit to any statuary but God: her shoulders and bosom were so faultless as to be admirable; 'a rare merit,' said Mr. Linley. She looked usually as though she were insensible, and her looks usually lied. Her neck, her arms, all her limbs, were white, clear, long; her eyes were attractive and dim. A statue elsewhere, she showed a soul there only, or rather seemed to show. Her hands were exquisite, soft and keen at once, made to caress and to repel. Her small rounded feet could curl up and strike out. She was a woman made to kiss, to resist, to laugh at, and to leave. Nothing in her was not pleasant; nothing was durable. She was full of life, and suggestive of change. She was active, and vital, and stupid. She despised intellect in women, and half understood that the stupidest or most amorous of her casual customers despised her, and was right.

This was Miss Leonora Vane Harley, otherwise Susan Farmer; a woman too stupid for vice or virtue; a victim given over to scurrility and success. She could not spell, and had never tried to think. She did not care more for one man than another; the watchword of her life was indifference. She was cold, slow, heavy; and therefore capable of worse things than a sensual woman abandoned to herself. She could neither love nor reflect; she could not even talk the bright false talk of women naturally dull. But for all this she was still one thing: a tower of ivory, roofed with gold.

CHAPTER X

ANOTHER PORTRAIT

THERE WAS A MAN IN LONDON THAT YEAR WHO IS NOW NO longer anywhere in our world, but somewhere (if his creed were true) where his work begun among men now goes on still and for ever; which seems improbable: [1] but assuredly, if anything on him is anywhere alive, it is at work somehow. A few years earlier, an Italian teacher had found employment at Ensdon; Lady Wariston had taken a fancy to read Dante; and this man had given Herbert a few stray lessons in holiday time. He learnt the teacher's language rapidly and roughly enough, and his politics in much the same fashion; as fast as he picked up words, he gathered up opinions. Carlo Speroni (no descendant of Tasso's traducer, the author Canace;[2] he could hardly have named his grandfather, and was much given to belief and adoration) taught his pupil to abhor Austrians at fifteen, and made him wish to be shot at sixteen if that could serve the cause. Once the boy asked him if it were not possible to see face to face some one of the great men of whom he spoke. 'I'd rather than anything, you know; I would,' he said, with fire in his cheeks and eyes. Speroni promised to present him when older to his chief friend, the exile who had found him out in exile and helped him on. 'Sono un niente io,' he said, 'ma lui!' At another time: 'There are men in the world still as well as swine; though one wouldn't think it when one looks round. And that is a man.' Herbert was in effect introduced to the man by Speroni, during one of his Oxford vacations: and found that his teacher had spoken truth.

Count Mariani was then about midway between thirty and forty. In 1849[3] he had received a shot in the left shoulder and a shot in the right hip, which disabled his left arm and right leg. He was thus incurably crippled, and in such a way that he might have moved more easily if the hurt limbs had been amputated in time. Born a rich man, he was now so poor that none but himself could have said how he contrived to assist and support Speroni and others. Some said that he wrote for English papers: which those who best knew him disbelieved, though he knew more than enough of English for that purpose. He talked the language with a small foreign accent, but without strange idioms.

After receiving his first wound (that in the shoulder) he had fought on till disqualified by the second. It was possible to fight with one arm and two legs; impossible, for him at least, to do any good fighting with but two left out of four limbs. Driven forth from Rome with other greater men by Oudinot and the titular⁴ Buonaparte, he had followed the great Dictator northwards, and when the campaign closed and all chances ended, he came to England and lived his life in silence. He was not eloquent or turbulent, and naturally made no mark there.

He was lean and sallow, with great eyes and heavy brows; his mouth was large and gentle. In his eyes there was always the likeness of a dream, in his lips there was always the look of a caress. His short heavy hair receded from his pale narrow forehead, and clustered behind in close masses without a curl. His voice and tone were beautiful, at once soft as a woman's and frank as a boy's. Many men, knowing his story and looking into his eyes, would have followed him into hell if he had bidden them. He was admirably narrow-minded and single-hearted; such men alone win to their cause followers worth having. And he was good beyond all words; sinless, as far as a man can see; which is probably as far as the rules of right and wrong extend.

His influence over young Seyton was great from the moment of their meeting, and became in time immeasurable.⁵ His manner was so quiet and his whole life so composed and reserved that strange things were now and then said of him.

Lady Midhurst for example said once to Herbert: 'I am quite sure, my dear boy, that your friend is—well! No Italian could be so placid; unless he were an Austrian spy. Upon my credit, I am convinced he takes German pay.' Whereupon Bertie, as she said afterwards to his sister, 'flashed and flew out at her like a mad kitten grown all at once into a tiger cat.' His creed for a certain time might have been resumed in four words: 'I believe in Mariani'. At his age he might have worshipped worse gods. His idol, if not superhuman in stature of intellect, was wholly pure and flawless. In his life (we must suppose) he had never consciously done wrong. That life, it is certain, he was ready to lay down at any moment in any manner, if that could serve or avail the cause of Italian unity.[6] He was called a rabid Republican and would not on any terms accept the presence or supervision of a king.[7] He had never felt but one passion, and that consumed his life. For he had never in his life loved any woman, not even in the way of lust; his country he had always loved. He was probably insane, and certainly admirable.

This was the Count Attilio Mariani, aristocrat and Republican, virgin and martyr. There are a few such men, it is hoped, in all times; equally laughable and adorable; but the hope savours of optimism.

CHAPTER XI

AN EPISODE

ON A SPRING DAY IN 1861[1] HERBERT SEYTON AND ATTILIO
Mariani were together. The elder man, usually tacit and
hopeless of alien sympathy, had taken a liking to the younger;
who was at least in earnest on the subject of Italy. Encouraged
by Mariani's kindness of manner, he had asked why his friend
was not then at home, with other patriots? Mariani smiled
and spoke softly in answer.

'They will not have us—yet: perhaps never, I do not know.
The General has Caprera;[2] well! He is also away, do you see?
It may be that he is right. His work is not done yet; for all[3] I
know, mine is. And he has faith in his kingdom.[4] Is there any
place for me? There is hardly room, it seems, for him. I do
not think now I shall ever go home.'

'But when you have done—what you have—' Herbert said
passionately, and broke down. The same fatal quiet smile
answered him again.

'My good boy, listen. I have done nothing. Those who have,
you know them. So do all men. They are dead, for the most
part. Some are in exile, or (what you call) under a cloud. It is
very well, if that shall help our Italy. But if these have not
reward, what am I that I should at all look for it? I have done
the little, very little stupid bits of work that I could. They
have done—look! you know of whom I speak. I do not say
his name. I think of him as of that boatman in Dante, you
know? "Fa, fa che le ginocchia cali; ecco l'Angel di Dio."[5]
Without him we should not be anything at all. And what is it
that your journals say of him? Assassin, conspirator? I know
not of French papers or German: but these; it is bad.'

'Yes, I have seen,' said Herbert, sadly, looking down. 'We

can't help it, you know. These writing men are what they are; they must live; at least they think so. And for bread and meat they would talk of their mothers I've no doubt just as they talk of him.' For very love and reverence and thankfulness neither would name the great name of Mazzini.[6]

'It may be,' said the other after this: 'but then, see, what am I that I should be angry? I had but only so very little to give; money, and lands and life and limbs. I am not clever, you see, not of genius. I can do not much good. But those who have more to give than I, I envy them; yes. And certain of mine have given more. I had three brothers. They are dead now; I hope. Of two I know it: I shall tell you of these. You English boys are children, good or bad, when ours are men. These all were younger than me. And Vincenzo was killed at Milan; he had a post to fill, what do I know of it? and got himself so shot down. He must have fought well while he could keep his legs; I remember him. And then Cesare got killed. Yes, at Novara. He had faith in Savoy, that one. And Lorenzo—look, this is what he was like.' He showed Herbert a queer sketch of a boyish head, roughly drawn and carefully framed: the features were curiously exquisite, like a Roman bust. This face had the singular dubious beauty distinctive of Italian boys; a loveliness that wavers and hovers between female and male; dark and soft, rounded and radiant.

'That was a martyr,' said his brother: 'my Renzino. He had not the luck to die or fly like the others. He was with us in a plot: I cannot say now any more; and he was taken. He was put in prison and examined; you know what that means with our Austrians? beaten to pieces till something comes of it; death, or madness, or confession. Eh! when they don't stop at women. There's Haynau[7] hardly warm in hell yet. Well, confession didn't come of it this time. I believe death did; I hope so. My little Renzo; he was good; loved me well, for one. What is it they call it, schlagen? Yes?'

'It isn't true! oh, do say it isn't!' Herbert actually screamed out with passion and pain, like a child. The other laughed a sad light laugh.

'My friend, there is nothing truer. This is what we have to
fight against. Think, Verona has to bear it all, even now; and
Venice. I don't grudge my little brother to the cause. What
are we, to care about this thing or that man? We have to die
somehow, or live; which may be worse. You can't save a lost
country by wishing; the price has to be paid. And it cannot
be too high. You don't think I wouldnt have taken this place,
teh poor boy? but each has his own bit of work to do. Now
if you or I were to be shot or hanged or beaten, would it help
Italy at all?'ᵇ

At this Herbert bowed his head, and understood. Naturally
sensitive and tender, Mariani was now harder than flint for
the sake of the cause.

'I dare say you would take it all, yourself, a stranger; eh?
if you had to be shot, now?'

Herbert raised his face again and looked him in the eyes.

'I thought so. And that is nothing. Who are you, and what
am I, that we should have the luck to serve Italy by our lives
or deaths? Understand that there is no higher reward, no
splendider crown attainable or conceivable by any man; by
our greatest. Be killed, by the Austrians, for Italy! as those
French say—vous n'êtes pas dégoûté. What on earth —what
the devil —is there in that to cause any hesitation, or any
compassion? Our betters would be glad of the chance, do you
see? Your betters and mine.'

'I know, death cannot be much to mind; but disgrace, or
what people call disgrace—being beaten and tied down—it is
too bad to think of, surely.'

'Child!' said Mariani, getting on his feet; his voice
deepened and thundered; his eyes moistened and lightened.
'You draw the line there? as if it were so great a thing to
give your poor little life, or mine! You must do more than
that, if you would do anything. You must be ready to give
your honour.'ᵉ See me, now: I am what you call a gentleman,
I suppose, and I would lie, and steal, and forge, and murder,
and betray men, and cut purses, if need were, and if this
could serve our cause. I would not grudge my honour and

my soul to Italy; not more than my flesh and bones and blood;
I grudge her nothing. I am one, and she wants so many. They
will come, I tell you; kingdom or republic, we shall get our
Italy; but first, mind, we shall pay for it. We shall not pay
down monies or lives to the Buonaparte; not to any thief or
any ruler in the world; but to fate, what you call Providence.
And then we shall do well enough.'

To reason with Attilio Mariani was like talking to a con-
flagration; Herbert knew better. Presently the flame broke
out again.

'For what is it that you call honour, and what is it that you
call Providence? My honour is to do my work, my Providence
is to shut my eyes. You now, you have a sister: well; would
you let her be sacrificed for the sake of Italy, and live, you,
still—because her death might be useful to us, and your life
also, see—and her life, not; and your death, not?'

After this Herbert felt as one cut off from answer; and
seeing him abashed and knowing him sincere, Mariani re-
lented for a little:

'You could not; you are not alone; and you are a good boy
to go so far as you do. I do see, or I do believe (it is one thing),
you would give yourself at least; well! It is something; I say
not, in face of what has been, I say not it is much. But some
would not give that. You shall see soon a man that would not,
who yet loves our cause in his fashion; and I respect him, and
his work; bad; but it is work. I say, bad; but it labours hard,
and it would fain be good. And perhaps one day it will, who
knows? not you.'

Herbert, in a loyal and credulous state of mind, waited for
the apparition of this dubious workman: he appeared before
long. Pierre Sadier was one of those men with whom honesty
is a passion, with whom belief is a lust. To him there were
but two kinds of men seriously hateful and condemnable; the
liar and the turncoat. All other sins in his view were sinless.
He would assert or would admit, according to place and time,
that a man might be libidinous, murderous, thievish, blasphemous, tyrannous, ineffably foul and infinitely cruel, and

yet possibly admirable; capable of redemption and deserving
of respect: but not the man who should commit theft and
murder by means of lying lips and hands pledged to a perjury.
As in modern days such crimes are of course unknown, it is
simply impossible to conjecture the source of this Frenchman's hatred. He had lived in exile since 1852; but how
should this explain his perverse antipathies?

The citizen Sadier (his former colleagues would assert) was
in appearance not unlike one of those 'republican blackbirds'
the last of whom was shot down, if newspapers may be trusted,
in October 1866.[10] This parallel had been drawn some six
years earlier. He was a dark, full-fledged, full-breasted sort of
man and speaker; and the one tune and tone of his mind was
set to the air of the Marseillaise. No apostle was ever more
candid and veracious. His figure was moderately protrusive
on either side; under the skirt and below the belt. He had
fine eyes and full lips: he had also clean hands and a sincere
heart. Proofs of his courage were not wanting; he had held
his own on various occasions, public and other.

He came in without a word, and without a word sat
smoking for twenty minutes. Both the others did likewise,
Mariani through courtesy and habit, Herbert through perplexity and respect. Before the half-hour was out Sadier broke
silence:

'Vous avez de la chance, vous autres': and refused for some
time to utter anything further, except inarticulate syllables
of scornful smoke. At last, being gently pressed by Mariani,
he explained; in somewhat piebald English:

'You have Italy made to your hand, cooked to a point;
enough; and you wash your hands of the world: of us; of all
things. You are admirable! One comes to you with full heart;
it is good; you make derive those ardours into your—
channels. We give you the hand that you may give it again
to the others—to all. It is not this that we want—not this that
you do; England is territorial, Italy provincial, France human.
Understand, then, the republic is not municipal. A nation is
a tyranny. On parque les troupeaux au profit du pasteur.

Where kingdoms are, there are kings. We will none of them—; we will the people, one and entire. That survives to many things. What then? You see but Italy alone, Hungary, Poland alone? I see not a certain number of men, a given number of years; I see humanity and time.[11] Is it worth the pain to work for anything of less?'

'I think it is,' said Mariani.

CHAPTER XII

LA BOHEME DEDOREE

TWO NIGHTS LATER HERBERT RECEIVED A NOTE FROM MR. Linley inviting him to a private supper. Feverish from the contact of Mariani and hungry for a chance of service, he felt not unwilling to win a little respite from the vexation of patience; to wait and to abstain were not yet among the virtues practical for him, adorable as they might be afar off in the silent and sleepless figure of his friend. The sage had never found him more amenable to the counsel he called reason. Miss Brandon had not lately crossed his way; and Italy would have none of him: how indeed was he fit for either service?

Over their evening Leonora Harley presided with the due graces of her professional art: no other friends intruded or intervened. Her chaff was temperate, and her demeanour up to a certain point not ungracefully imitative of a lady's.[1] It was not her fault if she could not help asking her younger friend when he had last met a darker beauty: she had seen him once with Lesbia.

'My belief in virtue totters,' said Mr. Linley, observing him silent: 'il doit y avoir anguille sous roche.'

'C'est une horreur que cette jeunesse-là', said Leonora with a delicate mimicry of his inflection and manner which made Herbert smile.

'It is true then,' said the sage; 'or something is true like it. Hein?' (Nothing would have made him say *Eh?* but *Hein?* was a delicate and Parisian sound in his ears.)[2]

'You might tell us, I think,' quoth Leonora, with a smile so palpably professional as to freeze any lover neither old nor brutish nor foolish; a hard dry smile, compound of conscious fun and repellent lust.

'I'm sure I would if I knew how,' said Bertie stupidly.

'But you don't, hein?—Now, is it worth giving this boy a chance?'

'Chance?' said Miss Harley, expanding her overgrown smile; 'what sort of it?'

'Dieu de Dieu!' said Mr. Linley; 'she calls that English— still! Stick to bad French, my love; to please me.'

Hereat Leonora blushed and winced naturally; and as the mask of her trade dropped off her face, it resumed the native and momentary beauty that could now return only by flashes. For an instant, seeing that sweet and superb face with the pure and simple charm upon it of a child's, Herbert felt the attraction of the woman, and was drawn to her without knowing it; she caught him round the head and kissed his hair.

'Isn't it a shame now?' she said in a longer whisper that hissed and gurgled through her lips as they parted.

'Herbert,' said Mr. Linley, 'I shall tell your tutor.'

But as Herbert's mouth was fastened under Leonora's left ear, and her neck was twisted in the attempt to revenge the kiss upon his neck, this jest of the sage fell wholly flat. At least, Leonora only heard it, and swung her head back, laughed at him with more of scorn than of sympathy.

'He is a boy—isn't he?' she said. 'You wouldn't be one— would you? at no price?'

Her voice had the clangor of metal in it, cold as iron and sharp as steel. It repelled and sickened him as the noise of drum or bagpipe might have done; his arms relaxed, and his lips released their hold.

'Are you cross with me—us?' said she, putting forth hands and face.

'How could I?' said Herbert, and took her kiss hastily; but the trademark had reappeared, and in his eyes could never be re-effaced. It is superfluous to say that he was thenceforward attractive to her and she repulsive to him.

She turned, with eyes and lips of sulky splendour, to the wine; and drank as much of a full tumbler of champagne as woman could without sneezing.

'Good,' said the sage; 'Ariadne was wise when she turned to Bacchus;[3] he is a safe card. Hein?'

Herbert grew at once hot from hair to heel with the sense of unintended discourtesy. He had still the full feeling in him of woman-worship.

'If you are not cross now with me—may I drink after you?' he said.

'Oh! if you like,' she said coldly;[4] and again kissed his wet lips after they had touched the leavings of her draught; and again repelled him. A face unlike hers[5] rose between her eyes and his; with close melancholy lips, full of meaning and of passion; with sombre and luminous eyes, with deep thick eyelids and heavy lashes that seemed as though sodden and satiate with old and past tears; with large bright brows, and chin and neck too sensitive and expressive to be flexible as these before him. This face, he thought—and thought untruly; but the error was excusable—would bend and expand to any man as to him.

'Are you going to be good children—you two?' said Mr. Linley, panting and chuckling and neighing and choking; 'because if not—I shall—go.'

Herbert had never felt more virtuous; but Miss Harley replied—'No; we ain't; so you, go.'

'Tiens, tiens, tiens,' said the sage, rising; 'but it seems to me a left-handed affair—one-sided—morganatic?'

Herbert disengaged himself, and sat looking sadly nowhither.

'Is it drink deadens him?' said their teacher. 'Give him more, then.'

Leonora put a full glass to his mouth; he sipped it and turned away.

'C'est l'amour, l'amour, l'amour!' said Linley in the wheeziest of false notes.

CHAPTER XIII

[FRAGMENT]

THE WICKED AND WEARY EYES TURNED UPON HER KINDLED AND hardened; a soft tremor shook the network of wrinkles about lip and eyelid.

'Can you remember poor Arthur?'

'Your son?'

'So I have always heard. Died in 1847, I know.'

'No,' she said smiling with cold lips at the equivocal echo.

'I assure you he did. Drowned, poor boy. It was a loss. Pardon, I see: you do *not* remember him. I fancied you meant to impugn my dates. He was drowned at Oxford. I paid his bills; a mournful consolation. His mother had left me to mourn her years before: if it be permitted to lament an angel, that is.' ('Killed her you know, my dear,' said Lady Midhurst afterwards: 'not a doubt of it: killed her by inches; and it took time, for she was a big woman!') Sneering with all his features and quivering through all his limbs, the husband and father looked once more like a satyr struck frigid and grown vicious.

'About the son?' said Lady Wariston.

'If you had remembered I meant to ask—do you see the likeness to your brother? A very nice boy. I went down to see him at Eton in '51 or thereabouts. Tutor told me I remember there wasn't an idler fourth-form in his house: I couldn't see him till after twelve; and then he came in red-hot from punishment. My boy never learnt anything there but swimming, and that river[1] was the end of him after all. If he had lived no doubt he would have come to harm.'

'Thanks; may I warn Herbert?'

'Ah, pray do. I believe in likenesses, and that they go deep.

118

I shall write a treatise some day on their meaning. It is significant of something, I am convinced, when two faces without a vein of kindred blood in them are so alike. I have endless superstitions, Lady Wariston. Better to believe too much than too little, isn't it? One hears so. Your brother was a very pretty boy; but that goes off in the male. You never see remarkable beauty in any one of a family where all are good-looking. What startles, what is perfect and exceptional, stands out single and allows no comparable beauty near it.

Lady Wariston permitted the delivery of this little essay with calm patience, accepting the necessity of attention and ignoring the implication of compliment. The old eyes had fastened on her averted face with covetous violence as wasps fasten on a fruit. Softly they fed upon the shapely splendour of her neck, the tender and stately grace of her recumbent hands and feet. Her beauty seemed to warm and enlighten the dim and weary winter of his senses, to fertilise a soil once fruitful of enjoyment, able now to bring forth only the cold grey sins of intellect. In these the dry keen nature of the world-worn tyrant still took a bloodless pleasure; he had grown into something of an idle Iago turned out as it were to grass, and doing evil (as the Scotchman swore) at large. He loved mischief as a child does, but his mischief was enormous. He took a childlike pleasure in the infliction of pain, but of pain at once acute and mental and durable. He knew not why, and Thersites-like would have bidden one 'make that demand of his Maker'.[2] His disposition was the work of nature, made perfect by practice. 'S'il l'effleure, elle doit pourrir', said Lady Midhurst to herself: meaning of course a moral contact and a moral decomposition.

'Among these children, now, the girl has absorbed—or she will soon—all the beauty: no law of primogeniture for that. I fear sometimes that nature is a democrat. Beauty you see is an exception; and exception means rebellion against a rule, infringement of a law. That is why people who go in for beauty pure and plain—poets and painters and all the tail trash[3] of the arts, besides all men who believe in life—are all born aristocrats on the moral side. Nature, I do think, if she had her own way, would grow nothing but turnips; only the force that fights her,[4] for which we have no name, now and then revolts; and the dull soil here and there rebels into a rose. We all grow into wall-fruit and vegetables; but some remember what they were like in flower. The nature of things beats us in the long run, and we grow old all over, inside and outside. The comfort is that there will always be flowers after us to protest against the cabbage commonwealth and insult the republic of radishes. It's the same with all exceptions, beauty which is best of all, and genius[5] and great wealth and capacity of happiness. Each of these is an insult, an outrage, an oppression and affliction to the ugly, the stupid, the poor and the despondent. Après? This only makes them gifts worth taking.'

Lady Wariston was neither stupid enough to misapprehend nor social enough to dislike the tendency of this elaborate improvisation. To wit and trivial forms of speech, such as the social novelist takes down by photographic process for his own uses, she had no leaning. Society she could only enjoy by fits, and in a somewhat intolerant way.[6] Nevertheless, being feminine, she preferred to take her philosophy in pills; and a draught like this was somewhat of an overdose, and drenched her understanding not pleasantly: so she answered, emphasising the word:

'Did you ever write moral essays? Mr. Linley?'

'I thought of it once,' he said simply and gently; but a friend suggested the addition of a syllable to the adjective, and of course I refrained.'

CHAPTER XIV

LES MALHEURS DE LA VERTU

ON THE SAME DAY DENHAM HAD COME UP TO LONDON, STILL undecided. He had gone at once to Mr. Linley, whose house was three doors off Miss Brandon's. Tired and soiled from travel, he was ushered somewhat too suddenly into a small delicate room, full of faint light and heat. As he entered, something swift and silken went out at another door in a rapid hustle: but Linley met him with bland grave smiles.

'You have been smoking. Pardon: I object. There is so much to talk over that we must have a suitable atmosphere.' He lit a few pastilles and let them burn out under his eyes, sitting sleepy and silent. Knowing his teacher of old, Denham waited opposite without a word.

'You will not eat or drink? no. Now then we come to close quarters. You mean to restore the letters.'

'Well—I don't know. How should you?'

'I can hardly say: but I do. It's on you somehow; you look good. They are all ready. But I wouldn't in your place. Even if you don't care for the woman it's something to keep in hand.'

'I'm not sure now that I care,' said Denham, with a sharp short sigh.

'Hein? a new light on the matter, is there?'

'No: but I think it's beyond me as yet to hurt her: somehow.'

'I see: the dawn of virtue. You are in the convertible mood. Now, do you know, this is dangerous. She can hardly love you.'

'How should she? look here. You don't understand. It's quite serious. I am really ashamed, but I care about her: and

121

of course it's too absurd—and not the less grave—for me. There are boys and girls on one hand; old men on the other.'

'Quorsum haec tam putida?[1] I don't see. At least there must be old women too on that hand.'

'Well, yes: but sex ends at a certain point—male and female coalesce. You won't deny it?'

'God forbid,' said Mr. Linley. 'Après?'

'Après, there's this. The old people are safe anyhow, good or bad. And the young have their own way. But we two are not children, and not old. If we come together—don't you see, the others do as they please.'

'I don't, but suppose they do?'

'I mean, there can be no question with her of pure passion. I think she rather hates me. She couldn't love me, but she might like, and fear. That's what I want. Now old people have struck into their own line and stick to it, right or wrong, and so all goes straight with them. And with boys and girls it's all plain sailing. But with us it's all mixed up. I don't want her to love me, and I don't want her to suffer too much. I want her not to hate me, and to fear, and to give way— and then to be as before.'

'You are a study: but I think now I do see. She has upset you.'

'Very likely. I always felt a fool there. But then, she is too beautiful.'

'Like her mother. Shall I tell you the story?'

The old man's eyes were soft and cold, a little cruel and a little kind. His subtle and reserved smile invited a question: but none came.

'It's not much to tell: and I always meant you should know some day. The father was dead before your time, I know.' Here his smile broadened and his eyelids sank. 'You may as well be told, after all. He was yours. I suppose people have done me the honour to imagine—never mind: I didn't. But you are not legitimate, nevertheless.'

'Well,' said Denham, looking down with angry eyes; 'I know that.'

'Your father was hers: when you went to Ensdon I gave you the charge of your little brother. There's the material about you of a bad novel and a good comedy. Your father was a very fair sort of man. But, with all apologies, I must say your mother was not of the better sort of woman. I ought to know, for I married her sister. They were co-heiresses—Irish: one good of course, and one bad. The latter produced you: the former married me. Both might have done better. But the fault in both cases lay with your mother: elle l'a voulu. Georgette Dandin[2] I called her. She married poor Charles Brandon: I always liked them both, and was glad when they came together. But I quite believe she never cared for any man but one—Fred Seyton: and the result we see. He was very poor and pretty,[3] your good father, and she ruined him; did it very well: beautifully. Light and slight, with weak hair. His eyes were the strong point. Now I think of it, he must have been a boy when they met: she was the elder. I had the honour to be his confidant, afterwards. I was related to the sisters: and the affair came off[4] a little before I married the younger. He wanted to marry her—the elder you know: and that happened to be impossible. Elle en avait vu d'autres, votre mère. You don't mind hearing the truth now? After you were born she ceased to care for him: queer, and true. Now I was in her confidence; she liked me. I was engaged to her sister as it was: the two marriages came off in the same month: I married Catherine, Charles Brandon married Margaret. (By the by, of course your father called his daughter after her—Margaret; of course.) She had been out of sight for two years. They were both talked about: blown upon:[5] more or less. I don't mean ruined; they were received. But after marriage the whole weight fell on my wife, who was incredibly innocent; I can answer for it. She was a saint, and had the fortune of saints. I might have ruined her and upset your mother: but I would not. In effect, I think now I was rather in love with my sister-in-law: a pleasure, I believe, prohibited.'

'One minute,' said Denham, collecting himself. 'How did

you come to take charge of me? And what about my father?'

'I tell you she ruined him, utterly. It was her style; she always did. As for you, Fred never knew you were in this world;⁶ it's a delicate matter to handle, but she threw him off rather too soon, do you see? She was very sharp and reticent, we had always been good friends, and I knew the worst; and perhaps something worse. When he found she was not to be married, he vanished, and took up in time with⁷ the mother of your old pupil and your present idol. She had sixpence, he threepence: at least they say so. It sounds improbable, I know. She was far more beautiful than your mother, and very unhealthy: I saw her once; a memorable sort of woman: she was in love with him. Whether he had ever cared for her I never could take the trouble to guess; I suppose one might have known. But he didn't after marriage: as a good son, you may console yourself with that knowledge. They fell out of sight at once: and I heard of the children first through Wariston. I really know no more of your father; he dropped out of my line, you see, when he married. As to you—I must go some way back to explain. My wife was fond of her sister. Their names got mixed up: you know at least what that is.⁸ When the younger married Lord Charles Brandon,⁹ all the world called him a fool; but my wife—an angel (I have reason to know it)—bore the blame. He was not a fool; not then. She brought him money enough to live on. They didn't live well; but a daughter was produced: a noticeable girl. I fancy your father and his wife hardly lived at all. Of course you'll tell me they had splendid chidren. I've no doubt they died most dismally. Well, I never exactly undertook to adopt you, mind: you owe me nothing: but I did make the best of it. Your father was turned off. Your mother had gone off. Both were my friends: she was my wife's sister. We took charge of you: she liked it: my wife I mean. There are women who are saints: pure and good: is it not written in the gospel of your modern writers?'

'Do you mean that harm came to her through me?' Denham asked this with a grave tone of vexation; then it struck

him that the whole involved story might be a a sudden fiction,
kindled by wine and lascivious fanciful humour in the labouring brain of this inventive cynic, this great *blagueur* of private
life. The change in his eyes betrayed him. 'I see,' said Linley;
'and this becomes pathetic. I have lived to hear my word
doubted by him who has been more to me than a son: how
much more he only knows; and God. But seriously, in all this
there is no *blague*—no chaff as you call it. I could show you
proofs, but it would take time and give trouble. Take what
I tell you on trust for the present, and act as if you knew it
to be true: will you?' Denham bowed his head and believed;
he sat now as one stunned by the rush of revelation. 'Then I
continue. First (I have reason to believe) people gave me the
credit of you, and called her Griselda. Then, when that grew
stale and out of date, they reversed the charge, which was ingenious; and likened me in turn—shall we say to King
Arthur? I suppose I was not designed for the part of an ideal
knight: at all events I set my face against that rumour. Still
you see it gave me a hold on her. And by that time we had a
son of our own; genuine.'

His cruel colourless old face brightened and quivered, as
he remembered the past pain he had given, and enjoyed the
pain his last word now gave.

'It did give me a hold on her. And we sent you to Eton
and to that tutor during the holidays: she never saw any
more of you. But her sister did; your mother.' The listener
started, and blushed slowly. 'Do you remember the lady who
called to see you at your tutor's? I was to have gone with her
down to Slough and waited: but when we got there I thought
I might as well go on to Eton too. She might have lost her
head. It was just six or seven months before your sister Lesbia
was born (named after your common grandmother[10] I think);
your sister Margaret on the other side was some years older of
course; about three I believe. And I naturally wanted to see
my own boy; and my nephew Sundon[11]—Wariston as he is
now, but my sister and her husband were both alive then; it
was in '33 I think. So I came on with her: now you remem-

ber. She kissed you rather violently for a distant relation. I suppose the future child made her soften just then towards the past. At least you must allow she tipped you handsomely. Women are the most eccentric of all God's inventions, I do think.'

The cynic's chatter took effect upon his hearer in a way unforeseen by the speaker. Though not' over tender¹² by nature or by habit, Denham was moved by the memories thus revived. He remembered the day well enough now; how he came with Lord Sundon into their tutor's room, one Friday after twelve, and there found waiting his old guardian or supposed father, and a pale large handsome woman who addressed and embraced him in the same moment: he remembered even the heavy folds of his colleger's gown pressed about him by her arms as they clasped his shoulders, and how he looked across her at the oppidan and saw him grin as he shooks hands with his uncle. He had no doubt now that this had been his one sight of his mother.

'She cried on the way back,' Linley went on: 'and I suppose the whole thing was unwholesome for her. Mais! tu l'as voulu, Georgette Dandin, I never knew such a stubborn nature: what she wanted she would have. Perhaps that was what I used to like in her. I know at least I never had felt before how little I liked my wife till her sister died; some months after that visit, it was; you know (or you don't I suppose) she didn't survive for two hours after Lesbia was born. Ah! she brought strange children into the world; don't you think? After her death I used to wonder if either of you would live long: they tell me Miss Brandon won't. However that may be, when she was dead I did begin to feel what a fool my good wife was to her. Now if you want an instance of suffering virtue, there is one I can commend to your notice. I never knew such a good woman. And I never cared for any one (that is, for more than half an hour) as I did for her sister. And when her sister was dead I set myself to torment her. There was nothing else left me; nothing of any serious interest. And I did torment her to some purpose, I fear. She was curiously fond of her boy; I used to scourge her through him. You never heard of such a thing? I thought not. However, you remember the boy at Eton? looked rather tame, did he not, and cowered through his schooldoys? Ah! he used to be flogged at home once a week.[13] I wonder he cared for an Eton switching. His mother—tiens! he used to go to her afterwards, crying and tingling. It drew blood of both at once. She couldn't stand it; not constantly. And I never would stand tears in my presence; she had to swallow them; and digest. I suppose they disagreed with her. Je lui faisais passer de mauvais quarts-d'heure. Et cependant je ne me pose pas en philosophe achevé; I don't see why any one should liken me to old Cenci; or to—or to the others. I can say truly I never outstepped the duties of a British parent, or the rights of a British husband. Never! I say it solemnly.' He said it also with an admirable subdued burlesque. 'When my good wife died, I can truly say I mourned for her. In fact, as a husband I was heart-broken; as a Christian I was resigned. She followed your mother to the grave in about six years. I presume there was ill-health in the family. I must say I never liked Arthur, but after that he was dear to me as her son. You recollect his death at college; it was lamentable; but you were left me; and you had always appeared to me preferable.' Here again it flashed upon Denham that this man might after all be his father; as to his mother he had no longer any doubt. But this fancy also, on reflection, he soon saw reason to resign. 'You were at college I think a year or two longer; then, being alone in the world I sent for you—home; my heart went out towards my old friend's child. That too I believe is natural, according to the authoresses now predominant. You came, having no other chance but the church, and stayed till I sent you down to Ensdon.'

Here there was a little interlude of suggestive silence, and each looked at the other. There was no reproach in Denham's look, but there was a certain repulsion. In Linley's there was a soft scornful inquiry, mixed with a sense of wider knowledge and deeper enjoyment; but under these, if the other could have seen it, lay hidden and veiled an expression of bitter and obscure despondency. Well fenced and hedged against feeling or suffering as he was, he was not upon the whole scornful; but he was not happy at heart.

'And now you see it has come to this.'

CHAPTER XV

VIA DOLOROSA

HE STOOD LOOKING AWAY FROM HER AND SPOKE SOFTLY, WITH head bent and fallen face, fixed as if held by hands: heavily sorrowful, not without pity; there was an air as of something at once feeble and noble about him. 'This ought to end. It is a great misery. Let us keep something like honour. We cannot go away together. You have broken my life between you; you two. I want to die sane. Do you think I can live? seriously. Look at me then. Ah! don't cry. It's not to set her free;[1] nor to spare you. I know it will hurt you: and if I lived you would come to no harm by me. Only to escape and have done with living. I think some die young by mistake; and others survive. I have got another man's life, and can't use it. Besides I will not live. But say something to me.'

She rose up, reeled on her feet, and sat down; stretched out her arms, and lifted up her lips and eyes. He bent down swiftly and seized her; their open lips, in meeting, shut and stung each other; fierce heavy kisses were pressed into them, wrung out of them by turns; her rare tears, quickening as they came, fell like fire down his cheek and neck. Lifting his head a little, he plunged his face into the relaxing heaps of her massive hair, kissing it with all his might and heart, crushing his lips upon the ripples in it, draining out of it the perfume of hot and hidden honey. She sobbed and sighed with love under her kisses; her fragrant glittering throat trembled, her veins felt fire, her eyes gathered tears; the wet lids and lashes blinded them; even her head quivered with the pulse and the pain of her passion: she clove to him with fluttering[2] body and vibrating hair. So for some moments they took the cruel pleasure left them as their love drew to a

129

close; they grew³ and hung together for a little, then divided slowly, one weeping. She, with hands still hanging upon him, spoke words that were like tears, and muttered names that sounded like sobs; to some such ineffectual effect as this.

'I will die instead. My love, my beloved; because you love me. Oh, I cannot have you killed: for I never was good to you. I have only harmed you and hurt you. You made me feel my life pleasant for a year.'⁴ Here she raised her face, with voice and eyes clearing in a second, and for a moment; then they filled and faltered again. 'You said things to me that make me shiver through and through to think of. You looked at me with such eyes that, if anyone had seen you look so she would have knelt down to thank you. All my days were delicious to me. I was good all through with pure gladness. She has no eyes and no heart or soul. Oh, I cannot let you go now. I shall not live at all unless I die. I shall be mad and lose my soul or my heart too. We are not two but one. If you die first there will be a wicked half of you alive till I die. I cannot lose you; cannot.'

'Yes,' he said, 'and our honour? what shall we get for that? Darling, you know nothing in the world stays after it. And it will go. We have not strength.'

'Ah, I could be quite happy,' she said. 'People might abuse me or forget me; I would swallow all shame, put up with all pain, resign all things and support all things. Children? what am I to them? I could hate them for love of you. I shall not be good to them even, now: my poor children.'

'Who knows?' he said, in a vague sad voice, speaking as if under a weight, looking as if through a cloud.

'I should not be happy. That is true: but I should live. Let me live; a little. I shall not, when we are cut in two. And because I shall breathe and speak they will not bury me. We will settle to see each other sometimes: no harm shall come of it. And you will be good to her: ah, but she will not let you; nor deserve it. And no one will be wronged; and no one come to shame. We shall live and grow old—I shall be soonest old you know, by so much—and keep alive each by knowing

that the other lives; alone, and each know that the other
loves. And we shall not have happiness, but honour and love
and life we shall have. No; none of them: no; not one. You
were right. I cannot bear it. But I could not bear living in
that way. No we must save something. There is only that to
hold by. Keep my honour for me; and yours. Ah, who could
touch yours? that is safe for ever. Do what you will now, and
tell me what to do. No, say nothing, please, now. It is best to
keep one's honour; that is all I have to remember: and I
have it by heart.'

'I have nothing to tell you; I don't know what will happen.⁵
Only I shall go away to-day and not come back to you: never
in my life. And now you see I could not with honour.'

'Never,' said she; 'never in my life or in yours any more:
oh, not once; never while we live any more.'

Then she let fall her head and hands together as if the life
in them had been drained out suddenly: then dropped her
face on her arms and trembled all through. Her voice with its
broken words was more piteous than a hurt child's. What she
said was hard to make out for the thin harsh undernote of
incoherent and sobbing sound. She called him all the most
tender names, gave him all the most loving looks that could
live upon her drowning eyelids and strangling voice. 'Not the
face, darling; ah, not your face': to which he answered with
some promise. 'You are too young. Oh, once more,' as she
held to him and fed on him with pungent kisses that tasted
of tears: 'I wish you had never come near me. Now go. I
wonder how she will bear it. I shall love you to the end of my
life. If you can see things you will be sorry for me. Oh, when
I think⁶ I shall see nothing—I shall not be sure of you—I
shall not know if anything is left that loves me. I hope they
will put me near you somehow again in time to come. I don't
know. I don't care for any other life if we are to lose this: why
should God have pity then and not now? Oh, all that I love
and all that I know of, all is taken out of my hands; out of
sight; out of hope. God? I don't know. What is all this for?
I love you and want you; go now, please, and let it come to

an end.' With which they parted, and she went to a couch and fell down on it, hiding her face. Her sides heaved and shook as if with violent laughter; her body labouring in the last throes of love, her soul travailing in the barren pangs of hunger, she endured the hour of her passion without sighing and without tears. Once or twice only she cried out under the extreme torment of desire and despair, calling upon his name in a dreadful pitiful note of pain.' The horror of her sudden want and intense love seemed to beat upon her nerves, and inflict rapid running strokes or cuts of conscious sorrow. Now dulled and now sharpened, her sense of grief seemed to come and go as in a fierce fluctuation of soul. The whole vision of her spirit was broken and blinded by pain; she felt her entire life beaten upon and driven about, sucked this way and dragged that, by the strong alternating tide of keener or fainter torture. She lusted after death with the violent desire underlying violent fear. The light pressed upon her painfully; her throat rose with loathing of life; all things were black to her eyes and bitter to her lips. She seemed to taste and see them now with acuter sense and intenser relish of their painful and hateful nature. Everything struck and stung her. As the hard dumb convulsion of suffering lifted and strained her body from foot to head, she crammed her hair into her mouth, bit and shook it, tore at her fingers, caught herself by the throat, strangled shriek upon shriek, crushed sob after sob. She writhed and wrung herself as for less grief she might have wrung her hands only. She beat her head and face upon the cushions; not upon the woodwork even in her utmost pain and passion; retaining always a luxurious loathing and feline fear of blind hard blows or bruises; but she would have taken sharp strokes thankfully. Indeed she bit her arms once or twice hard enough to indent and redden them: thrust her hands into her hair and plucked it as hard as she could—not very hard: it was not in her nature to tear it. Not the less she would have given her life for him; would have been burnt or scourged to death for his sake; but to save his life and his soul she could not for example have dashed

her head once against the wall and made an end. Suffering
these things and feeling them to the quick of her nervous life,
she endured greatly a great torment; conscious of herself to
the core of her sensitive and fervent nature, she crucified her
soul gradually, driving as it were through hands and feet the
nails of self-knowledge,[9] submitting her spirit as it bled and
quivered to a horrible vivisection, till she saw every nerve
naked and felt every drop of blood drawn from the several
wounds: till, when this cup also was drained and the very
dregs had left their loathsome arid savour of her tongue,
having exhausted all other sensations that could inflict pain,
she came upon the sense of pity and broke suddenly into
tears. This was the last stage of her passion; at this turning-
point of pain the torn feet paused,[10] the torn forehead felt its
crown of thorns soften and loosen. Weeping with intense pity
for him, she felt a hot and sharp sense of relief and release
as the supreme agony relaxed and the intolerable hour took
flight for ever. She could not again suffer this; the bitterness
of life and death was over with her. She wept piteously, knowing what must come, knowing what had been; but the fever
and convulsion of supernatural pain was done with. She rose
now and bathed her face and hands, turning up her sleeves to
plunge her bright white arms, round and tender as vigorous
stems of flowers, up to the soft carved elbows in cold water;
and laughed at her likeness to a laundress; she felt full of
laughter and tears, ready to tremble and overflow at a touch.
The pure sharp contact of the water steadied her head a little
and settled her blood; she looked across at a glass and started.
Colourless, with fixed bewildered eyes, and bright questioning lips, fairer from sighs and tenderer from tears, her face
confronted her, hot and white; white with old sorrow and hot
with new life. She arranged her hair and went down to the
children. A great desire to devour the time till nightfall impelled her, passive as before a wind. It was already but an
hour from twilight: she had suffered long, and lain long
torpid. In two hours it would be time to expect the end. That
all would not return who had gone forth she knew well

enough. At any minute some evil and horror nameless to herself might be at point to happen. Alone and silent, she would surely fall ill or go mad. She had impulses, bitter and strong, blind and imperious, to sing and play the time through: since somehow it must needs be lived over and lived through. Far out of sight, deep down in her sense of things, intangible to reason and invisible to thought, there lived a cruel fear of every instant, less this perhaps were the instant for him of agony and death. Such a one there must be, and soon. She did not fear a suicide, she did not fear a mischance; she felt a fate as one feels a blow. Whence or how it might come[11] against her she did not exactly guess, and would not. She awaited the stroke as though with bared breast and half-shut eyes.

The children saw only the bright face and swift step with which she entered. They came about her gladly, and she caressed them.

'What shall I sing you, children? we are left to our own devices; suppose you make the best of yours, and choose.'

She did not often sing to them, and they would have left any game to hear her; even the elders, aggrieved as Cecil especially was by the refusal of a gun.

'You would rather I chose, or made a start at random? Draw the curtains first, it's dark enough: I hate the dusk out of doors. Tell them not to bring lamps till we ring, and I'll play by firelight.'

She settled herself at the pianoforte and began playing as they stood round her; the eldest leaning on a chair, chin on fist, his thin sombre face brightened about the eyes as he took his pleasure sadly; Cecil opposite, with hands still restless but fixed face and feet; the second Bertie and Rosamond on either hand of her. At first she played short random tunes of rapid and brilliant sound; then fell as if by chance upon an old French air of softer music, and began singing the words; a double ballad of love, the first part April and the second February. This first part she sang in clear high notes, where a sense of pleasure and of fear seemed to hover and tremble as in a bird's song.

'Tressez ma couronne
 Des fleurs de roseau.
Tu me dis: Sois bonne,[12]
Je te dis: Sois beau.

'Ecoute: tu m'aimes,[13]
 La belle aux beaux yeux;
Allons par nous-mêmes,
 Allons deux à deux.

'Nous irons, ma chère,
 Au fond du verger:
Tu seras bergère,
 Je serai berger.

'Tais-toi donc, mignonne,
 Il faut s'apaiser
Quand on est si bonne,
 Si bonne à baiser.

'Le roseau qui penche
 Est moins doux, moins frais;
Moins belle, moins blanche,
 La rose des prés.

'Que dit l'hirondelle?
 Le jour va périr:
Aimons-nous, ma belle,
 Avant de mourir.

'Aimons-nous, ma mie:
 Viens, écoute, vois,
Songe que la vie
 Ne vient qu'une fois.

'*Veux-tu que je meure,*
Vraiment, sans amour?
Nous vivons une heure;
Nous mourrons un jour.'

Her voice sank here as a wind at evening, and she paused before saying: 'That was in early spring; this is in late winter; all but a year gone: and it's her turn to sing now.'

'*Tressez ma guirlande*
D'if et de cyprès;
Bien belle est la lande,
Bien verts sont les prés.

'*Faites-moi ma bière,*
Mettez-m'y ce soir;
Bien triste est la terre,
La tombeau bien noir.

'*Qu'il aille aimer Rose;*
L'amour lui sied bien;
Elle a toute chose,
Et moi je n'ai rien.

'*Des nattes de soie*
Qu'on rehausse en tour;
Des yeux pleins de joie
Et vides d'amour.

'*Quand son cou se cambre,*
Tous ses grands cheveux
Cousus d'or et d'ambre
Tombent sur ses yeux.

'*De l'Eure à Sambre*
On ne vit jamais
Si beaux cheveux d'ambre,
Si beaux yeux de jais.

'*Je n'ai rien à dire;*
   J'ai gardé ma foi.
Sa bouche sait rire;
   Je sais pleurer, moi.

'*La lune etait belle;*
   Mais le jour a lui.
Que nous voulait-elle
   Quand j'étais à lui?

'*Vous verrez éclose,*
   Quand mai le veut bien,[14]
Vous verrez la rose;
   Je ne verrai rien.

'*Les jours où l'on cueille*
   L'hyacinthe au pré
Et la chèvrefeuille,
   Moi je dormirai.

'*Que dit la colombe?*
   Vivez, aimez-vous;
Bien douce est la tombe,
   Le gazon bien doux.

'*Mais quand l'hirondelle*
   Chante aux champs de mai,
Va, lui dira-t-elle,
   Tu fus bien aimé.'[15]

She ceased, with the full firelight on her sad bright face, as the last note faded from her voice; and watched them with eyes that were tender and grew bitter as they watched.

'You look touched; all of you. I must give you something to take the taste out: a better song, and better sense.'

Combien de temps, dis, la belle,
Dis, veux-tu m'être fidèle?
Pour une nuit, pour un jour,
Mon amour.

L'amour nous flatte et nous touche
Du doigt, de l'œil, de la bouche,
Pour un jour, pour une nuit,
Et s'enfuit.[16]

'There, children, that's how people really look at things: but you don't understand. This hardly makes you laugh, and that hardly made you cry. Ethel, if you get between me and my arm, I can't play.'

The child withdrew his head from beneath her left elbow, and looked up hungrily, with a smile.

'That means you've had enough of French songs, and want something you can follow as well as feel? You small elf! you understand one thing as well as another, I believe. But you shall have a ballad if you like. I think I know it by heart now; Herbert was so fond of the scraps left of it, he wrote them out and added a verse or two. I used to sing him the fragment long ago: he was a child and I was a girl. His modern touches don't improve it.'

She spoke in a rapid vague voice, turning from one to another, with brilliant unquiet looks. The firelight played upon her pale cheeks, her shifting eyes and bright bound hair.

'It's in two parts like the French song; it's called the Weary Wedding.[17] The woman who nursed me taught me the old part, but I can't sing it now as she did.' (She drew her arm again round Ethel's head and went on, leaning over him.) 'Look here: at first there's a girl and her mother: that's all. Her lover—her first husband is just dead, you see, children, and they want to marry her again. They have driven her to it, and made her give up her little child. You needn't cry, and you needn't laugh; any of you.'

And what will you give for your father's love?
One with another.
Fruits full few and thorns enough,
Mother, my mother.

And what will you give for your mother's sake?
One with another.
Tears to brew and tares to bake,
Mother, my mother.

And what will you give your sister Jean?
One with another.
A bier to build and a babe to wean,
Mother, my mother.

And what will you give your sister Nell?
One with another.
The end of life and beginning of hell,
Mother, my mother.

And what will you give your sister Kate?
One with another.
Earth's door and hell's gate,
Mother, my mother.

And what will you give your brother Will?
One with another.
Life's grief and world's ill,
Mother, my mother.

And what will you give your brother Hugh?
One with another.
A bed of turf to turn into,
Mother, my mother.

And what will you give your brother Ned?
   One with another.
Death for a pillow and hell for a bed,
   Mother, my mother.

And what will you give to your bridegroom?
   One with another.
A barren bed and an empty room,
   Mother, my mother.

And what will ye give your bridegroom's friend?
   One with another.
A weary foot to the weary end,
   Mother, my mother.

And what will ye give to your bridesmaid?
   One with another.
Grief to sew and sorrow to braid,
   Mother, my mother.

And what will you drink the day you're wed?
   One with another.
But one drink of the wan well-head,
   Mother, my mother.

And whatten a water is that to draw?
   One with another.
We maun draw thereof a', we maun drink thereof a',
   Mother, my mother.

And what shall ye pu' where the well rins deep?
   One with another.
Green herb of death, fine flowers of sleep,
   Mother, my mother.

Are there ony fishes that swim therein?
One with another.
The white fish grace, and the red fish sin,
Mother, my mother.

Are there ony birds that sing thereby?
One with another.
O when they come thither they sing till they die,
Mother, my mother.

Is there ony draw-bucket to that well-head?
One with another.
There's a wee well-bucket hangs low by a thread,
Mother, my mother.

And whatten a thread is that to spin?
One with another.
It's green for grace and it's black for sin,
Mother, my mother.

And what will you strew on your bride-chamber floor?
One with another.
But one strewing and no more,
Mother, my mother.

And whatten a strewing shall that one be?
One with another.
The dust of earth and sand of the sea,
Mother, my mother.

And what will you take to build your bed?
One with another.
Sighing and shame and the bones of the dead,
Mother, my mother.

And what will you wear for your wedding gown?
One with another.
Grass for the green and dust for the brown,
Mother, my mother.

And what will you wear for your wedding lace?
One with another.
A heavy heart and a hidden face,
Mother, my mother.

And what will you wear for a wreath to your head?
One with another.
Ash for the white and blood for the red,
Mother, my mother.

And what will you wear for your wedding ring?
One with another.
A weary thought for a weary thing,
Mother, my mother.

And what shall the chimes and the bell-ropes play?
One with another.
A weary tune on a weary day,
Mother, my mother.

And what shall be sung for your wedding song?
One with another.
A weary word of a weary wrong,
Mother, my mother.

The world's way with me runs back,
One with another,
Wedded in white and buried in black,
Mother, my mother.

The world's wrong and the world's right,
  One with another,
Wedded in black and buried in white,
  Mother, my mother.

The world's bliss and the world's keen,
  One with another,
It's red for white and it's black for green,
  Mother, my mother.

The world's will and the world's way,
  One with another,
It's sighing for night and crying for day,
  Mother, my mother.

The world's good and the world's worth,
  One with another,
It's earth to flesh and it's flesh to earth,
  Mother, my mother.

'That's the first part; then they marry her to the new man, and his mother receives her—you see? Herbert stuck in a quantity of lines hereabouts; they're not good, but they tell the story.'

When she came out at the kirkyard gate,
  One with another,
The bridegroom's mother was there in wait;
  Mother, my mother.

—O mother, where is my great green bed,
  One with another,
Silk at the foot and gold at the head,
  Mother, my mother.

—Yea, it is ready, the silk and the gold,
　　One with another.
—But line it well that I lie not cold,
　　Mother, my mother.

She laid her cheek to the velvet and vair,
　　One with another.
She laid her arms up under her hair,
　　Mother, my mother.

The gold hair fell through her arms twain,
　　One with another;
—Lord God, bring me out of pain!
　　Mother, my mother.

The gold hair fell in the reeds green,
　　One with another.
—Lord God, bring me out of teen!
　　Mother, my mother.

She raised her eyes and seeing opposite the intent faces of the elder children laughed softly and turned to the youngest, who had drunk every note with eager lips and eyes full of fiery pleasure.

'Then you see, Ethel, the husband came and met his mother. It wasn't his fault. He didn't know where she was—or what like, as they say. All the last verses are old. You may come and stand close up to me as you did before; if you like. I mean the last twelve or so.'

O mother, where is my lady gone?
　　One with another.
—In the bride-chamber she makes sore moan,
　　Mother, my mother.

144

Her hair falls over the velvet and vair,
  One with another;
Her great soft tears fall over her hair;
  Mother, my mother.

When he came into the bride's chamber,
  One with another,
Her hands were like pale yellow amber;
  Mother, my mother.

Her tears made specks in the velvet and vair,
  One with another;
The seeds of the reeds made specks in her hair;
  Mother, my mother.

He kissed her under the gold on her head,
  One with another;
The lids of her eyes were like cold lead;
  Mother, my mother.

He kissed her under the fall of her chin,
  One with another;
There was right little blood therein;
  Mother, my mother.

('Bertie stuck all this in a year or two ago—I think it was better before; wait, and you'll see when the old verses begin again.')

He kissed her under her shoulder sweet,
  One with another;
Her throat was weak, with little heat;
  Mother, my mother.

He kissed her down by her breast-flowers red,
  One with another;
They were like river-flowers dead,[18]
  Mother, my mother.

145

What ails you now o' your weeping, wife?
  One with another.
It ails me sair o' my very life,
  Mother, my mother.

What ails you now o' your weary ways?
  One with another.
It ails me sair o' my long life-days,
  Mother, my mother.

Nay, ye are young, ye are over fair;
  One with another.
Though I be young, what needs ye care?
  Mother, my mother.

Nay, ye are fair, ye are over sweet;
  One with another.
Though I be fair, what needs ye greet?
  Mother, my mother.

Nay, ye are mine while I hold my life;
  One with another.
O fool, will ye marry the worm for a wife?
  Mother, my mother.

Nay, ye are mine while I have my breath:
  One with another.
O fool, will ye marry the dust of death?
  Mother, my mother.

Yea, ye are mine, we are handfast wed,
  One with another.
Nay, I am no man's; nay, I am dead,
  Mother, my mother.

'Crying? You ought to have something to cry for. Look at Cecil, how round his eyes are. And it's all a song; and silly.'"

People don't die; not women. Little bits of heart are tough: the girl was no such fool. And suppose she died, Bertie, you little white wild animal, do you know what that means? She is asleep and has forgotten it all; wouldn't know one from the other if they came and called her and kissed her—so. Your lips are very hot; and your head: what lithe hair you have; I shall get you shaved. She remembers no more about it now than you remember being born. You were redder then: your small scalp was a bald rose-leaf: you were hot like the heat of a flower. Eh! you don't remember. And when you began talking you spoke broad Northumbrian: you were just a pure borderer. You said *vai* for very: Italian.'

'I remember,' said Arthur[20] with implied self-applause.

'Yes: you remember. You are my changeling; I knew you as soon as the fairies put you in my bed. Because I was a witch, children; like the witch-mother.

> *She's set her young son to her breast,*
> *Her auld son to her knee;*
> *Says, 'Weel for you the night, bairnies,*
> *And weel the morn for me.'*

Then she killed them, Ethel, both, and put their blood in a little brass dish—ah! I heard somebody; no?—in some pot or pan, with the blood of a little white chicken, like you: and of a grey pigeon, like Rosamond; and of a yellow kite, like Cecil; and of a starling, like nobody—except another starling.

> *Says—Eat your fill of your flesh, my lord,*
> *And drink your fill of your wine;*
> *For a' thing's yours and only yours,*
> *That has been yours and mine.*

'You see that she didn't kill them for fun at all. It's not every witch that kills little unweaned babies; yes, it was hard, that. I might kill you if I tried; take care; be good. You are the auld son that stands at my knee. I shall never have a younger one again; no little red round fat fragments of babies: ah, you were all such fun once.

N 147

Says—Drink your fill of your wine, my lord,
And eat your fill of your bread;
I would they were quick in my body again,
And my body were dead.[21]

'Ah—ah—as if people could drink themselves back into love;
they try sometimes now: eating and drinking won't do it.
You can't make that verse out: you will some day, Ethie, my
small bad boy; when you and I and Elaine[22] go underground
and keep house with elves and learn witches' tricks. You don't
cry now? Yes, come close to me. You are more electric than
I am, child, I can comb sparks out of your hair with my
fingers. Things in verse hurt one, don't they? hit and sting
like a cut. They wouldn't hurt us if we had no blood, and
no nerves. Verse hurts horribly: people have died of verse-
making, and thought their mistresses killed them—or their
reviewers. You have the nerve of poetry—the soft place it hits
on, and stings. Never write verses when you get big; people
who do are bad, or mad, or sick. Herbert? but he doesn't
count; he scribbles now and then when I tell him, for fun: I
don't mean that. How your under-curls hiss and sputter on
the inside. It's odd that words should change so just by being
put into rhyme. They get teeth and bite; they take fire and
burn. I wonder who first thought of tying words up and
twisting them back to make verses, and hurt and delight all
people in the world for ever. For one can't do without it now:
we like it far too much, I suspect, you and I. It was an odd
device: one can't see why this ringing and rhyming of words
should make all the difference in them: one can't tell where
the pain or the pleasure ends or begins. "Who shall determine
the limits of pleasure?" that is a grand wise word:[23] you
ought to find out what it means soon. Listen now again.

'O where will ye gang to and where will ye sleep
Against the night begins?'
'My bed is made wi' cauld sorrows,
My sheets are lined wi' sins.

'*And a sair grief sitting at my foot*
And a sair grief at my head;
And dool to mak' me my pillow
And teen till I be dead.

'*And the rain is sair upon my face*
And sair upon my hair:
And the wind upon my weary mouth
That never shall kiss mair:

'*And the snow upon my heavy lips*
That never shall drink nor eat:
And shame to cledding, and woe to wedding,
And pain to drink and meat![24]

'I never knew the rest of that, but it should be something rather horrid to match the first lines.[25]

'*But what will ye have to your marriage meat,*
The day that ye are wed?'
'*Meat of strong crying, salt of sad sighing,*
And God restore the dead.'

'*But what will ye have to your wedding wine*
The day that ye are wed?'
'*Wine of weeping, and draughts of sleeping,*
And God raise up the dead.'

'But he won't now; he knows better. You would rather not see ghosts, children, would you? If they came back with white crying faces and no hands to touch you, you wouldn't thank God exactly: you'd rather let them be, under ground or under water.

The cockle-shells to be my bed
And the mussels in the sea;
And the easterin' wind and the westerin' wind
To mak' my sheets to me.

O when my bed was saft wi' silk,
Mine een were sair wi' weeping;
But now my bed is sair wi' stanes,
Minc een are saft wi' sleeping.

Its under faem and fathom now,
And fathom under sea;
And for a' gates the wind gangs,
The wind wakes na me.[26]

'But the sea-shells have sharp edges to lie down on the first time. Still, never to hear[27] any manner of wind that blows, that must be a comfort when one gets to bed: and we all shall some day: you remember that nursery jingle[28] that I wouldn't let them frighten you with twice, Atty?

Fair of face, full of pride,
Sit ye down by a dead man's side.

Ye sang songs a' the day:
Sit down at night in the worm's way.

Proud ye were a' day long;[29]
Ye'll be but lean at evensong.

Ye had gowd kells on your hair;
Nae man kens what ye were.

Ye set scorn by the silken stuff;
Now the grave is clean enough.

Ye set scorn by the ruby ring;
Now the worm is a sweet thing.

Fine gold and fair face,
Ye are come to a grimly place.

Gold hair and grey een,
Nae man kens if ye have been.

She had sung this with hands resting idle on the keys, never striking a note: as it ended, her hands dropped off them, and hung by her side; only the fingers quivered and curled. Then, having Ethelbert close and Rosamond near her, both silent and trembling with dim pleasure and soft fear, she looked towards the two elder[30] and seeing a whisper stir between them, laughed lightly and sadly. 'You schoolboys think the little ones are fools to cry? come, I know you do. Now listen, I mean to make you cry: as Ethel here did over the wedding song. I won't have my young birds pecked at. I'll do what the headmaster never did—at least you say so—make you cry. I don't care what you do at school, but you shall cry this time, and without being whipped. I know, Atty, Cecil did squeak the first time: I know, Cecil, it's an awful lie; never mind. Stand there now and let me sing.'

Her face altered as the smile went off, leaving for a moment a grave silent motion in the lips and eyelids: then, with a few rare touches by way of interlude, she began to sing.

There's mony a man loves land and life,
Loves life and land and fee;
And mony a man loves fair women,
But never a man loves me, my love,
But never a man loves me.

O weel and weel for a' lovers,
I wot weel may they be;
And weel and weel for a' fair maidens,
But aye mair woe for me, my love.
But aye mair woe for me.

O weel be wi' you, ye sma' flowers,
Ye flowers and every tree;

And weel be wi' you, a' birdies,
  But teen and tears wi' me, my love,
  But teen and tears wi' me.

O weel be yours, my three brethren,
  And ever weel be ye:
Wi' deeds for doing and loves for wooing,
  But never a love for me, my love,
  But never a love for me.

And weel be yours, my seven sisters,
  And good love-days to see,
And long life-days and true lovers,
  But never a day for me, my love,
  But never a day for me.

Good times wi' you, ye bauld riders,
  By the hieland and the lee;
And by the leeland and by the hieland
  It's weary times wi' me, my love,
  It's weary times wi' me.

Good days wi' you, ye good sailors,
  Sail in and out the sea;
And by the beaches and by the reaches
  It's heavy days wi' me, my love,
  It's heavy days wi' me.

I had his kiss upon my mouth,
  His bairn upon my knee;
I would my soul and body were twain,
  And the bairn and the kiss wi' me, my love,
  And the bairn and the kiss wi' me.

The bairn down in the mools, my dear,
  O saft and saft sleeps she;

I would the mools were ower my head,
  And the young bairn fast wi' me, my love,
  And the young bairn fast wi' me.

The father under the faem, my dear,
O sound and sound lies he;
I would the faem were ower my face,
  And the father lay by me, my love,
  And the father lay by me.

I would the faem were ower my face,
  Or the mools on my ee bree;
And waking-time with a' lovers,
  But sleeping-time wi' me, my love,
  But sleeping-time wi' me.

I would the mools were meat in my mouth,
  The saut faem in my ee;
And the land-worm and the water-worm
  To feed fu' sweet on me, my love,
  To feed fu' sweet on me.

My life is sealed with a seal of love,
  And locked with love for a key;
And I lie wrang and I wake lang,
  But ye tak nae thought for me, my love,
  But ye tak nae thought for me.

We were weel fain of love, my dear,
  O fain and fain were we;
It was weel with a' the weary world,
  But O, sae weel wi' me, my love,
  But O, sae weel wi' me.

We were nane ower mony to sleep, my dear,
  I wot we were but three;

And never a bed in the weary world
For my bairn and my dear and me, my love,
For my bairn and my dear and me.

Her singing rather than her song had fulfilled her threat; before she ended, the boys stood by shuffling, with cheeks that twitched and eyes that blinked, stung by the bitter sweetness of her soft keen voice. She lifted her face and laughed again; as though their tears had the power to dry her own.

'I said you would children: Herbert always cried over that, and he would have gone into seas where I should like to see Atty follow him: never mind crying, Bertie minor, your major did when he was older than Cecil. They call that song *The Tyneside Widow*,[31] I think; it never made me cry. But you are a set of children, and Herbert was the oldest baby: and is. I suppose it's the burden. I like it much better in that song of a border thief whom his wife or some other woman betrayed into the hands of justice—you know?'

'Oh, I know,' said Cecil, with eyes now dry and bright; "Willie's neck-song:[32] Bulmer[33] used to pitch into the maid for singing it. Oh I say, do sing that.'

She bowed to the boy, smiling, and played some loud rapid music as she sang: turning first towards the youngest with a word or two.

'You see, Ethel, this woman—his wife—he had come back out of hiding to see her. He was a reiver, you know what that is, and had lifted ever so many heads of kye; a thief, and they wanted to hang him. He was safe I suppose where he was, but he must needs have a look of her, poor man. Well, when she had him safe at home, she gave him up. And they made this song for him at the gallows. They say he made and sang it, but I doubt that.'

Some die singing, and some die swinging,
And weel mot a' they be:
Some die playing, and some die praying,
And I wot sae winna we, my dear,
And I wot sae winna we.

154

Some die laughing, and some die quaffing,
And some die high on tree;
Some die spinning, and some die sinning,
But faggot and fire for ye, my dear,
Faggot and fire for ye.

Some die weeping, and some die sleeping,
And some die under sea;
Some die ganging, and some die hanging,
And a rape and a tow for me, my dear,
A rape and a tow for me.

'There's a song for you; but you needn't laugh and make such eyes. I'd rather cry over that of the two. You look half frightened.'

As the fierce fragments rang from her lips, their eyes glittered and their lips moved; now they stood abashed and troubled. The brilliance of her voice and face became stronger at each note; her features assumed a fierce and funereal beauty, her eyes a look of insane and bitter foresight. The children began to flinch from her; all but Ethel, who clung to her side and caressed her face with his fixed eyes.

'Ah, children,' she began again, laughing only with the lips. 'Do you think she saw ghosts afterwards? I think not. They don't come to such people. I'm sure there was somebody just coming in. It must be fearfully late. I wish I knew more songs, but I forget them all now. And my voice is going; ah, not now: but I shan't sing a note much longer. Come over and kiss me, Atty my old first child. No, don't you all come. Are you afraid, now! you'll never be a man after all: but never mind. I can't sing any more. Oh!' she sighed and shuddered, sitting ith open hands and shining eyes.[34]

'It must be so late—ever so late. I ought to have sent you off. But I'll try and play to you. Do you ever dream now, Arthur? you did once; the trouble you gave with your dreams, and the frights you got! poor child. Do you remember the little woman in red shoes who sang songs that you knew were wicked without hearing the words? there was a notion for a child's head to get hold of. And the cruelties you used to invent in your sleep and cry over when you awoke! Don't be ashamed of dreaming. I dreamt once that I was very old, in an empty house in winter, and it snowed and blew outside, and there were trees torn up in the garden. And there was a secret about the place I had once known and forgotten long ago: not a good secret. And I was very cold, and I dreamt I fell asleep by the fire, and a little child came into the room and sat down on the rug and made faces at me; and I woke. I felt old for a day after. That was last week. Ah! keep where you are and listen. I thought so.'

Steps and voices came near the door, hurried and hushed. As she rose, her husband stood in the doorway, white-faced, with his right hand lifted.

'An accident,' he said, speaking low and fast: 'His gun went off in getting through a hedge.'

'Lodged where?' said Lady Wariston, as she paused between him and the children.[35]

'In the heart: killed on the spot.' Then she passed him, and going into the passage saw her dead lover carried in; made a few more steps towards the bearers, then reeled and fell with a great short cry.

CHAPTER XVI

LEUCADIA[1]

SINCE HIS RETURN FROM ENSDON, HERBERT HAD BEEN LIVING alone in chambers, a sad and fitful sort of life. His old friend's death had hurt him for a time; but the blow fell on senses deadened and a hardening skin. Inaction and inadequacy oppressed his conscience, and a profitless repugnance against things that were: he held on to his daily life with loose and empty hands, and looked out over it with tired unhopeful eyes. He did not seem effeminate or dejected, and hoisted no signs of inward defeat; but at heart he was conscious of weakness and waste. For some months he had fared unwholesomely, taking a painful pleasure through pure indifference, and vexed in all serious moments by the shadow of a hopeless hope,[2] the phantom of labour unperformed. Late on an afternoon, as he lounged or lay about angry and careless through mere fatigue, a note came to him. He had meant to dress early and dine out, to kill his fatigues and kindle his fancies with champagne and chatter; but the note made him cool at once and sensible of present pain. It had been posted that morning, and was pencilled in a faint thin handwriting, thus: 'Come now if you like, and see me through this: I suppose you may: I have done with doctors and all friends. I should like, if you did. Don't mind if not. They have done with me, of course you see that. Goodnight, if you fail me. Dear Herbert. This may miss you, and you would like a word. L.B.' He seemed to see face to face in each line the lean pallor of death. The last strokes were hardly legible, dim and rude as the scrawl of a child with shut eyes.[3] In twenty minutes' time he was inside her house. There was no man to admit him; a maid showed him in at once to her mistress. Had he been indeed her brother it would not have seemed more simple to all concerned; in all their eyes it was natural that she should so receive him.

He had never come near the dead or dying since his tenth year, when his father died at Kirklowes: but he knew there was a savour of death in the room: something beyond the sweet strong smell of perfumes and drugs. The woman's sad and slow suicide had been with time and care duly accomplished. She had killed herself off by inches, with the help of eau-de-Cologne and doses of opium. A funereal fragrance hung about all the air. Close curtains shut out the twilight, and a covered lamp at either end filled the room with less of light than of silver shadow. Along her sofa, propped by cushions and with limbs drawn up like a tired child's, lay or leant a woman like a ghost; the living corpse of Lesbia. She was white, with grey lips; her long shapely hands were pale and faded, and the dark tender warmth of her even colour had changed into a hot and haggard hue like fever. Her beauty of form was unimpaired; she retained the distinction of noble and graceful features and attitudes. She looked like one whom death was as visibly devouring limb-meal as though fire had caught hold of her bound at a stake: like one whose life had been long sapped and undermined from the roots by some quiet fiery poison. Her eyes and hair alone had a look of life: they were brilliant and soft yet, as she reached out her worn hot hands. Herbert came to her with a sense of pressure at his heart, and something like horror and fear mixed with the bitterness of natural pain. The figure and the place were lurid in his eyes, and less fit to make one weep than to make him kindle and tremble. There was an attraction in them which shot heat into his veins instead of the chill and heaviness of terror or grief.

'I'm dying, Bertie,' said Lesbia. He sat down by her, silent.

'I'm dying,' she said again, playing broken tunes with her fingers in the air.

'It's very like living, do you know? If you stay with me now, mind you don't cry. I've been out of tears myself for a long time—not a sob on hand at any price; and I hate them in others. You look so very sorry.'

'Is it quite a sure thing, then?' he said quietly, in a tone which pleased her.

'As sure as death, literally; I suppose the first time that was said it sounded serious. Both doctors told me—Luthrell you know and Sir Thomas Gage. It's a question of hours. I ought to have settled it before now: but I'm as bad a hand at casting up sums as you are. I'd have made an end to-day but I really care little about it and do want to see how long this will hold out—how far the life in me will go. I won't be beaten first—not till it gives in.'

'Your voice is clear enough; though you look—'

'Yes, I know. I'm dying upwards. My head is as clear as my voice. I could stand only an hour since, and I can move now. But I'm very hot and weak all through, like warm water running out. There's nothing for it; only I wish I were dying in Italy. Your friend never will. All mine are there—friends I mean; which is a touch of good luck for me. My cousins—those Burleigh people, I don't know if there are any in Ireland—never were much in my way even in my poor father's time. Poor man, if there were another life I might see him. It would be curious if each knew all about the other. Old Lady Midhurst was here last week: corbaccia.[4] I like her a little, too. It is something to be left alone and free to choose times and ways of dying. There's no one but you I should like to have by me, who would not disturb and upset me. I heard your sister had been quite ill after that shock.' She reared her head and set her eyes sharply on his face.

'She was quite ill for a time; it was horrid for her,' said Herbert, in default of other words. 'But ought not—' She lifted a hand and repressed him.

'One word, please. You are to let me go my way and follow if you like—I mean listen; I don't advise you to die.' He noticed how she still addressed him as a woman does a boy. 'For the bit of time I have to live, I want no nursing, and no guidance; I want company, and—well! I suppose, love. You

care for me; sit still and be a good boy to me, and brother.'
She reached him her hand, and let him kiss and keep it. 'Yes;
do stay, if you can. I thought of dying quite alone among these
women of the household. But they are servants, and I can't
turn them out, and so I thought as there must be people in
the house when I die there might as well be a friend.' Here
she raised herself and pointed, seeing a figure in the doorway
about to enter. 'Send her away—my maid there. I don't want
you to watch to-night, Grace.—You can let yourself out when
you like,' turning back to Herbert as the door closed. 'Are
you a good watcher? don't leave me. I might be afraid. I don't
know. I might think of things and hurt myself. Not that I
fear or care now, or need for that matter. Give me a little of
that—a spoonful in the glass: thanks. You don't mind all
this? No: I know; I see so much at least; now. My poor boy;
there.' She touched his hair and his cheek with the hand disengaged. Seeing him visibly torn and trembling with the
torment of a passion compressed for her sake, she felt deep
and warm pity for him, and something of a real sister's love,
sad and pure as a prayer without hope. 'Do you know a
clergyman wanted to see me; he knew my uncle Burleigh: a
Mr. Chaplin. I did think of seeing a Catholic priest; God
knows why—perhaps' she added with sceptical caution. 'I told
them to say I was a Catholic; for aught the man knew, I was:
like my mother. I shall be past it all soon, and the less said
the better: and perhaps the less thought, too.' There was
silence between them for a time, and when she spoke next
her voice was vague and strange.

'Do you believe in anything better than sleep? for I don't.
I shall be so glad to sleep and forget all the weary work of the
world. I feel inclined to die talking, do you know. Last night
I had a good dream; I suppose I shan't be troubled with
dreaming—at least—O, I hope not. But I wonder, I am
curious to find out what it can be like to sleep sound. I'm
only afraid I may not, even then. To have dreams underground and be restless after dying would be hard. Well, most
things are hard. I never found out the soft side of life yet.

There ought to be some soft place in one's fate, some weak point in the divine armour: never mind. Even by dying I suppose sometimes one can hardly escape what torments us, it would be too easy.'

Here she began to muse heavily, and her worn eyelids to draw downwards without meeting. He had nothing to say; and after a little she began again.

'If there is such a thing as sound sleep, it must be eternal. The difficulty is to believe in sleep at all.'

She stretched out her weary arms, and lifted herself from heel to shoulder, with a great sigh, bending her body like a bow, so that for a minute only the head and feet had any support: then slowly relaxed her lifted limbs, and relapsed into supine and sad prostration.

'I dreamt of the old stories; I was always fond of them. I saw Lethe; it was not dark water, nor slow. It was pale and rapid and steady; there was a smell of meadowsweet on the banks. I must have been thinking of your Ensdon woods. And when one came close there was a new smell, more faint and rank; it came from the water-flowers;[5] many were dead and decaying, and all sickly. And opposite me just across there ran out a wharf into the water: like the end of the pier at Wansdale.[6] I saw nothing anywhere that was not like something I had seen already. I can't get that out my head; as soon as I woke it frightened me: but I didn't wake at once. I remember the green ooze and slime on the piles of the wharf; it was all matted with dead soft stuff that smelt wet. Not like the smell of the sea, but the smell of a lock in a river. And no boat came, and I didn't want one. I felt growing deliciously cold inside my head and behind my eyelids and down to the palms of my hands and feet. I ought to have awaked with a sneeze, and found I had caught cold in fact: but I didn't. And I saw no face anywhere for hours; and that was like a beginning of rest. Then I tried to see Proserpine, and saw her. She stood up to the knees[7] almost in full-blown poppies, single and double. She was not the old Proserpine who comes and goes up and down between Sicily and hell; she had never seen the sun. She was pale and pleased; there was nothing in her like memory or aspiration. The dead element was vital for her; she could not have breathed in higher or lower air. The poppies at her foot were red, and those in her hand white.'

'Well?' said Herbert as she paused: her voice had filled him with subtle dim emotions, and he was absorbed at once by the strange sound and sense of the words.

'She had grey eyes, bluish like the mingling of mist and water; and soft hair that lay about her breast and arms in sharp pointed locks like tongues of fire. As she looked at me this hair began to vibrate with the sudden motion of her breast, and her eyes brightened into the brilliance of eyes I knew; your sister's; and I began to wonder if she would melt entirely into that likeness.[8] All the time I knew it was impossible she should, because she was incarnate death; and the other I knew was alive. And behind her the whole place all at once became populous with pale figures, hollow all through like an empty dress set upright; stately shadows with a grey light reflected against them; and the whole world as far as I saw was not in darkness, but under a solid cloud that never moved and made the air darker and cooler than the mistiest day upon earth. And in the fields beyond the water there was a splendid harvest of aconite: no other flower anywhere; but the grass was as pale, all yellow and brown, as if the sun had burnt it. Only where the goddess stood there were poppies growing apart; and their red cups, and the big blue lamps of the aconite, all alike hung heavily without wind. I remember, when I was little, wondering whether those flowers were likest lamps or bells; I thought any light or sound that could come of them must be so like the daylight and the music of a dead world. Well, I don't remember much more: but I was haunted with the fear that there might be nothing new behind death after all; no real rest and no real change. And the flowers vexed me. Only these, and no roses; I thought that white single sort of rose might grow there well enough. And I saw no men there, and no children.'

Herbert sat silent; there was nothing to be said in answer. She roamed on through strange byways of sickly thought and channels of straitened speech. Her sleepy delirious eloquence rambled and stumbled to right and left among broken fancies and memories. He saw that her dozing remembrance enlarged and explained the half forgotten dreams of which she spoke. She had not dreamt all this, but something partly like it; and beginning to remember she went on to imagine. There is nothing harder for a child of a sick person than to tell a dream truthfully; for only the clearest and soundest of full-grown minds can safely lay down the accurate landmarks of sleep. Something of this she seemed even to perceive herself as she flowed on fitfully, with sorrowful sudden pauses.

'I tried to sleep again and dream it out; I felt it all going wrong and slipping away from me before I woke; and then I shut my eyes and set my mind steadily upon the dream, but it wouldn't go on: I could only turn over in my head what was apst of it. But in a dim way I feel sure about the wharf, and the woman, and the flowers: and for the rest—well, I think it was like that. But I do hope it will not be the same thing afterwards. That would be a terrible sort of hell.'

The morbid and obscure fascination of obscure disease began to tell upon her listener: his nerves trembled in harmony with hers: he felt a cruel impersonal displeasure, compound of fear and pain, in the study of her last symptoms. Then by way of reaction came a warm sudden reflux of tenderness; and he clasped one pale restless hand with a sweet acute pang of physical pity.

'My dear brother,' she said sadly and softly; then changing her voice to a sudden sharp note of irony—'Bertie, you should have been my lover, sitting here like this. What else would people think if they knew?'

He wrung her hand in his, looking down silent.

'I wonder what it would have been like, to have loved you in that way. I missed of it somehow; I have missed of so many things. But mind I was always fond of you too: and never of any man else. You might give your old sister a kiss now.'

O   163

A bitter taste came into his mouth and made his cheeks tremble; the bitter water rose against his teeth; he felt his throat compress, and the moist heat of thickening tears swell and beat upon his eyelids. He bowed his face upon her face, his breast across her breast; plunged his lips into hers, hot and shuddering; and devoured her fallen features with sharp sad kisses.

'Lesbia—my dearest and first love in the world—if you could love me at last—you need not die at once surely—and I will go with you.—Oh, only try to love me for five minutes!'

These words came broken between his kisses and her sobs; but as his arms fastened upon her she broke from him sideways, trembling terribly, with widened eyes and repellent hands.

'No, no, Herbert! Let me go! let me die! will you?'

There was a savage terror in her voice and gesture; the hands that thrust him back, the eyes that shone with fear of him, might but have excited him further into a passion of bitter pity and love, but for the mad repugnance, the blind absolute horror, expressed in all her struggling figure and labouring limbs. He let her go, and she cowered away against the wall, moaning and shaking like a thing stricken to death.

When she spoke next her voice was clear and low, pitched in a soft equitable key; and never varied again.

'You have done me no harm; don't be vexed. Sit down and listen quietly. Or talk to me if you have anything to say: I like your voice. There is one thing that rather troubles me, the way I shall be buried. I hate all funerals, and all the words read over us: (I feel as if I were one of them, the dead, already;) all the flutter and fuss, all the faith and hope. I have none, and no fear. And if I were to repent of anything I would repent first of my birth. It was no fault of mine. But I think people repent more of their luck than of their faults, as a rule. God knows I repent of living,—if he knows anything about us, or cares. You were very like your sister once about the mouth and eyes. No, not again; when I am dead if you like. I dreamt once that I saw her fall over a cliff. I wish I

were dying out of doors, and by day. I should like my body
to be burnt and the ashes thrown into the sea. It is I who have
taken the leap now, not she. But in my dreams she didn't fall
of herself; somebody pushed her, I think I did. My head is
full of old dreams, full. I should like to see you as you were
that first time. You couldn't go and dress up' now, though I
have seen women with as much hair about the lips. I should
like to die acting; I've heard of people dying on the stage. It
would be some relief to have a good part to keep up. Here I
am going out by inches, and every minute I feel more alive
here, in the head, and less in the body. I think of so many
things, and wish I had one to think of: nothing seems worth
the trouble it gives.'

'I wish to God I could give my life for yours.'

'Don't; but I've no doubt you do just now and will for a
day or two. I wouldn't have it as a gift.'

'I know it's not worth taking,' said Herbert, 'but it might
be worth giving—though its not worth keeping either.'

'Try,' she answered smiling. 'As for me, I have done with
trying, thank heaven, and now I'll go to sleep.'

She drank again a shorter draught and turned over lightly
but painfully. But she could not sleep or die just yet. For an
hour or so Herbert sat by her, watching; her limbs shuddered
now and then with a slow general spasm, as though cold or
out-tired; but there were no symptoms of a sharper torment.
A faint savour of flowers mixed with the smell of drugs as the
whitening dusk with the yellow twilight of the lamps. The
place seemed ready swept and garnished for death to enter:
the light had red and yellow colours as of blood and fog. The
watcher felt sad and sick and half afraid; his mind was full of
dim and bitter things. He was not in heart to pray; if indeed
prayer could have undone things past, he might have believed
it could break and remould the inevitable future growing
minute by minute into the irrevocable present. The moments
as they went seemed to touch him like falling drops of sand or
water: as though the hourglass or the waterclock were indeed
emptied by grains or gouts upon his head: a clock measuring

its minutes by blood or tears instead of water or sand. He seemed in the dim hours to hear her pulses and his own. That night, as hope and trust fell away from under him, he first learnt the reality of fate: inevitable, not to be cajoled by resignation, not to be averted by intercession: unlike a God, incapable of wrath as of pity, not given to preference of evil or good, not liable to repentance[10] or to change.

It was after dawn when Lesbia spoke next. 'Keep the curtains drawn,' she said; 'I won't see the sun again. I mean to die by lamplight.' Then after a little: 'The room must be dark and warm still, as I like it; though I am getting cold; at last. It will be close and dark enough soon; when I have got to bed again. Keep the light out. There: goodbye.' With this she put her hand out, dropped it, turned her face into the cushion, sighing, opened her eyes, and died. He left her in half an hour to the women, having kissed her only twice.

And that was the last of Lesbia Brandon, poetess and pagan.

CHAPTER XVII

ATTILIO MARIANI DIED NEXT YEAR IN HIS LONDON LODGING, doubtful at last whether he had achieved much, certain only that he had always desired with his might to do what he could. Circumstance had twice shut him out from the council and from the army of Italy. The cripple could not follow Garibaldi, the fanatic could not sit down beside Rattazzi.[1] What with one bad chance and another, he never again saw Italy at all. 'She will do well enough without me now,' he said towards the last; that was his comfort. (Pierre Sadier, as sincere a man, could never have said, 'La France se passera bien de moi maintenant'; this marks the main difference between two perfect patriots.) After much suffering, his end was quiet and sad. He had no visions of opening heaven, no hopes of reward for the just man made perfect. Having lived with resignation, he died without repentance. It was one of the man's great merits that he never thought better of anything once designed or done. He was never sorry that he had not made his life brighter or better to live. Sitting at the feet of Italy, as Mary at the feet of Christ, he had given what he could: had broken upon them, not an alabaster box of very precious ointment, but the whole life and complete soul of a man worthier to live than most men: an offering which to him at least should have been precious. He had not looked for thanks; which was fortunate for him. Among his few legacies, he left to Herbert Seyton two books, dissimilar and incongruous enough; the Memoir of Orsini, and the *Chartreuse de Parme*. He had been likened to Palla Ferrante,[2] and felt flattered when near his death at the comparison. Even the sublime vanity of martyrs has its weak side.

Miss Leonora Harley made her way in time into the newspapers under a pseudonym, and consequently made a great match, with a great fool. She was called Aspasia (they spelt it Asp*a*tia) by penny prints, L'Innominata (which they did not spell at all) by threepenny journals; and her marriage came off a few months after. It is doubtful which of the two promotions gave her most pleasure. It is certain that her latter success enraged Mr. Linley, who could not accept it as a fresh and fortunate instance of the prosperities of vice, because (as he said) Leonora was not in his opinion properly vicious. Thus debarred from the last and surest source of philosophic consolation, he denounced the poor bride as 'an empty-headed and empty-hearted harlot, who because she was unfit for a cook-maid thought herself fit for a courtesan.' He was but partially avenged by the Divorce Court, whence the lady came forth with flying colours and overflowing pockets.

These two names are here again bracketed together, that the two extremes of nature may be confronted with each other, in their likeness and after their kind; soul almost without body, and body almost without soul: neither man nor woman complete in their own way. 'Courtisane manquée, patriote manqué,' Mr. Linley might have said. The one, I am told by men skilled in the science of erotics, was a failure in their eyes, a discredit to her calling, incompetent to fulfil expectations and respond to desires. The other, I am told by men skilled in the art of politics, was not less imperfect;³ inadequate to the pressure of the moment, contemptible to all trained statesmen. And thus after all she became a wife, and he a martyr. To such base uses may we return. Herbert in his first foolish youth preferred the patriot; at thirty he might have preferred the courtesan.

As for him, I cannot say what he has done or will do, but I should think, nothing. This may be certainly affirmed of his sister, whose husband, one of our happiest countrymen, is content to farm, to shoot, to vote in the House where he never speaks, and to adore his family.

APPENDICES

REGINALD HAREWOOD

[*Kirklowes* Fragment]

IN MARCH 1830, A FARM ON THE SOUTH-WEST FRONTIER OF
Westmoreland[1] called Kirklowes passed into the hands of one
Harewood. This man, himself a native of the county, a month
after his purchase married a woman born in the next village,
very handsome and of bad health. In February 1831 the name
of a daughter was inscribed on the church register; five years
later, that of a son. In 1837, the name of Margaret, wife of
Francis Harewood, occurs in the list of funerals.

The house[2] stood alone on its little estate, one of the fractions of a wide thinly-inhabited frontier parish. A low narrow
stone house, washed grey with rain, bleared and discoloured
with weather-marks, flecked with blue grey soft gold of
mosses: three lean rowans and a bent poplar in front, seven
aspens worried out of shape by the wind to the left. Behind,
a long slope of field, hoary and wet, fell back to a rapid
curved stream; beyond that a slope upwards, still grey and
damp. A small square garden with three sides walled and to
the south a low thick fence, green and white in the late spring,
black and waste before winter, and toothed with grim thorn:
hardly above leaping-height for a grown man. A mile lower
the burn runs sharply in between brown stones, and narrows
into a rapid; some way off one could hear the fretful chuckle
of the water ending in a clear sound among the pebbles.
Across this shallow bit a ruined floodgate hung and swung
dismally. Below this again there widens northward a long
valley broken into marshland and waste places where the
floods leave their deposit of stone and sedge. To the right of
the house a thick squat gathering of pine, alder and birch; all
about it the moors slope slowly, broken with fair green

171

waste land and dipping hollows spongy with well-heads.

The proprietor of 1830 was a kind shrewd man, with a quaint passion for miscellaneous reading, especially of Latin and French books; rather more indolent, when there was no special work to do, than most men of his kind; very just, courteous, and peaceable; hard and quiet, with habits and proprieties of his own to which he held toughly on occasion. A man whom no one would call whimsical out of his own family; sociable rarely and heartily, genial only upon great provocation, capable of being very merciless and good-natured.[3] He was very fond of his son, and usually flogged him four times a week till the blood ran.[4] He gave Reginald anything he asked for, and never spared him one cut of the birch. He took the tenderest care of him, and it would no more have entered his head to have mercy upon the boy as he roared under the rod than to deny him his daily bread. Having no theory as to his daughter, he made her learn all he knew in the world and loved her in a steady grim way. It was lucky the children were handsome, for he had a special and religious objection to ugliness of face or form; indeed this was his deepest moral feeling in the world.[5] In a certain way he was very speculative, and held some queer opinions on character.[6]

This was the father; of the two children, the boy was a fair average boy, strong, sharp, well broken in to the bearing of hard work and bodily pain, but with no love for either; a boy who used up enormous quantities of birch; on whom no rule grammatical or moral took the least hold, till it was well beaten in; the seat of intellect or conscience being to appearance by no means in the head.[7] He had[8] an animal worship of his sister's beauty and seldom rebelled against her: she in return[9] was decidedly fond [10] of him, but there was no weakness in her affection.

She was by nature untender, thoughtful, subtly apprehensive, greedy of pleasure, curious of evil and good; had a cool sound head, a ready, rapid, flexible cleverness. There was a certain cruelty about her which never showed itself in a harsh or brutal way, but fed with a soft sensual relish on the sight or conceit of physical pain. It was a nervous passion derived from her mother's weak blood and retained in the strong body given her by her father. She was a mixture of two breeds: of a sensual blood and quick nerves, but also of a steady judgment and somewhat cold heart. At bottom, she had no moral qualities at all; was neither good nor evil, and took no pleasure in helping or harming others.[11] Beyond the rule of habit she could see no rule in the world: that once removed by force or chance, she could not understand the existence of reason or right. She knew that murder for example was a theological sin, but except for that technical prohibition she knew no reason against it. She had instinct of a sort, but not the instinct of moral repulsion, she could not disapprove anything except by rote. This character of mind was born with her and grew up quietly, as her body grew in beauty. She was curiously beautiful; her features were clear, tender, regular; she had soft and subtle eyes, the shifting colour in them drowned and vague under heavy white eyelids and curled lashes. She had the sign given by Lavater[12] as typical of faces not to be trusted;[13] eyebrows and hair of a different colour. The hair was saffron-coloured, thick and sinuous, the neck large, polished,[14] and long. The shape of her cheeks and temples was of a singular perfection, which could only be understood when the hair was fastened up from the sides of the head.

She had some real admiration and liking for her father: she respected his cleverness and the absence of any sham or show from his nature. But her liking was for her brother Reginald; her interest for his affairs within doors and without, his misdeeds and misfortunes. Each of Redgie's floggings was a small drama to her: she followed with excitement each cut of the birch on her brother's skin, and tasted a nervous pleasure when every stroke drew blood; she analysed the weals, and anatomized the tears of the victim. Reginald roared profusely on these occasions, and his father was a strong and skilful workman, who flogged neatly and with a cunning hand. It is certain also that Helen felt real and acute enjoyment at the sight of her brother horsed and writhing under the rod; there was in her senses a sort of reversed sympathy with the pain of Reginald's tingling flesh. When the flogging was over she would comfort and coax him, being really grateful to him for the pleasant excitement she had gone thro': but it never entered her head to intercede for him,[16] or his to appeal to her. The boy knew well enough that Eleanor had no pity for him that would interfere with the delight of seeing him well flogged. I cannot say whether Harewood beat him oftener, or laid on the rod harder for his sister's sake; perhaps it was partly on her account that Reginald was always horsed more than once[17] in the week. Harewood was just the man to appreciate the oddity and quaintness of such a taste; doubtless he had himself a deep inward relish of his skill and strength, a keen flavour of the pain he inflicted, when Reginald, nicely adjusted on a farm-servant's back, or simply on a convenient bench or block, reddened and wriggled with smart and the birch drew fresh blood at every cut on the flesh of the roaring boy.

In 1850 Helen was married. The husband was a small gentleman, meek and weak, of a temper like that of grey sloppy weather. He had a fair estate and house, and hung about his woods in shooting time with a kind of futile pleasure. Personally he looked as if he had been half sponged out on his birth; his features had a sort of blotted outline as if they were effaced and worn off at the angles. This desirable male had met his wife in the following way. He had strayed out alone with gun, and fallen somehow off his own land and into the little barren Kirklowes property: and following the edge of the little burn till it grew into a fair-sized flow of moss-water, full of rapids and brown pools spanned with stooping birch and fir; and after a mile's walk he came upon this spectacle. A boy of fourteen or so was practising swimming in a long deep pool; a tall lady quietly contemplating him.[19] Her hair was knotted and wet, and water drops clung about her lips and chin. Her dress was stained at the knees and her naked feet were drying in the sun on warm and powdery moss. The poor man spoke to her[20] and six weeks later she had married him. Two months more and there came a day when Reginald Harewood found his father's hand heavier and the familiar birch-twig sharper than usual, and ran away[21] with the marks of four dozen cuts[22] on his flesh. Next day he turned up at his sister's, as tired, hot and dirty as could be wished. Frederick Ashurst received him kindly enough, and Helen[23] made much of him for a week. Mr. Harewood accepted his son's desertion with patience, and on his return flogged him as long as he could lay on the rod.[24]

It seemed as if his daughter's marriage had really affected him for the worse; his fondness for Reginald became weaker and his treatment of the boy harsher and rougher altogether. He left off training him; and hardly noticed him except for punishment. Both were unhappy enough,[25] and the first visit[26] they paid together began without much hope of pleasure. It was a curious society into which Helen had been thrown. The household consisted of old Mrs. Ashurst, a religious and torpid old woman who had just energy enough to take out and put in her teeth; Mr. Shore, her brother, a grey thin man with sharp eyes; and a rather singular French lady, Mrs. Ashurst's companion for the last six years.

[A BREAK HERE]

Both were unhappy enough; and in a few months Reginald had made his way again to his sister, and applied for help to her.

'Look here, Helen, you must do something for me,' he said; 'I can't make shift in this way, and the father's just mad if one comes across him. I wish you'd get him to send me somewhere to school—or to sea, I don't care.'

Helen offered him to stay with her. 'I'll get you leave and you can go about and shoot if you like.' So her brother was established in the house, and the father remained by himself. The year went on towards winter; Helen had married in February. It was a windy and heavy season before the snow set in. At Kirklowes Helen had gone out in all weathers; now she shut herself into the old library for days and sat by huge fires with her head fallen and her eyes black and large. She was tired all day; read the strangest books; made the weariest dreams, and wasted with the hard desire of pleasure. She wanted sometimes the Kirklowes life back again,[27] more of the days when she gathered cranberries out of the moss and went into the patched black plashes of reedy peat after the soft windy feathers of cotton-grass. Then she would take Reginald with her and make him help to saddle the horses, and ride for hours against the rain till the weariness and heat were drenched and blown out of her. She kept usually out of her husband's way; he employed himself mainly in managing the land, and began to think seriously of politics.[28] Reginald was the happiest; he made friends with the stablemen, rode all day, and shot as much as the gamekeeper.[29]

The winter thickened and grew threatening; Helen went hardly ever outside the park. Putting to profit her father's teaching, she began reading the old French books laid away in the library, all memoirs and novels of the eighteenth century: Mme. d'Epinay's correspondence, Grimm and Diderot letters, Faublas,[30] Crébillon, and all manner of minor historical works. She tried writing, and tore up six chapters of a story in the form of letters. Her beauty, which she used to enjoy and relish, was a thorn in the side of her eager ambition; she would have given it all for some distinction, some power and place like the women in her books: Mme. d'Epinay's for example;[31] she began to wish for the last century back.

Before the year of their marriage was out, there arrived at the house uninvited a Mr. Champneys, who was made so welcome that it was clear the master looked on his coming in the light of a windfall. He was rather handsome with some rapid power of talk which passed for[32] sense and humour among people who had no talent that way. Ashurst was an old friend, and stupid enough to be good company: and Mrs. Ashurst the most beautiful woman in the rough he had ever seen. He was kind enough to teach her riding on a less rude

principle than she was used to: also a little music, for he had
a smattering of many things, being a delicate accomplished
sort of person. He disliked boys and children, and might perhaps have ousted Reginald, but from regard for his friend's
wife, whose deep affections were evident to him; such evidence of sweet and noble character was precious in his
judgment. In February he proposed to go, but remained at
the request of his friend. Before March the household was
decidedly happier. 'I say, Helen, is that fellow going to stay
here for good?' Reginald inquired. Presently Mrs. A. became
awake to the waste of her brother's time and energies, and
sent him back to Kirklowes, where he was received with
patience by his father, who had a return of liking towards
him;[33] he took to teaching him again, and kept the boy about
him; Redgie was so quick to fend for himself, Harewood said,
and he was no fool neither at bottom. In fact, he wanted
Reginald all the more now, to make up for his sister. Still the
schooling he got was of a rough makeshift kind, and his father
used him at fifteen harder than most schoolmasters; but
Redgie was not mentally thin-skinned, and no more sensitive
than another boy. His mother had left none of her feeble
blood about him.

Presently there came a great scandal. The Ashursts were
gone to London; there had been violent quarrels, and Helen
had left the house after a fierce scene with her husband, who
was seriously ill. Thus far the news came direct; report added
that Mr. Champneys had joined Mrs. Ashurst at Folkestone
and they had crossed to France together. Harewood's fury was
excessive; fortunately he found it a vent, remembering that
Reginald was not too big a boy to be beaten. But for this
relief[34] he might have been in some danger. As it was, when
he had given Reginald such a flogging that the scars remained
for three[35] good months, Mr. Harewood was much better and
even became rather hopeful. He was tired out for that day,
but the next he walked sixteen miles to the nearest town, and
horsewhipped the propagator of the Champneys part of the
story. On his return home that evening, he was much as usual,

and was even at the pains to make friends with Reginald, who was naturally sore and sulky.

Next week came more news. Mr. Ashurst was dead, and his property left by will to a cousin; no mention was made of his wife's name. This time Harewood could have little doubt left about his daughter: but he was not the sort of man to die of horror or grief. He simply waited, and went about his day's work. Reginald was getting too tall to be idle, he said quite suddenly; it was late to set him to school at fifteen and he would learn nothing if he went.[37]

[A BREAK HERE]

A curious coloured light had filled all the space between sea and cloud, and the wind that drove inshore curled up the thin edges of water, showing a little reflected glitter on the west side of each, although the sea was dun and wrinkled, without colour or lights on it. The wind quickened rapidly and the side-lit ripples ran in harder and closer. Presently the boat came in sight. Helen drew a sharp sighing breath and stooped out a little to see it, as it caught the last colour from the west side, and slid inshore with the faint low light upon it. There came a quick squall of wind, so violent that she almost lost her footing, being taken unawares. Her brother's cap was blown off and he was after it along the sand at full speed. Looking again to sea, she missed the boat. It had gone down in the short gust of storm, which came before the rain set in. For the whole sky was dark now all but a thin wan slit above the water, and rain fell heavily. Lying down and grasping the rims of rock, she stooped and peered upon the pale-coloured sea, crossed now with slow serpentine streaks of moving foam. All under and round the rock it came in with a bubbling and gurgling noise, distinct from the kiss of the rain. In a little while she got sight of what she was looking for. Clearly there was a man swimming in from where the boat had gone down. She knew he could swim well enough, and began praying under her breath that God would never let him get safe to land. Still he was close in now, but she had good faith and hope. It was a rough sea and he must have had hard work.

In effect when the boat sank Champneys had disengaged himself with fierce efforts which had taken half the strength out of him, and had then set to work to slip off his boots, knowing the value of that move. This work again had beaten half the breath out of his body, fighting as he was with waves that grew heavier each minute. Still he was not a hundred strokes off shore. Whether he too prayed or not, at least he struck out with his best skill and strength. But the wind had raised the rollers and he was swimming now with short blind broken strokes in a heavier sea then he had ever ventured on, toiling up the greenish wrinkled back of one wave in trust to get past the full weight of its blow when it broke, caught and flung forward in the thick of the foam, breathlessly getting his chin above water with a sense of strangling hands upon the throat and a great weight in the body, suddenly seized by the next wave and hurled on a yard under water, level and helpless as he drove, hardly fighting with hands that let the water between their loose feeble fingers. Then at last as his feet sank under him, they felt the slipping shingle of a steep bank, and he got strength again for a minute and breathed between two waves. Then the sea caught him again and flung him in a feeble heap up the shingle-bank. Blind and beaten as he was, he grasped the sliding stones with hands dug in and knees tightened, to stand if he could the recoil. It loosened his hold but left him some slight grasp of the shingle as he drove backward. Then he was hurled further in, above the bank. For a second, he got his head clear and breathed hard. Then came the ebb and forced him out again, and the gripe of throttling fingers choked him and his eyes were filled with sea water. Again he was hurled in, too weak this time to help himself, his body and legs dragging as if dead, knees and toes grated on the shingle: and he felt on one cheek and temple the rapid lash and sting of small pebbles driven through the water. Still, when this breaker was spent, he was in shallow water, gulping and bruised, with miserable arms flung up for a moment. Then the ebb sucked him back, beat his feet from under him, and hurled him right down the bank. Here a strong groundswell took him and carried him sideways through the hissing water upon the black reef, which stove in two of his ribs. Clutching at the long sea-weed as the sea drove it straight in, he felt it slide through his fingers and uttered a last choking scream before the water poured into him. Then the next breaker dashed him doubled up against the ribbed sharp side of the reef, breaking his back and splitting open his skull. Afterwards one great wave hurled up out of sea-reach the hideous ruined body.

Helping herself with hands and knees, Helen crawled down the slant back of the great rock, and watching her time, when the recoil of the water left a little space between that and the next rock, leapt down, caught the swinging weed with both hands, and crawled and sprang up the rock-side out of harm's way. She was drenched through and stiff with keeping to one position, bruised too and grazed with the rough edges of rock. But her lips had the look of laughter and her eyes shone and smiled; all her face was warmed and lit with pleasure. Meeting Reginald, who came back wet and blown, but cap in hand, she took him round with her arms and kissed him, laughing.

'You have had a quarter of an hour's run, Redgie. Look here.'

'Eh!' said Redgie, frightened; 'it'll be one o' those in the boat!'

'Yes,' said his sister. 'The master. He must have sunk at once, and got those hurts after death. I wonder if the other has been cast up further on?'

[END OF THIS FRAGMENT]

HERBERT WINWOOD

Uses of Prosody

A LITTLE BEFORE EASTER THE SPRING BEGAN MOVING HERE AND
there, taking short breaths and feeling after doubtful
flowers.[1] At Ensdon it was sharp enough, but sweet; all went
well within doors and out. Present as guests:[2] two Winwoods,
three Lunsfords. On an average there were four riders a day;
Herbert, Margaret,[3] and one of the boys with Rosamond.
Miss Lunsford was a fair rider, but wanted practice: Arthur
had never shown her much patronage. Upon the whole she
was not the woman for love-making on horseback. Herbert's
eye matched her against the splendid grace and supple vigour
of the two other feline horsewomen he had known: and found
that his sister used to ride better and Anne[4] to enjoy herself
more. Lady Waristoun never rode now: she had turned soft
(as Cis[5] graciously expressed it) and sedentary: sitting
between fire and flowers in a heaven of heat and scent, she let
the day slide past through her eyes and Mrs. Lunsford's talk
slip through her ears without much notice or response.
Neither in effect appealed much to her. Her days were set
fast and firm now to the end of her unchangeable life. She
had bought off all her fears at the price of all her hopes.
Politics began to interest her as a practical form of dramatic
art always at hand; a big tragicomic play without a final fifth
act possible; very preferable to any stage ware. Her tacit
philosophy had now reached the point where inaction adores
fact and satiety takes to worshipping reality; a change significant in her case that action, even the small fine work of
domestic intrigue, was over for ever. Her nature was still
strong and wholesome enough to be secure against the barren
lust of self-examination, the dull folly of revising and re-

casting her past deeds and days that conscience or repentance
might label them as good or bad. She bought pictures, and
began decidedly to spoil the children; Bertie[6] especially, who
grew unbearable, though comic, whenever out of the shadow
of the birch. Incessant swishing might have kept him alive
and left him harmless; without the beneficent sting[7] and
daily curb of flagellation he was like a dormouse possessed
by the devil. The beauty of the birch, as Lord Waristoun with
grave pathos once observed, is that while it rouses the
heaviest-headed boy by the tickling and tingling vigour of its
pliant stimulant twigs, it tames likewise 'the lightest-tailed
fellow of feathers and fire' by the same pungent means. For all
his father's wisdom however Ethel[8] was not made to smart
half often enough that spring: he wore through his Easter
holiday 'with the loss of few tears and little blood': and the
place was at once cumbered and pestered with a boy who was
alternately a marmot and an imp. Lady Waristoun left Arden
and Cis mainly to their father's and tutor's handling; but the
young one she used as tenderly as Elaine[9] la blanche, who
fattened and whitened visibly as the days went. For hours the
boy and cat basked in supreme and shameless sloth at her
feet in the perfumed fever of the air which she now preferred
breathing. One blushes to say it of a twelve-year-old, but he
did actually read, fast as his first half had left him sticking
low down in the lower fourth: novels mainly of the bicipital
or muscular type:[10] much preferring, in the luxurious feline
fashion he had inherited, the fence-jumping and jaw-breaking
feats of ink and paper heroes to a healthier practical 'rooge'.[11]
I regret to believe also that this model reader of Messrs.
Horesleigh and Hurlstone usually fell fast in love with the
seductive and poisonous heroines whose deadly beauty
managed to soften the hero's nerve at the wrong time or send
him, a jilted heap of aimless muscle, a heart-broken mass of
whole bones, upon his final peril by fence or flood: also that,
in the Christian-muscular section of this stimulant class of
higher literature, he always blinked the prenuptial con-
versions, and collapsed in sleep at the point where 'one of

God's maids' appeared upon God's earth to reclaim a godless but desirable Hercules, from whom the Apollonian shaft of a cleric athlete had fallen blunted; to whom now Artemis comes in Christian habit, resistless, sweet, saintly; acceptable to the muscular fancy, yet not condemnable by the moral instinct.

One fine day, though, for the elder Bertie's misfortune, Ethel was of the riding set, Arden and Cis being kept in at their verses; and devoted himself to the aggravation of Rosamond's steed, a blood-mare too exquisite and too nervous for the rough work of child's play. Whereby the dialogue was kept up much as follows, at a cross-fire of cross-purposes.

HIC:[12] (winding up a small speech which had somehow begun itself). And it doesn't depend upon such things at all; you must see that. People don't get the chance of saying the right word. You know when one wants a thing one has never the heart or the face to say—

ILLA: Bertie major, tell Bertie minor not to make Zulma flick her ears.

ILLE: Because you know you can't sit her. Fancy you after the hounds. Bertha Brackenbury—

HAEC: If that child begins quoting novels—

HIC: Ethel, if you make yourself a nuisance, I shall have to lay you over the saddle and give you such a flogging as will save your father the expense of next half's bill for birch.

ILLE: —when she hunted with the Rivers pack and Fred Loring—and you can't, Herbert, for it doesn't depend on a fellow's being swished you know, if you weren't a fool—what a beastly chouse—

ILLA: Give him another cut; the boy is insufferable.

HAEC: Quelle moue d'impératrice!—Children, do give one some peace for a second or so. You were saying—

HIC: I think this is about the best view of Cauldhope Flats.

HAEC: How the wind has worried that line of firs.

ILLA: She said so: and that you were the stupidest laziest worst-bred—

ILLE: She wants her head punched. But you see a governess lives among girls till she thinks she can say anything.

HAEC: You can see to Greystead and Kirklowes almost. I wonder if Lieut. Halden has got his promotion.

ILLE: Frank Halden is the only fellow I know that's like Branks Musselston and that lot; the way he sat Nicette—

ILLA: Anybody can sit Nicette; any man. She's too much for boys.

ILLE: But he rides Isis. Isis is a clipper, but she pulls like anything. She's got no end of a hard mouth: and she shies. *I* wouldn't ride her.

ILLA: Cis said yesterday Lady Ethel was more of a girl than I am.

HIC: Otterton is getting ready for flower again. You know how that mile of bent-grass burns[13] and heaves in the wind and light on late summer afternoons: like a sea of pale red-brown flame and green ripples. I like the Latchburn way best. It's odd the way time gets wasted. When one has a chance—

HAEC: Herbert, please open that gate, or Ethel will certainly be off. Besides, the grass is just orange: like worsted.

ILLE: And you know Frank said Zulma was too much for you.

Whereat Rosamond, exasperated, lashed him sharply over the neck and cheek with her whip, raising a thick bright ridge of tingling red flesh. Startled by the unfamiliar sting of a cut in those upper regions, Ethel winced and jerked the curb-rein, his eyes and face flaming; then, as his horse reared, hit furiously at hers and caught it over the ears. Mlle. Zulma kicked; and after a confused and clattering minute the combatants were set straight again.

'Don't flog Bertie,' Rosamond said to Herbert, with much

184

heroism of tone, 'it was me set them off': for the wretched elder not inexcusably was aching with rage and the desire to give the boy a thorough good thrashing with a tougher whip than hers; did indeed lay one or two hard quick strokes over his shoulders, making Ethel catch his breath and suck his lips; after which they got home more quietly; for Margaret would go no further, and petted 'Bertie minor' all the way home, distinctly snubbing and cutting off the other two. So they were back early, and thus it fell out that the same afternoon saw a little play played out of the *proverbe* or drawingroom-comedy kind. In a quiet quick hour or two one may get to the catastrophe of such a play without knowing it:

Lady Waristoun had left the sliding-doors half open between her small close bright room and the wider public study; letting in some fresher sound and air upon the sweet heavy heat endurable only by herself, Ethel and Elaine. In the outer room the two elder boys still sat versifying, with interludes of weary qualified imprecation; Mrs. Lunsford poured upon if not into Lord Waristoun's patient ears a soft warm stream of articulate religion and social science; Mrs. Winwood, with emphatic or even equivocal relish, dilated to Margaret upon the infamies of French literature as embodied in *La Chimère*, which was then but a month old in London and two days old at Ensdon; Herbert was left afloat between the boys who kept begging for 'sense' for their verses and Rosamond who required hints for a moral tale of low life designed by her to benefit the poorer neighbourhood. Ethel, with Elaine's warm weight crushing his shoulders, lay flat on his breast reading, with chin propped on his fist or elbow. Lady Waristoun inhaled the heat, and took her rest sadly, after her manner.

CECIL: Is *imago* masculine? what's 'prince'?
MRS. W.: A most horrible book, really blasphemous; more offensive in detail too than I could have believed.
MRS. L.: The unassisted work of a most apostolic man; the Rev. William Swallow, curate of St. Tobias.

LORD W.:   Ah. A man of the name was chaplain, I recollect, to Lord Wearmouth and tutor to the boy.

MRS. W.:   And ended by robbing him of life as well as honour in a way too repulsive to think of.[14]

MRS. L.:   That was Robert. His influence with young men was wonderful

MRS. W.:   I don't believe it's natural, my dear. Even if it is, such things are improper to touch upon in public.

HERBERT: I say, Cis, you'll catch it if you make the 'i' in *ligustrum* long: what *are* fellows' quantities coming to at Eton?

ROSAMOND: And so his wife heard of him at the public-house, Herbert, and went up to see the clergyman and and found him—

MRS. W.:   La tête renversée dans les seins de Cécile, qui haletait comme une moribonde. Cette figure virginale écumait d'amour. La chair de ses joues prenait des tons violacés. On voyait sur la blancheur mate de son cou des taches presque jaunes. Tout son sang battait furieusement. Sa chevelure paraissait s'animer et siffler.[17] Son amant presque pâmé ne râlait plus que par moments.

MARGARET: Tiens. But what made her neck yellow?

MRS. W.:   Eh, ma chère! Tous ces gens-là font de l'anatomie. C'est une manie. Ca veut dire qu'elle pâlissait et rougissait énormément. Par exemple!

ARDEN: I say, give me some sense, Herbert; about Satyrs.

MRS. W.:   Here again.—La vibration de son sang lui faisait bruire dans la tête une musique voluptueuse. Ce corps de cygne semblait prendre des plis onduleux comme une étoffe blanche et chatoyante. Sa beauté morbide et venimeuse alléchait l'œil mais effarait l'âme. On entendait tout près d'elle comme un bruissement d'illusions qui s'envolaient à tire-d'ailes.[18] Ce sang musical et maladif qui toujours allait et venait semblait laisser ça et là des flaques malsaines à force de pâleur, des marbrures d'or ou de cuivre, des étincelles de flamme pourpre. On eût dit parfois que l'âme de cette belle couleuvre s'efforçait vainement de transpirer par sa peau.—You see.

MARGARET: Oh: metallic, serpentine, sick, musical, and poisonous. I quite see.

HERBERT: *Satyrique Camœnæque?* my good fellow, you can't well make an ending like that before a pentameter, I should say. And I think the Camœnæ never get to Thessaly. Besides, *nemores!* are you out of your mind? Lucky you won't show that up. Try something like this:

Infremuit subito sedes commota Lyæo,
Et nemora insolito consonuere Deo.

MRS. L.: His good work among those poor women has indeed been signally blessed of God and man. The night we know cometh, when no man shall work. But he labours all day in that one field. He is not of those who have put their hands to the plough and looked back. And they are so grateful. One poor creature said—'I couldn't have believed one man could do what he does among so many.'

MRS. W.: Bathilde hurlait. Une saline verte filtrait par ses gencives bleuâtres. Cette écome hideuse frangeait toute sa lèvre inérieure. Une bordure âcre et jaune estompait lentement sa lumineuse paupière. Les dents dechaussées, pareilles à des perles mortes ou rongées par l'acide cyanocéphalique, avaient pris des tons crus qui effrayaient, et faisaient songer à des dents de cadavre. Sa gorge ferme et frémissante appelait encore des morsures amoureuses. Même agonisante, elle eût su faire vibrer tous les nerfs d'un poète. Cette pourriture attrayait. Cette charogne faisait venir l'eau à la bouche. Ses pieds, qui se tordaient sur les draps déchirés, montraient des talons qui rappelaient des boutons de rose sauvage. Elle avait toujours des orteils à croquer. Par moments elle serrait les dents et blasphémait.

MARGARET: Merci. (Here she rose and crossed over to the boys.)

HERBERT: Mais mon Dieu, ma mère, qu'est-ce que c'est donc que ce livre-là?

MRS. W.: Ca? c'est un roman de moeurs. C'est de M. Flambeau—je me trompe, c'est de M. Verdier.

HERBERT: Ca me paraît un peu bien fort.

MRS. W.: Que veux-tu? c'est un genre.

HERBERT: De cannibale? Have you begun on the Mœnads yet, Arden?

ARDEN: I want full sense for six or eight verses about the river and wood. Look here, will *pharetratæ* do in this line? it's just the length I want.

HERBERT: Eh? Quàque pharetratæ—something—micat umbra corollæ? I should imagine not. What on earth do you mean?

ARDEN: Well, you see I thought pharetratæ might do for 'quivering'.

HERBERT: Ingenious. You should write on comparative philology: but the moods are shaky.[19] Better drop

[CHAPTER OBVIOUSLY UNFINISHED]

ARDEN MAJOR TO LADY WARISTOUN

Eton, June 5th, '62

Dear Mamma,

Arden[1] has got into the most awful row and my tutor talks of his having to leave. He is excessively cut up, and very sulky. It's something out of the way,[2] and he didn't steer well last night. Ethel knows more than I do but won't tell for fear of a licking. He (A. not E.) was swished after twelve.[3] It has made no end of talk among the fellows. Yesterday went off very well. I have got my remove[4] but it's a great bore living up to Barker. Herbert[5] came down yesterday with his wife, who was very jolly. Ethel[6] fell in love with her again. I like dark. She thought he was in lower remove,[7] and made him awfully cocky. He was near being late at Surley[8] for he stayed in their carriage till the boats were off and got up quite winded and had too much hock given him and got quite tight, and my tutor nailed him and he got such a jolly good swishing after nine[9] to-day as you never saw. She gave him a cigarette and it made him seedy. Item a £, *which didn't.* Herbert tipped me. He looks excessively happy but I suppose all fellows do when they first marry. She is so like a white cat that there *must* be *claws.* Ethel sends love and can't write; says it's because he's got a 100 lines but I *know* he can't sit down.[10] I am all right. Tell my father I have not been complained of[11] again this half. Make Rosamond look after the beasts for me.

With best love,
Your affec. son,
CECIL WINWOOD ARDEN.

189

COMMENTARY

La critique du roman est elle-même un roman dont les romanciers sont les personnages. Il y a une Comédie Romanesque *comme il y a une* Comédie Humaine.

ALBERT THIBAUDET

CHAPTER I

THE FRUSTRATE MASTERPIECE

or THE FINE ART OF SUPPRESSION

A history of the more external facts of *Lesbia Brandon*:
its inception, advance, arrest, and final elimination

T. J. Wise, in a *Bibliography of the Writings in Prose and Verse of Algernon Charles Swinburne*, 1919, gave what he would have considered a history of *Lesbia Brandon*: this he republished, with amplifications, in *A Swinburne Library*, 1925; and reproduced again, but without some of the necessary amplifications, in the *Bonchurch Bibliography* two years later.[1] This account, adopted in large part by Lafourcade in *La Jeunesse de Swinburne*, 1928, is practically the only one furnished so far, and may be assumed to have become universally standard: at least, it has no doubt been accepted as reliable as far as it goes by those who consult Wise for bibliographical and other elementary information on the writings of the poet. But almost everything Wise says on this as on most other subjects is doltishly wrong—incredibly wrong except to anyone who has seriously tested a few items of his work. One way of presenting the actual facts would be to cite Wise's 'facts' one after another and to negate them with the necessary corrections. I prefer to give the former directly, and to relegate notice of Wise's (and Lafourcade's) errors to foot-

---

[1] In what follows I shall refer to these as *Bib., S.Lib. and B.Bib.* respectively. The contents of S.Lib., with their hundreds of errors and absurdities, are incorporated in the famous that should be infamous Catalogue of the Ashley Library, where all Wise's spoils are inventorised to the most splendid advantage.

notes, where they can be ignored by those who do not wish to make acquaintance with stupidity, even when it is entertaining by a certain comicality in its grossness.

What follows is primarily the actual extant facts, news of *Lesbia Brandon* in correspondence and elsewhere, and secondarily commentary on this, the whole forming in the main the history of what may be called the external fortunes of the work: the other story, that of the progress or evolution of the book as an artistic creation, will be given in the next section, although some incidental reference to it is more or less inevitable here.

The earliest extant reference to *Lesbia Brandon* is in a letter written from Tintagel on the 2nd of October 1864 by Swinburne to his cousin Mary Gordon.[1] Describing a swimming 'adventure which might have been serious' he says 'I . . . had twice to plunge again into the sea, which was filling all the coves and swinging and swelling heavily between the rocks; once fell flat in it, and got so thrashed and licked that I might have been—in—'s clutches [alluding to characters in a story][2] . . .' (In *The Boyhood of A. C. Swinburne*, by Mrs. Disney Leith (née Mary Gordon) 1917.) There can be no doubt that Herbert Seyton—or simply Herbert—and Denham are the names in the blanks (why did the lady want to make a mystery of the thing?). The reference is perhaps to the beatings of Herbert by Denham in general, but more probably to the one administered when the boy was caught coming from his forbidden bathe in a dangerous sea. There is, *à propos* of a beating received by the poet at Eton, an

[1] Wise, in B.Bib., says, amplifying an earlier statement, that "Apart from a brief mention . . . in a letter to W. Rossetti on March 21st, 1866, the earliest glimpse we have of *Lesbia Brandon* is in a letter addressed to Sir Richard Burton, on January 11th, 1867'. Lafourcade cites the letter from Tintagel. But he simply quotes the sentence 'I got thrashed and licked . . . clutches', which gives the impression that Swinburne had really been flogged, and not that he was using metaphor. Also, he does not notice the other letter from Cornwall, nor what Swinburne's cousin says of the date and contents of the novel.

[2] The comment in square brackets is Mrs. Disney Leith's.

allusion to the novel in another letter written at about the same time from Cornwall to this much favoured cousin, to whom apparently Swinburne addressed himself as to one who would not find the subject of flagellation distasteful (it recurs significantly more than one or twice in such portions of these letters as she gave to the public[1]: one suspects there must be even more revealing passages in the part of this correspondence which has been kept private):

> 'And then I showed my verses indignantly (*after* the catastrophe) to another master, and he said they were very good, and there was but one small slip in them, *hard* as the metre was; and I told my tutor with impudent triumph (knowing he had done his very worst), and he was shut up I can tell you . . . but that did not heal the cuts or close the scars which had imprinted on the mind and body of—[a fictitious schoolboy character with whom he identifies himself here],[2] a just horror of strange metres.'
>
> (Mrs. Disney Leith, *op.cit.*)

(He had been flogged for the grave crime of bravely trying his hand at Galliambics, a difficult metre good enough for Catullus, but 'no metre at all' according to his tutor.) Here again Herbert may be taken to be the suppressed name.[3]

This same cousin, with whom he had earlier that year col-

---

[1] The simple-minded Professor Chew (for a more detailed reference to whom see the last footnote of this section), not observing this and other patent facts, thinks that the novel must have been quite nice and respectable at this stage, because Swinburne allowed this lady cousin of his to have knowledge of the contents!

[2] Here too the comment in square brackets is Mrs. Disney Leith's.

[3] It is just possible that it is that of one of the boys representing Swinburne (Algernon Clavering etc.) in certain of the flogging-pieces. In this case we should have proof that Swinburne had begun to write these pieces as early as the date of the letter in question; (1869 is the earliest of the relatively few watermark dates borne by the large mass of the manuscripts of these unpublished pieces). We should also have here the proof that the poet's cousin was made privy to these sadicomasochistic compositions; once again it is strange that she should withhold the name of the boy.

laborated in the production of a work in which full-blooded flagellation figures prominently (a fact that has never received due attention[1]), makes a further reference to *Lesbia Brandon*, and this time she is really a little informative. Still speaking of 1864, she says, in the same book on the poet with whom her kinship was evidently not only genealogical:

'The autumn of that year found us again both in London, and he was a frequent guest at my father's house at Chelsea. I think it was at that time that he wrote some chapters of a novel, which never saw the light, or, as far as I know, was completed. He used to read me bits of the MS. of an afternoon when he happened to come in. I do not know what was the plot of the story, but I recollect some of the characters—one being the bright young lovable schoolboy he delighted in portraying, in constant scrapes, but noble and honourable through all; and a tutor, who bid fair to be the 'villain of the piece'. There was a description of a bathing-place under the rocky cliffs, taken, no doubt, from the scenes of his Cornwall scrambles. The plot was in no way connected with his late novel, *Love's Cross Currents*.'[2]

It is clear from these passages that by the autumn of 1864 Swinburne had written the first two chapters and some part of the third; at least that portion of the work up to and including the installation of Denham as Herbert's tutor and the exhibition of his sadic proficiency in making the boy suffer. Mrs. Disney Leith's erroneous remark that the plot was 'in no way' connected with *Love's Cross Currents* (mistakenly

[1] I shall deal with this and related matters in *Swinburne: the Arcane Side*, a work that will be largely a supplement to the present volume.

[2] Mrs. Disney Leith was pretty certainly wrong in her belief that the seaside scenes in *Lesbia Brandon* are Cornish; they are undoubtedly more than anything else Northumbrian, and convey part of the neighbourhood of the poet's ancestral home on the side of his fathers.

and perhaps significantly called 'late' by her[1]) indicates that Swinburne had not yet written any of the sections in which Lady Midhurst appears or in which mention is made of her family. This conclusion is reinforced by the fact that Lesbia herself had apparently not yet come into the book: she is first referred to therein at about the same time as the characters of the earlier book.

It is not likely that the novel was begun before 1864. It was beyond any question written after *Love's Cross Currents* (to name only one piece of evidence, Swinburne's own reference, in the next letter to be cited, to the relative position of the two works is quite conclusive on this point.) And Swinburne himself gave '1862-3' as the period in which he wrote *Love's Cross Currents* (in a passage where he called it his 'maiden attempt at a study of contemporary life and manners'.). In the second half of 1863 he was very busy with *Chastelard*, *Blake*, *Atalanta* and other undertakings, which must have been more than enough to occupy all his creative energies. Altogether, then, it is not probable that he set to work on *Lesbia Brandon* in that year; it is just possible that he may have done so near the end of it.[2]

---

[1] By 'late' she cannot have meant 'recently published', for *Love's Cross Currents* came out in volume form in 1905, and 1917 is the date of her own book. If she saw it on its first (pseudonymous) appearance in *The Tatler* (1877) it can be taken for certain that she was ignorant of the authorship. But Swinburne's description of it in the 1905 preface as a 'bantling' of his 'literary youth' ought to have set her right as to the period when it was composed. She does not strike one as having a bright or alert intelligence—at least at the time she was engaged on this work concerning Swinburne (which, incidentally, in its epistolary —and far greater—part covers not only his boyhood but practically the whole of his life. The letters are very badly edited).

[2] On this as on other rudimentary points Wise falls into crass error. He dates it quite definitely 1859–1867, as if there was no room for doubt. Then later, on the very same page, he says with characteristic disregard of consistency: 'It was commenced in 1859 *or 1860* [my italics] and was continued at intervals until 1867'. His only reason for giving these dates is that 'the dated watermarks on the paper extend from 1859 to 1865' (even here he commits a gross elementary blunder,

The next mention of the novel is in a letter[3] written by the author to W. M. Rossetti on the 21st of March, 1866. Here he speaks of it as 'the unfinished hybrid book of which you have heard so much laely', and in which are 'hinted at or sketched retrospectively' 'one or two characters' who had received 'full development' in the earlier novel, for which he was at that time trying hard to find a publisher who would issue it anonymously. By now, then, the work had grown to include charac-

(*Note* [2] *continued*)—

for 1866 is the latest of the watermark dates). Of course a watermark date only indicates a year *before which* what is on the paper could not have been inscribed upon it; it does not indicate *when* it was inscribed; this may have been at any time after the paper was issued, and at any time after it came into the writer's hands. (The watermark date does not even indicate a time before which what is written on the paper could not have been *composed* in cases where it is a fair copy of work turned out previously.) Wise's constant reliance on watermark dates to determine the time of composition is grotesquely naïve especially on the part of one who was primarily and professionally a bibliographer—or aimed at getting the world to accept him as such. (Lafourcade, in whose eyes he is a great bibliographer, often follows him in this silly method of establishing when works were written.) In the present connexion, he never pauses to consider the *order* of the watermark dates in the sequence of the book. Now what is pretty certainly the earliest of the extant sections has a watermark date 1864; but a page of a manifestly later section has the watermark date 1859, and what is more, this follows pages *of the same section* of which 1863 is the date, and is followed by other pages carrying this last date; again, eight pages of what is plainly one of the latest sections have the watermark date of 1859—and so on: it is unnecessary to insist on the extent to which these facts make a fool of Wise.

[3] Cited by Wise, *Bib., S.Lib. and B.Bib.* I have not been able to trace the original of this letter. Letters or portions of letters published by Wise, or by him and Gosse in conjunction, are subject to the greatest caution. As I have mentioned in the Foreword, not only do this pair of literary miscreants leave out whole passages with no indication of any sort that they have done so, but even in what they do publish there are frequently errors of transcription. Where I have not been able to check their copies by collation with originals, I can only hope that I am giving what Swinburne actually wrote.

ters from *Love's Cross Currents*[1] and Swinburne had evidently begun to set great store by it, and was bringing it to the notice of his friends, largely no doubt by his favourite method (which was also D. G. Rossetti's) of reading aloud every instalment as soon as possible after he had turned it out.[2] And already he had recognised that the work was 'hybrid'; by which he very probably meant not only that it was in an unusual degree a compost of realism and poetry, but also that in its general structure and development it did not satisfy standards that were canonical. And apparently he had decided to let the work proceed on the line into which it was falling, however little conventional these might be. (It would be too much to say that he had decided to acquiesce in irregularity in the composition of the book, for there is no evidence—nor is it at all probable—that he felt there was irregularity from his artistic point of view; and indeed the work is irregular according to one only of a number of possible and acceptable views as to how a novel should or might be composed—but discussion of that question belongs to a later chapter.)

About ten months later, on the 11th of January, 1867, writing to his crony and fellow free-thinker, Sir Richard Burton, he spoke of it in terms which showed that he was well pleased with it as it had become some three years after he had first set to work on it:

'I have in hand a scheme of mixed verse and prose—a sort of *étude à la Balzac* plus the poetry—which I flatter myself will be more offensive and objectionable to Britannia than anything I have yet done. You see I have now a character to keep up, and by the grace of Cotytto I will

[1] Called *A Year's Letters* until the publication in volume form in 1905 I shall throughout use the better-known title which the work bears in all editions (except the pirated one brought out by Mosher in 1901).

[2] An entry in W. M. Rossetti's Diary, to be cited presently in a footnote, shows that he did not only 'hear of' *Lesbia Brandon*, or listen to a reading of it by Swinburne, but also read at least a certain part of it.

endeavour not to come short of it—at least in my writings.'[1]

A sort of *étude à la Balzac* plus the poetry: this, a good general description of it, suggests that Swinburne is increasingly conscious of its hybridity, and realises that it is a novel of no ordinary sort. And he is assured that, however abnormal it may be, all is well as regards the two main forces determining its growth; one is realism as practised by the greatest of all masters in that line; the other is poetry of the kind in which he himself is supreme. Further, he is more than ever insurgent against prescriptive and restrictive respectability, which his recently published *Poems and Ballads* had shocked into a rant of abuse against him. He is now writing in a spirit of challenge, delighting to overstep moralistic bounds to the freedom of art. Evidently not only Lady Midhurst, but the sinister sadist and Baudelairian Mr. Linley, and the sapphic Lesbia herself, and other scandalizing things now had their place in the novel.[2]

Burton, replying from Santos on April the 5th of the same

---

[1] Wise, *Bib., S.Lib., B.Bib.*

[2] It is possible that at this date Swinburne had written all that he ever produced of the book. The latest watermark-date of the manuscript is 1866 (it occurs in six chapters or sections, and one of these is fairly early, being the fourth—but it is nearly half-way through the book measured in terms of pages). The contents of these sheets, then, cannot have been composed earlier than 1866 (unless they are fair copies of material previously written, but this appears improbable in the case of all of them). Theoretically, they may, in the case of two of the chapters (IV and VII) have been written at any time between 1866 and the end of 1877, when Swinburne sent them to be set up in type. But as these are fairly early chapters, an earlier rather than a later date in this interval is far more likely. Narrower limits can be assigned in the case of three (IX, X, XI)—if not of all four—of the other chapters in question, as they were handed to Watts-Dunton by 1875. Since the three belong to the later part of the story, it is probable that the whole book was written before that date. This probability is considerably reinforced if the fourth too was sent to Watts-Dunton (a point that will be discussed later), for it is the last. Beyond that one can make no safe affirmation.

year,[1] after reference to other things, including a man who had written from Dublin to Swinburne threatening to castrate him because of the wickedness of his writings ('one can hardly believe', remarked Burton, 'in the existence of such a Yahoo so far removed from Australia!'), exhorted him to keep to the risky path along which he was advancing in this novel:

> 'Keep me au courant of the étude à la Balzac, which promises well. Remember Vestigia nulla retrorsum; you are bound to write for older and maturer men . . .'

The next extant reference to the book[2] is in a letter written by Swinburne on the 15th of November, 1870, to C. A.

[1] Letter in the British Museum.

[2] According to Wise, followed by Lafourcade (although not with absolute assurance), the next reference is in a letter written to Swinburne by Bayard Taylor from Pennsylvania on the last day of October, 1868. In this letter (now in the British Museum) Taylor speaks of a novel which he is trying to place for Swinburne in America:

> '. . . we have ascertained that Mr. Lippincott is willing to publish the novel anonymously, provided he finds nothing in it intrinsically objectionable. I think this is as good an offer as will be made, seeing that the author's name, and its corresponding service to the publisher, is withheld.'

Now it is certain that this work was not *Lesbia Brandon* (which Swinburne in any case could not have been trying to get published then, as it was not finished), but his earlier novel now known as *Love's Cross Currents*. From several letters it appears that Swinburne was anxious to publish this finished work anonymously. (Why anonymously? Was it because certain characters or events in it were too easily recognisable as coming from real life—perhaps from a circle which included relatives of the author, and maybe one person in particular? This is an interesting and perhaps profitable question that has never been so much as raised, let alone properly investigated.) Cf., e.g., an already mentioned letter of March 21st, 1866, on the subject of this novel: '. . . I think of bringing it out as it stands on the first occasion: not of course with my name appended . . .' Again, eleven years later, in a letter (now in the British Museum) written to Watts-Dunton early in 1877 he speaks as follows regarding the same work: '. . . an old MS. of mine . . . which has failed, as the anonymous work of an unknown writer, to find favour in the sight of any publisher. (I need not say

Howell, another crony and fellow in something beyond the abstract joys of freedom of thought. (To put it plainly, this one-time secretary of Ruskin was a connoisseur in the art of

(Note ² continued)—
that this . . . is in strict confidence "betwigst you and me" as Mrs. Gamp says . . .).' This insistence on 'strict confidence' is very striking. and when the work at last came out late in the same year in *The Tatler* (under the title of *A Year's Letters*) Swinburne resorted to a pseudonym. Anyhow, that it is the epistolary *Love's Cross Currents* that is referred to in Bayard Taylor's letter is decisively proved by the following passage from W. M. Rossetti's *Diary* for 1869:

'Monday, 25th January.—. . . Hotten . . . says Swinburne's novel in the form of letters (of which I have often heard, but never, I think, read any of it, only of a different and later novel) is being, or about to be, published anonymously in America. Swinburne offered it to Hotten himself; but he, thinking it would make little or no impression if anonymous, declined . . .'—(W. M. Rossetti, *Rossetti Papers*, 1903.)

The crass and ill-informed Lafourcade, although he cites the *Rossetti Papers* in his bibliography, missed this entry, or failed to see its importance for the point under discussion.

Another gross howler (and worse) of Wise to be noted at this stage is the following affirmation which immediately follows what he says about Bayard Taylor:

'It is evident that at a later date Swinburne submitted the novel, *Lesbia Brandon*, still unfinished, to the Cornhill Magazine. I have before me a letter, far too long to print, written by Leslie Stephen to the author, full of detached and kindly criticism, and declining the work . . .'—(*B.Bib.*, reproducing and enlarging entries in previous works of Wise).

This is richly characteristic of Wise. It is altogether wrong, and forgery is not absent from it. To begin with, there is no evidence whatsoever that the document (now in the British Museum), which bears the imprint of *The Cornhill Magazine* and is signed L. Stephen, is a letter to Swinburne, or that it is a letter at all: it has no 'Dear' anything at the beginning, no sort of epistolary opening, and no 'Yours' anything before the signature: it has all the appearance of a formal report on a novel that had been submitted to Stephen. But it was not a novel of Swinburne's; the report opens with the words 'Having read Mr. Brown's MS., I think that it shows much promise'. Mr. Brown was inconvenient for Wise, who had got it into his muddled head that *Lesbia Brandon* was the book in question. But this bibliographer who

flagellation and was ready to inflict and receive delight on and from others who liked that kind of thing.) Swinburne here makes the following remark *à propos* of a young Etonian cousin of his in whom he was chiefly interested as the recipient of a formidable number of sanguinary floggings at the school where he himself first became an addict of the birch:

> 'I didn't take Bertie Seyton's name from my cousin, who was too young for birch when I wrote that fragment six years ago or nearly(!) but you see a real live Herbert can wear out as much birch as any imaginary boy.'[1]

The 'or nearly' is probably uncalled for, as we know from the first of the letters cited in this conspectus that one if not all of the flogging-scenes in which Herbert Seyton figures was written before October 1864. The present letter not only helps to fix or confirm the date of composition of a portion of *Lesbia Brandon*, but it also indicates that that portion in

(Note [2] continued)—
was a forger as well as a fool, this worthy associate of Gosse, was not going to allow any inconvenience to stand in his way, even though it were the most solid of facts. So he simply suppressed Mr. Brown, and in his reproduction of the document gave the first sentence as follows: 'Having read the MS., I think it shows much promise'. Apart from this consideration, there is clear and ample evidence that *Lesbia Brandon* is not and can not be the work with which this report deals. To give only one or two examples, from passages not cited by Wise: Stephen criticises the character of an 'absent-minded uncle' in the book, but there is no such personage in *Lesbia Brandon*; again, Stephen animadverts upon the excessive use of the Devonshire accent in the book, but there is not a syllable of this accent in *Lesbia Brandon*. One knows that Wise was incapable of reading anything with more than asinine intelligence, but such things as this make one wonder if he ever read *Lesbia Brandon* at all. And this remark applies to Lafourcade, who refers to Stephen's document as a letter to Swinburne, and does not see that it can have nothing to do with *Lesbia Brandon*.

[1] Letter in the British Museum. It is dated only 18th November, but reference to another matter in it makes it pretty certain that 1870 was the year.

especial was well known to persons who were on particularly intimate terms with the author. In this connexion it is interesting to recall once again the letter of October 1864 in which he wrote to his cousin Mary Gordon as one who, like his fellow-flagellantist Howell, had been made privy to these passages.[1]

The next item in this catalogue is the following passage in a letter[2] dated the 23rd of June, 1873, from Watts-Dunton[3] to Swinburne:

[1] Probably they were both shown the passages in the same year, as it was in 1864 that Swinburne first met Howell. The latter's question, in 1870, about Herbert Seyton may of course mean that he had only recently become acquainted with the flogging-scenes. On the other hand, it may mean that he retained a lively memory of an exciting passage on one of his pet subjects read soon after it was written. And it is much more likely that, Howell being what he was, Swinburne brought it to his notice soon after he got to know him.

[2] Published by Mr. H. G. Wright in *The Review of English Studies*, Vol. X, No. 38, April 1934. Mr. Wright, in his comments on this letter, does not make any reference to the implications to which I draw attention; indeed he does not consider at all the question arising from mention of the two novels. Lafourcade gives the above-cited passage in *La Jeunesse de Swinburne*, but he omits the words 'in manuscript', with no indication that he has done so. It was only discovery of Mr. Wright's publication of a batch of letters from Watts-Dunton to Swinburne that enabled me to obtain the fuller text, for I had not found it possible to trace the original. One of the greatest difficulties with which the Swinburnian scholar has to contend is that items cited by Lafourcade as belonging to Wise's Ashley Collection when he had the run of it are no longer part of that Collection since its acquisition by the British Museum, and that Wise left no indication into whose hands they passed when, financially or otherwise, he feathered his already very comfortable nest by disposing of them: and thus they are almost as good as lost. Lafourcade does not realise the import of the date of this letter, following closely on Hotten's death; indeed he appears to know nothing at all of that side of Hotten's activities which I partially reveal in what follows. (Some years later, however, he was a little better instructed, and in his *Swinburne, a Literary Biography* (1932) he got as far as saying that Hotten 'was a publisher of dubious character', and that 'he was responsible for [sic] books dealing with flagellation etc'.)

[3] More properly Watts, who did not enlarge his name by the addition

'I saw Purnell[1] yesterday and he seemed to think that there are two novels of yours in manuscript lying at Hotten's place. What can this mean?'

The facts behind this letter, and the answer to the question of the evidently mystified Watts-Dunton, may be conjectured with a confidence not far removed from certitude.

Swinburne's publisher Hotten had died nine days previously, and Watts-Dunton (a solicitor among other things), who now looked after the business affairs of the poet, had been making enquiries as to how matters stood as between the latter and the firm that was perhaps going into dissolution. He had already enquired of Swinburne himself, in a letter dated the 19th:[2]

'Hotten is dead. Is there anything in connexion with the affairs between you and him which I do not know and which it may be important for me, now, to know? Has he any property of yours which should be demanded of the executors? You once mentioned some old plays . . .'

'anything between you and him which I do not know' may indicate that Watts-Dunton had a suspicion that certain matters had been kept back from him; but he may have had only the 'old plays' in mind, and had no *arrière-pensée* in

---

(*Note* ³ *continued*)—
of that of his mother's family till 1936. But I shall throughout use the appellation by which he is now generally known.

[1] Thomas Purnell, dramatic critic (under the pseudonym of 'Q'), of the *Athenaeum*, and founder of *The Tatler* to which Swinburne gave *Love's Cross Currents*. He was one of the more bohemian and (from a certain point of view) 'safe' of the poet's familiars.

[2] Cited by Mr. H. G. Wright, *loc. cit.* I have not been able to trace the original of this letter. Mr. Wright says that Watts-Dunton wrote 'with all speed' as a consequence of Hotten's death. But this event occurred on the 14th.

writing in these searching terms. Swinburne replied vaguely, not to say evasively, on the following day:[1]

'I do not remember that any property of mine was in the hands of Hotten except the copies of Chapman's different works, lent to him for use in his projected edition . . .'

The word 'property' is ambiguous here, and may be meant to cover only such things as books lent to Hotten, and not manuscripts of work written by the poet. But this is unlikely; and as Swinburne, if he had handed the manuscripts of at least any considerable compositions of the publisher, could hardly have forgotten the fact, one can only suppose that in this case there were things he wished to keep from Watts-Dunton's knowledge; and that this was indeed so in respect to matters of a certain category will be made clear presently.

After Swinburne's affirmation in his letter of the 20th, Watts-Dunton was naturally surprised to learn from Purnell, whom he had perhaps asked to investigate, and who evidently had not yet been put on his guard by Swinburne, that there were two novels of the latter lying in the publisher's office. And his words—'two novels of yours' and not 'your two novels'—show that he knew nothing about them.

They could only have been *Love's Cross Currents* and *Lesbia Brandon*. The former had been rejected by various publishers, including Hotten himself; as we have seen from a passage in W. M. Rossetti's *Diary*, he had declined it some years previously as being likely to 'make little or no impression if anonymous'. Perhaps Swinburne had urged it upon his attention again, or perhaps Hotten had spontaneously reconsidered his decision, and was taking another look at it. And it may well be that Swinburne had submitted the unfinished *Lesbia Brandon* to him, with a view to getting his ideas on it as far as it had gone, and not unnaturally expecting

---

[1] No. LXXXII of *Letters* in the Bonchurch edition; date June 20th [1873]. This is another letter of which I have not been able to trace the original.

that they would be favourable. For Swinburne's reputation was rapidly increasing, and it is altogether unlikely that he wanted *Lesbia Brandon* to come out anonymously; and even if he had done so this probably would not have been a serious objection with a publisher such as Hotten, and given the nature of certain parts of the book. Certainly Hotten would not have been put off by the *risqué* passages of either book, as doubtless other publishers had been in the case of the earlier of them.[1] For one of his specialities—a for the most part furtive side-line—was pornographic and cognate literature, and particularly works on the subject of flagellation; and more particularly fictional works in which it is treated as an erotic jollity with a luxury or riot of detail in which there is no kind of reserve. He may even be said to have been one of the chief London purveyors of this sort of entertainment, as I shall show, along with much other curious and novel matter, in my *Swinburne: the Arcane Side*, where many things that need only be glanced or hinted at in the present volume will be dealt with at greater length. It is enough to mention here by way of example, that in 1870 he had openly published *Flagellation and the Flagellants, a History of the Rod in all Countries*; and that two years later he more or less surreptitiously reprinted[2] *The Sublime of Flagellation, Lady Bumtickler's Revels, A Treatise of the Use of Flogging in Venereal Affairs*, the *Exhibition of Female Flagellants*, and, in addition to these four works, three others belonging to the same naughty tradition. Moreover—a point

---

[1] Cf. John Nichol's impression on reading the manuscript of *Love's Cross Currents*: '. . . I would be in favour of excising the passages I have marked . . . I think it inadvisable to mislead, possibly, the reader at starting into a hope or fear of a flagellation novel . . .' (Letter to Swinburne, Jan. 22, 1878; in British Museum.) Nichol was an old friend, liberal-minded, and a professor. The ordinary run of publishers would have been far more apprehensive than he about these passages; and there were much bolder things in *Lesbia Brandon*.

[2] For none of them were new or recent, and some had first appeared long before.

of more immediate concern—, when he was getting together
the materials for another work on the subject (apparently to
some degree his own this time: 'his abortive book on flagellation' says Swinburne in reference to it), he sought the aid of
the poet, who obligingly drew up for him a series of flogging
'scenes in school which he was to get sketched for me on
approval by a draughtsman of his acquaintance . . . , in which
list, though there was nothing equivocal or dirty in any way,
I had explained the postures and actions of 'swishing' to be
shown in detail, . . . with due effect and relief given to the
more important points of view during the transaction'. And
further on in the same unpublished epistolary passage Swinburne says: 'I see he advertises a new "Romance of the Rod"
as in preparation, to which I shall be happy to lend any assistance that I could, and so you might let him know if we are
to remain on terms.'[1] Hotten, then, was not the man to be
shocked or scared by any freedom in Swinburne's two novels;
it is only to be expected therefore that the poet should have
taken them to him for consideration (or further consideration
in the case of the one he had already refused); especially as
Hotten at this time was developing the above-mentioned side
of his business more actively than before; and it is very
probable that had he lived longer he not only would have
brought out *Love's Cross Currents*, but would have en-

[1] From a letter, now in the British Museum, to C. A. Howell, Feb. 6
[1873]. The incompetent and (in these matters) unprincipled Gosse
and Wise published this letter (with their customary errors of transcription) in the 1918 volume of the poet's *Letters* and later in the
Bonchurch edition of his works, but—with no sign whatsoever of
omission, according to their scandalous practice—they suppressed the
important section to which the passage we have cited belongs. As
already remarked, in consulting any letter of Swinburne's published
by these two loons one can never be sure that one is reading all that
the poet wrote nor even what he actually wrote in the passages which
their high-handed censorship thought fit to give to the world.

Lafourcade, in his *Swinburne, A Literary Biography* (1932) quotes
a portion of the unpublished section of this letter.

couraged Swinburne to complete *Lesbia Brandon* as a work that he would like to publish.[1]

His death at this stage was almost unquestionably a set-back to the fortunes of these two works, and in the cast of *Lesbia Brandon* a very serious one that was never retrieved. For his successor Chatto severely discontinued the *risqué* side of the business,[2] and it may be safely assumed that he was not encouraging about *Love's Cross Currents* (which had to wait another four years for publication elsewhere—and that not in volume-form), and that he was positively *dis*couraging about the unfinished bolder work, which, according to the author himself, was meant to be 'offensive and objectionable' to the moral standards of Britannia.

To return to Watts-Dunton in the present connexion: there is, in an unpublished letter[3] written by Swinburne to Howell three days after the last-mentioned one to the latter, a very significant sentence in reference to the 'swishing' scenes with which the poet had obligingly (and, we may be sure, not at all reluctantly) provided Hotten for one or other of his works on flagellation. 'As to the school list of course you will say nothing to anyone, least of all men to Watts.' That decisively gives Swinburne's attitude, in respect of certain of his activities and interests, and in particular on the subject to flagellation and the Sadist philosophy, to the legal adviser who gradually was to win acceptance as his best friend. If he had not already by this time (February, 1873) tested the

---

[1] I do not of course suggest that Swinburne's two novels were on the same level as the fore-mentioned publications; the latter are almost if not entirely worthless as literature, and are hardly even interesting to a reader who is not attracted by flagellation; in Swinburne's novels the flagellation is only incidental, and is always given the higher value of art.

[2] H. S. Ashbee, by far the best of the available authorities on these matters, records that 'immediately after his [i.e. Hotten's] demise all his books of a *doubtful* character, whether acquired or of his own publication, were at once disposed of . . . ; those gentlemen [i.e. his successors] have entirely relinquished that branch of the business'.

[3] Now in the British Museum.

latter's reaction to the doctrine of Sade and to hints on the attractions of flagellation, he had evidently at least sensed that in this quarter he would find no sympathy at all. Certainly, some fifteen months thence he had put the matter to the proof and had discovered that 'nothing was doing' where his very *bourgeois* solicitor was concerned.[1] For on July the 18th, 1874, we find him writing thus to Watts-Dunton:

'I deeply grieve at the incurable blindness and stiff-neckedness as of a new Pharoah which keeps you still in the gall of prejudice and the bond of decency, and debars you from the just appreciation of a Great Man—a bit of true human stuff (Carlyle) a deeper study of whose immortal work would have shown you

> *How charming is divine philosophy;*
> *Not harsh and crabbed, as dull fools suppose,*
> *But musical as is Priapus' pipe.*

I cannot but think that God must have hardened your heart—il en est bien capable; and nothing else *could* account for insensibility to the peculiar but surpassing merits of the Marquis . . .'[2]

More than that, Watts-Dunton, apparently, has been so shocked by what Swinburne had shown him of Sade that he had gone to the extent of putting his foot down and insisting that the subject must be taboo in conversation between them and also in a letter from Swinburne to him. Witness the following from another unpublished letter[3] written to him by the poet on the 27th of December, 1876:

[1] Lafourcade, in his *Swinburne, A Literary Biography*, says categorically that 'In July, 1874, Swinburne had introduced Watts to . . . the Marquis de Sade'. But he cites no evidence in support of this particular and improbably rather late date—for the good reason that there is none.

[2] Unpublished letter in the British Museum (or rather virtually unpublished: Wise gives a part of it in *A Swinburne Library*—and says with silly prudish exaggeration that much of the rest is 'unprintable').

[3] In the British Museum.

'. . . I must be allowed for once to mention the unmentionable and say how vividly I was reminded of the Marquis de Sade's attack on the memory of Mirabeau as—a writer of obscene and immoral works of fiction! . . .'

(Swinburne continued to slip in, from time to time, over a period of many years, and for long after his installation at Putney, mention of the unmentionable—'swishing' as well as the *opus Sadicum*—when writing to the friend who continued to be stiff-necked on this matter. It may be noted in passing that this is one of many things that show how absurd is the legend, coined by the malignancy of Gosse and sheepishly adopted by others, that Swinburne abdicated his independence after he became the friend of Watts-Dunton, and docilely followed or deferred to the opinion of the latter even in matters where he would naturally be of a different opinion. The truth is that he robustly maintained his independence—intellectual, moral and aesthetic—to the end of his life, and not least in opposition to the man whom for certain good reasons he regarded as his best friend (and who in other respects might be regarded as the opposite of that). But due explosion of this nonsensical legend, which ignorant fools go on repeating, must be postponed to a later occasion.

It is easy, then, to understand why Swinburne had not made Watts-Dunton acquainted with his two novels, in which flagellation and more audacious things had no small place; even though, being lodged with his publisher, they were part of the business matters in general over which he had given supervision to the lawyer of literary aspirations who was fast making himself indispensable as an agent or steward to him as well as to Rossetti in the boring practical side of life. But some four months after the poet's warning injunction to Howell, Watts-Dunton, owing to Hotten's death, and an indiscretion on the part of Purnell, got to know of the existence of the novels. Swinburne could not now very well withhold them from him altogether. Strangely enough, he did not let him see the milder of the two, and the one that was finished, *Love's Cross Currents* (about which he had previously shown himself mysteriously secretive, to the extent of insisting that he must not be known as the author of it).[1] But he did give him *Lesbia Brandon* to read. And if it was not immediately that he did so, it must have been—doubtless under pressure from Watts-Dunton—at no distant date in the future: for, writing to him less than four years later, in February, 1877, he speaks of having let him have it 'some years ago'. But before considering this letter further, there is a previous one that demands our attention. On the 21st of June, 1875, he wrote to Watts-Dunton as follows:

'On arranging my papers I find that many leaves and some whole chapters are wanting to the MS. I lent you, which you returned in several packets. (1) The first five leaves, numbered by you in pencil. (2) Two entire consecutive chapters, 'Turris Eburnea', and 'Another Portrait'. (3) Two incomplete chapters, 'An Episode' (I think that was the name) and 'La Bohême Dédorée'. As I have no copy of any part of the MS., I must ask you to find and send me these strays.'[2]

Watts-Dunton, then, had sent back parts of the manuscript by mid-1875, but still had other parts in his keeping. This letter

---

[1] Watts-Dunton, it appears, never saw it till it was published (pseudonymously) in *The Tatler* in the last five months of 1877. In a letter to him (now in the British Museum), dated the 14th of February of that year, Swinburne, speaking of the idea of bringing it out in that paper, says 'you have never seen nor I presume heard of it'. If he had never even heard of it (apart from vague mention by Purnell of its nameless existence), Swinburne must have carefully kept from him all knowledge of it as a work additional to *Lesbia Brandon* when, after Hotten's death, he got wind of 'two novels' lying in the office of the latter.

[2] Letter in the British Museum. Cited by Wise with an error—or rather a liberty—of transcription: he takes it upon himself to change a bracket of Swinburne's into dashes: gratuitous impudence of this sort is frequent on the part of this uneducated huckster who was much less than a tyro in the lowest stages of the art of writing.

also makes it clear that if *Lesbia Brandon* had been laid aside, it was only temporarily, and that Swinburne continued to think of it as one of his living enterprises.

In spite of Swinburne's request, becoming insistent and even peremptory with 'I must ask you to find and send me . . .', Watts-Dunton did not return the missing chapters. Such slackness was odd, very odd, on the part of a solicitor. He could not have ignored this letter; he must have put Swinburne off with some plea or other, such as that he had not yet had time to read the missing parts, or that he had yet to draw up his comments on them, or that he had mislaid them and would have a good look for them . . . But I have not been able to discover any answer from him to Swinburne's demand (and of course he may have replied orally when they next met). However, other activities intervened to divert Swinburne's attention from the matter, and, as far as can be seen from the extant correspondence, it was more than eighteen months before he returned to it. Beginning to occupy himself again with *Lesbia Brandon* in February 1877, he realised that Watts-Dunton had still not complied with his request, and he renewed it in terms even more pressing than on the previous occasion:

'I hope you will not curse me as a dun of a new and deadly kind if I reiterate an urgent request for the "missing links" of my old unfinished MS. story—*five* half-sheets of foolscap at the beginning, and two or three etc. chapters (complete and incomplete)—"Turris Eburnea', "Another Study", "An Episode" (study of characters of exiles and talk on foreign politics), and "La Bohême Dédorée"[1]—belonging

[1] Swinburne at first wrote: '. . . and one or two chapters—'Turris Eburnea' and 'An Episode' (or 'Another Episode')—belonging to another and late part of the design. It is of great moment to me . . .' Then, with erasures, substitutions, and interlinear additional matter, he altered it to what we have given in the text. Adding 'Another Study' to 'Turris Eburnea' and 'An Episode', he had to change 'one or two' to 'two or three'; then further adding 'La Bohême Dédorée', he had to extend the limit 'three', and he did so by writing 'etc.' after

to another and late part of the design. (There may be more, but I think not; these I know were parts of the MS. I lent you some years ago.) It is of great moment to me that I should have these fragments gathered together, though it may not be on such economical grounds as actuated the Founder of Christianity in his desire that nothing should be lost. The mutilated MS. is a constant fidget to my nerves, and an open sore in my memory.'[2]

(Note [1] continued)—

'La Bohême Dédorée' and joining it by a line to 'three'; the point is that he meant it to follow 'three' and not 'La Bohême Dédorée' (which completed the list); but he wrote it after the latter to indicate that it was this that made necessary a further extension of the original number. He really ought to have changed 'two or three' to 'three or four', but he had got to the end of the line and was hard up for space. Wise, and Lafourcade following him, take 'etc.' as readily following 'La Bohême Dédorée'; this—besides raising a (non-existent) problem—is at variance with Swinburne's own statement a couple of lines down that he does not think there is anything further to add to the list.

This is a good example of the difficulties one has to contend with if one has to rely on Wise and Gosse and Lafourcade for rtanscripts of anything written by Swinburne. Nearly if not absolutely always there are errors in their transcripts; and it is not always possible to check the latter, for, as I have already observed, in many cases the originals are no longer in the Ashley Collection, and are so hard to trace, if traceable at all, that for practical purposes they are lost.

[2] Letter dated February 11th (1877 on envelope); now in British Museum; cited by Wise (and by Lafourcade slavishly following him) with errors and gross liberties of transcription.

Keeping in mind the chronological order of documents, we may note here two very crass errors on the part of Wise. In the *Bonchurch Bibliography* he cites as referring to *Lesbia Brandon* passages of two letters from Nichol to Swinburne: one dated January 22nd, 1877, and the other January 28th of the same year (Wise wrongly gives 1876). But both these passages quite manifestly refer not to *Lesbia Brandon*, but to *Love's Cross Currents*, of which Swinburne had sent the manuscript to Nichol with a view to getting his opinion on it. What is more, Wise himself, in his own *A Swinburne Library*, had already rightly given the two passages (with the correct date of the later letter) as referring to the earlier of the two novels!

This letter is valuable as confirming the previous list of the missing parts ('Another Study' is undoubtedly the same as 'Another Portrait' of the earlier catalogue, Swinburne's memory going slightly astray here);[1] it is also valuable as indicating the probable if not certain order of the chapters named, and a stage of the composition at which the story is drawing to an end; and it is even more valuable as showing that Swinburne still, in 1877,—some fourteen years after beginning it—, thought of the work as being on the stocks, and attached so much importance to it that it was now an obsession with him.

What plausible or supple reply the solicitor sent this time we again do not know; but, as will appear from a letter to be cited later, he still failed to restore the missing parts to the anxiously expectant poet! Slackness was perhaps the wrong word; one's suspicion grows that there was something deeper in the extraordinary failure of this provincial man of law and respectability to return to his client and friend property so urgenty demanded on more than one occasion . . .

Three days later, in a long letter to Watts-Dunton *à propos* of his projected handing over of the manuscript of *Love's Cross Currents* to Purnell for publication in *The Tatler* Swinburne makes the following remark; 'I have been writing to you . . . rather in the spirit and style of Master Herbert Seyton, if you do him the honour to remember anything of the name or nature of that young gentleman'.[2]

---

[1] As we have already seen (the last footnote but one), he wavered over this title, and at first wrote 'Another Episode', as a possible alternative to 'An Episode'; then he remembered that 'An Episode' was indeed the right title of *that* chapter, but that there was 'Another' something: here however he was unable to recall the noun.

[2] Letter dated February 14th (1877 on envelope); now in British Museum. Although Wise cites this letter in connexion with *Love's Cross Currents*, he fails (and so does Lafourcade after him) to give the reference in it to *Lesbia Brandon* in his no doubt would-be exhaustive section on this latter novel. I do not know what Swinburne was thinking of when he said 'I have been writing to you . . . rather in the spirit and style of Master Herbert Seyton'. For Master Herbert Seyton never

Herbert Seyton, of course, is the central character of *Lesbia Brandon*, and has a place in no other work. It is curious that, having mentioned him, Swinburne did not further reiterate his request for the portions of the novel which were still in the tenacious keeping of Watts-Dunton: but perhaps he considered that enough time had not elapsed for the sending and reception of a reply to so recent a communication.

Certainly there was no falling-off in his lively concern and enthusiasm for the work; it continued to be an obsession, something central to which he constantly swung back, and compared to which all other work was no more than marginal. This is well shown by a very interesting entry in Gosse's journal, describing Swinburne as the critic found him four months after he had addressed the last-mentioned of his reclamations to Watts-Dunton:

'June 11th, 1877. A.C.S. having summoned me to go to his rooms on Saturday evening for the particular purpose of hearing a new essay he had written on Charlotte Brönte, I duly arrived at 3 Great James Street about 8. Algernon was standing alone in the middle of the floor, with one hand in the breast of his coat, and the other jerking at his side. He had an arrangement of chairs, with plates and glasses set on the table, as if for a party. He looked like a conjuror, who was waiting for his audience. He referred vaguely to 'the others', and said that while they delayed in coming, he would read me a new poem he had

(Note ² *continued*)—
writes anything, and he does very little talking, in *Lesbia Brandon* as we have it. Can it be that there is a lost part of the novel that would dispose of this difficulty? Or did Swinburne use 'style' very loosely and mean only 'spirit'? Other words of the same letter indicate that this may be so: 'exuberance of gushing chatter on all subjects of personal and egoistic excitement that may spring up to right or left', which he fears he may have dropped into on this occasion, could no doubt be regarded as a tendency of the autobiographic hero of *Lesbia Brandon*, however little that tendency is actually expressed in the novel as far as it was carried by Swinburne.

just finished, called "In the Bay", which he said he should
solemnly dedicate to the spirit of Marlowe. He brushed
aside some of the glasses and plates, and sat down to read.
The poem was very magnificent, but rather difficult to
follow, and very long. It took some time to read; and still
no one came. As the evening was slipping away, I asked
him presently whether the reading of C. Brontë should not
begin, whereupon he answered, "I'm expecting Watts and
Ned Burne-Jones and Philip Marston, and—some other
men. I hope they'll come soon". We waited a little while in
silence, in the twilight, and then Swinburne said, "I hope I
didn't forget to ask them!" He then trotted or glided into
his bedroom, and what he referred to there I don't know,
but almost instantly he came out and said cheerfully, "Ah!
I find I didn't ask any of those men, so we'll begin at
once." He lighted his two great candlesticks of serpentine
and started. He soon got tired of reading the Essay, and
turned to the delights, of which he never wearies, of his
unfinished novel. He read two long passages, the one a ride
over a moorland by night, the other the death of his heroine, *Lesbia Brandon*. After reading aloud all these things
with his amazing violence, he seemed quite exhausted, and
sank in a kind of dream into the corner of his broad sofa,
his tiny feet pressed tight together, and I stole away."[1]

[1] Cited in Gosse's *Life* of Swinburne. The two passages referred to
are in the seventh and the sixteenth chapters, and are probably the
whole of those chapters. The fact that he read these to Gosse suggests
the possibility that he had recently written or completed them, or had
to some extent been working on them; for it was his habit to read to
his friends compositions which he had just, or not long since, finished,
and about which the first flush of enthusiasm was still upon him. I do
not know of any case where he thus read work written some time
previously—so far back that there could be no question of the heat of
creation being still astir in him, and prompting him to communicate
what he had turned out. The available watermark dates are of no
assistance here; the sole one of the sixteenth chapter—1863 on one
sheet—may be very misleading to those who, like Wise, depend on
this evidence for fixing the time of the actual composition.

'The delights, of which he never wearies, of his unfinished novel: thus Gosse, who after the author's death impertinently and gratuitously took it upon himself to withhold the novel from publication, testifies to the dominant degree to which it counted in Swinburne's life. 'Of which he never wearies' implies that he constantly referred to it in conversation with his friends—much more than he does in such as of his correspondence as is available.

The mention of Watts in this passage reminds us that Swinburne, being now more or less permanently settled in London since the death of his father in the previous March, was by way henceforth of seeing him personally, and could get at him more effectively about what he had failed to return of the novel. But whatever he did—and he certainly must have done something—Watts-Dunton still managed to maintain himself intractable. The situation is very curious—something of a mystery, and no light is thrown on it by any documents accessible to research. Partial explanation may once again be found in the fact that Swinburne was usually occupied by more than one creative venture at a time, and thus his attention may really have been distracted from the novel even in this period, when it had become the greatest thing in his life. A more satisfying explanation of his not bringing Watts-Dunton to heel is that in the latter part of this year (1877), as in the summer and autumn of the previous year, his health was very bad, and was to be so intermittently until the end of 1879, when Watts-Dunton carried him off to Putney. Thus on September 18th, 1877, he tells Gosse in a note that he 'can just manage painfully to scrawl a line . . .'[1]

Howell, writing to him on the 2nd of October, says 'I am truly sorry to hear you are so seedy';[2] he informs Howell on the 8th of that month that he has 'been prostrate for weeks . . . days together in bed . . .';[3] and in January 1878, writing to an

[1] Letters 1918 and Bonchurch *Letters*.
[2] Unpublished letter, now in British Museum. I have failed to discover the note from Swinburne to which this is a reply.
[3] Letter in British Museum.

American correspondent of whom he had come across an un-answered letter dated October 12th, he excuses himself on the score of 'an intermittent illness of some months' duration', which is probably that referred to in the other letters mentioned here. 'During my illness', he proceeds, 'my books, papers and parcels have got into such confusion that for two days I thought I had lost the most important manuscript I have of unpublished verse and prose combined. That has turned up . . .'[1]

Thus—but this only increases our difficulty—even through-out this bad period and after it he continued to think of *Lesbia Brandon* as 'the most important' of all his unpublished works.

The next discoverable item of information in the history of the novel is that Swinburne decided to have it set up in print. Why?[2] Partly no doubt, because he wanted to see how

---

[1] Letter to P. H. Hayne, January 15th, 1878, cited in part by Lafourcade in *Swinburne, A Literary Biography* (Lafourcade also cites a smaller portion of the same section of this letter in *La Jeunesse de Swinburne*, but here he omits—with no indication that he has done so—one of the important words). I have not been able to trace the original. The tense of 'has turned up' is odd; one expects a preterite in a letter written in January 1878, since the manuscript must have turned up at least by mid-November of the previous year, for, as we shall see presently, it was round about that time that Swinburne handed it to Chatto to be set up in type. Query: is 1878 the right date of this letter?

[2] Lafourcade, in his *Swinburne, A Literary Biography*, referring to the latter months of 1875, says that Swinburne 'was now again thinking of publishing' 'the long-forgotten novel *Lesbia Brandon*'. This is one of the more silly of the portentous number of inexcusable errors committed by this master of *bêtise*, for whom other dunderheads naturally have the highest esteem. In fact, there are no grounds for saying that the work was long forgotten; Swinburne had never before thought of publishing it, and he could not have done so, as it was unfinished (he himself describes it as such in one of the afore-cited letters to Watts-Dunton—which Lafourcade gives in his jumbled array of evidence!); and for the same reason he could not have thought of doing so at any time in the period to which Lafourcade refers.

it looked in print (being perhaps like Rossetti, who said 'I can never see my work clearly till in print',[1] a feeling that is no doubt common to the great majority of writers). Partly also, doubtless, because, after his recent scare, he feared the manuscript might really get lost, and wished, against this eventuality, to have copies of it on hand. This was not the first time he had had unfinished work set up in type before there was any question of publishing it; for instance, he had done so in the case of the first act, and part of the second, of *Bothwell*, three years before the play first came out.[2]

While he was about it, he decided to have printed also all that he had done of *Mary Stuart* (Act I and part of the first scene of Act II), and *John Jones*, a parody of Browning that was not published till some twelve years later.[3]

---

[1] Unpublished letters to Swinburne, now in the British Museum. It was a habit of Rossetti's to have 'trial-sheets' or 'trial-books' of his poems printed, and Swinburne may have caught the idea from him.

[2] Frederick Locker-Lampson wrote the following note on the fly-leaf of his copy of this imprint: 'I got these pages printed for Swinburne by Davey from his MS. as he feared he might lose it; he had half a dozen copies printed . . .' Cited by Wise, *S.Lib.* and *B.Bib.*

[3] There is no reason at all to suppose, as do Wise, and Lafourcade meekly following him, that Swinburne got his manuscripts mixed up and inadvertently sent those of these two latter works instead of other sheets of *Lesbia Brandon*. No evidence exists that he had any other sheets of the novel at the time (it must be remembered that Watts-Dunton still had a good part of it). Moreover, Swinburne, in a complaining letter to Chatto—to be cited presently—regarding the printing, does not indicate that he had found absolutely missing any section of what he thought he had handed over; when he does specify missing parts, he only names portion that were actually printed but of which he had not received the 'slips'. Again, he twice in letters to Lord Houghton (July 11th and November 21st, 1879) says that 'the first act of *Mary Stuart* has been some time in type'; which does not suggest that it was due to inadvertence on his part; if anything, it rather suggests that he had meant to have it done. A final clinching consideration: the idea—implicit in Wise's and Lafourcade's theory—that he was so obfuscated, for whatever cause, when putting his sheets together for the printers that he mistook pages of blank verse and

What follows in the next few pages will no doubt seem at
first sight excessive attention to a number of tiresome details
that might have been passed over, or dismissed in a couple of
sentences. But it is necessary for two reasons to go somewhat
closely into this particular transaction. In the first place, the
only hitherto available account (that of Wise and Lafourcade
in his wake) of this part of the history of *Lesbia Brandon* is
almost entirely wrong, and it is desirable that even in record
of the humblest matters error should be replaced by truth.
Secondly, there are certain points involved which have a not
unimportant bearing on one of the main themes of this
chapter—the mystery or problem of the frustration of a work
that was one of Swinburne's most cherished designs for a large
part of his life. We have here further elements of a sort of
detective story—in which unfortunately there is more conjecture and probability than sure detection of the ways of the
criminal.

Swinburne very probably gave this lot of manuscripts to
Chatto and Windus in the first week of November.[1] Some of

(Note³ continued)—
other pages of humorous lyrical verse for parts of *Lesbia Brandon* is so
ludicrously fantastic that it is not worth serious examination.

Lafourcade says that Swinburne 'sent the manuscript of *Lesbia
Brandon* to the printers in the teeth of Watt's opposition'. But there
is not the least evidence that this was so. In no document is there
any sign that Watts-Dunton tried to dissuade the poet from having the
work set up in type. What arguments could he have used against Swinburne's decision? It is true that it was in the teeth of his opposition
that Swinburne published *Love's Cross Currents* in *The Tatler*, but
that is another matter, and probably Lafourcade got the two cases
confused.

[1] Lafourcade, with characteristic looseness, says 'a la fin de 1877'.
According to Wise, 'In the autumn of 1877 Swinburne one day entered
the office of his publishers, Messrs. Chatto and Windus, and handed to
the late Andrew Chatto a parcel of manuscript, informing him that
this contained the MS. of an unfinished novel, and instructing him
to have it at once set up in type.' Wise offers no evidence in support
of this richly circumstantial story (adopted in part by Lafourcade),
and it appears that in all its details it is an invention of the irresponsible fancy of this forger.

the galley sheets bear a small adhesive printers'[1] label, and on a few of these[2] is written a date; the earliest of these dates is November the 14th, and it is on a label attached to the first of the sheets. Indicating the day on which that sheet was printed, it suggests that the whole set of manuscripts was received not long before that date. There was no delaying crisis in the printing business in those good old days.

The last of the dates is December the 21st,[3] and the label bearing it is affixed to a sheet about midway through the work. The printers evidently were far from considering the job urgent; at this rate it was probably finished in the second or third week of January. Anyhow, it is towards the end of the third week that we find Swinburne occupied with the outcome of the job. The following letter from him carries no address, no date, not even the name of the person addressed, but, as we shall see presently, it was as good as certainly written in London to Chatto on the 20th of the month:[4]

[1] Spottiswoode and Co., not Eyre and Spottiswoode, as Wise says.

[2] Six, to be exact; which Wise's mind registers as 'many'.

[3] Wise says December 5th! This is one of a vast number of almost incredible blunders which show that Wise cannot be trusted to get even the most rudimentary matters right. The dates I give are on sheets in the set in the Ashley Collection (now in British Museum), which was Wise's own property, and to which he refers in his wildly erratic historic survey of *Lesbia Brandon*.

[4] In British Museum. Wise speaks of it as if it actually bore Chatto's name; and, failing to see its connexion with other letters, and misled by the 'care of . . .', he says it was written from Glasgow. Had this been the case, Swinburne would have written Nichol's address in the normal place at the right hand top of the paper before the actual letter. (He was on the eve of going to stay with Nichol for a month.)

It may be mentioned in passing that the *Cyril Tourneur* and *The School of Shakespeare* of which Swinburne asks for copies, and which in the context have the air of being works of his own, are the *Plays and Poems of Cyril Tourneur* by Churton Collins and *The School of Shakespeare* (a collection of plays, *Nobody and Somebody, Histrio-Mastrix, Faire Em*, etc.), edited by Richard Simpson. The former, dedicated to Swinburne 'with respect and affection', came out in 1878; the latter bears the same date, but the rubber stamped date of the British Museum copy, indicating time of acquisition, is November 2, 1877.

'Dear Sir,

Please send me by return of post if possible a set of the proofs of my new series of poems (including the last sonnets printed)—and the remaining sheets of my unfinished novel, of which the MS. is still in your hands, as you reminded me when I last called and was afraid it had been lost or mislaid. I want these at once for a particular and important reason. Send also copies of Cyril Tourneur and the School of Shakespeare.

Yours truly,

A. C. SWINBURNE.

(Care of John Nichol, Esq.,
14 Montgomerie Crescent,
Kelvinside,
Glasgow).'

There is a difficulty at the outset here: to which noun, 'sheets' or 'novel', does the pronoun 'which' in the phrase 'of which the MS.' relate? If to the former, then only a part of the manuscript that had gone to the printers is in question; if to the latter, then Swinburne means the whole of the manuscript he had sent to be set up in type. Fortunately a sentence in the next letter to be cited settles this difficulty: it is there made evident that the pronoun relates to 'sheets', and so it is only to the manuscript of the text on those sheets that Swinburne is here referring. This point disposed of, the following may be gathered from this letter. At the time it was written Swinburne had received *some* galley sheets and the corresponding part of the manuscript; he thought he had also received on this occasion the manuscript of the as yet undelivered galleys as well (i.e. the whole of the manuscript he had given to his publishers), and finding this latter portion missing, he feared it had been 'lost or mislaid', but, calling on Chatto and Windus, was informed that they still had it. The 'particular and important reason' for which he wanted the remaining galley sheets was that he intended to show the work to Nichol, whom he was about to visit, and who had given a highly gratifying verdict on *Love's Cross Currents* when, about a year previously, he had seen it in manuscript.

Much—and what is most essential—of this interpretation of the letter is confirmed by part of another letter which Swinburne wrote in London to Watts-Dunton on the 20th of January:[1]

'I was in hopes to have seen you yesterday by or before 1 o'clock, as I thought we had agreed, but I suppose you found it impossible to keep the engagement. I stayed in some time over the hour, and consequently when I did go out I found Chatto's shop shut—whereat, like the heroine of Gabriel Rossettis poem 'The Bride's Chamber', I 'cursed God and lived'. He (Chatto, not God) had promised to send me yesterday the MS (and the proofs in slips) of the part still remaining in his hands[2] of my fragmentary novel (or whatever you call it—by any other name it would smell quite as sweet) containing some of the best verses in the book, which I particularly want to show to Nichol. May I ask you to be good enough to take him by the throat (morally) and make him *at once* send me proofs at least to Nichol's address which is 14 Montgomerie Crescent

Kelvinside,

Glasgow.

[1] In British Museum. Partially cited, with errors of transcription, by Wise; ignored by Lafourcade, in spite of its importance as a document in the history of *Lesbia Brandon*. The letter is dated only January 20, and there is no address on the note-paper. But the year, '78, is given by the postal stamp on the envelope; and London W.C. is stamped on the front, and London S.W. on the back, of the envelope: the former of these is Swinburne's postal district, and the latter Watts-Dunton's.

[2] These words, 'the MS. . . . of the part still remaining in his hands', prove that 'which' in the ambiguous clause 'the remaining sheets of my unfinished novel, of which the MS. is still in yours hands', in the preceding letter, goes with 'remaining sheets' and not with 'novel'.

'You will pardon me bothering you once again about the missing chapters and fragments of my "novel" aforesaid—I could not possibly re-write them, and as I certainly mean to complete the book some day their loss or destruction would be a serious business to me. Especially I should regret the chapters respectively describing a woman of the demi-monde (a chapter most warmly and generously applauded by George Meredith), and an exiled[1] Italian Patriot, of whom William Rossetti inaccurately remarked that he was the only adult of tolerably decent character in the whole book. It is the fate of all great moralists like myself to be misunderstood in this world. Happily (as the Very Rev. Richard Burton would say) we know that there is a reward laid up for us in another.'

It appears, *inter alia,* from this important letter than Swinburne thought 'the remaining sheets' (mentioned in the previous letter) were only those of the long chapter where Lady Wariston sings a number of verses while waiting for the news of her lover's death (unless 'containing' here means 'containing among other things', which is not at all likely); that he had tackled Chatto about them; and that, the latter having undertaken and failed to let him have them by the 19th or the 20th, he had arranged that he and Watts-Dunton should go together to get them from Chatto's office. This arrangement having fallen through, he wrote to ask Watts-Dunton to bring pressure to bear on Chatto. But, to make doubly sure, he also wrote to Chatto at the same time. That is how I situate and interpret the former of these two letters (the one without date, address, and the name of the recipient), taken in conjunction with that of the 20th. This conjecture is borne out by a letter written the following day (the 21st) by Chatto and Windus to Watts-Dunton:

---

[1] This appears as 'excited' in Wise's copy of the letter!

'Mr. Swinburne asks us to return the manuscript of his novel, which we sent to you with the proofs. Will you kindly let us have it back, that we may do so.'[1]

The publishers would have been more accurate if, instead of 'the manuscript of his novel', they had said 'the manuscript of the part which he has not yet received'; and they should have mentioned that he had asked for proofs as well; but they doubtless dashed off a note with more haste than care in their bewilderment before two sets of instructions so confusingly at variance. For evidently Watts-Dunton had intimated to them that what they still had of *Lesbia Brandon*, proofs and manuscript, should be delivered to him.

Swinburne, meanwhile, arrived in Glasgow, further examined what 'proofs in slips' he had of the novel, and wrote another letter to his publishers specifying exactly what he had not yet received. This letter is apparently not extant, but there is a reference to it in yet another one he wrote to Chatto on the 31st of January, doubtless because the former had been ineffective; and also because he had by this later date discovered that eleven other slips were not among those he had:

'Dear Sir,
    Please send me at once a copy of my Essay on Blake; also another proof of pages 17-32 (inclusive) of my new volume of poems . . . I must again beg you to let me have with all possible speed the remaining slips of my unfinished "novel" which I specified in my last note and which I particularly want at once. The slip numbered 49 breaks off in the

[1] In British Museum. Wise only gives a paraphrase of this letter, ignoring the statement that proofs as well as MS. had been sent to Watts-Dunton. And Lafourcade, failing to take account of this communication, which was among the materials to which he had access, only mentions proofs as having been sent to the latter, and, moreover, he says 'Il me *semble* [my italics] que . . . l'imprimeur ait envoyé certaines épreuves à Watts au lieu de Swinburne'.

middle of a sentence, at the words "and he would"—the next page of the MS. begins "have gone into seas where" etc.*

With thanks for the other books and magazines received.

I am,

Yours very truly,

A. C. SWINBURNE.

* I want also the slips 32-42. The whole is well printed, with few errors, but most carelessly arranged."[1]

The words 'the next page of the MS. begins . . .' apparently indicate that he had taken part of the manuscript with him, as well as the proofs of that part (for it is hardly likely that he was quoting from memory). It also appears that he had with him part of the afore-mentioned chapter where Lady Wariston is waiting to hear of her lover's death, but that one or more other parts of it were missing; for slip 49 is one of those that belong to this chapter. The poor publishers of course could not satisfy his demand, as Watts-Dunton had the rest of the slips (as well as the corresponding part of the manuscript). They doubtless passed Swinburne's urgent letters on to him, and took it for granted that he would do the right thing. They certainly, as is clear from the next letter to be quoted, sent Swinburne at an indeterminable date a note, no longer available, telling him that the remaining proofs and the corresponding manuscript had been despatched to Watts-Dunton before the first of his demands reached them.

But Watts-Dunton behaved here with the same slackness (and, the conviction still grows, more than slackness) as he had shown about restoring certain of the chapters of the novel some four years before; (and Swinburne, chafingly alive again to this fact, especially as he had not been able to send these chapters to the printers, had once more, in his letter of the

[1] Letter now in the possession of Mr. J. S. Mayfield, Washington, U.S.A., to whose kindness I am indebted for a correct copy of it. Wise partially cites it with the errors and liberties that are to be expected of him.

20th, pressed him to render up what he was unconscionably hanging on to). He had not acquiesced in the publishers' request that he should return proofs and manuscript to them so that they could send them to the agitated poet (this, deducible from the preceding letter, is evident from the one that follows); nor had he himself sent the latter the proofs named as missing in the letter of the 20th; he had not even, by the end of the month, apprised Swinburne of the explanatory letter written to him on the 21st by the publishers when the poet's impossible demand came in. In short, he had done nothing at all. He did, finally, however, tell Swinburne of the publishers' communication, but it was more than a fortnight after he had received it, for the missive giving news of it did not reach Swinburne till the 7th of February, the date of the following letter, in which the poet replies to him from Glasgow. (It also appears from this letter than in the interval since the 31st of January Swinburne had received the rest of the slips of the chapter in which Lady Wariston is waiting for news of her lover's suicide. Whether he got this from Watts-Dunton or from the publishers is not clear; probably it was from the latter, for he speaks as if Watts-Dunton still had the slips of this chapter which he had received from the publishers (there were several sets of slips, and the publishers no doubt still had one or more from which they could let him have this chapter). That so precious a document should 'somehow have got mislaid' after reaching him may be taken as an indication of the sort of good time he was having at Glasgow in the convivial company of his old Balliol crony Nichol and other congenial spirits—the young John Davidson was one of them—with whom Nichol had brought him in contact.[1] It was no doubt because of the perilous chances of

---

[1] Lafourcade, speaking of the bad effects of this month on Swinburne's health, says that during it 'he had enough energy to . . . put together the scattered fragments of *Lesbia Brandon*' (*Swinburne, A Literary Biography*). But he had already done this, as far as possible (Lafourcade forgets that Watts-Dunton still withheld a part of the

this 'boisterous month', as Gosse calls it, that he went as dangerously far in another direction as to request Watts-Dunton to keep in his possibly all too retentive custody all of the manuscript that had reached him from the publishers.

'I am especially glad of the note just received as it gives me occasion to assure you that I was (and expressed myself) as much astonished as yourself at Chatto's truly unaccountable conduct in sending you the proofs and MS. of my unfinished book. Please don't on any account send any part of the MS. hither; but if you have by you the proofs of the chapter where the heroine, waiting to hear of her lover's death, sings songs (French and North-English) to her children, please send them at once. I had them here, but somehow they have got mislaid.'[2]

And so Watts-Dunton had told Swinburne he was 'astonished' at Chatto's action in sending to him, Watts-Dunton, the slips and what remained of the manuscript . . . One cannot help having very serious doubts as to the sincerity of this astonishment . . . This solicitor is a wily bird, is one's gathering impression. It is most improbable that a publisher would, spontaneously and uninstructed, send proofs and MS. to anybody save the author himself. There is only one person from whom Chatto could have received the instructions on which he acted . . . And Watts-Dunton did not keep his appointment with Swinburne (another strange thing on the part of a solicitor). Had he done so of course Swinburne would have got to Chatto's in time, and would have secured slips and manuscript; and then of course he, Watts-Dunton, would not have received them. Or alternatively, Swinburne would have

(*Note* [1] *continued*)—
work), in the previous November, with a view to having it set up in type.
   [2] Cited by Wise (in *B.Bib.* only). I have not been able to trace the original. The letter in which Swinburne had 'expressed' his surprise was probably the no longer extant one in which he had specified what slips he had yet to receive.

discovered (at an earlier date than suited Watts-Dunton) that
Chatto had already sent them to the solicitor, in spite of his
recent promise (which proves that Swinburne's own instructions had been) to send them to Swinburne himself, and
Swinburne would have insisted that Watts-Dunton should
give them up . . . In any case, it would be awkward for Watts-
Dunton if Swinburne saw Chatto on the 19th; and if he did
not see him then it was a fairly safe assumption that he would
not be able to do so before his departure within the next
twenty-four hours or so for a long stay at a conveniently
remote place in the North. The essential facts are that slips
and MS. were in Chatto's hands when Swinburne 'last called'
on him, that he had undertaken to let Swinburne have them,
that before the 21st they had been sent to Watts-Dunton, and
that on the 19th the latter did not keep his appointment with
Swinburne. Whichever way one looks at these facts, and the
more one looks at them, the whole affair has a decidedly fishy
appearance.

This is the last available letter or other analogous document
in which there is any mention of this particular matter, or any
specific or direct reference to *Lesbia Brandon*. The book
never came out. What really happened? What is the true
story, the exact explanation of the external facts we have
given and of the non-appearance of the work in the long
years that remained to the poet? With the evidence at one's
disposal, it is impossible to get at the precisely exact truth,
impossible to do more than approximate to it: but (the evidence being what it is) there can be no reasonable doubt that
one is really on the way to it and pretty close to it.

We have seen from more than one letter that for Swinburne
himself the work was one of his dearest, most important,
undertakings, and he stated categorically in his letter to
Watts-Dunton of the 20th of January, 1878, that he 'certainly
meant to complete' it at some time in the future.[1] Even as

---

[1] One of Wise's most asinine pronouncements is the following: 'The
manuscript is quite complete [it certainly is not, and that on more
than the count we are at present considering], and the story is brought

late as 1884, in an indirect epistolary reference to it, he speaks of it as something still dear to him which he had not yet come to think of as abandoned:

'. . . Some day perhaps I shall take heart of grace to ask for your frank opinion on certain crude attempts of my own at novel-writing, or more properly at studies of life and character in our own day. Among the two or three friends who have seen anything of them Watts thinks little, but Nichol thinks much of them, so that *I* know not what to think . . .'[2]

But he never completed it; and the fact that five years later

(Note [1] *continued)*—

to a conclusion with the death of Lesbia. When Swinburne spoke of it as "unfinished" he meant that the work had still to receive its final polish.' That in spite of Swinburne's own description, in letters cited by Wise himself, of certain of the chapters as 'incomplete'; and of serious lacunae or gaps in the story obvious to the most cursory inspection of any intelligence higher than that of Wise, his associate Gosse, his follower Lafourcade, and later numskulls who can make no advance beyond this trinity.

[2] Letter to Mrs. Lynn Linton; in Bonchurch *Letters*. I have not been able to discover the original of this important letter, of which both Lafourcade and Wise take no account at all in their sorry attempts to give the history of *Lesbia Brandon*. Swinburne must refer particularly to the latter work in it, for *Love's Cross Currents* had been seen by more than 'two or three friends', and anyhow it had appeared some years before in *The Tatler*, and the authorship of it was an open secret.

Mrs. Lynn Linton (1822–1898), a novelist, and a very popular one in her own day, had been closely associated with Landor; this was the chief reason of Swinburne's very friendly feelings for her. It is perhaps also worth while recalling that in 1870 she wrote thus to W. M. Rossetti: 'All my life I have been ridiculed for my love of Shelley, and told how his poetry has been my ruin . . .' Three years previously she had parted amicably from her husband. A very interesting short book might be written on her and her set.

he took a large number of the verses[1] from it and published them in the third series of *Poems and Ballads* (1889) may be regarded as indicating that at this date he had indeed given it up for good.[2] This, then, is the last item in the history of this frustrate work in the lifetime of the poet. Even after his death the frustration continued with the scandalously absurd embargo which Gosse, strangely endowed with plenary rights, took it upon himself to impose on the publication of a novel that had in it masterpieces of beauty.

It is possible (but not probable) that the fact that Swinburne did not complete the work was partly because he could not do so in a way to satisfy himself. As in the case of *Bothwell*,

---

[1] Wise says that the poems of *Lesbia Brandon* were 'introduced into the text as being said or sung by the several characters' (*B.Bib.*1; they were said or sung not even by several, let alone by *the* several, characters, which in ordinary English means all those that appear in the book.

[2] Wise, in his barbarous speech, and with his usual blundering confidence says: 'It is evident that in 1878 he certainly made a commencement at revising and arranging the novel before renouncing it for ever'. And Lafourcade, at his heels, gives the same year as that in which the work was 'définitivement abandonné'. Lafourcade also tries to make out that there was an earlier, practically definitive, abandonment, in 1867, owing to the influence of Mazzini. He has a theory that under that influence Swinburne made a 'complete' break with his artistic past, one consequence of which was that he gave up work on *Lesbia Brandon*; the theory is so palpably ludicrous that refutation of it is scarcely necessary. In any case, part of *Lesbia Brandon* itself, and not only that dealing with Mariani and Sadier, is written under the influence of Mazzini. Lafourcade, suddenly recalling this inconvenient fact, says that Swinburne tried 'to reconcile Mazzini and "l'art pour l'art" '—but found that it was useless. Even with this qualification Lafourcade's contention remains untrue. 'As early as October 1866 . . .' says Lafourcade, 'Swinburne had *spontaneously* turned from Rossetti and his followers in art (l'art pour l'art) to Italy and Mazzini'. But (to name only one thing) it was after this, in 1867, that he wrote his enthusiastic letter to Burton on *Lesbia Brandon* as a work à la Balzac, with poetry thrown in. And by poetry here, he meant poetry of the purer sort.

'Its motto must be Caesar Borgia's—Aut Caesar, aut nullus'.[1]
And he might also have said of it, as he said of *Bothwell*, 'Very
likely it may be years in hand before it is (if ever it be) completed to my liking and satisfaction'.[2] *Bothwell* was finished
and published three years after that. *Lesbia Brandon,* like that
other masterpiece on the Borgias that was a dream lasting all
his literary lifetime, a design to which he kept returning, was
never brought to completion, and, excepting the verses, was
never even published in part, as was the work on the Borgias.

The chief, if not the only, reason for the hold-up was
apparently, and even evidently, very cautelous opposition on
the part of Watts-Dunton. As we have seen, he obstinately
failed over some four years, in spite of reiterated urgent
demands from Swinburne, to return parts of the work which
had been lent to him. He certainly had not returned, by the
time the work was set up in type, the four chapters of which
Swinburne had given the titles, for they are not among those
that make up the galley-proofs; not to mention the fact that
in his letter to him of the 20th of January, 1878, by which
time the galleys had left the printers, Swinburne once again
put in an urgent demand for them. Moreover, the following
facts make it pretty certain that he never let them out of his
clutches. Wise, in his extremely muddled account of the
manuscript and galleys and his acquisition of them, says that
'early in 1910' he bought 'from Watts-Dunton Swinburne's
own set of the galley-proofs, accompanied by the MS. of the
matter carried by them'. (The last part of this statement is
inaccurate, for, as I show later in the section on the manuscript, and galleys, portions of the manuscript of 'the matter
carried by' the galleys were not acquired by Wise, and are
missing.)[3] But Wise did not at the same time purchase the

[1] Letter to F. Locker-Lampson, August 4th, 1871.
[2] Letter to F. Locker-Lampson, November 7th, 1871.
[3] If they are still extant somewhere, Watts-Dunton probably sold
them to some collector other than Wise. It is possible that he did send
them to Swinburne in Glasgow, and that the poet lost them during
the hectic month he spent in that place.

four chapters in question. For 'later in the same year', he proceeds, 'I bought the four chapters cited in Swinburne's letters'. (Here again is inexactitude of the kind common in the work of this man who got himself accepted by 'experts' among others as a master in the menial profession of bibliography. He did not buy the four: the one named 'Another Portrait' never came into his possession.[1] Wise's chronic inaccuracy, a form of immorality not unrelated to his exploits as a forger, infects even his records of his own business deals.) It would appear that these latter chapters had always lain apart from the portions of the manuscript that were in Swinburne's keeping. The most probable—and as good as certain —explanation of this is that Watts-Dunton had carefully hidden them, and only came across them after for unneeded lucre he had betrayed into the forger's hands the great mass of the unpublished and other literary remains of the recently deceased friend who had left him a considerable fortune. (*A propos* of this crime, one cannot help recalling Whistler's dig, 'To Theodore Watts, the Worldling', the inscription on his presentation copy to the latter of his *The Gentle Art of Making Enemies*.[2] Even now, as we have already indicated, one of the four chapters ('Another Portrait') was not forthcoming. Why? Was Watts-Dunton withholding it in the hope of getting a higher price for it elsewhere?[3] Did he come

[1] The grounds for this statement are given in the section on the manuscripts and the galleys, where also are more fully discussed other matters mentioned in the present argument.

[2] There is something pathetic in the adoring unintelligence of Watts-Dunton's wife, who missed the point of this altogether, and quoted it as a tribute to the sociability of her late lord: 'He was very fond of society—no one was less of a recluse. Whistler took note of this fact when he inscribed on the fly-leaf of a presentation copy of *The Gentle Art of Making Enemies*: "To Theodore Watts, the Worldling".'

[3] This question is suggested by such facts as the following. Wise records that in May 1909 (that is, only a few weeks after Swinburne's death—it would be hard to beat this for indecency) the MS. of *Under the Microscope* 'was sold by Watts-Dunton to a London bookseller'. About the same time presumably (for it was on sale in America in

across it later, and, for whatever reason, sell it or give it to another person, being indifferent to (or even gratified by) the fact that thus he was helping to impair the manuscript? The most probable explanation is that, as an extra precaution against Swinburne's ever recovering the missing portions of the novel, he had hidden it apart from the rest, and hidden it so well that he himself never came across it after Swinburne's death, and it was only found after his own demise in 1914. Even what happened to it after it had come to light is another mystery. Described as 'the property of' an unnamed 'London collector', it was sold in America in 1916.

Watts-Dunton had also not returned, by the time the work was set up in type, nor by the time the galleys had left the printers, 'the first five leaves' which Swinburne had mentioned in his letters. At least, the first three of them (Chapter I) are not in the galleys, and immediately following these three were others—almost certainly two, as I shall give reasons for believing in a later section—which apparently Wise never obtained (and which, although, according to Lafourcade, they were extant towards 1928, I have found impossible to trace). Wise does not say when he acquired the three; perhaps it was 'early in 1910'; or it may have been when he bought three of the four missing chapters; or it may have been at a later date still. As for the missing sheets following the three, we do not know when or to whom they passed out of Watts-Dunton's keeping. In any case, it is practically certain that Swinburne never recovered the 'first five leaves' mentioned in his list.

(Note ³ continued)—
1910) the manuscript of *A Note on Charlotte Brönte*, Wise also records, 'was sold by Watts-Dunton to a London dealer'. Nothing is more certain than that Wise himself, who was quickly on the spot for spoils after Swinburne's death, would have liked to add these very important manuscripts to the treasury or stock of the Ashley Collection, of which the Swinburnian section was a chief glory. That he did not do so may well be because Watts-Dunton obtained elsewhere higher prices than those he offered: after a few experiences of this kind Wise could be depended on to make liberal initial bids for anything Watts-Dunton dangled before him.

And even this does not complete the tale of the missing parts. Wise further records that in 1920 he 'obtained the balance of the manuscript from' a sister of Watts-Dunton. He does not specify of what this balance consisted. But it could only have been (of the manuscript now in the British Museum) the chapter I have numbered XVII, and also *Uses of Prosody* and the epistle from Arden major; these two latter, as I shall show elsewhere in the commentary, do not belong to *Lesbia Brandon*, but Watts-Dunton probably thought they did, being misled, like Wise and Lafourcade later, by the fact that certain of the characters of that novel, or characters of the same name, come into them. What is the explanation of the long-deferred appearance of these things? Here again the most probable one is that Watts-Dunton, having acquired them somewhen and somehow in Swinburne's lifetime,[1] secreted them apart from the other portions of the manuscript in his possession, in yet a third hiding-place, and so well that they were discovered only after the others.[2] There is no sort of indication as to how Miss Watts got hold of them.[3]

All the evidence then goes to show that during the whole of Swinburne's lifetime after about 1874 Watts-Dunton hung

[1] Chapter XVII of *Lesbia Brandon* at least may have been lent to him by Swinburne along with the four chapters named in Swinburne's letters. In the second of the letters, having enumerated the four chapters, Swinburne added 'there may be more', although, as he went on to say, he did not think there were.

[2] It would have been easy for Watts-Dunton to conceal things all too effectively in *The Pines*, where in addition to his own study and other parts of the house allocated to him, there were 'certain rooms encumbered with a lumber of books and papers'. Wise records this, speaking of a deal he did there with Watts-Dunton some twelve years before Swinburne's death.

[3] Watts-Dunton himself no doubt gave them to her as things convertible into hard cash. Cf. his injunction to the donatory of *The Chronicle of Tebaldeo Tebaldei* (which now, alas, had been abandoned to America) that she should take great care of it, as it was worth at least £200. These manuscripts were not the only items of the spoils of Swinburne that passed into the possession of Miss Watts, and thence into the hands of Wise.

on to the four chapters and the five leaves of the novel specified by Swinburne, and also to another chapter, and to other
portions of manuscript which in all probability he thought
were parts of the novel.[1] As already remarked, this is in no
small degree intriguing. One would like to know, but one
never will know now, how Watts-Dunton diddled Swinburne,
what answers he made to put him off, time after time, as the
period of non-compliance was ever more prolonged to an outrageous extent. Swinburne was not easily put off; there was
nothing of the simpleton about him, and the soft virtues of
the Sermon on the Mount had no place in his composition.
He was one of the most robust, forthright, straight-speaking,
hard-hitting characters in all literary history. Chicanery or
humbug of any kind he would tolerate as little as Dr. Johnson
or anyone you like to name. Of this one could give pages of
evidence. 'I take unasked advice from no one, friend or not'—
this declaration to Hotten[2] indicates the temper, the forceful
independence, that were always his. Even to Watts-Dunton
himself, although he had come to rely a good deal on him as
an adviser and agent in the business matters that he always
found tedious, he could speak very sharply when occasion
demanded it. We have already seen an example of this in one
of the foregoing letters; here is another, where he administers
a snub to the man of affairs who had presumed too much in
offering him gratuitous advice on a purely literary matter:

'I am simply astonished—excuse me saying so—at your
suggestion that my volume of 'Studies' should omit all

[1] Wise stupidly says that 'During the interval between 1867 and the
autumn of 1877 Swinburne made repeated efforts to recover the manuscript of *Lesbia Brandon* from Watts-Dunton'. But Watts-Dunton met
Swinburne for the first time in the summer of 1872!—and, as we have
seen, he evidently knew nothing of the work till about a year later.
Furthermore, Swinburne's 'efforts to recover the manuscript' extended
—in writing—till at least the early part of 1878, and they were probably
renewed orally more than once in after years.

[2] In an undated letter now in the British Museum.

articles on contemporary poets. What on earth would it contain, after omitting . . . The points on which I am un-decided are those only on which I asked your advice in my last letter.[1]

And this sharp-wittedness, this alert and at need very blunt and far from gullible independence (in spite of what the afore-mentioned ignorant fools say to the contrary) persisted intact and entire after he settled at *The Pines*, right up to the time of his death.

The only excuse, plea or pretext acceptable by Swinburne that Watts-Dunton could make—at least after a certain in-

---

[1] From a letter dated June 20, [1873]; in Bonchurch *Letters*. Also cited in Hake and Compton-Rickett's *The Life and Letters of Theodore Watts-Dunton*, where the year is wrongly given as 1874. Watts-Dunton took the snub with due meekness:

'I fear that you have taken amiss my suggestion . . . My view of the matter was that, valuable as are, undoubtedly, the articles in question, your generous enthusiasm has often led you into expressions of admiration which your cooler judgment might now induce you to withdraw . . . If, however, I have been mistaken in this, I have no more to say upon it, and (as you say) you certainly did not ask my advice upon it.' (Letter dated June 23, 1873; printed in *The Review of English Studies*, vol. X, No. 38).

Cf. also, in this connexion:

'. . . I particularly want you just now to send me as soon as possible the MS. or copies (as long since faithfully promised but faithlessly unperformed) of my parodies "John Jones" and "The Poet and the Woodlouse". I have no full copies . . . I want a sight of the complete original text of these works at once.' (July 17th, 1875. Unpublished letter in British Museum.)

Here too, Watts-Dunton did not comply with the request, and Swinburne renewed it some six weeks later in a letter of which the peremptoriness is relieved by a note of jocularity. (Unpublished letter dated August 27, 1875; in British Museum.) Was non-compliance here merely due to slackness? Or did Watts-Dunton retain the manuscripts, prudentially thinking it would be inadvisable for Swinburne to publish burlesques of people like the Brownings? Whatever the explanation, in this case he ultimately did hand the manuscripts over, and Swinburne published them five years later.

terval—was that he had lost the missing parts.

This pretext for non-return of them was one in which Swinburne would have to acquiesce. The more especially as he was perfect in the matter of friendship.

If Swinburne were ever gullible or over pliable it was only because he was too generous, too noble, in his conception of friendship. Once a friend it seems, he gave practically un-limited trust, in a way that might almost be called childlike, and was not open to such feelings as suspicion; it is perhaps not too much to say that he abdicated, *vis à vis* the other person, something of that detached judgment which wisdom, or at least the worldly wisdom of a Polonius, would prescribe.. ('He was courteous and affectionate and unsuspicious, and faithful beyond most people to those he really loved', says Lady Burne-Jones of him in her *Memorials of Edward Burne-Jones.*) This was all the more so when he had reason to be grateful to the friend; his gratitude was large and liberal, and could never be munificent enough. More than once—in the cases of Rossetti and Howell, for instance—he was severely disillusioned, and he expressed his contemptuous disgust in forcible speech equal to the occasion (and perhaps rather in excess of it); but these tendencies do not seem to have acted as a corrective on his tendency to be unguardedly generous wherever he gave himself as a friend. Now he had reason to be grateful to Watts-Dunton; and more and more the latter succeeded in advancing himself in his regard from the status of a very useful professional adviser to that of a friend in the highest sense of the term.

If therefore Watts-Dunton told him he had lost the missing parts of *Lesbia Brandon*, Swinburne would automatically believe him, and the more so as time went on.

Now it is exceedingly difficult to write again work—at least highly creative work, depending a good deal on inspira-tion—that has once been composed to a more or less definitive degree, and then completely lost: it is more difficult than to write something entirely new, where inspiration is not hampered by fragmentary reminiscence and the desire to recover the lost integrity. This certainly was the case as regards *Lesbia Brandon*, and Swinburne was acutely conscious of it; in the very passage of the letter to Watts-Dunton in which he had declared that he 'certainly meant to complete the book some day' he had also said that he 'could not possibly re-write' the parts that were missing. This statement (but Swin-burne could not have realised this) was only calculated to make Watts-Dunton hang on to them all the more. That is, if he had a reason for wishing to do so; and that he must have had, and did anyhow pertinaciously fail to return them, we have given more than enough evidence. The reason could only have been that he strongly disapproved of certain of the themes of the novel and Swinburne's treatment of them.

The disabling loss of the missing parts, then, would go to explain why Swinburne never carried out his firmly-expressed intention of completing the novel.

He might, however, in spite of all difficulties, have set about re-writing these parts, and then doing what was still necessary to bring the work to its proper completion. But the wily Watts-Dunton forestalled this possibility: whenever Swinburne, regretfully, hopefully, reverted to the derelict masterpiece the solicitor assured him that it really was a failure. This is clearly indicated by the passage from Swin-burne's letter to Mrs. Lynn Linton which we cited a few pages back. 'Among the two or three friends who have seen anything of' the work, 'Watts think little but Nichol thinks much of' it, 'so that *I* know not what to think.' Another clear indication to the same effect is furnished by words in the afore-cited letter written by the poet to Watts-Dunton on the 20th of January, 1878: '. . . my fragmentary novel (or what-ever you call it—by any other name it would smell quite as sweet)', which also show that Watts-Dunton had begun this line of dissuasive attack some time before Swinburne settled at *The Pines*: he probably had resorted to it from the very outset. And no doubt Swinburne's placing of the word 'novel' between inverted commas even in a letter to Chatto (31st January, 1878) is another sign of Watts-Dunton's insidious

disparagement of the book—and perhaps not only to Swinburne himself, but also to the man whom Swinburne would
regard as a prospective publisher of it, so that the latter,
when Swinburne had recently sounded him about it, had
questioned whether it qualified for publication as a novel. It
would have been like Watts-Dunton to take the precaution of
getting at Chatto. Anyhow, there can be no doubt that he did
his best to arouse dubiety in Swinburne. It is easy to guess the
arguments he used; one can almost hear him (and see him,
with his heavy dogged jowl, his scraggy walrus moustache, his
dark eyes, shrewd at once and dreamy—but dreamy with
defeated dream), driving them home to the poet who was all
too perfect as a friend. 'Ah yes, those missing sheets . . . I've
hunted high and low for them time and again . . . I can't
think what became of them . . . Could I have left them in a
cab? . . . But after all . . . I'd like to be quite frank with you
about this—to talk to you as a friend has the right to talk . . .
You know, it isn't really a novel at all . . . not a *novel*, mark
you . . . You yourself call it bybrid, and that perhaps shows
you are quite sure about it . . . And if it were only hybrid,
that wouldn't matter so much; even hybrid elements might
be hammered into some sort of unity. But what unity is there
here? what composition? what ordering of parts so that they
all harmoniously contribute towards a whole? . . . Of course,
there are excellent bits; first-class poetry . . . You should
exercise that in its own proper domain, and not waste your
time expending it where it is like a flower choked by a lot of
weeds . . . And the characters . . . they are really queer . . .
there may be such people, but . . . No, I can't believe in
them . . . Decidedly, my dear fellow, this is *not* a novel—and
you know I'm talking to you as a friend . . .' And so on (not a
word about moral offensiveness, of course—the main if not
the only reason for the opposition—: that would have been
maladroit, and would at once have been effectively countered
and squashed)—repeated, with variations, as often as the subject came up, year after year. Gosse too (who, as we have seen,
had knowledge of parts if not of the whole of the work at

241

least as early as 1877[1]) very probably was far from encouraging. (This is a safe inference from the fact that, many years later, he rigorously suppressed the work when he had a chance of bringing it out.) He no doubt, for much the same secret reason, adopted the same line of attack as Watts-Dunton; used the same stock pedantic arguments (still common in journalistic, periodical and other criticism), derived from a standard of the novel which really is only one of a number that might be considered valid. But, although in the actual history of the novel as practised up to that time by masters there was much that might be cited in cogent defence of the pretended faults of *Lesbia Brandon*, there was not nearly so much as at the present time. The charges were more plausible then than they would appear to-day. They certainly made Swinburne hesitant, as his letter to Mrs. Lynn Linton shows.

The afore-mentioned ignorant fools and their kind would no doubt pounce on this and say 'Ah, here is another proof that Swinburne after his installation at *The Pines* lost his true individuality, meekly followed Watts-Dunton in everything.' (These noodles follow Gosse,[2] the arch-author of this nonsense). 'Swinburne submitted to everything that Watts-Dunton suggested' he said in his *Life*, writing out of the lying malignant jealousy of a mediocrity of whom Swinburne had got rather tired, and who would have liked to make him a sort of prize of his own. As I have already remarked, I shall annihilate this legend in a later book. Here, with regard to the matter in hand, I will only observe that Swinburne (like many other writers—and artists in general—of distinction) was in the habit of consulting and paying attention to the opinion of friends on his work long before he came across Watts-Dunton.

[1] The words 'of which he never wearies' in the afore-cited passage from Gosse's journal, suggest that Swinburne had often brought the work to Gosse's notice before the night of which Gosse speaks.

[2] His sycophancy, apart from his mediocrity, must have got on Swinburne's nerves. He 'used to follow' the poet 'about like a dog', as he himself told Lafourcade. The more one learns of Gosse, the more one finds him contemptible.

He was always glad to have confirming approbation (although to nothing like the same morbid degree as Rossetti), even in the years when he was most challengingly and truculently individual—the years that are usually contrasted with the Putney period. Even W. M. Rossetti, a man of many sterling qualities, but not a literary genius, was among those to whose opinion he was not indifferent. Witness the following from an unpublished letter to this friend written early in 1870:

'I cannot tell you how glad I am to find you like my "Eve of Revolution" so much. I never took such pains with any poem, and I thought it was a good one, but I wanted an opinion—and I hadn't the chance of showing it to Gabriel the day he was in town.'

And again, towards the end of the same letter:

'I *am* so glad you like the "E. of R." that I must say so again. Ellis has in hand the "Prelude" which comes before it, just finished. I shall like to know your opinion on that too before the book appears.'

This is only one testimony of many that might be cited. Now, as already observed, Watts-Dunton was very much a friend in Swinburne's eyes. And the more he got himself accepted as such, the less Swinburne—being what he was in the matter of friendship—would discourage the intrusion or rather insinuation of his opinion on purely literary questions, even though here Swinburne was immeasurably his superior; indeed, the more Swinburne would be inclined to accord hearing to his opinion—while never abating his independence in anything fundamental (there were many things on which they remained divided to the last).

Friendship, then, accounts a good deal for the influence of Watts-Dunton's animadversions respecting *Lesbia Brandon*. But that is not all. I have more than once referred to Watts-Dunton as 'the solicitor', but that gives an incomplete, a wrong, idea of the man as he more and more came to stand in the view of the great mass of his contemporaries, including

T   243

not a few of the most distinguished. It must not be forgotten
that all this time he was steadily building up a reputation as
the greatest English critic of his day. 'Greatest' here is not
exaggerative, although it will doubtless appear wildly so to
readers of this generation. The leading reviews, the *Academy*,
the *Examiner*, the *Athenaeum* competed for his work; he was
chosen to write the article on Poetry for the ninth edition of
Encyclopaedia Britannica; 'Our ablest critics hitherto have
been 18-carat; Theodore Watts goes nearer the pure article'
said J. R. Lowell; Stevenson 'would rather read your blame
than most men's praise' wrote Henley to him in a letter
begging him to review *Kidnapped*; and Stevenson himself, in
a letter thanking for the review (from which blame was not
absent) wrote 'A critic like you is one who fights the good
fight'—and so on: it would be easy impressively to extend a
list that already is impressive. Whether the reputation was
really deserved is another matter; but the reputation was
there.

Moreover, as an artist himself and not only as a critic Watts-
Dunton managed to win no small praise in quarters that cannot be dismissed as negligible. He was 'the most original
sonnet writer living' in the opinion of Rossetti, himself one
of the world's masters in this line. Even as a novelist he got
pretty good testimonials from some of the elect. Meredith
wrote of one of the characters of *Aylwin* (a book that has
hardly been rescued from oblivion by its inclusion in 'The
Worlds Classics'): 'I am in love with Sinfi. Nowhere can
fiction give us one to match her, not even the "Kriegspiel"
heroine, who touched me to the deeps . . . The sun comes to
me again in her conquering presence. I could talk of her for
hours. The book has this defect—it leaves in the mind a cry
for a successor.' Once again, whether this and further similar
praise was really deserved—was much more than a *gentillesse*
of friendship—is another matter; but the praise was actually
there.

Furthermore, it was not only as a reviewer that Watts-
Dunton the critic held a position of authority. He was con-

sulted as an expert, his approval and sanction were sought,
by different writers as to the quality of their work before they
sent it for publication. Thus Tennyson himself read to him
Becket while it was yet in manuscript. But Rossetti is the
most striking case in this connexion. He deferred to an extraordinary degree to the critical opinion of Watts-Dunton even
with regard to some of his better work. There is no exaggeration in what A. C. Benson wrote on this matter: [1]

'Though singularly independent in judgment, it is clear
that, at all events in the later years of his life, Rossetti's
taste was, unconsciously, considerably affected by the critical
preferences of Mr. Watts-Dunton. I have heard it said by
one who knew them both well that it was often enough for
Mr. Watts-Dunton to express a strong opinion for Rossetti
to adopt it as his own, even though he might have combated
it for the moment.'

I will give only one of many illustrations, and choose this one
the more especially as it provides an opportunity of publishing a very notable and valuable piece of Rossetti's work that
has remained unknown to the world. The important poem
Cloud Confines ('his highest effort in the field of contempla-
tive, not to say, philosophic, verse', as Franz Hueffer rightly
said[2] contains only five stanzas in the published text; but
Rossetti wrote two others as well: [3]

> *The present is but one coil*
> *Of a snake wherewith we strive:*
> *It clings to all things alive*
> *But drops them dead to the soil:*
> *And yet it keeps as it goes*
> *Some point of our moulding throes,*

[1] In his book on Rossetti in the 'English Men of Letters' series.
[2] In the Tauchnitz edition of Rossetti's *Ballads and Sonnets*.
[3] They are contained in an unpublished letter from him to Watts-
Dunton, dated 23rd February, 1873; the letter is now in the British
Museum.

Some change from the vanished foes
Whose crown it wears for a spoil
    Still we see as we go, etc.

Even as we writhe and strain,
    The future is onward roll'd
In the snake's course, fold on fold:
Yet ah! do we 'scape the chain?
    Or shall not each life forth-hurl'd
    Again in new flesh be furl'd
    And what we made of the world
Fall back on ourselves again?
    Still we say as we go, etc.

These two are at least not inferior to any of the five published, and may even be adjudged superior to certain parts of the latter, if not to anything in them. The second of them in particular is, apart from its quality as pure poetry, noteworthy for its gnomic felicity, the effective economy with which it expresses the most reasonable view of the condition or status of the human soul in a future existence, if there be any such thing. Now Rossetti submitted these stanzas to Watts-Dunton for approval or condemnation; Watts-Dunton decided against them, and so they were never given to the world, which indicates that Watts-Dunton's reputation was not precisely the measure of his critical faculty. But, yet once again, the reputation and the influence were there: Watts-Dunton's prestige was a very solid fact. (Gosse, who had an enormous itch for prestige and proprietorship, never had anything like this influence, a fact that would chafe him into the ugliest jealousy.)

As we have brought in Rossetti, we may in passing cite—it is only fair to do so—Rossetti's opinion of Watts-Dunton as an offset to that of Whistler, who summed him up as a 'Worldling'. Rossetti, who had earlier described him[1] as 'the most companionable man I know', said as he lay dying

---

[1] In an unpublished letter now in the British Museum.

'Watts is a hero of friendship'. Whistler, of course, might have retorted that even in his devotion—or adherence, as Whistler would no doubt have preferred to put it—to genius he was still very much a worldling. (Watts-Dunton is rather a complex character, and so far no adequate portrait or estimate of him has been put forward. I shall attempt one in my *Life* of Swinburne, developing certain suggestions I have thrown out in this volume. The absence of anything satisfactory in this direction is particularly marked in the work of the dim-witted ignoramuses who, following Gosse, have grossly mis-represented Swinburne's life at *The Pines*.) But, once more, whatever be the truth as between Rossetti's and Whistler's opinion of him. Watts-Dunton had a prestige as a friend that reinforced his considerable standing as a literary figure.

It was not then exactly to a literary nobody to whom Swinburne listened when Watts-Dunton gave his opinion on *Lesbia Brandon*.

I have already said that Watts-Dunton's main if not sole objection to *Lesbia Brandon* was a moral one. We have no specific expression of his opinion of the book, but we know enough of him to be quite certain that he must have dis-approved of it very strongly on moral grounds. Take, for example, his criticism of *Dr. Jekyll and Mr. Hyde*. He has nothing but condemnation for this able story which it is very hard, nay impossible, to find other than innocuous and in-offensive from the point of view of the most austere type of morality. He pronounced it a 'great mistake', 'coarse', and 'worthless in the world of literary art'; but he hardly considers it from a literary point of view.[1] He attacks it on the grounds that are almost exclusively moral, in a way that is astonishing to sense and education. 'It was', he says like some primitive evangelist, 'left for Stevenson to degrade' this theme 'into a hideous tale of murder and Whitechapel mystery.' That Stevenson should have been impelled to write the story shows

---

[1] Contrast Swinburne's strictures on Stevenson: they are nothing but literary.

what the 'Suicide Club' had already shown, that 'there was in Stevenson that morbid strain which is so often associated with physical disease'. The mark of the beast, it appears, is not always visible in Stevenson's books; in his other works he 'for the most part succeeded in keeping down the morbid impulses of a spirit imprisoned and fretted in a crazy body'. And this, it seems, was due solely to the influence upon him of Scott, 'the healthiest of all writers since Chaucer'. But for the blessed beneficence of this influence what might have become of Stevenson won't bear thinking about: he 'might have been in the ranks of those pompous problem-mongers of fiction and the stage who do their best to make life hideous'.[1] Then the grand principle of Watts-Dunton's own artistic creed slips out: 'all art is dedicated to joy'; 'to make men happy' is the supreme function of the artist . . . What he thought of *Hamlet*, *Lear*, and much else of the great art of the world on this principle must be left to melancholy conjecture.

What is quite certain is that he would have found in *Lesbia Brandon* little of the 'joy' he desiderated; little, or rather nothing, to make people 'happy' with the happiness he sought of the artist. On the contrary, with his standards, he would assuredly have found a 'morbid strain', 'morbid impulses', a terrible amount of morbidity, unredeemed, alas, by any healthy influence whether of Scott or of himself, who had done his unavailing best against what was 'evil' in Swinburne.

In short, much of *Lesbia Brandon* could only seem to Watts-Dunton 'to make life hideous', and therefore he would do his best to secure its suppression.

As already suggested, the line of attack he would resort to would be aesthetic, as being the only one likely to have any effect on Swinburne and not immediately antagonise him; nor would be necessarily adopt this line without real convic-

[1] There is a hit here at Ibsen among others: Watts-Dunton considered him a monster of depravity.

tion and the force accompanying it; on the contrary, it is more than probable that he actually held such views on the 'right' structure of a novel as we have supposed him expressing in his effort to discredit *Lesbia Brandon*.[1]

All things considered—Watts-Dunton's position as a friend together with his position in the literary world, and the fact that Swinburne was to a certain extent experimenting with the novel in *Lesbia Brandon*—, it is not suprising that Swinburne was not indifferent to any critical strictures made by Watts-Dunton. Had they been the only impediment, he might well have overborne them and got on with the novel. The more especially as the competent Nichol and the still more considerable Meredith had praised it highly.[2] But there was also the very serious handicap imposed by the loss of the missing parts. Had that too been the only impediment he might have completed the work in spite of it. The two in

[1] One fact makes it quite clear that he was bent on frustrating *Lesbia Brandon* at all costs, and that any aesthetic arguments he used were primarily in the service of moral considerations. Reverting to Swinburne's letter to Mrs. Lynn Linton, if the plural 'attempts' is taken at its face value, it follows that Watts-Dunton had disparaged *Love's Cross Currents* as well as *Lesbia Brandon*—in other words, had tried to persuade Swinburne that he had no power at all as a novelist. But this was disingenuous, to put it very mildly; because he really had a high opinion of *Love's Cross Currents*. For towards 1905— having now quite definitely brought about the abandonment of *Lesbia Brandon*—he spoke very eulogistically of the earlier novel and urged Swinburne to bring it out. It would not have been safe to do this—that is, to tell Swinburne that he had the makings of a good novelist in him—while there was a possibility that he might try to complete *Lesbia Brandon*. Of course, with his usual wiliness, it would have been easy for him to make out that he had changed his mind about *Love's Cross Currents* (which anyhow had appeared in print). Watts-Dunton's aesthetic lie about at least one of these novels is one of the ugliest things in his career.

[2] The hopeless Wise, who possessed and published the letter to Mrs. Lynn Linton in which Swinburne says that 'Nichol [who, incidentally, had expressed enthusiastic admiration of *Love's Cross Currents*] thinks much of' the work, suggests that Nichol 'dissuaded the poet from continuing the book'!

combination proved too disheartening—as Watts-Dunton counted on their doing—and so *Lesbia Brandon* was never completed.

Watts-Dunton perhaps had no vision for so much that is great even in the book in its unfinished state. Or if he had he refused to admit it in the interests of his petty morality, in the interests of 'joy' and 'happiness' and 'health' and the rest of the things that he put above beauty and the adventure of mind into places beyond prescription.

There are at least two crimes from which Watts-Dunton can never be absolved: the sale of his dead friend's manuscripts to the unlettered pedlar and the forger Wise, and the frustration of a work that had in it the makings of a masterpiece.

As I have related in my Foreword, the work was further suppressed after Swinburne's death by Gosse, abetted by the probably not very willing Wise. Thus the two enemies, Gosse and Watts-Dunton (at least the former had for the latter a furtive sly hatred arising from petty jealousy), piquantly appear as collaborators in the history of a crime.

AN EXCURSUS THAT DEVELOPS INTO
AN IMPORTANT DIGRESSION

A titre de curiosité, and as an example of the extent to which the grotesquely incompetent Wise has been slavishly followed by others, I give the two following compendia of the main facts in the history of *Lesbia Brandon*. The first, from *A Study of Swinburne* by T. Earle Welby, a superficial work that has in it nothing of value:

> 'Begun in 1859-60; taken up again with the naughtiest intentions in 1867, as appears from a letter to Burton: put into type from a muddled manuscript in 1877 . . .'

(It does not appear from any letter to Burton, nor from anything else, that work was 'taken up again' in the year named. And practically all the rest is wrong.)

The second, from *Swinburne*, by Professor Samuel C. Chew, a very American production, detestably bad from all points of view:

'The history of its composition . . . had best be disposed of at this point. That in its earlier form it was—or at least parts of it were harmless enough is indicated by the fact that in 1864 Swinburne read aloud some chapters to his cousin Miss Gordon [I have already touched on this point]. But later his intentions changed, for in January 1867, he writes to Sir Richard Burton: "I have in hand a scheme of mixed prose and verse . . . which I flatter myself will be more effective and objectionable than anything I have yet done'. Yet in this same year some chapters were set up in type and in 1868 Swinburne tried to find a publisher for it. Through the good offices of Henry Stoddard and Bayard Taylor the manuscript was submitted to Lippincott and was rejected by that firm. In 1877 it was again sent to the printers and reached the stage of proof sheets; and in 1878 it was submitted to Leslie Stephen for publication in *Cornhill*. Obviously the version which Swinburne allowed Stephen to read could not have been so naughty as that described to Burton. In the opinion of Sir Edmund Gosse and Mr. Wise the work should never be published!'

(Here errors on errors accumulate . . . The naive Professor Chew dedicates his volume to Wise, whom he hails as a 'scholar'. *Sans commentaire,* as they say across the Channel.)

I add here a sort of stop-press P.S., after my work has gone to the printers. This is in reference to Mr. Humphrey Hare's *Swinburne, A Biographical Approach* (H. F. & G. Witherby Ltd., 1949). Mr. Hare is very scrappy on the subject of *Lesbia Brandon*, and the little he does manage to say is almost without any exception wrong. He emits the astonishing statement that 'when Swinburne wrote it he was honestly endeavouring to recapture the emotions of his dead self'. 'Dead' is the last word that should be used here, and it isn't even that, for it is completely out of place; and 'recapture' very nearly is too. In no period of his career was Swinburne more intensely alive that he was in that when this book was written. Even if it be supposed that 'dead' is a clumsy and illegitimate equivalent of 'past', the statement would still remain untrue; for even in portraying his boyhood Swinburne was conveying essentials of that boyhood (passionate love for the sea, etc., etc.) which were still active in him, and which indeed persisted well into his middle years and beyond; and as for the early manhood of his hero, here of course he was simply reproducing himself as he was at the time of composition.

One cannot help having very strong doubts as to whether Mr. Hare really read *Lesbia Brandon* before starting to write about it. For he does not even know the surname of the hero; he calls him 'Bertie Leyton'; the first time we meet 'Leyton' we think it must be a printer's error; but when it occurs again this charity can hardly be invoked. He also affirms that the said 'Leyton' was 'the victim of an irresistible love for his sister'. Bertie certainly had a strong, even an incestuous, love for his sister during a part of his boyhood, and it might rhetorically be called irresistible, although this perhaps suggests more than we are told in the story; but it subsided as he grew towards manhood, there is no hint of any incestuous feeling on his part towards his sister in the later years, and most assuredly it cannot with any exactitude be said that in the upshot he was a 'victim' of this early passion. He *was* in the true sense of the word a victim of his passion for Lesbia; perhaps Mr. Hare (even if he really read the work) confused Margaret and Lesbia—and also Herbert and Denham, who was a victim of his love for Margaret: this would not be unlike Mr. Hare, to judge from other things in his very queer volume of his. Is an example of these other things required? Well, he describes 'Reginald in *A Year's Letters*' as 'torn between resentment of [sic: Mr. Hare might with advantage take a correspondence course in elementary English] his

252

father, Captain Harewood, and love for Eleanor Ashburst'. This takes the bun, cake, or whatever first prize may be going for the wildest inaccuracy. There is no character named Eleanor Ashburst in *A Year's Letters* (*Love's Cross Currents*) or in any other work of Swinburne. In a fragmentary composition (which evidently in Mr. Hare's skull was muddled into conflation with *A Year's Letters*, from which it is quite separate in actual fact) there is a Helen Harewood—once, and once only—inadvertently called Eleanor by Swinburne—who takes on the name of Ashurst by marriage. Here again, on first meeting Ashburst one passes it as a printer's error; but here again also one has to forego this charity when the absurd name recurs. But the failure to get even names of chief characters right is only incidental and symptomatic; it is part of a larger failure. Even had Mr. Hare said Helen Ashurst instead of Eleanor Ashburst he would still have been ridiculously wrong. Reginald Harewood of *A Year's Letters* could have had no feelings of any kind for Mrs. Ashurst, for he never came across her. It is not even for a sister of another name that he has a passionate love: it is for a cousin, and not a first cousin, so that technically there is no question of incest. (One may enquire parenthetically how it is possible to be torn between resentment against one person and love for another. Torn—to the point of laceration, if Mr. Hare likes— between love for two different objects, or between love and hatred in the case of one, yes, but between sweet feelings for one and bitter for another?—unless the situation is such that the two sets of feelings are mutually exclusive, but the situation imagined by Mr. Hare does not appear to be of this kind. Did the two feelings—in the story that shaped itself in Mr. Hare's head—compete like two carrots, so that the poor donkeyish Reginald was forced to choose between them; being unable to accommodate both of them at once, or at least to dismiss one into abeyance while he devoted himself to the other? Are we to understand that when his attention and energy were nicely set towards love they were jerked away towards resentment, and then bafflingly back towards love, and so on, to and fro, so that the unfortunate fellow was for all the world like a pendulum? The picture is a curious one, and has a certain originality—but it or anything remotely like it is not to be found in anything ever written by Swinburne.) Once again, on meeting such a passage, one cannot help strongly doubting whether Mr. Hare really read the works about which he discourses; *really* read them, and not merely acquired a hasty and not even sketchy knowledge of them (if knowledge it can be called)—and that, in the case of a fair number of them, not at first hand, but (one shrewdly suspects) at bad secondhand in the untrustworthy pages of Lafourcade, for whom he has sentiments that do not stop short of idolatry. In this particular case, it is impossible to avoid the conclusion that Mr. Hare simply does not know what he is talking about; and this conclusion is imposed on one again as one makes one's painful way through a book that is a big evil even though its bulk is not big.[1]

There are even wilder things. 'It is difficult', writes Mr. Hare, 'to refrain from reconstructing the classic situation by substituting Lady Jane for Lady Wariston and Eleanor Ashburst, and the Admiral for Denham and Captain Harewood'. (Lady Jane is Swinburne's mother, and the Admiral his father.) It is no doubt difficult, nay, quite impossible, for Mr. Hare to refrain from such nonsense. The Oedipus Complex has been so much misapplied or overdone by shallow fools that one is sick to death of it. (Why, incidentally, call the situation 'classic'? Is it *par excellence* classic compared to many others? Does it occur so frequently in literary and scientific history in the vast interval between Sophocles and Freud that it enjoys this status as a matter of course?) Dragging it in here is ludicrous in the extreme. There is not the least particle of evidence to give even plausible support

[1] *Τὸ μέγα βιβλίον ἴσον, ἔλεγεν, εἶναι τῷ μελάλῳ κακῷ* (Callimachus, in Athenaeus.) I give this reference because I have found that many people even of humanistic education do not know the Greek tag of which I have made use.

to this antic, which Mr. Hare no doubt thinks clever and delightfully up-to-date. If one seeks autobiographical explanation of Bertie's incestuous love for his sister Lady Wariston, there is no need to perform the desperate feat of substitution by which Mr. Hare hopes to distinguish himself. One is not under the necessity of foisting in Swinburne's mother; there is more promising material in another quarter; but Mr. Hare has no eye for this—if he has run up against it: he frequently has no eye for truth or probability when it sticks out pretty prominently.

For the rest (as regards *Lesbia Brandon*) Mr. Hare says little more than the following. Pierre Sadier 'was very likely modelled on Louis Blanc'; the novel 'was abandoned' shortly after and as a consequence of Swinburne's first meeting with Mazzini, which took place in 1867 (moreover, at the same time, and under the same influence Swinburne executed a '*volte-face*' and 'abandoned the theory of Art for Art's sake' as a whole and not only this particular expression of it); but in 1877 the novel (definitively abandoned in 1867 along with all the heresy of Art for Art's sake!) 'in face of opposition and though incomplete was sent to the printers' (there is not a word in explanation of this apparent apostasy from the religion towards which the author had allegedly performed his *volte-face*, nor as to why such of the manuscript as he had 'was sent to the printers': the reader, especially in view of the words 'and though incomplete', will naturally understand that it was in order to get it published there and then, in spite of the fact that it was far from publishable in such a state of incompleteness. That is to make a sorry fool of Swinburne. But then most, if not all, of Mr. Hare's book, furtively or overtly, has the belittlement and vilification of Swinburne as one of its central aims. Another is doubtless to establish Mr. Hare himself as a man of shining parts.) Now all these affirmations of Mr. Hare are wrong; well-nigh everything he says about *Lesbia Brandon* is a blunder, a blunder that could not have been committed by anyone who had a real knowledge of the subject (and such real knowledge as is easily derivable from evidence no less available to Mr. Hare than to anyone else working on Swinburne).

One reason why Mr. Hare has gone so grievously wrong here (where not opinions but hard facts are in question) is that he has simply been content to repeat statements of Lafourcade, instead of troubling to get down to real things himself. At least, all these affirmations of his are to be found in Lafourcade. (I have cited them from the French critic and exploded them in various parts of the present work.) If there is no docile reproduction (others would more tersely say plagiarism) here the then amount of concordance between Mr. Hare and Lafourcade is nothing short of a miracle; and miracles no longer receive credence. As already mentioned, Mr. Hare has for Lafourcade a veneration that may be mildly called excessive (but which after all is perhaps only natural on the part of one who would be helpless without what he receives— or takes—from this source of blessings for intellectual poverty). He fervently declares that 'It would be effrontery to pretend to supersede his profound and detailed studies', and 'vanity' 'to hope to supplement them'. This is hugely comical in the light of the irrefutable results of due and strictly just examination of much of these 'profound studies' in the present work (and also in the *Lucretia Borgia* volume). Supplementation and, still more, supersession are in actual fact one of the most crying needs in the field of Swinburnian studies, which Lafourcade bedevilled to a woeful extent: of all the interlopers into this field he is perhaps the most noxious (which is saying a lot, in view of certain of the others, and particularly of the one who is now and will assuredly remain his arch-thurifer, the most devout of all those quiring him). But Mr. Hare is right in one respect: it would certainly be effrontery and vanity on his part to attempt or hope to do any of this corrective work. (One cannot, incidentally, help enquiring why, if it is impossible even to do as much as supplement Lafourcade's masterly labours, Mr. Hare bothered to perpetrate a book which, on his own showing, must be quite superfluous.)

He sometimes—nay, often—is so slavish in his dependence on Lafourcade that he merely translates him (and with no acknowledgment). Examples? I will give only three here out of a foison that I have noted in a first rapid reading of his book:

1. Mr. Hare: 'The Pre-Raphaelites—whose philosophy Jowett was constitutionally incapable of appreciating . . .'

Lafourcade: 'Jowett était constitutionnellement incapable de comprendre les P.R.B.' [i.e. the Pre-Raphaelite Brotherhood.]

2. Mr. Hare on John Nichol: 'Having already spent four years at Glasgow University, where his father was Professor of Astronomy . . . He was a logician of parts: had travelled: admired Mill, Carlyle and Goethe, had met Kossuth and Mazzini, was free-thinking and republican . . . His austere and ruthless intelligence was allied to a certain melancholy, a capacity for satire and sardonic wit.'

Lafourcade on John Nichol: 'Il a passé 4 ans à l'université de Glasgow où son père est professeur d'astronomie; il est très versé dans l'étude de la logique; il a voyage . . .; il admire Mill, Carlyle et Goethe; enfin et surtout il est libéral avancé en matière de politque et de religion; il a rencontré . . . Kossuth et Mazzini . . .'

3. Mr. Hare pronounces that *The Chronicles of Tebaldeo Tebaldei* is 'a paraphrase of Burchardus'.

Lafourcade had written: 'La source principale où le poète a puisé est le Diarium Burchardi . . . Swinburne en paraphrase des passages entiers'. (This is almost entirely asinine error, as I proved in *Lucretia Borgia*; but Mr. Hare could have had no inkling of the error, as he makes no investigations on his own account, never goes near things where truth may be found: so implicit and entire is his faith in Lafourcade that anything he finds in Lafourcade is for him gospel and the richest cream of the word.)

I have cited only a few of the mistakes and howlers in Mr. Hare's book; but they abound throughout it, they are the main constituent of it, they are its chief distinction for anyone who has more than a smattering of the subject. And of course in most cases they come straight from Lafourcade. It would take a book almost as large as Mr. Hare's own to show up all of these. I can only give a few additional examples here (and the reader can quite safely take it for granted that they are typical—representative of the whole of Mr. Hare's contribution to the subject, which exactly amounts to nil). On the subject of Nichol: he begins by saying that the latter 'was some years older than Swinburne and indeed of [sic: Mr. Hare really should take that correspondence course] most of the rest of the set of which he was the leader'; and then, contradicting himself as regards 'most', he goes on to say 'he was not only in age but . . . already much more formed than the others' ['formed in age' is queer, mais passons]; here 'the others' in normal English can only mean 'all the others'; but this is not true, for another member of the set, G. R. Luke, had, like Nichol, spent four years at Glasgow University, was coeval with him, and had the same seniority as he. But Mr. Hare knows nothing of this—nor does Lafourcade, whence he draws all his facts or fancies regarding this group. (Mr. Hare, by the way, in his section on Swinburne at Oxford says not a word of Swinburne's college essays, which are important as providing valuable material for the poet's intellectual biography.[1] 'A Biographical Approach' is the sub-title of Mr. Hare's volume. In fact, Mr. Hare does not even begin to enquire what Swinburne got from the educational system at Oxford; what—to name only one thing—the philosophical

---

[1] Wise, with his usual vandalistic indifference to the integrity and fate of his spoils, disposed of many of these in various directions, and they are now difficult to trace. But I have unearthed some thirty of them altogether—including several not mentioned in Lafourcade's 'liste aussi complète que possible de toutes les œuvres ou lettres publiées ou inédites de Swinburne (jusqu'a à la date de mai 1867)'—and it is my intention to publish the set within the next couple of years. There are still some half-dozen missing, and I should be greatly obliged to any library or private collector who could give me news of them.

poet who wrote *Hertha* learned as an undergraduate of the ideas of Heraclitus, Plato and other thinkers with whom he had to make some acquaintance. But here Mr. Hare is not singular (at least in one sense of the word): he is in what by his standards is no doubt the best company. (Previous incompetents have not thought of opening up this important line of enquiry.) He asserts, with no supporting evidence, that Swinburne 'read Froissart and Joinville' 'with Morris'; this may be; but it is more important to note that Swinburne studied Joinville in detail with Stubbs, and wrote for the latter a long essay on the French historian which is still extant; and among the work which he did with Stubbs (of which Mr. Hare apparently knows nothing) there are other exercises and notes which are a first source for *The Chronicle of Queen Fredegond* and other of Swinburne's compositions in the same line. He quotes Swinburne as writing 'of the *Chronicles of Charlemagne*' 'that is the sort of history I like'. What Swinburne actually wrote was 'I am taking . . . either Charlemagne or St. Louis . . . That is the sort of history I like'. What are the *Chronicles of Charlemagne*? Has Mr. Hare come across them? Or should he not have said Eginhard's *Life and Annals*, which was the work on Charlemagne prescribed for study in the year Swinburne was working for his final examinations?[1] He says that the invocation to love which forms the prelude of Tristram of Lyonesse was written in 1871; as a matter of fact Swinburne was writing it in 1869: for duncery in the lowest branches of scholarship Mr. Hare almost equals Wise himself, whose eminence in this matter can scarcely be overtopped. This is a small thing? But one was hoping that Mr. Hare might at least be able to show competence in small things even though he was so grossly incompetent in the handling of large ones.

Mr. Hare is so intent on proving that Swinburne, for a

[1] If he substituted *Vita Caroli Magni* and *Annales Francorum* for the term used by the University it would get him no nearer the *Chronicles* which he assures us were read with predilection by Swinburne

long period before going to *The Pines*, was a victim of 'alcoholic poisoning' that he makes the rash statement that the poet's bilious attacks (why not also his frequent attacks of influenza?!) were due to this, and that he suffered from them 'only in London' (where he always committed excesses), 'never in the country' (by which Mr. Hare means more particularly his family home, where he could not go in for excesses). Note the 'only' and the 'never': sweeping and absolute: the effect must be as damnatory as possible. Now the state of Swinburne's health 'in the country', as reported in many letters of his written thence, was by no means always what Mr. Hare would have us believe. There is record of illness from time to time, more especially in unpublished letters; Mr. Hare should do a little research for once, and acquaint himself with this record, which he will find rather inconvenient. (This thesis of his, of course, like so much else, is borrowed from Lafourcade. E.g.—in the latter's *Swinburne, A Literary Biography*—, 'But he was back in town . . . and he was promptly laid up with one of those bilious attacks'; and 'A week or so later he was back at his old lodgings of [sic] Dorset Street after an absence of nearly four months; bilious influenza was not long in overtaking him . . .')

Even the other half of Mr. Hare's indictment is not true. In London itself the bilious attacks were not always due to excessive drinking; the poet suffered from them even when he was leading a regular life in that as well as in other respects; I will give here only one item in proof of this, the following passage from a letter written by him in 1867 to W. M. Rossetti from his London address:

'If you haven't seen or heard from me for such ages it is because I am still half dead with bilious influenza. It's very hard lines . . . as I have abstained from sitting up or drinking or any irregularity in a way worthy of a better cause and effect.'

(W. M. Rossetti was one of the friends to whom he spoke freely of his peccadilloes and excesses, and—apart from the general fact that he was not given to lying—there is not the least ground for doubting the accuracy of anything he says here.)

Of course Swinburne drank, and, like many good (including many of the best) men, he sometimes in his earlier manhood drank to excess, drank till he was three sheets in the wind, as the saying goes. But it's a bit thick (as Arnold Bennett would have said—who, by the way, although the most regular and steady of men, suffered sometimes from bilious attacks, and also from neuralgia and insomnia, two other things of which Swinburne was often the victim) if one's biliousness is to be regarded as being always or even generally a consequence of drinking on an immoderate scale; if it and alcoholic poisoning are to be viewed as synonymous, or two members of an equation from which there can be no sort of appeal. Many readers who, like the present writer, are subject to this ailment, but rarely have the consolation of knowing that it results from a festive occasion, will no doubt share an amused resentment at this piece of silliness.

Mr. Hare might be prevented from rushing into (or even merely borrowing) such extravagant conclusions if he kept a few simple facts in mind. Swinburne (like Arnold Bennett: the medical history of the two has much in common) obviously was cursed with a weak stomach (with Nietzsche, another fellow-sufferer, he might have exclaimed 'Give us good stomachs and we shall become as gods'); this sometimes leads to biliousness even when one is living in the most respectable seclusion in the country at its most bucolic. Next, Swinburne (as was natural with one so eminently a poet) was exceedingly high-strung; this sometimes leads to headaches of the kind called nervous, and biliousness frequently goes with these. In this connexion, Gosse's testimony is apposite; in his Introduction to Swinburne's *Letters to the Press* he records that when the poet was roused by 'evil and ugly things' he 'was possessed with sacred rage and divine indignation to such a degree that his sleep was broken and his appetite impaired'. It is a fact of common experience that

261

loss of sleep and impairment of appetite frequently result in nervous and bilious headaches; and in Swinburne's case they would also be caused by other forms of spiritual excitement—altogether independent of alcohol—besides that mentioned by Gosse: strong ecstasy of any kind would disturb his physical euphoria: the poetic temperament had to be paid for pretty heavily by him. Further, hot weather acted very adversely on him; it affected him in a way very likely to lead to the condition that Mr. Hare facilely diagnoses as due to alcohol. The following illustrative passage—one of many that might be cited—occurs in a letter of his written not only from his mother's home in the country but also some three-and-a-half years after he had begun to live the almost ideally regular life of his Putney days:

'It has been parchingly hot here . . . The agony of starch in my new shirts has made me physically irritable and morally impotent for days, at a time when I want all my powers . . . Who could write—prose or verse—with a sense of chalky grit rubbed into every pore, stopping all perspiration, chafing the cuticle, and drying up the blood?'[1]

Mr. Hare ought also to ask himself whether a man suffering from alcoholic poisoning (in the real and no rhetorical sense of the term) could have turned out so much work of such high quality in the period when he is supposed to have been most severely affected by the poison. Lafourcade, after assert-

---

[1] And it was not only heat that upset his health when he was in the country; he suffered there also in cooler seasons of the year. For example, in a letter written form his mother's country home in October 1882 he complains that his condition is such that his 'working faculty seems actually benumbed'. He had sometimes made the same complaint when ill in London—from alcoholic poisoning, according to Mr. Hare—in the course of the twenty years that preceded his new life at *The Pines*. It cannot be argued by Mr. Hare and his kind that in October 1882 he had not yet recovered from the effects of the alleged poisoning; for six months previously—in April of that year—he had written (from London): 'I have been stronger and harder at work . . . than ever I was in my life'.

ing that he was then (circa 1867–1870) 'drinking himself to death', might well say that 'the way in which for about twenty years Swinburne sustained the strain of his many activities and vices is a puzzle to modern doctors'. It *would* be a puzzle to them if Lafourcade's thesis (appropriated in its entirety by Mr. Hare) were true: but it is highly questionable if any doctor would, on the face of it, accept it, and it is pretty certain that none would after considering the evidence.[1]

Mr. Hare ascribes not only Swinburne's bilious attacks, but also his fainting fits to alcoholic poisoning. Here he is even more absurd, more grossly ignorant of or indifferent to important facts that bear upon the case and point to a far other conclusion. Even the revered Lafourcade, the source—one might almost say the author—of so much of his book, shows a little more sense when he touches on this subject. At least he does in one place, where he writes that these fits 'semblent avoir été independantes de ses excès alcooliques'. Mr. Hare would have been wise to transfer this prudential statement to his book, but he probably thought the dubitative *semblent* left room for adventurous affirmation in a contrary direction. Moreover, Lafourcade himself, 49 pages further on, commits one of his characteristic acts of self-stultification and writes the following: 'il [Swinburne] tombe de bonne heure dans l'Ivrognerie, qui semble déterminer bientôt les crises de plus en plus fréquentes d'une sorte d'épilepsie'. In the fact of this flagrant self-contradiction, perhaps we can hardly blame poor Mr. Hare: what is the acolyte to do when the master behaves thus? Anyhow, the latter statement suited his main thesis, the general tenor and bias of his detractive book, and so he made it his own; moreover, he scrapped any hesitancy denoted by *semble*, and with him the statement becomes splendidly absolute. He no doubt thought that was a way of being original

---

[1] Of the doctors among whom Lafourcade had found puzzlement—no doubt amounting to scepticism—he names only one: in a footnote to the above-cited remark from his *Swinburne, A Literary Biography*, this was a member of the Faculty who reviewed his *Jeunesse de Swinburne* in a French medical journal.

and shining with greater lustre. Like a cocksure matamore of comedy, he flatly contradicts Gosse, in so far as the latter says that the fits were a form of epilepsy. 'In fact', pontificates Mr. Hare (as if he were speaking out of special and privileged knowledge), they were a 'symptom of alcoholic poisoning', just as much as the bilious attacks were. But he didn't read his Gosse carefully enough; for Gosse himself says that these 'epileptiform' fits 'seemed to be exclusively brought on by the excitements of London life'—which might be taken to support the nonsense Mr. Hare is anxious to bring to the notice of the world. Mr. Hare, had he been a little cleverer, might have argued that epileptiform attacks could be brought on by alcoholic poisoning; in fact that whether they were epileptiform or not was a matter or no importance.

But Gosse—although not to the same ludicrous extent as Lafourcade—stultifies himself in the statement we have quoted. At least, he himself in other places gives information which points to the radical cause of these fits, a cause very different from that which the spheterizing Mr. Hare proclaims as a grand discovery. He records that Swinburne occasionally suffered from 'a disturbance of his nervous system' even in his childhood—in other words, Mr. Hare will note, long before he had any opportunity of absorbing strong drink—, and that a doctor his mother consulted about this reported that it 'resulted from "an excess of electric vitality".' Gosse also records Lord Redesdale's testimony that Swinburne was 'a bag of nerves' in the earlier of his years at Eton. These facts are quite enough to explain the fainting fits, altogether independently of alcohol (as Lafourcade suggests in the saner of his two contradictory statements). Alcohol could of course be an incidental or subordinate cause, but it was not a primary one, and there was no need for it to come into play at all. The previously mentioned states of poetic and other strong ecstasy would be enough to produce the fits.[1]

[1]Cf. the case of Burne-Jones, whose nervous constitution was in certain respects very like that of his friend Swinburne, and in par-

Overwork too would help to bring them on; in fact Gosse appears to suggest that this is so, for after writing the following *à propos* of the poet's creative activity in 1868: 'All this labour, all the fury and flame of intellectual productivity, could not be indulged in without manifest danger to his health', he goes on to record a fainting fit into which Swinburne fell while working one day in the British Museum. Gosse is sometimes a wobbly writer, but here it look as if the sequence were one of cause and effect; anyhow, the judgment expressed in the cited sentence, and its important corollaries, remain unquestionable.

In this connexion one may also cite Gosse's testimony (in another publication) to the poet's condition in the autumn of 1874: 'It was my privilege to see Swinburne almost daily [in London, Mr. Hare will note] during the months of September and October of this year [1874] . . . His energy and his ardour were unsurpassable; they even affected unfavourably his health . . .' Here Gosse (who was not concerned to vindicate Swinburne in this matter) is quite categorical: enthusiastic overwork was a cause of ill-health during this time. Even Mr. Hare, it may be remarked incidentally, will agree that a man suffering from (not to say almost dying of) alcoholic poisoning could not be possessed of 'energy and ardour' in an 'unsurpassable' degree. But in the face of even such facts (in the unlikely event of his having knowledge of them) he would no doubt defer to the infallibility of the supreme Lafourcade. According to the latter, the autumn in question was part of the period when 'Swinburne's health, and perhaps life, were miraculously preserved on several occasions by lack of money more than by anything else'. Lafourcade says not a word of the unsurpassable ardour and energy of which Gosse speaks from the personal and first-

(*Note* [1] *continued*)—
ticular the following incident of his schoolboy period: 'He once . . . carried off an armful of prizes home, rolled them in the doormat, and then fainted upon them.' (*Memorials of Edward Burne-Jones.*)

hand knowledge of one who was in 'almost daily' contact with the poet in that part of 1874. Nor does Lafourcade (nor consequently does Mr. Hare) say a word of the admirable work produced (in London, Mr. Hare will go on noting) by the poet during that time; work notable for intellectual strength no less than for artistic qualities. (According to Gosse, Swinburne's 'extraordinary powers of analysis and his distinguished erudition' receive in it fuller expression than in any 'previous production'; and Gosse further characterises it as 'perhaps the finest exercise in pure criticism, the most learned, the most searching, and even the best balanced which he [Swinburne] ever presented to the world'. However all that may be in respect of details, the 'exercise' is quite certainly first-class. It is indeed phenomenal that such work should be producible by a man so infected by alcoholic poisoning that he would have died but for an insufficiency of funds.) Such is the value of Lafourcade's biography—and such is the value of Mr. Hare's, which derives from it (and 'derives' is a polite word) to an extent which is more than remarkable.

Presumption, sense, and facts, then, are all against this ill-informed and leaden-witted twaddle about alcoholic poisoning, and henceforth it should be left on the rubbish-heap where it properly belongs.

I have gone into this particular matter in some detail (and I could do so to a much greater extent) to show with a sufficiency of evidence the value of the chief charges against Swinburne reformulated (and intensified) by the latest of a long line of detractors. I will also with the same intention touch on one other matter—one item among many of another of the chief and stock charges which this company of calumniators have repeated *ad nauseam*, and which is now universally (it seems) accepted as being unquestionable as a law of nature. I refer to the legend that for the long period after Swinburne went to *The Pines* he abdicated intellectually, and was nothing but the creature of Watts-Dunton. Discussion of this matter here is not flagrantly digressive, for it is one I have more than once had occasion to allude to in the preceding section regarding the history of *Lesbia Brandon*.[1] I shall here further substantiate certain counter-assertions put forth in the course of arguments there.

Mr. Hare—it goes without saying—rehashes (and 're-hashes' is hardly the right word, for there is nothing new in his presentation) all the old rot about Swinburne's abdication, servitude, effacement etc. under the sway of Watts-Dunton for considerably more than half of the long years of his manhood. As I have said, I will examine here only one of the so-called facts he gives as an example of this surrender on Swinburne's part, but it may in its probative worth be taken as typical of all the others that go to form this stupid legend. Expatiating on what he obviously regards as Swinburne's absolutely unqualified admiration of Whitman before the period of enslavement at *The Pines*, he writes, in reference to the essay entitled *Whitmania*, which first appeared in 1887: 'But in 1887, under the influence of Watts-Dunton, Swinburne was to repudiate his youthful enthusiasm'; and further, '*Whitmania* disposed of one "unhealthy" admiration (Watts "hated him most heartily").' This is simply a *précis* (accompanied by no acknowledgment) of a passage in Gosse's slyly malignant *Life* of Swinburne (only antiphrastically can it be referred to by this title):

'. . . the essay, written in 1887, in which Swinburne, who had been one of the earliest to welcome Walt Whitman as a "strong-winged soul with prophetic lips hot with the blood-beats of song", enounced a full recantation. Even as lately at February 1885 he had written, 'I retain a very

---

[1] Of course the securing of the suppression of *Lesbia Brandon* by Watts-Dunton cannot be cited as an example of 'tyranny'; it was nothing more than trickery, in other words, the action of a man who knew quite well that he had not the least hope of imposing any sort of sway over a mind so unlike his own and so independent as Swinburne's but generous enough to have no suspicions of anyone accepted as a friend and not openly showing that in this matter he was very far from being that.

267

cordial admiration for not a little of Whitman's earlier work" . . . But now the Muse of Walt Whitman was nothing but "a drunken apple-woman, indecently sprawling in the slush and garbage of the gutter amid the rotten refuse of her overturned fruit-stall". This was an interesting example of the slow tyranny exercised by Swinburne's judgment by the will of Watts, who have never been able to see merit in the work of Walt Whitman, and who frankly admitted that he "hated him most heartily".[1]

Now let us look at the actual facts. In 1867, long before he met Watts-Dunton, and when, according to his ignorant and/or unscrupulous detractors, his admiration for Whitman was entire and unqualified, he used the terms 'very feeble' and 'frothing and blatant ebullience' in the course of a

---

[1] This passage affords a good example of Gosse's dishonesty when he is up against facts that don't happen to suit him. Anyone reading the passage would gather than Swinburne, against Watts-Dunton's pressure, succeeded in maintaining entire his 'cordial admiration' for Whitman up to 1885, but that by 1887 Watts-Dunton's tyranny had got its way and brought about a complete reversal of the poet's opinion. But the words quoted by Gosse: 'I retain a very cordial admiration for not a little of Whitman's earlier work' (there is, by the way, already something of qualification in this sentence), are followed by others which Gosse is very careful not to quote. They are: 'but the habit of vague and flatulent verbiage seems to me to have grown upon him instead of decreasing'. This sentence (which, incidentally, indicates that Swinburne had always thought there was a certain amount of 'vague and flatulent verbiage' in the American's effusions) expresses, in 1885, a very considerable qualification of Swinburne's 'cordial admiration' for Whitman's work, which Gosse, to suit his own ends, threw out into solitary relief. It cannot be pleaded in Gosse's favour that he perhaps did not know of this second sentence, for it occurs in a letter written to himself (he does not reveal that he is drawing on such a document in presenting this part of his vilifying case against Swinburne—and at the same time against Watts-Dunton as the pretended villain in this tragedy of a great man degraded into the lowest servitude).

criticism of the American's work;[1] these terms, expressive of critical reserve and disapproval, are as strong as any employed in the essay he wrote twenty years later. Moreover, in 1871— again before he had met or so much as heard of Watts-Dunton —he wrote the following passage, which Mr. Hare and other detractors won't like at all:

> 'I perceive that, *à propos* of Gabriel's poems, a son of Sodom, hitherto unknown except (I suppose) to Whitman's bedfellows the cleaners of privies, has lately "del cul fatto trombetta" in a malebolgian periodical called the *Contemporary Review* . . .'[2]

The contemptuous terms in which he speaks of Whitman here are not only as strong as, they are stronger than, any in

---

[1] In a letter to W. M. Rossetti, who was preparing a selection from Whitman's poems; he incorporated Swinburne's remarks into his Introduction (as being those of 'a friend highly entitled to express an opinion'), but toned down 'very feeble' to 'feeble' and 'frothing and blatant ebullience' to 'blatant ebullience'. He, then, considered that Swinburne even in these early days was too hard in the condemnatory part of his criticism of the American's work; but his brother Gabriel would not have done so, if—as is very probable—his opinion then was what it was some ten years later; 'By the bye', he wrote in a letter to William, 'I am sorry to see that name [i.e. Whitman's] winding up a summary of the great poets: he is really out of court in comparison with anyone who writes what is not sublimated Tupper; though ou know that I am not without appreciation of his fine qualities'. Which, put in other words, is pretty well Swinburne's opinion on the same matter from first to last.

[2] From a letter to W. M. Rossetti. The phrase 'Whitman's bedfellows' etc. suggests that Swinburne, who detested homosexuality (between men) already at this date had some knowledge of the homosexual proclivities of the American poet. In which case even the 'pathological study published on Whitman the man, which', according to Rickett and Hake in their *The Letters of A. C. Swinburne*, Watts-Dunton and he 'read' (presumably at *The Pines*) gave him no fundamentally new information on Whitman and was of no decisive effect on him, as Rickett and Hake, following a suggestion of Watts-Dunton, would seem to believe.

the essay supposed to have been written almost under the dictation of the nefarious Watts-Dunton.

And so this item of the nonsensical legend[1] turns out not only to have no basis in fact, but also to be directly counter to facts which give the whole truth of the matter. And with the same ease one could dispose of the rest of the dishonouring fable—but this is a pleasant task that I must reserve for a later work. I can promise the cads a very uncomfortable time.

[1] A good example—one of decades or scores—of how this rubbish is propagated and consecrated by people content mere to repeat like parrots is provided by the following extract from a book on the Rossettis:

'In the sixties Swinburne was as ardent an admirer of Whitman as William Rossetti could wish . . . and as late as 1885 [he] wrote that 1887 he recanted completely.'—*Three Rossettis*, by Janet Camp. Troxell, 1937. This afflictively superficial American production carries the imprimatur of Harvard.

Troxell, 1937. This afflictively superficial American production carries the imprimatur of Harvard.

Another and more recent example of the same unintelligent parrotry in respect of the legend in general is to be found in Professor O. Doughty's *A Victorian Romantic* (1949). In this very unsatisfactory book on Rossetti, which is largely a detestable denigration—detestable because so wide of the truth as regards essentials—of that exquisite poet and still more of his gifted and unfortunate wife, we are informed that Swinburne 'had sunk into futility' in 1879; that in that year 'the heroic Watts' 'descended upon him' 'and—to the amazement of the Town, for since the Rape of the Sabines there had been nothing like it' [such cheap Brummagem rhetoric, utterly unrelated to anything real, is not uncommon in the work of this Professor of English Literature]—carried him 'triumphantly' off to his residence in Putney; where the poor captive wreck of a man and a poet—this is all the history of the rest of his life—was henceforth "the prisoner of Putney", a shadow of a shade, devoted to the reading of the Elizabethan dramatists and the occasional writing of a "poem" from which all inspiration had fled.' And so there is the old story once again, with its belittling and dishonouring stupidity and absurdity (and colossal ignorance!) raised to a still higher power, if that be possible—but it remains doubtful if Mr. Hare here as elsewhere isn't the winner of the first prize.

Mr. Hare might have been saved from howling error here had he read his sacrosanct Lafourcade with a little more attention. Lafourcade contradicts (or all but contradicts) himself here, as he so often does elsewhere; in one part of his *Jeunesse de Swinburne* he says that the poet 'répudiera en 1887 cet amour de jeunesse', which 'semble pur et sans mélange'; but later in the same work he records that this love was qualified by serious reserves even at an early date. And in his *Swinburne, A Literary Biography*, questioning if not actually rejecting the theory that *Whitmania* was 'suggested if not dictated by Watts', he states that 'the poet's dislike of Whitman's most glaring defects can be traced back to a much earlier date.'[1]

Mr. Hare's handling of this matter is typical of his procedure in general. In the work of others (he depends entirely on others) he seizes on what is most detrimental to Swinburne's reputation and ignores anything corrective of this, even if it is put forward by the most cherished of those without whom he would be nothing at all.

I have exposed only a fraction of the errors and absurdities out of which his book is made. (But I have, I think, sufficiently annihilated the most serious part of his monstrous misrepresentation of Swinburne, that summed up in the sentence: 'in 1879, weakened by alcoholic poisoning, he surrendered in his life as he had capitulated in his art'. More than once in the future I shall have occasion to return to this book and its enormities—unless I disregard it as being absolutely valueless and unworthy of any sort of attention. For it brings forward nothing new (except in the way of badness)— the author frankly admits that he can make no advance

---

[1] He gives no evidence here in support of this statement, but he refers the reader to an article of his on the subject in the *Revue Anglo-Americaine*. I have not seen this article, nor another on Swinburne and Whitman in *The Modern Language Review* to which he refers the reader in his *Jeunesse de Swinburne*. After the latter work and the *Literary Biography*, one feels that one can't stand any more of the *bêtise* that is his speciality.

beyond Lafourcade—and it serves up the worst of the worst that has gone before it. Its bias is revealed, consciously or unconsciously, by the fact that it has as a frontispiece Pellegrini's caricature of the poet: the book itself is, in sum, a sorry caricature that has not even the virtue of being funny. (And perhaps 'caricature' is too ambiguous a word to apply to it, for a caricature may be an exaggeration of truth, but this is an exaggeration of falsehood; an emphasising into further and cruder grotesquerie of lineaments daubed by malevolence and squint-eyed ineptitude.) For anyone who has a due regard for Swinburne it can only be an abomination—and a very dreary one.

It may be asked why, if I think the book utterly worthless, I have given attention to even a few of the offences of various kinds with which it superabounds. The reason is that the favourable reception accorded it on all hands by critics (who manifestly were not competent to deal with the subject) will help to consolidate still further the demeaning fictions and misconceptions of which Swinburne has been a victim for all too long a time. With this book and the approving pats given it by influential ignorance, the situation has ceased to be merely farcical, it is outrageous, and must be treated as such. The legend, instead of meeting with its due refutation and extinction, has become more vigorously current. Things are really desperate for those who care for the truth. Kill the legend here, in this its latest trumpery avatar, and there is a chance (but, alas, no more than a chance, so ready is stupidity always to welcome stupidity, in spite of all demolishing evidence) that it will not raise its silly head again even in the lowest quarters of literature.

THE STORY

Le romancier authentique crée ses personnages avec les directions infinies de sa vie
possible, le romancier factice les crée avec la
ligne unique de sa vie réelle. Le vrai roman
est comme une autobiographie du possible.

ALBERT THIBAUDET.

CHAPTER II

THE STORY

ITS GENESIS AND EVOLUTION INTO *Lesbia Brandon*

> *Le romancier souffre parfois
> de découvrir que c'est, en effet,
> toujours le même livre qu'il
> cherche à écrire et que tous ceux
> qu'il a déjà composés ne sont
> que les ébauches d'une œuvre
> qu'il s'efforce de réaliser sans y
> atteindre jamais.*
>
> —FRANCOIS MAURIAC

WHAT FOLLOWS IS TO NO SMALL AND UNIMPORTANT EXTENT different from existing opinion as initiated by Wise and Lafourcade and up to the present uncritically adopted by other writers on Swinburne in so far as they have given any attention to his work as a novelist.[1]

Lesbia Brandon is not isolated and alone: Swinburne advanced to it by tentative stages, each of which is a distinct novel or fragment of novel: altogether there are four of these, and the following is a brief synoptic view of them. (The titles in the case of the first and third are my own, in default of any provided by Swinburne. They are the names of the male characters who are prefigurations of the largely autobiographical Herbert Seyton of the final novel. The second, on this principle, would, like the first, have been called *Reginald*

---

[1] I do not include in this survey Swinburne's other fictional work— mostly of the short story order—as it does not belong to the cycle I am considering here. I have already published a study of *The Chronicle of Tebaldeo Tebaldei* (*Lucretia Borgia*), and the other stories I shall examine on some future occasion.

Harewood; but Swinburne entitles it *A Year's Letters*, and later *Love's Cross Currents*. The fourth also had no title; *Lesbia Brandon* was the name given it by Gosse and Wise, and this was adopted by Lafourcade and others, and has become so well established that it cannot be changed now. This is unfortunate, as the name is far from appropriate: Lesbia Brandon is by no means the chief or central figure of the story, and her appearances are on the whole sporadic. *Herbert Seyton* would have been a more, if not the most, suitable title for this ultimate draft of the story.)

I. *Reginald Harewood*

The extant text of this work immediately follows that of *Lesbia Brandon* in the present volume[1] (and is itself followed by the fragments of the third novel, which I have called *Herbert Winwood*). In this first novelistic essay[2] there are several features that will characterise the cycle as a whole—and some if not all of them are present in a fair number of other compositions. Here we have the sadistic elder who appears so often in Swinburne's work, especially in that which remains to be published; in this case it is the father, Francis Harewood; then the other frequent Swinburnian figure, the victim, a lovable or likable boy on the way to adolescence; his older sister, physically attractive, to him as well as to others, so much so that he has 'an animal worship' of her beauty, and with this comes in the hint of incestuous love that

[1] The word *Kirklowes* was written by Swinburne at the head of this text. It was almost certainly meant as the title, not of the whole work, but only of the first of its chapters.

[2] It may be dated circa 1861-2. There is only one watermark date 1861, and this is on one of the last sheets of the manuscript. The work borne by that sheet, then, cannot have been written on it earlier than that date. *Love's Cross Currents*, which followed the first attempt at a novel, and probably fairly closely, was composed in 1862-3, according to Swinburne himself.

is another element of not a little of Swinburne's work; her husband, whom she marries at an early age, a man of little or no distinction for whom she has little or nothing in the way of love; and the other man, installed in the household, a fellow (in this case) of dilettante accomplishments that appeal to her fallow and unsatisfied aspirations, and whose disturbing presence can only break up the marriage if the situation develops to its natural end. One may also notice another figure that is more or less a constant part of Swinburne's novelistic world, although here, as more than once elsewhere, she receives only retrospective and incidental mention, for she is already dead by the time the story begins: the mother of the boy and girl, a contrast to the physically healthy father, a woman who is 'very handsome' but of 'feeble blood', and dies long before her time. Thus the children are 'a mixture of two' very different 'breeds', and this is especially emphasised in the case of the daughter, who gets a streak of sensuality, and keen nervous sensibilities, with sadistic tendencies, from the mother's weak blood, while from the father she inherits a robust body and a certain coldness both of heart and head.

Swinburne might have made out that her nervous organisation and her capacity for sadistic enjoyment came at least in part from her father, who was an active sadist (she only liked *watching* the infliction of pain) to something like a maniacal extent. He beat the boy mercilessly, terribly, with a relish of connoisseurship as he made the tortured flesh break into gouts of blood. Four days a week . . . four dozen cuts at a time . . . cuts so savage that the scars were still there three months later: this is well on the way to the ghastly scale of punishment that we find in the unpublished *Flogging Block*, where the mania runs riot and becomes epical. To act thus is in some sort a necessity of his nature, a vent for something perilous in his system that would have a wrecking effect on him if it did not receive this expression. This reinforces the impression that the urge to hurt is something like a fever, a disease irruptive into an organism that is otherwise sound or not abnormal to any unhealthy extent.

A very noteworthy thing in connexion with the sadism of this work and its congeners is the statement that there was in the daughter's senses 'a sort of reversed sympathy with the pain of Reginald's tingling flesh'. Thus her gloating over the weals and blood and tears of her brother was not altogether sadistic (perhaps it was not really sadistic at all): there was something of masochism in it: she in some degree put herself in her brother's place, and vicariously enjoyed the pain which made him writhe and roar. This, as I have pointed out elsewhere,[1] is really Swinburne's own attitude even in the case of passages that seem altogether sadistic, and where the sadism is extreme to a state of fury. Always he is a masochist, receiving sympathetically the pain of the victim conjured up by his imagination; and the greater that pain the greater the 'kick' he gets out of it, because of self-identification, not with the inflictor, but with the victim, and further because he imagines himself as putting up resistant endurance against the terrible increase of agony. For if there is sometimes sexuality in this masochism where Swinburne himself is concerned, there is also—and more frequently—something else in it, and this is a spirit of heroism: an obvious enough fact that has escaped the dim vision of Gosse, Lafourcade and others who have taken it upon themselves to convey a portrait of him.

The Reginald of this work does not show much heroism; does not conceive the flogging as a duel between the punisher and himself, as Bertie Seyton will do in the final stage of this novel-sequence. Indeed he is not a very remarkable character; he gives no signs of cleverness, shows no intellectual promise,

---

[1] In my commentary on Swinburne's *Lucretia Borgia* (*The Chronicle of Tebaldeo Tebaldei*). See also, in this volume, the 69th note on the second chapter of *Lesbia Brandon*. I consider that Lafourcade is very seriously wrong in making 'une tendance à la cruauté', sadism in the strict sense of the word, one of the fundamental and cardinal elements in Swinburne's nature. I merely glance at this difficult and important matter here; I shall discuss it more searchingly in my *Swinburne: The Arcane Side*, which will follow this volume. Further reference to it in the present work will be found in the next section of the Commentary.

and is not even sensitive to any degree above the average. In short, he is scarcely an autobiographical creation, as young Seyton will be to no small extent. His education, of course, was far from propitious; (here, it may be noted, there is an inconsistency: at one point we are told that he was sent to school—not to Eton, as he successors will be—, but more than once we are given to understand that his father educated him). What his rôle would have been in the fully developed story it is hard to see—apart from that of an incidental figure with no place in such intrigue as there was. The faintly suggested incest *motif*[1] could hardly have been taken further, for his sister was preoccupied in another and less illicit direction over the main part of the story as far as we can see it from the fragment. (Besides, Swinburne—unlike Shelley, for instance —never carried the incest theme, when the incest theme would have been conscious, beyond the initial stage of possibilities, never took it as far as consummation. If there is an exception to this, it is only in the—rather adumbrated than fully explicit—relationships of Lucretia Borgia with members of her family; and here Swinburne was giving history and not events in the world of his own imagination.) Perhaps, as far as Reginald was concerned, Swinburne, as elsewhere in his early tentative work (especially in his unpublished incomplete plays) had a situation on his hands with which he would not deal with an effectiveness satisfactory to himself; but the work as we have it is too fragmentary for anything definite to be said in this regard.

The central interest of the work as conceived—or at least in as much of it as was presumably finished, of which only a

---

[1] Helen's watching of her brother—aged fourteen and presumably quite naked—swimming may seem rather overbold. But cf. in the relatively respectable Meredith's *The Ordeal* the scene Lady Blandish 'to the scandal of her sex' similarly watches Richard, now 'tall, strong, bloomingly healthy), in his swimming match against a boy of his age. They too are no doubt quite naked, and Richard is so flabbergasted when he catches sight of a female presence that he makes a bad start and thus loses the match.

portion is extant—most probably lay in the character, the behaviour and the fortunes of the sister, particularly in relation to the lover with whom she eloped from all claims on her as a wife. From this point of view, *Helen Harewood* would be a more apt title for the first of Swinburne's novel-series. In her chafing dissatisfaction with her married life, her multifarious reading of unorthodox books, her aspiration after place and power, her febrile or atonic moods when she was 'wasted with the hard desire of pleasure', she makes us think of Emma Bovary. (And Mr. Ashurst, Helen's husband, in his dull worthiness recalls Charles Bovary. Swinburne had a great admiration for Flaubert's masterpiece,[1] and perhaps it more than any other work is a source or model of this his earliest venture in the novel—which, however, like its successors, is much more original that derivative from what had been done by other men.) But Helen Ashurst, née Harewood, in one important respect is very different from Emma, and very much a Swinburnian creation. She has a sinister side to her nature to which there is nothing comparable in the provincial Frenchwoman vainly seeking evasion from commonplace reality in adulterous loves that lead her nowhere. For Emma is not a strong woman, and will dominate nothing. But Helen is not like that; there is in her a strength, an overmastering something, which will make a very devil of her. Her coldness of head and heart, her moral insensibility, comes out when she abandons her husband suffering from a mortal illness which she herself has no doubt helped to bring on. It comes out still more, and horribly, as she gloatingly watches her shipwrecked and half-drowned lover being gradually swept to the iron reef where his life will be knocked out of him; she praying the while that he will not be saved, and having a glitter of pleasure in her eyes when she finds that her prayer is answered . . . No, she must have been a real and full sadist.

[1] He was reading it—no doubt for the first time—with great enthusiasm as early as February 1860, as he remarks in an unpublished letter of that date. 'I regard it', he then said, 'as one of the most perfect and complete books I know.'

Even Swinburne's Lucretia Borgia, for whom 'the taking of
life seemed a small thing, compared with a little pleasure',
was not so deadly as she; for Lucretia would hardly have
watched with eager delight the helplessly struggling drift of a
lover to the fatal rocks, and the smashing and cracking of his
body when he was at last beaten upon them. Helen, more
than Lucretia, is like the Venus that is 'a perilous Goddess, a
deadly lady; and the savour of destruction is on her lips'. She
has more in common with Mary Stuart, another avatar of the
most specially Swinburnian woman, on the elaboration of
whom the poet was engaged at the time when he wrote this
fragment. Mary Stuart, too, as seen by an ordinary woman,
has

> some blood in her
> That does not run to mercy as ours doth:
> That fair face and the cursed heart in her
> Made keener than a knife for manslaying
> Can bear strange things.[1]

Or as she herself freely admits, 'her heart is close and cold';[2]
and again

> I have
> No tears in me; I never shall weep much,
> I think, in all my life . . .
> *   *   *
> God made me hard, I think . . .[3]

And she too can watch the death of her lover—whom, having
it in her power to save him, she allows to go to the scaffold—
with shining eyes and a face of ecstasy.

---

[1] *Chastelard*, Act. V, scene III.
[2] These words occur in an unpublished fragment of an earlier draft
of *Chastelard*.
[3] *Chastelard* III, scene I.

This account of the death of the shipwrecked Champneys¹ in a strong sea (which, with the description of the Kirklowes dwelling and surroundings in their grey and somewhat grim desolation, is the best thing in the fragment) is very powerful, full of progressive tragic force secured by touches of economical realism. It shows that, in the matter of tersely effective narrative, ordinarily reckoned one of the requisites or desiderata of the novel, Swinburne, already at this early age, had a sufficiency of competence should he have occasion to use it. Just as what we can see of the character of Helen gives promise, and more than promise, of faculty in another of the constituents of the highest kind of novel according to the most general standards.

What led up to this last scene? How did the relations of Helen and Champneys evolve?; (did she marry him and had he come into an inheritance?: she calls him 'the master' at the end); by what gradations and through what vicissitudes did her love for him turn into the strong feeling that could pray that he would not live? Who was 'the other' person who had been in the boat with him? Was it another woman—like the strange unknown other woman in Denham's life in *Lesbia Brandon*—, who had come in as a complicating force (a probability, as Swinburne was very fond of complications)? There is no answer to these questions, for the pages on which this chief and crucial part of the story was written (if it was written, and most probably it was, for Swinburne would hardly have passed to the shipwreck scene without giving antecedents upon which this was consequent) have disappeared, and there is no hope that they will ever be recovered. We can be sure of one thing, and that is that there would have been a good deal of subtlety in the full story, and especially in the evolution of

¹ Perhaps 'shipwrecked' is too strong a word; it may be that Champneys was not escaping in a small boat from the wreck of a ship (as were people in the fragmentary ch. VI of *Lesbia Brandon*), but had been in a small boat all along. 'The sail too had', a cancelled portion of text, perhaps indicates that he had gone out from the shore in a yacht or some vessel of that description.

Helen's feelings in their final state. As much, perhaps, as in *Love's Cross Currents*, which is one of the subtlest books in the world.[1]

II. *Love's Cross Currents*

Although *Love's Cross Currents* is not an unpublished work, we shall discuss it almost as if it were, and at what may

[1] On the back of the first page of the manuscript Swinburne jotted down at random groups of names and other words, one below another; the following is a table of these:

Reginald	Reginald Harewood	Lucrezia	After death
Etsi	Ernest	Estense	Et
me	Arthur	Borgia	me
	Frank		E
Lucrezia			P
			R
	Edmund		Never
			Edmund Hazlehurst
			Et q quem
			Never any more while I live
			LB

These do not throw any light on the possible contents of the lost part of the story. Almost certainly, in fact, none of the jottings have anything to do with this first story at all. The names in the second group are very probably those of characters in *Love's Cross Currents*, with the conception of which Swinburne's mind was no doubt beginning to play before he had carried the first story to completion, or after he had decided to give it up. There is a Reginald Harewood in *Love's Cross Currents*, and the four Christian names are those of characters in that novel. 'Edmund Hazlehurst' in the fourth group is the name of a character (with the surname spelled Hazlehurst) in a play of Swinburne's that was probably written in this period (circa 1860-1862). I have seen only one act of this play (it is part of my own collection of Swinburne manuscripts). It was once in Wise's Ashley Collection, but Wise mentions it nowhere, nor does Lafourcade, who had access to all the Swinburne items possessed by Wise. The letters E P R seem at first sight a rather disproportionate length. There are sound reasons for this: it is very ill known, and may be said to be as good as unknown: it receives no attention at all in standard histories of the English novel, and in works on Swinburne written in English (or American) there is no adequate account of it, nor anything like due appreciation; and it may be regarded as having been out of print for a number of years:

(*Note* [1] *continued*)—
in the fourth group are all joined together in a direction slanting from the vertical; the middle one, which I have taken to be P, may be Q or O. Other jottings show that Swinburne was also more or less preoccupied with his work on the Borgias at this time. 'LB' at the end of the fourth group almost certainly stands for Lucrezia Borgia and not for Lesbia Brandon. But 'never any more while I live' is strangely like Lady Wariston's 'never in my life or in yours any more . . . never while we live any more', in the XVth chapter of *Lesbia Brandon*.

Neither Wise nor Lafourcade mentions these jottings. Lafourcade, with characteristically gross carelessness, gives 1836 and (twice) 1837 as the dates of the births of Helen and her brother respectively. But it is stated quite plainly and legibly in the manuscript that she was born in 1831 and that Reginald came into the world 'five years later'. Lafourcade also says:

Il semble . . . que le bateau portant Eleanor et son complice Mr. Champneys ait fait naufrage en face de la ferme du Northumberland, et que Reginald ait réussi par son courage et sa science de nageur à sauver sa sœur de la tempéte. Ceci formerait un digne *finale* à notre roman.

All this is moonshine or worse, and shows that those whose gait is a blundering stumble cannot even read what is writ large. Nothing of what Lafourcade says is to be found in or deduced from Swinburne's very clear text. 'Le bateau' should be 'un bateau'; there are no grounds for saying that it capsized off Kirklowes or in any particular locality; Helen (whom Lafourcade miscalls Eleanor) had—it is quite plain from the narrative—not been in it with Champneys, and so had not been rescued by her brother or anybody else, but had been safe on the shore since the beginning of the accident . . . And whether this tissue of fantastic errors or anything else would be 'un digne *finale*' to the story it is quite impossible to say without knowing what the main lines of the story were.—All this is a good example of the average quality of Lafourcade's mental powers, which is less than third class: and declension from this average is not at all uncommon.

if it is in print to-day it is only in the many-volumed, limited and very expensive edition that goes by the name of *Bonchurch*. Moreover, being the only novel Swinburne completed, it is the only work that gives an opportunity for arriving at a more than partial idea of what he could do in this line; coming before *Lesbia Brandon*, it enables us to say what were the proved capacities of the man who addressed himself to that larger enterprise. Furthermore, it contains several of the themes, and not only one of the chief personages but also some of the types, of the later novel and this alone would make necessary a fairly close examination of it. But our survey will by no means be exhaustive: it is designed primarily and mainly as helping to introduce *Lesbia Brandon*.

Here we still have the ultra-severe, not to say sadic, father, with only a change of Christian name and of profession (Captain Philip Harewood), and the pleasant son, who is still called Reginald; and the theme of conjugal ties disrupted or threatened by attraction of the wife of a worthy but dull husband towards another man, with resulting elopement if things are allowed to pursue their natural course. But there is no daughter, no Harewood girl this time; and so there is no opportunity for the incest *motif* in that quarter (but it turns up incidentally elsewhere). In this novel the principal amorous relations are simply between cousins (but, although no conventional stigma attaches to them on the ground of consanguinity, it is pretty certain that Swinburne felt—and relished —them as approaching incest in the technical sense). It is these relations that constitute the adulterous situation mentioned above; but there are two sets of them, and thus the intrigue is wider than in the fragment I have called *Reginald Harewood*; and it is also much more complicated, as all four lovers and one of the husbands are interrelated by ties of blood, and move and have a good deal of their being in the same family group. The evolution of these two affairs, and the thwarting of their progress, furnishes the chief business of the story.

The following is a rapid account of the family, in so far as it is necessary to an intelligence of the situation as a whole.

There are the three elder Cheynes: Helena (born 1800), who becomes (1819) Lady Midhurst, and her two brothers, Lord Cheyne and John Cheyne, who are both her seniors. Lady Midhurst has a daughter Amicia (b. 1820); Lord Cheyne has a son Edmund (b.1830), who succeeds to the title in 1858;[1] and John Cheyne, who marries rather late in life, has a daughter Clara (b.1836) and a son Francis, generally called Frank, born four years after his sister. The only sign of a possibly more than family relationship, licit or illicit, between these children was in the case of Edmund and Clara; he was attracted to her and she was not averse—indeed she tried hard to get the man and the future title when she became marriageable, but Edmund's father put a stop to this, having a strong prejudice against union between cousins (perhaps Swinburne means us to understand that old Lord Cheyne regarded it as incestuous. This would be a touch helping to create a suggestion of incest in the case of the affairs between cousins that are the main matter of the book).

The interesting relationships—the *liaisons dangereuses*—arise with children of the next generation, but between them and members of the group of offspring mentioned in the preceding paragraph. This possibly sounds strange, but the following are the clarifying details. Amicia marries (1837) Captain Philip Harewood, and they have a son, Reginald (b.1838); but Amicia elopes with a Mr. Stanford (this recurrent *leit-motif* is not developed here, but is merely given incidental mention as part of the background of the story); and she marries him (1840) after Harewood has divorced her, and by him has a daughter (1841), who is also called Amicia. Thus Reginald is the half-brother of Amicia II; they naturally are not in the way of meeting as children, as they live in separate and enemy households; on the one occasion on which she does meet him in childhood—he being fourteen and she eleven—she 'falls in love with him on the spot', but this is

[1] For a short account of him see the 111th note on Ch. III of *Lesbia Brandon*.

probably meant to convey nothing that is not perfectly innocent; and when they meet in later years there is no hint of
anything even remotely resembling passion between them.
Although these two, the grandchildren of Lady Midhurst,
belong to a younger generation than Clara and Frank, her
niece and one of her nephews, they are almost coeval with
them owing to the late marriage of the father of the two
latter: Reginald is only some two years younger than his
first cousin once removed[1] Clara, and Amicia II is only one
year younger than her first cousin once removed Frank: and
each of these two pairs, Reginald and Clara, Frank and
Amicia II, are in process of falling in love with each other
when the story opens. (There are some 37 pages of explanatory
and scene-setting *Prologue*, and then, in January 1861, begins
the story proper in the form of letters between the chief
characters, and it continues in this form to the end of
February of the following year.)[2]

But Amicia[3] had married her first cousin once removed
Edmund, now Lord Cheyne, in 1859, on her eighteenth birthday; and Clara, in 1857, had become the wife of Ernest Radworth, 'a slow, unlovely, weighty, dumb, grim sort of fellow',
an able scientist, interested particularly in bones (including
their use as manure) and beetles and other creeping things
that made her shiver; moreover, well-reputed professionally
and enjoying independent means—which no doubt made him
seem a good match to the shrewd side of Clara after she had
failed to win the larger and more distinguished affluence of
the Cheyne estates. But there is still at the beginning of the
epistolary story some sentimental interchange between her
and Edmund: even he, dull as he is, is more exciting than
her husband, who is a very desert of boredom for one of her

[1] Swinburne, adopting more popular but less correct parlance, uses
the term 'second cousin' for this degree of relationship.

[2] Whence the title *A Year's Letters* borne by the work when it came
out serially in *The Tatler* in 1877

[3] Henceforth 'Amicia', unless there is an indication to the contrary,
will mean 'Amicia II'.

287

aspiration and dreams; possibilities in this direction, however, decline and cease with the intervention, or rather coming to a head (for it had begun when he first met her as a boy), of Reginald's passionate interest in her, which gives her something much more attractive with which to engage her attention; something exciting, in fact, real fire for the starved romantic in her complex make-up to play with (but not beyond the limits of safety). Besides, as Lady Midhurst tells Amicia, when the latter lets her see that she has misgivings about her husband and Clara, 'any pleasant sort of woman can attract him *to her*, but no human power will attract him *from you*'. For Amicia, like Clara, is a very winning person, but in quite other ways. She has a 'strange grave beauty and faultless grace'; her grey-green eyes are luminous and soft; her abundant hair is deep-gold and it curls very prettily. Grave and soft: these two words sum up the chief effect of her personality. There is nothing hard about her, nothing very strong even, no calculating vision such as Clara's, no wild-fire that might lead her into recklessness (something of the sort, one suspects, is latent beneath the prudence that is a controlling force in Clara). Reginald's disadvanatgeous comparison of her with Clara has to be discounted, coming from so biassed a source, but it has in it a core of truth: 'She has a pliable, soft sort of mind, not unlike her over-tender, cased-up, exotic sort of beauty'. Frank's version of her qualities is far more enthusiastic, of course. As Amicia is a contrast to Clara, he, though in a lesser degree, is a contrast to Reginald. Altogether he is a very likable person; Lady Midhurst, who had not been very well disposed to him in his boyhood, and was much more a friend of Reginald, had formed a more favourable opinion of him by the time at which the epistolary story begins: 'I see he is a nice boy; very faithful, brave and candid; with more of a clear natural stamp on him than I thought.' And long before that she had allowed that he had a 'quality of always doing well enough under any circumstances'. On the whole, he is quieter, less headstrong, more practical than Reginald; but even he is 'somewhat excitable'

—excitable enough to be swept off his feet by Amicia—, and although not primarily a poet as Reginald is, he can pass into poetry scarcely inferior to Reginald's once he lets himself go on the subject of Amicia, as he does occasionally in letters to his sister:

'Your praise of Mademoiselle de Rochelaurier is, of course, all right and just. She is a very jolly sort of girl, and sufficiently handsome . . . Does Madame really want me to take such a gift at her hand? Well and good; it is incomparably obliging; but then, when I am looking at Mademoiselle Philomène, and letting myself go to the sound of her voice like a song to the tune, unhappily there gets up between us such an invincible exquisite memory of a face ten times more beautiful and loveable to have in sight of one; pale when I saw it last, as if drawn down by its hair, heavily weighted about the eyes with a presage of tears, sealed with sorrow, and piteous with an infinite unaccomplished desire. The old deep-gold hair and luminous grey-green eyes shot through with colours of sea-water in sunlight, and threaded with faint keen lines of fire and light about the pupil, beat for me the blue-black of Mademoiselle de Rochelaurier's. Then that mouth of hers and the shadows made almost on the chin by the underlip— such sad perfect lips, full of tender power and faith, and her wonderful way of lifting and dropping her face imperceptibly, flower-fashion, when she begins or leaves off speaking; I shall never hear such a voice in the world, either. I cannot, and need not now, pretend to dissemble or soften down what I feel about her. I do love her with all my heart and might.'

By way of comparison, here is Reginald in the same strain on the subject of Clara (and incidentally the passage throws light on more of the latter than was intended by Reginald):

'I found her yesterday by herself in the library here, looking out references for him [her husband]. The man was by way of being ill upstairs. She spoke to me with a sort of sad laugh in her eyes, not smiling; and her brows winced, as they never do for him, whatever he says. She is so gentle and perfect when he is there; and I feel like getting mad. Well, somehow I let her see I knew what an infernal shame it was, and she said wives were made for that work . . . I daresay I talked no end of folly, but I was regularly off my head . . . Nothing hurts me now but the look of her. She has sweet heavy eyes, like an angel's in some great strange pain; eyes without fear or fault in them, which look out over coming tears that never come. There is a sort of look about her lips and under the eyelids as if some sorrow had pressed there with his finger, out of love for her beauty, and left the mark. I believe she knew I wanted her to come away. If there were only somewhere to take her to and hide her, and let her live in her own way, out of all their sight and reach, that would do for me. I tell you, she took my hands sadly into hers and never said a word, but looked sideways at the floor, and gave a little beginning kind of sigh twice; and I got mad. I don't know how I prayed to her to come then. But she turned on me with her face trembling and shining, and eyes that looked wet without crying, and made me stop. Then she took the books and went out, and up to him.'

We have, then, a pretty entanglement of cousins (a thing that always had a sort of fascination for Swinburne) and illegitimate loves, with promise or menace of a good deal of trouble out of which might come disaster. The trouble develops, but the disaster, or the worst of it, is averted by the firm, and at need high-handed, intervention, the very skilful diplomacy, of Lady Midhurst, who takes it on herself to keep within prudential bounds the scattered family of which she regards herself as the head. It is a measure of the strength and subtlety and prestige of this 'beautiful old woman' from whom the two Amicias get their looks and carriage, that she can handle these difficult young relatives of hers and direct them in accordance with her decisions. Frank speaks of 'her passion of intrigue and management'; he of course is not an unprejudiced witness; but the omniscient author himself tells us in the Prologue that 'Education, superintendence, training of character, guidance of habit, in young people were passions with the excellent lady'. It is she who makes all the matches in the family—or so she believes, and apparently not without reason. 'I married Edmund to Amicia'; 'I don't know why I made him or let him [Captain Harewood] marry your mother' are samples of her self-assurance regarding her exercise of matrimonial authority. Indeed the extent of her arrogation is astonishing not only here, but with respect to things in general, as the following few examples will show (she is writing to grown-up people, one of whom has been married for pretty nearly two years). To Amicia: '. . . on that ground *only* I authorise you to invite her and Ernest while Redgie is still with you'. To Reginald: 'If there was any real danger for your cousin you don't suppose I would let Amicia have you both in the house at once?' To Frank: 'I would not have you write to Amicia about . . .' To Amicia again: 'I shall have to extricate your brother, half-eaten, from under her very teeth . . . Frank is very nice and sensible; I would undertake to manage him for life by the mere use of reasoning'.

It is even more astonishing that these grown-up people should be amenable to her pressure. But there is nothing incredible in this; it is a corollary from her clever force of character—all the more so as they have been subject to it in varying degrees from childhood, and thus predisposing habit tells in her favour. And anyhow they do show some natural recalcitrance. Clara speaks of 'her grey fierce old face' (she is 'clear-skinned, with pure regular features', we are told in the Prologue); and Clara pits her rebellious shrewdness against the dictatorial power, which handles her with a superb cunning that is always friendly and makes a show of moving in alliance with her. 'She is rather of the vulturine order as to beak and diet' writes Frank to Clara; and again, 'I am

certain that Lady Midhurst means venom'—and imagines
that his perspicacity will enable him to deal with her.

But she is too artful and forceful for them all, she imposes
her will and keeps things within the limits she prescribes, she
breaks or thwarts their loves—at least to the extent of pre-
venting their culmination in scandal. And scandal, or rather
scandal to no worth-while purpose by her standards (for had
she not favoured the elopement of her daughter?) was all that
she was concerned to stop. Commonsense, long-view values,
and not conventional morals, were her only criterion in the
matter of these loves; she even tells Reginald that she would
'allow' him '*any* folly' on account of an Athénais de Montes-
pan, but that Clara is not this sort of woman. Clara is worth
the generous and hazardous extravagances into which his
poet's imagination is all aflame to run; so at least she assures
him, and perhaps she is right—but she never gets him to believe
it. Besides she thinks, or professes to think, that these loves
are little or nothing but sentiment at bottom, and sentiment
she scorns as an unhealthy thing that has no greatness in it; a
thing that she would cut out of the world if she could. 'I wish
to Heaven there were some surgical process discoverable by
which one could annihilate or amputate sentiment. Passion,
impulse, vice of appetite or conformation, nothing you can
define in words is so dangerous.'

She gets her way, then, as far as what is most essential to her
is concerned. (We cannot here trace all the subtleties she
deploys, the actions and reactions, the gradual stages, of the
drama, which constitute the high interest of one of the most
delicate intrigues ever invented.) She gets her way; but she
cannot prevent Frank and Amicia from committing adultery,
and Amicia from becoming *enceinte* as a consequence.
Scandal, however, is averted, for Amicia's husband is drowned
in the course of a yachting-party during which the adultery
takes place, and so he can pass as the father of any issue of
this clandestine love.[1] And Lady Midhurst, of course, sees that

[1] This is the only case of questionable artistry in the whole of the

he does. (To her sharp eye the truth soon becomes patent from signs of wasting remose on Amicia's countenance.) She keeps the lovers rigorously apart during the crucial period after Edmund's death, and indeed indefinitely, till they are set on separate ways that will never join.

Frank, in the meantime, as the next in line, succeeds to the Cheyne title; but when, some eight months later, the child is born it is a boy—and so the very infant Frank himself has begotten turns him out of the inheritance! But all this is conveyed so subtly, by such tenuous hints, that ordinary wits, and even wits better than ordinary, may not be aware or at least quite sure of it. Joseph Knight, a very intelligent person, wasn't quiet sure as to what had really happened. 'If, as I suspect,' he wrote to Swinburne after reading the work in manuscript, 'Frank has robbed himself of his own inheritance the idea is wonderful'. Why, the reader of blunt sense will ask, should Frank lose Amicia too? Why can't they come together, at least by the respectable way of marriage, after the not so very long interval prescribed by social usage? But that is to reckon without Lady Midhurst and her values and the serene power of her authority over this little clan of hers. 'I will confess to you', she writes to Amicia at the end of it all, 'that if the child had been a girl I meant to have brought you together at some

(Note ¹ continued)—
book. Events not arising from the initial premises and the characters of the personages are illegitimate in drama or novel or any work that belongs to the category of art. Such things of course are common enough in life, and therefore are not out of place in the very inferior class of work that is merely representational and is content with 'being true to life'. But the truth of art is much stricter and narrower than that of life, as Balzac (following Aristotle and Corneille and other masters of aesthetic wisdom) proclaimed when he attacked 'la faute que commettent quelques auteurs, en prenant un sujet vrai dans la nature qui ne l'est pas dans l'art'. Still, the history of even novels of the higher kind is full of accidents of this sort that do not arise from the logic of the story. A signal case is the drowning of the protagonist in *Beauchamp's Career* (written long after *Love's Cross Currents*, which Meredith had read in manuscript).

293

future day'. But as it was a boy, her sense of fitness decided otherwise, and perhaps there is something to be said for her point of view. Anyhow she is quite supreme in the end.

As she cannot stop Frank and Amicia from committing adultery, so she cannot check the course of Reginald's ever more ardent (and ever more idealistic) love for Clara. Her letters to him, with their clever depreciatory hints about the latter, have nothing of the desired effect on him—rather they intensify his championship. And Clara too, in spite of prudential hesitations, seems at last ready to fall in with his desires. By January 19th, 1862, eleven days before the birth of Amicia's child (discomfiture enough for Lady Midhurst), things have come to a head between them, in a way altogether to the liking of Reginald. She may even have given herself to him: but here Swinburne's technique of indirection (a technique common with him and in spite of the current belief that he preferred headlong emphasis) is so delicate that one cannot get beyond conjecture. In the last of his letters to her, Reginald is waiting for her to join him, and some of his expressions might mean that she has already yielded to him what moralistic writers of a former age would have called her pearl or the most inestimable of her treasures. 'We have counted all and found nothing better than love'. '. . . you . . . *my love that is now*'. 'Are you ever going to be afraid of the old king in Cornwall *after this*?' 'The whole world has no claim or right in it *any longer* to set against mine'. I have italicised what seem crucial words; but she may only have written him a letter of acquiescence, and there is nothing in the way of confirming evidence. Lady Midhurst is faced with defeat here; but here, with diabolical cunning, she plays a trump card that is disastrous to their love. She has managed to get hold of some very compromising letters written by Clara a few years before to a dissolute French amorist who has not been gentleman enough to keep them from the eyes of others. It would have been interesting to know what was in them that could alienate such a fervent and yet unjealous and broad-minded passion as that of Reginald for his cousin.

('What is it to me', he writes to her when he has got wind of
the letters—Lady Midhurst has seen that he does—, 'if I am
to be the man fit to match with you by the right of my delight
in you, that you have tried to find help or love before we came
together, and failed of it? Let them show me letters to disprove that I love you, and I will read them.) But the author
sagely refrains from giving the damning contents, and we have
to take Lady Midhurst's word for it that 'one of these letters
would fall like a flake of thawed ice on the most feverish of a
boy's rhapsodies'. With exquisite craft, she writes to Clara,
affects to assume that the latter must be worried and annoyed
by Reginald's attentions, and suggests that she, Clara, should
write to him and tell him firmly that they must come to a
stop. Otherwise, she, Lady Midhurst, will be obliged to make
him privy to the letters. 'If you don't like writing to silence
him, I can but use them faute de mieux—for, of course, the
boy *must* be brought up short; but I think my way is the
better and more graceful. Do not you?' For suave grace of
devilish cunning that is quite matchless in literature.

Clara, of course, is cornered and has to agree. And so that
is an end of the loves of Reginald and Clara, and once again
Lady Midhurst comes out victorious. There is something in
this highly cultivated Victorian English gentlewoman of the
dread power of the tribal matriarch in primitive times.
'Grande, spirituelle . . . toujours vraie . . . Elle ne revient
jamais sur ses résolutions . . . La persistance, cette qualité de
son caractère impérieux, imprime je ne sais quoi de terrible à
toutes les scènes de ce drame fécond.' These words, written by
the enthusiastic Balzac of Stendhal's duchesse de San-
Severina, might have been written of Lady Midhurst. Stendhal's duchess is the only woman in fiction who enters into the
same class with her.

And so the whole thing—the two love affairs with their out-
reaching ardours and wistful passions and dreams—peter out
into nothingness and pure waste. As so often, if not always, do
the main affairs in Swinburne's fictional creations, dramatic
and other—and as they do in all the great truly tragic dramas

and in most of the great novels—being therein not at variance with actual life taken as a whole, at least in so far as it is an aspiration after fineness. (The fact that the greatest art is for the most part tragic is probably not without metaphysical significance: it may be an indication that tragedy belongs to the essence of things, that fundamentally and ultimately the universe, optimistically called the cosmos, has in it the dis- order of tragedy.) 'It is a dull, empty end; a blank upshot', as Lady Midhurst herself says, summing everything up when she has brought about the conclusion on which her heart was set. One cannot help wondering (although it is not probable that this was Swinburne's intention) whether she does not in these words condemn herself; whether it was worth while her work- ing to produce mere blankness, mere negation, nothing but a barrenness all the more dreary because it led nowhere; whether, in other terms, it would not have been better to allow things to pursue their course, and the lovers to go on to such happiness as they might have had. The question remains even if what she said about the loves being nothing but sentiment was sincere (as is perhaps possible) and true (but there does seem to be more to them, and a good deal more in the case of Reginald), and if the story is viewed as an illustra- tion of the dangers attending that rather cheap emotion (although it is the opposite of likely that Swinburne had any such sermonising intention in mind).[1] Certainly, the only

---

[1] Lafourcade thinks he had: 'Ce sentimentalisme morbide . . . Swin- burne l'a subtilement saisi et condamné'. But then Lafourcade sees nothing but that small thing 'le flirt' in these passions, including that of Reginald, which is as strong and full as that of Swinburne's Chaste- lard or Tristram or any other of the characters whom the poet un- questionably meant to present as great lovers. Lafourcade fails to see that Lady Midhurst *sometimes* writes not necessarily or entirely out of her heart—and still less as the mouthpiece of Swinburne—but in order to weaken or disturb a valuation held by the person she is addressing; and crafty denigration—whether of a character or of a situation—is one of the most common of her weapons. (It is a weapon very skilfully employed by Valmont and still more so by Madame de Merteuil in *Les Liaisons dangereuses,* and we may be certain Swinburne

consolation she has to offer (in a letter to Clara) is bleak, and is a further desolation: 'You see, my dear, the flowers (and weeds) will grow over us all in good time. One thing and one time we may be quite sure of seeing—the day when we shall have well forgotten everything . . . The years will do without us . . . In good time we shall be out of the way of things, and have nothing in all the world to desire or deplore . . .'

'Much incident', we are informed in the Prologue, 'is not here to be looked for', and indeed there is scarcely any in the ordinary sense of the word (how different in this—and other—respects is *Love's Cross Currents* from the work of Dickens, Wilkie Collins, Charles Reade, Meredith, Dumas, Hugo, Balzac and other contemporary or earlier novelists whom Swinburne greatly admired and by whom it might be expected that he would be influenced in various ways: but to a remarkable degree he has and maintains an individuality of his own even in this first completed essay of his in the novel, which was rather a side line for him). Lady Midhurst remarks on this when she summarises matters at the end:

'But for poor Edmund's accidental death, which I am fatalist enough to presume must have happened anyhow, we should all be just where we were. Not an event in the

(*Note* ¹ *Continued*)—
learned something from these two dread tacticians.) Lafourcade here also loses sight of the fact that Reginald is very largely a portrait of Swinburne himself—a consideration that makes it certain that Reginald's love is much bigger than anything of 'le flirt' order.

In Lady Midhurst's attitude to sentiment (apart from the question of her sincerity in classifying the loves of the cousins as such) there may possibly be something of a French tradition extending in various forms from Corneille to Laclos (and entering in a certain measure into what is known as 'beylisme'); a tradition according to which intelligence and will should have predominance over what comes from 'the heart'. Laclos' book is one of the influences behind Swinburne's novelistic work; and he admired Stendhal; he also had no small admiration for Corneille. But in his most immediate or essential self his sympathies were on the side of the great lovers.

whole course of things; not, I think, so much as an incident;
very meagre stuff for a French workman to be satisfied
with . . .'

For certain—and even many, more or less famous—French
workmen, yes; but it is in the distinguished tradition of other
French workmen that Swinburne created this masterpiece of
which the incidents, the interest, the excitement are almost
exclusively psychological: the adventure is simply that of
processes in minds dynamically in relation to one another in
a situation that is arriving at a point of crisis. This—to mention no more than two of the latter class of workmen—is the
technique of Racine aiming at making high tragedy out of
something that for most people would be nothing; and that of
Constant undertaking to make an interesting novel with only
two characters in a situation that never in any way varied.

One of the most striking things in *Love's Cross Currents*
is the writing, which is always consummate, always style in the
strictest and very highest sense of the word. It frequently
takes on powers of poetry, as will have been seen in some of
the passages we have quoted, but its virtue as style does not
depend on a context that easily rises into poetry. Even when
it is not poetical (or emotionally imaginative), even when it
is most workaday or 'prosaic', it never fails to be governed by
that form which is the ultimate and irreducible element of
what I have called style in its strictest sense. It has that perfection of grace or harmony that most essentially differentiates
style from writing that merely serves as statement. And this
is the real test of a stylist as distinct from anything else that
workers in words may be: he instinctively endows with
musical or architectonic grace or harmony whatever he writes,
even the most pedestrian or non-poetic information, so that
his sentences have a value over and above that of any function
they perform merely as instruments of statement. (Judged by
this test, Ruskin, for example, who has a great reputation as a
prosaist, is less than first-class; for, in general, his writing has
true and sure form only when it is poetic; elsewhere it is

information, organised syntactically etc., but not organised into something further exceeding all its utilitarian powers—a plus-value that may be called a *super*-fine art. This description of it carries the implication that it is a spiritual force, and no mere plaster-work or otiose decoration or decorum added to what is a substantiality without it: it is itself substantial—just as metre and other formal elements are in poetry of the highest kind.) Style, then, in this sense, is constant throughout *Love's Cross Currents*; and this fact is really notable, for the presence of style in a novel is a very exceptional thing. As Saintsbury says, 'if the novel writer attains to style it is almost a marvel. Of the four constituents of the novel,—plot, character, description, and dialogue,—none lend themselves to any great degree to the cultivation of the higher forms of style, and some are distinctly opposed to it. The most cunning plot may be developed equally in the style of Plato and in the style of a penny dreadful. Character drawing, as the novelist understands or should understand it, is almost equally unconnected with style. On the other hand, description and dialogue, unless managed with consummate skill, distinctly tend to develop and strengthen the crying faults of contemporary style'; and again, 'It is a pity that a novel should not be well written: yet some of the greatest novels of the world are, as no one of the greatest poems of the world is, or could possibly be, written anything but well'. It is indeed hard to find English novelists (to mention those of no other country) who are stylists in the narrowest but greatest, in the most specific, sense of the term, masters of unfailing form, of distinction and felicity, of a certain rightness in sentence and paragraph structure even when the subject-matter is most humble. Hardy, for example, is often a very able novelist; but he is a very poor writer; even the admired descriptive passages of *The Return of the Native* are not style in the esoteric sense; and as for Hardy's writing outside the novel—in his essays—, it is so wanting in style, so much the opposite of style, that it may properly be called detestable. This judgment concerning novelists may, as Saintsbury indicates, be generalised (with due qualification in particular cases): it is a rule proved by the exceedingly few exceptions to it. (Goethe makes a useful distinction between style and manner; Saintsbury makes a still more useful one between style and what he names 'handling'. The majority of the authors spoken of as great writers by schoolmasters, University lecturers and critics are not in the strict sense writers, they are no more than highly efficient handlers in various departments.[1]) Swinburne, on the other hand, is infallibly a stylist, whatever he is treating—in letters, in essays on the most sober subjects, in the most business-like textual criticism, as well as on occasions which contain an invitation to poetry. Saintsbury says somewhere that from the *Blake* onwards one might cull passage after passage unsurpassed in the whole history of English prose; he might well with little or no risk of exaggeration have used the words 'unequalled' of some at least of these passages; and he might certainly have taken as a starting-point *Love's Cross Currents*, which is anterior by some years to the best things in the *Blake*.

But, to quote Saintsbury once again, 'the ordinary Briton resents with angry impatience anything esoteric, fastidious, or fine', and so it is probably idle to insist on stylistic felicity, constancy of form, as a recommendation of any sort of book; especially in an age which takes Mr. T. S. Eliot (rightly included by Mr. Wyndham Lewis in his *Men Without Art*) and James Joyce as masters of the Word, not seeing that they represent a regress to a stage of chaos preceding anything in

[1] To give a few more crucial examples: J. S. Le Fanu, Conan Doyle, Mr. Algernon Blackwood, Mr. Somerset Maugham and G. K. Chesterton, are all short-story writers; it would be generally admitted that in varying degrees they are all masters in this line; but the first four are very mediocre stylists, or no stylists at all, whereas Chesterton, whatever be the relative value of his stories as stories (I rate them high myself), is always a stylist, always a master of the art of the Word as well as a very efficient handler. But his greatness in this respect has hardly ever been duly recognised. For some time past, indeed, British journalistic and other criticism as a whole, has shown itself indifferent (or impervious) to the quality of works from a stylistic point of view.

the way of cosmos.[1] (The gentle reader, of course, is not an ordinary Briton. But in that case, in face of these melancholy facts, he is probably very ungentle.) One is no doubt on more profitable ground in calling attention to the versatility of the writing of this novel, of the very different effects of which it is capable. That of humour or satire, for example, of which the following is only one of several species that the book offers:

'Had fate or date allowed it,—but stern chronology forbade,—he would assuredly have figured as president, as member, or at least as correspondent of the Society for the Suppression of Anatomy, the Society for the Suppression of Sex, or the Ladies' Society for the Propagation of Contagious Disease (Unlimited).'

Or this, analytic, anatomical, where physical portraiture merges into psychological and renders the inner springs of a character:

'She has edges in her eyes, and thorns in her words. That perpetual sardonic patience which sits remarking on right and wrong with cold folded hands and equable observant eyes, half contemptuous in an artistic way of those who choose either—that cruel tolerance and unmerciful compassion for good and bad—that long tacit inspection, as of a dilettante cynic bidden report critically on the creatures in the world, that custom of choosing her point of view where she can see the hard side of things glitter and the hard side of characters reflect light in her eyes, till she comes (if one durst say so) to patronise God by dint of despising men—oh, it gets horrid after a time!'

[1] In case this seems a mere fling of unsupported and unsupportable prejudice, I would briefly say by way of apologia that I consider to be a gross aesthetic error what is most plausible in the doctrine advanced in justification of the poetic (or rather the antithesis of poetic) of these two *sommités* of the world of letters to-day; fundamentally, it proceeds from a supposition that even the best art is representational, as distinct from creative in the most literal sense; and anyhow, the result, the actual work, has no high qualities of beauty in it

And, as illustrations of the resources of this style, one could cite many instances of dry terse comment and cool irony, very unlike the dithyrambic exuberance which alone is associated with Swinburne in the general if not universal misconception of his temperament and literary gifts; but they can only be fully appreciated in the context to which they belong.

Being so versatile, this style is capable of adapting itself in the letters to the various personalities of those writing the letters. And this is a very rare thing, much rarer than is no doubt commonly supposed. The idiom of the letters in the epistolary parts of, say, *The Ordeal* and *Evan Harrington* is very well differentiated; but Meredith is very much an exception as regards this matter. Differentiation, and so verisimilitude, is often wanting even in the longer passages of conversation of even novelists of high repute. To take only one example, compare, in Stevenson's *Olalla*, the conversational passages between Olalla and the narrator 'hero' near the end of the story; there is absolutely no variation of idiom at all in the utterances of these two very different persons.

The fact that the characters in Swinburne's novel are sufficiently well diversified in their epistolary expression is one of the marks of their reality. For they are very real people, they have authentic life, one does not feel them as puppets. Swinburne himself, judging the book, in a letter to W. M. Rossetti,[1] some forty-three years after its composition, and therefore as nearly as possible in a spirit of detachment, felt that this might be claimed for it. 'I think the people are real flesh and blood', he wrote; and he singled out with predilection Lady Midhurst as a person of special quality and also as being quite unique in the world of creative history (as he called fiction on its higher levels). 'I want you to like the presentation of Lady Midhurst—who is entirely a creature of my own invention . . .' About forty years earlier, in a letter to the same friend,[2] he

---

[1] August 21st, 1905. The letter accompanied a copy of the work that had just been volumed for the first time.

[2] March 21st, 1866.

had even more emphatically given her primacy and pride of place as a character that was a tie-beam for the book as a whole:

'This book stands or falls by Lady Midhurst; if she gives satisfaction, it must be all right; if not, chaos is come again.'

We have perhaps already sufficiently indicated for this summary sketch the extent to which she is the mainstay of the work, in her shrewdly exercised authoritarian control over the actions of the personages whence the story gets its dramatic elements; or rather, the latter—the vicissitudes of the two love-affairs apart from her interference—are the raw materials of a higher drama of which she is not only one of the forces, but an arch-force acting compulsively on the others.

We may consider her a little further as an individual (for she is going to re-appear in *Lesbia Brandon* and will have more than a minor place there). She is not merely a force, a strong personality, an exemplar of a fairly common one-piece type. She is distinctive in various ways that belong to her alone. If her mind is somewhat masculine, she is by no means unwomanly; she is certainly feminine enough to be viciously cattish on occasion—although this is not always with her a mere expression of idle feeling, as it is with most females who go in for this weakness: it sometimes proceeds from her clear-sighted outspoken critical faculty, and at other times it is no more than a form of the tactical denigration which is one of the arms she uses in furtherance of her designs. Moreover, it appears now and again that she is not without a tender side in which there is much sweetness. On the whole, however, any tenderness she shows is, or seems, the softening of a hardness—a hardness that is her very nature.

But there is nothing small or mean or narrow about her hardness. On the contrary, there is bigness in it, and the makings of heroism, and a clarity of vision that looks steadily at the severe reality of things as experience shows them. From it comes the courageous wisdom of her pagan or stoic self-sufficiency, part of the utterance of which will be found in the tenth note on the last chapter of *Lesbia Brandon*. In this, of course, and in certain other matters, she and Swinburne are at one; and Swinburne indicates this in the last of the letters to which we have referred:

> 'From the Galilean . . . point of view, I am aware that she and it [i.e. the book] and I must be all together condemnable, but we do not appeal to that tribunal.'

But it would be a mistake to regard her in matters of religious and other opinion as a mere mouthpiece of Swinburne; even where she is most markedly in unison with him she retains her own individuality and speaks with the voice that belongs to it. And she is not always on his side: on the contrary, her keen critical realism is very disrespectful towards certain things about which he is most fervorous. Thus, she pronounces that 'Mary Stuart' was 'admirably and fearfully foolish for such a clever cold intellect as she had'; and again, she laughs at Reginald's (i.e. Swinburne's) 'sudden engouement for foreign politics and liberation campaigns, and all that sort of thing', and goes on to say 'I should quite like to enrol him in real earnest in some absurd legion of volunteers, and set him at the Quadrilateral with some scores of horrid disreputable *picciotti* to back him'. The derided 'engouement' and the 'absurd volunteers' are the subject-matter and the inspiration of *Songs Before Sunrise* and much else of Swinburne's poetry in these early years. Any suggestion that even here, in her mocking treatment of his enthusiasms, she is not really at odds with Swinburne—in other words, that he could see the funny or lesser side even of the things that moved him most—would doubtless be regarded as an extravagance. But it is altogether true. Contrary to the prevalent idea of him, this supreme lyrical poet was capable of detachment even in respect of what made him most lyrical. He really had in him the makings not only of a humorist (as many passages of *Love's Cross Currents* show), but also of an ironist *vis-à-vis* things in general, including those which were the objects of his devotion. A sufficiency of evidence could be adduced in support of this statement (which to many will come as very strange news); and of course the very fact that he could put into the mouth of Lady Midhurst, a *sympathique* character and one of his pet creations, derisive remarks of the sort in question is in itself fairly probative. Swinburne, had he wished, could, in poetry and elsewhere, have been as much an ironist as Laforgue (the greatest of all) and other French poets of the last two or three generations.[1] But he preferred to keep his poetry pure, to remain absolutely at one with it and not, as did Laforgue, Lautréamont, etc., to stand apart from it every now and again in the *esprit gouailleur* which makes their irony; and he gave only sporadic or very occasional exercise outside poetry proper to this side of his personality. To return to Lady Midhurst: even although it is possible to bring her into line with Swinburne here, here too she retains her full separate individuality and does so over all the extent of the story.

Lady Midhurst, in sum, is one of the most striking characters in the history of fiction.

Clara, Captain Harewood and Reginald, as recurrent figures or types in Swinburne's work, including *Lesbia Brandon*, call for a little more attention before we finish with *Love's Cross Currents*.

Clara is another avatar, although on a relatively much lower, and far less heroic level, of the peculiarly Swinburnian woman, the Swinburnian woman *par excellence*, of whom Lucretia Borgia and Mary Stuart may be taken to be the extreme types. She is this woman caught in the confines of English domesticity and conventionality, and she has not enough bigness of any sort to escape from them even when her desire is met by opportunity.[2] In certain respects she is Helen Harewood over

---

[1] I do not mention the bastardising English, American and Anglo-American imitators or *démarqueurs* of these French (and other) writers, for their work is contemptible and of no account for anyone properly acquainted with European literature.

[2] It is not improbable that Swinburne found materials for her—as for other things in the book—in his own family *milieu*, which, I suggest, is the reason why he was so insistent that the work should come

again, but she is much more complex than her predecessor, as far as we can take stock of the latter in the short fragment where she makes her appearance. Like Helen, she is a sort of Emma Bovary romantically aspiring after an existence much ampler and grander than the grey mechanic life to which she is condemned (partly at least by an error of judgment on her part and other flaws in herself); a better educated Emma Bovary, of course, with an imagination nourished from higher sources of culture. 'I will tell you what I would have done, and would do if I could', she writes to Reginald. 'I would begin better; I would be richer, handsomer, braver, nicer to look at and stay near, pleasanter to myself. I would be the first woman alive, and marry the first man : not an Eve though, nor Joan of Arc nor Cleopatra, but something new and great. I would live more grandly than great men think . . . I would have all I wanted, and the right and the power to feel reverence and love and honour of myself into the bargain. And my life and death should make "a kingly poem in two perfect books".' A fine vista, and well calculated to stir into response such an imagination as Reginald's!

But she has another side; she is prudential, and that in a worldly way that serves no larger ends, and is not in accord with the splendour of these grandiose dreams. Part of her vision is for the main chance—the main chance that is so petty. She plays for safety, she who would adventure out into greatness. She would have the best of two contrary worlds, a feat prohibited by a fundamental law of things, and the attempt to achieve which means the ruin of the better of them.

Lady Midhurst clearly sees this side of her, and tries (in vain) to make Reginald see it. Clara, she tells him, 'is one of the *safest* women alive. Not for other people, mind; not safe for you; not safe by any means for her husband; but as safe for herself as I am, or as the Queen is. She knows her place

(*Note* ² *continued*)—
out anonymously; but this is part of the history of his private life that must be reserved for discussion in a later volume.

and keeps to it . . . She is a splendid manager in her way—a bad, petty, rather unwise way, I must and do think; but she is admirable in it'. And again: 'She never for an instant steps aside from the strait and narrow way, while she has all the flowers and smooth paving of the broad one . . .' But is Lady Midhurst, a subtle tactician with an axe to grind in this matter, a reliable authority in the case of Clara? Well, if she exaggerates at all, she only exaggerates what the omniscient author states in the Prologue. 'At thirteen', he informs us 'she had good ideas of management, and was a match for her father in most things . . . There was the composition of a good intriguer in the girl from the first; she had a desirable power of making all that could be made out of every chance of enjoyment. She was never one to let the present slip.'

But Reginald goes on seeing her as 'a great angel' and dreaming, among other of her lures, on her 'rich, reserved hair', the hair that while they were riding together, 'was blown down and fell in heavy uncurling heaps to her waist', while 'her face looked out of the frame of it, hot and bright, with the eyes lighted, expanding under the lift of those royal wide eyelids of hers.' He could not have been wrong about her beauty: and perhaps he was not altogether wrong in his estimate of the rest of her; no doubt there were possibilities in her that might have risen to the fineness whither his poetry was bent on taking her. And at last, as we have seen, she was almost won to his invitation, and was near the point of setting off to Cytherean places with him. She would not go all out, in spite of everything, and overbear even the damning evidence of the letters, as we feel she might have done with a man of Reginald's character. And so in the end she stands out as a small person who has let beauty run to waste. And that simply because of a weakness of character, although conventional morality is served by her failure. The profound 'immoral' doctrine of Browning's *Statue and the Bust* might have been written for her. And it was for such a woman as she that Swinburne wrote all the heartbreak of *The Triumph of Time*:

z

But you, had you chosen, had you stretched hand,
Had you seen good such a thing were done . . .

Is she a sadist like Helen Harewood? No; but in the way
she plays with Reginald and love there is perhaps discernible
a certain cruelty like that shown by Mary Stuart towards
Chastelard and his all too perfect devotion.

If, however, she is not on a par with Helen Harewood here,
there is an enormity of sadism in another woman in the book.
This is a Lady Cheyne of the seventeenth century, the central
figure of a story—a superb little *conte*—which Reginald
relates in one of his letters. She had a lover, a Reginald Harewood of those days and a member of the family to which his
Victorian namesake belongs. This young fellow, a poet as well
as a soldier and a great man of his hands with the sword, was
one night received into the house by her, and they had their
sweet hour of love. Then, on leaving him, she went to her
husband and bade him come and avenge a great wrong she
had suffered. She took him to where the soldier-poet was lying
asleep, and said that he had been let in by one of her gentle-
women suborned by him to betray her into his hands during
the night, and that she had just got wind of this. Let him therefore do what he should do as her lord. So he, although somewhat loth, so struck was he by a nobility in the handsome face
of the youth, roused him and bade him defend himself; which
the youth rose to do, but Lord Cheyne began before he was
well ready, and ran him through the heart. 'Then he took his
wife's hand and made her dip it into the wound and sprinkle
the blood over his face. And the fellow just threw up his eyes
and winced as she wetted her hand, and said "Farewell, the
most sweet and bitter thing upon earth", and so died.'

This woman's action is surely the most monstrous piece of
sadism, and the man's response the most extreme case of madly
noble masochism, in fictional or other record.

While in the domain of the so-called pathological, we might
notice occurrences of the theme of real or full incest in this
work. There are two of these, and they are quite incidental.

Lady Midhurst, telling Clara that she appreciates how regrettable will be the rupture with Reginald, upon which she insists, says that she herself is very susceptible to his charms, and adds with mock seriousness that 'it is simply the canon of our Church about men's grandmothers which keeps me safe on platonic terms with our friend'. Then she goes on humorously to give the outlines of a possible novel in the French manner in which a grandmother has an affair with a grandson, and at last, seeing him cooling off, contrives to pass him on to an aunt, her own daughter, part of the process being the seduction by herself of the latter's husband, so that the field may be clear for the young man. It is a piece of fun, of course, not meant to be taken seriously, but it is not without significance. It betrays preoccupation with the theme; here, under the guise of humour, Swinburne has given riotous development to one of his pet subjects, as he gave riotous development to another of his tastes in *The Flogging Block* and other pieces. Particularly notable is the wealth of that entanglement of family, and especially consanguineous, relations, which had a peculiar attraction for him, and which will be one of the cardinal elements of *Lesbia Brandon*. (It may be remarked, by the way, that the idea of a *liaison* between a nephew and an aunt does not belong solely to the category of the burlesque: it is one of the chief themes of *La Chartreuse de Parme*; at least, in Stendhal's masterpiece—which Swinburne greatly admired—the duchesse de San-Severina has a more than licit love for her nephew Fabrice, although she never succeeds in arousing that young man to reciprocity. And with a Ninon de Lenclos, even a *liaison* between a grandmother and a grandson would be quite verisimilar.)

The second incidental case in *Love's Cross Currents* concerns Octave de Saverny, the man to whom Clara had written the compromising letters, and the daughter of a Madame de Rochelaurier: these two had secretly plighted troth, but the engagement was broken off as soon as it came to light, the reason being, it is obscurely but unmistakably hinted, that he was an illegitimate son of the girl's mother. This is precisely the situation of Denham and Margaret in *Lesbia Brandon*, and one of the sources of tragedy in the book. (There, too, we may observe in passing, compromising letters were designed to come into the plot.)

With Captain Philip Harewood we return to the theme of sadism. According to Lady Midhurst, his treatment of Reginald was 'horrible, disgraceful for its stupidity and cruelty'. 'He spent his time, under cover of seclusion', she says again, 'in voluptuous pastime of torturing his unlucky boy'. Her testimony, however, is subject to caution: she was no friend of the captain after her daughter had left him for another man; and the author remarks that 'nothing could be falser than such an imputation; he was merely a grave, dry, shy, soured man . . .' But even the author adds that 'perhaps he did enjoy his own severity and moroseness'; and Reginald told his cousin Frank when the two first met as boys that his father really 'liked to swish' him, and that he could draw blood at the third or fourth stroke, so expert was he in the handling of the birch. Altogether, Captain Philip Harewood is a reproduction of the father in the first story—the somewhat sinister father who enters largely into Swinburne's work, particularly that which is yet unpublished. But his flogging activities, unlike those of his predecessor, and still more unlike those of Denham in *Lesbia Brandon*, are kept in the background; there are no scenes in which we see him actually at work.

Reginald is in some ways like the Reginald of the earlier story. For instance he 'revelled about the stables all day long' when he visited his great uncle old Lord Cheyne; and he once, after a severe beating, ran away from his father to his mother's home, where Lady Midhurst also lived. But he is far more attractive than the former Reginald—partly, no doubt, because we have far more knowledge of him. He is much livelier, and much cleverer (but then he had the advantage of an ordinary education, whereas his precursor apparently had no schooling at all). 'He was quite the nicest boy I ever knew,' wrote Lady Midhurst, 'and used to make me laugh by the hour; there was a splendid natural silliness in him, and quantities of *verve* and fun . . .' And at school he was capable of turning out 'a decent set of verses' (Latin and Greek) when, sporadically, he got down to that task. Physically, too, he was a very engaging boy: lithe and compact of build, and his significantly full red under-lip enhanced the 'impudent and wilful beauty' of the rest of his face.

Physically, no doubt, he is not at all points a portrait of the juvenile Swinburne. But on the whole he is a faithful representation of the poet in his boyhood and particularly in the early part of his manhood. We have Swinburne's own word for this; in an already cited letter to W. M. Rossetti, acompanying a copy of the book, he wrote: 'I think you may be reminded of a young fellow you once knew, and not see very much difference between Algie Harewood and Redgie Swinburne'. Even physically there is a certain amount of resemblance; the full under-lip was his; and so was the 'pale bright skin', the golden hair, the 'mass of rough curls', and the slight build. Intellectually, temperamentally, the similitude, or rather identity, is very striking. Of Reginald his half-sister says: 'I never saw anybody so excited or so intense in his way of expressing admiration'; and Lady Midhurst speaks of his 'ardent ways and eager faiths and fancies'; that is altogether Swinburne as he was during his springtide years. Like Reginald, he could turn out decent Latin and Greek verses at Eton, where too he was not noted for regularity; like Reginald, he went riding with a female cousin, boated, wrote verses in his own language, and was more than anything else a poet; at Oxford, his career, like Reginald's, came to 'a disgraceful finale'; like Reginald, 'he was 'inflammable on European matters', and was especially combustible on the subject of Italy—in short, Algernon Harewood is as much the young Swinburne as is the Herbert Seyton of *Lesbia Brandon*, who is only a more faithful likeness because more of the poet goes to his making

There is another point on which there is a good deal of resemblance between them. Reginald has an extraordinarily keen interest in flagellation; he gloats over the bloody torture of the most brutally severe flogging scenes. He discourses (in the Prologue) at learned length on the subject to Frank on the occasion of their first meeting. (He is already at Eton, and Frank has not yet gone there.) It was 'with a dreadful unction' that he went into details. 'He talked of *"cuts"* with quite a liquorish accent . . . The boy was immensely proud of his floggings, and relished the subject of flagellation as few men relish rare wine'. He staggers the younger boy with a gruesome account of an Eton flogging (which we may take as coming from Swinburne's own experience), savagely cutting at a laurel bush to make the thing more realistic. Finally, he coaxes, or rather goads, Frank into giving him as hard a cut as he can, and it is so successful that he jumps and yells—and then expresses his appreciation of it. Frank himself, we may further note, during Reginald's recital had 'shivered deliciously', and his nerves had 'tingled with a tremulous sympathy': here we have Swinburne himself in his true and unvarying position and spirit in this matter—he is the masochist, the imaginary (and sometimes more than imaginary) recipient of the pain, which strangely stirs him to ecstasy.[1]

And this *penchant* does not cease with Reginald's boyhood —and here again he and Swinburne are identical. Years later, talking in the course of a letter of the probability of his taking up a diplomatic appointment where he would have over him Arthur Lunsford, one of his seniors at Eton, he jocularly wonders whether the latter would still be able to lick his

[1] Seeing that these flagellation passages of *Love's Cross Currents* (not to mention other things in Swinburne's published writings) have been in print for some 45 years (and more than 70 if one counts the appearance the novel in *The Tatler*), there is no point in keeping suppressed the unpublished *Flogging-Block* and much else of the same kind. *The Flogging-Block* (from whichI have given extracts in the Notes) is only a series of ingenious variations (in admirable verse) of the theme fully brought out into the open in *Loves' Cross Currents*; it is absurd to describe it and its congeners as unpublishable, as so many people have done. It is among the things that I have in mind to bring out in a Corpus of the unpublished writings of Swinburne.

subordinates. 'I suspect he might thrash me still if he tried:
you know what a splendid big fellow he is.' Behind the jocularity, we may be sure, there was a seriousness of a hankering
after the pain he had suffered as a schoolboy . . .

Particularly noteworthy is the passage from the part of the
Prologue where Reginald shows that he is a connoisseur in
this line:

> 'As for shame, he had never for a second thought of it. A
> flogging was an affair of honour to him; if he came off
> without tears, although with loss of blood, he regarded the
> master with chivalrous pity, as a brave enemy worsted.'

Here, as I indicate elsewhere,[1] we have a very important
pointer to the correct interpretation of Swinburne's masochism in the matter of flagellation. It is by no means merely
a sensual experience for him, something in the way of sexual
pathology. To a considerable extent, it is the expression of a
severely moral attitude; a discipline; a response to challenge;
the acceptance of an opportunity to prove that one is capable
of heroism.

Here the masochism is positive, a declaration of independence, a rising into superiority; but in another connection it is
precisely the opposite of this. This is in the matter of love.
Here, the desire to suffer pain on behalf of, or better still at
the hands of, the beloved one is normal with Swinburne; it is
only to be expected therefore that Rginald should show something of it. He goes only as far as expressing a wish to be hurt
for Clara; but we divine that this is not his limit; (and in
Lesbia Brandon this comparative modesty or restraint will be
greatly exceeded into a longing for hurt received from the
object of adoration). Moreover, with masochism of the Swinburnian kind, there is subjection of another sort; the urge
even to undergo humiliation as a sign of one's devotion. Here
Reginald is a perfect exemplar; he would like to be Clara's
'footman or groom, and see her constantly'; 'I would clean

---

[1] The 69th Note on Chapter II of *Lesbia Brandon*.

knives and black boots for her'; nay more, he would even let her husband (whom he despises) 'insult' him 'and strike' him 'if she wanted it'; humiliation, the masochism of perfect devotion, there goes to its utmost limit.

Here also we have a key to the rationale of this very strange phenomenon. 'When I see a great goodness', says Reginald, 'I know it—when I meet my betters I want to worship them at once . . . When I fall in with a nature and powers above me, I cannot help going down before it.' Once again, the attitude is primarily moral; however excessive it may seem, there is nothing mean or dishonourable about it.

Love's Cross Currents, then, as *Lesbia Brandon* will be, is valuable as providing important data for a true biography of Swinburne (those perpetrated by Gosse and later interlopers in this field are—by reason of suppression, distortion or witless ignorance—lacking in truth to a degree sufficient to turn one into a Timon).

And altogether, as we have perhaps said enough to indicate, *Love's Cross Currents* is one of the most interesting and markworthy, yes, and one of the greatest, productions in the history of the novel. It is much greater than many works that far exceed it in reputation. But it has practically no reputation, and it can hardly be said to belong to history. The widely but ill-read Saintsbury, for instance, makes not the least reference to it in his lengthy tome on *The English Novel*, nor anywhere else in the gargantuan range of his works; nor is there so much as a mention of it in A. E. Baker's somewhat wooden *History of the English Novel* which runs to ten large volumes, of which some eighty pages go to Meredith. Even from Swinburne's commentators or biographers, with the exception of Lafourcade, it has obtained nothing like the recognition it deserves—if it has elicited any recognition at all. Gosse, for example, in his misnamed *Life,* merely mentions the date of its composition (which he gets wrong) and of its publication in volume form in England (he apparently was unaware of its previous publication in *The Tatler*). The wonderful Professor Samuel Chew, who had the temerity (and worse) to write a volume of over 300 pages on the poet, 'finds it impossible to take' *Love's Cross Currents* 'very seriously'; it is 'thin and wearisome' to his finely cultivated taste. Here—and throughout the whole of his volume—he gives the impression of a Caliban emitting confident opinions on things which lie quite beyond his perception. It is a relief—exceptionally—to turn from him to Lafourcade, who sometimes manages to talk sense; here indeed he so far exceeds his average self that the sense is really excellent. He very rightly says[1] that it is time *Love's Cross Currents* was given its proper rank, which is 'très élevé', and pretty close to *Vanity Fair* (he might have gone even further than this without being guilty of extravagance); that taken as a whole, it, and certain parts of *Lesbia Brandon*, are far superior to anything Meredith had done up to the time of their composition, with the exception of what is best in *Shagpat and Feverel*; that Swinburne is not only much more of an artist than Meredith, but much more subtle in his dialogues and conversations between people of breeding; that his characters have an ease and a gift of life that are lacking in Meredith's aristocrats;[2] and that Lady Midhurst is at once simpler and subtler, more intellectual

[1] In his *La Jeunesse de Swinburne.*
[2] Lafourcade also says of Swinburne, comparing him with Meredith, that he is never vulgar; he might also, and with more reason, have given absence of vulgarity as one of the things differentiating Swinburne from Thackeray. As H. G. Wells truly observes in his excellent essay on *The Contemporary Novel*, 'there was something profoundly vulgar about Thackeray'. Swinburne, of course, unlike Thackeray, was essentially and wholly an aristocrat and a gentleman (although he was far from being a 'Christian gentleman', a type for which he had a healthy disesteem : Thackeray would pass as a very creditable specimen of that type). It is not a mere *boutade* to say that Dickens, who, like his admirer Swinburne, was not a conventionally exemplary person, and is commonly supposed not to be able to depict a gentleman, was really more of one than Thackeray, who may be called a very genteel man.

On the question of the real aristocrats or gentlemen among writers, and of Thackeray's position as an outsider in this regard, the following additional opinions may be quoted. They are more striking as coming

and more alive, than anyone in the whole of the Meredithian world. In short, concludes Lafourcade, 'même dans le domaine du roman et de l'esprit comique Swinburne avait le droit de considérer en 1860-64 qu'il n'avait pas à recevoir de leçons de George Meredith'.

Meredith himself, after reading it in manuscript, praised *Love's Cross Currents* 'more or less highly for different qualities, especially the leading idea of the tragicomic catastrophe.'[1] Meredith here simply confirmed the praise of other contemporaries before it was published in *The Tatler*. Joseph Knight, for instance, spoke of it thus:

> 'The work has wonderful power, originality and individuality. Characters were never more distinctly marked or stood out more plainly on the canvas . . . I think the letters are fuller of character than those in the work which first suggested to you the idea, and the characters are every whit as life-like as those of Choderlos de La Clos . . .'[2]

And Professor John Nichol wrote to much the same effect:

(*Note* [2] *continued*)—

from men who are not only very different from Wells, but are also very unlike each other.

MACAULAY: 'Thackeray . . . lives on a countess's sneer.'

D. G. ROSSETTI: 'Thackeray is the Valet of Society to whom not one of his masters is a hero. He lives upon small advantages which he exacts from all alike.'

W. BAGEHOT: Thackeray 'could not help wondering what the valet behind his chair would think and say'.

Saintsbury's attempt (in *The Peace of the Augustans*) at ridiculing refutation of Bagehot's opinion is very weak (Saintsbury himself was a Christian gentleman, with a strong strain of genteelness, and this often disqualified him as a critic, especially of French literature, on which his pronouncements were often very funnily inept. It is not surprising that Thackeray was his favourite author).

[1] Unpublished letter from Swinburne to Nichol, 2nd January, 1877; cited by Lafourcade.

[2] Letter to Swinburne, February 25th, 1866; in British Museum.

'. . . it has the truth to detail of Richardson and the subtle analysis of Balzac . . .'[1]

'I hesitate to express my full feelings about the book, lest the simplest expression should seem inflated . . . The surface is a sparkling picture of a phase of Society with which the writer is evidently familiar.[2] But how many will detect the darts of satire in every page, and the lurid scorn that runs through the whole?[3] . . . Its subtlety, humour, and intense pathos are out of the ken of the British Public. God bless them! they will say that it wants interest and Christian principle. Some very knowing ones will say it recalls *Les Liaisons Dangereuses*, to which appropriate epithets will then be applied. There are of course some points of contact, but your leading characters and plot, which seems a very natural one, are wholly original. Lady Midhurst is as strikingly English as Madame de Merteuil is French . . .'[4]

Love's Cross Currents, then, in spite of the misprision of it by historians of the novel and others, and of the oblivion into

[1] Letter to Swinburne, January 22nd, 1877; in British Museum.

[2] 'And indeed', commented Swinburne, quoting this in a letter to Watts-Dunton, 'as I told him in replying to this, the writer never had sufficient confidence in his own imaginative genius to attempt, like the lady novelists of the period, a study of any phase with which he was not.' (February 14th, 1877; letter in British Museum.)

[3] 'I didn't mean it for a satire', comments Swinburne again in the same letter, 'but I suppose the reader *would* hardly infer on the writer's part as warm and conscientious a regard for the British institutions of marriage, divorce, and inheritance as ever animated the chaste pen (for example) of the judicious Thackeray.'

[4] Letter to Swinburne, January 28th, 1877; in British Museum. We may note here that this favourable reception was renewed in reviews of the book when, in 1905, it came out in volume form. 'Nothing in all my literary life', wrote Swinburne in an afore-cited letter to W. M. Rossetti 'had ever so much astonished me as the reception of this little old book. The first (small) impression, I am told, was sold out on the day of publication; and the chorus of praise from reviewers has hardly been broken by more than one or two catcalls.'

which it has fallen, is in many ways a great book. Moreover, it gives us an adequate idea of Swinburne's powers as a novelist. It shows not only that he could introduce into the novel a beauty of sheer poetry higher than any that had ever been seen there[1] (a thing that might be taken for granted in the case of one who was primarily a poet of consummate gifts, and, unlike so many masters of verse, could retain his distinction outside the bounds of metre); and that, for novelistic purposes, he could write excellent prose in provinces other than those of pure poetry; but also that he could create living and well-diversified characters and make them express themselves with verisimilitude, and could construct a plot or intrigue as shapely, economical and severe as could be demanded by any canonical standards. In short, he showed in this work (written at about the age of twenty-five), which he wrongly called a 'maiden attempt', forgetting the *Kirklowes* fragment, that he was well able to turn out a novel in the strictest or most specific sense of that term.

We know now the novelistic endowment of the man who undertook *Lesbia Brandon*; whatever else may be said, it cannot be said that he was congenitally incapable of writing a novel. Thus one judgment that may be made on *Lesbia Brandon* is initially ruled out.

The way is now clear for an examination of this latter work; but it first remains to take brief notice of another fragmentarily realised project that precedes it, and is not unrelated to it.

---

[1] I am speaking of the English novel; but even if one extended the range of reference, very little qualification would be needed, and that would be almost if not altogether entirely with regard to the novel in France. And even there, apart from Hugo and Gautier and Musset (in the *Confession*), and Nerval (if one can bring *Sylvie* and *Aurélia* within the category of the novel). What is there that is notable for high poetic quality? The two most outstanding things in this connexion in the second half of the century are Flaubert's *Salammbo* and the Goncourts' *Madame Gervaisais*, but the latter did not appear till six years after *Love's Cross Currents* was finished, and the former was published in the year when Swinburne had made a start on his novel.

III. *Herbert Winwood*

Among the documents of the Ashley Collection in the British Museum there is in Swinburne's handwriting the following plan, which is obviously that of a novel:

1850–1860 1) Kirklowes.[1]	2) Ellerstone.[2]
	Vol. 2[4]
1862 1. The Red Mouse	9. After Confession[5]
2. Characters	10. Fairy Tales
3. Retrospect and	11. At Sea
Prospect	12. Anima Anceps[6]
4. Work and Wages	13. A Chance[7]
5. Fiat Rosa	14. Hic breve plangitur[8]
6. Letting out of waters	15. Misfortunes of Virtue
7. Non perde ventura	16. Uses of prosody
8. Three Studies of	17. A Choice
Cats[3]	18. Correspondance[9]

Swinburne himself wrote concluding strokes at the end of both the columns.

[1] Swinburne first wrote 'Kirkalton' and then altered the '-alton' to 'lowes.

[2] Ellerstone replaces a heavily scored through word, which appears to be 'Laughton'.

[3] This replaces a cancelled 'Cats and Dogs'.

[4] There is no 'Vol. 1' at the head of the corresponding column on the left.

[5] No. 9 was originally in the first column, immediately under No 8, and had the (cancelled) title 'Kites and Crows'. In transferring it to 'Vol. 2' Swinburne upset the numerical symmetry of the two 'volumes'.

[6] This replaces a cancelled 'Sub Rosa'.

[7] 13 was originally 12, and 12 was originally 13.

[8] This replaces a cancelled 'A waif and stray'.

[9] It is more probable that Swinburne inadvertently wrote 'a' here than that he meant the word to be French. He misspelt thus what is certainly the English word in a passage of *Lesbia Brandon*.

On the same piece of paper (half a sheet of blue foolscap) there are also the following nomenclative, chronological and schematic notes, which as good as certainly belong to the same project as the foregoing list of chapters:

45.[1]

2. Cecil-Winwood, b. '47.[2]

3. Rosamund, b. '48.

4. Ethelbert, b. '50.

Francis
  Edward[3]
  Catherine[3]   reystead[4]
  Anne

1 Herbert, b. 1837
Herbert Winwood + Margaret Lunsford.
Anne Halden + Edwd. Wycombe (intrigues[5] with Arthur L.
                                                    ad fin[6]
Frank Halden + Cath.   do.

[1] The preceding part of this jotting (l., name, etc.) was on a torn-off part of the sheet.

[2] The 7, which replaces a cancelled 6, is, from its base, continued upwards, in a slanting direction to the right, into what appears to be a small birch, an emblem that Swinburne, in an idle—or grim—mood, sometimes drew on the manuscript of pieces dealing with flogging.

[3] Swinburne drew a line of cancellation through this name.

[4] There is a long downward stroke before the r, which is undoubtedly the lower part of a capital G: Greystead is a place in *Uses of Prosody*. The upper part was on a cut-off portion of the sheet.

[5] 'intrigue' replaces a cancelled 'elopes'.

[6] 'fin' apparently, to be completed by -em or by an abbreviating full stop. The rest of the bracketed section was on a cut-off part of the sheet.

Also written on the same page are Flumen ubi multâ lilia lambit aquâ, and the beginnings of three other Latin sentences or phrases of which the completing sections were on a torn-off part of the paper.

The discovery of this very interesting document,[1] which is nowhere mentioned by Wise, although it was in his Ashley Collection, was most important: it confirmed a strong suspicion, a quasi-certitude, of mine that the chapter *Uses of Prosody* and the letter *From Arden Major to Lady Waristoun*, incorporated by Wise in *Lesbia Brandon*, and accepted by Lafourcade docilely following in his wake as being parts of that work, do not belong to it at all.

If they are taken as belonging to it, we are faced by formidable and insuperable difficulties (and there is already enough that is enigmatic in the indubitable parts of *Lesbia Brandon*!). To name only the principal *cruces*, who is Frank Halden mentioned in *Uses of Prosody*? He is mentioned in no other chapter. Who, in the first paragraph of *Uses of Prosody*, is Anne. She also is mentioned in no other chapter, and yet here it is indicated that she had some place in Herbert's life, had engaged his appreciative attention in no small degree. When we read that 'Herbert's eye matched' Miss Lunsford 'against the splendid grave and supple vigour of two other feline horsewomen he had known', we expect one of them to be Lesbia, who was a very good horsewoman, even if she was not strikingly feline. But the two are Herbert's sister (who has not elsewhere been described as feline, or even as a good rider) and the mysterious Anne! It is as though Lesbia had never come into the story. And 'Margaret' elsewhere is always Herbert's sister, but here she confusingly turns out to be Margaret Lunsford, who also is mentioned in no other chapter. Then Mrs. Lunsford is among the guests here: but in one of the early chapters of *Lesbia Brandon* we are told that 'being invalided many years since' she 'never went out'. The 'Arthur' in the first paragraph is no doubt Margaret's brother; but there is no Arthur Lunsford in other chapters; Walter

---

[1] It was only long after first reading the manuscript of the novel as arranged and luxuriously bound by Wise that I came across it. It was not among the available Ashley material in the British Museum before the war, and during the war, and during the war nothing of this kind was accessible. Even now it is nowhere catalogued.

Lunsford is the only son of the family named elsewhere (in one chapter a mention is made of two brothers of his, but their names are not given). 'Waristoun' and not 'Wariston' is in both *Uses of Prosody* and the latter the spelling of the name of the nobleman who is the husband of Herbert's sister. A much more serious matter is the fact that Herbert's mother is also one of the guests in *Uses of Prosody*; but from two chapters of *Lesbia Brandon* we learn that she was dead before the beginning of the story, and in one of them that she had died 'when' Herbert 'was born'. More serious still is the fact that Herbert's surname here is not Seyton, as it is everywhere else, but Winwood (and this reappears as the second name of the boy who writes the letter: presumably it was his mother's surname before she married). And in this letter was are unpleasantly astonished to find that Herbert is married. Nothing prepares us for this; no woman but Lesbia has had any place in Herbert's sentimental life since his first meeting with that strange person; his marriage (that is, if *per impossible* it is a part of *Lesbia Brandon*) is terribly out of harmony with everything that we know of him since that encounter, and indeed with his character from the beginning; it really does jar and shock; an attempt might be made (transferring the letter right to the end of the book) to explain it away as a piece of cynicism concluding a story of waste, but that would be far from convincing.[1]

---

[1] Things are made much worse by Wise's stupid placing of the letter in the chapter sequence. He puts it about half-way through the book, thus making Herbert a married man while he is still passionately in love with Lesbia, and a good way before his meeting with Leonora Harley, engineered by Mr. Linley with a view, apparently, to curing him of his infatuation for Lesbia, and also a good way before he goes to see the latter on her death-bed. Which is absurd; other considerations apart, he is undoubtedly meant to be regarded as single on these two occasions. Besides, the date of the letter is June 5th, 1862; but the time of *An Episode*, which Wise puts after it, is the spring of 1861; and the events of others of Wise's later chapters pretty certainly belong to this year too. (This is one of hundreds of cases which show that Wise was a blockhead even in rudimentary matters that a normal

Lafourcade, who is lost in admiration for the acute perspicacity, the 'patience infinie', with which Wise 'a reconstitué le MS', naturally swallows holus-bolus this masterpiece of reconstruction; and so for him too *Uses of Prosody* and the letter are parts of *Lesbia Brandon*: no doubts on this score ever visit the hebetude which is his natural condition. He is not alive to any of the glaring resultant difficulties; or, if he is, he conveniently refrains from mentioning them in his very unsatisfactory account and discussion of the plot; in fact, even apart from these two chapters, he does not deal with any of the serious problems presented by the story as we have it in its unfinished state.

On the face of it, then, there are very good grounds for believing that *Uses of Prosody* and the letter are not parts of *Lesbia Brandon*.[2]

All the above-specified difficulties disappear if these two

(*Note* [1] *continued*)—
infant could be trusted not to go wrong about; and this stricture applies to Gosse as well, who as a rule revised Wise's work on Swinburne's manuscripts, besides supplying him with scholiastic information from his own very superficial erudition.) Wise's placing of *Uses of Prosody* is also blockishly wrong; it too he put near the middle of the book, making it about the sixth chapter; but in doing so he closes his eyes to the plainly written chapter number 16 which Swinburne prefixed to the title. Moreover, Herbert's sister is here shown as having passed through a stage of crisis by which she has been profoundly affected; 'she had bought off all her fears at the price of all her hopes', had 'turned soft' in an apathy consequent upon the loss of something that was principal in her life. So that if—again *per impossibile*—*Uses of Prosody* did belong to *Lesbia Brandon* it would have to follow the late chapter of that work in which Margaret's adulterous love-affair comes to a tragic conclusion.

It need hardly be said that Lafourcade crassly accepts, along with everything else in Wise's 'reconstruction', this palpably wrong order.

[2] A further ground for this belief is the fact that Swinburne did not send them to the printer with what was available of the rest of that work when he desired to see it in type. They could not have been, like certain other chapters, withheld from him by Watts-Dunton, for he makes no mention of them in the list of these latter chapters which he twice drew up in letters asking for their return.

sections are taken as belonging to a different work; and the strong presumption that they do belong to a different work is confirmed conclusively enough by the plan and schematic etc. notes which we have reproduced. *Uses of Prosody* is one of the chapters named in the plan; moreover, the number 16 precedes the title in the MS. chapter, and 16 is the number of the chapter in the plan. The letter is almost certainly the chapter or (more probably) part of the chapter of the plan entitled *Correspondance*. All the puzzling names in *Uses of Prosody* are those of characters in this other novel.[1] Frank Halden occurs in the notes; and the mysterious Anne is almost beyond a doubt the Anne Halden we find there. There too we find Margaret Lunsford, and Arthur L. may be taken to be Arthur Lunsford. Most important of all, the name Winwood has a place there; Herbert in that scheme is Herbert Winwood; and the Christian names Cecil Winwood (those of the writer of the letter) also occur there.[2]

That the novel of the plan is really another novel, and not *Lesbia Brandon*, is sufficiently clear from the plan itself, apart from the consideration of the names we have just discussed. Disregarding *Uses of Prosody*, of which we have disposed, the only chapter titles that might certainly appear to belong to *Lesbia Brandon* are 'Kirklowes' and 'Misfortunes of Virtue' (identical with 'Les Malheurs de la Vertu'). As for 'Kirklowes', it might occur in more than one work; and as a matter of fact

[1] Or, to speak quite strictly, they are those of characters in a work to which the schematic notes appertain. But it is practically certain that this work can be no other than the novel whose chapters are listed on the same page as the notes; and several of the names in the notes occur in a written chapter—*Uses of Prosody*—whose title is that of one of the listed chapters: whichever way one looks at it, one arrives at the same conclusion.

[2] It is true that this boy, the eldest of Lady Waristoun's children according to the letter, is apparently the second in age in what is evidently, among the notes, a list of these children; but Swinburne easily went wrong in such matters even where his own characters were concerned; in *Uses of Prosody* Cecil appears to be, as in the list, the second of the children of this family.

we have seen that it is the title of one of the chapters or sections of Swinburne's earliest attempt at a novel, which I have thought fit to call *Reginald Harewood*.[1] 'Misfortunes of Virtue', or 'Les Malheurs de la Vertu', might also belong to more than one work; it is a phrase from the Marquis de Sade, and Swinburne was fond of it, and, especially in his letters, made frequent use of it. The rest—that is very nearly all—of the titles in the plan have no clear, let alone certain, connexion with *Lesbia Brandon*.[2] On the other hand, none of the titles (with the exception of 'Les Malheurs de la Vertu') given by Swinburne to chapters which undoubtedly belong to *Lesbia Brandon*—'A Day's Work', 'On the Downs', 'Turris Eburnea', 'Leucadia', etc.—appears in the plan.

From those which do appear there it is impossible to gather any indication as to the story to which they belong. A certain meaning may be conjectured from some of them. E.g. 'Three Studies of Cats' no doubt refers to the three 'feline horsewomen' mentioned in *Uses of Prosody*. But what can one get out of 'non perde ventura' (even though one knows that it is the second part of a Tuscan proverb: Ragazza che dura, non

---

[1] That the fragment of that novel entitled 'Kirklowes' is not the chapter of the same name in the plan of *Herbert Winwood* is proved by the difference in the names of the characters.

[2] Lafourcade saw the plan, and, misled by the names 'Kirklowes', 'Misfortunes of Virtue' and 'Uses of Prosody', he jumped in his usual blundering way to the conclusion that it was 'no doubt intended for an early version of *Lesbia Brandon*.' This conclusion was the easier for him, as with his chronic gross inaccuracy he found that it consisted of 12 chapters (the number he wrongly assigned to *Lesbia Brandon* as 'reconstructed' by Wise), whereas it really consists of 18 (the figures were plainly written by Swinburne), apart from the preliminary section, where there are at least two more. But he did not see any of the difficulties arising from this assumption. Moreover, so little was he alive to the importance of the plan and notes that he did not even mention them in his long chapter on *Lesbia Brandon*, but only referred to them incidentally in a section on variant readings of *Dolores*, of which fragments happen to be written on the back of the sheet containing them.

perde ventura¹)? Or out of 'The Red Mouse', 'Letting out of waters', and most of the others?

The following is all that is certain. The novel was to be in two main parts, each subdivided into two sections: (1) A preliminary portion (corresponding roughly to the Prologue of *Love's Cross Currents*), covering ten years; this was to consist of a first section relating to life at Kirklowes (as in *Reginald Harewood*), and a second relating to life at another place called Ellerstone (which, changed from Laughton (?), may have changed again to the Ensdon of *Uses of Prosody*). These sections in all probability dealt with the boyhood and youth of Herbert Winwood (born in 1837), from the age of twelve or thirteen till the years of his early manhood. (2) The novel proper, or the part containing the intrigue, corresponding to the epistolary section of *Love's Cross Currents*, and dealing with events all taking place within the space of 1862 (a year later than the time of the main story in *Love's Cross Currents*).² This was sub-divided into two books, called volumes by Swinburne; the first consisting of eight and the second of ten chapters (originally there was symmetrical division into two sets of nine chapters.

¹ It is more probable that Swinburne had in mind not the adage as here cited, but the sentence from Boccaccio which Rossetti wrote on the back of his picture *Bocca Baciata* (1859): 'Bocca baciata non perde ventura, anzi rinuova come fa la Luna'. He saw the picture at Rossetti's studio in November or December 1859, and speaks of it in an unpublished letter dated Dec. 16, 1859.

² 1862 is written by Swinburne opposite the first of the 18 chapters of the two 'volumes'. 'A little before Easter' 1862 is the date of the events of *Uses of Prosody*, a very late chapter; the year here is indicated by the age of the boy Ethelbert: we are told that he is a 'twelve-year-old', and in the chronological notes 1850 is given as the year of his birth. So that a very short period of time has been covered up to the 16th chapter, And Arden major's letter, which may be taken as part of the last chapter, is dated June 5th, '62. Once again, the interval is short, and things must have moved pretty rapidly to the *dénouement*: altogether, the story proper extends over less than half a year. Of course, Swinburne, who was shaky on figures, may have gone wrong about his dates, but there is no strong reason to think that he did so.

In addition to this the following may be gathered from the schematic notes, *Uses of Prosody*, the letter from Arden major, and the table of chapters. There were three sets of sentimental relationships ending sooner or later in marriage: those between Frank Halden and Catherine Wycombe, between Anne Halden and Edward Wycombe, and between Herbert Winwood and Margaret Lunsford. There was probably here some entanglement of cousinships of the kind Swinburne was so fond of, but of this we have no evidence. And in the case of only one of these sets is there a definite indication of what is the main element of plot in Swinburne's other novelistic work, that of the disturbing attraction of a wife towards a man who would like her to become his mistress; Anne is to 'intrigue' if not actually to 'elope' with Arthur Lunsford; she, a woman of 'splendid grace and supple vigour', with a large capacity for 'enjoying herself', was probably to be the chief if not the only type of the Swinburnian *femme fatale* in this work (it is perhaps significant that Swinburne first wrote 'Helen' when he referred to her in *Uses of Prosody*: he may have more or less identified her with the heroine of that name in his earliest tentative in this line). There is no indication of any such person or situation in the case of Herbert. In *Uses of Prosody*, it is true, there is what might be a hint of sentimental interest on his part in Anne; but it appears from Arden major's letter that he was really and deeply in love with the woman who became his wife: 'he looks excessively happy'; she, who is 'like a white cat', is undoubtedly the 'feline' Margaret Lunsford of *Uses of Prosody*, whom he was to marry according to the table of alliances. Of any relationship in his case with any woman such as Lesbia Brandon there is not the slightest hint of any kind. It is very much more than probable that there was no Lesbia Brandon in the story. For this reason, it cannot properly be said that the plan and notes were 'intended for an early version of *Lesbia Brandon*', as they were thought to be by Lafourcade.

But one set of characters of the latter work does come into

Herbert Winwood.[1] That is Lord and Lady Wariston (Waristoun in this earlier work) and their children. Here too she is Herbert's sister. Of anyone corresponding to the Denham of *Lesbia Brandon* in her life there is no indication in the notes.[2] But her condition in *Uses of Prosody*, and especially the sentence 'She had bought off all her fears at the price of all her hopes', can hardly signify anything else than that there had occurred some tragedy in her life similar to that which she undergoes in *Lesbia Brandon*. Beyond that nothing can be said.

Did Swinburne write any of this work besides *Uses of Prosody* and Arden major's letter? It is impossible to say. The fact that right at the end of the last extant page of the manuscript of *Uses of Prosody* there are the two opening words of an incomplete sentence makes it pretty certain that at least one sheet of a further written part of this chapter was lost, and this makes it likely that other written parts of the book disappeared; but that sixteen and more whole chapters did is not very probable. Alternatively, did Swinburne—by way of experiment—write no more than the 16th chapter (or part of it) and one of the letters that were to constitute the final chapter? There is something of an experimental air about *Uses of Prosody*; for instance, in the parts where the conversation is disposed as in a play, and especially where Latin pronouns are used instead of the names of the speakers. This surely would not have been left in a definitive draft of the chapter. And, apart from this, *Uses of Prosody*, on the whole, is not very satisfactory as it stands; it is not well organised; there is little development in it, no really progressive interest. As a picture of manners, it is competent as

[1] Which is a reason—not the only one, of course—for placing *Herbert Winwood* immediately before *Lesbia Brandon* and not before *Love's Cross Currents.*

[2] These, however, while affording a list of various characters and their relationships, cannot be regarded as complete in this respect. The paper is torn or cut more than once. Lady Waristoun herself and her husband do not appear.

far as it goes, but little more, if anything, can be said for it: in spite of merits by the way, it never gets a secure hold on our attention. It even goes perilously near to being dull in parts; especially in that relating to the floundering efforts of schoolboys to turn out Latin verses. The incidental literary criticism—the satirising of 'muscular Christian' novels and of ultra-Romantic French fiction—is not dull—in the latter case at least it is amusingly successful—but it tends to develop too much on its own account. Altogether, we are far here from the finished technique to which, in *Love's Cross Currents*, Swinburne had shown it was within his power to attain. Of course many if not all the more likely in view of the following two sentences: '. . . the same afternoon saw a little play played out of the *proverbe* or drawing-room-comedy kind. In a quiet quick hour or two one may get to the catastrophe of such a play without knowing it'. In the larger scheme here adumbrated, such things as the scenes of frenetic passion from the imaginary French novel, and even references in the Latin verse exercise, would probably, by a system of ironic parallelism, have had dramatic value in a movement towards the 'catastrophe' of which there is no sign in what we have of the chapter. (Just as, in a similarly fragmentary or incomplete chapter of *Lesbia Brandon*, the characters take part in a real play—or play adapted to a charade—, which was doubtless intended to serve the same technical purpose in a larger design which does not appear in what is extant of the chapter.) But, as it now stands, *Uses of Prosody* leaves a lot to be desired, and even when all allowances have been made, one comes back to the probability that it was written as an experimental sketch. Still, the composing, even as a *coup d'essai*, of the 16th chapter before any of the others had been undertaken would have been strange—no less strange than the alternative supposition that some eighteen other chapters were written but were destroyed or lost. About this book, as about *Lesbia Brandon*, there is a good deal of mystery.

To sum up: We have here again, as far as can be seen and conjectured, the main themes of the two earlier works: a pleasant lad in his boyhood and early manhood (and, as in the case of the first but not the second of the preceding works, his sister, older than himself, and very attractive—but whether he himself is incestuously attracted by her at any stage cannot be inferred except as a possibility from such evidence as is available); at least one woman of the *femme fatale* type; and marriage disrupted or threatened by relations on the part of a wife with an actual or potential lover; and here, as in *Love's Cross Currents*, this situation occurs twice—in the case of Anne and of Lady Waristoun; but no tragic force of sentiment or passion appears to be at work in the life of the hero himself; the subject of flagellation is touched on in both the chapter *Uses of Prosody* and in the letter from Arden major, and was probably designed to receive more ample, more realistically detailed, treatment elsewhere in the book; and the peculiarly Swinburnian agent of this infliction, a sadistic father or his analogue, of whom there is no visible trace in the plan or in the extant portions of this novel, almost certainly must have had a place in it according to the full conception of the author.

We have now surveyed all the ground that may be regarded as an approach to *Lesbia Brandon*.

IV. *Lesbia Brandon*

We may begin by noticing that Swinburne brought into this work certain of the characters of *Love's Cross Currents*. Lady Midhurst has a prominent place in it (but not a cardinal one, as far as can be seen from what Swinburne completed of the story); and there are references to her brother Lord Cheyne and his wife and their son Edmund, to her husband, to her daughter and granddaughter (the two Amicias), and also to Reginald Harewood and Captain Philip Harewood; but these references are made at a date some eleven years before that of the crucial part of the story in both books; whether Swinburne intended to make later and fuller use of members of this family in *Lesbia Brandon* cannot now be determined. It is not at all likely that he meant to give them any main part in the actual plot of *Lesbia Brandon*; for one thing, the dates would hardly allow of this, as 1861 is in both works the year in which the chief drama is enacted or draws to its close.

From *Herbert Winwood* also Swinburne transferred certain things to this novel: Lord and Lady Waristoun (with the name modified to Wariston), their four children, with the same names, except that that of the eldest was changed from Arden to Arthur, and also the family cat, which kept its name Elaine; the Lunsford *ménage* (but the only member of it who really appears here is Walter, probably the Arthur of the Winwood story, and perhaps also the character of that name who is incidentally mentioned in *Love's Cross Currents*): and the place names Ensdon and Cauldhope, besides Kirklowes, which had been also used in the first of the works of this series.[1]

So much by way of preliminary. In addition to these matters of detail—some of which, especially the reappearance of Lady Midhurst and her family, give an air of continuity and larger and more various unity to Swinburne's novelistic world (Balzac uses the same procedure to the same effect)—, certain fundamental elements were taken over to *Lesbia Brandon* from the author's earlier work in fiction.

Here, in some respects to a greater extent than in *Love's Cross Currents* and perhaps in *Herbert Winwood*, reappear the Kirklowes family of the work with which this cycle opens. Once more we have the gentleman farmer, married to a handsome woman of feeble health who dies young, and their two children, a daughter and a boy some years her junior. But the surname is again different; it is neither Harewood nor Winwood, but Seyton; and there is once again a change in Christian names: the father is Frederick and the daughter is Margaret, as she probably was in *Herbert Winwood*, but the boy's name remains what it was in that work. Another

---

[1] In *Love's Cross Currents* Plessey had been substituted for it.

difference is that there is no sadistic father here; he is not available, as Frederick Seyton dies when the son is only nine. But his place is taken, and his *rôle* more than adequately fulfilled, by the tutor Denham, and also in a supplementary way by Mr. Linley. To return to common elements: the original Reginald 'had an animal worship of his sister's beauty'; Herbert, at the age of thirteen, manifests a strong incestuous passion for his sister, to which she gives signs of being responsive in kind, if not with anything like the same vehemence (and probably she hardly realises the full import of her kisses). But nothing comes of this, and quite different amatory interests occupy their attention in what may be called the story proper. Denham not only takes the place of the sadistic father, he also takes that of Champneys of the first work, the addition to the household who is attracted by the wife, and thus is a potential disrupter of the domestic establishment of the friend who has received him. The wife is Margaret; she, like Helen Harewood—or rather ultimately like her, for during a long time she is apathetic or acquiescent in her condition—is (with considerable qualifications) a sort of Emma Bovary who chafingly feels that she is receiving no fulfilment.[1] Apparently

---

[1] The same type reappears yet again and much later in Mauriac's *Thérèse Desqueyroux* (1926). Thérèse is married to a rich man whose main interests are rustic: hunting and pine-forests from which he derives most of his wealth. She has no concrete reason for being unhappy; but, like Lady Wariston, she is a prey to a vague, and yet at times anguishing, unrest which she is unable to understand. She comes to realise (or believe), however, that what is wrong with her is that she is not fulfilling herself, that she has no life, no personality, that is really her own. She feels this particularly when she is on the way to becoming a mother; she chafes at the idea (cf. the description of Lady Wariston in the *rôle* of mother) that she is a mere vessel or instrument for the propagation of a family which for her has no intrinsic importance. In the end she pertinaciously tries to destroy her husband by means of poison. She cannot give, even to herself, a satisfactory reason for doing so (which is somewhat strange, as rebelliousness against her condition would seem to provide at least some explanation). It may be that the author wishes us to understand that her action was an expression of mere perversity, in which, possibly, there was a certain amount

she becomes in time the clandestine lover of Denham; but it turns out—and thus the incest *motif* is reinstated—that she is his half-sister; he is the illegitimate son of her father by a woman who had been the latter's mistress; because (still apparently) he has learned this, he goes and takes farewell of her, and lets her know that on leaving her he will commit suicide, which he does, and thus this affair and two lives go down in waste. As in *Love's Cross Currents*, there is a second love-affair, although here there is involved no married woman and no possible break-up of a family. Herbert, with high poetic idealism, and also with a hunger for strong physical passion, loves Lesbia Brandon. She is the legitimate daughter of the woman who had been his father's mistress and had thereby become Denham's mother (but this secret is not revealed till near the end of the story, and it is not certain that Herbert and Lesbia were ever made aware of it). But Herbert's love is hopeless; for Lesbia is 'queer'; in fact her tendencies are exclusively homosexual; there was something of prophecy and fate in the Irish name imposed on her by her mother; it is absolutely impossible for her to return Herbert's love, but it is pretty evident that she has for his sister Margaret the feelings he has tried in vain to arouse in her: her chief interest in him is vicarious: in certain ways he recalls his sister.

Thus there is once again a pretty tangle of relationships, partially or approximately incestuous, and it is even more complicated than in the case of *Love's Cross Currents*. Den-

(Note ¹ continued)—

of sadism. Swinburne's Helen Harewood perhaps, and his Mary Stuart certainly, could not have given a clear reason, a rational explanation, of why they enjoyed seeing their respective lovers come to a violent end. The similarity of this 'heroine' of Mauriac to those of Swinburne is very striking; but of course there can be no question of influence of the earlier upon the later writer: here there is nothing more than coincidence. Which shows how circumspect one should be in the hunt ing out of influences, a favourite occupation of perpetrators of academic theses, one of the curses of what passes for education in these days.

ham (unwittingly) is in love with his half-sister, and is the
tutor of his half-brother, whom he punishes with a sadistic
rigour all the greater because of his seemingly frustrate love
for her: his maladive repressed passion strikes savagely at her
through the cruel wounds he inflicts on the boy. The latter in
his adolescence and early manhood is desperately in love with
Lesbia, who is in love with his sister, who is the daughter of a
man who had been the lover of Lesbia's mother, and is herself
loved by (and later becomes the lover of) a man who is not
only her half-brother but also the half-brother of Lesbia: it is
difficult to state the situation without getting into a dreadful
tangle! There are still further reaches of ravelment, but their
importance is only marginal. (One here recalls Swinburne's
own remark concerning similar intrications in *Le Paysan
perverti* of Rétif de la Bretonne: 'Nobody but the gifted
author could possibly remember how to unravel the complicated webs of reduplicated and intertangled incest': [1] In the
case of Swinburne's novel, however, the relationships are not
hugger-mugger or capriciously haphazard, but are strictly
organised, worked out and maintained according to an initial
plan, as nicely calculated, as psychologically pregnant and
just as any devised by Racine or any other master of what may
be called the mechanics of construction.)

Lesbia's love is as hopeless as Herbert's, for his sister is as
much beond her reach as she herself is beyond his, and probably Margaret is not even conscious of Lesbia's desire for her.
Life, in some respect that is essential and central, is barren

[1] Letter (in British Museum) to Watts-Dunton, July 27th, 1896. Swinburne had then 'just got through', with unexpected admiration, *Le
Paysan perverti*, of which, as he said, 'rape, incest, and the pox are the
three hinges', so that there is no question of his having been under the
influence of that work when he elaborated the complications of *Lesbia
Brandon*: these originated from something peculiar and fundamental
in his own nature, and also from the family *milieu* in which he moved
as a youth. I do not imply by these last words that incest went on in
that *milieu*. I merely mean that he received from it suggestions and
possibilities.

for Lesbia, there is an embargo, a strange doom upon her, and she too, like her half-brother, makes her way out of an intolerable situation by suicide; not, as he does, instantaneously with a fire-arm, but by slow poisoning, which allows her time for a long last talk with Herbert, who sits by her and watches her gradually sink into death. He is left desolate in a world from which even his hopeless hope has gone. And so, once again, two lives and two loves come to waste; as in *Love's Cross Currents*, a tragedy of waste is the upshot of the work.

Such is the story in its broad outlines, of which we get something like a full view only in chapters XIV, XV and XVI, and particularly in XIV, with Mr. Linley's revelations to Denham. But there are other elements, other intricacies and complications, and of these we are made aware only by incidental references, which are very obscure as they stand; instead of providing elucidation, they raise problems, and these problems are insoluble with such data as we possess. It is rather ironical that chapter XIV, which is evidently meant to be a clarifying chapter, contains most of these enigmatic references, and thus mystifies almost as much as it explicates.

The chief additional element is another woman in Denham's life. There are definite references to her in the first part of chapter XV, when Denham sees Margaret for the last time. Margaret says of some unnamed person 'She has no eyes and no heart or soul'; and again, referring to the alternative possibility of his breaking with her, Margaret, and going on living, 'And you will be good to her: ah, but she will not let you; nor deserve it'; and yet again, 'I wonder how she will bear it', referring to his intention, now accepted by her, of doing away with himself. And Denham says in the course of the same conversation 'You have broken my life between you two', where it is obvious that the second of the two persons referred to is another woman, to whom he alludes a few lines down when he says 'It's not to set her free' (that he thinks of making away with himself).[1] All this indicates that there was

[1] Another very puzzling thing in this speech of Denham's is 'I have

335

a tie of some sort between him and another woman; either she was his mistress or his fiancée or his wife ('It's not to set her free' would most naturally point to the last of these connexions). But there is no mention or sign or hint of this in any other part of the book. And there is a further difficulty here: from his conversation with Mr. Linley, upon which this scene presumably follows very closely, it would appear that the only complication in his life was the fact that he was in love with a woman (Margaret) who had been revealed as his half-sister.

Who could this other woman have been? Lesbia? Of all the women who have come into what we have of the story she is the only one that at first sight might appear likely. (The Fieldfare and Chalford young women of chapter III certainly are not: they are presented as being in no way attractive.) It would have been in accord with the rest of the plot, and with the general spirit of the story, as well as with Swinburne's tendency in these matters, to have a further strand of incestuous complication; and it would have been particularly piquant to have two half-brothers, Herbert and Denham, in love with the same woman, who, moreover, was the half-sister of the latter, he at the same time being in love with another woman, his rival's sister, who also was his half-sister in a different family: that would have been a masterpiece of subtle entanglement that Swinburne could never have bettered! But the possibility of Lesbia's being in Denham's life as wife or fiancée or mistress, apart from the difficulty that there has been no indication of it in the story as we have it, would appear to be ruled out by the fact that she is con-

(*Note* ¹ *continued*)—
got another man's life, and can't use it.' The only likely meaning I can attach to this is the following: it continues the thought of 'I think some die young by mistake; and others survive'; he had survived his real or legitimate self, the self that ought to have come to an end by now, and thus he was virtually another man, but he could not enjoy the extension of life he had thereby acquired. I do not think that the meaning is that possession of the mysterious letters of which we shall speak presently gave him power over some other man.

stitutionally incapable of being sexually interested in men. This seems to be quite clear; is it not, indeed, a central and pivotal supposition of the story, the thing that more than any other gives it the quality of tragedy wherein it is most appealing? Moreover, in chapter VIII ('On the Downs') she assures Herbert that if she could love and marry any man it would be he; and in chapter XVI (Leucadia') she reinforces this assurance by telling him that she had 'never' been 'fond' 'of any man else': for her he could be the only man if the doom on her were lifted, and we acquiesce in this as being true.

This possibility therefore is not available. The only other conjecture left open, apparently, is that there was something between Denham and the governess in the Wariston household. This governess, it is true, is not so much as mentioned in any of the existing chapters of *Lesbia Brandon*, but there is a reference to her in *Uses of Prosody*, one of the chapters in the immediately preceding story; and Swinburne may have meant to take her over to *Lesbia Brandon*, as he had taken over other characters that figure in that chapter. It would not be improbable that Denham, living in the same establishment as she, should have contracted some relationship with her, in spite of his passion for Margaret (which at first seemed hopeless, and had to wait so long before receiving anything in the way of satisfaction). But this is put forward only as a forlorn hope of conjecture.

The trouble is that, apart from lacunae due to disappearance of sheets of manuscript (as in the case of the last section of chapter I and the first section of chapter II), there are at least two serious gaps in the story, resulting from the absence of chapters which apparently Swinburne had not yet written:

1. What took place between chapters IV and V, i.e. in the nearly four years between 'after Christmas' of 1850 and September 1854, the time of the charade play, when Lesbia paid her first visit to the Waristons? Had Denham and Margaret become lovers in this interval?[1] (if they had not, they

---

[1] It had been decided that he should stay on in the family 'as

were an extraordinarily long time about it: it was now some six years since he had first come into the establishment). There is what appears to be a significant change in Margaret, which no definite remark or allusion in the chapter accounts for. 'She was seemingly warmer and really brighter. A delicate rapid grace, soft and keen as the play of light flame, moved now with all her motions. She spoke more and trod quicker than in past years.' And again, 'She was singularly animated all that week, and acted . . . with exquisite power and grace'. This would be natural if she had just reached a happy crisis in her life: if she and Denham had come to conclusions at last, and she had found fulfilment in a passion of real love. We expect, then, Denham to be acting with her in the charade play, and to be taking a *rôle* more or less parallel to that which he has in very reality; but we are disconcerted to find that there is no mention of him as having any part at all in the acting; indeed he is not once referred to in the chapter as far as it goes, which is a fairly long way!

In the missing (or, more probably, yet to be written) section of it Lesbia doubtless, *via* Herbert dressed as a girl, falls in love with his sister, who has his beauty in a higher degree, and carries no sexual disqualification.

2. What happens, as regards Denham and Margaret, in the seven years between 1854 and Mr. Linley's revelations to Denham of family secrets? The two must have come to conclusions in this space, if they had not already done so in the time preceding it. She tells him at their last meeting 'You made my life pleasant for a year' (a relatively short time, by the way), and they kiss and otherwise behave like people who are lovers to the fullest extent; and—a clinching fact—he is referred to as 'her dead lover' when his body is carried in at the end of this chapter. They had evidently planned, just before Mr. Linley's disclosures, to elope: 'We cannot go away to-

(Note ¹ *continued*)—
librarian, manager, friend of the house' when his duties as tutor were over.

338

gether' he says to her in their last conversation. (Helen Harewood and Champneys, Clara Radworth and Reginald Harewood, Anne Halden and Arthur Lunsford, and now Lady Wariston and Denham: the theme of elopement is persistent through all four works.) It is now at least twelve years since Denham became a member of the household (to mention only one thing, her two elder boys are now at Eton: Herbert was thirteen when he began his school life there). Thus, apart from a few passages in chapters II and III (and these refer only to his feelings before she is aware of his love), there is no record at all of relations between Margaret and Denham over this very long interval. This fact alone would make it almost certain that there were intermediate chapters which Swinburne had still to write (there is no grounds for supposing that they were written and lost. He doubtless, in accordance with his usual practice, had a pretty full plan worked out before he started, and it is not unlikely that he executed chapters or sections of this, as the fancy took him, in no regular sequence. The non-availability of this plan, which would have made so much clear, is even more unfortunate than the loss of parts of the manuscript). It is probably in the space between 1854 and the divulging of secrets that Denham becomes involved with the other woman; and during that time no doubt Lesbia's passion for Margaret deepens and takes on the despair that leads to suicide. The key to the chief enigmas of the book is almost unquestionably contained in absent chapters falling within this period.

We have taken for granted that Denham is the lover who in chapter XV sees Margaret for the last time and then commits suicide. Who else could it be? If one had any reason to look for a different person, there is just a faint possibility that it might be Walter Lunsford. To begin with, one might take as perhaps significant that in chapter IV, after Herbert's quasi-incestuous effusiveness, Margaret 'made less of him than before', and on the other hand 'was more than kind or gracious to young Lunsford'. Then, in chapter V, it was with the latter 'as a cavalier' that she played the part of Lucrezia Borgia.

Moreover, in the dramatic charade, he is not only a 'cavalier' to her, his *rôle* is that of Gennaro, the *jeune premier*, the attractive hero of the piece, for whom Lucrezia has a love that is perhaps more than maternal (he is the doubly illegitimate son of incestuous passion between herself and one of her brothers).[1] It is in acting to his Gennaro that she showed 'exquisite grace and power'; and the information that 'she was singularly animated all that week' is given in the same sentence. Here there is much more substantial ground for regarding the facts as significant of some more than merely social *rapport* between herself and Walter Lunsford, now an adolescent approaching manhood. It may be, of course, that her new charm and animation came from something that had happened between her and Denham, whose absence from the theatrical proceedings may be accidental or else a matter of prudence. But this, it seems, would be to leave her part in the play empty of significance, and this is hardly probable with Swinburne: he liked to establish a parallel in these cases between events in the play and others in the actual life of certain of the actors. Again, Margaret says to her lover at their last meeting 'I shall be soonest old you know, by so much'. There is a difficulty about this statement if she is comparing herself with Denham; for he is some twelve years older than she. And the difficulty is no more than reduced—it still persists—if she is taken as referring to the fact that a woman ordinarily ages—or at least becomes *passée*—much more quickly than a man. The remark would certainly be more natural addressed to Walter Lunsford, who was five years younger than herself. The difficulty recurs later in the same conversation when, talking of his suicide, she pleads with him not to damage his features: 'Not the face, darling . . . You are too young'. Would she be likely to say this to a man of over forty? But to one of only about twenty-six it is a thing she might very well say. Finally, in the second sentence of chapter XVI ('Leucadia') we read that Herbert had been hurt for a

[1] Cf. the last sentence of the 11th note on Ch. V.

340

time by 'his old friend's death'. If, as appears very probable, the reference is to the suicide of his sister's lover, the term 'old friend' might apply either to Denham or to Lunsford, but it would fit the latter—his comrade, his 'one friend', before his school days, his friend at Eton and after—better than the former, whom he might have come to regard as a friend after he had passed out of his hands, but who in his early years had treated him in a way that must always have seemed unfriendly to him.

A not implausible case, then, could be made out for Walter Lunsford in this mater. But is there any strong reason for doubting that Denham is the lover? He appears cast for that *rôle* from the outset, and it would *prima facie* seem to be somewhat awkward if he were replaced by Lunsford at a later stage of the story. Whereas, if any interest Margaret and Lunsford may have had in each other were only passing, an incidental and commonplace event in the social background, and came to nothing, that would not be objectionable from any point of view. Furthermore, it is quite clear from chapter XIV, which must be temporally very near chapter XV, that Denham is still very much in love with Margaret (Mr. Linley refers to her as his 'present idol') and it is surely only in connexion with this fact that Mr. Linley discloses the blood relationship between them. It may be regarded as a difficulty that in the lovers' last talk there is no mention of this matter, no indication that they have learned that their love is incestuous. Indeed, there is no allusion at all to the conversation with Mr. Linley. But it may be that an earlier part of chapter XV is missing, or else that the chapter begins in *mediis rebus*, it being left to the reader to assume that the conversation has been already mentioned. Moreover, the obscure harping by both of them on 'honour' may have to do with the question of incest (they shrinking from making explicit reference to it). 'Let us keep something like honour', he says; and further on, 'And our honour? what shall we get for that?' And she, soft, collapsible, facilely suggestible in her pitiful if not contemptible weakness, echoes with 'We shall not have happiness, but honour . . . we shall have', and 'Keep my honour for me; and yours. It is best to keep one's honour'. More notable than any of these is his 'And now you see I could not with honour' [i.e. come back to you], where 'now' strongly suggests some recent happening or information that has given a different complexion to things. And what could this be but the disclosure that theirs is an incestuous passion? Again, when she says 'And no one will be wronged; and no one come to shame' (i.e. if we part, but see each other sometimes), the second clause might very well refer to incest, the first doubtless referring to her husband and to the woman to whom Denham has contracted obligations. (Commonsense may object that sexual love between a man and his half-sister is not a very serious degree of incest, not sufficiently grave a matter to be taken thus tragically as meaning a loss of honour. But the conventional evaluation of it, especially in Victorian England—cf. the terrible scandal caused in an earlier and less strait-laced period by the fact or rumour that Byron had been the lover of his half-sister—was part of the social or ethical data that Swinburne had to accept as a novelist. And he had chosen not to make recalcitrant to it the two characters who judged by it had rendered themselves guilty. But it does not follow that he accepted it himself: probably his private opinion on this matter was no different from Shelley's.)

The mystery of the other woman in Denham's life is increased by passages of the conversation between him and Mr. Linley in chapter XIV (Les Malheurs de la Vertu'); and here, also, certain very enigmatic letters are mentioned for the first time and are a further source of confusion. What was Denham 'undecided' about (first sentence) before seeing Mr. Linley? Eloping with Margaret? Why are we told that Mr. Linley's house 'was three doors off Miss Brandon's'? Does it imply that Denham was going to see her too? If so, what for? Who was the unspecified female who left Mr. Linley's room 'in a rapid rustle' as Denham entered it? Leonora Harley? . . . 'You mean to restore the letters' says Mr. Linley. What letters? From whom to whom? The most natural assumption is that in some way they are incriminating for Margaret. 'They are all ready' says Mr. Linley. How did he come to have them? (if he does refer to the letters, as apparently it must). Then the two speak of an unnamed woman, and much of what they say is extremely baffling. E.g. Mr. Linley's 'Even if you don't care for the woman', and Denham's 'I'm not sure now that I care'; Mr. Linley's 'She can hardly love you', and Denhams 'How should she?', and 'there can be no question with her of pure passion. I think she rather hates me. She couldn't love me . . .' At first one is inclined to think that they cannot be talking of Margaret here; for there appears to be not the slightest doubt that Denham has all along been in love with Margaret; and that he is still is made plain—as we have already indicated—by Mr. Linley's calling her his 'present idol', and is made still more plain in the farewell scene of the following chapter (assuming he is the man in that scene), where it is also evident that his love is returned by Margaret. Surely, then, one thinks, the reference must be to the other woman in his life. And, continuing in this supposition, one wonders whether the other woman might not be Lesbia after all, in spite of the apparently decisive arguments one has brought against this possibility. In this case it would be natural for Mr. Linley to say, if he knew of her homosexuality, that she could 'hardly love' Denham, and for Denham, if he knew of her tendencies, to agree, and to say further 'there can be no question with her of pure passion'. Moreover, her peculiar constitution need not have prevented Denham from being attracted by her (any more than it prevented Herbert), nor her from playing with him up to a point that may have had awkward consequences; and, if this were so, the mention of Lesbia's house being so near, and the precipitately vanishing woman, and Mr. Linley's possession of the letters, presumably—in this case—left by that woman, might seem a little less obscure (but there would still be a mystery about the letters). Mr. Linley's 'Like her mother' in reply to Denham's 'she is too beautiful', might as it stands refer to Lesbia's mother, the attractive woman who had wrought on

343

Fred Seyton and brought Denham into the world. But the practically immediate transition to Mr. Linley's 'The father was dead before your time' excludes this hypothesis almost beyond any possibility of doubt. The father, it turns out, is Fred Seyton; he is not Lesbia's father (who anyhow died long after Denham had reached manhood); therefore the mother, unless the sequence of language and thought is incredibly unnatural, must be Margaret's and not Lesbia's—Seyton's wife, who 'was far more beautiful than' Lesbia's mother, Mr. Linley says later on in the conversation: a remark that accords with his testimony to the exceptional beauty of the mother mentioned in this earlier passage. And so the woman they have been discussing up to this point can be no other than Margaret. This is further borne out, a few lines down, by Mr. Linley's 'Her father was yours'. But all the aforementioned difficulties remain, and they are not the only ones. The woman being Margaret, why should Denham say not only that he hardly expected love from her, and that there could be no question of pure passion on her part, and that he thinks she rather hates him, but also that he 'wants her to give way'? Had she not already—as the following chapter shows pretty clearly—become his lover (and, it seems, arranged to elope with him), and so 'given way' as much as he could possibly wish? And again we are faced by the question of the letters. If he means, as he appears to do, that he contemplates using the letters (as Lady Midhurst uses correspondence in *Love's Cross Currents*) to make her 'give way', what can these letters be, what could there be in them that would give him a hold over her? They can hardly be letters between her and himself: no likely sense could be got out of that. Once more one is confronted by the hypothesis, already rejected as most improbable, that it was not Denham who was her lover, but some other man, who would be Walter Lunsford, according to all the evidence we have.

As already suggested, some of the afore-mentioned difficulties disappear if we adopt this hypothesis. Denham's feelings towards Margaret are no longer enigmatic. Of a woman whom

he loves with a great love (his 'idol'), but who does not return
that love, and on the contrary loves another man, he might
at almost one and the same time say 'I'm not sure now that I
care' and 'I'm really ashamed, but I care about her'. The
despair of passion would lead to the former feeling, and even
to something like hatred; there had been the same ambivalence in his feelings towards her—love, and hatred arising
out of hopelessness—in the early part of the story, soon after
he had met her for the first time. The letters, too, lose a good
deal of their mystery. They might well be compromising
letters from Margaret to him, showing that there had been
something of an affair between them, or at least an approach
to it. In his despair of getting her full love and his anger at her
having taken Lunsford as a lover, he had (on this hypothesis)
had thoughts of using the letters to force her to 'give way';
'not to hate' him (although that would seem impossible) but
'to fear' him, and to yield to the extent of giving herself fully
to him, if she had not already done so, or, if she had, to go
on doing so (cf. 'and then to be as before'), even though she
could never love him with 'pure passion'. But at the time of
his arrival at Mr. Linley's he is 'still undecided' as to whether
he will make use of the letters. Margaret's feelings too are
very much less problematic. She had been in a muddle with
regard to Denham; had never loved him properly, but perhaps, in rebelliousness against her unsatisfactory existence,
had not altogether rejected his advances; and because of this,
and still more because she now had a passionate love for
Lunsford, had come to 'hate' him. Her *rôle* in the charade-
play, that of a woman in love with the character acted by
Lunsford, now has the further significance we expect to find:
there is full Swinburnian parallelism between the play-acting
and something in actual life. The references in Chapter XV
to the man's age are also no longer mysterious. So far so good;
and that is a fair amount. But there still remain very teasing
obscurities. The other woman is as much a problem as ever;
the only difference is that she is now in Lunsford's and not
in Denham's life; no other woman has been mentioned in

connexion with the former, any more than in connexion with the latter; in fact, we know much less of Lunsford than of Denham: his appearances in the story are very incidental, and we are told hardly anything about him. (A very curious and perhaps—for the present hypothesis—awkward thing, if he is in love with Margaret, is that there is not the least hint of it in Chapter VII, which he has all to himself with Herbert, and the date of which is some years after the time he and she acted together. Moreover, while Herbert is there presented as being madly in love, there is what appears to be a definite suggestion that Lunsford has no such preoccupations and is quite fancy-free: whereas he 'slept well enough' that night, Herbert had a dream lurid and terrible with symbols of deadly sex and love turned into a great desolation.) Lesbia of course is ruled out in his (Lunsford's) case no less than in Denham's: the same precluding argument holds good here too . . . And other things: the mention of Lesbia's house being so near Mr. Linley's, the quickly disappearing female, Mr. Linley's possession of the letters: all this remains obscure . . . On the supposition we are following, the incest motive disappears from the scene between the two lovers. The 'honour' mentioned there can only refer to Margaret's duty towards her husband and children; and this perhaps (and even very probably) is, from the Swinburnian point of view, less interesting as a crux, and somewhat out of harmony with the general tenour of the book, and therefore—in this calculation of pros and cons—hardly a thing to be placed on the credit side. (Mr. Linley's disclosure of the blood relationship between Margaret and Denham can now only be taken as an effort on Mr. Linley's part to cure the latter not of a passion which has got its way but of one which has turned out to be hopeless.) If Lunsford is the lover, Swinburne transferred to *Lesbia Brandon* part of the plan he drew up for *Herbert Winwood*; it will be remembered that there Arthur Lunsford was to 'intrigue' (replacing a cancelled 'elope') with one of the married women; here Lunsford (become Walter) intrigues with a wife and mother, arranges (apparently) to

elope with her, but finally decides not to do so, but to go
and take his own life. (This—intrigue that does not get to
the point of elopement—is the situation in all four stories of
the cycle except the first: only in *Reginald Harewood* is
there elopement in the case of one of the chief sets of
lovers.)

On the whole, this hypothesis leaves more difficulties
settled than unresolved, and no doubt most readers will be
inclined to accept it. But when all is said, there is a problem—the main and key problem of the story—and I think
no solution of it can be offered with full confidence. We
(those who really know him) expect Swinburne to be very
subtle (he is as subtle as any writer in the whole of
literature); but here his subtlety is so fine-drawn that it is
impossible to do more than tentatively guess at it in its
main lines (and only in its main lines) from what appears
of it in the portion of the story he actually wrote—even
though that portion is pretty large and very probably
much more than half the book. This is very disappointing,
of course. But the problem at least has the virtue of being
very inviting in its interest. I do not know of any similar
literary enigma which is nearly so baffling and attractive:
the mystery of the disappearance of Edwin Drood, the
classic case in this line, is simplicity itself compared with it,
and so is far less engaging.[1]

There are in Chapter XIV certain subordinate difficulties
more or less related to the main problem we have just been
considering. What does exactly Denham mean by saying
'There are boys and girls on one hand; old men on the other'?
If he had Margaret and her ties in mind, one would expect
him to be alluding to her one daughter and three boys (who
might roughly be referred to as 'boys and girls') and her
husband, who could not have been put into the category of

---

[1] As a matter of fact, the real or central mystery of this novel in very
large part vanishes once we know that *Edwin Drood in Hiding* was one
of the alternative titles invented for it by Dickens.

'old men', as he was of about the same age as Denham himself, who, like Margaret, belonged to neither of these groups. But Denham is apparently driving at something else: what it is is not made any clearer by his following remarks.

Again, why could not Fred Seyton marry Denham's mother? 'Elle en avait vu d'autres' is the only explanation afforded us. The probable meaning of this is that she aimed higher; that she had Lord Brandon in sight, or perhaps his elder brother the Marquis of Burleigh, of whom, it is hinted in Chapter III, she had at one time been the mistress. From Mr. Linley's story, which Denham not unnaturally thinks 'involved', one is no doubt meant to gather that the latter was born before his mother married Lord Brandon; that she 'had been out of sight for two years' before the marriage came off; that in this interval both she and her sister were 'talked about, blown upon' because of her liaison with Seyton;[1] and that her sister, who became Mrs. Linley, finally took charge of the inconvenient Denham (of whose birth Lord Brandon presumably had no knowledge) and thus incurred and nobly bore the suspicion that he was an illegitimate child of her own—it having been first supposed that her husband was the father of the boy by some woman other than herself. Such, then, appear to be the facts behind the 'involved' story. A further complication of inter-relationships, with an approximation to incest, may be noted here. Denham's mother is connected with four of the elders in the story: Fred Seyton, her lover; Lord Brandon, her husband, and brother of the Marquis of Burleigh, who also had probably been a lover of hers; and Mr. Linley, her brother-in-law, who had feelings for her that were definitely illicit.

One may ask here what is the purpose of the fragmentary Chapter XIII in the economy of the story. Had Mr. Linley gone to give a hint to Margaret of the secret he conveys to Denham in the following chapter? This seems to be the only point of his asking her whether she had noticed a likeness

[1] As to why both of them were, see Note [5] on Chapter XIV.

to her brother in his late son Arthur; and of his comment: 'I believe in likenesses, and tha tthey go deep . . . It is significant of something, I am convinced, when two faces without a vein of kindred blood in them are so alike.' What was in his mind, it may be conjectured, was this, or something of the kind: while there was no kindred blood in Arthur and Herbert, there was in Denham on the one hand and Herbert and Margaret on the other; now Denham and Arthur were first cousins, Arthur being the son of the sister of Denham's mother, the one-time mistress of Herbert and Margaret's father; being cousins, there was a certain likeness between them; if, therefore, Herbert resembled Arthur at all, he also, and even more, would resemble Denham, who was not only first cousin to Arthur but also half-brother to himself . . . This could set Margaret thinking along the required lines . . . True, it is all very indirect, roundabout, distant, tenuous; but that is Mr. Linley's way (and Swinburne's way too when-ever he has to deal with crucial matters). Having thus thrown out his hint, Mr. Linley, again characteristically, goes off into other considerations, and finishes up with a philosophical dis-quisition (very cogent) on aristocracy as something divergent from and struggling against Nature. Thus, what at first sight seems a purely otiose chapter is in reality part of the organism of the work. It is germane to the plot, and it helps to convey the subtlety of one of the subtlest characters in the whole of fiction. (It may be asked whether the foregoing explanation holds if Lunsford is Margaret's lover. Why in this case should Mr. Linley wish to put her on the track of the secret? The only answer is that this was part of his plan of keeping Den-ham and her apart—of curing Denham of a passion for her that was all the more hopeless if she was in love with another man. For it was still on the cards that Denham might try to use the letters to make her give him some sort of satisfaction. And Mr. Linley, corrupt as he is, has solicitude of a kind for Denham: his heart, he told him had gone out towards him as his 'old friend's child'; and again, Denham had been 'more than a son' to him, he told him in a burst of feeling that

349

appears to be genuine—and adds pathos to his cynicism, thus increasing his complexity.)

So much for the difficulties, principal and minor, connected with the main part of the plot. There are others concerning less important matters, and we shall do no more than glance at one or two of these. The most puzzling is in Chapter IX ('Turris Eburnea'): what precisely was Mr. Linley's purpose in thrusting himself into the affairs of Herbert? That he should design to 'launch him imperceptibly into life', 'purge' his 'head of puerile fumes and fancies', 'lift' him 'out of the slough of sentiment and despondency', and that he should use the demi-semi-mondaine Leonora Harley as a means thereto—that offers no difficulty. But he also designed to 'start this boy', 'follow, catch him up, distance him', and 'supplant him at the right time'; and this is very far from clear. 'Catch him up', 'supplant him' etc. in respect of what? Surely not of Leonora: there can be no doubt that already he had access to all he wanted there: he was her 'patron', with usufruct of anything that she could offer. In any case, most men could have got her for a price. Could it have been in respect of a political career? This might be the implication of 'It was rare to find a boy of his age and rank so passionate on political matters as young Seyton; who, besides, was not exactly a fool, and therefore might be worth laying hold of'. And in Chapter III we are told that he 'had tried political life in his youth', but had sagely given it over 'as a barren nuisance'. Had he relapsed to this fancy of his youth? This would seem to be the most natural, not to say the only possible, interpretation of 'A certain recrudescence of personal ambition rose, subsided, and revived within him' (a part of the context at present under discussion). But how could he possibly make use of Herbert to advance himself in this direction? How can one push another man to a political position one is incapable of reaching oneself and then simply dislodge and supplant him with as much ease as a conjuror produces a rabbit? It may be feasible, but the process is so darkly tortuous that nothing of it is visible. Here as elsewhere the subtle Mr. Linley is very much a Prince of Darkness.

Of one thing we can be quite certain, and that is that it was not part of his intention that Leonora, who was bent on making a profitable marriage, should capture Herbert as a husband. That would be altogether intolerable; and Mr. Linley could not have thought of it: cynically amoral as he was, he had a certain refinement, and was too delicate to entertain an idea that was as preposterous as it was ugly. Besides, he was a man of shrewd sense, and would know that Herbert could never be brought to decline to this extent on a woman so hopelessly beneath the idealistic side of his nature. All that he could look for was that she might by exciting Herbert sexually help to detach him from his futile and unhealthy passion for Lesbia. And the main purpose of the almost certainly unfinished Chapter XII ('La Bohême Dédorée') was doubtless to show that this was a vain design: that other face, 'with close melancholy lips, full of meaning and passion', and 'with sombre luminous eyes', would always rise between him and any siren that might be produced by Mr. Linley.

I have now dealt with all the major difficulties of the story; other minor ones I have considered elsewhere, in the Notes and in the chapter devoted to the text. Before passing from the story or plot to other matters, I will briefly review Lafourcade's presentation of it, as it is the only one in existence, and has no doubt been unquestioningly accepted as trustworthy by those wishing to have information on the subject. It will have been taken for granted that anyone can be relied on for accuracy in so simple a business. But this natural assumption is never safe in the case of Lafourcade. As I have already said, he is alive to not one of the many difficulties on which I have touched, and so he nowhere considers any of them. (For instance, he states, without any qualifying doubt, that Margaret's lover is Denham.) His account, then, of the story is very far from being adequate. That is not all: even in this very inadequate account he makes a number of mistakes that one would have thought impossible. He says, for example, that Denham is the brother of Lesbia and Herbert, and that Margaret is his half-sister; not realising that if Margaret is his half-sister (as she is), then he must be the half-brother of Herbert, and of course he is the half-brother of Lesbia.

He makes Margaret—in an apparently would-be exhaustive genealogical table—the mother of only three children: he failed to notice the existence of the eldest boy Arthur (Atty); moreover, the table is so ambiguously constructed that, according to it, Denham rather than Lord Wariston is the father of the three children who are named in it.

Summarising the first part of Chapter XV, he says 'les deux amants décident de se séparer pour jamais': that is all: no mention of the man's intention to commit suicide, and of Margaret's final acquiescence in this desperate way out of a situation which somehow has now become impossible. Again, summing up the last scene of this chapter, he says '. . . soudain son mari entre précédant Denham porté mort sur une civière: Lord Wariston s'est vengé.' Evidently, having failed to see that the lover (who he still has no doubt was Denham) was going to commit suicide, he believes that Lord Wariston, knowing of the *liaison* (a supposition for which there is no warrant in the book) had murdered the lover! This in spite not only of the latter's sufficiently clear decision to take his own life, but also of the husband's words of explanation when the dead man is carried in: 'An accident . . . his gun went off in getting through a hedge'. Before such density, on croit rêver, as Lafourcade's fellow-countrymen would say, giving mild expression to their surprise.

To continue with our florilegium of insipience: he puts a love for Balzac among Herbert's enthusiasms: evidently he has read as the boy's (aged thirteen) certain very characteristic pronouncements of Lady Midhurst on this writer.

We get back to more serious crassness with his statement that Mrs. Linley 'accepte de reconnaître' Denham. This can only mean, in good French, that she acknowledged herself, or passed herself off, as the mother of the child, admitting

furthermore that it was illegitimate: all that she really did—
in Swinburne's text—was to 'take charge of' Denham, in conjunction with her husband. Lafourcade also says of Mr. Linley
that 'sa cruauté envers le fils illégitime de F. Seyton en faisait
"an instance of suffering virtue" '. The illegitimate son of
F. Seyton of course is Denham, and it is nowhere stated or
hinted that Mr. Linley was ever cruel to him. It was towards
his own son Arthur (who is never so much as mentioned by
Lafourcade) that he was cruel, and it was Mrs. Linley who for
that reason (among others) became 'an instance of suffering
virtue'. Mr. Linley himself, talking to Denham, applies these
words to her, and then, explaining how he set himself to
torment her, says 'I used to scourge her through him' (i.e.
Arthur): nothing could be clearer, but obviously nothing
can be guaranteed fool-proof.

Once again, all this is typical of Lafourcade: at least, where-
ever I have examined and tested his work I have found it to
be a compost of errors, often so extraordinary that one has
the uncomfortable feeling that one is in the presence of
cretinism.[1] And yet his tome on Swinburne passes as standard
and authoritative in academic and other circles in all parts of
the world!

I shall now go on to a brief consideration of some of the
characters. Lady Midhurst is much the same as she was in
Love's Cross Currents (except that here she is not one of the
controlling forces of the story). She is still fearsomely clever,
and her victims still speak of her 'fangs' and her 'venom'; she
has 'gone all to brain and tongue', says one of the more able
of them, who is her rival in the field of destructive scorn. The
frequent play of her 'sharp-edged paradox', especially in
alliance or in collision with that of Mr. Linley, is one of the
things that give quality to the lengthy third chapter (or, as
some would no doubt say, that save it from being merely a
longueur). But her soft side is more in evidence here than in

---

[1] See, in particular, my examination in *Lucretia Borgia* of his chapter
on *The Chronicle of Tebaldeo Tebaldei*.

the earlier work; the kindly gentle tact, the sympathetic understanding, with which she handles the wounded Herbert —one of the best things in the book—shows that there is something very lovable behind the sardonic sharpness she usually displays. We can well believe that 'many children were drawn to her', and that, as Lord Wariston testified, she could be 'delicious'—towards those who met with her approval. She is not only tender towards Herbert, she talks excellent sense to him; her wisdom, her austere, courageous, non-Christian wisdom, is the same here as it was in the earlier book. 'Don't get any notion of providential justice into your head; it doesn't pay except in Carlyle—and the Bible of course . . . I advise you to adapt yourself to the nature of things'. Here she expresses one of the cardinal articles of Swinburne's creed (and of the creed of Spinoza, Goethe, Taine and other of the better spirits of the world). But she is also again soundly critical of certain of the enthusiasms of Swinburne on his lyrical side (which once more shows that the poet was perfectly capable of critical detachment even in the case of things by which he was most profoundly stirred). 'I don't believe in revolution or what they call peoples et tout ce fatras . . . As for democracy and the illuminated masses, I hate the very smell of such cant.' That (spoken, be it observed, by a character very 'sympathetic' to the author, if not his mouthpiece at times)—that, and especially the second sentence, is admirable—and healthily corrective of much in the glorious *Songs Before Sunrise* and other political poetry of Swinburne before and after that collection. Still, she pays something of a tribute to Mazzini, declaring that he 'is worth many a Derwentwater'; even so, there is a corrective here too: 'I don't say' his and his kind 'are not mad, or not fools', a concession to sense that Swinburne never made in his lyrical moments. She is even critical of Hugo, another of Swinburne's gods, about whom she herself had spoken in exclusively superlative terms in *Love's Cross Currents*. Her 'philanthrope malgré Dieu et poète malgré lui', is an excellent statement, unsurpassable for epigrammatic concision, of the great French

354

poet's two chief faults: his stubborn optimism with regard to things in general and with regard to human nature in particular, in the face of contradictory facts in the Creation, and his didactic tendencies, which militate against true poetry— but in spite of which he always keeps himself on the level of true poetry. On the other hand, she refuses to see any faults in Balzac, and here it is Mr. Linley who provides the corrections; and they are quite just, although he is not a 'sympathetic' character. Wholesale acceptance, failure of critical judgment, in this one case, perhaps makes more feminine a woman of such a masculine mind.

Lafourcade, vainly seeking for originals or sources of Lady Midhurst in real life, naïvely remarks that she frequently drops into French, as did Swinburne's mother. It is hardly worth while to observe 'And so did hundreds of other ladies in English society.' The pagan Lady Midhurst of course is almost the opposite in essentials of Swinburne's pious mother. Lafourcade, not satisfied with this essay in identification, elsewhere asserts that Lady Midhurst has something of the intellectual charm of Lady Trevelyan. Here again, however, as it would be very easy to show, there is opposition rather than community where essentials are concerned. And Lafourcade himself, some 450 pages later, seems to have changed his mind, and rather self-stultifyingly declares that it is 'probably' wrong to see in Lady Trevelyan a prototype of Lady Midhurst. There is no prototype; and even if one succeeded in tracing resemblances here and there (as in, say, Swinburne's lively or energetic Aunt Julia[1]) the adding of them up would not result

---

[1] Or in such a person of the mid-Victorian age as the Lady Cowper described by Lord Ronald Gower in his *Reminiscences*. She 'had a rich vein of motherwit'; she talked much, but 'never for a second became wearisome'; 'although seeing people and things from a sarcastic point' (just like Lady Midhurst), 'she never said an ill-natured or unkind word' (it is to be feared that Lady Midhurst did at times); and in spite of her 'plain and modest' widow's attire 'she was thoroughly *grande dame.*' Her kind—the Lady Midhurst type—is not to be found in English society in its present declension.

in a Lady Midhurst. She is *sui generis,* holds of nobody, is a new and unique personality—and she is very much more alive than most people in what is generally but erroneously thought of as being the only real world. In other words, she is a true creation, with the fuller reality that belongs to art of the greater kind; and she proves decisively that Swinburne was capable of producing original or novel (and not merely autobiographic) characters as well as poetic beauty and wit and other things that give distinction to *Lesbia Brandon.* To sum up what should have been an unnecessary discussion: she 'is entirely a creature of my own invention' said Swinburne himself, and that is the whole truth of the matter at least as regards essentials.

The demi-semi-mondaine Leonora Harley is only a minor character, but she merits a few words, if only because Meredith singled her out for special praise. In the chapter that takes its title from her ('Turris Eburnea') she is simply described; it is good epigrammatic portraiture; in 'La Bohême Dédorée' she comes into action, but not to any great extent, and unfortunately the chapter is left incomplete just when it is working up to a climax; but her active part in it has the truth of life—of such poor inferior life as creatures of her kind possess. Lafourcade also vainly and unnecessarily tries to find originals for her, and in the process achieves further records of absurdity. She owes something he affirms, to 'a character' in *The Ordeal of Richard Feverel.* This unspecified character can only be Mrs. Mount. Mrs. Mount! The brilliant, manifoldly gifted, highly seductive fallen woman of 'An Enchantress', the best chapter of *Feverel,* and perhaps the best chapter in the whole of Meredith! 'Various as the serpent of old Nile, she acted fallen beauty, humorous indifference, reckless daring, arrogance in ruin', and many other things, and did it superbly. It is rank nonsense to represent the dull witless Leonora Harley as owing anything whatsoever to such a woman (doubtless Lafourcade thought the fact that they were both of humble birth was enough to make sisters of them). He flounders into almost worse nonsense when he says

that Leonora also probably owes something to Adah Isaacs
Menken (Swinburne's mistress in the period when this part
of *Lesbia Brandon* was probably written). Just think of the
two! Leonora, a woman of 'no mind whatever', uncommonly
'stupid', 'cold, slow, heavy'; 'coarse or fine, she never in her
life said a good thing. She had not even the harlot's talent of
discernment'. Adah, a woman of very lively intelligence (even
when all probable or possible exaggerations or legends concerning her have been subjected to discount); not without
education (according to one report she taught Latin and
French at a girls' school when she was young); an amateur of
literature who tried very hard to be a poet; a talented actress;
an entertaining *raconteuse*; in short, a woman of real brains,
by which as well as by her lavish physical charms she won
the friendship of men of the calibre of Bret Harte, Dickens,
Charles Reade, D. G. Rossetti, Gautier, Dumas *père*, and
Rochefort (and even—but only by the former of the qualities
mentioned—of a woman—George Sand—who belonged to
the higher reaches of the intellectual *élite*). And—but the
contrast is already sufficiently enormous, and there is no need
to go any further with it.

If one must find an original for Leonora, the most likely
place to look for one is among the *demi-mondaines* and models
who were associated with Rossetti and other members of the
Preraphaelite set, and with whom Swinburne was well
acquainted. And the most likely one of all these is the Fanny
who was the model for Rossetti's picture *Bocca Baciata* and
was for many years his mistress. William Bell Scott, writing of
'ladies who came within his [Rossetti's] orbit', said 'Among
these the most important was one who must have had some
overpowering attractions for him, although I never could see
what they were. He met her in the Strand. She was cracking
nuts with her teeth, and throwing the shells about. Seeing
Rossetti staring at her, she threw some at him. Delighted with
this brilliant naïveté, he forthwith accosted her, and carried
her off to sit to him for her portrait'. Rossetti's brother
William, commenting on this, gives the following account of

Fanny, which may be taken as being sober and objective, for William was a very fair-minded man, whose chief quality was integrity with regard to anything he touched upon. If, as is very probable, he found Fanny very tiresome, and did not approve of the extent to which she entered into Gabriel's life, this would not lead him into misrepresenting her in any way:

'If Mr. Scott "never could see" what were the attractions of Mrs. H— [i.e. Fanny], his eyesight must have differed from that of many other people. She was a pre-eminently fine woman, with regular and sweet features, and a mass of the most lovely blonde hair—light-golden or "harvest yellow". *Bocca Baciata*, which is a most faithful portrait of her, might speak for itself. If Mr. Scott meant not so much to deny that Mrs. H— was "fair to see", but rather to intimate that she had no charm of breeding, education, or intellect, he was right enough.'

The physical attractiveness, combined with 'no charm of breeding, education, or intellect', fits Leonora Harley exactly, and it may be safely assumed that Fanny more than anybody else—if there was anybody else—is the original from which she derives. Further corroborative evidence is found in the following line of Rossetti's poem *The Song of the Bower*:

Large lovely arms and a neck like a tower.

The 'a neck like a tower' of this verse may be the immediate source of Swinburne's 'Turris Eburnea' (of course the primary source of both his and Rossetti's phrases are two verses in The Old Testament); and Leonora's arms are among those of her physical charms to which Swinburne gives special praise. Now it was practically certain that *The Song of the Bower* was addressed to Fanny. William Michael Rossetti took it 'as relating to Miss Siddal' (Lizzy, the lady whom Gabriel finally brought himself to marry). But Swinburne corrected him on this; 'I am almost sure', he wrote,[1] 'that the *Song of the Bower* was not written with reference to Miss Siddal, but rather—if with any direct reference—to a creature—you call her "Mrs. H"—at the other pole of the sex. In fact, I may almost say I know it, from Gabriel's own admission—implied when he and I were discussing that as yet unfinished poem, which in the early days of "Bocca Baciata" may not have been so comically exaggerative as it seemed to me even when I first met the bitch". The terms in which he refers to Fanny (he was strongly on the side of Lizzy): 'a creature at the other pole of the sex', 'the bitch', further reinforce my supposition that he had her in mind when he created Leonora, who is by no means a 'sympathetic' character.[2] One last point: the latter was a daughter of a labourer and her real name was Susan Farmer; Fanny Cornforth was the daughter of a blacksmith and her real name was Sarah Cox. We may, therefore, write Q.E.D. Lafourcade knew the period very ill; had he known it as he should have done before attempting to write on Swinburne this demonstration would not have been necessary. Of course, in taking Fanny as a model, Swinburne did not simply copy her: like a true creator, he did no more than receive suggestions from her: but there were not a few of them, and in the creation we can see her likeness. But she is one of the minor figures. The more important the characters are, the less is the likeness of any original to be seen, and the more true is it that they are 'entirely creatures of' Swinburne's own invention', to quote once again a claim he made for one of them: I believe this can be taken as a general rule. There is, of course,

---

[1] Letter to W. M. Rossetti, December 4th, 1895 (in British Museum).

[2] Apparently Swinburne was not so unfavourably impressed when he first met her. Talking of Rossetti's painting *Bocca Baciata* in an unpublished letter written in December 1859, he says: 'I daresay you have heard of his head in oils of a stunner . . . She is more stunning than can be decently expressed.' The stunner was Fanny. The word 'decently' indicates that Swinburne was struck by more of her charms than appear in the head of the picture, and nothing that he says suggests that he did not approve of her. It was only later that he met Lizzie and realised that Fanny was part of the tragedy of her life.

an exception in the case of the autobiographic Herbert and previous avatars of him.

As we have already noted, the fundamental type of the specifically Swinburnian woman is seen in Helen Harewood (of the *Kirklowes* fragment): in whom 'a sensual blood and quick nerves' are combined with the very different and almost contrary qualities of 'a steady judgment and somewhat cold heart'. The formula applies, on the whole, to Mary Stuart; and Clara Radworth in *Love's Cross Currents*, who is 'at once excitable and cold', is an examplar of it, although in a lesser degree and on a lower plane. Margaret, Lady Wariston, also has the two somewhat opposed sides, well differentiated, of course, as in the case of Clara and others, to suit a new personality, which has the diversity of its uniqueness. But Margaret, unlike Clara, who is pretty well the same from beginning to end, goes through stages of development. (And this adds to the impression that she is a real person—although, for the matter of that, there are lots of people in real life— perhaps the immense majority—whose personality remains stable once they have passed into their adult years.) At first, there is nothing striking or salient about her except her beauty. In the matter of feelings, she is curiously undeveloped, not to say, subnormal; her life appears to be arrested in an apathy. She seems to be capable of nothing but a rather placid affection; although a 'wife and mother from her girl-hood', she has no strong love—if any love at all—for her husband nor even for any of her children; for him she has 'a dutiful and temperate' something that certainly has no touch of passion in it; and as regards the children, we are told that they 'had no hold on her', that she 'was not by nature a specially maternal woman', and that her first-born was the off-spring of a passive mother who was no more than an instrument of propagation. 'Of any possible passion', then, 'she seemed to give but slight promise.' Indeed, things could hardly be more unpromising; there is a terrible dearth of exciting or even interesting possibilities with such a woman: that at least is one's first impression. But we are incidentally informed that she has a 'strange and subtle nature'. And there is a good deal to her (which a keen eye might have divined from her physical portrait in the opening pages of the book). Only it is dormant or stagnant or blindly and confusedly reaching after expression. She has 'a vague and violent thirst after action and passion'; her affections, we are told, were 'less excitable and fervent' than her brother's, which implies that they were excitable and fervent up to a point, and it appears to be a pretty high point, judging from the scene at the end of Chapter III, where she does not leave altogether without return Herbert's passionate feelings for her. Even so, however, she is in some sort unawakened: she is quite unconscious of Denham's violently strong love for her up to about a year after his arrival (and it is not certain that she ever becomes pervious to the psychic force that must emanate from it). Early in 1851 she 'has never thought of love'. How long she continues in this state does not appear; but nearly five years later, by Chapter V, something has happened, there has been a change, and she is now well on the way of development away from the unpromise of this early condition. A 'rapid grace, soft and keen as the play of light flame', informs all her actions, and signifies that passion has come into her life. We next see her between six and seven years later, together with her lover, and now her development is complete. Her 'throat trembled, her veins felt fire . . .; her head quivered with the pulse and the pain of her passion'. Her potentialities have run their full course and received their utmost expression.

The first of the two constituent sides of the type of which she is an example is seen in the last part of the preceding paragraph. Its opposite, the second, is seen in her tendency to recede or fall away from high feeling; 'her instinct' was to 'grow less tender', while Herbert's was 'to become more loving' once passion or sentiment had entered upon its course. This indicates a certain deficiency, and may be equated with the 'somewhat cold heart' of the formula. Here she is like Helen Harewood and Clara Radworth; but there appear to be no grounds for putting down to a certain amount of shrewdness or calculation any failure on her part where passion is concerned, and here she is quite unlike Clara. It is nothing but deficiency with her. When the time comes, in Chapter XV, for decision, for forthright and thoroughgoing resolution, she cannot rise to it. She wavers woefully. She loves her lover passionately, but for the sake of their love she cannot bring herself to brave the world. And herein she somewhat resembles Clara: like her, she does not 'care to fight for' what she values (even although her love for her paramour is stronger than Clara's for Reginald, and has already been proved to be an avenue to the highest happiness she has known). Still, it was Clara herself who made the negative decision; she had the strength to impose her weakness; but here all resolution is left to the man. Margaret weakly follows or rather collapses into all the fluctuations of his thought. She even at last acquiesces in the most desperate of alternatives: that he shall bring everything between them irretrievably to an end by committing suicide.

There is nothing sadistic about her; the author expressly says that 'there was no cold undercurrent of sleepy cruelty in the flow of her blood'. She would not, like Helen Harewood, take an eager pleasure in watching her lover die. But she does show a terrible coldness of heart even in this connexion. Referring to the place where he will inflict death upon himself, she says: 'Not the face, darling; ah, not your face'; and when his dead body is brought in her only question is: 'Lodged where?' in reference to the bullet that killed him and love and all that she had known of felicity: a purely aesthetic consideration seems to have driven all pity out of her.

Margaret is partly conceived as a contrast to Lesbia: 'she had never made friends of her own sex' is given as one of her characteristics. This makes Lesbia's tragedy: to be in love with such a woman. Her name of course indicates her constitution. But it does not necessarily do so; as Margaret tells Herbert, it is Irish, and as such it is quite respectable and might be borne by the very strictest of nuns. (Cf. Lesbia Burke in Henry Kingsley's two novels *Geoffrey Hamlyn* and *The Hillyars and the Burtons*.) The fact that it was given in all innocence to her was a kind of irony; and also a kind of fatality, she herself might have thought in her moments of bitterness.

Her homosexual nature is never explicitly emphasised; it is not even definitely stated anywhere that she belongs to that class; the fact, in Swinburne's usual manner, is conveyed by hints or suggestions, some of which are so tenuous that they might pass unobserved. Her unsuspecting father's impression of her (imparted to Herbert) is that she has always wanted to be a boy and, he says, everybody thought she would be until she was born;[1] she had (he goes on) always insisted on having the training and lessons that are reserved for boys. 'She's half male as it is I think sometimes', naïvely comments this father, who otherwise is a fastish man of the world (but it is the world of the turf and its adjuncts rather than of sexual psychology). In her poetry she always writes from the man's point of view, a fact that strikes him as strange; he sees nothing of its significance. The unusually close relation between her and her governess, which he mentions, also have a significance of which he is not aware. The first time she meets Herbert, he being dressed for a female part in a play, she says (still thinking he is a girl) that she would like to act Guanhumara (of *Les Burgraves*) to his Régina, and she asks 'Could we rehearse in private?': the fact that the question slips out incidentally only makes it the more significant.

Just as Margaret's nature is subtly conveyed by her physical portraiture, so is Lesbia's in the same manner. 'She was warm and wan as a hot day without a sun'. This marvellously renders the very essence of her personality—her ardours and their sterility, consequent upon a frustration that defeats all

[1] Did Swinburne mean to suggest that a strong desire on the mother's part to have a boy, and her conviction that she would have one, determined to some extent the child's homosexual tendencies? If so, this is an acute idea, and (as far as I am aware) a novel one, and it deserves to be taken note of by those who deal in abnormal psychology.

her life. Again, to the same effect, there is 'trouble' as well as 'power' in her face; and 'the face was one to attract rather than to satisfy' sums up her nature from the point of view of any man unfortunate enough to come under her charm. The inner truth of her personality is further wonderfully conveyed in the sinister beauty of Herbert's dream, a masterpiece in that kind of literature.[1] This inner truth there strikes through, from subconscious impressions, and afflicts Herbert before he knows of it consciously. 'The torture of the dream' was that everything was 'unfruitful and barren'. And this is what she, and love for her, turn out to be when, soon after, Herbert passionately, tragically, makes his declaration and offers her devotion perfect beyond the utmost bounds of reason: perfect so that there is madness in it. She gently, obliquely, but categorically forces the disastrous truth upon his full consciousness. She realises the sincerity and beauty of what he says, but she is so completely homosexual that she cannot understand it. (The completeness of her homosexuality is a thing to be insisted on. It differentiates her from, say, such an historical personage as Alcibiades on the male side; and, in fiction, from the numerous lesbian women in the work of the Marquis de Sade. These latter are almost, if not altogether, all perverts; that is, they are not innately homosexual, and most, if not all, of them have commerce with men as well as with members of their own sex. Perverts call for no pity and can hardly be tragic figures (merely as perverts); for normal sexual and cognate possibilities are not closed to them; Lesbia is a genuine invert, is innately homosexual, and that gives a quality of tragedy to her life. In which respect she is far superior in interest to any of Sade's women: and, in general, Swinburne's erotic work is immeasurably superior in psychological as well as in aesthetic interest to that of the somewhat crude Marquis, which has little diversity and no *nuances*, and

[1] A masterpiece not only of beauty, but also of psychological insight—even from the much later point of view of the Freudian school and derivatives from it. See Notes 10 and 11 on Ch. VII.

364

is absolutely lacking in subtlety.)[1] His talk is quite 'senseless' to her, Lesbia tells Herbert with a candour that wrecks his dreams. Then, in a vain effort to soften the blow, she says that if she 'could love or marry' he would be the man of her choice. But she can't, and she herself is baffled by the embargo —but not on the practical side: 'I don't know why, at least I don't wholly know': what she does not know about it is metaphysical: a question of ultimate forces, Law and Chance, Order and Disorder, the problem of 'the mystery of the cruelty of things'; but she knows well enough that in spite of her body she has not a woman's nature. Whatever the cause, whatever the mistake of which she is the victim, she knows quite well that she is a homosexual. She is 'not marriageable' she tells him, putting the hard truth nearly in its fullness. And the sight of the immensity of his love and his despair makes 'her eyes grow dim for once. But the woman was all but incapable of tears'. In this respect she is perhaps of the same class as Helen Harewood and Mary Stuart; but her coldness of heart has not the same origin as theirs.

The death-bed scene—one of the most beautifully and movingly sad things in literature—shows that she is hopelessly homosexual to the very last. In the land of death, with its pale desolations, of her dream fantasy, it was only a woman she wanted to see, and it was only a woman, Proserpine, whom she finally saw, no men, and no children even: and Proserpine herself became Margaret . . . Thinking of Herbert as a brother, and loving him as such, which is all she can do, she wonders what it would have been like had she loved him the other way. The way that was impossible . . . but she insists that she was always fond of him—giving him ghostly comfort which she does not realise can only sharpen his bitterness. And, going deeper into this mood, she imprudently says that he may kiss her. Which he does, in the only way he can, as a real lover, giving her the ardour of his manhood—and the result is

---

[1] I am speaking particularly of character, and psychological *finesse*; in other respects, of course, there is plenty of diversity—among other merits, some of them considerable—in the works of the Marquis.

ghastly. She is horrified, terrified, recoils as from some dread and loathly incubus of nightmare, and pushes him back with panic savagery: so alien is she from normal love, so utter in her homosexuality.

Then her thoughts swing back to her real affinity. She tells him that he was once very like his sister 'about the mouth and eyes' (which of course is why she had sent for him, to be the last thing she should see on earth). In another dream, she says, she saw Margaret fall over a cliff. Then, after a while, 'It is I who have taken the leap now, not she (a covert reflection on Margaret's weakness in going on living after frustration and disaster in her love-affair). 'But in my dream she didn't fall of herself; somebody pushed her; I think I did' (an expression of a subconscious wish to kill Margaret—just as Denham had at times wished to kill her in his paroxisms of despair exacerbated into deadly hatred of her). And what was virtually her last wish was an expression of her homosexuality: that Herbert might dress up as a girl again and appear as he did at their first meeting: thus she would have some sense of Margaret's presence as she passed into death.

Lesbia is a very real, a very convincing, character, and in her Swinburne has presented, out of his intuitive knowledge, a very successful portrait of a fully homosexual woman in whom are realised the tragic possibilities resulting from her state. (Successful—that is, as far as another man, normally sexed, can say, relying also on intuitive imagination, as well as on knowledge of 'cases' derived from standard works on abnormal psychology and from other sources.[1]

[1] What Arnold Bennett says of 'the psychological picture of the type-pederast' in Proust's *Sodome et Gomorrhe* is, *mutatis mutandis*, true of Swinburne's presentation of the female counterpar,t and true in a higher degree, for Swinburne had a command of poetic beauty much greater than anything of the sort that Proust could command: 'An unpromising subject, according to British notions! Proust evolves from it beauty, and a heart-rending pathos. Nobody with any perception of tragedy can read these wonderful pages and afterwards regard the pervert as he had regarded the pervert before reading them.' But the pervert, as I have observed above, is not really a tragic figure.

Among the male characters, Attilio Mariani and Pierre Sadier are no more than incidental figures; they are well contrasted types of political idealists, and, within the limits allowed them, they have life and verisimilitude. Lafourcade, without any supporting argument, identifies Sadier with Louis Blanc, but I see no good reason for doing so; he is simply an example of the cosmopolitan-minded political thinker who rises above mere nationalism and delimited patriotism; a type of which France, although ordinarily the most 'insular' of chauvinistic of nations, furnished in Montesquieu, Voltaire, and others, more signal representatives than any other country in the modern world. This latter fact was probably in Swinburne's mind when he conceived this character.[1] Still more is Lafourcade wrong in identifying Mariani with Mazzini. A sentence in Chapter XI (which Lafourcade read) proves this decisively: 'For very love and reverence and thankfulness neither [Mariani nor Herbert] would name the

---

[1] See Note 11 on Chapter XI. In the history of political ideas Louis Blanc's distinctive place is a founder of monopolistic State socialism as against private enterprise or economic individualism in general; he is not notably—if at all—associated with universal humanitarian idealism, with something bigger than nationalism, nor did Swinburne ever make any sort of reference to him as such in his correspondence (where there is mention of him) nor in the three obituary sonnets in which he celebrated what he regarded as the outstanding qualities of the French thinker. It is interesting to note that Mazzini, in a letter to Lamennais, expresses disapproval of the view of which Swinburne's Sadier is the upholder in opposition to the merely patriotic republicanism of the Mazzinian character:

'On ne peut jamais assez se tenir sur ses gardes. Nous avons ici, parmi les ouvriers français surtout, des échantillons de toutes vos fractions du parti . . . Nous avons des hommes qui votent par assis et levé l'abolition de toute nationalité, c'est-à-dire qui veulent briser le point d'appui du levier dont ils prétendent vouloir se servir . . .'

This passage—of a letter which was not published till 1922—shows that in point of historic actuality as well as in a general or symbolic sense Swinburne's two idealists are true to life: to the political life of the generation of which they are fictional representatives.

great name of Mazzini'. That of course clearly differentiates him from the latter.[1] He is meant to be no more than an example of one of the more fervent Italian exiles; these were disciples of Mazzini, and as such of course resembled him in certain ways. Mariani naturally did so as an out-and-out nationalist, an intransigent republican, and an opponent of any sort of monarchy. He was also like Mazzini in that he was 'admirably narrow-minded'—but it is highly doubtful if Swinburne, speaking in his own name, would have thus described the Italian leader—although the detached side of him that sometimes spoke through Lady Midhurst might very well have done so.

In the few short paragraphs of Mariani's simple and noble eloquence the hard high-souled loyalties and the epic energies of the Risorgimento are conveyed as effectively as in any part or in the whole of Meredith's very long novel on the subject.[2]

[1] And in the preceding chapter ('Another Portrait'), which Lafourcade had not read, there are other details which confirm this sufficiently conclusive piece of evidence. There, we are told that Mariani was only aged thirty-five in 1858 or thereabouts, that he was a cripple, and that he probably did not write for the English press. None of these facts is true of Mazzini.

[2] A reference in the text shows that Swinburne certainly wrote 'An Episode'—or at least a part of it—after October 1866. By that date he could have read a good deal of *Vittoria*, which first appeared in the *Fortnightly Review*, from January 15th, 1866, to December 1st, 1866. He certainly had read it before March 1867, for on the 2nd of that month Meredith wrote to him about it, and said that he 'alone had hit on the episode of the Guidascarpi', one of the best things in it. (Letter in the British Museum. There is also, in the B.M., another letter from Meredith to Swinburne in which he speaks of the latter's opinion of *Vittoria*: ' "*Vittoria*", as I am told . . ., is not liked; so you may guess what pleasure your letter has given me. For I have the feeling that if I get your praise, I hit the mark'. This letter is undated, but a reference in it to Swinburne's essay on Byron makes it probable that it was written soon after March 1866, when the essay appeared.) Of course Swinburne admired *Vittoria*, but there are no grounds for supposing that he was influenced by it in writing his two chapters on the same theme; his enthusiasm for the Risorgimento dated from his undergraduate days, if not from an earlier period.

It may be asked where Swinburne got raw materials for his two idealists—if anywhere apart from sources of political ideas in various writings, and the working of his imagination to provide characters animated by opposing theories. He first met (on one and the same occasion) Carl Blind and Mazzini in the early spring of 1867; and through Carl Blind certainly, and through Mazzini probably, he came in contact with other political exiles after that date. That would pretty certainly have given him enough material for the two chapters dealing with exiles. Were these chapters written after the time in question? It is very likely that they were. They were certainly not written before 1866 (unless they were copied from other sheets, and that is not at all probable), for 1866 is the water-mark date of two sheets of the former of them and three of the latter. Moreover, a reference in 'An Episode' shows that it must have been written after October of that year. For work composed in 1867 paper manufactured the previous year might very well have been used. And it is more than probable that Swinburne wrote the two chapters in the flush of the enthusiasm consequent upon his first meeting with 'the Chief'. It may be enquired whether he was in touch with political exiles (Italian, French etc.) in London before this latter meeting. An unwary answer would be that he surely had contacts with men like Sadier and especially Mariani through the Rossettis. It is well known that the house of Gabriele Rossetti was frequented by refugees of the most divers kinds. And Although Gabriele died in 1854, a good while before Swinburne met Dante Gabriel, it is likely (one might argue) that the latter and his brother William maintained contact with the exiles after their father's death. But the opposite is the case, as William himself makes quite clear: 'I regard it as more than probable that the perpetual excited and of course one-sided talk about Luigi Filippo and other political matters had something to do with the marked alienation from current politics which characterised my brother in his adolescent and adult years'; and again: 'Since the close of my father's life my knowledge of Italians in England is practically a blank; and the same was the case of my brother'. So that if Swinburne had had any first-hand acquaintance with political refugees before 1867 it cannot have been through the Rossettis. Were there any other possible intermediaries? One cannot reply with any certainty here. That Ford Madox Brown may have been an intermediary is apparently all that can be safely affirmed. A passage in Lafourcade's *Swinburne, A Literary Biography* would lead one to believe that he must have been. Swinburne, says Lafourcade, speaking of the period 1860–61, 'was taken to the house of Madox Brown . . ., and found there, much to his satisfaction, a bracing atmosphere of political activities and Italian agitation: radicals from all over Europe congregated at Brown's . . .' But Lafourcade gives no authority for this statement. The only one, apparently, that he could have given is the following passage in *The Whistler Journal*:

'Once in a while I would take my gaiety, my sunniness, to Ford Madox Brown's receptions. And there were always the most wonderful people—the Blinds, Swinburne, anarchists, poets, musicians, all kinds and sorts, . . . and Howell with a broad red ribbon across his shirt front . . .'

And Lafourcade cites this passage, with the heading 'Une soirée chez Madox Brown (1863)' in his earlier work *La Jeunesse de Swinburne*. If this passage was his sole authority, he multiplied the contents of it considerably in the above-cited portion of *A Literary Biography*. Moreover, *The Whistler Journal* is not really a journal at all. It is a somewhat loose or haphazard record, by E. R. and J. Pennell, of things said by Whistler in conversations with them in the last years of his life. (The conversation in which mention was made of Brown's receptions took place in 1900.) The time to which the passage in question refers is very vaguely indicated thus by the Pennells: 'It was at the time the large fair person Rossetti painted as Lilith, and called The Sumptuous, presided at Rossetti's, when Swinburne and Meredith and Sandys were living there' [i.e. at Tudor House]. The period thus characterised may be dated 1863 (but not 1860–61, the time to which the passage of *A Literary Biography* refers. Incidentally, the unreliability of Whistler's memory, or—more probably—of the Pennells' capacity as recorders, is indicated by the mentions of Sandys as an inmate of Tudor House: he was never a part of that establishment).[1] But there could have been no reception of Brown's in 1863 at which Whistler saw (if he meant—which is not at all certain—that he did) both Swinburne and Blind, for the poet had never previously met the German exile when he went to his house in 1867 to be introduced to Mazzini; moreover, Brown did not know the Blinds before 1870.[2] However, there is no evidence to show that Whistler could not have seen both Swinburne and 'anarchists' at Brown's in 1863 (but here again he may not have meant that he did so: he may merely have been recalling the kind of people he met at the painter's house over a number of years); but on the other hand there is no evidence to prove that he could have done so. Even assuming that he did, however, we are not very much advanced; for men of the type of Swinburne's two idealists cannot be brought under the head of 'anarchists'.[3]

Among the other minor characters, old Mathison, Herbert's 'first friend', calls for a few words of mention. He is 'a bit of true human stuff' if ever there were: Carlyle's words have never been more apt than in the case of this rapidly-sketched figure, of whom we have little more than a glimpse on the rare occasions when he comes into the story. In spite of this

[1] I mean of the Rossetti-Swinburne-Meredith establishment. Sandys was an inmate of 16 Cheyne Walk for some fifteen months long after Meredith and Swinburne had left it.

[2] According to F. M. Hueffer (later Ford). It may also be noted that Howell could not have been at a *soirée* of Brown's in 1863, for he was not in England then. He had left the country round about the end of 1857 and did not return till 1864.

[3] Mrs. H. Rossetti Angeli, who doubtless had access to special and private sources of information, says in her *Dante Gabriel Rossetti* (1949) that Ford Madox Brown's 'sympathies', in spite of his being 'something of an old Tory in politics', 'were strongly on the side of many rebels against the powers that were. I remember how warmly he

exiguity he remains alive in one's memory; simple, plain, direct, elemental, and all this in a lovable way, he indicates that Swinburne had it in him to create at need characters very different from the complex natures who are the chief personages of his work in fiction. He reminds one of old Mr. Peggotty; and the shipwreck scene in which his son sacrifices his life to save another person's recalls that in which Ham Peggotty does likewise. Dickens was one of Swinburne's favourite authors from boyhood to old age, and might be expected to have exercised some influence on his work as a novelist. But it is only here, in respect of old Mathison and his son, that I can detect what might pass as a trace of it.[1]

Denham gives a strong impression of being life-like, as a man of a certain neurotic class (but, while a type, he has plenty of singularity—apart from that of the class itself: which is singular in both of the more ordinary senses of the word) and also as a tutor (here Swinburne was able to draw uopn a good deal of first-hand personal experience, for he had a tutor to prepare him for Eton, and at least two others in the interval between his departure from Eton and his going up to the University. And no doubt he also drew upon his impressions of one or more of the masters with whom he came in contact at Eton.) Denham is certainly, in his own way, as life-like and individual as Adrian Harley, who, as the tutor and 'fixture' in the family, has an analogous position in the best of Meredith's novels. As a possibly disturbing addition to the household, he corresponds to Champneys of the *Kirklowes*

(*Note* [3] *continued*)—
encouraged our youthful socialistic and anarchistic leanings, and how genially he welcomed the Russian revolutionaries of different shades of opinion—Stepniak, Kropotkin, Volkhovsky. In the early 'seventies his house bristled with Communards.' But there is no specific reference here to the time before Swinburne's first meeting with Mazzini, nor even to Italian exiles.

[1] And perhaps—but much less surely—in one or two places of *La Fille du Policeman*; which is meant to be a parody, not of anything Dickensian, but of certain French authors, and in especial of Hugo, writing on the subject of England.

fragment, but he has much more strength of character than the latter, and, with his strange mixture of the contrary qualities of excessive emotionality and extreme reserve, he is much more complex than Champneys is or promises to be in the little we see of him. In some respects he closely resembles another character of the *Kirklowes* fragment: the father, Francis Harewood: like him, he finds a certain 'relief' in the cruel floggings he gives Herbert, and in the intervals he can show himself very amiable.

Buffon, in his *Histoire Naturelle*, speaks of the gravely untoward consequences of sexual abstinence, and Denham, who had 'visibly been abstinent' from his boyhood, might, in his pathologically erotic moods and the accompanying sadism, be taken as a forceful illustration of this far from orthodox judgment. In more modern terms, he is an example of neurosis following upon repression. Swinburne himself actually uses the Freudian word: 'Life repressed and suppressed strength' is one of the pregnant formulas in which he sums up his state and the forces producing it. And again: 'He was passing through quiet stages of perversion': more than once in *Lesbia Brandon* Swinburne, writing some half-century before Freud, gives the impression of having read the latter and other writers of the same school. Anyhow, whatever its remoter causes, Denham's pathological condition is presented with cogent verisimilitude and much acuity of analysis. In its duality, its ambivalence ('intense attraction' and 'intense antipathy' are co-present in it), it might be summarily rendered by the brief terse words in which Catullus threw off the agony of his bitter despair:

Odi et amo . . . et excrucior.

But if the love is as great in Catullus' case, the opposed feeling is not nearly so strong, or at least so extensive, as it is here; where it becomes maniacal in its desire to inflict disintegrating torture and death on the being with whom love cannot have its way. (And, it may be noted, as there is nothing like this sadism in Catullus, so there is nothing like Denham's alternating and contrary mood, the wish to 'die crushed under her feet': to this masochism there is nothing comparable in the erethism of the Roman poet. And, with very little qualification—as, for example, in the case of Goethe—this remark may be generalised and extended to the greater love-poets of all ages.)

Altogether, in Denham Swinburne has portrayed the sadistic-masochistic type far better, more fully, than anyone else in literature. Even Sade, who allows himself unlimited licence of allusion and description, has not presented the type nearly so successfully; as already observed, he has nothing of the psychological *finesse* which is constant in Swinburne; and, anyhow, masochism of the kind expressed in the words cited above has no place in his amorists or rather lusters after extremes of sensation (and it is utterly at variance with his philosophy, which with them is translated into action); *their* masochism (the reception of a certain amount of pain) is very narrow in range, and is largely a different thing, being merely one of many extra fillips to sexuality suffering, not, as in Denham's case, from complete lack of satisfaction (and because of that excessively and idealistically ardent) but on the contrary from too much satisfaction. With them it is a whip to jaded powers: it is nothing of the sort here.

In Mr. Linley we have the full sadist. With him there reappears the cruel father of the *Kirklowes* fragment and *Love's Cross Currents*; and he is not only cruel towards his own son, he is, or would like to be, cruel towards Herbert and, further, towards children and adolescents in general—if (and in proportion as) he finds them comely. This differentiates him from Francis Harewood and Philip Harewood; as also does the fact that in intention they were no more than severe disciplinarians; however much pleasure they took in inflicting punishment, they were not consciously and systematically cruel, they did not cause pain gratuitously or apart from any sort of pretext. He did so; we can be sure that he tortured his son as he had a lust to torture Herbert; and we know that in flogging his boy he was deliberately wounding his wife, against whom he had no grounds for displeasure—on the contrary, he recognised her excellent qualities and proclaimed them with something like fervour (of course the contrast gave piquancy to the delight he received from her tears). In all this he differs from Denham too. Denham, in the fevered despair of his thwarted love, had some reason for wishing to strike at Margaret through Herbert; moreover, he did not do anything of the sort in reality, for she remained unaffected, and he made no further attempt to cause her pain (unless the possible project, towards the end of the story, of threatening to use compromising letters to her detriment, may be regarded as such).

Mr. Linley's sadism is well conveyed in the words contrasting him with Lady Midhurst, who sometimes hurt in the exercise of her gift for sharp satirical comment:

> 'Here was the main difference between her and Linley; she was not a bad woman for a cynic. Cruel she certainly was on occasions; cruelty amused her and she liked to make her cuts tell; but she was not, like some, impregnated with cruelty as a sponge with water.'

The fundamental contrast between these two masters of afflictive observation, these two countertypes of Christian benevolence, is expressed more explicitly and more revealingly in the following sentence: 'When rare beauty . . . came in her way, despite all the humorous violence and sharp-edged paradox in her talk, she was impelled to touch it tenderly; not', as he was, 'to strike and hurt it with a furious amorous admiration and rage of angry delight'. In this last phrase we get sadism at its fullest and also at its most specific (as distinct from mere cruelty)—with sex coming into play; the sadism properly so-called, that lusts to torment and mar the very beauty by which it is attracted, and gets sexual satisfaction in the process. Mr. Linley is the perfect sadist; is much more of one than any other character in Swinburne. His sadic completeness is further seen in the fact that he likes to inflict moral as well as physical pain: this 'torturer had a little pack of questions ready which he used to apply to every boy who came in his way, secure that one or two must always hurt'.[1] In this, again, he is quite unlike Denham, who never indulges in anything of the sort. Yet another point of difference is that there is nothing of Denham's masochism in him: and here again he is the perfect sadist: as we have already remarked, true masochism is contrary to the essential teaching of the Marquis.

Of Mr. Linley's esoteric and fully satisfying activities as a practising member of the latter's sect we are told nothing. He would take care of course to keep them dark (as Swinburne kept very private the practical side of his masochism). But the fact that although 'no special scandal clove to his name' 'many abhorred him as a thing foul and dangerous' indicates that there was an inavowable clandestine part of his life of which something found its way into rumour. (Sade would have given a complete account of Mr. Linley's occult doings: Swinburne compared with him is a very model of respectable restraint.)

But there is much more to Mr. Linley than his sadism. He is one of the most complex of the many complex characters created by Swinburne. He is the opposite of a 'Christian gentleman', and he is equally little 'one of nature's gentlemen' (a democratic phrase he would have detested), and yet he is certainly a gentleman in a traditional sense of the word which is worthy of high esteem. If he is something of a satyr, with a leer of ribaldry never long absent from his face; if he allows himself a freedom of rakish appraisal when women (including ladies) are mentioned over the wine—in short, if he does many things that conventionally are 'not done'—still there is a certain delicacy about him, he is a highly-civilised

---

[1] It may be asked whether his moral or mental torturing of his wife was sadism in the stricter sense, as he was apparently not attracted by her. But certain of Sade's characters commit what appear to be acts of pure cruelty on a person in whom they have no sexual interest, and then, in the resulting mood, indulge with another person in a frenetic act of sexuality.

person (although the civilisation he represents would by many be called a decadence). He is a true scholar and man of taste. And he is not, like many scholars and most collectors, of very small range intellectually; he is not without philosophical capacity, and he bases his practical life (or at least the unorthodox side of it) on principles, and is not content to let it pass as mere instinct. He can argue effectively in favour of aesthetic hedonism, of beauty for beauty's sake—or rather (where human comeliness is concerned) for the sake of those to whom it causes a titillation. More than this, he can formulate a very cogent philosophy of aristocracy as something out of line with, and running precariously counter to, struggling against, the democratic mediocrity or worse of Nature as a whole.

A further element of complexity in his case is that there is a certain kindness in him. And with this and the rest, behind it all, there is the cark of a great dissatisfaction, a melancholy of defeat. A 'bitter and obscure despondency', a 'heavy sorrow', a 'fatal fatigue' . . . Captain Philip Harewood, in *Love's Cross Currents*, was troubled by some underlying 'bitter doubt and regret': the much more sadistic and otherwise self-indulgent Mr. Linley, with no similar material cares (e.g. his wife had not deserted him), was in the same case, but to a much higher degree. Moralists will no doubt draw an edifying moral from this.

Mr. Linley is in his own way as remarkable as memorable, a character as Lady Midhurst, and that is giving him the highest praise. He can only seem unlifelike to those who know very little of life. He is somewhat strange, of course, like those other very real characters Lesbia and Margaret and Denham —and like many people in history (not to mention that truer history which is fiction of the higher kind). Strangeness is a part of life, and he authentically belongs to life.

We have seen how crassly wrong Lafourcade is in regard to the minor characters. He is even more crassly wrong about these major ones. In a preliminary sweeping statement he says that there is nothing searching in the presentation of the characters, that they are not independent of the author, in other words that they are not real people with an existence of their own. (This, be it noted, with no qualification, is affirmed of 'the characters' and so it applies to Lady Midhurst, whom elsewhere Lafourcade has properly saluted as one of the greatest creations of fiction: she has 'une grandeur balzacienne', she is more alive than any character in Meredith, etc., etc.). Then, proceeding from the nameless all-embracing general to a certain amount of specification, he says that not only Herbert but also his nephews, and Denham and Linley and Lesbia 'ne sont que divers reflets de la sensibilité du poète—ou de sa fantaisie . . . Ils sont autant de modalités du génie de Swinburne.' Consequently, the Zoilean Lafourcade affirms that he cannot 'take' these characters 'seriously', thereby sinking altogether to the nadir-level of the mirific Professor Samuel Chew, who proclaims the same inability with regard to the characters of *Love's Cross Currents* (not even excepting Lady Midhurst from the sweep of his damnation).

In what way and to what degree *all* characters in art are or may be 'reflets de la sensibilité' of the artist and 'modalités' of his genius, is a very difficult question of aesthetic philosophy that cannot be properly examined here. It may well be that, as Arnold Bennett says, all 'first-class fiction is, and must be, in the final resort autobiographical'. But this does not prevent Arnold Bennett from talking of the 'convincingness' of characters, their 'authenticity', their 'reality', their 'being true to life', and regarding this quality as a norm by which they should be evaluated. And he makes this consideration primary: 'The first thing is that the novel should seem to be true. It cannot be true if the characters do not seem to be real'; all the rest, 'style . . . plot . . . invention . . . originality of outlook . . . wide information . . . wide sympathy', is of inferior importance compared with this. And by this criterion Bennett finds that Virginia Wolf's novelistic work is not first-class because 'the characters do not vitally survive in the mind'. Now, in all this Bennett does not mean 'real', 'authentic', simply in reference

to the author's personality; when he says 'true to life' he does
not mean simply true to the author's own life; and he would,
no doubt, have agreed that Virginia Woolf's unsatisfactory
characters are true to her life in the sense that they are expressions of her personality. No, he means something more
than this, in spite of the first-quoted of his statements. That
statement only holds if due importance is given to 'in the final
resort', which must be taken as being backward in its reference. In its origin, its remotest beginnings, all first-class fiction
is autobiographical, but in the final resort in a forward direction the character of that fiction (or some of them) have a
life which is not merely a part of the author's biography even
in a very loose sense;[1] they (or some of them) are not even
potential or ideal selves of the author given being and scope
in a verisimilar world of the imagination; in some real sense
they have a life of their own, an existence independent of
their creators, an identity no more to be equated with his
than is that of anyone in what is called the world of 'reality'.
In other words, personages in first-class fiction grow into something no less distinct from their author than are children from
the father in whom they have their origin. (Pirandello's conception of 'Six characters in search of an author' is only an
exaggerated expression of this truth.) Now Bennett was un-

---

[1] One might add that it can only be in a very loose sense, so loose as
to be almost without significance or value, that *all* characters are autobiographical even in their first origins; that Fagin and Squeers, say,
are as much so as David Copperfield. Bennett, apparently, felt this
difficulty and tried to meet it by saying that in the first-class novelist's
'own individuality there was something of everybody'. It may be so:
but this seems to be a desperate solution of the problem in which
Bennett had landed himself; and it calls up other problems by no
means easy to answer. Bennett may have been feeling his way towards
the view (I would say the truth) expressed by Thibaudet in the following: 'Le romancier authentique crée ses personnages avec les directions
infinies de sa vie possible, le romancier factice les crée avec la ligne
unique de sa vie réelle. Le vrai roman est comme une autobiographie
du possible . . .' But even this truth calls for qualification in respect
of the characters of a novelist in their whole range.

379

doubtedly thinking of the life, the authenticity, etc., of characters in this sense; and it was because Virginia Woolf's
characters were not real in this sense, however real they were
autobiographically, that he did not give them a high mark.
And this no doubt is what Lafourcade vaguely had in mind
as opposed to the 'reflets' and 'modalités' to which he reduced
Swinburne's characters, not realising that in doing so he was
raising a very debateful question, the answer to which might
not necessarily help him in his work of denigration. In
this more testing sense the Swinburnian personages under
discussion are real, and not merely reflections of this or that
side of Swinburne. Of course this, like all aesthetic judgments
—in other words, like all appreciations of quality—, is dogmatic, and cannot but be so for ever and ever. If A finds that
characters are real, but B does not, there is nothing more to
be said; any more than there is if A thinks a picture or a wine
or a woman delightful, whereas B has nothing like the same
opinion. There can be no demonstration one way or the other
here, no appeal to anything beyond the impression of the
individuals concerned. We are up against the old commonplace of *De gustibus*, and I will not attempt the impossible
in defence of my opinion as opposed to that of Lafourcade and
those who are congenitally like him. These characters, and
especially Lesbia and Mr. Linley, in addition to Lady Midhurst, do 'vitally survive' in my mind, and I am confident that
here I shall not be singular.

One, however, is not reduced to being simply dogmatic in
this matter; one may advance a few facts which go to invalidate
Lafourcade's thesis that not only Herbert, but his nephews,
and Denham, Mr. Linley and Lesbia are no more than aspects
of the personality of Swinburne. How could this be true of
the eldest nephew, for instance, not merely an 'unlovely and
unhealthy' infant, but a 'sluggish fellow' as he grew into
adolescence? Can he represent any side of Swinburne? Can
he and the 'excitable and fervent' Herbert be reflections or
expressions of any one and the same person, however complex? Are they not so much at variance as to be mutually

exclusive—as much so as 'puny' and 'robust', 'a bright lad' and 'a dullard' would be as general descriptions of one and the same person? Again, can both Denham and Linley be representative of Swinburne? In some ways they are fundamentally different types; as I have shown, the former is far from being a thoroughgoing sadist, and is very largely a masochist; while the latter is an out-and-out sadist, and has nothing of the masochist in him. Once more, can Lesbia, a female homosexual, be expressive of Swinburne, a male who not only was not in the least homosexual, but detested what (on non-colloquial occasions) he derisively called 'Patonic' or 'Spartan' love?[1]

[1] His unvarying attitude on this matter is forcibly expressed in the following words from a letter to Watts-Dunton which is now in the British Museum: 'I will do Rétif the justice to add that . . . neither Anytus and Meletus, nor you and I, could have felt heartier and more abhorrent loathing for Platonic love, whether imbued with 'sweetness and light', by philosophic sentiment [doubtless a hit at J. A. Symonds in particular, an apologist—and practitioner—of uranism of whom Swinburne always spoke with contempt] or besmeared with blood and dung by criminal lunacy'. It may be objected that he chose to depict homosexuality in Lesbia, and that he betrayed not the slightest disapproval or repugnance in handling this case. The answer is that here he was viewing the thing with the objectivity of art or science, as a psychiatrist does an abnormality or a dramatist a villain, and he kept up his objective attitude. (Cf. the following from the third chapter of *Lesbia Brandon*, on the moral detachment of the greatest artists with regard even to the most monstrous characters in the world of their creation: 'Bah! look at the great man and say which side he favours when you find out; let the world know when you catch Shakespeare condemning the moral state of Iago, or Balzac deploring the perversity of Madame de San-Réal'.) One may add that many normally sexed men who have a horror of male homosexuality have no such feeling about homosexual relations between women (Baudelaire, for example, who wrote a poem of over one hundred lines on the emotions etc. of two lesbians lying together, and obviously did so with complacency, not to say with zest, would never have written anything such—or anything at all— on two male homosexuals: he had no stomach for 'Spartan' love in any of its manifestations). I note in passing that an interest in hermaphroditism, which Swinburne certainly had, is not necessarily a sign of homosexual tendencies; Théophile Gautier, who had this interest— and, like Baudelaire, was by no means averse from dwelling on lesbian

The first of the three preceding observations (that concerning the nephew) is a matter of elementary sense that may be left as irrefutable; and the others are too really, but as they are perhaps less obviously so at first sight it may be well to give a little more attention to the points which are the subject of them. With respect to the second, Lafourcade, and those who take their cue from him, would reply that Denham and Linley, however much they differ, are not incompatible as representing different sides of Swinburne; for Swinburne was at once a masochist like Denham and a sadist of the kind typified by Linley. Lafourcade asserts this several times in the course of his Bœotian volume; it is one of the main elements in his analysis or diagnosis of the poet's character. 'La double tendance à la cruauté et à la soumission'; 'Sa cruauté latente'; 'le sadisme actif [i.e. the desire to inflict pain] . . . la profonde intensité du sentiment chez Swinburne'; etc., etc.: these are a few examples of the extensive anthology of error that one might draw up. For there is a good deal of wild error here. There is much confusion, and an ignorance not only of Swinburne's personality, but also of what is strictly meant by sadism. The truth is that Swinburne was a masochist, but nothing of a sadist. He had no tendency to cruelty; on the contrary, he hated and loathed it, as it would be very easy to prove by many facts both in his life and writings. But this is a matter that I am reserving for adequate treatment in my *Swinburne: the Arcane Side*, which will follow this volume. I will merely remark here that the fact that there are sadists such as Mr. Linley in Swinburne's *work* is no proof that Swinburne himself was a sadist (any more than the fact that there is such a character as Darnley, say, in the work is a proof that

(*Note* ¹ *continued*)—
love—was one of the most robustly normal of men sexually, and to him, as to Swinburne, the very idea of uranism was in no small degree abhorrent. I shall touch on this point at greater length later on in this section. Perhaps, as regards terminology, it should be mentioned that I follow those writers who limit the word 'uranism' to homosexuality between males.

Swinburne must have been like Darnley). If one is going to establish equivalences or approximations, one should take account of Lady Midhurst, with whom Swinburne has far more in common than with Mr. Linley (if he has anything at all in common with him) and whom he definitely presents in contrast to the latter as being rather the contrary of a sadist; or of Herbert, with whom Swinburne has more in common than with any other character in *Lesbia Brandon* (or in the whole of his works), and who is strongly a masochist with no trace whatsoever of tendencies towards sadism.[1] And, as I pointed out in *Lucretia Borgia*, and have again pointed out in the Notes to *Lesbia Brandon*, in describing sadistic scenes, especially those in which extreme physical pain is inflicted, Swinburne's constant tendency to put himself in the position of the sufferer; in other words, where he is most likely at first sight to appear to be giving expression to sadistic impulses, he is nothing but a masochist, the very opposite of a sadist in the ordinary as well as in the most technical sense of the term.

Lafourcade goes badly wrong in his definition of sadism: 'C'est en cette alliance intime des deux formes de souffrance, trop souvent dissociées par les psychiâtres, que consiste pro-

---

[1] Lafourcade is wrong, therefore, when he says that 'le sadisme est étroitement uni au sentimentalisme dans l'œuvre de Swinburne—le besoin de faire souffrir au besoin d'adorer'. There is no such union in the case of Herbert (not to mention others), who is the type *par excellence* of those in whom 'le besoin d'adorer' is a master instinct.

I use 'sadist' in the sense of one who has a lust to inflict pain on others, particularly, if not exclusively, as a means, sole or partial, of arriving at sexual satisfaction. Lafourcade, to give plausibility to his infirm thesis, lumps sadism and masochism together as varieties of the same thing; calling the former active and the latter passive sadism. This classification is quite abitrary, is no more than a gratuitous assumption in which there is no element of certainty or anything on the way to it. It seems to me that McDougall (to cite only one modern psychologist who would reject this classification) is much nearer the truth in holding that sadism and masochism are expressions of two 'independent' and 'quite different' instincts, which may or may not co-operate with the sex-impulse. Unquestionably this view of the matter

prement le sadisme'.[2] As I have already indicated, in the most extreme form of sadism known, that of which the Marquis de Sade is the chief exemplar and exponent, masochism of the specifically Swinburnian kind has no place at all, and indeed is at variance with the fundamental teachings of the master.[3] And those 'psychiatrists' are right who regard the two things as being essentially different, and make no attempt to 'associate' them within the artificial unity of a facile formula that is in no sense scientific.

As for the third point, Lafourcade (and those who docilely follow him), unable to refute fact and sense in the matter of homosexuality, would say that Lesbia is expressive of Swinburne's 'sterility'. This is another of the capital errors in Lafourcade; another of the cardinal elements in his fantastic analysis of the personality of the poet. 'Celui qui devrait demuerer seul et stérile'; 'Cette stérilité froide qui retranche des plaisirs humains'; etc., etc.: here is the beginning of another anthology of *bêtise*. On the face of it, the charge of

---

(*Note* [1] *Continued*)—

fits Swinburne's case much better than does Lafourcade's theory—which indeed does not fit certain facts of that case at all, and is rather glaringly at odds with them.

[2] 'Les deux formes' are 'la souffrance active' and 'la souffrance passive', his names—in addition to 'sadisme actif' and 'sadisme passif'—for what are commonly—and in standard text-books—called sadism and masochism. Other considerations apart, the phrase 'souffrance active' is very unhappy: it is more than inaccurate, for the two words are incompatible, containing notions that are not far from contradictory. Certainly the person inflicting pain in these situations—the sadist properly so-called—experiences in the process no feelings that can be described as 'suffering'. A term of exactly the contrary import is required. It may also be remarked that even 'souffrance passive' is a doltish expression: in the very nature of things—not to mention etymology—there is no suffering that is not passive.

[3] I would emphasise the words 'specifically Swinburnian'. Flagellation undergone by sensation-hunters in Sade is not the masochism of Denham and Herbert. But this is a point with which I shall deal fully in *Swinburne: the Arcane Side*, where I shall give an abstract of the works of the Marquis.

sterility is laughable in the case of a personality so robust, so forceful, so bountifully alive and so plenteously productive as the man whom Meredith rightly called the greatest lyric poet in the whole of literature. The charge might not implausibly be brought against Mallarmé, say. But Swinburne!—who in this matter might be taken as the exact opposite of the French poet who was tortured by the blank sheet on to which he could rarely project the world of his imagination.

But Lafourcade, unable to meet this weighty consideration, would shift his ground, and say or hint that Swinburne was sexually sterile. He does so in the phrase '*impuissant* a réagir aux stimulants ordinaires de l'instinct', giving particular emphasis and significance to the first word by the use of italics. Again, on the face of it, the idea that a man who was a *babilan* or a sort of eunuch could produce what Swinburne did is nothing short of comical. It is all the more so when we are told that the 'sterilité *froide*' was accompanied by an 'intensité de *passion* inassouvie' (my italics in both cases)—a sublime paradox or oxymoron, which for Lafourcade and his kind is perhaps resolvable into sense by mental processes not available to the rest of humanity. (He probably got the idea and the formula from Baudelaire: cf. the two following lines from the latter's lesbian poem mentioned in the last note but three:

Jamais vous ne pourrez assouvir votre rage . . .

*　　*　　*

L'âpre sterilité de votre jouissance . . .)

But apart from this general consideration (the improbability—to put it mildly—of a sexual impotent being so productive),[1] which we cannot stop to develop here, it may be asked on what precise grounds is this charge brought against Swinburne? What is the evidence that he was really impotent sexually? The story of the relations between him

---

[1] What about Ruskin? it may be asked in this connexion. But the full truth about Ruskin has yet to be revealed.

and Adah Menken? But there is a good deal of legend, and nonsensical legend, in that story that has been uncritically accepted as fact open to no sort of doubt. This, however, is another of the many important matters that I reserve for treatment in the book (*Swinburne: the Arcane Side*) that will follow this volume. In the meantime I do no more than suggest that the so-called evidence be looked at again; if it is, narrowly and without preconception, it is more than probable that a surprising amount of it will turn out to be exceedingly flimsy. It should not be necessary to remark that the mere fact that Swinburne was a masochist is no proof at all that he was sexually impotent.

One may incidentally enquire with what accuracy it can be said that Lesbia (who in this matter is supposed to be representative of Swinburne) as well as Baudelaire's two tribades, is sterile, and that the passion of such women can never receive satisfaction. Surely they get as full specifically sexual satisfaction from their intercourse as normal people do from theirs? Surely Lesbia would have been *assouvie* had she been able to make Margaret her lover? As much so as any woman with any man (within the limits of the sexual act throughout its whole gamut up to the final *jouissance*); as much so as Sappho was, which presumably was in the fullest degree; as much so as the numerous tribades in Sade's works, who are nearly if not quite all sexual dualists, and proclaim that intercourse with their own sex is much more satisfying than with the highly expert males to whom they occasionally turn for the sake of a little variety? (Indeed more than these last women, from the fact that she is exclusively homosexual, and therefore would find a profounder gratification if the lesbian delights which leave them with no feeling that they have not reached fulfilment.) The whole and the only tragedy of Lesbia is that she cannot get her native satisfaction with the only woman whom she loves supremely.

Such love, of course, is sterile—but only in the sense that it does not result in procreation; and fully normal love is sterile too in this sense, when effective measures are taken to obviate procreation. And, I submit, it is in this sense only that Swinburne can be said to have been sterile: those of a contrary opinion must bring forward something really worthy of the name of proof.

Lafourcade's view of the characters under discussion, then, is very largely absurd. Whether these characters are alive, real, and otherwise successful is a matter of opinion; but it is a matter of demonstrable fact that they are not mere reflections of Swinburne—who is not what he is represented as being by Lafourcade and the general run (if not the whole) of those who have undertaken to give an account of his personality.

Herbert, on the other hand, is more than a reflection of the poet: to a considerable extent, if not altogether, he is a faithful portrait of the latter in his boyhood, youth and early manhood (here even Lafourcade could hardly fall into error). To begin with, the physical portrait, as far as one can check it from reliable testimony, is more than tolerably exact. The hair, for instance: Herbert's 'had much more of brown and red mixed into it [i.e. into the gold] than' Margaret's, 'but like hers was yellower underneath'; here are the 'three different colours and textures, red, dark red, and bright pure gold' of Swinburne's hair at Eton, according to Sir George Young, the most intimate of his school friends. The eyes: Herbert's, 'except for the green in them', were 'best definable as citrine . . . Looked well into and thro', they showed tints of blue and grey', and they were 'full of daring and dreams'; Sir George Young remembered Swinburne's eyes as 'green'; as Gosse saw them they were 'greenish grey'; in Rossetti's 1861 portrait they are light blue (Gosse speaks of this as though it were a bad mistake, but the account of Herbert's eyes suggests that Rossetti was right, and had what Gosse had not, a vision for more remote delicacies of colour); as for the 'daring' and 'dreams', they are the chief feature of Swinburne's eyes as they were painted by Watts. Herbert's eyelashes were 'longer and wavier than his sister's'; Swinburne's cousin, Mrs. Disney-Leith, says that a 'peculiarity' of the poet's face was 'the length and thickness of the eyelashes, which he used to complain would get entangled in a high wind'. Skin: Herbert's was 'so thin and fair that it glittered against the light as white silk does'; Swinburne's in his Eton days was 'very white . . . a transparent tinted white' records Lord Redesdale, another of his cousins, and another of those who knew him best at school. The latter also records that 'of games he took no heed'; therein being like Herbert, who 'preferred stories to sports'.

Herbert's reactions to life at Eton are also Swinburne's, who was much less happy there than is generally supposed. Even Herbert's 'blind passion of pain' on leaving home, his 'sense of perplexity and exile' at school, his impression that he was a 'seagull in an aviary' and that this was 'no life for him', which may seem to extreme to be autobiographical, are more than probably a transcript from the poet's own experiences when he passed through the same period. Mrs. Disney-Leith records that 'sea-gull' was 'one of his home nicknames'; Lord Redesdale says that he was 'shy and reserved' at Eton, and Sir George Young that 'he was not at home among Eton boys'; and there is unpublished matter (which I shall bring out in a further volume) which confirms even more decisively that this part of *Lesbia Brandon* gives the quintessential truth regarding his Eton days.

The description of Herbert as 'wilful and idle and exigent in a noticeable degree' during his boyhood may also be confidently taken as autobiographical: it is a key to Swinburne's as yet unexplained irregular departure from Eton about two years before the normal time upon what Gosse discreetly calls 'representations' from the authorities who had found him too much of a handful.

Furthermore, Herbert's temperament in general is that of the young Swinburne.[1] One of the words used to describe him

[1] One may say of Swinburne altogether: as the poet himself observed, 'as in some points . . . I found myself at thirty very much what I was at thirteen, so I have some reason to fear that if I live so long I shall find myself on the same points (like Landor) very much the same at seventy as I was at seventeen . . .'

is 'excitable'; indeed, it occurs again and again. 'His affections' were 'excitable'; and 'fervent'; he was 'quiet usually and excitable always' (this rather oxymoronic combination is repeated in 'by nature idle and excitable'); etc., etc.: evidently this quality was the most remarkable or prominent in his character. And he was 'not ashamed of excitement', he made no attempt to put an embargo on this tendency even when he reached what in worldly wisdom should be years of discretion: he 'actually screamed out with passion and pain' at Mariani's story of his brother's heroic death under Austrian torture. All this might be a description of Swinburne. His mother was so concerned at his excitability, his capacity for rapture, in his childhood that she sought the advice of a specialist. The latter's verdict was that he was endowed with 'an excess of electric vitality'.[1] But with this quality, as in Herbert's case, there went a somewhat opposite quality, for which the word 'quietness' might be used. We have already quoted Lord Redesdale as saying that he was 'shy and reserved' at Eton; but there, too, according to the same witness, he was 'a bag of nerves'. However, this latter side of the poet is so well known, so much in evidence in his work, that there is no need to cite this kind of testimony. If he had, following the rather silly English convention (or rather the Victorian convention, for it is not really traditional), been 'ashamed of excitement' and put an embargo on his excitability he would not have been the greatest of all lyric poets.

It goes without saying that the immense attraction and obsession of the sea in Herbert's boyhood is entirely autobiographical. 'The magnetism of the sea' . . . 'All his soul saluted it through his senses' . . . 'His heart opened and ached with pleasure' . . . 'A violent and blind affection' . . . 'The soul of the sea entered him' . . . 'Its incessant beauty maddened him with pleasure . . . filled him with a furious luxury of the senses that kindled all his nerves and exalted all his life'—

---

[1] Reported by Gosse in *Life*.

this is found in his verse, from first to last, giving it power and magnitude and strange elemental beauties as from some wild beyond the cosmos. And yet there is cosmos in it too; form brought to its furthest pitch. For Herbert was 'conscious all over' not only of 'the beauty' but also of 'the law of' the things of nature. And—a fact that has never received due recognition—all his life Swinburne had a profound instinct for, and preconized, law, and served it faithfully in his own particular labour of literary creation.

The beauty of things and the law at work in them were enough for the young Herbert; he was 'a small satisfied pagan'; his real development was apart from the orthodox religious instruction which he received as a matter of routine, and which was not oppressive enough to prevent his 'growing straight in the strength of his spirit'. Is this autobiographical too? Not entirely this time; it is rather nostalgic, an idealisation towards a completeness in this regard which was denied to Swinburne in his boyhood. As he himself confessed, he was brought up on the strictest Anglican principles, 'as a quasi-Catholic', and this diverted him so much from his natural course that he 'went in for it passionately'. And so we find him writing to his mother as late as the age of eighteen: 'How I do trust that some day all will be able to worship together and no divisions and jealousies "keep us any longer asunder" '. And in the same letter he uses the expression 'Our Saviour'. He must, in retrospect, have been rather ashamed of such things when he was emancipated into his true religion a few years later. This explains his educational dictum à *propos* of the growth of children like Herbert: '. . . his relish of things will probably be just and right, his faith and his taste wholesome, if not twisted round and disfigured by the manipulation of fools, preached out of heart and moralised out of shape'. There is a note of bitterness here: 'the manipulation of fools' had thwarted his own progress towards the truer light.

I have spoken of three stages in Herbert's life: boyhood, youth or adolescence, and early manhood; but it will have been observed that, compared with the first and third, the

middle period is presented very exiguously (and in all probability would not have figured to an appreciably larger extent
had the book been completed). Technically, or from the point
of view of the psychology of fiction, this is interesting, and
bears out Thibaudet's judgment that adolescence does not
lend itself to treatment in a novel. The opposite, says this
acute critic, is the case with the period of childhood; which,
compared with that of adolescence, is clear, perspicuous,
spontaneous, and has a life and logic of its own which are
harmonious and complete. And so it is not beyond the grasp
of the novelist. But adolescence is not clear-cut and well-
defined; it is turbid; it is made up of unrevealed secrets, of
difficulties, of half-shades that shift into a blur. In other words,
childhood is a definite state, but adolescence is a period of
transition. Thibaudet instances *The Mill on the Floss*, which
he thinks the most abundant and the most beautiful of the
epical novels of the nineteenth century: here the infancy of
Tom and Maggie is presented on an ample scale, whereas
their adolescence gets very summary treatment. And Thibaudet generalises, and says that with the exception of *Jean
Christophe*, where the temperament of the hero and the
author's mode of procedure are exceptional, there is no novel
in which adolescence receives satisfactory treatment. As I have
said, this is borne out by *Lesbia Brandon*. Here also childhood or early boyhood is presented on an ample scale and
convincingly, but adolescence is presented hardly at all. Again,
Thibaudet says that it is extremely difficult for a novelist to
render love in the case of an adolescent; to convey love with
the differentiation that belongs to it at that period. When the
novelist attempts it, he conveys love pure and simple, *l'amour
éternel*, love as it is known to those of adult age like himself.
This also is borne out by *Lesbia Brandon*. Herbert's love for
Lesbia on his first meeting with her in his adolescence is not
sensibly different from that which he experiences for her as a
young man. It is true of course that we see relatively little
of his feelings in the former case (but that very fact is perhaps
a proof of the thesis that adolescence of its nature can get no

more than scanty treatment[1] in a novel). And it may be that Thibaudet exaggerates here: that the love of an adolescent does not (at least in all cases) differ essentially from that of a grown man: that *l'amour éternel* can be present in its fulness when the lover is no more than a youth.

That Herbert's lively interest in European, and particularly Italian politics is Swinburne's is so obvious to anyone who knows the poet's work even superficially that demonstration can here be dispensed with.[2]

---

[1] This judgment of Thibaudet's was first published in 1912. In that year there was also published Alain Fournier's *Le Grand Meaulnes*, which would no doubt have been cited by Thibaudet, had he been writing at a subsequent date, as constituting in some degree yet another exception; as would also certain later works: e.g. Jules Romain's *Les Copains*, parts of Roger Martin du Gard's *Les Thibault*, Gide's *Les Faux Monnayeurs*. Cocteau's *Les Enfants terribles*, and more than one of Mauriac's novels. It may be noted incidentally that in *Les Enfants terribles* there is an incest (brother and sister) situation; but it does not come to the point of consummation.

[2] The silly old idea that Swinburne lived a mindless life in a tower of pretty (or the opposite of pretty) dreams remote from the world of everyday reality is still strong, and it will probably take a long time for truth to consign it to the rubbish-heap. The latest expression of this absurdity is Mr. Henry Treece's *Introduction* to a brochure of 'Selected Poems of Algernon Charles Swinburne' (London, The Grey Walls Press, 1948). It is with melancholy amusement that one reads here that in contradistinction to Swinburne's attitude to such matters, certain people 'presumably' found it 'important that the 1914–18 War happened when and where it did'. As if it were not of tremendous importance to Swinburne that things of the same kind happened in his own lifetime! But this *Introduction* is full of the traditional nonsense. 'Swinburne was a man of only slight intellectual force', 'he was impervious to any sort of intellectual pressure', etc., etc. Practically everything Mr. Treece says in this *Introduction* is glaringly wrong, and is no more than a docile re-hash of what is worst in the stagnant incompetence of past critics. Even Lafourcade was immeasurably better than Mr. Treece; he at least met and refuted what should have been once for all certain of the nonsense that Mr. Treece serves up again. It is as though Lafourcade's and other work in this direction had never been done.

What chiefly strikes one in Mr. Treece and other traducers of the

Herbert's masochism too is very largely Swinburne's. Of this I have said enough for present purposes in this section and in the Notes; that is one of the matters I shall discuss more fully in a later work; where also I shall examine to what extent other things in Herbert's history are also taken from Swinburne's. For example, Herbert's sister Margaret and his attitude towards her. And Mr. Linley: is he, as Lafourcade suggests, in part a portrait of Lord Houghton?; does he in part derive from certain personages in the work of Sade? (In discussing sadism and masochism here I have been rather concerned to indicate *differences* between Swinburne and the latter; in *Swinburne: the Arcane Side* I shall estimate the poet's debt to the boldest and most thoroughgoing historian and philosopher of sexual ways and means that the world has ever seen—or ever will see, it may be pretty safely predicted: at least it is hard to imagine how anyone could go further in the presentation of the whole range of sexuality from the normal to the abnormal in its most extreme reaches. D. H. Lawrence and James Joyce are innocent infants compared to the Marquis once he moves into his own stride.) And taking Swinburne's novelistic work as a whole, I shall in this later supplementary volume deal with the following points and enquire to what degree, if any, they are autobiographical: the sadistic father; the entanglement of cousinships; other consanguineous relations (such as the one mentioned above), and, connected with these, the question of incest; and such other matters as are common to the novels, recur in them as *motifs*[1] that may be called obsessional, and give them homogeneity,

---

(*Note* [2] *Continued*)—
poet is their amazing ignorance—ignorance not simply of Swinburne but of many other things of which knowledge is essential if Swinburne is to receive his due assessment.

[1] I will say here, in connection with the elopement theme, that I do not accept as true the story—circulated by two wildly irresponsible and (to use a polite word) mythpœic writers—that an elopement of Swinburne with Rossetti's wife was possible or had actually been arranged.

make them so many variations of one and the same work—a work that was always in the background of Swinburne's mind, but which he never brought forth in its fullness.[1]

But there is one question of this class that I will deal with here, and that is the provenance (apart from Swinburne's imagination) of Lesbia—the influences, if any, that went to her making (and consideration of this matter will develop into an enquiry respecting influences in general with regard to the book as a whole). Lafourcade sees autobiography here suggesting that the relations between Herbert and Lesbia are in some measure a 'transposition de l'épisode de "Boo" (Jane Faulkner, qui inspira le *Triumph of Time*).' This can be dismissed as an impossibility, for the story of Swinburne and 'Boo' is a piece of impossible nonsense, as I shall prove irrefragably in my next work on the poet.[2] In any case, as it is not part of the 'Boo' myth that this female was a sapphist there is not much point in trying to find in it a parallel or an analogue for the situation between Herbert and the sexually impossible Lesbia.

Lafourcade, blindly groping after the truth, emits another idea notable for fantasticality: that 'a whole side' of Lesbia's character is 'directly copied' from Christina Rossetti. Lesbia, the complete pagan, eager and ready for passionate experience (with an affinity of her own sex); of 'warm' temperament, 'wan' only because it has never been properly satisfied: Christina practically the opposite of all this, an ultra-devout

---

[1] The latest of the projections of this work was a novel in verse, *The Sisters, A Tragedy*, which appeared in 1892.

[2] Gosse, it appears, was the arch-agent in the propagation of this balderdash. For the story, see his Bonchurch *Life* of Swinburne, p.78. The latest retailer of the legend is Mrs. Rossetti Angeli in her *Dante Gabriel Rossetti* (1949). My suspicions regarding it began many years ago, but I had nothing factual to bear them out; and, in spite of misgiving, I provisionally referred to the fable as though it were history in an article entitled *Unpublished Swinburne* which appeared in *Life and Letters* in January 1948; since then, however, I have obtained definite evidence proving that my intuitive feelings were altogether sound.

Christian ascetic who was a full nun except for the official part of the business . . . Irrespective of this decisive consideration, their mere physical qualities show the enormous difference between them. Lesbia with 'the fiery beauty of her face', her 'fine and close mouth with small lips', etc.: compare this with the portrait of Christina executed by her brother in 1848, when her charms were at their freshest . . . Lafourcade's reasons for equating the two are funny in their flimsiness. (1) Lesbia also was a poetess; (2) she also shunned men; (3) she also admired Sappho. Apart from the fact that on a basis of this kind Lesbia might be equated with lots of cloistered spinsters, it may be remarked that (1) the 'pulse and play of the blood' of Lesbia's poetry is hardly a quality of Christina's; (2) the latter shunned men for a reason the very contrary of that which made Lesbia do the same (and can it even be said that Christina shunned the opposite sex?—seeing that she was at least once engaged, and only broke off that engagement because the man was a Roman Catholic, she herself holding very strong Protestant views); (3) it is more than probable that Christina never read Sappho, except possibly in some translation in which inevitably there was no touch or note of the real Sappho; for, if she was a Greek scholar at all, it is practically certain she was not one to the extent required for an appreciative reading of the Mytilenean poetess; but this point is really irrelevant, for nowhere in the novel is there any indication that Lesbia admired the latter! (According to her father, she wrote 'sapphics', which Herbert, probably quite rightly, took to be Latin—and anyhow 'sapphics' is no more than a certain kind of metre; and, according also to her father, Lady Midhurst predicted that 'she would be the real modern Sappho' in English; that this should in Lafourcade's pate take on the meaning that she admired Sappho would simply be a matter of course.)

Lafourcade is as wrong on the negative as he is on the positive side: he dismisses contemptuously the possibility that the *Fragoletta* of Henri de Latouche is a source for Lesbia and the situation arising from her peculiar character. Yet in

actual fact this now-forgotten or misprized work is one of the
chief sources—indeed the chiefest—for all this part of Swinburne's novel. A few of the apposite facts will be enough to
indicate this. Fragoletta (Camille Adriani) is an Italian hermaphrodite (with, one gathers, rather more of the male in her
than the female), and from this proceeds the plot, or the main
matter, of the sentimental part of the book.[1] She (or/and he:
a bisexual pronoun is required) is passionately loved by
d'Hauteville, a young French officer; he loves her 'comme on
aime cet être adorable ou maudit qui doit faire le destin de
notre vie': Lesbia is an accursed person whose influence is
fateful in Herbert's life. But Fragoletta meets and falls in love
with d'Hauteville's sister Eugénie: this is exactly the situation of Lesbia in reference to Herbert and his sister; the only
difference is that Eugénie reciprocates Fragoletta's love,
whereas Margaret is apparently not so much as aware that she
is loved by Lesbia. Fragoletta, even while making her love
plain to Eugénie, warns the latter against herself:

'Moi, j'ai la honte à offrir pour l'impossible amour que
je demande. La honte, l'inanité, les dangers stériles . . .
défendez-vous de moi!'

Such things as the following, said by her to the brother, recall
even more closely Lesbia's repelling words to Herbert when
he is making love to her:

'Voulez-vous regretter la mobile affection d'une être
bizarre? Viendrez-vous dans ce pays des fables . . . chercher,
comme Orphée, une ombre?'

Fragoletta's bitterness at her constitution, her feeling that she
is the victim of some mistake, is very much like Lesbia's:

(*To the sister*): 'Savez-vous ce que je suis . . .? Erreur,

---

[1] In part it is also an historical, or a political, novel (Latouche
claimed that he was an initiator in this regard). Its republicanism and
anti-clericalism would give it a further claim on the sympathies of
Swinburne.

crime ou rebut de cette nature qui vous a tout départi . . .'

(*To the brother*): 'Qu'y a-t-il de commun entre moi et les créatures humaines? je ne suis pas de leur espèce.'

(*To the brother again*): ' . . . Dieu, que j'accuse d'inconséquence et de méchanceté. '

(Cf. Lesbia's words to Herbert: 'I have missed of so many things . . . God knows I repent of living,—if he knows anything about us, or cares'). She too, like Lesbia, feels that death is the only way out of an impossible situation; she will welcome the mortal stroke from d'Hauteville's sword that will give her release:

'Otez-moi, comme un fardeau, cette vie qui m'a tourmenté sans but; aidez-moi à sortir d'un monde où je ne puis être aimé!'[1]

Enough has doubtless been said to show that, if one is going to look for external origins for Lesbia, this is a patent one, and the most important of all. The central idea is the same: the tragic situation—for herself and others—resulting from the fact that a woman is radically abnormal in her sexual constitution, a victim of some strange error on the part of forces that order—or fail to order—the world. And, especially with regard to the brother and sister, there is a striking parallel in certain of the developments. Lesbia, of course, as a personality, is Swinburne's own creation; she is very different from Fragoletta (although no more different—one might even say less different—than some other figures of fiction who cer-

---

[1] d'Hauteville thinks that Fragoletta in her male character and costume has fully seduced his sister (and the ingenuous Eugénie also thinks that, having ceased to resist the ineffectual ardours of the hermaphrodite, she has lost her 'virtue'). He pursues her to Italy, finds her, and gives her a choice: either she marries Eugénie or else she must fight a duel with him. (In her masculine capacity she had passed as a twin-brother of herself; d'Hauteville, who finally kills her, never discovered that the supposed young man was Fragoletta; never knew that he had slain his love, whom he imagined lost somewhere in the world; this is the crowning touch of tragedy in a work that is charged with tragedy in all of it that has to do with the unfortunate heroine.)

tainly derive from the latter and who are also influences that go to the making of Lesbia). She is much more gifted, educated, civilised and complex than the Italian girl, who, albeit there is aristocracy in her lineage, is rather a primitive creature. But the latter and her fate is undoubtedly part of Lesbia's ancestry, and the part of it that most appears in her.

Lafourcade, asininely anxious to prove that Swinburne owed nothing to Latouche's far from contemptible book, says that he was well aware of its 'énormes défauts'. The only thing he could have had in mind here is a remark of Swinburne's in *A Note on Charlotte Brontë*, which he cites elsewhere:

> '. . . the Rhadamanthine author of "Fragoletta"; who certainly, to judge by his own examples of construction, had some right to pronounce with authority how a novel ought *not* to be written.'

But this, as the context clearly enough indicates, only refers to a defect of construction in *Fragoletta* (a defect that occurs in more than one other of Latouche's nine or ten novels). As I have already remarked, *Fragoletta* is partly a historical or political novel, and partly a story of sentiment or passion of which the hermaphrodite is the moving cause. Now these two parts are not fused so as to make a unity. (Of this defect—one common to many well-reputed novels, historical and other— Latouche himself was fully conscious. Cf. the following from a letter written by him to his cousin Charles Duvernet on the subject of his novel entitled *Aymar*: 'Ta remarque critique est pleine de justesse. Il y a interruption d'intérêt, solution de continuité, entre la philosophie du livre et sa fable. Je n'ai pas le malheur d'ignorer ce défaut . . . Ce défaut est inhérent à ma manière de traiter un sujet. J'y veux toujours un peu de portée et j'y cherche quelque intérêt. Il n'y a que l'image du caducée antique qui ait encore parfaitement réalisé mon problème, celui d'enlacer autour du même rameau deux serpents qui font symétrie, se séparent avec grâce et se rejoignent harmonieusement. Le même défaut est dans *Grangeneuve*, dans *Fragoletta*'.) But each of the two non-fused parts may be of high quality in itself. And it does not follow from Swinburne's awareness of the lack of unity that he did not admire one or both of them. And as a matter of fact he did greatly admire the second part (that having to do with the hermaphrodite). He may have admired the other, too, as Balzac did (cf. the latter's words: 'Lorsqu'il [Latouche] aborde l'histoire, tout devient net, brillant, clair et sonore'); but of this there is no positive evidence, as there is in plenty of enthusiasm for the story of tragic passion. The fact that Lafourcade was a dullard does not secure him from a charge of bad faith in not citing this other judgment of Swinburne on one of the most notable[1] novels of the period that might take its name from Balzac:

'. . . the *Fragoletta* of Henri de Latouche . . . that singular, incoherent, admirable novel, so various and vigorous in manner of work; full of southern heat, and coloured as with Italian air and light to the last page of it.'[2]

---

[1] What does Saintsbury say of it in his *History of French Literature* (620 pages)? He does not so much as mention Latouche!—although he gives liberal space to Janin, Sandeau and other *minores* or *minimi* of the same period. But then Saintsbury, who is vastly and ludicrously wrong in much if not most of what he does say about French literature (he was not fitted to deal with it), does not so much as mention Laclos either in his misnamed 'History': it is incredible, but there is not a word in it about *Les Liaisons dangereuses*, which Swinburne rightly called the greatest book in the century in which it was produced. For the still more extraordinary (and very funny) treatment of Laclos by Saintsbury in his *History of the French Novel* see Note 159 on Chapter III.

[2] *Les Abîmes. Par Ernest Clouët* (MS. in British Museum). There is factual mis-statement in the concluding words, for parts of the story are set in France, and have the corresponding atmosphere.

It must be to this judgment that Lafourcade refers when, *à propos* of Swinburne's poem *Fragoletta*, he says that 'l'admiration de Swinburne pour ce livre [Latouche's work of the same name] était en grande partie ironique'. This statement is altogether and impudently gratuitous; there is not the slightest reason for regarding this expression of admiration as in the very least ironical; it is true that it occurs in a piece of work that in its general intention is a burlesque; but in certain parts of it, as (for instance) here and in a passage on the Marquis de Sade,

Latouche's *Fragoletta*, indeed, and especially the eponymous character with her ambiguous sex haunted the imaginaiton of Swinburne for many years. Another witness of this is the piece entitled *Fragoletta* in the first *Poems and Ballads*:

> *O Love! what shall be said of thee?*
> *The son of grief begot by joy?*

> *   *   *

> *Being sexless, wilt thou be*
> *Maiden or boy?*

> *I dreamed of strange lips yesterday*
> *And cheeks wherein the ambiguous blood . . .*

> *   *   *
> *   *   *

> *What fields have bred thee, or what groves*
> *Concealed thee, O mysterious flower,*
> *O double rose of Love's . . .?*[3]

(Note [2] *continued)*—
Swinburne enunciates views that are completely his own. Lafourcade failed to see that he does not cite this judgment as an extravagance of the fictitious Clouët; but formulates it incidentally, in his own name as a commentator on a subject handled by Clouët. Besides, had the passage been ironical, it would not have contained the restrictive 'incoherent' along with purely eulogistic words. 'Incoherent', it may be noted, expresses the unfavourable criticism conveyed in the aforementioned passage from *A Note on Charlotte Brontë*, which Lafourcade disingenuously cites as though it represented Swinburne's entire opinion on the book in question.

[3] Lafourcade, brutishly bent on traducing Latouche and denying that Swinburne owed anything to him, says: 'il m'a été impossible de découvrir le mondre rapport entre l'affligeante production de l'éditeur des poèmes de Chénier [i.e. Latouche] et la *Fragoletta* de Swinburne'. This in spite of a declaration (which he cites) by W. M. Rossetti (who

Even more eloquent of this *hantise* is the passage in the *Dedication* of the same volume, where Fragoletta has her place among the women who have chiefly moved the poet's imagination:

> *O daughters of dreams and of stories*
> *That life is not wearied of yet,*
> *Faustine, Fragoletta, Dolores,*
> *Félise and Yolande and Juliette . . .*[1]

'Livre terne et banal', 'affligeante production': if Lafourcade's estimation were right Swinburne must have been something of a fool to have had an enthusiastic admiration for so poor a thing. Something of a fool he evidently was, in Gosse's eyes, who, contrary to Lafourcade, frankly admits the admiration, and characterises it as 'violent and inexplicable'. The judgment implied in the later epithet is typical of Gosse's

(*Note* [1] *continued*)—
was in very close touch with Swinburne at the time in question) that the poem 'Fragoletta' was inspired by Latouche's book. Lafourcade, having thus dismissed Latouche, affirms that the poem is 'sans doute' founded on a sketch of three heads by Giorgione (which Swinburne cursorily mentions in his *Notes on Designs of the Old Masters at Florence*). It is unnecessary to say that this is nothing but gratuitous nonsense.

[1] It would be difficult even for Lafourcade to maintain that the *Fragoletta* of these lines is merely one of three heads in a sketch. Of course she is a 'daughter of story', and the story is that by Latouche which the poet found 'admirable'.

We may note here that, apart from Lesbia herself, a reminiscence of Latouche's novel in *Lesbia Brandon* occurs in a passage, towards the end of Chapter III, describing Herbert's beauty as he lay sleeping. '. . . a head to be caressed by Bacchus and carved by Polycles'. This Polycles (so little known in England that even his name is not to be found in many standard books of reference such as Smith's *Smaller Classical Dictionary of Biography*) is the sculptor of the statue of the Hermaphrodite which d'Hauteville, Fragoletta and another character see in Chapter IV of Latouche's book: the sight of the statue first awakens in Fragoletta a full consciousness that she herself is an epicene.

radical incompetence as a man of leters. 'Man of letters' indeed is a misnomer; in very reality, and in spite of his adroitly decorated façade (and in spite of all other things, including the strange—or perhaps not so strange—fact that he was appointed to a lectureship in literature by the University of Cambridge) he was almost as unlettered as his very congenial companion Wise. (It must be remembered that he was not educated even in the ordinary sense, and that he never succeeded in educating himself.) In the matter of *Fragoletta* I find the opinion of men of the calibre of Balzac (not to mention Swinburne) infinitely more authoritative than that of nullities such as he and Lafourcade and others of their kind. I have already cited part of Balzac's judgment; a little more of it will not be out of place here, and it will have relevance to later sections of our argument.

'Cet ouvrage est destiné à un grand éclat,' he proclaimed in the article of 1829 from which the just-mentioned citation comes. In another article (still on *Fragoletta*), in 1831,[1] he saluted Latouche as 'Un des hommes chez qui une haute raison s'unit à une grande puissance d'imagination'. Here too he well summed up the central theme of the book, the drama of passion, and its inevitable advance into tragedy:

'Faites poser devant vous cet être inexprimable, qui n'a pas de sexe complet, et dans le cœur duquel luttent la timidité d'une femme et l'énergie d'un homme, qui aime la sœur, est aimé du frère, et ne peut rien rendre à l'une ni à l'autre, voyez toutes les qualités de la femme rassemblées dans cette intéressante Eugénie, et toutes celles de l'homme dans ce noble d'Hauteville; placez entre eux l'effrayant et gracieux Adriani, comme la transition de ces deux types; jetez sur ces trois figures de la passion à pleine main, torturez ces trois cœurs avec des combinaisons dont l'idée ne se rencontre nulle part; puis, ne pouvant trouver de baume à ces indicibles souffrances, élevez ce malheur à son comble,

[1] Both these articles appeared in *Le Mercure du XIXe siècle*.

imaginez un dernier, un épouvantable sacrifice, épuisez
enfin toutes nos facultés, et vous aurez créé un chef-
d'œuvre, vous aurez fait *Fragoletta*.'

Again, in 1831, in his *Lettres sur Paris*, he spoke of 'les ravis-
santes pages de *Fragoletta*'.

Those who have not read the book will at least see from all
this that it is more than an 'affligeante production', and that it
is far from 'inexplicable' that it should have been admired
by Swinburne.

Now Balzac not only had a great esteem for Latouche
(tempered, of course, as in Swinburne's case, by a certain
amount of reservation); he was considerably influenced by
him, and not merely by him as the author of the work on the
hermaphrodite. But as the influence of this work on him is
what concerns us particularly, we shall limit our attention to
it. *Seraphita*, one of his most ambitious undertakings, proceeds from it in very large measure, a fact of which he made
no secret: on the contrary, he very explicitly drew attention
to it. '*Seraphita*', he said (to give only one supporting citation),
'serait les deux nature en un seul être, comme *Fragoletta*'.
Seraphita, then, like Fragoletta, is epicene; moreover she
(or/and he) is loved by a man and a woman, although in this
case they are not brother and sister. Thus (all due deductions
being made, of course) to the influence of Latouche on the
author of *Lesbia Brandon* is added that of Balzac, and we have
here one indication of what was in Swinburne's mind when
he described that work as being Balzacian as well as an essay
in poetry.

(Swinburne was steeped in Balzac before he left Oxford. I
have drawn up a list of the French books borrowed by him
from the library of the Taylor Institution between March
1859 and May 1860 (that given by Lafourcade is incomplete),
and it includes over forty of Balzac's works. *Seraphita* is
among them. He also had a copy of his own of at least one
volume, containing *Seraphita* and two other stories, for it
appears from an unpublished letter of his that he sent this

volume to a friend in February 1860. In this letter he speaks of Seraphita as 'a lusus naturae, hermaphrodite, quasi-eunuch, or — something. You know I cling to physical interpretations.' It may be taken for granted that he knew intimately all the works of Balzac mentioned in these pages.)

Seraphita is not the only work of Balzac which to some extent has its origin in *Fragoletta*. An earlier story, *Sarrasine*, is also derivative from the same source. Sarrasine is a young French sculptor who, during a residence in Rome falls passionately in love with Zambinella, a *prima donna* of one of the chief opera-houses in that city. For him, she is the *beauté idéale* after which he has always sought, and so far always in vain; the artist in him—and the man as well—is roused to extremes of ecstasy by the wonder of her many qualities. In her are the 'exquises proportions de la nature féminine' which satisfy all his exigencies. Perfections which he has hitherto had to be content with finding, one in one woman, another in another, and so on, he now finds combined in one and the same creature. Hands, legs, neck, shoulders, breasts—everything, as far as it is revealed on the stage, is just as it should be . . . After watching her night after night from a stage-box (not unobserved by her), he secures access to her, and presses upon her the fervour of his love, which, like Herbert's for Lesbia, is ready to run to mad excesses of devotion: if she wished, he tells her, he would even give up his sculpting, the thing through which he expresses his genius. He offers what to an artist is more than life itself—is not this masochism pushed to its furthest point? The following is part of her response to this love whose greatness takes it beyond sanity:

'J'abhorre les hommes encore plus peut-être que je ne hais les femmes . . . Le monde est désert pour moi. Je suis une créature maudite condamnée à comprendre le bonheur, à le sentir, à le désirer, et . . . forcée à le voir me fuir á toute heure . . . Je vous défends de m'aimer. Je puis être un ami dévoué pour vous . . . J'ai besoin d'un frère . . . Elle sourit

tristement, et dit en murmurant: "Fatale beauté!" Elle
leva les yeux aux ciel. En ce moment ses yeux eut je ne sais
quelle expression d'horreur si puissante, si vive, que Sarrasine en tressaillit.'

Is there not something in this of the response of Fragoletta
to d'Hauteville—and also of Lesbia to Herbert: the same
recoil, the same bitter sadness, the same thrusting away of the
man into a perplexed despair?

Sarrasine decides to abduct Zambinella with the help of
some friends; but just before doing so he is informed that she
is a castrate male: for in the Papal States women are not
allowed to appear on the stage, and female *rôles* are taken
by males whose sex has been ablated . . . Nevertheless, he
bears 'her' off to his studio, and finally proceeds to kill her,
when he himself falls under the daggers of three agents of a
cardinal who is politely called her 'protector'.

Zambinella is virtually an hermaphrodite. The operation
he had undergone had set going in him forces that made him
very largely a female. (Doubtless, tendencies or potentialities
in this direction were part of his original constitution. Medical
science knows of cases in which a person's sex begins to change
spontaneously. I make this remark with a view to indicating
that Balzac's Zambinella is not an impossible character.) And
so to some extent we have here again the central idea of
Fragoletta.

There is no hermaphroditism in Balzac's *La Fille aux yeux
d'or*, and so from this point of view it cannot be said to show
the influence of *Fragoletta*. But there is something analogous
to hermaphroditism in it, dual love on the part of the principal
character; and the sapphism, and other things, connect it with
Lesbia Brandon (Swinburne refers to it in more than one
passage, with which I have dealt in the course of the Notes).
And so, particularly as we have, *à propos* of the provenance
of Lesbia, been led into speaking of sources or influences
from which Swinburne's novel proceeds, we may as well deal
here with this powerful story of the great romantic-realist.

Paquita Valdès, la fille aux yeux d'or, is a mysteriously guarded young woman, born of a Georgian mother (the wife or mistress presumably of a full or half-caste Spaniard) in Havana, and brought thence to Paris by the Marquise de San-Réal, the wife of a Spanish grandee too old to be of any concern to her in her sexual life. Henri de Marsay, a *blasé* young man of singular beauty and commanding personality, passes her more than once as she is walking with a duenna in the Tuileries; and from the beginning each of them is strongly attracted to the other. He sees in her the most adorably feminine person he has ever met; a creature who, Asiatic by her mother, tropical by her birth, and European by her up-bringing, presents a rare variety of charms. As Sarrasine did in the case of Zambinella, he finds combined in her perfections that hitherto he has only found separate in different women (and in the matter of women he is a connoisseur with a very extensive experience). He manages to get to her beyond the formidable barriers by which she is enclosed. All his expecta-tions were realised; her body was superb, there was no part of it that was not voluptuous; she was a magnificent love-machine, 'the richest organisation' that Nature had ever made for love; any other man than de Marsay (a character of iron) would have been frightened by her powers as an amorist . . .[1]

She was evident far from innocent; but (to his astonishment) she was technically a virgin.

She told him that from the age of twelve she had been shut away from the world,[2] and taught to hate men; and that she

[1] I faithfully report Balzac, whom certain readers will no doubt find extravagant. But Baudelaire, for example, an expert on these matters, would not have done so.

[2] How did she come to be in the Tuileries? it may be asked. She had got out of her confinement, during an absence of the Marquise de San-Réal by threatening her duenna with immediate death (which she had the means of inflicting on her) if the latter would not let her see as much of the world as was possible in the course of a walk. The Marquise's absence lasts over the time she and de Marsay are in touch with each other.

had been loved only, and had never loved anybody. That was all of her secret that he was able to get out of her.

At their first *rencontre d'amour* she cajolingly makes a strange request: that he should begin by dressing up as a woman.

The second time, at the height of their ecstasy, she calls out a woman's name. He is at once disenchanted; feels that he has been made a fool of, used as a mere substitute, and in his anger he attempts to kill her. She is able to press a button before he does so, and he is foiled, but he determines to get back somehow and take his revenge upon her.[1]

He does get back, but only to find the room in a terrible state; there is blood everywhere, and other signs of a desperate struggle. Paquita, pierced with dagger-wounds, is at the point of death, and another woman is standing over her. This woman is holding a blood-stained poniard; her garment is all ripped, her half-naked body is covered with scratches and bites, and, like some dreadful creature of prey, she is so intent upon her victim that at first she is not conscious that de Marsay has come into the room and is watching her. The Marquise de Rèal (having learned that she had been supplanted by a man during her absence) has had her revenge, and robbed de Marsay of his.

She is so like de Marsay that she might be his twin sister. After a look at each other they both exclaim: 'Lord Dudley must be your father?' They were illegitimate children, by different mothers, of a member of the English peerage.

'She was faithful to the blood' says de Marsay, pointing to the lacerated corpse of the woman whose consummate charms both of them have enjoyed.

(Melodrama, all this? No more than certain scenes in highly reputed works of Shakespeare and of many other

---

[1] He is a man who puts to death, or has put to death, people who have seriously incurred his displeasure. As I have said elsewhere, this character (who comes into some fifteen of Balzac's novels, and was evidently a favourite of his creator) is a sort of Caesar Borgia in nineteenth-century Paris.

writers considered great or classic. The important thing is that melodrama should transcend itself and assume the powers of tragedy. And with Balzac it does no less than with Shakespeare. Cf. Swinburne's description of Balzac, in the first paragraph of *Lesbia Brandon*, as 'the greatest analyst of spirit and flesh that ever lived': and it is *à propos* of—although, of course, by no means exclusively in reference to—*La fille aux yeux d'or* that Swinburne assigns to the French novelist this œcumenical and unshared primacy in one of the most important matters of the art of the kind to which tragedy belongs.)

We have here certain of the elements of *Lesbia Brandon*: illegitimacy, offspring of the same father by different women, sapphism, the call of the blood: and we have further explanation of what Swinburne meant when he said his work was an 'étude à la Balzac'. (Another notable thing in *Lesbia Brandon* that is probably a reminiscence of *La fille aux yeux d'or* is the desire of Paquita to see de Marsay dressed as a woman.)[1]

Although I am reserving consideration of Sade for the volume to follow this, I may parenthetically note at this place the probable influence of this writer on the intrigue of *Lesbia Brandon*. I have already said that the complication of 'intertangled incest' in that work cannot be ascribed to the influence of Rétif de la Bretonne, and that it originates in Swinburne's own nature and also in certain suggestions received from the *milieu* in which he moved as a youth. But this needs to be supplemented. Intertanglements of this sort are to be found in Sade, by whom Swinburne was strongly influenced. I shall give only one example here. In *Florville et Courval, ou le Fatalisme*, one of the stories in *Les Crimes de l'Amour*, a man commits incest with his daughter, and she commits incest not only with her brother, but also (seventeen years later) with her son, the issue of this latter union (a crime of another order in this history of a family is that she kills this son—having already been the cause of her mother's death). In

[1] See Note 9 on Chapter XVI.

this rich complication of triple incest (which no doubt roused competitive feelings in Swinburne) there is no real crime, no vice even by conventional standards except that of love outside the holiness of wedlock. None of these people know that he or she is committing incest (and the daughter does not know the identity of the persons whose death she brings about). Everything is done in innocence. Only at the end does the truth come out, and it is shattering in its effect. The same innocence and the same late revelation, as well as similar entanglement, is part of the plot of *Lesbia Brandon*.

It is perhaps worth noticing that there is another point in common between this story of Sade's and Swinburne's novel. It is that indicated by the subtitle of the former: 'ou le Fatalisme' (which is a solecism: the Marquis should have written 'ou la Fatalité). All these innocent people are the victims of some sort of Fate; their 'criminal' actions are not willed by themselves, do not really proceed from them, but are errors into which they are led, as it were, by circumstances or forces external to themselvs, just as Oedipus was. I have remarked that Lesbia is the victim of a fatality; and so, from another point of view, or for different reasons, is Denham (and Margaret too if she is his lover); and Herbert also is a victim of the fate that defeats Lesbia. From still another point of view, Emma Bovary (a character by whom I have suggested Swinburne was influenced in more than one of the tentatives of his cycle) is a victim of something that might be called Fate. That is the name her husband gives it: 'C'est la faute de la fatalité' is the poor man's comment ('un grand mot' Flaubert calls it) when the lamentable history is closed by her suicide. But the operation of Fate is less external here than in Sade's story and in the part of *Lesbia Brandon* of which ignorance is an element making for tragedy. Emma is never in what may be called the Oedipean situation. Her actions are wholly willed by herself, she knows what she is doing (relatively, of course; for absolutely every human being acts in ignorance, is driven by forces of which he has nothing like clear or full knowledge, and so may be called a victim of fatality. A fact which Kafka, it seems, tried to convey—clumsily, or anyhow abortively, far from successfully—in allegorical or symbolical fashion in *Der Prozess*). But we have the Oedipean situation in Balzac's *La fille aux yeux d'or*, which in virtue of that situation is more tragic that *Madame Bovary* (and *Lesbia Brandon*, too, in the relevant parts, is for the same reason more tragic than Flaubert's work).

Thibaudet, one of the most penetrating and suggestive critics of modern times (no British—and still less American—critic of this century is anything like his equal) affirms that the French novel in general (he even says 'tout le roman français') since *Madame Bovary* has proceeded from that work, just as all French classical tragedy proceeded from the *Cid* and from *Andromaque*; like *Madame Bovary*, all novels subsequent to it have been 'romans de la fatalité', works in which a fate or destiny runs its course, and in which a character or characters are passive victims of its operation; whereas in the preceding period—that between 1830 and 1857—the opposite is the case: all the great novels of this period—*Les Misérables*,[1] *La Comédie humaine*, *Le Rouge et le Noir*, etc.—are novels of will, of resistant and forward-driving energies that cannot acquiesce in passivity. On the whole, no doubt, this is true.[2] But it does not apply to *La fille aux yeux d'or* and other parts of the *Comédie humaine*, which are eminently 'romans de la fatalité (as is *Lesbia Brandon*, which is Balzacian in this and not in the other direction). Lesbia herself, it may be further remarked, suffers from a fatality greater or worse than those we have mentioned so far. She is much more of a victim than Emma, or even than characters like those of Sade's story or of *La fille aux yeux d'or*, whose tragedy is the result of ignorance. She does not suffer because of ignorance; but because of some

---

[1] If any sciolist objects that *Les Misérables* was published in 1862, one can answer, on behalf of Thibaudet that most of it was composed within the period named.

[2] Up to the time—1920—when Thibaudet first published his essay on this subject; and, at least in so far as better or more genuine French novels are concerned, one need not stop at that date.

radical error in her very constitution (and against which she could hardly be anything but passive); and this makes her more tragic than any of the other characters—Sade's, Balzac's, Flaubert's—and their kind, to which we have referred in what immediately precedes. Beyond any doubt, she is a far more tragic figure than any character in Flaubert; and one might go further—but that would shock literary superstition and be of no service to Swinburne.

I pass over the influence of Latouche on Stendhal, Hugo, George Sand and others (which would have astonished the contemptibly ignorant Gosse and Lafourcade) and come to his influence in work of Gautier which made a strong impression on Swinburne. Gautier, like the latter, was obsessed by *Fragoletta*, and especially by the idea of ambiguous sex. His poem *Contralto*, for example, is a transposition into verse of the part of Latouche's novel dealing with the statue of the hermaphrodite:

> *On voit dans la musée antique,*
> *Sur un lit de marbre sculpté,*
> *Une statue énigmatique*
> *D'une inquiétante beauté.*

> *Est-ce un jeune homme? est-ce une femme,*
> *Une déesse, ou bien un dieu?*
> *L'amour, ayant peur d'être infâme,*
> *Hésite et suspend son aveu.*

> * * *

> *Pour faire sa beauté maudite,*
> *Chaque sexe apporta son don.*
> *Tout homme dit: 'C'est Aphrodite!'*
> *Toute femme: 'C'est Cupidon!'*

Sexe douteux, grâce certaine,
On dirait ce corps indécis
Fondu, dans l'eau de la fontaine,
Sous les baisers de Salmacis.

*   *   *

Swinburne's four sonnets entitled *Hermaphroditus* (which form a companion-piece to his *Fragoletta*) derive part of their inspiration from these verses of Gautier, and also, directly, from the chief source of the latter:[1]

. . . To what strange end hath some strange god made fair
The double blossom of two fruitless flowers?

*   *   *

Beneath the woman's and the water's kiss
Thy moist limbs melted into Salmacis . . .

This predilection for sexual ambiguity, or a twofold sex transcending each of its constituents, which Swinburne shared with Gautier, is expressed more than once in prose in the latter's *Mademoiselle de Maupin*; the following will be sufficient as as an example:

'C'est en effet une des plus suaves créations du génie païen que ce fils d'Hermès et d'Aphrodite. Il ne se peut rien imaginer de plus ravissant au monde que ces deux corps tous deux parfaits, harmonieusement fondus ensemble, que ces deux beautés si égales et si différentes qui n'en forment plus qu'une supérieure à toutes deux, parce qu'elles se

---

[1] Notwithstanding the note 'Au Musée du Louvre' written after the sonnets. Of course, the inspiration from Gautier and Latouche may have been reinforced by the piece of sculpture in the Louvre; but the influence of the latter is no more than secondary. Lafourcade is not aware of the important influence of Gautier's poem in this connexion.

412

tempèrent et se font valoir réciproquement: pour un adolateur exclusif de la forme, y a-t-il une incertitude plus aimable que celle ou vous jette la vue ce dos, de ces reins douteux, et de ces jambes si fines et si fortes, que l'on ne sait si l'on doit les attribuer à Mercure prêt à s'envoler ou à Diane sortant du bain?'

There is something of the thought and spirit of this passage in a section of the eleventh chapter of *Lesbia Brandon*:

> This face had the singular dubious beauty distinctive of Italian boys; a loveliness that wavers and hovers between female and male . . .

Ambiguity, divergence from or transcending of the normal, in the matter of sex is the most important if not the all-governing conception of *Mademoiselle de Maupin*. The central figure of this novel, which is almost entirely epistolary, is a young person called Theodore. Theodore is masterfully virile; he is a dare-devil rider, a dashing hunter, a duellist of very formidable powers. He has so hardened himself that he has risen superior to a respect for human life as such. Altogether, he has exceptional force of character. He has, too, exceptional beauty of face and figure, as well as distinction, grace, and charm; altogether, there is about his masculinity an attractiveness that is far from usual. Rosette, a young woman of aristocratic birth, falls in love with him, but he does not show himself responsive. In desperation, she offers him all sorts of opportunities (in secluded places) of enjoying her charms, which are considerable: but she can never bring him to the desired conclusions. All the same, Theodore is pleasantly stirred by her manifestations . . . She at last takes the extreme step of coming, in night-attire, to his bedroom, and makes advances that even St. Anthony could hardly have resisted. But he is resistant; again, however, he is stirred, and something seems on the point of happening, when her suspicious soldierly brother bursts into the room, and tells Theodore that he must either marry the lady or else fight a duel on the spot. Theodore chooses the latter alternative, disables the hefty brother, and then rides away.

Rosette discovers his whereabouts, and begs him to visit her at a castle of hers in the country, which he does. She in the meantime has become the mistress of d'Albert, a cynical but earnest and quite pleasant young man who has all Gautier's anti-Christian pagan philosophy, and especially his fervent aestheticism, and has long been looking for a woman who shall satisfy his very exigent ideas of what constitutes the right sort of lover. Rosette, in spite of her many qualications, does not come up to the required standard; she is not the woman sought by the poet and idealist in him. In fact, he feels that he must continue the search elsewhere, and is becoming somewhat irked by his association with her. He is at the castle when Theodore turns up, is immediately impressed by him, and before long is horrified to find that he is falling deeply in love with him. (This horror, expressed several times, is a proof—if any were needed—that Gautier—of whom d'Albert is largely a self-portrait—was the very opposite of homosexual, in spite of his predilection for hermaphroditism and sexual ambiguity: as was Swinburne, who had the same predilection in much the same degree. Sade, on the other hand, and his most typical characters, would have been the contrary of shocked had they discovered they were conceiving a passion for a personable young man.)

Rosette again comes to Theodore's room—although not after bedtime on this occasion—, and he tells her that 'an unsurmountable obstacle' prevents him from returning her love in the only way that would be satisfying to her.

With the deepening of his passion, d'Albert has an increasing suspicion that Theodore is really a woman in disguise; he is more than ever convinced of this when, in a performance of Shakespeare's *As You Like It,* Theodore, playing the part of Rosalind to his Orlando, has to appear in a woman's dress. He finds Rosalind bewitching, and he has the impression that, addressing him in the amorous interchange of the play, Theodore is speaking directly to him as d'Albert, and not only to him as a character in Shakespeare. From now on he is absolutely certain that he has at last found the ideal lover for whom he has hitherto sought in vain; Theodore-Rosalind, in personality as well as physically, satisfies all his exigencies is for him the one and only Companion in the whole universe—and so on: all the old romantic Platonic fancy of a complete darling, pre-elect immemorially, known before she is met, and now found and recognised as the presence that has always been missing. To this effect he writes a long letter to her, not as Theodore but as Rosalind, and, waiting till her room is empty, goes and leaves it there.

Theodore is indeed a woman, and her real name is Madelaine de Maupin. As she explains in her part of the correspondence (to a woman-friend), she set out disguised as a man (after due training in the use of a sword, etc.) in order to gain the largest experience possible of the world—an experience much more extensive than she could acquire if she showed herself as a female. In particular, she wants to make a thorough study of men, to get to know them as they really are in themselves and in the company of their own sex, when there are no ladies about, before giving herself to any one of them as a lover (for she is boldly emancipated in her ideas, in spite of her strict conventual upbringing. In fact, she is really shocking judged by the standards of orthodoxy. But so far she is absolutely 'pure' physically). 'The solution of the great problem of a perfect lover' is the ultimate goal of her quest: from an opposite direction she is making for the same objective as d'Albert.

But in the course of her adventures, her nature undergoes a curious change—or potentialities in it which in her ordinary life would have remained in abeyance are educed and developed by the experiences through which she passes in her masculine disguise: she finds that her femininity or womanhood is being replaced by something else, or at least is no longer single in her, that something of the opposite sex has come into her nature, and yet she is not simply a woman plus a man, but something beyond both of these things:[1]

'Je perdais insensiblement l'idée de mon sexe, et je me souvenais à peine de loin en loin, que j'étais femme ... En vérité ni l'un ni l'autre de ces deux sexes n'est le mien; je n'ai ni la soumission imbécile, ni la timidité, ni les petitesses da la femme; je n'ai pas les vices des hommes, leur dégoûtante crapule et leurs penchants brutaux:— je suis d'un troisième sexe à part qui n'a pas encore de nom ...; j'ai le corps et l'âme d'une femme, l'esprit et la force d'un homme, et j'ai trop ou pas assez de l'un et de l'autre pour me pouvoir accoupler avec l'un d'eux ... O Graciosa, je ne pourrais jamais aimer complètement personne ni homme ni femme; quelque chose d'inassouvi gronde toujours en moi ... Ma chimère serait d'avoir tour à tour les deux sexes pour satisfaire à cette double nature ...'

Here we have in full the idea of a double or, more than a double, a further, sex transcending the male and female elements of which it is composed. And this person 'of a third sex apart' is different from those we have met so far; she is not physically hermaphroditic like Fragoletta and she has not been mutilated to incompleteness like Zambinella; and Paquita, if she is really bisexual in temperament, is rudimentary compared to Mademoiselle de Maupin, who is a very accomplished creature, capable of living the life of a man of superior parts in more ways than one. Still, as her experiences with Rosette show, she remains fundamentally much more a woman than

[1] The following observation of Havelock Ellis may be cited as apposite here: 'We may not know exactly what sex is; but we do know that it is mutable, with the possibility of one sex being changed into the other sex, that its frontiers are often uncertain, and that there are many stages between a complete male and a complete female. In some forms of animal life, indeed, it is not easy to distinguish which is male and which female.'

a man; and yet she is not left altogether unaffected by advances
here . . .[1]

We have referred to as much of this work as is germane to
the subject under discussion, but those who have not read it
may like to be told parenthetically how the story ends. No
answer comes to d'Albert's letter, and the poor fellow is left
in suspense for a fortnight; then Theodore goes to his room
dressed as Rosalind again, and tells him that she has decided
to give herself to him for a night, but that on the morrow she
will resume her life as a male. They have a perfect night of
love. 'L'amour de d'Albert monta à un chiffre formidable . . .
Rosalinde avait de prodigieuses dispositions . . .' Then, when
he at last falls asleep, she dresses, and goes—not to her own
room but to Rosette's; and it is midday before she leaves it . . .
She does not appear at either of the following meals, retires
early, and next day at dawn rides away from the castle, and
never comes back.

She writes to d'Albert, telling him that they have had one
perfect night, and that she has gone away before the experience can decline in quality, as it is bound to do sooner or
later—in six months, two years, even ten years—, however
strong may be his feeling to the contrary. They will each go
their own way now—and one day perhaps—who knows?—
they may meet on the other side of the world. Let him live in
this hope, and not go after her, for all search for her will be
in vain. In her final words she bids him give the best consolation he can to poor Rosette, who (she says) must be upset at
least as much as he by her unexpected departure: let them
love each other in memory of their love for her. 'Aimez-vous
bien tous deux, en souvenir de moi, que vous avez aimée l'un
et l'autre et dites-vous quelquefois mon nom dans un baiser.'

In the same way the bisexual Seraphita of Balzac left the
man and the woman who loved her passionately—but without

---

[1] As I have already remarked, Gautier, who has a horror of male
hemosexuality, has no such feeling about lesbianism; and many men
are like him in this.

giving either of them so much as a few consummating hours of love. And if she had done so she would not have continued, and for the same reason as that which made Mademoiselle de Maupin break off: in order that love may remain perfect, she said (anticipating the attitude of the Wagnerian Tristan), it must end in death when it comes into its perfection.

The general theme of sexual ambiguity makes *Mademoiselle de Maupin* a descendant of Latouche's *Fragoletta*; among resemblance of detail one may cite the alternatives of mariage or a duel imposed by Rosette's brother on the heroine for the mistaken reason that the latter has been guilty of seduction.

Gautier's novel made a profound impression on Swinburne. For him it was

> ... *the golden book of spirit and sense,*
> *The holy writ of beauty; he that wrought*
> *Made it with dreams and faultless words and*
> *thought* ...

In prose he gave it even higher praise: it was 'the most perfect and exquisite book of modern times'. And superlative laudation of it is not at all surprising. Its charm (no idea of which is given in the foregoing rapid summary[1] is one of the most delightful things in literature. The style is as pellucid and easy (and at need, witty) as tha tof Voltaire at his best; and it has a quality of supple and poetic life that is never found in Voltaire; and its atticism rises on occasion into passages of Asiatic grandeur.[2]

---

[1] And—inevitably of course, as it is consubstantial with the very texture of the French words—it is lost completely in any of the English translations.

[2] There is, however, a rather serious fault of structure. The letters are not duly sequent, and this results in a disunity that is awkward apart from any abstract theory of structure in the novel. The narrative in 'Theodore's' letters to her friend is temporally a good deal behind that in d'Albert's and in the parts of the story given by the author. For example, in Ch. XI 'Theodore' (in d'Albert's account of events) is

This work confirmed[2] Swinburne's interest in the theme of sexual ambiguity or abnormality and the artistic virtualities contained in it: there is no need, after what precedes, to give elaboration to this point. The following declaration of d'Albert (or Gautier) might serve as an epigraph for *Lesbia Brandon*:

'Moi-même, qui ai le commun en horreur, qui ne rêve qu'aventures étranges, passions fortes, extases délirantes, situations bizarres et difficiles . . .'

Especially 'situations bizarres et difficiles': and these are provided in an eminent degree by the theme named in the last paragraph. Swinburne's originality was that, while keeping to

(*Note* [2] *Continued*)—

acting the part of Rosalind; but in her own account in Ch. XII she still has not reached the castle, and it is not till Ch. XV that she herself gets up to the play-acting. The disadvantage of this is not offset by any psychological gain in having the same events reported by different personalities.

[3] The temporal order of the afore-cited French works on this subject is: *Fragoletta, Sarrasine, La Fille aux yeux d'or, Séraphita, Mademoiselle de Maupin.* It is impossible to determine with certitude in what order they were read by Swinburne. As already mentioned, he was acquainted with Seraphita and the greater part of the rest of Balzac's works in 1859. He made enthusiastic mention of Latouche in a letter to Monckton-Milnes in 1860 (if one can trust the date given by Gosse and Wise). He probably read *Mademoiselle de Maupin* last of these very influential books.

It would be interesting, but there is no space for it here, to trace the history of the conception of hermaphroditism or sexual ambiguity from ancient to modern times. I will only recall that it was common in the Greek world, to judge from such things as male-female divinities worshipped in different regions, and the fact that men wore women's garments, and women men's, at certain religious ceremonies. Cf. also the myth of the original male-female sex related by Aristophanes in the *Symposium*. The idea, indeed, seems to have been something of a *hantise* in the Greek imagination; it may be, as Licht suggests (in *Das Liebesleben der Griechen*), that this was due to a dim subconscious memory of the original bisexual state of the human species, and also to a knowledge that the human foetus is androgynous in its earlier stages.

the general subject of sexual abnormality, he chose, not (as his predecessors in this line had done) an hermaphrodite or a castrate or a person of ambiguous or bisexual tendencies, but a woman who was entirely homosexual;[1] and he had here to handle a new psychological situation, with possibilities more genuinely tragic (if less melodramatic) than those offered by the cases treated by the French writers from whom he got his *nisus* in this direction. That he handled this new situation successfully, and educed moving tragedy from it, even in a work that remained incomplete, will, I think, be admitted by most readers. Certainly the chapter entitled Leucadia is, in tragic and imaginative beauty, and in intuitive psychological insight, superior to anything in the French works to which we have referred.

To return to *Mademoiselle de Maupin*, the following observation of the heroine sums up the situation of Lesbia:

'Il arrive souvent que le sexe de l'âme ne soit pareil à celui du corps, et c'est une contradiction qui ne peut manquer de produire beaucoup de désordre.'

And a remark of the unfortunate Rosette epitomizes the situation of Herbert:

'Si vous savez. Théodore, combien il est profondément

[1] What about the possibility that Lesbia is an hermaphrodite? Is not, for instance, what her father says of her: 'she's half male as it is I think sometimes' a pointer in this direction? All things considered, I reject the possibility. Almost everything goes to show that she is nothing but a woman who is fully homosexual; there is nothing epicene about her; she is sexually interested only in women, and is positively repelled by any intimate contact even with the man in whom she sees something of the woman for whom she has a passionate desire.

I do not know of any work previous to Swinburne's novel in which there is a fully homosexual female comparable to Lesbia; but there is one in Lacretelle's *La Bonifas,* which appeared some sixty years after the time in which Swinburne's work was written. It is one of the more notable French novels of the past quarter of a century.

douloureux de sentir qu'on a manqué sa vie, que l'on a passé à côté de son bonheur . . .'

There is even something of Herbert's wild masochism in one passage of d'Albert's letter to the woman in whom he has discovered his ideal: 'Je me prosterne, je m'anéantis devant vous'. We may also cite the eonism of transvestism in Gautier's novel as (together with the same thing in *Faublas* and several other works[1]) one of the details by which Swinburne was influenced. Not only is Mademoiselle de Maupin in the dress of the opposite sex, but her page is too; and Mademoiselle de Maupin is alternately dressed as female and male in the play in which she performs. It was perhaps under the influence of Gautier's book that Swinburne introduced the amateur theatricals, the charade-play, in the fifth chapter of *Lesbia Brandon*;[2] and almost certainly, had he finished the chapter there would have developed a sort of play within the play, an inner drama expressing something in the private life of two or more of the actors, as in the case of d'Albert and Mademoiselle de Maupin when they played Shakespeare:

'C'est en quelque sorte une autre pièce dans la pièce, un drame invisible et inconnu aux autres spectateurs que nous jouions pour nous seuls . . .'

Mr. Linley seems to have read *Mademoiselle de Maupin*; his aestheticism certainly recalls that of d'Albert, as when, for example, he says that 'any sort of beauty is good at all times', whoever possesses it and quite independently of whether or not it has any practical use. And again, when he answers young Fieldfare's question, 'Good for what?', in re-

---

[1] Reference will be found in the Notes. See in particular Note 75 on Chapter III for Louvet de Couvray's *Faublas*; and see Note 159 on the same chapter for the puritanically squeamish Saintsbury's ridiculous exclusion of *Faublas* from his *History of the French Novel*.

[2] Cf. also the 'comédies *dell 'arte*', the charade-plays in the *Chartreuse de Parme* (Ch. XXIV); but here only the outline of the plot was given, and the actors invented the dialogue as the action unfolded.

spect of Herbert's looks, by 'To give pleasure while they last to others; as a singing bird does, or a flower'. He constantly seems on the verge of saying things as bold as any said by d'Albert in the freest moments of his pagan cult of beauty; had he let himself go, one feels, and given full expression to his creed or values, he would have thrown off (preferably in French, and with the most natural air in the world) heterodoxies such as the following:

> 'Le Christ n'est pas venu pour moi; je suis aussi paien qu'Alcibiade et Phidias . . . Je pense que la correction de la forme est la vertu.' 'Le précieux don de la forme anathématisée par Christ . . .' 'Ce qui est beau physiquement est bien, tout ce qui est laid est mal.' 'Je préfère une épaule bien modelée à une vertu, même théologale; je donnerais cinquante âmes pour un pied mignon.'[1]

On the other hand, d'Albert would have been mightily pleased to have composed Mr. Linley's tirade on behalf of distinction and aristocracy against the dull democratic tendencies of Nature:

> 'I fear sometimes that nature is a democrat. Beauty you see is an exception; and exception means rebellion against a rule . . . Nature, I think, if she had her own way would grow nothing but turnips . . . It's the same with all exceptions, beauty which is best of all, and genius . . . Each of these is an insult, an outrage, an oppression and affliction to the ugly, the stupid, the poor and the despondent.'

In this part of his philosophy, which is a fine challenge to the spirit of the Sermon on the Mount, or at least in this attack on Nature, Mr. Linley has more affinity with Baudelairean doc-

---

[1] Cf., in *A Treatise of Noble Morals* (a section of *Lucretia Borgia*), 'A beautiful soft line drawn is more than a life saved; and a pleasant perfume smelt is better than a soul redeemed'; and many other things in the *Treatise* which might have been written by Mr. Linley and by the character in *Mademoiselle de Maupin* through whom Gautier expresses the boldest part of his philosophy.

trine than with anything formulated by Gautier's apostle of Beauty. Mr. Linley of course may have reached his conclusions by original ways of his own (and certainly his manner of putting things in the passage under discussion is not wanting in originality). But it is interesting to note that in his *Salon de 1845*, and also in his *Salon de 1846*, both of which Swinburne had read when he wrote *Lesbia Brandon*, Baudelaire speaks (and primarily if not entirely from an aesthetic point of view) very scathingly of Nature, which both Romantics and Realists in their different ways regard with immense respect. 'Bête comme la nature', he says in the former of these works; and, in the latter, 'la première affairs d'un artiste est de substituer l'homme à la nature et de protester contre elle.' And Mr. Linley's defence of feminine make-up reads like an echo of Baudelaire's proclamation of 'la haute spiritualité de la toilette', and of his assertion that 'la mode doit être considérée comme une déformation sublime de la nature, ou plutôt comme un essai permanent et successif de réformation de la nature.' (See Note [105] on Ch. III of *Lesbia Brandon*.) But it is very doubtful whether Swinburne had read *Le Peintre de la vie moderne* (in which Baudelaire's apologia of make-up occurs) when he wrote this chapter of *Lesbia Brandon*. *Le Peintre de la vie moderne* appeared in the *Figaro* towards the end of 1863, and was not published in a volume till 1869. It is most unlikely that Swinburne saw the numbers of the newspaper in which it came out; and it is pretty certain that Chapter III of *Lesbia Brandon* was written before 1869. It looks therefore as if here Mr. Linley had reached Baudelarian conclusions quite independently of the French writer.

Continuing our investigation of certain or probable influences,[1] we may note that the use of incriminating letters (in

---

[1] Lafourcade is very unsatisfactory here. For instance, he vaguely mentions Gautier's *Mademoiselle de Maupin* and Balzac's *La Fille aux yeux d'or* (but no other works of this writer) as influences in the case of *Lesbia Brandon*, but he does not specify any details, he gives nothing in the way of evidence; and he completely fails to see that both these

Love's Cross Currents as well as in *Lesbia Brandon*) was perhaps suggested by *Les Liaisons dangerouses*, where this device is one of the chief elements in the evolution of the plot.

But Swinburne's own description of *Lesbia Brandon* as 'a sort of étude à la Balzac plus the poetry' indicates that in his own eyes the author of *La Comédie humaine* was a principal —if not *the* principal—influence in respect of the more novelistic part of the work, as distinct from anything purely poetical in it. (As regards 'the poetry', his own by now independent and sure genius had no need to receive lessons from anybody.) Is any Balzacian influence traceable beyond that (far from negligible) to which I have already drawn attention? There is in the important matter of physical portraiture (which at the same time is meant to be psychological). Now it may well be that this part of what Chesterton calls 'the task of giving an account of a human being' is feasible to no more than an extent so small as to be derisory compared to what can be done by other arts in this direction. And this can be enlarged to a general doubt whether, as is usually if not universally supposed, it is one of the functions of literature to describe: whether description in the strict sense of the word can be effected by the resources that belong to literature. It may be that, as Mérimée said, no words can exactly describe the qualities of a work of art (nor, therefore, he could have added, the qualities of a human body or anything else that may be the 'object' of a work of art). Bourget was pretty certainly right when he said that the roughest sketch can reproduce any object whatsoever far more successfully than the most masterly piece of writing. ('But,' Bourget added, 'no picture, however masterly, can render, as writing of a certain kind can, the *impression* produced on a human mind by an object'—and that re-establishes literature in its own province

(Note ¹ *Continued)*—
French works, as well as much in Swinburne, have as a grand source the novel of Latouche which he crassly dismisses as unmeritable and of no importance.

with the glory of its own powers.[1] And in this province, we may say in passing, Swinburne is excelled by no-one.) Arnold Bennett was beyond any doubt right when he affirmed that 'Descriptions of facial detail are almost invariably quite futile.'

Perhaps a feeling, more or less clear, on the part of writers, that literature was ill-equipped for work of this kind, and a consequent failure to attempt to make any progress in the matter, accounts for the extreme poverty of physical portraiture in fictional and other compositions before Balzac came along with different ideas. In any case, the extreme poverty is a thing that cannot be denied. The Marquis de Sade's portraiture, for instance, is factually terribly superficial and banal, and it is sometimes eked out by the cheapest of metaphors. 'Her features were sweet and delicate, her skin had the whiteness of the lily, her mouth, fresh and most pleasantly embellished [with teeth], was like a rose in spring-time'. Or, 'She had very white skin, beautiful blue eyes, and a welladorned mouth'. Or, 'She had beautiful fair hair, large blue eyes full of tenderness and modesty, and skin white as a lily and fresh as a rose'. And so on: he never gets beyond that. But Sade, it will be said, isn't a first-class writer, and his performance doesn't count as evidence. But Sade in this matter is really representative of practice in general, effects such as his are common to the great mass of literature before the period of Balzac. Diderot, for example, who may be regarded as the founder of modern art criticism,[2] and who tried hard to render effects secured by painters, is, in his *Salons* and also in

[1] How wrong, in the light of the former of the truths enunciated by Bourget, is Gide when he says: 'A vrai dire, en art, il n'y a pas de problèmes—dont l'œuvre d'art ne soit la suffisante solution'.—And how right he is in the light of the second. (I am fully aware of the philosophical difficulties inherent in Bourget's word 'impression', which raises the knotty question of subject-object relationship, and of the whole process of perception. The point would be less debatable if one replaced 'impression' by 'spiritual emotions'.)

[2] I mean of the best kind, which conveys with beauty as well as competence the beauty of the work of art which is under consideration.

his novelistic work, scarcely, if at all, superior to Sade when he has to describe faces. Nor is Bernardin de Saint-Pierre, who did so much to advance the description of scenery (in which he was one of, and probably the chief, of Ruskin's masters, a fact that has never been duly recognised).[3] This general observation may be extended from French to English and all the other literatures of Europe.

Now Balzac, more than anybody else, changed all this; for Balzac, rightly or wrongly, did not have the pessimistic view of the capacity of literature for portraiture held by the eminent critics and practitioners whom we have cited. His attitude, his belief in the possibility of disengaging and conveying significant facial details, is well summed up in the following:

'Le visage de la femme a cela d'embarrassant pour les observateurs vulgaires, que la différence entre la franchise et la duplicité, entre le génie de l'intrigue et le génie du cœur, y est imperceptible. L'homme doué d'une vue pénétrante devine ces nuances insaisissables que produisent une ligne plus ou moins courbe, une fossette plus ou moins creuse, une saillie plus ou moins bombée ou proéminente. L'appréciaiton de ces diagnostics est tout entière dans le domaine de l'intuition . . .' (La Bourse.)

Hence the very detailed, the carefully elaborate or analytical description of physical and especially facial qualities in book after book of the immense production of Balzac; there is nothing comparable to it in the work of any of his predecessors. Take, for instance, the portrait of Camille Maupin in Béatrix;

(Note [2] Continued)—
Lessing and Winckelmann do not lead to the Goncourts and the other masters in this high line of literature.

[3] For the novelty and recency of the full consciousness of the problem and the attempt to tackle it (but only so far as scenery was concerned), cf. the following sentence, written by Bernardin de Saint-Pierre when, rather late in life, he was beginning to practise the craft of writing: 'L'art de rendre la nature est si nouveau, que les termes mêmes n'en sont pas inventés'.

in my edition no less than some twenty-four lines are given to the eyes, ten to the nose, eleven to the mouth, and so on.

To give an adequate idea of Balzac's powers as a facial portraitist alone would require the space of a small book; and adequate treatment of the whole subject would require a fairly large one. (This important branch of literary technique has never received due investigation; most books on literature never deal with essentials. And this is still more true of articles of the review order, particularly in what the French all too loosely call the 'Anglo-Saxon' world.) I shall limit myself here to his rendering of eyes, and shall give only a very few samples out of the *embarras* that present themselves:

'Des sourcils noirs et fins, dessinés par quelque peintre chinois, encadraient des paupières molles où se voyait un réseau de fibrilles roses. Ses prunelles allumées par une vive lumière, mais tigrées par des rayures brunes, donnait à son regard la cruelle fixité des bêtes fauves et révélaient la malice froide de la courtisane. Ses adorables yeux de gazelle étaient d'un beau gris et frangés de longs cils noirs, charmante opposition qui rendait encore plus sensible leur expression d'attentive et calme volupté; le tour offrait des tons fatigués . . .'—(*Une Fille d'Eve.*)

'C'est le dernier effort de la nature que ces plis lumineux où l'ombre prend des teintes dorées, que ce tissu qui a la consistance d'un nerf, et la flexibilité de la plus delicate membrane. L'œil est au repos là-dedans comme un œuf miraculeux dans un nid de brins de soie. Mais plus tard cette merveille devient d'une horrible mélancolie, quand les passions ont charbonné ces contours si déliés . . . Ses yeux, dont la couleur était un gris d'ardoise qui contractait, aux lumières, la teinte bleue des ailes noires du corbeau . . .' —(*Splendeurs et misères des courtisanes.*)

'L'arc des sourcils, tracé vigoureusement, s'étend sur deux yeux dont la flame scintille par moments comme celle d'une étoile fixe. Le blanc de l'œil n'est ni bleuâtre, ni semé de fils rouges, ni d'un blanc pur; il a la consistance de la corne, mais il est d'un ton chaud. La prunelle est bordée d'un cercle orange. C'est du bronze entouré d'or, mais de l'or vivant, du bronze animé. Cette prunelle a de la profondeur. Elle n'est pas doublée, comme dans certains yeux, par une espèce de tain qui renvoie la lumière et les fait ressembler aux yeux des tigres ou des chats: elle n'a pas cette inflexibilité terrible qui cause un frisson aux gens sensibles; mais cette profondeur a son infini, de même que l'éclas des yeux à miroir a son absolu. Le regard de l'observateur peut se perdre dans cette âme qui se concentre et se retire avec autant de rapidité qu'elle jaillit de ces yeux veloutés. Dans un moment de passion, l'œil de Camille Maupin est sublime; l'or de son regard allume le blanc jaune, et tout flambe; mais au repos, il est terne, la torpeur de la méditation lui prête souvent l'apparence de la niaiserie; quand la lumière de l'âme y manque, les lignes du visage s'attristent également. Les cils sont courts, mais fournis et noirs comme des queues d'hermine. Les paupières sont brunes et semées de fibrilles rouges qui leur donnent à la fois de la grâce et de la force, deux qualités difficiles à réunir chez la femme. Le tour des yeux n'a pas la moindre flétrissure ni la moindre ride. Là encore, vous retrouverez le granit de la statue égyptienne adouci par le temps.'—(*Beatrix*.[1])

Compare now Swinburne's account of Margaret's eyes in the first chapter of *Lesbia Brandon*: once more it will be seen what he meant when he said that he was writing 'un étude à la Balzac'.

In this matter, it is doubtful if anyone has gone beyond Balzac in France; it is certain that in English literature no-one has exceeded Swinburne, or even touched him at his best.[2]

---

[1] For another specimen, that of the eyes of Paquita Valdes, to which Swinburne refers in the first paragraph of *Lesbia Brandon*, see the 5th Note on Ch. 1.

[2] Gautier is generally more summary, less resourceful, more traditional, in his portraiture; but on occasions he does work comparable to Balzac's, probably under the influence of the latter; and it is likely

And his best is better than Balzac's best; the latter's descriptions often produce the effect of a congested catalogue, a pell-mell accumulation, and their final impression is rather turbid. Swinburne's are never like this: each item is effective, and the sum-total is no less decisively so on its own larger scale.

Another point in which Swinburne followed Balzac's procedure was in such conversations or discussions as those in Chapter III, on literary and other matters; these may seem overlong, and not to be relevant to such plot as the book possesses, but that is quite in the manner of Balzac. Compare, in *Illusions perdues*, the talk between Lucien de Rubempré and Daniel d'Arthez on Scott, Richardson, and the novel in general; the long dinner-party conversation, in the same work, on journalism; and, also in the same work, the even longer discussion, at a dinner-party give by Lucien, of journalism and literary matters. Compare the same thing in *Un prince de la bohême, Les Comédies sans le savoir*—and in a fair number of other works.

It may be said in defence of such talks that they are not really excrescences, or gratuitous additions; that they, as much as action, are an expression, a further illustration, of the characters who engage in them. This is especially true of Balzac; and it is true of Swinburne to an even greater degree. Moreover, Swinburne's conversations of this category are not nearly so long on any one subject as are most of Balzac's. And it is not Swinburne's habit to go off into essay-like digressions, usually terribly long, as Balzac frequently did. For instance, there is one of over a dozen pages in *Les Employés* on the French Civil Service; there is another long one in *Illusions perdues* on the French banking system; and, in the same book, yet another on the paper industry, tracing its development from its earliest beginnings in China! This last might be a parody of this bad habit of Balzac's: it pre-

(Note ² Continued)—
that he reinforced Balzac's influence on Swinburne in this part of the novelist's craft.

cedes a long conversation (between two lovers!) on the same subject, and is introduced with these words: 'This long parenthesis between a lover and his beloved will no doubt gain by being summed up in a preliminary statement'! There is only one case of this Balzacian abuse in Swinburne; this also occurs in the third chapter of *Lesbia Brandon*; but on revision, although excellent in itself, it was too much for Swinburne's sense of fitness, and he drew a line of deletion through it.[1]

Another of the Balzacian *longueurs* that Swinburne avoided was the lengthy preliminary section, the prolegomena in which are presented the main characters and perhaps something of the situation. The introductory part of *Lesbia Brandon*, which some may consider too protracted, is tiny compared with a typical initial presentation from the works of the French writer. The first part of *Béatrix*, for example, entitled 'Les personnages', runs to 131 pages; it is only on p.132

---

[1] See Note 120 on Ch. III. It may also be noted that Swinburne's literary, etc., conversations are never as long (and dull!) as are frequently those of Proust, who, like Joyce and others, has been elevated by ignorant or perverse *snobisme* to a place altogether beyond his due. What Arnold Bennett says in this connexion (*à propos* of *Du Coté de chez Swann*) does not call for much qualification:

'The *longueurs* of it' are 'insupportable, the clumsy centipedalian crawling of the interminable sentences inexcusable. The lack of form or construction may disclose artlessness, but it signifies effrontery too. Why should not Proust have given himself the trouble of learning to "write" in the large sense? Further, the monotony of subject and treatment becomes wearisome. (I admit that it is never so distressing in *Swann* as in the later volumes of *Guermantes* and *Sodome et Gomorrhe*.)'

And again, *à propos* of Proust's work in general:

'He will write you a hundred pages about a fashionable dinner at which nothing is exhibited except the littleness and the naïveté of human nature . . . Again, he cannot control his movements; he sees a winding path off the main avenue, and scampers away further and further and still further, merely because at the moment it amuses him to do so.'

Bennett of course rightly finds also in Proust things worthy of no small praise.

that the story proper, with the part called 'Le drame', really begins; of 'Les personnages', the first forty-two pages consist practically altogether of descriptions and what follows is pretty well all descriptive.

Of course most of these *longueurs* are an inevitable part of his grandiose design 'to paint the dress, furniture, houses, interiors, and the private life, as well as the spirit of the epoch' which was the setting of his various novels. They are bound up with his ambition to be a Cuvier, a Geoffroy Saint-Hilaire on the subject of modern man viewed as a resultant of environmental forces, of the society in which he has his being. But Swinburne did not follow him in this line of activity, which really is history, sociology, and a species of natural science, rather than literature in the more specific sense of the word.

But in the course of his work Balzac gave a large place to passion, which for him was of capital importance; he introduced 'faits étonnants', 'choses effrénées', and a good deal that was pathological; moreover, he sometimes (happily) forgot his theory of the *milieu* (which is a kind of Marxist determinism), and presented characters not as products of environment (which is never more than *conditioning*), but as they were in virtue of certain inner forces which belonged to them at birth. In all this he is, in a general way, a large influence on Swinburne. And he is, again, through the fundamental drive of his nature. In spite of his frequent pratings of the Throne and the Altar (which superficial critics take at their face value), he was not really orthodox, he was very far from being a Christian in the true or essential meaning of the word. His temperament was revolutionary, and his work, on the whole —in its spirit, if not always in the letter—is a powerful negation of the values that go by the name of orthodoxy.[1] Here he

[1] Certain more or less conservative or traditional critics have been very conscious of this. Philarète Chasles, for instance, called his *Comédie humaine* 'monstrueuse'. Pontmartin said that he had 'assaisonné de maximes légitimistes ses peintures équivoques, comme un

was a master of Swinburne, and his influence in this respect is not limited to *Lesbia Brandon*.[2]

I have now, I think, sufficiently indicated what Swinburne meant when he said that *Lesbia Brandon* was an 'étude à la Balzac'; and sufficiently indicated also the other influences which went to its making. It only remains to enquire what, in the upshot, is the value of this work. I have already done this in respect of the characters; the chief of them at least, I have tried to show, are original and largely unique, and I am confident that many readers will find them truly alive: a thing one cannot establish by debate. I have also discussed the plot, as far as it can be seen in what we have of the book; it will no doubt be agreed that it is well conceived and highly ingenious—and ingenious not only in the superficial or external way in which those of most stories of the mystery-type are, but in such a way—the Racinian way—as to be revealing of character in the play of its dynamics.

The charge most likely to be brought against the book is that it is wanting in unity. What, for example, have such chapters as 'Another Portrait' and 'An Episode' to do with the plot or the main theme? Certain things must be kept in mind here. In the first place, Swinburne could not have lapsed or departed from any canonical standard because of mere ignorance of the principles of the craft. He knew all about the art of the novel—as much as Saintsbury, say, or Henry James (and indeed much more than the latter, for he had a much better mind than this rather fumbling and somewhat old-womanish American who tried to make himself a European). His various essays on novelists—from which one could

---

(*Note* ¹ *Continued*)—

pharmacien halluciné qui délayerait de l'arsenic dans le l'eau bénite'. According to Thureau-Dangin (*Histoire de la Monarchie de Juillet*), 'La chasteté même chez lui est corrompue'.

[2] Was there anything positive as well as destructive in Balzac's revolutionary side? This question, as far as I know, has not even been raised in any of the large mass of studies devoted to him; the answer to it, as I see it, I shall postpone to one of my later volumes.

collect a pretty complete aesthetic of the novel—are decisive proof of this.

Secondly, he was as little deficient in actual capacity as in knowledge of the craft; he had shown in *Love's Cross Currents* that he could write a novel as strict and shapely in its unity and general economy as any that has satisfied the most canonical standards; that is, within the limitations and with the handicaps imposed by the epistolary form; here he is as competent as Laclos, who was—and still is—the master *par excellence* in this domain of the novel. Let us admit, however, that such seemingly transgressive chapters as 'Another Portrait' would have remained as they are, and would not have been modified in their effect, had Swinburne completed the book. They are not really foreign to the main theme; for the main theme is not Lesbia Brandon, as the title most inappropriately given to the work by Wise and Gosse suggests, nor the love affair between Herbert and Lesbia together with the other love affair which has some organic connexion with it. The main theme is Herbert Seyton much more than Lesbia Brandon and anything else, Herbert Seyton and his development and fortunes, intellectual and spiritual no less than sentimental; 'Another Portrait', then, and 'An Episode' are fully in place from this point of view.[1] *Lesbia Brandon* is

---

[1] Because of a failure to see these facts and others to which I am drawing attention, Lafourcade emits such crudely wrong judgments as the following on *Lesbia Brandon* as a novel:

'Le récit est dépourvu du minimum de vraisemblance [!] et du minimum d'unité qu'il faut pour faire un roman.' '*Lesbia Brandon* n'est pas un roman au sens propre du mot.' 'Ce demi-chaos . . .' '*Lesbia Brandon* n'est pas sous sa forme actuelle un roman mais plutôt un journal intime.' '*Lesbia Brandon* sera purement et simplement un réservoir commode où Swinburne va déverser le trop plein de son génie.' 'Tout ce que Swinburne ne pouvait introduire—pour des considérations diverses—dans ses œuvres publiées il l'a déversé dans le cadre commode de ce qu'il appelle un "livre hybride".'

This last pronouncement is particularly inept; for Swinburne put what was then unpublishable—at least under his own name—into such compositions as *The Flogging Block*, which might well be called a 'réser-

primarily a novel of character; and as Swinburne himself rightly says in his *Note on Charlotte Brontë*, things that would be 'damning flaws' in a novel of mere incident, and other things that would be ruinous in a novel of mere manners, are of only minor importance in a novel of character; and Stevenson, an excellent critic of the craft,[2] has the same right idea and goes as far as to say that 'a novel of character requires no coherency of plot'.

Flaubert gave expression to the same principle—that a novel of character is not amenable to the same requirements as other types of novel—in connexion with the structure of

(Note [1] *Continued)*—

voir' (or a 'déversoir'); and anyhow, while writing *Lesbia Brandon*, and long after, he fully intended that it should have the fullest publicity. If, as is unlikely, Lafourcade only means that any of the contents of *Lesbia Brandon* could not have been fitted into the structure of other works, Swinburne could easily, with additions where necessary, have published these as prose sketches or vignettes, or something of the sort (as later he did in fact publish separately the sections in verse). But Lafourcade's main contention is absurd. So far from being a sort of rag-bag, a hotch-potch of odds and ends, as Lafourcade believes. *Lesbia Brandon*, to any but purblind or squint-eyed vision, has, in spite of its multiple elements and variety, no small traces of design. It was obviously conceived as an entity with its own particular or peculiar unity, and it is not merely a haphazard collection of parts that are altogether discrete. We can be certain that, as in the case of *Love's Cross Currents* and the Winwood story, Swinburne followed his usual practice and began by writing a plan. It is unfortunate that nothing of this survives. (Cf. the explicit expression of Swinburne's belief in the imporance of planning: ' "How greatly it is all planned!" [he is citing Goethe], the first requisite of all great work . . .' This principle governed the structure of his work over the whole of his career. Of course he often modified a plan as the composition proceeded; but he never departed from design, for which he had a strong instinct, as he had for law in general in truly spiritual matters.)

[2] One of Saintsbury's numerous howlers is his disparagement of Stevenson as a critic. It seems to me that the latter's work in this line is superior to most of his achievement in fiction and to the whole of his achievement in all other lines. Saintsbury accuses him of ñot having 'fixity or grip', but that is just what he had: a firm grip of what is fundamental in the novel.

his *Madame Bovary*. Having reached page 260, he was some-what worried to find that so far he had not yet got to the true action of the novel, that in all this space there was nothing but presentation of characters, description of places, scenery, etc.: nothing but preparatory matter, in short. The narrative of the death of Emma, her burial etc., was going to take up at least sixty pages. So that only one hundred and twenty, or at the most one hundred and sixty, pages would be available for the action proper—and this disproportion, Flaubert re-flected with dismay, was a very serious fault (he was writing the letter containing these details at night, when after a hard day's work, he was apt to be pessimistic and to lose sight of the book as conceived when his mind was in a healthier state). But on further reflection he brightened up, for, he said, the work was 'une biographie', or a novel of character, and not a 'péripétie développée', or a novel of dramatic action with its parts organised accordingly—indeed of drama in the strict sense of the word there was very little in it. And so what would have been a fault in a novel of this latter category was not one in a novel dealing for the most part with character.

Far too much novel-criticism explicitly or implicitly has as a criterion an ideal type of novel, to which I have applied the word 'canonical'. What is this ideal type? It has frequently been defined, and the definitions all agree in essentials. I shall give a few English examples. Hardy desiderates 'a well-rounded tale', one that is 'an organism'; and the meaning he gives to this latter word is rather superficial, for if a story is to be organic 'nothing', he says (citing Addison on the epic), 'should go before it, be intermixed with it, or follow after it, that is not related to it.' Stevenson, a much greater writer than Hardy (who is scarcely a writer at all) or Addison, puts the same thing very much more attractively. According to him, there should be 'a series of impressions all aiming at the same effect, . . . all chiming together like consonant notes in music or like graduated tints in a good picture'; there should be 'one creative and controlling thought; to this must every incident and character contribute . . .' Arnold Bennett lays it down that 'Every episode must directly assist the progress of the tale'; and, not content with that, he makes the astonishing, or at least very contestable, statement that 'It is useless to urge that such and such an episode, though it does not help the actual story, illustrates a character or confirms an atmosphere.'

To these English examples there might be added numerous French. (Indeed, in the modern world France is more than any other country the home of the ideal, the place whence it has been diffused and where it has been upheld and applied with the fullest consciousness.) Of these numerous examples I will cite only one: Bourget, one of the subtlest of French critics, and a novelist of a good deal of technical competence. He is a stout champion of the ideal: a novel of any kind, he maintains, must, like a drama, be 'composed', must be proportioned and organised so that it constitutes a true unity, its parts must be subordinate and contributory to an effect larger than themselves that is a harmony. This 'beauté de composition', this quality of ordered and harmonious unity, is, proclaims M. Bourget, pre-eminently a French quality, it is the chief glory of French literature, and it should never be given up. It is present in, for example, Corneille, Racine, Molière, La Fontaine; in *La Princesse de Cleves, Candide, Manon Lescaut, Eugéne Grandet, Colomba, Madame Bovary, Germinal, François le Champi, Le Nabab*: in the greatest or most notable of French works from the seventeenth century classical period to the time (1921) when Bourget was writing his essay. But it is not present in, for example, *Don Quixote, Robinson Crusoe, Wilhelm Meister, Rob Roy, David Copperfield, The Mill on the Floss, L'Education sentimentale, War and Peace, Anna Karenina, Crime and Punishment,* all of which Bourget counts as masterpieces. But the lack of it in them is a flaw, a source of weakness: each of them is less of a masterpiece than it would have been had it been 'composed' as are the works cited in the other list.

Now even some of those who formulate and sponsor this ideal admit in other places exceptions or qualifications which rather damn it. Stevenson, for example, in his affirmation that 'a novel of character requires no coherency of plot'. I would impugn the ideal as a canon to which novels in general are amenable; it is exceedingly narrow and particular, and only defines one out of many estimable kinds in the world of the novel. (It could be perfectly realised in a yarn of external adventure, a common-or-garden detective story, and other sorts of trivial compositions that might be called the dregs of literature.) There have been cogent protests against it; one of the best of these is that of H. G. Wells, from which the following are a few extracts:

'If the novel is to be recognised as something more than a relaxation, it has also, I think, to be kept free from the restrictions imposed upon it by the fierce pedantries of those who would define a general form for it . . .'

'The underlying fallacy is always this: the assumption that the novel, like the story [i.e. the short story] aims at a single, concentrated impression. From that comes a fertile growth of error. Constantly one finds in the reviews of works of fiction the complaint that this, that or the other thing in a novel is irrelevant . . .'

'Nearly all novels that have, by the lapse of time, reached an assured position of recognised greatness, are not only saturated in the personality of the author, but have in addition, quite unaffected personal outbreaks . . .'

'The novel I hold to be a discursive thing; it is not a single interest, but a woven tapestry of interests; one is drawn on first by this affection and curiosity, and then by that . . .; and I do not see that we can possibly set any limit to its extent.'

Wells rightly goes on to say that the greatest of the English traditional novels, so far from conforming to the canonical ideal, are in no small degree discursive. There is in them a 'lax freedom of form', a 'rambling discursiveness' and a 'right to roam'. The greatest of these sinners is Sterne, and Wells proclaims that he is 'the subtlest and greatest *artist*—I lay stress upon that word artist—that Great Britain has ever produced in all that is essentially the novel'.

Hardy is constrained to admit that the 'fewness' of the novels satisfying what he takes to be the ideal standard 'is remarkable'; and he feebly explains this (being a person of very limited literary vision and information) as due to the fact that the art of novel-writing is still in its infancy. There's a good time coming (is the thought of this mediocre artist) when all first-class novels will conform to the facile exigencies of the orthodoxy which to him was definitive.

Arnold Bennett, too, in spite of his draconian laying down of the law, had (in a later book) to allow that the facts of the novel in its greatest examples were against his grand principle:

'I now have to admit that the modern history of fiction will not support me. With the single exception of Turgenev, the great novelists of the world, according to my own standards, have either ignored technique or have failed to understand it.'

(What he ought to have said of course was that they understood and observed a technique different from the canonical one which he, like Hardy, imagined to be valid and requisite for all novelistic work—for all sorts and conditions of novels.)

It is unquestionable (except by incompetence) that Bennett and Wells and Hardy are right in their affirmation that the immense majority, the quasi-totality, of great English and other novels are far from satisfying what is generally accepted by criticism as the ideal. To take only one English case, Sterne, whom Wells proclaims the greatest artist of all, he is so much at variance with the canon that, as Saintsbury observes, 'many, if not most of his letters might have been twined into *Tristram* without being in the least degree more out of place than most of its actual contents'. One could cite equally notable cases in the history of the French novel. Proust, for instance, who has had an enormous vogue, and still passes as a master novelist. His work is eminently and flagrantly a negation or flouting of all that is most holy in the canon.

Even among Bourget's typical exemplary French novels there are some which are offences against the canon, are not 'composed' in the sense to which he lent his powerful advocacy. Zola's *Germinal*, for instance, and Daudet's *Le Nabab*: these consist of a series of episodes, which are not interdependent and indispensable parts going to form a harmony. Other episodes could be added—and even certain of the existing episodes might be suppressed—without any substantial impairment of the general aesthetic effect of the work, without any disturbance of the economy governing its construction. This is not true of a play of Racine or of Ibsen, say, which might be taken as models of 'composition' according to Bourget's ideal. And is not *Madame Bovary* itself, which is another of Bourget's exemplary novels, and is generally regarded as a model of novelistic construction, rather a work of the same class as *Germinal* and *Le Nabab*? Is it not a sequence of episodes in the same way as (although in a lesser degree than) is *L'Education sentimentale*, which Bourget includes in his black list of novels which, although of high merit, are relatively inferior because they are not constructed according to the grand principle? (Cf. Flaubert's own account, cited a few paragraphs back, of the construction of *Madame Bovary*.) Furthermore, Bourget's claim that 'composition' (in his and Stevenson's and Hardy's and Bennett's sense) is a distinguishing feature and glory of French novelistic as well as other literature is subject to considerable qualification even as regards the classical period up to the nineteenth century. In this, no doubt the safest of epochs in Bourget's eyes, there are so many exceptions to the rule that the rule is rather itself an exception. Not only novels, like *L'Astrée*, anterior to Corneille's *Le Cid*, which may be said to have introduced or at least to have firmly established the canon in modern Europe, but novels coming after *Le Cid*, such as *Cassandre*, *Le Grand Cyrus* and *Clélie*, are far from being 'composed'. They are eminently (and from the point of view of Bourget, Hardy, etc.) terribly episodic; any number of episodes could be added to them, and almost any number subtracted from them, and they would remain fundamentally the same. Things are no better after *Le Princesse de Clèves*, which *is* 'composed' (but, like *Manon Lescaut*, another of Bourget's models, it is not a novel, but a *nouvelle*, or a long short-story, which has a special technique of its own). Typical chief novels after *La Princesse* are Lesage's *Gil Blas*, Marivaux's *La Vie de Marianne* and *Le Paysan parvenu*, Voltaire's *Zadig* and *Candide*, and Rousseau's *La Nouvelle Héloïse*: all these, too, are episodic in structure. Thus the principal French novels of the classical period, as well as many of the major ones of more recent times, are in architectonic a series of episodes. In other words, their construction is additive and not organically unitary, as is demanded by the canon. Moreover, Bourget, like Bennett, recognises as great works written by men who 'have ignored or failed to understand technique': the canonical technique which for him is the one and only norm and ideal after which all novelists must strive.

In view of all this, one may well wonder whether the ideal is legitimately enforceable on the novel; and not only that, but also whether it is germane to, congenial with, or implicit in the true and specific nature of the novel. Is there not some radical mistake on the part of those seeking to impose it? The above-mentioned fact (I think it is a fact, in need of little qualification) that the canon was introduced or established in modern Europe by *Le Cid* suggests that perhaps it is proper to drama, is valid and essential only in the case of work dramatic in its nature, or subject to the same conditions as drama.

For this tentative conclusion, reached some time ago, I am glad to find strong confirmation in two essays of Thibaudet, read only after I had sketched the preceding paragraphs. Thibaudet says, in effect, that the canon, the ideal of an organic unity whose parts are the elements of a harmony, belongs to drama, and to drama he adds oratory of the kind cultivated by the Greeks and Romans and such modern masters as Bossuet. The canon arises from the very conditions governing a play or an oration; both these kinds have at their disposal a limited time, and for them the primary problem is to produce the maximum of effect within this very small temporal space. The problem is more imperative for drama than for oratory, because drama is severely selective: it chooses for treatment only certain moments: moments in which a situation has reached a critical point. But in the case of both kinds the most effective solution of the problem is found in a certain grouping of parts, so that they reinforce one another; in an order which is a steady progression towards the producing of a master effect. This grouping, this order, is the 'composition' that is an article of the gospel of novelistic technique according to Stevenson, Hardy, Bennett, Bourget and other literary magnates. This is the canon which the good Hardy thinks will govern the novel more and more as it gets beyond its 'infancy'. In varying degrees, it was formulated by Aristotle for drama, and by Aristotle, Cicero, Quintilian and others for the art of oratory. At the Renaissance it was recovered from these writers, and so has become a force in the modern world. But in casual origin it belongs only to the play and to the oration; from these it derives its *raison d'être*; and by extension it belongs to any kind of writing that has to meet the same problem as these two forms of art. It is valid therefore in the case of the *conte* or short story, and of the *nouvelle*; for these have to get a maximum of effect within an area of time that is sensibly limited. But it is not valid or necessary in the case of any kind of literature which is not at the mercy of time. The epic is one such kind (although the shallow Addison, uncritically followed by Hardy, thought it was governed by the canon). The *Iliad*, the *Odyssey*, the *Aeneid*, etc., are episodic or additive in their structure. The novel, too, is not subject to temporal limitation. That being so, there is no imperative reason why it should observe the canon; nay more, a technique of another order may be more apt, more natural to it on account of this large fundamental difference. Here one might write Q.E.D

Thus, a little hard thinking, a little investigation into first principles, in other words a little real philosophy, is enough to enable Thibaudet to show that an ideal which many critics would erect into a law is for the most part an error. (But philosophical thinking—which simply means getting down to essentials—is exceedingly rare in English criticism; there is very little of it in Saintsbury and still less in most of the rest of the academic and other pundits who pass as having authority. As for the great majority of journalistic reviewers, who every week cry up noteless ephemeral trash and give it the label of genius, their knowledge of fundamentals, and cerebration concerning them, come to exactly nil.)

These more or less dialectical conclusions are borne out by facts (which indeed started the line of sceptical thinking at the end of which lay the conclusions). In spite of strenuous attempts to impose upon it the 'composition' proper to drama, the novel has always tended to adopt another form of technique. It has always tended to be episodic rather than, or instead of, organic as is drama of the stricter sort. Of course, as a general rule, the principles of the canon come—or should come—into play to a certain extent in each of the separate episodes of a novel; the point is that they have no *a priori* authority over a novel in its whole development, apart from each of these constituents. And of course there are notable novels which in their entire or general structure observe the canon, but there are exceedingly few of them: as is more or less dolefully admitted by the most fervent supporters of the canon. Moreover, the technique proper to drama—designed to get a maximum of effect within narrow temporal limits— may lead to unfortunate results if used in the novel. Swinburne, a first-class critic and aesthetic philosopher—although he is often content to throw off profound observations without systematically developing them—notices this danger. Thus, speaking of Charles Reade, he says that 'if some of his best effects were due to his experience as a dramatic aspirant, not a few of his more glaring faults as a novelist are traceable to the same source'. And, talking of *Griffith Gaunt* in particular, he says that Reade 'saw, with the quick eye of a cunning playwright, the splendid opening for stage effects of surprise, anxiety, and terror, supplied by means of' a certain incident 'to the future progress of the story: he could not forego such magnificent opportunities: he would not see, he could not consider, what a price he would be obliged to pay for them: no less that the inevitable destruction, in the mind of every reader worth having, of all sympathetic or serious interest in the future fortunes of his hero'. Contrariwise, he observes, Scott 'was hampered as a dramatist either by his habit of narrative writing or by his sense of a necessity to be on his guard against the influence of that habit'. Again, Richard Brome, he thinks, 'in our own day would have won higher distinction as a novelist than he did in his own as a playwright . . . In fact, his characters are cramped and his plots are distorted by compression into dramatic shape: they would gain both in execution and in effect by expansion, dilation, or dilution into the form of direct and gradual narrative'. These passages, and the last in especial, indicate that Swinburne well understood that—and in what respects and for what reasons—the technique most natural to the novel differs from that most appropriate to drama. 'Expansion, dilation', etc.: here we have the cardinal point: the novel is not confined within limits as in drama, and can range at will, and—among other processes—can adopt the mode of growth that I have called additive. And, boldly entitling one of the chapters of *Lesbia Brandon* 'An Episode', Swinburne showed that he was alive to this point: the novel of its nature is episodic rather than organic in the manner of drama, particularly when it is to a large extent a biography. (But, in *Lesbia Brandon*, he did not limit himself to the episodic technique. *Lesbia Brandon* is not simple but complex in its structure; as I have stated in an earlier part of this chapter, it contains besides the episodes a plot which in its psychological mechanics is of the Racinian order; and this plot (as far as can be judged from the work in its unfinished state) is not dissonant with the episodic structure: it merges with it in a way that is perfectly harmonious. This, if not unique, is one of the several things that give no small distinction to *Lesbia Brandon*.)

So much, then, for the canon.

In the light of all this, any charges of discursiveness, laxness of structure, want of unity that may be brought against *Lesbia Brandon* from the canonical point of view are of no weight at all; especially if it be remembered that it is first and foremost a novel of character and also an 'étude à la Balzac', and not a work according to the more canonical standards of Laclos, which Swinburne had already shown he could satisfy in a masterly degree.

From the foregoing considerations, also, it matters not at all that the work is 'hybrid', as he himself described it. By this he chiefly meant that there was poetry in addition to the Balzacian elements, prose poetry and also poetry in verse.[1]

Altogether, the one and only serious defect of *Lesbia Brandon* is that it was never brought to completion. On the whole, it is a masterpiece awaiting consummation, like certain of the great statues of Michael Angelo.

This judgment will doubtless come as a surprise and perhaps an offence to prejudice unused to thinking of Swinburne as having any capacity as a novelist.

As for the matter of the work, as distinct from its structure, there is little to be said here. Critics of the poor Matthew Arnold type, who want such things as messages, will not find them in *Lesbia Brandon*. Great art does not deal in goods of that kind (or if it does it gets none of its greatness thereby). *Lesbia Brandon* is a tragedy, a tragedy of waste arising from error in the constitution of things (called by optimism an order) to which human life and all its aspiration is subject. 'The mystery of the cruelty of things', 'sunt lacrimæ rerum',

---

[1] Cf., to name only one example, Peacock. In the latter's work—where, by the way, the story is a very minor matter—there is a lot of inset verse. Swinburne may also possibly (but not probably) have meant by 'hybrid' that in addition to being a novel of character the work was in places a novel of manners (as are most, if not all, works dealing chiefly with character).

'vanitas vanitatum': all the great cries of despair incriminating the cosmos might serve as an epigraph to it—as they might to so much of what is best in the literature of the world. To ask what it means is the same as asking what *Hamlet* or *Othello* or any other of the great stories of tragic waste really signifies. The answer to the question may well be that the tragedy *is* a tragedy, from any point of view, and that, as Glycon's epigram has it, everything is dust and nothingness and a derision, for everything comes out of unreason. But that takes us into metaphysics.

For the rest—the prose-poetry (the verse needs no special advocacy)—there will probably be less predisposition to contest that it is of the highest order. There is much more of it than in *Love's Cross Currents*, and much of it is greater than any in the latter; where there is such a foison of excellence it is difficult rather than easy to choose a few examples. Among the scenic descriptions I would mention in particular that of the suave amenity of the country around Eton as opposed to the wild vigours of the land by the North Sea; that of *Kirklowes* (in the second chapter), so remarkable for the sparse economy with which it suggests abandoned desolation; and the marine pieces, where economy gives way to an opulence that conveys the beauties and moods of the sea in the fulness of its multitudinous powers.[1] Two other prose poems that cannot be kept out of any set of examples—they are indeed the best of all—are the magnificent dream at the end of Chapter VII, which equals and surpasses anything that has been achieved by any worker in *surréalisme* (which did not begin with the on the whole abortive efforts in that line of the present century); and the other dream-piece, in Chapter XVI, describ-

[1] There are traces of Ruskinian influence here. But Swinburne, while easily equalling Ruskin's most successful pictorial feats, is far superior to him in grace, as well as in effects of sheer poetry. With Swinburne, grace, sure concinnity of form, is constant and unfailing in all sections of his writing. With Ruskin, it is precarious and intermittent, and for the most part informs his prose only when his imagination is touched into poetry.

445

ing the ghostly underworld and the pale sovereignty of Proserpine.

Proceeding from glories of general effect to details, one might cite numerous instances of triumphant phrase-making.[1] From this abundance I give only a few:

> Margaret 'grew troubled as a water grows without perceptible wind'.
>
> 'sense unawakened and the dubious heat of dormant blood.'
>
> Lesbia 'was warm and wan as a hot day without a sun'.
>
> Of Prosperpine: 'she had grey eyes, bluish like the mingling of mist and water'.
>
> 'his bitter and wrathful despair of delight.'
>
> 'in an exquisite agony of virtue'.
>
> 'the murmur of unseen motion in the long quiet of profound noon.'
>
> 'the blue horror of remote darkness.'

Sometimes the chief potency of these remarkable phrases resides in an epithet, used somewhat unconventionally:

> 'noble *gradual* rivers'
> 'the low remote chime of the *regular* sea'
> 'a stately *recluse* beauty'
> 'with clenched *instinctive* hands'

Swinburne's style is apt not only for poetic purposes; it is multi-competent, and can work effectively in practically all domains; here are examples of homely phrase-making far removed from the heights of poetry:

> 'She would afterwards drop the victim as a sheep with its owner's mark well singed into the fleece.'

---

[1] On this and cognate matters see also my centenary article on Swinburne in *The Nineteenth Century* of June 1937.

'A woman's consistency . . . stamped with the domestic trademark.'

'A love of durable homespun quality, good as a working or a walking dress.'

If it be said that stylistic excellence is not of much importance in the novel, it can be answered, not only that this is very contestable (Flaubert, for instance, would have contested it strongly), but that Swinburne used his style very effectively to secure results that belong altogether to the novel. I have tried to show this in much of what precedes; to what I have already said I will merely add as instances two other things: in Chapter XV, the last meeting of the lovers, and the agonised wait of Margaret, while talking and singing to her children, for the news of the shot that has killed all her happiness; and, in the following chapter, the last of Herbert's frustrate interchanges with Lesbia, and her slow lapse into death, through desirous dreams of fever, and bitter regret and wonderment grown into a great weariness. This is novelistic work in the highest. In view of it, and of other things of a like quality, one cannot help regretting a little that Swinburne did not devote to the finishing of *Lesbia Brandon* and to other work in the novel some of the large amount of energy he expended in writing his dramas in verse. The latter are full of noble poetry and subtle psychology, and I have a great love for them; but they are largely in the idiom of another age; had he completed *Lesbia Brandon* and gone on to other work in the same line, not only would he have certainly taken a place in the first rank of novelists, but he would have had much more influence on his age than he had as the writer of most of his dramas. I would rather have a finished *Lesbia Brandon* (or even *Lesbia Brandon* as it is) than the greater part of *Mary Stuart*; and more work like *Love's Cross Currents* than *Locrine*, with all its virtuosity. One of the several things for which one can never forgive Watts-Dunton is that he thwarted the progress of *Lesbia Brandon*, denigrated Swinburne's capacity as a novelist, and discouraged him from doing

447

more in this direction. This damns him as a critic (if not also as a friend), in spite of the considerable reputation he managed to acquire.

Even so—everything adverse notwithstanding—, one can make large claims. In *Lesbia Brandon* (as well as in other prose works) Swinburne is consummate as a master of style, and not only of style that has in it the powers of poetry. In the whole range of the English novel there is no-one who excels his in this respect, and it can even be said that there is no-one who reaches his level. And as a novelist pure and simple, on the basis of *Love's Cross Currents* and what is best in *Lesbia Brandon*, he is entitled to a place in the first class. This judgment will more than probably be disputed and ridiculed, especially in an artless age which salutes the crudities of the contemporary American novel as estimable, and has an *engouement* for much else that might have been composed by Caliban. But those who attack *Lesbia Brandon* as a novel must define what for them is the norm of the novel; they cannot condemn it in the name of what I have called the canonical standards, for, as I have shown, those standards are not applicable here. (They cannot even say that Swinburne was incapable of satisfying those standards, for *Love's Cross Currents* shows that he could.) In general, they must refute the aesthetic arguments I have advanced in this matter, and I venture to believe that this is no easy business. More particularly, they must prove that the many clinching excellencies to which I have drawn attention are not excellencies at all; this is even harder, and indeed impossible, and a dogmatism of blank negation will be the only course here. (Blank it will be in more senses than one, and good men will know it for the utterance of that thing, 'énorme', with its 'front de taureau', on which Baudelaire exercised his scorn.)

Whatever the immediate upshot of the inevitable quarrel, I am convinced Swinburne's place among the greater English novelists will be assured in time, in spite of superstitious obscurantism, which is as obdurate in literature as it is in the religious field.

THE TEXT

CHAPTER III

THE TEXT

1. *The Manuscript*

THE FOLLOWING IS A BRIEF TABULAR ACCOUNT OF THE manuscript as, arranged and bound by Wise, it exists at present in the British Museum. The initial numbers are mine:[1] they indicate the order of the chapters or sections in this disposition of the text, accepted as definitively right by Lafourcade, and hitherto questioned by no-one:

1. My chapters I and II, conjoined by Lafourcade (probably with Wise's concurrence) as though they were unquestionably one chapter. The title, *A Character*, is inscribed at the top of the first page; it is more than a little doubtful whether it is in Swinburne's handwriting. The last extant word of my Chapter I is right at the end of the first page of the third sheet, and the sentence is unfinished. The first extant word of my Chapter II is right at the beginning of the fourth sheet and necessary antecedent words are wanting. Obviously[2] an uncertain number of pages are missing between the present third and fourth sheets. Two small concluding strokes in Swinburne's handwriting after the last words of Chapter II show that the chapter finishes with them.

[1] Wise nowhere gives any systematic enumeration of the chapters; he does not even state what he thinks is their total number.

[2] Only 'seemingly' to Lafourcade's mentality: 'Quelques pages manquent tout au début, et aussi, semble-t-il, entre 3 et 4'. There is no reason at all for supposing that anything is missing 'tout au début'. Further discussion of this point will be found in the fourth of the footnotes in Section III of this chapter on *The Text*.

2. *A Day's Work*. My Chapter III. The title, which is in Swinburne's handwriting, follows, on the same page, immediately after the concluding strokes of the second chapter. A concluding stroke in Swinburne's handwriting after the last words shows that the chapter is complete.

3. Chapter beginning 'After that day's work' and continuing as far as 'without colour in her life'. No title. About the first four-fifths of my Chapter IV. The first words are at the top of a fresh sheet and are probably the beginning of the chapter. The three words of the last line of the MS. (in her life.') are right at the bottom of the page. They are followed by no concluding stroke and the section is almost certainly incomplete. The first paragraph of galley 28 (the MS. of which is not extant), manifestly a fragment and belonging to a different chapter from that of the paragraphs succeeding it in the galley, follows more naturally here than anywhere else, and I have detached and transferred it to this position. Even with this addition it is doubtful whether the chapter is complete.

4. Chapter beginning 'The house had by this time'. My chapter V. No title. The first words are at the top of a fresh sheet and are probably the beginning of the chapter. The last words are not quite at the bottom of the page. No concluding stroke. The chapter is obviously unfinished.

5. Section beginning 'He woke his father'. My chapter VI. No title. The first words are at the top of a fresh sheet. The last are about four-fifths down the page, of which the rest is blank. No concluding stroke. The section is obviously unfinished and is no more than a fragment of a chapter of which a preceding part was probably written but is missing, and of which the remainder was never composed.

6. *On the Downs*. My Chapter VIII. The title is not absolutely certain; it is in Swinburne's hand, but it is written not at the top of the first page, but on the otherwise blank

back of the last sheet turned upside down, about three inches from the bottom. The first words are at the top of a fresh sheet and are probably the beginning of the chapter. The last words are about a quarter down the page, of which the rest is blank. No concluding stroke. The chapter is probably unfinished.

7. *Uses of Prosody*.[1] I have rejected this from *Lesbia Brandon*. Title in Swinburne's handwriting at the top of a fresh sheet. The last extant word of the chapter ends right at the end of a page and the necessary grammatical sequence is wanting; therefore an uncertain number of sheets of the manuscript are missing at this point.

8. Chapter beginning 'Dis-moi-donc'. My chapter VII. No title. A concluding stroke in Swinburne's handwriting after the last words shows that the chapter ends with them.

9. *Arden major to Lady Waristoun*. I have rejected this from *Lesbia Brandon*. Title in Swinburne's handwriting at the top of a fresh sheet. A concluding stroke after the signature, which is more probably meant to be the author's than that of the writer of the letter. This may be part of a larger chapter or a little chapter in itself.

10. *An Episode*. My Chapter XI. Title in Swinburne's handwriting at the top of a fresh sheet. The words are about four-fifths down the page, of which the rest is blank. No concluding stroke. The chapter is obviously unfinished (and it is described as incomplete by Swinburne in correspondence with Watts-Dunton).

11. *Turris Eburnea*. My Chapter IX. Title in Swinburne's handwriting at the top of a fresh sheet. A concluding

[1] This title is preceded by the chapter number 16 in Swinburne's handwriting; how, in view of this (apart from other serious considerations), Wise justified the position of the chapter here must remain a mystery to commonsense or anything in the way of reason.

stroke in Swinburne's handwriting after the last words shows that the chapter ends with them.

12. *La Bohême Dédorée.* My Chapter XII. Title in Swinburne's handwriting at the top of a fresh sheet. The last words are near the top of a page, of which the rest is blank. No concluding stroke. The chapter is obviously unfinished (and it is described as incomplete by Swinburne in correspondence with Watts-Dunton).

13. Two chapters with disgracefully inexcusable stupidity mixed up, so that over some twenty pages one has an impression of lunacy. Disentangled, they are:

(*a*) *Les Malheurs de la Vertu.* My Chapter XIV. Title in Swinburne's handwriting at the top of a fresh sheet. The last extant word is right at the end of a page, and the necessary grammatical sequence is wanting; but it is given in the corresponding galley, and another sentence follows there. So that this is another case where Swinburne sent to the printers manuscript that has disappeared. Even with the additional matter in the galley the chapter is probably incomplete.

(*b*) Chapter beginning 'He stood looking away from her'. My Chapter XV. No title. The first words are at the top of a fresh sheet, and the chapter may begin here. A concluding stroke in Swinburne's handwriting after the last words shows that the chapter ends with them.

14. Chapter beginning 'Attilio Mariani died'. My Chapter XVII. No title, but '(For penultimate chapter)" is written in Swinburne's handwriting near the top of the page. As I show later, in Section III, these words in brackets almost certainly do not refer to the text that follows them. The last words are about three quarters down the page, of which the rest is blank. No concluding stroke. The chapter is perhaps unfinished.

15. *Leucadia.* My Chapter XVI. Title in Swinburne's handwriting at the top of a fresh sheet.[1] A concluding stroke in Swinburne's handwriting after the last words shows that the chapter ends with them.

* * *

As incidentally noted in what precedes, in the case of some chapters parts that were written are certainly missing, some chapters are (and always were) unfinished, and others are more or less probably unfinished. These facts may be tabulated separately as follows:—

MS. certainly missing	*Extant MS.* Ch. certainly unfinished	*Extant MS.* Ch. very probably unfinished	*Extant MS.* Ch. perhaps unfinished
1. (i) Last sentence of my Ch. I incomplete.	4.	3.	14.
(ii) Beginning of first sentence of my Ch. II lacking.	5. An earlier as well as a later portion lacking (perhaps sheets of MS. missing).	6.	
7. Last sentence incomplete.	10. (Described as incomplete by Swinburne.)		
13a. Last sentence incomplete.	12. (Described as incomplete by Swinburne.)		

These facts make nonsense of Wise's assertion that 'the manuscript is quite complete'—in however wide or however narrow a sense we take it. So also does the fact that there is no manuscript of the contents of two of the galleys—28 and 29

[1] *Leucadia* (cf. On the Downs of 6) is also written on the otherwise blank back of the last sheet turned upside down, about three inches from the bottom.

(which were in Wise's possession: evidently he never collated the galleys and what he had acquired of the manuscript).[1] Moreover, not only are certain of the extant chapters incomplete, as Swinburne himself declared in correspondence quoted my Wise, but parts of the novel as planned were never written, as Swinburne himself again made clear in the course of this correspondence. This renders ridiculous Wise's affirmation, already noted elsewhere, that 'when Swinburne spoke of' the novel 'as unfinished he meant that the work had still to receive its final polish'. Another point to be noted in the present connexion is that of the four chapters named by Swinburne in this correspondence (which we have cited in a preceding section) that which he calls *Another Portrait* or (alternatively) *Another Study*, is not among those of the British Museum manuscript. Yet Wise says that he purchased all these four chapters, and, if we are to believe him, *Another Portrait* is part of the manuscript in the British Museum![2]

[1] Had he done so he would not have been able to assert without any qualification that as the first step of his acquisition of *Lesbia Brandon* he 'purchased from Watts-Dunton Swinburne's own set of the galley-proofs . . ., *accompanied by the MS. of the matter carried by them*' (my italics). The second step, we may note here, was the purchase of three (wrongly given as four by him) chapters to which we shall refer presently. The third was the purchase of 'the balance of the manuscript from . . . Miss Theresa Watts' (this last lot can only be the section above which '(For penultimate chapters)' is written, and *Uses of Prosody*, and the letter to Lady Waristoun from her eldest son).

[2] Lafourcade, who had access to Wise's possessions long before they went to the British Museum (and even before Wise printed the statement in question) notes that this chapter is not one of those constituting the manuscript as it was acquired by Wise. Lafourcade's suggestion that *Another Study* or *Another Portrait* may be *A Character* (his Ch. I, my Chs. I and II) is far from happy. For Swinburne himself says that the former followed immediately on *Turris Eburnea* and, with it, belonged 'to a late part of the design'. Now *A Character* is obviously an early, indeed the earliest, part of the book—and the result is grotesquely chaotic if one thinks of it as following *Turris Eburnea*. But this would not arrest Lafourcade: we have here a good measure of his judgment in matters that are quite elementary.

In short, neither all of what Swinburne actually wrote, nor even all of what he sent to the printers is comprised in the manuscript which Wise finds complete.—Still less is it complete when viewed as representative of the novel which Swinburne purposed to write.

The shocking confusion of parts of *Les Malheurs de la Vertu* and of parts of the following chapter would be well nigh incredible in the case of anybody but Wise. The some twenty intermixed pages, one would have thought, must strike the lowest intelligence as being a mess and a muddle, intolerable, and probably rectifiable if only a little care were spent on it. (And as a matter of fact a little care does set it right.) And yet in the face of this (not to mention other glaring things) Lafourcade admiringly speaks of the 'patience infinie' with which Wise 'a reconstitué le MS., presque feuillet par feuillet'! The significance of the *presque* is not apparent: if the fellow didn't do it sheet by sheet he ought to have done: how else could he properly reconstruct the text? but perhaps the adverb is idle (that would not be astonishing on the part of Lafourcade) and is not meant to modify this superlative tribute to the genius of Wise. Anyhow, Lafourcade swallowed Wise's reconstruction whole, including this sense-defying confused section, and he also accepted here as one chapter what are evidently two. His resulting comment on this blockish conflation: 'texte très corrompu', is one of the most comical of many comical things in his Bœotian volume.[1]

At this point, before concluding discussion of the incompleteness of the British Museum manuscript, it will be

---

[1] Even the humble printers did much better here than Wise and his acquiescent panegyrist: they sorted out and put into the right order and gave as a separate chapter the sheets making up *Les Malheurs de la Vertu* as an entity distinct from what follows it. We have here another indication that Wise—and Lafourcade—did not discharge the elementary duty of collating the text of the manuscript with that of the galley-proof: had they done so they could not have allowed sheets of *Les Malheurs de la Vertu* to remain jumbled up with sheets that belong elsewhere.

convenient to deal with the sheets and the way in which they are paginated.

There are 184 sheets altogether; 19 of these (all my Ch. XIV and the first part of the following chapter) are quarto (white); the rest are foolscap of various colours (white, very light greyish blue, light blue, dark blue). Almost always Swinburne writes on only one side of a sheet; in four cases he continues the text on the back of a page; in nine other cases he utilises the back, but only to jot down additional matter for insertion in the text of the first page of the following sheet.

The first three sheets are numbered 1, 2, 3 in black ink, probably by Swinburne. They are also numbered in pencil; 2A is plain on the second; 3A is almost illegible on the third; there was presumably a 1A on the first, but it is now so faint that it is practically indiscernible even under ultra-violet rays. These pencilled numbers are pretty certainly Watts-Dunton's, for in an already cited letter to him Swinburne speaks of 'the first five leaves, numbered by you in pencil'. As we have noted, a portion of the text is missing after page 3. The next extant page and all those following it up to *An Episode* have no number in black ink; but as far as the end of my Ch. IV (beginning 'After that day's work') these pages are numbered consecutively 6a to 89a in pencil. Thereafter there are no pencilled numbers with little *a* attached. It is natural to assume that these further pencilled numbers, 6a–89a, are also Watts-Dunton's. Probably the alphabetical letter was used by him to indicate a sequence of pages composing a chapter. 6–89 (ignoring for the moment 1A, 2A, 3A) makes a very long chapter, of course. Swinburne, it would seem, at first went on continuously, with no division into chapters or sections, as far as the 89th page. (Why shouldn't he do this if his thought carried him on from point to point over however long a distance? Breaking up into sections, and even into chapters, is frequently felt as artificial: on the other hand, Joyce, e.g. in *Ulysses*, has huge sections, and, whatever else may be said about them, their length does not seem unnatural.) Watts-

Dunton, however, being, like most editors and publishers, mechanically conventional, and thinking frequent paragraphic and chapter segmentation essential, probably objected and persuaded Swinburne to introduce divisions into the lengthy section which he had distinguished by the letter *a*. It is pretty clear that Swinburne at least made one division *après coup*: he wrote in (the ink is of different colour) between two lines that were evidently continuous, the chapter heading *A Day's Work*.

We may note here that one of the sheets of this *a* set, that which should be 19a, is numbered 19–20a, and is followed immediately by 21a. This is curious. Looking at the text (p.   of this edition), we see that p.18a originally ended with 'rigorous hand and eye', and that the following page begins 'hardly over-strict': there is no continuity of sense. But in the exiguous space remaining at the bottom of p.18a Swinburne added, obviously later (the ink is different), 'he began to learn his paces bit by bit; a breaker who', and inserted 'was' above the line before 'hardly' on the next page. This restores a sequence of sense; but it looks as though Watts-Dunton had found a sheet missing after 18a (if he did not deliberately lose it!), and had indicated this by writing '19–20a' on what was really 20a; and it further looks as though Swinburne, faced by this *contretemps*, had on the spur of the moment replaced the contents of the missing sheet by inserting the words we have just cited. (These contents need not have occupied a whole page: he sometimes used only part of a page and then, still continuing the section, passed on to a fresh sheet.)

There is confirmation of the assumption that these *a* numbers are the right ones of the part of the manuscript distinguished by this letter. On the otherwise blank back of p.55a Swinburne wrote 'pp. 6–55' in black ink (no doubt when he sent the manuscript to be set up in type; and it was very probably then that he inserted the words we have noted above). This can only mean that there was here a batch extending from p.6 to p.55, both numbers inclusive. One thing is quite certain, and that is that the page on which he wrote these numbers could have been none other than 55. Now it is numbered 55a in pencil; and it may be safely assumed therefore that all the other pencilled numbers of the *a* series are correct. It follows, then, that 6a being really 6, to should be preceded by five pages to make up the tale of the series. The question now arises, are 1A, 2A and 3A part of these five? that is, did Watts-Dunton begin by using capital A and then inadvertently, at a now indeterminate point, go on to use little a? If this is so, then only two pages are missing between 3A and 6a. The portraits of the brother and sister might well have ended at some point of 4A (or a), and the part of the story introducing the father, with mention of the dead mother, and leading up to the father's death, might just possibly have been got into what space remained up to 6a. On the other hand, it is unlikely that Watts-Dunton would thus inadvertently or capriciously change from A to a; it seems more probable that Swinburne had a clearly indicated chapter or section division somewhere between 3A and 6a, and that Watts-Dunton designated the first chapter or section by the use of the capital. But in this case considerably more than two pages are missing; there are five of the *a* series, and an indeterminate number of the section marked with the capital. Perhaps Swinburne's already cited words 'the first five leaves, numbered by you in pencil' give the number of the sheets carrying A. That would mean that there are seven ($2 + 5$) missing sheets altogether in this part of the manuscript. This seems rather a lot; at least, while one feels that the A series is near its end, one does not feel that five whole foolscap pages of a new chapter preceded the matter of 6a.

It is possible, of course, that the *a* numbering was not done by Watts-Dunton; that it was done by Swinburne himself, who, remembering that Watts-Dunton had numbered the first five sheets in pencil with the addition in each case of the initial letter of the alphabet, but forgetting that it was a capital, carried on the process up to p.89 on the sheets that were in his possession.[1] All things considered, I strongly incline to think that this was the case. Swinburne's list of what was missing from the manuscript may be taken as complete; apart from the 'first five leaves', the items he gives (excepting *Another Portrait*) are precisely those portions of the British Museum manuscript which were not set up in type (I ignore *Uses of Prosody* and the *Letter from Arden major*, which I have given reasons for rejecting from *Lesbia Brandon*; and he does not mention these). It is safe to suppose, therefore, that 'the first five leaves' is an exact and exhaustive mention of all that was missing in addition to these other items. Had more than five been lacking, Swinburne would surely have said so. Now 1A, 2A, 3A like *An Episode*, etc., did not go to the printers. It looks then as if they were a part of the missing five; in which case only two sheets are wanting before that which bears 6a; and when Swinburne wrote 'pp. 6–55' on the back of 55a he meant they were pages 6 to 55 of the whole book and not simply of one of its parts. (Elsewhere, as we shall see presently, he did paginate chapters afresh, starting with 1 again on the first page of those in question.)

In any case, Lafourcade's affirmation that 'les 4 ou 5 premières feuilles semblent encore manquer' is an absurd error; as we have already remarked *à propos* of another of his affirmations to the same effect, the very first sheets are not missing at all: 1, 2 and 3 are quite plainly the opening of the book.

Lafourcade says in a footnote to the former of the two statements just referred to: 'Mr. de V. Payen-Payne possède dans sa collection 1 ou 2 de ces feuilles' ('1 or 2': the imprecision is curious coming from one researching on doctoral levels; it must have been very easy at the time to ascertain the correct

---

[1] It is not easy to pronounce on the handwriting where these pencilled numbers are concerned. The A series, as far as one can see them, *seem* to be in the larger, rather sprawling, hand that was frequently Watts-Dunton's; and the *a* series *might* be in the smaller and neater hand that was sometimes Swinburne's in his more composed moments.

number, and even to secure a copy of the sheet or sheets, and indeed it was nothing less than a duty to do so). I, unfortunately, have not been able to trace these 1 or 2 sheets (which, oddly enough, are not mentioned anywhere by Wise); if there were really two of them they almost certainly were the two which we have given reasons for supposing are the only ones missing between the third and fourth sheets of the manuscript as it exists to-day.

To return to and finish with the pagination. There are numbers in black ink (which may be Swinburne's) only in three other chapters: *An Episode, Turris Eburnea* and *La Bohême Dédorée*; the numbers are, respectively, 1 to 7; 1 (only); and 1 to 4. The only other chapters that contain pencilled numbers—which are more or less partially erased—are *An Episode* and *Turris Eburnea*; the visible numbers, in the case of the former, are 9, 11, 12, 14, on the sheets numbered 1, 3, 4 and 6 in black ink respectively (in what sequence of conjoined sheets the first page of this chapter became 9 is now beyond determination); in the case of *Turris Ebernea* there are visible 2, 3, 4, 5 on the corresponding sheets that make up that chapter.

In addition to the afore-mentioned numbers in black ink and pencil, there are numbers in red ink running continuously from 4 on the fourth sheet (6a pencil) to 195 on the 184th sheet. These red ink numbers were almost certainly written in by Wise in the blundering fashion that is characteristic of him. The order of the chapters, and even of sheets in chapters, is wrong, but he stuck in his red numbers as if the text thus huddled together by him were *ne varietur* for all time; and he had it firmly (and sumptuously) bound so that it should be consecrated for ever . . . . The disparity between 195 and 184 is accounted for by the fact that in some (not all: such is Wise's inconsistency) of the cases where Swinburne used both sides of a sheet Wise numbered both sides.

Besides all the foregoing numbers there are written on the text itself of the sheets of all but three of the chapters which were sent to the printers numbers in large characters which were presumably inserted by the printers. These numbers, which are sometimes in red ink, and sometimes in blue pencil, run thus: A1, A2, etc., B1, B2, etc., and the last of them is 118. Their sequence is erratic; thus the B series is on pages of one of the later chapters; moreover, the sequence is erratic even as regards the order of the galleys established by the printers themselves; thus E is on the sheets corresponding to the third set of galleys, and B on this corresponding to the 6th set. There is no F series: this was probably on the sheets (no longer extant) corresponding to the second set of galleys.

It perhaps should be mentioned for the sake of completeness that near the left-hand foot of an otherwise blank portion of the last page of *La Bohême Dédorée*, at right angles to the text above, there is written in faint pencil the following, in a hand that is pretty certainly not Swinburne's:

Comes in before No. 6 and before Shooting scene.

This is mysterious. What is 'No. 6'? And what is the 'shooting scene'? There is nothing such in the work as we have it; it may possibly be a loose description of the chapter (my XVth) in which Lady Wariston's lover leaves her to commit suicide by shooting himself; but the shooting takes place 'off stage' and cannot properly be called a scene.

On the same page, in the opposite direction to the text, there is also written in very faint pencil, again in writing that is not Swinburne's:

Original
MS
A.C.S.

Also, on the otherwise blank top of the first page of my Chapter XVII at right angles to the text, there is written in very faint pencil, in a hand that is probably Swinburne's:

Notes for last chapter.

463

The cancelled L is no doubt the first letter of *Leucadia*.[1]

It only remains to mention the watermark dates. All the chapters of the British Museum manuscript except *On the Downs, La Bohême Dédorée, Uses of Prosody* and the letter from Arden major carry watermark dates. The following is a table of these; the chapter numbers are those of the text as I have established it; I have not thought it necessary to give the page numbers of the sheets being the cited dates; this would have required considerably more space; but the order in which the batches of sheets follow one another is that of the text which they contain; thus, in Chapter III, the one sheet dated 1859 follows, in the text, four dated 1863, and is followed by 23 others dated 1863; but the sheets in each batch, when there is more than one, are not always immediately consecutive one upon another: there may be among them sheets that bear no date; thus, in the third batch of the third chapter (the second 1863 group) the second sheet immediately follows the first, but between the second and the third there are two sheets on which there is no date; and, of course, there may be undated sheets between any two of the groups (*see Table on p.*465).

As I have remarked elsewhere, the only sure inference to be drawn from any of these dates is that the text contained on the sheet bearing it could not have been written on the sheet earlier than the year in question. Those who, like Wise and Lafourcade, take a watermark date as indicating time of composition, should notice that in Ch. III one sheet dated 1859 comes after three issued four years later; and there can be no doubt that the text on the 1859 sheet was written after that on the three younger sheets. Again, the text of the eight 1859 sheets of Ch. XV belongs to a part of the book that follows as a consequence from Ch. XIV, which contains seven sheets dated 1865; and, what is more, the first eight sheets of Ch. XV, which precede those (foolscap) dated 1859, are white

---

[1] I shall discuss this pencil jotting further in section III of this chapter on *The Text*.

Chapter	Sheets	Date	Chapter	Sheets	Date	Chapter	Sheets	Date
I	2	1864	V	2	1864	XI (An Episode)	3	1866
II	8	1864	VI	1	1864	XIV (Les Malheurs)	7	1865
III (A Day's Work)	4 1 23 2	1863 1859 1863 1864	VII	1 (separate draft of ballad quatrain)	1866 (1864)	XV	8	1859
IV	1	1866	IX (Turris Eb.)		1866	XVI (Leucadia)	1	1863
						XVII	1	1866

quarto, precisely the same as those of Ch. XIV dated 1865, and (like the other sheets of Ch. XIV, also white quarto, which they follow immediately) they are probably the same age as these latter, particularly as this is the only part of the book where white quarto sheets are used.

If Wise had been alive to these elementary considerations he would not have boldly written 'Commenced in 1859 and completed in 1867' on the title page of his grandly caparisoned redaction of the sheets of *Lesbia Brandon*. (Why 'completed in 1867'?: consistently with his own stupidity, he ought to have said 1866, the latest of the watermark dates borne by the manuscript.)

Bound up with the manscript are two pages of drawings by Simeon Solomon; one, 'Lesbia Brandon 27'; the other, 'Lady Midhurst aged 35' and 'Bertie aged 15'. The former of these pages has the watermark date 1812: one wonders what monstrosity of deduction would have been drawn from this by Wise.

So far I have spoken only of the British Museum manuscript. It is not however all that is extant of the novel in manuscript; only recently, after completing practically all that seemed possible of my work on the text I discovered that the MS. of the chapter entitled *Another Portrait*, which I had given up as lost, was really in existence. The discovery was accidental and incidental: I happened to enquire of the authorities of the Huntington Library, California, if they had, or knew anything of, the 'one or two' missing sheets of my Chapter I which Lafourcade recorded as being in the possession of Mr. Payen-Payne (who died some years ago). The Huntington authorities replied that they had the manuscript of a piece of prose by Swinburne, entitled *Another Portrait*, which might be the sheets I was looking for. They were not of course; but they were a welcome recovery of another part of the work which I had not even hoped might still be available; and I readily accepted the kind offer of the owners to let me have a photostatic copy of them for publication with the rest of the work.

They consist of three folio sheets of blue paper, of which the versos are blank. There is no concluding stroke, but the chapter appears to be finished. Two of the sheets have the watermark-date 1866.

Mr. Harmsen, of the Department of Manuscripts of the Huntington, informs me that *Another Portrait* was acquired on January 7, 1916, from the American Art Association in New York. The books and manuscripts which were sold that day came from various sources. *Another Portrait* was one of eight Swinburne manuscripts, identified simply as being the "property of a London collector". Who this person was, I have not been able to determine.'

All this is very mysterious. Who was this 'London collector' and how and from whom did he acquire *Another Portrait*? And what were the other seven Swinburne manuscripts that were in his possession? In spite of enquiries in many directions, I have so far received no enlightenment on these questions.

As regards the former, it is pretty certain that the 'collector' was not Wise; for, incompetent and conscienceless as he was, it is incredible that he would, for however tempting a sum, have parted with the chapter had it come into his possession. For he already had the bulk of the manuscript of the novel, which he regarded as one of his greatest treasures, and he would have been anxious to retain anything that helped it towards completion. His monetary cupidity was now so well satisfied that if it came into competition with his vanity as a prince of collectors, vanity would be sure to win.

Another part of the mystery is why Wise did not acquire this missing chapter. Is it at all probable that he, a professional collector, and in touch not only with all likely auctioneers etc., but also with all likely owners (such as Mrs. Watts-Dunton) of Swinburne material, was not aware that it had become purchasable? And, being aware, would he not have been prepared to pay as much or more than anybody else to secure this highly desirable addition to a work of which he already possessed the greater part of the manuscript? This is indeed a mystery, and very likely it will remain one.

Another question is why this chapter was not available as part of the second lot of the manuscript sheets which Wise, as he himself records, purchased from Watts-Dunton 'later in' 1910. In other words, why it was not procurable along with what may be called its companion pieces, *Turris Eburnea, An Episode*, and *La Bohême Dédorée*; (Swinburne, it will be remembered, named the four together in letters to Watts-Dunton when he vainly tried to recover parts of the manuscript retained by the latter). If the other three chapters were then at hand, why was this one not too?[1] Had Watts-Dunton

---

[1] Wise affirms that he bought 'the four chapters cited in Swinburne's letters'. But—assuming that he means the four I have named, and not three of these and some of 'the first five leaves' also mentioned by Swinburne (of which he says nothing)—this cannot be true, as I have already shown in this section. We may further note that he nowhere speaks of *Another Portrait* as being, or having been, in his collection; and Lafourcade, who was in close contact with him and the collection,

hidden it separately, and so well that it remained undiscovered for some time after his death? Few detective stories are more intriguing than this enigmatic affair—stretching from about 1875 till after Watts-Dunton's demise in 1914—of the suppressive retention and concealment of parts of *Lesbia Brandon*; here, alas, the only detection has been that of the crime itself; the mystery in which it is involved has only increased with the appearance of fresh data.[2]

The only other portions of manuscript that I have been able to see are not really additional, but merely duplicative; they are those of two ballad quatrains of Chapter VII, and are described in the 7th of my notes on that chapter.

It is convenient to give here a few particulars of the manuscript of the *Kirklowes* fragment, a first tentative out of which *Lesbia Brandon* grew. It is written on seven sheets of white foolscap followed by a double sheet of blue foolscap. Except in the case of the second white one, Swinburne used the backs of the sheets, very irregularly at times; for example, page 8, which is on the back of sheet 5, is a continuation of page 7, which is on the other side of that sheet; but $3\frac{1}{2}$ lines on the back of page 1 are a continuation of page 8; and $2\frac{1}{2}$ lines on the back of page 9 (sheet 6) are a continuation of the text of page 11, which is on the back of sheet 7 turned upside down. The only watermark date, 1861, is on the first of the brace of blue sheets containing the last part of the fragment.

<hr>

(Note [1] *Continued)*—
definitely refers to the chapter as lost, and evidently had not the least suspicion that it had ever been in Wise's hands. Of course if Wise really did purchase the chapter along with the three others, there would arise a hypothetic possibility that he was the 'London collector' in question above, or that he disposed of the chapter to the latter; but I have already dealt with this possibility, and shown that it has all probability against it. Whatever the approach, one reaches the same conclusion: the chapter could never have come into the possession of Wise.

[2] I have modified my views on this matter in the light of information acquired since this work went to the press. See the *P.S. Note* that is an appendix to the Commentary (pp. 484-488).

As already stated, there are watermark dates on none of the sheets of *Uses of Prosody* and the letter from Arden major, parts of what I have called *Herbert Winwood*, another tentative on the way to *Lesbia Brandon*. Nor is there a watermark on the stray unattached sheet (unrecorded by Wise and as good as unrecorded by Lafourcade) containing a plan of this Winwood story.

As *Love's Cross Currents* belongs to the same cycle as the three works just mentioned, it may be interesting to note here that of its 39 watermark dates 37 are 1862 and the other two 1860; and each of the 1860 sheets is preceded as well as followed by sheets bearing the later date (Swinburne himself gave 1862–3 as the period in which this work was composed).

II. *The Galleys*

I have given introductory information on these in Section I. The set in the British Museum is complete. It is made up thus:

Nos. 1–24   : part of *Mary Stuart*.
„   25–97B : *Lesbia Brandon*.
„   98–101 : *John Jones*.

Thus there are 103 slips altogether in the set, No. 97 of *Lesbia Brandon* being followed by Nos. 97A and 97B.

The print is on one side only of large white sheets. In principle, there are two columns to a sheet; but sometimes there is only one column, or a portion of one, or one and a portion of a second. Each column which contains print is numbered; and galley-proof, or galley-slip, or galley, or slip is its technical name.

As Swinburne said in a letter cited elsewhere, the material printed in the galleys was 'most carelessly arranged'. It does not seem worth while to give an account of the whole series of the galleys; the following few details should serve by way of example. There are twelve lots or groups; the first lot, 25, 26, 27 contain my Chapter VII (Wise's Chapter 8), a section that certainly is nowhere near the opening part of the story. The fifth lot, 37 to 41 (inclusive) contains *Leucadia*, the last of Wise's chapters and the second-last of mine. Worse still, the first part of my Chapter XV (Wise's Chapter 13b) is contained in lot 12 (97–97B), the second part of it is contained in lot 6 (42–49), and the last part is given in lot 10 (91–92)! Here we have chaos emulative of that of Wise at his most characteristic.

As already noted elsewhere, there are no galleys for the following parts of the British Museum manuscript, as Swinburne did not send them to the printer: the first three pages (my Chapter I), *Uses of Prosody*, the letter from Arden major, *An Episode, Turris Eburnea, La Bohême Dédorée*, and my Chapter XVII (Wise's Chapter 15). *Uses of Prosody* and the letter did not go to the printer because (as I have argued in a previous section) they do not belong to *Lesbia Brandon*.[1] The rest did not go because Swinburne could not extract them from Watts-Dunton (at least this is true of the first three of them; it may also be true of Chapter XVII, but of this we cannot be sure; Swinburne, in the second of his extant requests to Watts-Dunton for return of the missing chapters says 'there may be more' than those included in his list).

On the other hand there are parts of the galleys which are not in the British Museum manuscript: the whole of the contents of galleys 28 and 29, and the following words at the end of galley 96:

> *he was not upon the whole scornful; but he was not happy at heart.*
> *'And now you see it has come to this'.*

The chapter to which these words belong, *Les Malheurs de la Vertu*, is the same in manuscript and galleys up to these

---

[1] And so it does not matter whether they were in Watts-Dunton's keeping or not; it is not probable that they were, any more than that the *Kirklowes* fragment was: like it, they belonged to an abandoned scheme superseded by *Lesbia Brandon*, and Swinburne would not have submitted them to Watts-Dunton.

words; the manuscript stops with the word preceding them; they provide the grammatical and other sequence which is here required. The contents of galleys 28 and 29 are printed as though they were a continuous chapter or part of a chapter, but this is clearly a mistake. The first paragraph does not cohere with what follows it, all of which is evidently part of another chapter. I have adjoined the first paragraph to the manuscript contents of my Chapter IV (Wise's Chapter 3), where it seems to follow naturally. Of the rest of galley 28, together with the whole of galley 29, I have made a new chapter[1] (which is more than probably incomplete at both ends), as it does not naturally take its place in any of the existing chapters of the manuscript.

What happened to these missing portions of the manuscript can be no more than a matter of conjecture. Perhaps Swinburne lost them at Glasgow; perhaps they went to Watts-Dunton and were carelessly or otherwise lost by him; or perhaps, as *Another Portrait* was until very recently, they are still extant, but cannot be traced. The incompetent Wise and Lafourcade do not so much as mention them, never (although they had access to all the evidence) having even become aware of the patent fact that they had once existed. It is passing strange (or perhaps it isn't) that they did not realise that a not inconsiderable part of the galleys was not in the text which they imagined was complete.[2]

Wise affirms (*S.Lib.*) that 'with the exception of *A Day's*

---

[1] That numbered XIII. That the printers could make the mistake of printing in a continuous block sections that do not go together is definitely proved by, for instance, galley 36, where the end of Chapter V and the fragment of Chapter VI are thus given, although they are on different sheets in the manuscript, and the latter obviously belongs to another chapter.

[2] As noted elsewhere, Wise states that he purchased, along with the galleys, 'the MS. of the matter carried by them'. Which—once again—shows with how little care he compared the printed with the manuscript text, and how little he can be relied on in even the most rudimentary matters of the business in which he palmed himself off as a master.

Work, galley 60, none' of 'the printed chapters' 'are supplied with individual titles as are those in manuscript';[1] that 'the text' of these galleys 'is corrected throughout in' Swinburne's 'handwriting';[2] that 'throughout the whole of the proofs the name of the lady [sic] is misprinted *Leslia Brandon*', and that 'in the present set Swinburne has altered *l* into *b*'. Every one of these statements is wrong. The title of another chapter, *Les Malheurs de la Vertu*, is given in the galleys. The only section of the text of these galleys that carries corrections in Swinburne's hand is the chapter *A Day's Work*, and even here only seven of the thirty galleys composing this chapter bear corrections by him. *Lesbia* is not misprinted *Leslia* throughout; it is given correctly in four of the galleys; and nowhere in the eight where *Leslia* occurs has it been changed by Swinburne.

Swinburne's emendations in these galleys are for the most part corrections of real printers' errors or omissions; but twice he makes additions to the text of the manuscript: in galley 71 ' "Cranberries", said Lady Midhurst' is expanded to ' "Three cranberries, you mean", said Lady Midhurst'; and in galley 72 'enjoined by the moralist' is enlarged to 'enjoined by the Roman moralist'; and sometimes he modifies punctuation or inserts punctuation where there is none in the text. I have incorporated into the text of this edition all the corrections which he made in the galleys.

The British Museum set of the galleys, which has been under discussion up to this point, was not the only one that was printed, and is not the only one that exists at present.

There is one in the Brotherton Library at the University

[1] 'As are those in manuscript', taken in the normal sense of the words, can only mean that all the chapters in the manuscript are provided with titles; but only a few of them are; in *B.Bib*. Wise modified the clause to 'as are the four still in manuscript', but this doesn't mend the muddle, for more than four 'are still in manuscript', and they are not all provided with titles.

[2] Here, too, Wise modified in *B.Bib.*, and said 'carry numerous corrections in Swinburne's hand'. But there still remains considerable error.

of Leeds; many slips are missing from it, but many more slips than in the British Museum set contain corrections in Swinburne's hand; I have taken note of these in establishing the text of this edition. (It may be remarked that the misprint 'Leslia', as in the British Museum set, is nowhere corrected in the Brotherton set.) I am much obliged to Mr. A. Whitworth of that Library for helpful information, supplementary to that acquired by myself, with regard to these galleys.

Another set was sold in October of last year (1948) in London, to the Library of Harvard University; the Librarian of this institution has obligingly informed me that this set is complete, but that it contains no corrections at all.

Wise records (*S.Lib.*) that a set was sold 'in the American Art Galleries' in 1922; this set, according to him, is uncorrected, but he does not say whether it is complete, nor does he say by whom it was acquired. The authorities of the Huntington Library, California, have, however, kindly given me the following information on this set. 'It contained forty folio leaves numbered consecutively from 25 to 97B' (in other words, it was complete). 'There was no mention in the description of any corrections on the slips. The purchaser of this set is not marked in our copy of the sale catalogue.'

The Huntington Library itself has a set, 'purchased from Pickering and Chatto in 1920'; it is complete, but contains no corrections.

Mr. J. S. Mayfield, of Washington, D.C., has another set, from which are missing galleys 28 and 29, and also 73–97B (both inclusive). (It is strange that 28 and 29 should be missing from both this set and that of the Brotherton Library.) Moreover, there are here duplicates of ten of the sheets, and also of half of another sheet: that containing galley 42 (the other side, that on which was printed 43, had been cut away). In other words, there are here two incomplete sets, one more incomplete than the other. Mr. Mayfield had the extreme goodness to send me a photostatic copy of this double set. There are corrections on a number of the sheets; some of them are in Swinburne's hand, others in another hand, which

I identify as Nichol's; the different scripts are on different sheets, except in the case of one, where there are some of one and some of the other: probably these were two sets of the galleys which Swinburne had at Glasgow, in 1878, when he was staying with Nichol there. On one slip Swinburne altered 'Leslia' to 'Lesbia'; in all other cases where 'Leslia' appears (two of these are on sheets where Nichol made emendations) it is left uncorrected. (Which, incidentally, indicates that Nichol did not know the name 'Lesbia Brandon', and may be taken as a proof that Swinburne had not given the work that title.) For the rest, the only noteworthy correction of Swinburne's (apart from modification of such things as punctuation) is the deletion of '-proverb' in the MS. expression 'show-proverb' (galley 33, chapter V). I am informed by Mr. Mayfield that this double set once belonged to Wise.

Messrs. Pickering & Chatto Ltd. (London) have two further sets (April 1949). I am indebted to this firm for permission to inspect them: they are both incomplete, and neither carries corrections by Swinburne.

Another two sets are in the possession of Mr. E. H. W. Meyerstein, of London, who kindly placed them at my disposal. Two persons owned them before Mr. Meyerstein, and the former of these purchased them from Wise. Neither set is complete: one contains forty-two galleys (including Nos. 28 and 29), and the other only two. In both sets there are corrections by Swinburne; these I have adopted when they modify the text of the manuscript. As noted elsewhere, the fragment I have numbered Chapter VI and part of the preceding chapter are lumped together in galley 36. This latter galley is in both Mr. Meyerstein's sets. Someone (not Swinburne) drew a line down the right-hand margin of the fragment in both copies of this galley, and wrote 'Out of order'. Underneath these words Swinburne wrote 'rather!' in both cases. There is another confirmation of my text as given in the galleys. In No. 28 there is a small ink mark in the margin opposite the words 'The wicked and weary eyes turned upon her here', which are the beginning of a new paragraph. (I have assigned this paragraph and all that follows it in Nos. 28 and 29 to a separate chapter (XIII), and all that precedes it I have transferred to Chapter IV.) The marginal mark was very probably made by Swinburne; it was almost certainly meant to signify that there was something wrong here. There are other particularly noteworthy points in Mr. Meyerstein's galleys:

1. On the otherwise blank back of the sheet containing Nos. 91 and 92 Swinburne wrote 'Via Dolorosa' (with two strokes beneath it). This is very probably meant to be the title of the chapter (XV) to which 91 and 92 belong. I have placed it at the head of that chapter.

2. At the top of the set of verses beginning 'God send the sea sorrow' (towards the end of Chapter III) Swinburne wrote 'The Watcher' (galley 87). I have not put this into the text, as it is not likely that Lady Wariston, breaking into song as she did, would have given the title of the piece. Swinburne probably wrote it in many years later when he was thinking of bringing out the songs of *Lesbia Brandon* separately (this one however was never published by him).

3. On a blank space of galley 92 Swinburne wrote an extra stanza for *Willie's neck-song* (Chapter XV); this is the second stanza of the poem as it is published in *Poems and Ballads* III (under the title of *A Riever's neck-verse*). This stanza, like the aforementioned words 'The Watcher', was probably jotted down much later, when Swinburne was contemplating separate publication of the *Lesbia Brandon* poems. There are cancelled tentatives in the fourth line of the stanza. Following this stanza, there are tentative portions, all cancelled, of another stanza, which does not belong to *Willie's neck-song*. 'A weary weird to dree' and 'For ye sauld my life' are two of these portions.

There is also in the British Museum, in addition to the complete set, a portion of galley 43 (containing the poem now known as *Dolorida*—'Combien de temps, dis, la belle . . .', and other French verses of my Chapter XV, as well as English prose), and on it there are corrections in Swinburne's handwriting. This is very probably a part of the galley 43 that was cut away from one of the sheets of one of Mr. Mayfield's two sets. This is indicated by the fact that there are also alterations in Swinburne's hand on the half of the sheet in Mr. Mayfield's possession. Wise no doubt removed the half on which 43 was printed because it contained 'Dolorida', in which he had a particular interest.

It looks, then, as if (not counting the just-mentioned fragment) at least eleven sets were printed; I have made enquiries of Swinburne's publisher and also of the printing firm, but no information is now available as to how many were turned out.

In view of the fact that there are corrections by Swinburne in the Brotherton set, and also in one of Mr. Mayfield's (ignoring once again the fragmentary 43) it is absurd of Wise to distinguish as 'Swinburne's own set' that which he possessed (or retained), and which later went to the British Museum. For in the sense meant by him the Brotherton lot and Mr. Mayfield's were equally 'Swinburne's own set'. The poet apparently made use of different sets at different times; if there was another set or sets in which he made further corrections, it or they are not on record, as far as I can ascertain, and probably they have ceased to be extant.

III. *My Chapter Arrangement*

As a preliminary it may be noted that Lafourcade, who accepted Wise's sequence of the text (which, as I have more than once indicated, is absurdly wrong), failed to distinguish in that sequence the right numbers of chapters, plain enough to the most cursory inspection of ordinarily competent intelligence. I have given Wise's order of the sheets at the beginning of my section on the Manuscript; the sheets, thus arranged, form the chapters as there numbered by me (Wise attached no numbers to them): there are fifteen of them, but according to Lafourcade there are only twelve. There is no excuse for this blunder; he read the text so carelessly that he took as one continuous chapter 3 and 4, which are obviously quite distinct; he did the same with 7 and 8, which are no less manifestly quite separate; and he ignored 5 altogether, even omitting from his table[1] (as though it were missing) the number of the page on which it is written. Thus to his vision the fifteen chapters of the text as presented by Wise appear as only twelve. (Moreover, as we have already noted, he did not see that Chapter 13 of Wise's text is really a grotesque muddle of two chapters that could not possibly form a unity. Again, he gives no place in his table—he does not mention them anywhere—to the text of galleys 28 and 29; it is as though he had never seen them; but he must have done so, for—apart from the fact that they are in Wise's set of the galleys, to which he had access—he quotes a passage from the second of them.

I now pass to my own arrangement. Chapters 7 and 9 (*Uses of Prosody* and the letter from Arden major) of the text as presented by Wise I have rejected altogether from *Lesbia Brandon*, for reasons set forth elsewhere. The section given by Lafourcade (doubtless with the assent of Wise) as one chapter (the 1st), under the title of 'A Character',[2] I have given as two chapters, the first and the second, each of them without a title.[3] It would not be unusual for Swinburne to devote a relatively short chapter of a few pages to nothing or little but portraiture (cf. 'Turris Eburnia' and 'Another Portrait').[4]

---

[1] This table, giving his chapters and the pages composing them, will be found as part of a footnote on page 304 of text II of *La Jeunesse de Swinburne*.

[2] In the Bonchurch *Bibliography* (but not elsewhere) Wise applies this title to the text of the first three pages of the manuscript; so that it is just possible that he did not, conjointly with Lafourcade, regard this portion of the text and that of the following thirty pages as belonging to one and the same chapter.

[3] As I have already noted, 'A Character', written at the top of the first page of the manuscript, does not appear to be in Swinburne's hand.

[4] Lafourcade, as I have already mentioned in the section on *The Manuscript*, affirms that the first pages of this opening chapter are missing; but, as I remarked in that section, there are no grounds for this assumption. On the contrary, as I have shown in the same section,

The second, of which the first part is missing, doubtless opened with some brief account of Kirklowes and the father and the early stages of his death; the rest, the extant portion, continues without a break to Chapter III, by the title of which its final line is followed immediately on the same page: so that there can be no doubt of the sequence here. Chapters IV and V are in no need of discussion. The fragmentary VIth is, in the galleys, printed (in the same column) immediately after the last words of the incomplete Vth, with which it obviously has no connection. It is on a separate sheet of the manuscript. I have placed it between V and VII for the following reason. In Chapter III old Matheson's son is 'a small boy', 'about a year younger' than Herbert; i.e. he was then about 12. In this fragment he is a 'young fellow', and he acts as if he were not far from manhood. The date therefore may be placed between that of Chapter V (1854), when he would have been about 16, and that of Chapter VII, when Herbert was a young man (aged 24, if, as is probable, the events of this chapter and those of Chapter VIII take place in the same year). There seems to be no room for doubt as to the location of VII. I have placed VIII after it, as in VII Herbert's love for Lesbia

(*Note* ⁴ *continued*)—

there are the best of reasons for believing that of 'the first five leaves' which Swinburne in afore-cited correspondence with Watts-Dunton lists as missing, only the fourth and fifth have not yet been recovered. One thing alone would give colour to Lafourcade's affirmation, and that is that Swinburne in the second of the letters in question to Watts-Dunton speaks of 'five half-sheets of foolscap at the beginning' as among the parts missing. We have no *half*-sheets at the beginning. But it is pretty certain that Swinburne's memory betrayed him here. Examples could be given to show that it was fallacious regarding his past work, and the more so the further he was from that work. A cogent and opportune example is provided by this very correspondence; in the first of the two letters he mentioned 'Another Portrait' as one of the missing chapters; in the second letter, written only about a year and eight months later, he had forgotten its title, and called it 'Another Study'! The important thing is that in the first letter he spoke of 'the first five leaves', and did not call them *half*-leaves.

⁴ In afore-cited letters to Watts-Dunton.

is apparently not yet hopeless; after the talk with Lesbia in VIII all his hopes must be dashed, and he could not light-heartedly fling off songs. Chapter IX ('Turris Eburnea') can only come where it does, and Swinburne himself[4] says that X ('Another Portrait') comes immediately after it; he also indicates that XI ('An Episode') and XII ('La Bohême Dédorée') are the next in order. The fragmentary XIIIth is part of the text in galley 28 and the whole of galley 29 (the manuscript corresponding to these two galleys is apparently lost). The rest of the text of galley 28 is manifestly part of another chapter; I have added it to the manuscript text of Chapter IV, where it appears to be in place. Apart from this transferred portion, the text of galleys 28 and 29 seems to belong to a chapter close to XIV, and preceding it (see my remarks on this matter in the fourth section of my chapter entitled *The Story*). Chapter XV calls for no comment, but the relative positions of Chapters XVI and XVII is a matter of some difficulty. At first sight Chapter XVII is the second last chapter, for at the top of the sheet the words 'For penultimate chapter', enclosed in brackets, are written in Swinburne's hand. But there is a certain note of finality, something like a summing-up and dismissal, in the last paragraph, which would only be proper to the end of the whole book. This is particularly true of what is said of Herbert: 'As for him, I cannot say what he has done or will do[1] but I should think, nothing'. It is hard to imagine this sentence as coming before another chapter, concerned with Herbert as a lover of Lesbia. But, it will be objected, Chapter XVII records the death of Attilio Mariani, and in the second sentence of Chapter XVI we read that 'his old friend's death had hurt' Herbert 'for a time'. Surely this determines that the latter chapter should follow the former. Besides (it will further be argued), what about Swinburne's own words 'For penultimate chapter'? The objections appear formidable;

---

[1] A curious statement from the omniscient author, but one could cite hundreds of cases of this inconsistency from works of the best-known novelists.

they are not insuperable however. To take the first point first.
As I have suggested elsewhere, the phrase 'old friend' most
naturally refers to the dead lover of Margaret. If this lover
were Denham the phrase would fit him; if the lover were
Walter Lunsford it would apply to him still more; but
Mariani was a comparatively recent friend of Herbert's; and
the term 'old' in the other sense, that of advanced in years,
would not apply to Mariani either, for he was only about
thirty-five when Herbert first met him, a few years before the
time of his death. That the 'old friend' and the dead lover
are the same person seems to be indicated by the opening
words of the preceding sentence: 'Since his return from Ensdon'; which seems to imply that Herbert had been there in
connexion with the death of the person in question. Another
thing: Lesbia, in Chapter XVI, says to Herbert 'Only I wish
I were dying in Italy. Your friend never will'. Who other than
Mariani can 'your friend' be here? Evidently then he is still
alive (for Lesbia surely cannot mean 'he will never die in
Italy, because he has already died in England'), and so this
chapter cannot follow that containing the news of the Italian's
death. But 'For penultimate chapter'? Notice, to begin with,
that Swinburne did not write 'Penultimate chapter'. Now if
he had meant this chapter to be the penultimate one, would
he not have written no more than these two words? The addition of the preposition 'For' (and, it may be further said, of
the brackets) rather indicates that what was to follow were
notes for this chapter. But Swinburne evidently changed his
mind, and on this sheet wrote the last chapter instead of notes
for that preceding it. This hypothesis is reinforced by the
following fact: at the top of the sheet there is a blank of about
two inches in depth, and in the left-hand corner of this, at
right angles to the text of the chapter, there is written in
pencil that is now barely discernible:

Y

Notes for
last chapter

480

The cancelled L may be the first letter of 'Leucadia' (Chapter XVI) If this is so, it looks as though the intention of jotting down notes for 'Leucadia' was replaced by that of writing them for another chapter, which is described as the last. 'Leucadia', therefore, cannot be the last. In any case, independently of this fact, I think I have effectively disposed of objections and given sufficiently cogent reasons for my placing of these two final chapters.

The preceding chapter-order will be found to accord with the date-order as far as the latter is stated or is deducible from the context. For example, 1854 is given as the year of V. 1861 is deducible as that of VIII, for here Herbert tells Lesbia that he is twenty-four: from the fact (Chapter III) that in September 1850 he was thirteen, and from other concurrent facts, he must have been born in 1837. Further, the time here must be early spring, soon after Herbert's birthday, for 'Spring 1861' is given as the time of Chapter XI. And so on throughout: there are no temporal difficulties where chapter-order is concerned. But there are incidental difficulties of dates here and there, and of these I will note and discuss only the two following, which are the most important.

1.   The date of Denham's arrival at Ensdon in Chapter II. 'Twelve next month, is he?' says Denham of Herbert the day he arrives. In Chapter III Herbert tells Lady Midhurst that his birthday is 'in the spring'. The month is nowhere specified, but it was probably April, for Herbert is in large part Swinburne himself in his boyhood, and April was Swinburne's birth-month. Denham, then, must have arrived in, or very close to, spring 1849, and most probably in the second half of March. This is borne out by the statement in Chapter II that 'the last month or two of' Herbert's 'free childish life' is placed in the early part of the year: it is 'under March winds' that he runs wild by the sea during the final period of liberty before his tutor arrives. But Swinburne says in the same chapter that Denham 'arrived a month later [i.e. later than the previously mentioned 'towards the end of 1848'], in 1848'.

But this is inconsistent with preceding facts, and it can only be a slip. So bad a slip may seem scarcely credible, but it is not surprising in the case of Swinburne, who was very weak on dates, as numerous examples could be quoted to show. (Cf. Lesbia's remark to Herbert in Chapter XVI: 'I'm as bad a hand at casting up sums as you are'.) Even here he first wrote 'Mr. Denham arrived early in 1848'; then, no doubt realising that he was talking of a time later than 'towards the end of 1848', he struck out the work 'early'. But he ought to have further realised that still more correction was required, or rather that he had made a mistake in the correction. The 'early' which he had in his mind was right; it was the year that was wrong: 'early in 1849' was the correct date.

2. The date of Chapter III. The events of this very long chapter (which covers no more than two days) take place only 'a month later' than the time of the close of the preceding chapter; and as we read on we are surprised to find that we are in September 1850. This is absolutely certain. 'September' is in the text; and several allusions (Balzac's recent death etc.), as well as the words 'some two years after this, in 1852', fix the year more than once. But we have not the impression that anything like some eighteen months have elapsed since Denham's arrival early in 1849. September of *that* year would rather seem to be the right date. It is as though an intervening section of the story were missing; but this is not so in fact: Chapter III follows Chapter II immediately and on the same page of the manuscript (which shows how easy it is to draw wrong conclusions about missing sheets from difficulties in the story). We can only conclude that Swinburne failed to give any adequate indication of the longer space of time—if he was really conscious of it. 'Every Friday for some time', 'after some months had gone': a few vague phrases of this kind are all that we find to mark temporal advance in the period we are discussing. Swinburne, always a little hazy about such matters (in spite of carefully drawn-up preliminary plans or synopses)

did not trouble to see if he had sufficiently observed the calendar.[1]

---

[1] Such carelessness is not uncommon in the English novel; Thackeray in particular is a great delinquent here, as even Saintsbury, his most fervent thurifer, has grudgingly to admit: 'Thackeray's sins (if in novel-writing it be no blasphemy to say that Thackeray sinned at all) are gross, palpable . . . In particular, if anyone will try to arrange the chronology of the various Pendennis books, and if his hair does not turn white in the process, he may be guaranteed against any necessity for a peruke arising from similarly hopeless intellectual labour'.

A P.S. NOTE

ON THE PROVENANCE OF THE MS. OF
ANOTHER PORTRAIT

IN SPITE OF ALL THE COMMONSENSE REASONING TO THE contrary in the immediately preceding section—reasoning that would have been perfectly valid if anyone of normal intelligence were concerned—I now believe that Wise was, or at least may well have been, the London collector to whom *Another Portrait* belonged before its sale in the American market. The following is the reason for this change of an opinion based on presumption apparently so strong that it had all the force of certainty.

I recently saw (and acquired) at the establishment of Messrs. Maggs Bros., London, a number of Swinburne manuscripts purchased by that firm from Wise a long time ago. One of these items I had immediately recognised as belonging to an unpublished play of Swinburne of which 121 pages are now in the British Museum. Before the Museum acquired it this play was in the possession of Wise and is listed and described in more than one of his catalogues. The description is crudely incompetent, but it shows that Wise had at least glanced at the play and must therefore have seen the names of the characters. Some of these names appear in the fragment which is now in my possession. Moreover, 121 pages is a large amount: it is very nearly the whole of the play. The arguments therefore I have used in the case of *Another Portrait* are fully applicable here. Wise, having, and keeping, very nearly the whole of the play, could not have been the person who owned and sold the manuscript pages that very clearly belong to it. But he *was* that person: he did own and he did sell these pages . . . The argument therefore, sound if one were dealing with a person of normal intelligence and morality, is defeated by facts that lie beyond the normal. It is no more valid for *Another Portrait* than it is for this fragment. If Wise could sell the latter and thereby spoil one of his treasures, he could equally sell the former and thus harm another of his treasures.

Was he criminally indifferent to the integrity of his possessions? We know that this close associate of Gosse was a criminal; not only was he a forger, but he certainly in some cases did break up manuscript wholes and sell the pieces. But he was also a prize dullard; and here it seemed that he was merely stupid to an unbeatable degree (I say 'seems', for it is always possible that in cases like the present the criminal, the conscienceless money-grubbing vandal, was also at work. But in what follows I shall give him the poor benefit of the doubt, and assume that he was a donkey pure and simple as regards the manuscripts we are discussing). Not only did he fail to recognise these sheets as belonging to the play in question; but he lumped them together with other sheets containing quite different work, put them into a folder (which I obtained with the manuscripts), and on this wrote the following:

> 'This is evidently a Poem, or a portion of a poem, belonging to the "Undergraduate Papers" period. I know nothing at all about it, and can make nothing out of it.'

In a florilegium of literary asininity there could be no choicer bloom than this.

I have also recently ascertained what were the other seven Swinburne manuscripts sold at the same time as *Another Portrait* by the American Art Association on January 7th, 1916. One of these was a composition of ten pages entitled *Les écoliers britanniques*. Now this is a chapter of *La Fille du Policeman* (although it was not recognised as such by those who drew up the catalogue of the items for sale in which it was included). The title is one of those in an extant table of chapters of that work written by Swinburne himself. Now this table and a large portion of the work were in Wise's possession up to the time of his death. Here again, then, he apparently, not to say evidently, let go a section of a fairly large whole which he retained among his possessions. Probably here too—particularly as he could not read French and so very likely did not attempt to examine anything of Swinburne's written in that language—he had failed to recognise this section as belonging to this whole, although the fact was made quite clear by the table of chapters which was part of his Ashley Collection. This confirms the conclusion suggested by his selling of the section of the play. He was quite capable of selling a chapter—*Another Portrait*—of a novel of which he had acquired, and might as a collector be presumed to value highly, pretty nearly the whole of the manuscript. That he did so is not far from certain. He, very much more than anybody else, was likely to have acquired the chapter from Watts-Dunton or from the latter's sister. Here again (if it was he who sold it) stupidity more than anything else is the most probable explanation of why he let it go and thus spoilt his collection. He must have failed to see that it was a part of *Lesbia Brandon*. It is true that this is well-nigh incredible; for even if he had not before the time of the sale seen Swinburne's letters to Watts-Dunton in which *Another Portrait* is named as one of the chapters of *Lesbia Brandon*, the most cursory inspection of *Another Portrait* would (or ought) to have shown him that it was a part of the novel. To mention only one thing, the names Herbert and Lady Wariston occur in the first few lines of the chapter. But we have frequently seen that with Wise even the incredible is possible and achieves actuality. We have seen that his knowledge of *Lesbia Brandon* was very slight and highly imperfect; he said things about it so grotesquely wrong, and arranged the parts of it in such an absurdly wrong order, that it is natural to doubt if he ever really got as far as reading it. And, in the case of the dramatic fragment, we have seen that the argument (the strongest that can be advanced) that the sight of the names of characters must have set him right has no validity where he is concerned.

486

We may revert here to Wise's curious statement that 'later in' 1910 he 'bought [from Watts-Dunton] the four chapters cited in Swinburne's letters' to Watts-Dunton. These four chapters include *Another Portrait* (inadvertently called *Another Study* in the second of the two letters). The statement is curious because this chapter was missing from Wise's manuscript of the novel (which is now in the British Museum), and Wise nowhere records this fact. Did he (assuming he was the mysterious London collector) only see the letters in question after the sale of *Another Portrait*, and only then realise that it belonged to *Lesbia Brandon*? (He, presumably, in one or more documents, had a record of the eight items he had sold, and could refer to this record if his memory was in need of confirmation.) Did he then, having thus discovered that he had stupidly let one of the chapters go, decide to conceal the fact by writing that 'the manuscript' in his possession was 'quite complete'? For that is what he did write (some years after the chapter had been sold). But in the same paragraph he also wrote that he had acquired 'the four chapters cited in Swinburne's letters'—and it was patent that one of these chapters was missing from the manuscript which he had described as 'quite complete" only a few lines previously! The self-stultification is flagrant: the only possible explanation of it is that his forger was too much of a duffer to engage successfully even in sharp practices of this lowly nature. (And even if he were not the person who sold the chapter the self-stultification remains in all its enormity.)

Once again it has become plain to what a grievous extent Swinburnian studies—and, more than that, the fortunes of Swinburne's unpublished work—have been bedevilled by Wise's dullness, if not also (in this case) by his criminal proceedings. It was only by luck that I came across *Another Portrait*; it was only by luck that I learned of the existence of, and acquired before it became untraceable, the fragment belonging to the unpublished play; by luck at the same time, I may note here, I learned also of the hitherto unrecorded existence of, and redeemed from possible loss, an act of another—nowhere mentioned—play of Swinburne and also a fairly long fragment of a story by him that likewise is mentioned nowhere;[1] but I have not yet had the luck to discover the whereabouts of the missing chapter of *La Fille du Policeman*, which passed from anonymous hands into anonymous hands more than thirty years ago. And so on and so on. There is no sure and ready means of locating the numerous Swinburne manuscripts that Wise (after discerption in some cases) unconscionably allowed to be dispersed, without due record, that he might add a little to his large pile of lucre or otherwise gain worldly advantage[2] (useful to his prestige and so calculated to provide extra disguise for the seamy side of his life). Chaos has come again (and in more ways than that just mentioned) as regards Swinburne: and to bring this chaos to cosmos and truth is a thing of formidable difficulty.

[1] All these finds will be duly printed in the Corpus of the unpublished writings of Swinburne that I have already begun to prepare.

[2] I refer, in particular to his gifts of manuscripts etc. to certain places of learning.

NOTES
ELUCIDATIONS
PARALLEL PASSAGES
CANCELLED PORTIONS OF THE TEXT

NOTES AND CANCELLED PORTIONS
OF THE TEXT

IN THE CASE OF CORRECTIONS, ALTERATIONS, ETC., WORDS IN small capitals are those of the printed text; the immediately following words in italics are cancelled portions of the manuscript at this particular stage. When there is more than one variant they are separated by double colons. Cancelled variants occurring in a passage which is itself a cancelled variant are enclosed between square brackets. Deletions offering little or no interest—e.g. 'from the iris' replaced by 'from an iris', in the fourth line of the first chapter—are not given.

Notes are in normal Roman type, preceded by the parts of the text (small capitals) to which they refer.

CHAPTER I

[1] BEAST OR BIRD: *animals.*

[2] PURE: *absolute.*

[3] THE GREATEST ANALYST OF SPIRIT AND FLESH THAT EVER LIVED: Balzac. It is refreshing to find Swinburne, whose admiration of Shakespeare ordinarily ran to extremes of idolatry, elevating Balzac above him in the highly important matter of the analysis of the human spirit, in which, as in so many other things, the Elizabethan is superstitiously reputed superior to anybody else you care to name.

[4] HIS GEORGIAN GIRL: Paquita Valdès, La Fille aux yeux d'or (the third of the three novelettes in *L'Histoire des Treize*). Swinburne is not strictly correct in calling her a Georgian.

Her mother was a Georgian, but she herself was a native of the West Indies, and she is called 'l'Espagnole' more than once in the story. The coloration of her eyes and of her personality in general is thus described:

> Elle appartient à cette variété féminine que les Romains nommaient *fulva*, *flava*, la femme de feu. Et d'abord, ce qui ma le plus frappé, ce dont je suis encore épris, ce sont deux yeux jaunes comme ceux des tigres; un jaune d'or qui brille, de l'or vivant, de l'or qui pense, de l'or qui aime et veut absolument venir dans votre gousset!

For Swinburne's mastery (following and generally outdoing that of Balzac) in the difficult business of rendering the distinctive subtleties of eyes, cf. the following from *Love's Cross Currents*:

> 'The . . . luminous grey-green eyes shot through with colours of sea-water in sunlight, and threaded with faint keen lines of fire and light about the pupil . . .'

[5] FAIR AND FLORAL: *exquisite*.

[6] THEY COULD DARKEN . . . SPLENDID CHANGE: *they could darken and lighten with delicate and splendid alteration.*

[7] OF A GOLDEN BROWN: *brown* : : *yellowish brown.*

[8] CURVED AND DEEP: *decided.*

[9] Deleted after CUTTING AND COLOUR: *as a small conch for sea-fairies*: : *as a small sea shell lined with live rose.*

[10] FROM THE LOWEST RIPPLES OF THE SPRINGING HAIR TO THE FRESH FIRM CHIN: *from chin to hair*: : *from the round chin to the hair.*

[11] AS A FRUIT, PLANTED AS WITH TENDER CARE: *as a white fruit, or orb-shaped blossom*: : *as a fruit tenderly and carefully planted.*

[12] LANGUOR AND LAUGHTER: *languors and laughters alike delicious.*

[13] PERPETUATE: *reproduce.*

[14] THE VENUS OF THE TRIBUNE: The Medici Venus, in the Tribuna of the Galleria degli Uffizi at Florence.

[15] THE HYBRID HEAD AND PATCHWORK ARMS: *the restored head and arms.*

[16] ATTACHED: a very French use of the word; cf. Balzac: 'La fille aux yeux d'or avait ce pied bien attaché'.

[17] THE SAME: *identical.*

[18] HIS EYES: cf. the description of them on p.95, including the cancelled words.

[19] LIKE BRILLIANT SEA-WATER: *and deep and brilliant.*

[20] VAGUE SURFACE: *glass.*

[21] HIGH: *open.*

[22] AND HIS HANDS . . . SUN AND WIND: *and his hands were the same: : and his hands were hers.*

[23] AT HIS FINGER TIPS, . . . BLUE: *in thick blue threads at the.*

[24] IN SECRET: *at root.*

[25] ONE BORN WEAKLIER: *sickly plant.*

[26] UNTEMPERED AND UNALLAYED: *without mixture or allay* ('Allay' is an archaic form of 'alloy'.)

[27] Deleted after NERVOUS AND FEARLESS: *sensitive and daring.*

CHAPTER II

[1] HE HAD SAID LITTLE: What he does say, in the broken fashion of delirium or semi-consciousness, is partially enlightened by Mr. Linley's revelations to Denham in the chapter entitled *Les Malheurs de la Vertu.* But even so it remains exceedingly obscure. 'Wouldn't hear of it': the

apparent meaning of 'it' is Herbert's being allowed to go to or into the water; but there is probably a further meaning: his (the speaker's) marriage to the woman with whom he was passionately in love. 'His own' apparently means his father's father; but it may mean some woman loved by his father. 'Lost at land for all that' most probably refers to himself; he made shipwreck on land, owing to the breaking up of his love affair. 'Not your fault, sir': 'sir' is probably Lord Charles Brandon, who comes into the story later. 'She thrives, though': there is no doubt that Lady Brandon is referred to here. 'The little thing': his illegitimate son, who appears later.

[2] BUT I SHOULD . . . FOR ALL THAT: *but her child was mine.*

[3] LOW: *grey.*

[4] QUIVERING UNDER CLOUDS AND SUNBEAMS: *quivering with weary beauty and infinite excess of life*: : *quivering under clouds and sunbeams: infinite and variable smiles of weary beauty on its immortal face, soft sighs and heavy murmurs under the laughter and dance-music of its running stream.* The part of the second version after the colon is used at the end of the next sentence, with one of the adjectives altered.

[5] INFINITE . . . SMILES: Cf. Aeschylus (in whom Swinburne was steeped): ποντίων κυμάτων ἀνηριθμον γέλασμα (*Prometheus Vinctus*); Swinburne's phrase is almost a literal equivalent of this.

[6] TROUBLED WITH STRENGTH AND VEXED WITH LOVE: *troubled with love.*

[7] SOUL: *heart.*

[8] SOUL . . . THROUGH THE SENSES: A pointer to one of the cardinal articles of Swinburne's philosophy, here in line with that of Blake: cf. '. . . the five Senses, the chief inlets of Soul in this age'. (*The Marriage of Heaven and Hell.*)

[9] ENSDON: The house probably and the landscape and sea-

scape certainly are a reproduction of Swinburne's ancestral home on the male side at Capheaton in Northumberland, which he visited every year from his infancy till about 1860. The place and its environs frequently appear in his work. Herbert's life there, and especially his fervent contact with the sea, is undoubtedly in large part that of the poet during his sojourns at Capheaton in his boyhood.

[10] INCONSISTENT: *mixed.*

[11] THE ENSDON LIBRARY: The library at Capheaton was famous as one of the best in the North of England, being particularly well furnished with Spanish and French works.

[12] AND FRENCH VERSE AND FICTION: This seems ultra-precocious in a boy of nine (Herbert was in his tenth year when his father died, we are told in a later chapter); and especially in a boy who had apparently received little education up to that date. But it could have been true of Swinburne himself (who sometimes loses sight of superficial verisimilitude when his fiction becomes autobiographical.) His mother taught him French as well as Italian when he was very young; in one letter to her he recalls that they read Goldoni together when he 'was a little chap', and in another that he was only 'a little boy' when she helped him 'to enjoy and understand' Molière as well as Shakespeare, Dickens and Scott.

[13] IMPRESSIBLE: *sensitive.*

[14] POURING STEAM: *underwood.*

[15] FOR THE SUN TO FILL: *and full of heavy sunlight.*

[16] WERE FRIENDLY TO HIS FEET: *made him welcome.*

[17] IMMEASURABLE BEAUTIES, etc.: Cf. 'The immeasurable tremor of all the sea' (*Anactoria*), and the afore-quoted phrase of Aeschylus.

[18] ITS SACRED STRENGTH: For the epithet cf. 'The sacred spaces of the sea' (*Songs before Sunrise*).

[19] THE SHARP DELICATE AIR . . . GRACIOUS GOD: *the delicate air about it, sharp as the taste of pleasure*: : *sharp like the breath and the nostrils of the god peculiar.*

[20] SEMITONES . . . STRUCK OUT . . . EXTENDED . . . IN EXTREMITY AND EXHAUSTION: *semitones made by the exhausted and extreme.*

[21] FINGERS OF FOAM: *hands of weary foam.*

[22] GALE: *wind.*

[23] CRYING OUT TO THE SEA . . . AS TO A MOTHER: This conception recurs frequently as a sort of dominant in Swinburne's work, e.g.:

> I will go back to the great sweet mother,
> Mother and lover of men, the sea . . .
> > (*The Triumph of Time*)
> But when my time shall be,
> O mother, O my sea,
> Alive or dead, take me,
> Me too, my mother.
> > (*Ex-voto*)

[24] THROWING AT IT ALL THE SCRAPS OF SONG: cf.

> Yours was I born, and ye,
> The sea-wind and the sea,
> Made all my soul in me
> A song for ever . . .
> > (*Ex-voto*)

[25] HOW MANY LIVES WENT YEARLY TO FEED, etc.: Cf. 'Thou art fed with our dead, O mother, O sea . . . (*The Triumph of Time*).

[26] OPEN: *living.*

[27] SENSE OR PERCEPTION OF THINGS CERTAIN: *sense of unmistakeable things.*

[28] BY INFINITE INFLUENCES AND EFFECTS: *by all effects and influences.*

[29] HE MAY BE: *he is.*

[30] NOT INCOMPETENT . . . HIS THOUGHTS . . . FANCIES PERVERSE AND SUBTLE: *Not incompetent to think [subtly and perversely], he is incompetent to [of the] use his [of] thoughts.*

[31] APART AND NOT AVERSE FROM THE DAILY RELIGION TAKEN AND TAUGHT ON TRUST: *apart [from] and not in [conseq] averse from the daily religion taught and taken on trust.*

[32] IMPREGNATE WITH COLOURS: *dye.*

[33] Deleted after IRREGULAR OUTLINES: *as of a disorderly rosebud.*

[34] THE RED AND RIDICULOUS LUMP: Cf. 'The boy does us as much credit as anything so fat and foolish, so red and ridiculous, as a new baby . . . can do.' (*Love's Cross Currents,* Letter XXVIII.)

[35] LAY HARDER . . . ANOTHER'S: *lay hold of his finger with a double violence.*

[36] HIS BROTHER: properly his brother-in-law.

[37] WHO SHOULD UNDERTAKE . . . PURPOSE: *if he was to bring the crude mind to fruit or flower.*

[38] IN 1848: *early in 1848.* Here, and earlier in this paragraph, the galleys wrongly give 1849. Swinburne's '8' is sometimes not as plain as it should be, but it is unmistakable for anyone used to his handwriting. On the inconsistency, and hence the impossibility, of the date here see the third section, ad. fin., of my chapter on *The Text.*

[39] BIRCHEN: *birchrod.*

[40] Deleted after SCHOOLROOM TO DO: *and he knew well enough in what manner and upon what material it was likely to act.*

⁴¹ Deleted after GOT YE HORSED: *he'll whip ye till the rod wears out, and ye'll be let down crying and roaring, and [your skin all bloody and smarting] covered with blood and all over [great] weals.*

This, the last (40), and the two following (42 and 43) passages were plainly cancelled (in ink of a different strength) at a time later than that of composition—doubtless when the manuscript was revised before going to the printer. This happened almost exclusively—and almost always—in the case of passages relating to flogging. (Where necessary, there was modification and/or insertion of words or phrases to connect what preceded and what followed the cancelled portions.) Swinburne presumably thought that certain details of flogging would be too much for the general public of that day; and reluctantly sacrificed part of the text in its integrity as he conceived it. But he made up for this restraint by incorporating them, and others much more gruesome, in the unpublished *Flogging-Block* and other similar compositions. Cf.:

> Every fresh cut well laid on
> The bare breech of Algernon
> Makes the swelled flesh rise in ridges
> Thick as summer swarms of midges;
> Every stroke the Master deals,
> Every stripe the schoolboy feels,
> Marks his breech with fresh red weals;
> How he blubbers, how he bellows!
>
> On those broad red nether cheeks
> That their own blood scores and streaks,
> That the red rod streaks and dapples
> Like two great red round streaked apples
> That the birch-twigs cut and slice! . . .
>   (*The Flogging-Block*. Algernon's Flogging.)

498

. . . Quite a harvest of tingling thick throbbing long fresh
Great bloody red smarting sore weals on his flesh.

> (*Ib.* Charlie's Flogging.)

How those great big red ridges must smart as they swell!
How the Master does like to flog Algernon well!
How each cut makes the blood come in thin little streaks
From that broad blushing round pair of naked red cheeks!

> (*Ib.* Algernon's Flogging.)

ALGERNON. Oh! Oh, sir! Oh, please, sir! Please, please, sir!
Oh! Oh!

MASTER. No crying, sir, here! I won't have it, you know.

> (*Ib.* Ib.)

MASTER. . . . Charles and yourself shall be both double-
flogged.
First, hoisted, and whipped on the back of the
porter
—And, when horsed, you know, boy, the birch
gives no quarter . . .

> (*Ib.* Charlie's Flogging.)

[42] Deleted after 'NO CRYING HERE': *and 'Hold him.*

[43] Deleted after OR—': *and he'll hold up the rod.*

[44] EAGER: *high.*

[45] THAT THE HOUSEKEEPER'S FERVID ELOQUENCE: *by the eloquent wrath of the housekeeper.*

[46] Faintly deleted after CHAFF AND BRAN: *It was a quite [purely]
unbroken and virgin ground which was now to be ploughed
and harrowed in the approved fashion [for the reception of
seed] by [the] scholastic instrument of husbandry.*

Cf. 41, deletion and comment. Subsequent cancellations
to which this comment applies will be followed by the words
'A later deletion'.

[47] A LONG-LIMBED, DARK SKINNED BOY: *a long, dark boy, amiable
and quiet.*

[48] LOW: *rooted.*

[49] THE REEFS CLASHED . . . THE BANKS CHAFED . . . THE WATER RANG . . . WAVE BY WAVE, etc.:

> Cf.　　With chafe and change of surges chiming,
> 　　　　The clashing channels rocked and rang
> 　　Large music, wave to wild wave timing,
> 　　　　And all the choral water sang.
> 　　　　　　　　　　　　　(*At a Month's End.*)

[50] FIERCE FLEET LIFE: *beautiful life*: : *barren life*: : *loud and fruitless life.*

[51]　　And wave by wave roared out its heavy heart
　　And lost its fierce fleet life in lavish foam
　　Beyond the yellow labouring space of sea
　　That heaved and wallowed close inshore . . .

Although Swinburne was primarily a poet, and ran with native ease into numbers, his prose very rarely forms a continuous passage of a blank verse as in the above case. Even isolated lines of pentametric or greater length are rare in his prose: much rarer than in that of Dickens, Trollope, Stevenson, Hardy and many other writers who worked exclusively or primarily in that medium.

[52] BEYOND THE SUDDEN GREEN LINE OF PURER SEA: *above the greener*: : *beyond the sudden line of greener.*

[53] AND HIS EYES OF DREAMS: *and his head full of dreams*: : *and his eyes of visions.*

[54] ALL ITS AIRS AND LIGHTS . . . UPON HIM: *all the light of the sea shone into him*: : *all the colour and savour and all the light and shadow of the sea hung about him.*

[55] YEAR TO COME: *the next few years.*

[56] RATHER A TRAINING ATHLETE THAN TRAINED STUDENT: *rather a type of athlete than a sample of the student.*

[57] LIFE REPRESSED AND SUPPRESSED STRENGTH: Cf.

> With care inappreciable and invaluable fidelity . . .
> *(William Blake)*

> . . . under other heavens, on another earth, than the
> earth and heaven of material life.   *(Ib.)*

> It needed no exceptional acuteness of ear or eye to
>   see or hear that . . .   *(Essays and Studies)*
> . . . the spring and the stream as of flowing or welling
> water . . .   *(Ib.)*

> etc., etc.

Swinburne was fond of chiasmus. One gets the impression that he fell into it naturally under the impulse of an idiosyncrasy of his mental structure; perhaps it was because there is a certain subtlety about it, a departure from the straightforward obvious, that satisfied his tendency towards complexity. Saintsbury, talking of Swinburne in his essay on *Modern English Prose*, opines that 'the . . . dangerous licence of the figure called chiasmus has been to him even as a siren, from whose clutches he has been hardly saved.' There is more ineptitude than justice in this ill-written remark. Playing commentator on himself years later, Saintsbury wrote: 'I cannot think what I was about!', *à propos* of another of his deliverances in this essay: he might well have said it of much else in that paper (and in not a little of the rest of his work).

[58] Deleted after IN HIS FLESH: *the first of many sharper tinglings soon to be felt.* A later deletion. Cf.

> Don't the thought make you tingle before the
>   strokes come?
>   *(The Flogging-Block.* Algernon's Flogging.)

> How each lash leaves its mark well cut into the flesh!
> How each cut must make Algernon tingle afresh!
>   *(Ib.* Ib.)

[59] WINCED: *recognised a tormentor.*

[60] TIME OF IT . . . PUNISHMENT: *time of it. He was [usually] not infrequently hoisted [about] three times in a wee; and the floggings he received were no [fleabites: : light] joke to him, fresh.* A later deletion. Swinburne at first tried to tone the passage down to the extent of replacing 'usually' by 'not infrequently', then he regretfully drew two vertical lines of cancellation through it; this preliminary attempt at compromise occurred in many of these cases.

[61] UPON HIS PUPIL, AND IT WAS: *upon his pupil, whose delicate cuticle readily took and long retained the red impression of birchen twigs. It was.* A later deletion. Cf.

> Well, to judge by the old cuts we see, and the fresh 'uns,
> I should say that the birch has made lots of impressions
> On Willie's unfortunate bottom.
> > (*The Flogging-Block.* Willie's Flogging.)

[62] Deleted after AMIABLE ENOUGH: *the one way to get work out of Herbert was to fix a certain quantity for the day and apply the birch instantly and unsparingly if he fell short. Idle.* A later deletion.

[63] AS FRIDAY WAS CONSECRATED: *On Friday the weekly arrears of flagellation were usually paid up; but it was also and especially consecrated.* A later deletion.

[64] Deleted after FOR SOME TIME: *He might pull through six days without a whipping by dint of good luck and good work; but on the seventh he was sure to be well flogged.* A later deletion.

[65] Deleted after EXPECTED OF THE BOY: *who certainly did want whipping now and then.* A later deletion.

[66] Deleted between DENHAM HAD ALWAYS A FAIR PRETEXT and HERBERT HAD LEARNT: *at hand for laying on the lash, and was not unjust or unkind, though he might have hit less hard and less often without absolute error on the side of*

indulgence: but as he got used to flogging, Herbert got used to being flogged, and the torture had to be increased in quality or frequency, until the tutor's growing appetite outran the pupil's growing endurance. In a school this gradual relish of his work on the headmaster's part is less visible and terrible to the sufferers; but here there were no other boys to halve the infliction and turn it to matter of jest or emulation; all the gathering storm broke over one victim and descended in stinging showers on the head of a single boy [one boy al]. By this time however. Swinburne at first wrote 'not on the head of a single boy', and omitted to cancel the 'not' when he went off into another construction. A later deletion. The 'growing appetite' of the master (or father) in the unpublished flogging pieces reaches ghastly proportions. Forty-eight cuts is moderate there; five dozen is an average number; sometimes the total goes beyond one hundred. Ordinarily Swinburne carefully noted the increments of mounting torture in the margin. Thus, in the *Flogging-Block,* Reginald's Flogging, 21, 32, 38, 44, 48 and '60 in all' at the end. For 'matter of jest or emulation' cf.

> I hear my Cousin whispering to my Brother—
> 'This was a good tough Rod—but see the other!
> See, Charlie, what a lithe fresh, sappy one!
> I call your Brother's flagellation Fun! . . .
> (The Flogging-Block. Prologue.)

> Well, I'm sorry for Algy, but still it's a spree;
> And his floggings are always so jolly to see.
> (Ib. Algernon's Flogging.)

> (Headmaster)   . . . I fear
> He's proud of the fact that no other boy here
> Gets punished as often as he . . .
> (Ib. Charlie's Flogging.)

'He' in this last quotation is Algernon, with whom Swinburne identified himself.

⁶⁷ Deleted between RETICENCE and BEAR ANYTHING: *Once or*

twice Lord Wariston, on entering the library now used as schoolroom, had found Herbert roaring under the rod, and begged him off an extra cut or two; but the boy's agony of shame at being seen in tears and disgrace and shameful naked submission taught him to. A later deletion. For 'agony of shame' cf.

ALGERNON. Though it stings like the devil—and marks like
the deuce—
Yet he shan't make me cry any more—what's
the use?
Next time I won't cry—and I wish, oh, I wish
I had borne the first dose of it pluckily!

[68] Deleted between CONTEMPTUOUS and AND THUS EVERY FLOGGING. *When after some months he took hold of his courage with both hands, heaved his heart into his mouth and begged [with moist eyes and fiery cheeks that he might not be] [hoisted or held down by a servant, promising: : hoist across the whipping-block by a servant, promising] to be no longer hoisted, promising to keep quiet and take his due allowance of cuts without wincing, Denham acceded with a sharp laugh, and thus [thenceforth] chair or sofa [became substituted for the wooden horse] served the purpose of a school block, and every flogging.* A later deletion.

[69] A DUEL . . . BETWEEN THE MAN AND THE BOY: Cf. A flogging was an affair of honour to him; if he came off without tears, although with loss of blood, he regarded the master with chivalrous pity, as a brave enemy worsted. A real tormentor always revelled in the punishment of Reginald. (*Love's Cross Currents.* The reference is to Reginald Harewood, another boy in whom Swinburne largely portrayed himself.)

Who will flinch and wince and shrink?
What unmanly fool can think
Birch must make a boy's heart sink? . . .

———

Make the brute who flogs us know
You and I won't blub, although
Blood should run at every blow!
Yes: it hurts: but what care we?

(*By Robert Birks*, one of the unpublished
flogging pieces.)

This conception of the flogging experience as a duel, an
affair of honour, is a chief key to the proper interpretation
of Swinburne's extensive production on the subject of
flagellation, and sharply differentiates it from the general
run of work, and especially the Marquis de Sade's, on that
rather nauseating theme. However extreme and gruesome
it is as treated by the English poet, there is always in it a
moral element, in the highest sense of the work. It is—
among other things at times, no doubt—an expression of
heroism; and the more the agony is piled on the more call
is there for heroism. And Swinburne's attitude is never that
of the sadist or tormentor: he is always in the place of the
sufferer.

[70] ECSTASY: *violent delight.*

[71] THAT AFFLICTION WAS POSSIBLE ON LAND: *that there was
birch growing on land, or any affliction possible in the
world;*

[72] THE BRIGHT AND VIGOROUS DELIGHT, ETC.: This and all that
follows down to HIS APPRENTICESHIP BEGAN at the end of the
paragraph is marked for deletion in the Brotherton galley-
proof, but not in that of the British Museum, nor in the
manuscript.

[73] CHAFFS ONE ABOUT GETTING SWISHED: Cf.

Ah, the man! how he'll chaff! he can, I know, chaff, awfully,
won't he too!
'Well, sir, how do your cuts feel now? You've had it hot, sir—
they've given it *you!*'

(*Cuckoo Weir*, an unpublished flogging-piece
relating to Swinburne's life at Eton.)

OLD ETONIAN. Where are you going now?

REGINALD. To Cuckoo Weir, Sir.

OLD ETONIAN. Your schoolfellows will laugh to see you there, sir,
Stripped for a swim; . . .
(Epilogue to *Reginald's Flogging*.)

[74] CHOUSE: a term of contemporary slang frequently used by Swinburne's juvenile characters.

[75] Deleted after TUTOR: *birch in hand*.

[76] A TOUGH AND SUFFICIENT ROD: *a rod*.

[77] GRASPED HIM ROUND THE WAIST . . . AND LAID ON: *laid him wet and naked across one knee, and pinioned his legs with the other; held him down with the left hand and flogged him*.

[78] Deleted after LUXURY: *The sting was doubled or trebled; and he was not released till blood had been drawn from his wet skin, soaked as it was in salt at every pore: and came home at once red and white, drenched and dry. Nothing in his life had ever hurt him so much as these.* A late deletion. Swinburne replaced it by 'He did not care to face again [after this taste of such [an overplus of] superfluity of infliction] [of] the sharp superfluous torture of these'.

[79] Deleted between MOIST FLESH *and* FROM THAT DAY: *a boy less thin-skinned [sensitive] would have winced under such delicate excess [overplus] of torure. It fairly cowed him for a time and he did not run the same risk again. From.* A later deletion.

[80] NOTICE: *notice and manner*.

[81] ACRID: *acid*.

[82] PASSING . . . PERVERSION: *undergoing perversion*: : *passing through silent stages of perversion*.

[83] HE COULD NOT ACT OUT, etc.: This and all that follows down

to HE HAD NOT STRENGTH ENOUGH is marked for deletion in the Brotherton galley-proof, but not in that of the British Museum nor in the manuscript.

⁸⁴ SCORN OF THE EFFECT: *scorn of himself.*

⁸⁵ WAS READIER TO HELP AND AMUSE: *opened out more when in private.*

⁸⁵ COLENSO: This much attacked bishop, who according to Swinburne's friend Jowett 'made an epoch in criticism by his straightforwardness', wrote in his twenties, when heavily oppressed with debt, manuals of arithmetic and algebra which were widely used in England.

⁸⁷ BE FLOGGED: *be soundly flogged.* A later deletion.

⁸⁸ Deleted after ANYHOW: *if you compel me to punish you every day, every hour.*

⁸⁹ Deleted between A FLOGGING WHICH and WHY DENHAM: *which made him sore for three days and left marks for a month. He could not guess what he had done to bring down such a storm of stripes. That he should be whipped before getting through any sum in division seemed to him quite natural and fair; punishment was part of his work: but.* A later deletion. Swinburne replaced it by [*he did wonder*] [*made him wonder*] *left him incapable of any sense but wonder.* SORE FOR THREE DAYS, etc. Cf.

He couldn't sit down for three days.
His bottom was perfectly flayed—as one flays
A carcase: the sight of his broad nether cheeks
Was a warning: he couldn't sit down for three weeks ...
(*The Flogging-Block. Edward's Flogging.*)

⁹⁰ TWO SHARP CUTS EXTRA WHICH TOOK: *extra. The swift stinging lashes took.* A later deletion.

⁹¹ GASP AND SOB: Cf.

The Master leaves off flogging Algernon for a few

minutes, during which not a sound is heard but Algernon's sobs, as he writhes . . . in a perfect agony of smart.

(*The Flogging-Block*. Charlie's Flogging.)

The last cut left poor Reginald's bare bottom covered with blood. He rose . . . crying and sobbing like a child.

(*A boy's first flogging*, published anonymously in *The Whippingham Papers*.)

[92] FIERY CHEEKS BLOTTED BY TEARS: Cf.

. . . The face that turns red at each stroke, and gets hot,
And smarts till a fellow can't bear it, and cries,
And feels the tears stream down his cheeks . . .

(*The Flogging-Block*. Charlie's Flogging.)

[93] Deleted after ONE DAY: *before Herbert's scars were healed.* A later deletion.

[94] FOR A WEEK OR SO: *since his last flogging.*

[95] WAS IN THE MOOD TO ENCOURAGE: [*began to think he had*] *had for once felt a sort of pity on seeing that the red impressions of his rod were yet uneffaced. He even let the boy see this, by encouraging.* A later deletion.

CHAPTER III

[1] STEEP HILLSIDES OF WATER: *steep waves like a small sea-beast.*

[2] THE GROUNDSWELL: Cf. *Love's Cross Currents*, when Reginald Harewood dives into the sea in a vain attempt to save Lord Cheyne from drowning: '. . . jumped in after him . . ., but he could hardly make the least way because of the ground swell'. Swinburne himself in his youth deliberately—and gratuitously—courted danger in the same spirit in which he faced in imagination (and unquestionably in reality) the floggings on which he was so fond of dilating.

[3] IT WAS A CHANCE . . . WOULD HAPPEN OR NOT: *it was all in the game, and fair fighting.*

[4] WAVE ABOUT TO BREAK: *curving unbroken wave*:: *wave yet unbroken.*

[5] A HAND CLUTCH . . . AND SLIP OFF: *arms close about his waist, and legs fasten on his.*

[6] AND FLEW INTO FOAM: *in a cataract.*

[7] STUNNED BY THE HARD WET BLOWS AND BLIND WITH RETURNING FRIGHT: *stunned and mazed with fright.*

[8] FELLOW: *gentleman.*

[9] SPOTTING AND SALTING . . . CLOTHES: *making homewards briskly under the weight of his wet clothes.*

[10] CERTAIN OTHER: *certain other transverse.* A later deletion.

[11] Deleted after CUTS WHICH: *told elsewhere of past flagellations. These faint red seams and small impressions of twig and bud Herbert, who could not see them, had forgotten.* A later deletion. For 'red seams' etc. and 'a sharp fire of chaff' a few lines down, see Chapter II, Note [73] and cf.

> . . . Strange that his bare bum showed no seam or fleck,
> No sanguine sign or imprint of the rod . . .
> (The unpublished *Edgar's Flogging.*)

[12] SMALL REPLICA: *[pocket] small edition.*

[13] DAMNATORY PROOF, etc.: Cf.

> You have climbed, swum and ridden in places forbidden;
> You have played truant with Edward to bathe on the Witches' Down;
> So take down your breeches! . . .
> (The unpublished *Frederick's Flogging.*)

[14] Deleted after THE BOY'S VOICE: *some shade of impudence in his bearing.*

[15] WAS IN THEIR DARK GREY GLOBES, LATENT AND TACIT: *was latent in their dark grey globes.*

[16] Deleted between THOUGH and HIS WILL: *the boy felt by instinct that something had intensified tenfold, had heated to a white glow and whetted to a fine point, his tutor's native* [*native relish of pain*] *and severe appetite for perfection in the matter of punishment.*

Denham was composed enough before he began operations. His. A later deletion. Here the printers ignored Swinburne's vertical lines of cancellation, and the passage appears in the galley-proofs. For 'severe appetite for perfection in the matter of punishment.
chapter.

[17] Deleted between NERVES and THE LIKENESS: *Feverish hands, he knew, would deal but inadequate strokes: and he was on all accounts inclined to give Herbert something to remember for life.* A later deletion. Here again the printers ignored the vertical lines of cancellation and the passage is in the galley-proofs. For 'something to remember for life' cf.

> You feel, and we see, how the birch makes you bleed:
> And I hope I shall make you remember it, Reed.
> > (*The Flogging-Block.* Willie's Flogging.)

> All his life he'll remember this flogging, and wince
> > as he thinks of it, when
> Old schoolfellows meet and remind him—by Jove,
> > how the birch was laid into you then.
> > > (The unpublished *Rupert's Flogging.*)

[18] PLEASE, SIR, . . . I PROMISE I WON'T etc.: A frequent cry of the victims in the unpublished flogging-pieces. Cf.

> Please don't sir,—don't whip me, sir, please, any more!
> O, I'll never not look at my lesson again—
> No, never, sir! Please, sir! Next time, sir—oh then . . .
> > (*The Flogging-Block.* Willie's Flogging.)

ALGERNON. Oh, please, sir, I'll never be late again.

MASTER (raising the birch to the utmost height possible).
    Pish!
ALGERNON. Oh, I'll never be caught out of bounds again—
    Rod. (whipping his bottom again). Swish!
                        (*Ib.* Algernon's Flogging.)

[19] I DON'T THINK YOU WILL . . . I MEAN TO MAKE SURE OF THAT:
Cf.

WILLIE. Oh please, I'm so sorry, sir!
MASTER.   Yes, Master Willie;
    I'm certain you are . . .
                    (*Ib.* Willie's Flogging.)

[20] 'GO DOWN' . . . 'WENT DOWN' . . . AT THE BLOCK. Cf.

Go down on the whipping-block—down on your knees, sir
           (*The Flogging-Block.* Willie's flogging.)

Go down, sir! Go down when I tell you! Go down, I say,
                     Wentworth! Go down!
    (*Rupert's Flogging.*)

[21] Deleted after SAID THE BOY: *Then his tutor took up a long cutting rod, and laid it on smartly; lashing him till the supple twigs bent round upon the flesh.* A later deletion. This passage was replaced by the following, which was also sacrificed: *His tutor fell vigorously to work, lashing him till the supple twigs bent round upon the flesh, biting well into the tenderest part and stinging with all their buds.*

For 'the supple twigs bent round' cf.
    How the birch-twigs bent round at each fresh cut
      afresh . . .
        (*The Flogging-Block.* Willie's Flogging.)

[22] Deleted after SHARP SOB: *At the next he reddened with a double blush; the third cut left traces raised in red relief on the smooth pale skin; and after another cut or two the boy could hardly keep his tears in.* A later deletion. For 'double blush . . . red relief . . . pale skin' cf.

See, boys, how he blushes! how red his cheeks are!
But his other end soon shall be redder by far.

(Ib. Algernon's Flogging.)

. . . the delicate boyish skin grew gradually into a
mass of red ridges . . .

(A prose piece published anonymously
in *The Whippingham Papers.*)

[23] DENHAM KNEW BETTER . . . PAUSED AFTER EACH CUT: *Denham
took his time and left a pause after each blow.* On the facing
blank page of the preceding sheet Swinburne wrote and
later cancelled the following passage, no doubt meant to
replace part or parts of the last few lines of the paragraph:
*A few words or warning menace and sharp reproach were
intermixed between the stripes; and after each pause of the
kind a long switching cut was laid on which left deeper
marks on the boy's smooth skin [which made the room
echo, answering upon].* 'Intermixed words' from the tormentor are a common element of the flogging-pieces. Cf.

MASTER.   Does it hurt? (whipping Willie) does it
          hurt you, my lad?
          I'm glad that you feel it (whipping Willie again)—
          I'm heartily glad.   5 cuts.
          It will help you, I trust, (whipping Willie again) if
          you're not quite a fool,
          To behave rather better in church and in school.
          (whips Willie severely)   6
          For in school you're a dunce (whipping Willie
          again), as you know—and in church,   7
          (whipping Willie severely) You know how your
          sleepiness merits the birch.   8
                    (The Flogging-Block. Willie's Flogging.)

[24] THE CUTS STUNG LIKE FIRE, AND BURNING? Cf.

the burning and fiery Pain of his whipped Posteriors

(Notes to *The Flogging-Block*)

. . . the pitiless rod seems to search
All the tenderest hind parts out, and leave them on fire—
set on fire by the birch.

(*Rupert's Flogging.*)

You don't mean—you, who know how the birch makes
one's skin burn—
That this cousin of yours, Redgie—what's his name?—
Swinburne,
Gets whipped more severely than this?

(*The Flogging-Block.* Charlie's Flogging.)

[25] Deleted after HIS FINGERS: *his underlip.*

[26] HIS TEETH DREW BLOOD AS WELL AS THE BIRCH: *his teeth drew blood from the underlip as the birch drew blood elsewhere.* A later deletion. Cf.

. . . Shewing how sharp the pain must be
That at each fresh cut laid on
Makes the breech of Algernon
Flinch and quiver, wince and shrink—
Makes him bite his lips and wink!

(*The Flogging-Block.* Algernon's Flogging.)

Swish!—Swish!—Rupert pants, catches breath, takes his
under-lip tight in his teeth . . .

(*Rupert's Flogging.*)

[27] Deleted between GLITTERED WITH PASSION and A FRESH ROD: *Two dozen was Herbert's usual allowance, and till the twenty-fourth cut he held out pretty well in hope of an end; but when Denham applied.* A later deletion. For mounting number of cuts see Note [66] of Chapter II.

[28] Deleted after A FRESH ROD: *to his quivering flesh.* A later deletion.

[29] Deleted after WAS APPLIED AND: *stripe followed hard on stripe.* A later deletion.

[30] TEARS STREAMED . . . IMPLORING LIPS: Cf.

> *Algernon* (looking up in the Master's face with streaming
> eyes): Oh, sir! Oh, dear sir!
> > (*The Flogging-Block*. Algernon's Flogging.)

[31] IT WAS NOT . . . TRANSIENT ANGER: *It was no mere lust of
torture, no mere brutal habit or transient anger.* A later
deletion.

[32] COLD FURY . . . WHITE HEAT: There is plenty of cold fury and
white heat in the unpublished flogging-pieces, and it is hard
to avoid the impression that 'mere lust of torture' is the
main impulse behind the blows of the schoolmtster in the
all too vivid scenes of this arcane part of the poet's work. Cf.

> 'What made you late, sir?' with a smile and frown
>   Of outward wrath and cruel inward joy,
> Replied the master . . .
> > (*Arthur's Flogging*; published anonymously
> > in *The Whippingham Papers*.)

MASTER. Hold your tongue! you don't mind me, then,
eh, you young dog, you?
Then I'll flog you—O Algy, my boy, how I'll
flog you!

ALGERNON. Oh please, sir—oh dear sir—O pray sir—O,
don't—

MASTER. What, you won't hold your tongue, then—you
won't sir—you won't?
You defy me, then Algernon—eh, you young
rip, you?
Then I'll whip you—I'll whip you—I'll whip
you—I'll whip you!
> (*The Flogging-Block*. Algernon's Flogging.)

Swinburne's depiction of public-school flogging, more than
probably drawn in large part from his own unfortunate
experience, bears out Mr. Bernard Shaw's forcible observa-

tions on this very unpleasant subject. Cf., e.g., in the Preface to *Misalliance*, the whole of the section *Under the Whip*, in which the 'frantic excesses of this disgusting neurosis' are dealt with at some length.

(And Gosse, in his grossly misrepresentative *Life*, which has practically imposed itself as standard, shows us Swinburne as peaceably happy at Eton!)

[33] Deleted after SIGHT OF IT: *Don't roar like that.* A later deletion.

[34] HIMSELF: *his deranged apparel.* A later deletion.

[35] NERVOUS SULLEN BEAUTY OF OUTLINE: *angry*:: *nervous anger*:: *nervous sullen beauty of their outline.*

[36] EMOTIONS INVERTED AND PERVERTED: Cf. 'inverted love', p.46; he was passing through quiet stages of perversion', p.30.

[37] Deleted after WITH INFINITE PRECAUTION: *uttering a sharp suppressed cry as he came in contact with the one hard seat in the room, reserved for his use: easy chairs in schooltime, his tutor justly thought, were inadmissible.* A later deletion. Cf. Chapter II, Note [89].

[38] INDIGNANTLY PLAINTIVE: *of plaintive indignation.*

[39] Deleted after HE HIT RATHER HARD, BUT: *the cuts don't hurt very much when a fellow's used to them. (This he said while still tingling to the very bone, and too sore to bear a touch with flinching.)* A later deletion.

[40] Deleted after PRESENTLY: *he concluded with a splendid assurance-feeling as he spoke that for three or four days at least a chair would be to him an object of horror and avoidance.* A later deletion. The printer did not see that Swinburne's vertical strokes of cancellation were carefully drawn so as not to include 'That is, he hit rather hard, but I shall be all right presently', and these two sentences do not appear in the galley-proof.

[41] Deleted after HAD ONLY KNOWN: *but you've been such a brave boy all through.* A later deletion.

[42] Deleted after COURTEOUS ENOUGH: *the fisherman was a royal sample: : the gaunt old man had hair flecked lightly with grey as with foam: : heavy flakes of splashed foam: : heavy sprinkles and flashes of foam.*

[43] ALTERED: *alarmed: : dimmed.*

[44] REPUGNANT MODESTIES AND PUERILITIES: *modesties and repugnances.*

[45] Deleted after PUT TO SHAME: *in presence of this grey [great] gaunt sea-waif [sea-growth] that seemed.*

[46] 'WE COULDN'T SPARE . . . JUST NOW': *'We couldn't get on without our torment in the house.'*

[47] MOVED TO PRUDENCE BY PAINFULLY PRIVATE CONSIDERATIONS: *moved by private and prudential considerations.*

[48] Deleted after FELLOWS: *and have no end of larks.*

[49] Deleted after READING: *Petronius.*

[50] NOTICED WHAT LAY AT HAND: *noticed the print of his knees on the couch, the tumbled cushion, and among other significant minor indications sundry broken twigs of birch lying about, bruised buds and frayed fragments of a very sufficient stout rod. That well-worn implement, no longer fresh and supple, with tough knots and expanding sprays, but ragged, unsightly, deformed and used up, lay across a chair close at hand, not without [specks] marks of blood [about] on it.* A later deletion. For 'broken', 'frayed', 'worn', 'marks of blood on it' Cf.

> . . . the twigs that on this one were lately so fresh
> Are all frayed and worn out . . .
> (*The Flogging-Block.* Algernon's Flogging.)

> I'm afraid
>
> It won't hurt: and the twigs are all broken and frayed.
> (*Ib.* Reginald's Flogging.)

> These twigs are all broken: there's hardly a bud left:
> And I see on the tips some of Collingwood's blood left.
> (*Ib.* Percy's Flogging.)

[51] WAITED, HALF SMILING: *made part of a group too beautiful to bear:* : *looked more than ever too beautiful to bear.*

[52] OF DYING CRUSHED DOWN UNDER HER FEET: *to die at her feet:* : *for a chance of dying at her feet.* One of the first and inevitable impulses of extreme Swinburnian devotion (which is one of the main elements of the poet's masochism). Cf.

> I charge thee for my life's sake, O too sweet
> To crush love with thy cruel faultless feet . . .
> (*Anactoria.*)

> All things were nothing to give
> Once to have sense of you more,
> Touch you and taste of you sweet,
> : :   : :
> Trodden by chance of your feet.
> (*The Oblation.*)

[53] LASHED TO FIERCE INSANITY . . . A PASSION OF VEHEMENT CRUELTY . . . DESTROY HER . . . SCOURGE HER . . . ABSORB THE BLOOD . . . LACERATE HER LOVELINESS . . . WOUND HER OWN WITH HIS TEETH . . . INFLICT CAREFUL TORTURE: Cf.

> I would my love could kill thee . . .
> : :   : :
> I would find grievous ways to have thee slain,
> Intense device and superflux of pain;
> Vex thee with amorous agonies . . .
> : :   : :
> O that I
> Durst crush thee out of life with love . . .
> : :   : :

Would I not hurt thee perfectly? not touch
Thy pores of sense with torture, and make bright
Thine eyes with bloodlike tears and grievous light?

      : :   : :

. Take thy limbs living, and new mould with these
A lyre of many faultless agonies?

      : :   : :

Cruel? but love makes all that love him well
As wise as heaven and crueller than hell.
Me hath love made more bitter toward thee
Than death toward man . . .

(Anactoria.)

[54] In the manuscript these four stanzas were written in the following order: 1st, 2nd, 4th, 3rd, but Swinburne inserted a 2 above the 3rd and a 1 above the 4th, to indicate that these two stanzas should change places; but the printer did not notice the inserted numbers, and the original order is maintained in the galley-proof. Swinburne published these verses, with slight variations, under the title of *The Winds* in *Poems and Ballads* III (1889).

[55] SUNKEN: *taken* (which Swinburne restored in the published version, changing 'a seven score' to 'an hundred').

[56] AND LET MY LOVE'S GANG FREE: *And left my love's for me.*

[57] These verses were published by Gosse and Wise, with mistakes of transcription (one of them inexcusably stupid), under the title of *The King's Ae Son* in *Posthumous Poems of A. C. Swinburne,* 1917; and again, with the same mistakes, in the ludicrously designated 'complete' Bonchurch edition of the poet's works, 1925; and also by W. A. Mac-Innes (M.A.) in *Ballads of the English Border,* 1925, with the mistakes (now consecrated) of the previous bunglers, whose incompetence is a curse in the field of Swinburnian studies.

[58] HAVE: *get.*

⁵⁹ HEAVY: *weary.*

⁶⁰ 'WHAT TO HIS LEMAN, THAT GARR'D HIM BE SLAIN?' *'What shall come to his leman again?'* This is an alteration in a variant of the whole couplet, of which the first form was

> 'What shall come to his light leman?'
> 'Hell's pit and the curse of man'.

⁶¹ SLAYERS: *woman.*

⁶² I BEG YOUR PARDON: 'Birk', 'birken' is Scots and Northern English for 'birch', 'birchen'; hence Margaret's apology. 'Dr. Birkenshaw' is the name of the flagellant Headmaster in a number of the unpublished flogging-pieces (and also in *Love's Cross Currents*); one of the flogging-pieces, a parody of a poem of Burns, is entitled *By Robert Birks.*

⁶³ ANY MAN OR WOMAN AS A fera naturae: *all men as game* : : *any man or woman as fair game* 'ferax naturae' in galley-proof.

⁶⁴ WITH ITS OWNER'S . . . FLEECE: *with the red letters safely on his fleece.*

⁶⁵ Deleted after MOBILE AND SIGNIFICANT: [*and in them a look of*] *a cruel cunning melted into a lighter look of desire that* [*mocked*] *despised and contemned itself.*

⁶⁶ FOUL AND DANGEROUS: *unclean and nameless*: : *unmentionable.*

⁶⁷ HAD RANGED HERSELF AGAINST HIM . . . ONLY: *who professed of late years to detest him*: : *who professed of late years to violent hatred of him.*

⁶⁸ DOG-KENNEL: i.e. cynic.

⁶⁹ M. BEAUHARNAIS: Louis-Napoleon, later Napoleon III. Swinburne, speaking through Lady Midhurst, here, as in all this passage, closely follows Victor Hugo in his contemptuous references to the son of Hortense de Beauharnais and certain of his associates. Cf.

> Quand Monsieur Beauharnais fait du pouvoir une auge.
> (*Les Châtiments.*)

The point of using his mother's name is that he was reputed a bastard: only on his mother's side was his parentage certain, although there was a rumour that the Dutch admiral Verhuell was the lover who had begotten him on the notoriously unstable wife of the King of Holland. Cf.

> . . . Bonaparte apocryphe,
> A coup sûr Beauharnais, peut-être Verhuell . . .
>
> (*Ib.*)

And Swinburne's echo of this in *The Saviour of Society*:
> O son of man, but of what man who knows?

To accuse him of bastardy was not as petty and irrelevant as it might seem; for his chief credential was his name: the word Bonaparte still had a magical effect, and it gave him immense prestige.

[70] BOULEVARDS . . . LEROY . . . SAINT-ARNAUD: General, later Marshal, Armande-Jacques Leroy de Saint-Arnaud, Minister of War in Louis-Napoleon's Ministry of October 1851, and one of the chief organisers of the *coup d'état* of the 2nd of December of that year. On December 4th he launched cavalry brigades on the boulevards against the resistance organised by Victor Hugo and others, and an ugly massacre took place. Of course, he frequently comes under the lash of the greatest masterpiece of invective in the whole of literature. Cf.

> Morny, Maupas le grec, Saint-Arnaud le chacal . . .
>
> (*Les Châtiments.*)

> J'appelle Saint-Arnaud, le meurtre dit: c'est moi.
>
> (*Ib.*)

> Hyènes, loups, chacals, non prévus par Buffon,
> Leroy, Forey, tueurs au fer rongé de rouilles . . .
>
> (*Ib.*)

There was no sense in refusing to call him by the nobiliary part of his name, for it was no less patronymic than

Leroy, and there was no question of his legitimacy. (Of course (taking 'severe accuracy' at its face value) the reference may simply be to nomenclative purism: the strictly correct way of referring to Jacques Henri Bernardin de Saint-Pierre, for example, is 'Bernadin' (apart from Bernardin de Saint-Pierre') and not 'Saint-Pierre' (and still less 'de Saint-Pierre'). But it is probably that Lady Midhurst's objection had further reach than this.)

[71] DURING THE CRIMEAN WAR: in which Saint-Arnaud was one of the two Allied commanders.

[72] FIALIN: Jean-Gilbert-Victor Fialin, comte, then duc de Persigny. The most devoted of all the followers of Louis-Napoleon from an early date in the latter's political career. He became Home Secretary soon after the *coup d'état*, and was twice ambassador in this country. There was some reason for refusing to call *him* by the nobiliary part of his name, for he added it himself to the Fialin he had received from his obscure origin. Cf.

> C'est pour Monsieur Fialin et pour Monsieur Mocquart
> Que Lannes d'un boulet eut la cuisse coupée . . .
>
> *(Ib.)*

[73] ET CIE: Louis-Napoleon's other Ministers, particularly Troplong, Flahaut and Rouher, against whom Hugo frequently inveighs.

[74] TALLEYRAND-BRIDOISON: Talleyrand, the type of the sharp-witted resourceful diplomat; Brid'oison (*Le Mariage de Figaro*), the type of the ignorant doltishly formalistic judge ('J'aime la fo-orme avant tout'): the later comparison, even if it is not altogether excluded by the former, seems more than a little strained in the case of Mr Linley: the oxymoron misses fire, and is unworthy of so clever a person as the speaker.

[75] MADAME DE FAUBLAS: The meaning, presumably, is a female edition of the Chevalier de Faublas, and not the girl who

became the wife of the latter. The reference is to the novel *Les Amours* (in some editions *Les Aventures*) *du Chevalier de Faublas*, by Louvet *de Couvray* (Paris 1787–89). This work, which the idealistic Madame Rolland thought 'joli' and 'de bon gout', but which shocked the prudishness of the strait-laced Sir Walter Scott, had an immense vogue in its own day and for many years after. (As late as 1852, Flaubert, who thought it 'inepte', notes with disgust that its annual sale, and that of *L'Amour conjugal*, exceed that of all other books.) The humorous passages are amusing enough, and those dealing with adventure move with smooth and rapid ease, but it is the ease of superficiality, and the whole book may be summed up thus. Faublas, whom one admirer describes as 'une idole du boudoir, un héros de bonne compagnie, libertin quelquefois sensible, toujours spirituel et Français', is nothing or little but a facile amorist, and the book (there are 1,500 pages of it) is made up of the succession of his affairs with various women. Bed-scenes predominate; they are often interrupted by intrusions which have a perilous sequence, and this provides a good deal of the 'plot'.

Swinburne appears to have had a soft spot for the book. The transvestism, which is one of its features, doubtless had a particular attraction for him. (In one section, Faublas, disguised as a nun, seduces a real nun—and in a most un-nun-like way she is very grateful to him.)

Here again, it is difficult to see the aptness of the comparison: in virtue of what could Lady Midhurst be assimilated to a *coureur* of this sort?

[76] Deleted after HIS MARRIAGE: *with the twin-sister and co-heiress.*

[77] BATTUE: *massacre.*

[78] THE BITTER RELISH: *the energetic enjoyment*: : *a sense of the bliss.*

[79] OF THE MOST INCREDIBLE: Mr. Linley imports his French into his English here.

[80] THE BLACK OX, etc.: See Brewster, *Dictionary of Phrase and Fable*, under Ox.

[81] BALZAC . . . EYES: See Note [4] on Chapter I.

[82] 'THREE CRANBERRIES, YOU MEAN': Swinburne expanded the 'Cranberries' of the MS. to this in the British Museum galley proof.

[83] THERE WAS MORE . . . HARMONIES OF HER TALK: Swinburne later (the ink is different) lightly traced brackets at the beginning and end of this sentence, and put a dubitative question-mark after the second of them.

[84] ROMAN: inserted by Swinburne in the British Museum galley-proof.

[85] AT THE SIGHT OF . . . RUMOURS: *at once when the boy came up, remembering the rumours of three rough herdboys.* The reference here is to 'two or three boys I seem to have heard of, fresh from the paternal plough', .73.

[86] BRUSHING . . . TICKLE: Common expressions in the unpublished flogging-pieces. Cf.

> I'll remember to tickle him well, and pick out
> A good cutting fresh rod for him . . .
> *(The Flogging-Block.* Charlie's Flogging.)

> . . . And see me unsparingly brushing your bum.
> *(Ib.* Reginald's Flogging.)

[87] SENT UP: i.e. 'sent up for good': at Eton, work of a certain merit was (and still is) 'sent up' to the Headmaster's notice as being 'good'.

[88] THE BILL: a list of boys who have to see the Headmaster for some reason, usually (as in *Lesbia Brandon*), but not always, of an unpleasant nature.

[89] CELA VAUT LA PEINE DE VEXER: Cf. the following, from an unpublished part of a letter to C. A. Howell, dated Nov. 18

[1870]: 'I had a note yesterday from Eton which I send you a copy of . . . The boy whipped is a young cousin of mine, a very handsome youngster "et qui vaut bien la peine de vexer" as the dear and great Marquis has it'. 'The dear and great Marquis' of course is the Marquis de Sade, of whom Swinburne and Howell were practising disciples.

[90] COMPRESSED . . . NECESSARY MOVEMENT: *could have yelped with pain like a whipped hound*: : *drew together his lips and eyebrows as in sharp pain at every necessary movement which deranged his uneasy seat.*

[91] Deleted after BORN CLEVER: *or dumb, the boy said inwardly.*

[92] STILL TINGLED AT THE WORD 'BLOCK': *still had marks of the birch on his person and tingled instinctively at the very mention of a flogging-block.* A later deletion.

[93] UNMISTAKEABLE: *and at once divined what the boy's drawn forehead and manner of sitting could not but make evident.* A later deletion.

[94] I AND ANOTHER FELLOW, etc.: Cf.

In the days when your father and I went to school—
When we used to be sent for each morning, and
    stripped . . .
                    (*The Flogging-Block.* Edward's Flogging.)

[95] THE DUE MURMUR: *a duly low.*

[96] AFTER TWELVE: there was a free period after 12 o'clock, and it was then that the boys in the bill went to the Headmaster.

[97] PRAEPOSTOR: prefect. The duties and powers of prefects at Eton were more extensive formerly than they are now.

[98] SHOW UP: hand or send to (the Headmaster in this case). 'Bill' here appears to have the special meaning of flogging-list. Cf.

DR. BIRKENSHAW. Let us just look the flogging-lists over:
　　　　　it's pleasant
　　　　　And useful—amusing and helpful—to
　　　　　search out
　　　　　The names of the boys whose backsides
　　　　　wear most birch out.
　　　　(*The Flogging-Block*. Charlie's Flogging.)

99 . . . FIRST AND HAVE IT OVER: Cf.

'I'd rather come first, and have it over', said Ernie . . .
　　(*A Boy's First Flogging*, published anonymously
　　　　　in *The Whippingham Papers*.)

100 THEIR BABY . . . STORIES, etc.: The references are to characters and events in *Love's Cross Currents*. Miss Helena Cheyne married Sir Thomas Midhurst in 1819; their baby daughter was Amicia; there was a scandal in the latter's life, for she ran away from her husband, Captain Philip Harewood, and after he divorced her she married Fred Stanford, with whom she had eloped.

101 HER DAUGHTER: also called Amicia (b.1841). She too was to have a sentimental aberration after her marriage, thus confirming Lord Charles's distrust of 'the race'.

102 GREAT LIGHTS: *swells*.

103 MRS. LEMONS: Probably 'Mrs. Lemons' is a satirical corruption of Mrs. Hemans, who would be a 'great light' among female poets to Lord Brandon and other of the literary profane present at this typical dinner-party of the 'educated' classes.

104 PINK PERFECTION: *coarse-grained comeliness*.

105 ART'S ABOVE NATURE IN THAT RESPECT: Mr. Linley is very Baudelairian. Cf. the French poet's *Eloge du Maquillage* in *Le Peintre de la Vie Moderne* (1863), and especially ' . . Louis XV (qui fut non le produit d'une vraie civilisation, mais d'une récurrence de barbarie) pousse la dépravation jusqu'à ne plus goûter que la *simple nature*!', and 'La femme . . . doit emprunter à tous les arts les moyens de s'élever au-dessus de la nature . . .'

[106] WITH KING LEAR'S LEAVE: *Lear*, 4, VI.

[107] FOURTEEN: *eleven*: : *twelve or*. This is a good instance of Swinburne's shakiness in the matter of dates.

[108] THAT GIRL'S MARRIAGE, etc.: Cf. Note [100] of this chapter.

[109] WHY, GOOD HEAVEN, . . . THE GIRL'S STEP-FATHER: A passage in one of Lady Midhurst's own letters shows that the insinuation was not quite gratuitous: '. . . Captain H. told me so; he was one of *my* friends at that epoch; he was courting your mother, and in consequence hers also. Indeed, I believe he was in love with me at the time, although I am ten years older . . .'(*Love's Cross Currents*. Lady Midhurst to her granddaughter.)

[110] HER BROTHER: 'old Lord Cheyne, the noted philanthropist.' (*Ib.*)

[111] DIED OF THAT PORTENTOUS ASS THEIR SON: Edmund Cheyne. 'Educated in the lap of philanthropy, suckled at the breasts of all the virtues in turn, he was even then the worthy associate of his father in all schemes of improvement . . . Mr. Cheyne was a Socialist—a Democrat of the most advanced kind . . . The wrongs of women gave him many a sleepless night . . . the moral-sublime of this young man's character was something incredible. Unlike his father, he was much worried by religious speculations—certain phases of belief and disbelief he saw fit to embody in a series of sonnets, which were privately printed under the title of "Aspirations, by a Wayfarer". Very flabby sonnets they were, leaving in the mouth a taste of chaff and dust; but the genuine stamp of a sincere and single mind was visible throughout . . . The wife of Lord Cheyne, not unnaturally, had died in giving birth to such a meritorious portent.' (*Ib.*)

[112] HER LORD WAS THE ONE MAN IN LONDON: 'Malignant persons, incapable of appreciating the moral-sublime, said that she died of a plethora of conjugal virtue on the part of her husband.' (*Ib.*)

[113] A FAIRE CREVER UN OCTOGENAIRE: A variant of a commonplace in French erotic literature. Cf. 'Elle était la reine du plaisir, comme une image . . . de cette joie qui transforme . . . les vieillards en jeunes gens'. (Balzac.)

[114] LES GENOUX . . . LISSES, RONDS: Commonplaces again. Cf. 'les genoux polis . . . la rondeur prestigieuse du cou . . .' (Balzac); 'Ce qu'on voyait de la jambe était rond . . . poli.' (Gautier).

[115] UNE SAVEUR PLUS FEMME . . . CETTE ODEUR D'AMOUR: Here, too, Mr. Linley is very Baudelarian. Cf.

Je confondais l'odeur de la fourrure avec l'odeur de la femme. (Baudelaire, *Fusées*.)

Je respire l'odeur de ton sein chaleureux.
(Id., *Les Fleurs du Mal*.)

Et, des pieds jusques à la tête,
Un air subtil, un dangereux parfum
Nagent auteur de son corps brun.
(Id., ib.)

[116] BETWEEN THE TWO RACES: If this is meant to imply that old Lord Cheyne's wife was English while Savigny was French, Swinburne forgot that he had made her a Frenchwoman in *Love's Cross Currents*.

[117] PROVOKED: challenged, a sense obsolete in 1850. But in Mr. Linley's mouth it is a gallicism and not an archaism.

[118] IL RAFFOLAIT . . . TASTE: In the Brotherton galley-proof a line is drawn through the sentence, but Swinburne did not delete it in the manuscript nor even put a dubitative question-mark against it.

[113] CHANGING: *softened.*

[120] Deleted between PHYSICAL PHILOSOPHY and JUST NOW SHE HAD: *Perhaps the highest compliment that can be paid to pleasure or to beauty is indeed this: to compel or persuade them into a fierce but unreluctant union with their apparent opposites, so (if it at all may be,) to satiate and relieve, to express and fulfil, the overbearing aim which directs and the overwhelming sense which absorbs the soul through the body in seasons of vehement and mutinous ecstasy of flesh and spirit; and to torment may be a form of thanksgiving, to oppress an act of homage. On the same principle lovers and mothers use fierce and violent words in the extreme agony of tenderness, in the desperate energy of love. To draw tears also into her service who delights in laughter, to bow down pain also under the yoke of pleasure, would seem to be the final tribute wanting to final triumph. Torture and rapture, hatred and love, lie surely as closely together, are perhaps at root as inextricable and indissoluble, in essence as simply one and identical, as evil and good.*

It can hardly be necessary for an editor to intimate his fervent disbelief and disapproval of the especial paradox above set forth. In compliment to the perspicacity of judicious readers he has not enclosed within brackets or commas any part of this exposition; it will be understood that one of two parties must be supposed to have spoken in self-defence. Leaving behind with due disdain both hypothesis and apology we may look again with comparative tolerance upon a form of cynicism less ruinous and less rare. Swinburne indicated this deletion not by drawing lines through the passage, but by putting brackets round it and writing 'Just now she had' and '(Dele) (   )' above 'philosophy. Perhaps the highest'. The printer ignored these indications, and the passage appears in the galleys; Swinburne deleted it again in the Brotherton set. The passage is awkwardly intrusive coming where it does; and the author's disclaimer of the sentiment, and description of it as 'spoken in self-defence' by 'one of two parties' is more than awkward.

[121] A FELLOW ABOUT YOUR AGE: Reginald Harewood (b.1838), the hero of *Love's Cross Currents*; son of Captain Philip Harewood and Lady Midhurst's daughter Amicia. See Note [100] of this chapter.

[122] Deleted after SUNSHINE ABOUT IT: *green-grey with flakes of gold.*

[123] THE HAND: *the academic hand.*

[124] SLIGHT: Wrongly printed as 'light' in the galley-proofs. In the Brotherton set 'light' is deleted, but a question-mark is placed against it in the margin. This would seem to show that Swinburne did not have the manuscript by him to refer to when he went over this set.

[125] SNOB: *sneak.* In the Brotherton galley Swinburne altered 'snob' back to 'sneak'. He probably would not have done so had he been able to see from the manuscript that he had already advanced from 'sneak' to 'snob'.

[126] WHIPPED FOR DOING A YOUNG ONE'S VERSES, etc. Cf. a similar incident in *Love's Cross Currents*: 'I wonder if Frank remembers what a tremendous licking he got once for doing Lunsford's verses for him *without* a false quantity, so that when they were shown up he was caught out and came to awful grief'. The Frank here is Frank Cheyne (son of Lady Midhurst's other brother), who was eighteen years younger than his cousin, the 'nephew Cheyne', who has just been mentioned. No doubt this benevolent action, introduced into two works by Swinburne, was one of his Eton memories; and perhaps he himself (a good verse-writer at school) was the boy who suffered so heavily for the benefaction.

[127] SENT UP FOR GOOD: See Note [87] of this chapter.

[128] ARDEN: In the manuscript, what may be 'Arden' is apparently changed to 'Harden'; the galleys give 'Horden'; in the Brotherton set Swinburne altered this to 'Arden'.

Arden is therefore the family name; but in a later chapter
(*Les Malheurs de la Vertu*) Mr. Linley speaks of a visit he
made to Eton in 1833 to see 'my nephew Sundon ——
Wariston as he is now'; and Denham, in the same chapter,
refers to him as 'Lord Sundon'. Swinburne could be as
shaky on names as he was on dates or anything arithmetical.

[129] THE MISFORTUNES OF VIRTUE . . . THE PROSPERITIES OF VICE:
The sub-titles of the two best-known works of the Marquis
de Sade: *Justine ou les Malheurs de la Vertu* and *Juliette
ou les Prospérités du Vice*, which had a sort of fascination
for Swinburne over many years of his literary career. Of
course Lady Midhurst would not know these works (as she
indicates later, even Rabelais is closed to her). But she
would have heard the phrases from Mr. Linley—an accomplished Sadist in all senses—and she cites him as one with
whom they were commonplace. In a subsequent passage of
this chapter, later deleted, he uses the words 'ou les malheurs de la vertu'; and in the chapter entitled *Les Malheurs
de la vertu* he speaks of his own wife as 'an instance of
suffering virtue' (under the moral or mental tortures to
which he subjected her).

[130] Deleted after WOULD TELL YOU SO: *in his favourite French*.
See preceding Note.

[131] VOYEZ DONC CE SCELERAT QUI RICANE: This and the large
section that follows up to and including 'entangled uncle
and nephew' (p.106) are deleted in the Brotherton galleys,
and there, in the margin, is written in pencil 'They came
together'; so that the text becomes '. . . and exchange a
pass or two. They came together in the mazes of a discussion . . .' Swinburne evidently thought that, with this
section, there was too much harping on the subject of flagellation, even after he had made considerable deletions. But
he passed the passage when he revised the manuscript
before it went to the printers.

[132] GOBEMOUCHARD: A good pun. 'Gobemouche' of course

(literally 'a fly-catcher') means 'an easily gullible simpleton', and 'mouchard' is a popular word for 'a policy-spy' or 'detective'.

[133] CALEMBOUR: Swinburne wrote 'calembourg'; surely a *lapsus calami,* and not an attempt at another pun.

[134] HE ENFORCED THIS . . . ON THIS OCCASION: This sentence was inserted later, replacing the following passage, deleted by two downward strokes: *This sentence was sportively enforced by a sharp stroke with the flat hand which made the boy cry out and catch his breath: the secret pinch that followed brought the tears full into his eyes, and his teeth pressed his underlip hard: these caresses had literally enough touched a tender part.*

[135] I WANT TO KNOW WHEN YOU WERE FLOGGED LAST?: *'I want to know if you ever get whipped?'* Silence. *'Now, my boy, I will know. When were you flogged last?'* A later deletion.

[36] Deleted between IN THE FACE and SAY: *even with those great hazel eyes stolen from some girl, and say you are not whipped now and then.* A later deletion.

[137] BUDS, etc.: Cf. *The Flogging-Block, passim.* e.g.:
The supple Twigs, the swelling Buds I view,
That once too well my burning Buttocks knew.
(Prologue).

There are just seven twigs, and each twig is in bud—
And I'll bet you the very first cut will draw blood.
(Algernon's Flogging).

[138] AND THEY STING, DON'T THEY: Cf.
Master. Does it sting? does it hurt you, my boy? does it tickle?
(*Ib.,* Ib.)

'And how do you like it, Fane?' he says, 'does it sting? does it sting you Fane?'
(*Reginald's Flogging,* Part II, published anonymously in *The Whippingham Papers.*)

And for gloating sadistic taunts in general see Note [28] of this chapter.

[139] RITES OF MARRIAGE . . . BETWEEN YOUR PERSON AND THE BIRCH: Cf.

How the birch seems to love Master Wilfred's backside!
How it kisses and clasps and embraces it!

> (*The Flogging-Block*. Willie's Flogging.)

Arthur. Algernon's bottom and Birkenshaw's rod—
    A'n't they a couple of lovers, by God!
Reginald. Lovers? the banns have been spoken in
    church . . .

> (*Ib*. Algernon's Flogging, Chorus, Str. I.)

[140] Deleted after THIS BOY HAS HAD! *He had found out by means of a fresh blow with the hand, which brought such exquisite pain into Herbert's face as could not be mistaken or controlled: the cheeks were contracted and the whole body quivered.* [This sentence was incorporated in the foregoing paragraph when Swinburne revised this part of the manuscript] *but he did not appeal.* A later deletion.

[141] SMALLEST FOR A BOY: *prettiest*.

[142] Deleted after SPOIL THEM: *Better have the marks where no eye can see them, your own included.* A later deletion.

[143] HE WILL LIVE TO BE THANKFUL TO YOU: For this Pecksniffian humbug, a common additional infliction from sadistic punishers on their victims, cf.

Master. . . You'll live, sir, to thank me for whipping you
    well.

*   *   *

You'll remember your numberless floggings with
    with gratitude.

> (*The Flogging-Block*. Edward's Flogging.)

[144] Deleted after I CAN SEE: *if your tutor were not to tickle your hide now and then with birch twigs.* A later deletion.

[145] A TOUCH OR TWO OF THE OLD SCHOOL: *details of school flagellation.* A later deletion. It is such 'details' that furnish the epical bulk of *The Flogging-Block* and the other pieces belonging to that cycle.

[146] Deleted after THE BITTERNESS OF BIRCH: *interlarded with further queries as to his recent flogging.* A later deletion.

[147] LET HIS VICTIM SLIP: *reserve for the present his intended tales of the whipping-block.* A later alteration.

[148] ADDING A PROMISE WELL UNDERSTOOD: *with a promise well understood that she would come late to his room to console him.*

[149] ALL DAYLIGHT HAS GONE OUT OF THE WORLD WITH HIM: Cf. Baudelaire:

> ... depuis la disparition de Balzac, ce prodigieux météore qui couvrira notre pays d'un nuage de gloire, comme un orient bizarre et exceptionnel, comme une aurore polaire inondant le désert glacé de ses lumières féeriques, —toute curiosité, relativement au roman, s'etait apaisée et endormie.'
>
> (Article on *Madame Bovary*, pub.
> in *L'Artiste* in 1857.)

[150] BLONDET, LOUSTEAU ET CIE.: Characters in Balzac. Emile Blondet (in *La Vieille Fille, Le Cabinet des Antiques, Un Grand Homme de province à Paris* and other works), journalist; a critic of no moral delicacy, one of whose specialities was denigration of even the best-assured reputations. Etienne Lousteau (in *Splendours et Misères des courtisanes, Illusions perdues, Une Homme d'affaires, Les Comédiens sans le savoir,* etc.), a multifarious journalist, a sponger, an exploiter of women—in short, a man whose living by his wits was restricted by no over-niceness of principle.

[181] HUGO'S ORATION: At the graveside. Praise of Balzac's work could not have gone higher: 'Tous ses livres ne forment qu'un livre, livre vivant, lumineux, profond, où l'on voit aller et venir et marcher et se mouvoir, avec je ne sais quoi d'effaré et de terrible mêlé réel, toute notre civilisation contemporaine; livre merveilleux, que le poète intitule *Comédie* et qu'il aurait pu intituler *Histoire*, qui prend toutes les formes et tous les styles, que dépasse Tacite et qui va jusqu'à Suétone, qui traverse Beaumarchais et qui va jusqu'à Rabelais; livre qui est l'observation et qui est l'imagination; qui prodigue le vrai, l'intime, le bourgeois, le trivial, le matériel, et qui, par moments, à travers toutes les réalités brusquement et largement déchirées, laisse tout à coup entrevoir le plus sombre et le plus tragique idéal.' Etc.

[152] PHILANTHROPE MALGRE DIEU: (i.e. in spite of human nature and the sorry state of the world viewed as the workmanship of a God); a good description of Hugo in his obstinate optimism regarding things in general. 'La vie et les hommes me faisaient horreur' says the solicitor Derville in *Gobseck*; 'Le monde est infâme et méchant' says Mme. de Beauséant in *Le Père Goriot*; and these two evaluations sum up the pessimism of Balzac, who unlike Hugo saw no remedy and had no kind of hope. (The Christian religion for him was no more than a political instrument to keep the vile herd in order.) He could never have written

> God's in His heaven—
> All's right with the world!

but such facile faith is one of the cardinal elements of Hugo's creed.

[153] POETE MALGRE LUI: i.e. in spite of the non-poetic didactic which his conscious self aimed at being.

[154] ENOUGH TO MAKE HIM TURN IN HIS GRAVE: If this means that Balzac would have been shocked at the idea of *Eugénie*

Grandet being taken as representative of him at his best, it remains true that he was very well pleased with this work. E.g. *'Eugénie Grandet,* un de mes tableaux les plus achevés . . . J'en suis très content.' (*Lettres à l'Etrangère.*) And again: 'Eugénie Grandet est une belle œuvre.' (*Ib.*) But Swinburne would prefer the stronger meat of such works as *La Cousine Bette and La Fille aux yeux d'or*: things lurid and dealing with the fierce reach of passions.

[155] MADAME MARNEFFE: In Balzac's *La Cousine Bette.* Valérie Fortin, the wife first of Jean-Paul-Stanislas Marneffe and then of Célestin Crevel ('le représentant du parvenu parisien'). A woman of consummate depravity, intelligent and very beautiful. 'La fine, l'élégante Valérie', whose unclothed charms 'offraient des beautés surnaturelles', was the property at one and the same time of Marneffe, Crevel, the Brazilian Baron Henri de Montes, the Pole Count Wenceslas Steinbock, and the Baron Hulot . . . 'C'est madame de Maintenon dans la jupe de Ninon!' says of her one of the more respectable characters of the book, an ex-professor of Greek who had won distinction as a critic; 'Lui plaire, c'est l'affaire d'une soirée où l'on a de l'esprit; mais être aimé d'elle, c'est un triomphe qui peut suffire à l'orgueil d'un homme et en remplir la vie.' She came to a nasty end: Montès, terribly jealous, paid a prostitute to get herself infected by one of his negroes with a horrible disease, which he himself contracted from her, and then passed on to Valérie, who (and Crevel also) died of it in a most repulsive fashion: she was an 'amas de pourriture' some days before she cease to live. (Montès—and presumably the prostitute —hurried to Brazil, where alone the disease could be cured.)

[156] MADAME DE MERTEUIL: The Marquise de Merteuil, the central female character of Laclos' *Les Liaisons dangereuses* (1782). The central male character is the Vicomte de Valmont, the Don Juan of eighteenth-century France, well summed up thus by one of the most competent historians of the French novel: 'Il est un gourmet et un artiste en

vice; il est le génie du mal, Satan en habit à la française';
which is an abridgment of what Sainte-Beuve had said in
the last batch of his *Lundis*: 'Il existe dans ces caractères
[of which Valmont is the representative] une base d'orgueil
infernal qui se complique de recherche sensuelle, une féro-
cité d'amour-propre, de vanité, et une sécheresse de cœur
jointes au raffinement des desirs, et c'est ainsi qu'ils en
viennent vite à introduire la méchanceté, la cruauté même
et une scélératesse criminelle, jusque dans le plus doux des
penchants, dans la plus tendre des faiblesses.' Madame de
Merteuil is the admiring and admired associate of Valmont,
and at the end his deadly enemy (deadly in the literal
sense, for he met his death through her). She is the perfidy
of woman brought to a terrible perfection; the perfidy of
woman deployed against the predatory selfishness of the
male—and against anything else that happens to stand in
her way. She is cleverer than Valmont even—and so more
diabolical than this pattern of elegant satanism. The best
summary of her is that of the Goncourt brothers: '. . . la
femme que Laclos a peinte et à laquelle il a attribué tant
de grâces et de ressources infernales . . . Ainsi formées,
secrètes et profondes, impénétrables et invulnérables, elles
apportent dans la galanterie, dans la vengeance, dans le
plaisir, dans la haine, un cœur de sang-froid, un esprit toujours présent, un ton de liberté, un cynisme de grande
dame, mêlé d'une hautaine élégance, une sort de légèreté
implacable. Ces femmes perdent un homme pour le perdre.
Elles sèment la tentation dans la candeur, la débauche dans
l'innocence. Elles martyrisent l'honnête femme dont la
vertu leur déplaît; et, l'ont-elles touchée à mort, elles pous-
sent ce cri de vipère: 'Ah! quand une femme frappe dans
le cœur d'une autre, la blessure est incurable . . .' Elles font
éclater le déshonneur dans les familles comme un coup de
foudre: elles mettent aux mains des hommes les querelles
et les épées qui tuent. Figures étonnantes qui fascinent et
qui glacent! On pourrait dire d'elles, dans le sens moral,
qu'elles dépassent de toute la tête la Messaline antique.

Elles créent en effet, elles révèlent, elles incarnent en elles-mêmes une corruption supérieure à toutes les autres et que l'on serait tenté d'appeler une corruption idéale . . .'

(*La Femme Au* 18e *siècle.*)

[157] THAT SMALLPOX: After Valmont's death and the revelation of her crimes, Madame de Merteuil was ignominiously cold-shouldered and avoided and even hooted at the theatre, but she remained superbly self-possessed throughout this public reprobation; the following night, however, she fell into a heavy fever, and this was followed by an attack of smallpox.

[158] THE BOSTON LADIES IN DICKENS . . . HOMINY . . . TOPPIT . . . CODGER, etc.: *Martin Chuzzlewit,* chap. XXXIV. The two 'literary ladies', Miss Toppit and Miss Codger, are cited by Lady Midhurst as proficients in the art of rhapsodising. We give a specimen of their typical American vacuous gush (in the best manner of the Transcendentalists of the Boston school):

'To be presented to a Pogram,' said Miss Codger, 'by a Hominy, indeed, a thrilling moment is it in its impressiveness on what we call our feelings. But why we call them so, or why impressed they are, if impressed they are at all, or if at all we are, or if there really is, oh gasping one! a Pogram or a Hominy, or any active principle to which we give those titles, is a topic, Spirit searching, light abandoned, much too vast to enter on, at this unlooked-for crisis.'

'Mind and matter,' said the lady in the wig, 'glide swift into the vortex of immensity. Howls the sublime, and softly sleeps the calm Ideal, in the whispering chambers of Imagination. To hear it, sweet it is. But then, outlaughs the stern philosopher, and saith to the Grotesque, "What ho! arrest for me that Agency. Go, bring it here!" And so the vision fadeth.' (The style of Henry James in its most developed state has, notwithstanding all differences, a curious affinity with the former of these two masterpieces of utterance: he always remained a true, and somewhat anile,

Bostonian, in spite of his strenuous efforts to make a European of himself.)

[159] THE GREATEST AND GRAVEST BOOK OF A CENTURY: An opinion that would not be shared by the orthodox, for whom this book would be horribly wicked, a creation of the Devil. But true intelligence has always on meeting it saluted it as one of the greatest things of the world. For Stendhal, who derived in large part from it, it was a sort of Bible. The Goncourts, who also owed much to it, spoke thus of it and the age which it expressed: 'La corruption devient un art égal en cruautés, en manques de foi, en trahisons, à l'art des tyrannies. Le machiavélisme entre dans la galanterie, il la domine et la gouverne. C'est l'heure où Laclos écrit d'après nature ses *Liaisons dangereuses*, ce livre admirable et exécrable qui est à la morale amoureuse de la France du dix-huitième siècle ce qu'est le traité du *Prince* à la morale politique de l'Italie du seizième.' No less enthusiastic—in spite of moralistic prejudice—is Le Breton, who may be taken as typical of the better academic criticism of France: 'L'œuvre est faite à la perfection. Je ne parle même pas des qualités du style: cela est écrit avec un stylet d'acier. Mais entre tant de romans par lettres . . . il n'en est aucun . . . où l'intérêt soit aussi bien conduit, aussi gradué, aussi continu . . . On n'a jamais eu plus d'adresse, et les *Liaisons dangereuses* peuvent être regardées comme le premier roman bien fait qui ait paru en France.' My own copy of the book once belonged to Arnold Bennett, and at he end of it this master wrote a note in pencil (dated 14.7.16): 'When you read this you are apt to think it is the only really realistic novel ever written. It is very great in parts, and some of the character drawing is very great. La canaillerie becomes beautiful.' The next sentence shows that he shared Swinburne's opinion on a point of detail as well as on the value of the book as a whole. 'Realistically the blot on it is that Madame de Merteuil should be disfigured by smallpox at the end, and, in a less degree, that Valmont should be

killed in a duel. Too much poetic justice. However, these things are trifles, because they are at the end, they do not influence the plot, and they occupy such a little space.'

Léon Daudet also had the same opinion as Swinburne of this work and expressed it in particularly the same words: '. . . *Les Liaisons dangereuses*—le plus grand livre du XVIIIᵉ siècle . . .' (*Action Française*, 22 novembre, 1938.)

The Goncourts, in a passage quoted in Note [156], say that Madame de Merteuil overtops the Messalinas of the ancient world. It could further be said that she and Valmont overtop Lady Macbeth and Iago and any of Shakespeare's evil characters. In fact, Iago and Lady Macbeth are crude pygmies to the two protagonists of the greatest book of the eighteenth century.

I have elsewhere in this work stated that Saintsbury does not so much as mention Laclos in the 620 pages of his *History of French Literature*. Things are even worse in his large two-volume *History of the French Novel*. Here once again, in a work dealing specifically and exclusively with *the novel* in France, and professing to deal with it comprehensively, Laclos is given no place at all in the book proper! Saintsbury does mention him in the miscalled history, but it is only to proclaim his Grundyish intention of keeping him severely out of the highly respectable exhibition run by Saintsbury. 'Others may ask,' he says, in reference to the indecorous, the wicked Rétif de la Bretonne, whom, after what must have been long and worried hesitation, he decided to admit (and relegate to an obscure corner)—'Others may ask why he is let in and Choderlos de Laclos and Louvet de Courray,* with some more, kept out, as they most assuredly will be.' 'As they most assuredly will be': there is almost something savage in this; here is the martinet Bible-

---

* Sic; and—to make matters worse—'Coudray' in the Index: Saintsbury was an ignoramus even about certain things of which in his professional capacity he should have had a better than the pitiful knowledge he exhibits here.

class teacher speaking, and not a man who has a right to give opinions on French literature. 'However', goes on Saintsbury, somewhat naïvely, 'on representations from persons of distinction I have given Laclos a place in an outhouse. And I have made the place as much of a penitentiary as I could.' Penitentiary! Again a note of savagery, of heavy-witted prejudice, of prepense condemnation that is the very opposite of criticism, in which Saintsbury plumed himself as being one of the elect. (And 'outhouse': has this the—shall we say nasty?—meaning it has in certain parts of England and elsewhere? If so, Saintsbury is cruder than Laclos ever is; in fact Laclos is never crude; he was always a gentleman compared to Saintsbury, who never managed to get beyond genteelness.) Well, the outhouse is among the *Addenda and Corrigenda.* 'I am aware,' Saintsbury there says, 'that persons of distinction' [there is an ill-concealed sneer here] have taken an interest in it.' (They have done very much more than that! But you never get honesty from your orthodox polemist.) Dowson, he 'understands' (note the sneer again, the detachment of the superior person who won't bother to get or verify information on certain matters), 'wasted his time and talent on translating the thing.' Saintsbury, accordingly, overcoming his prudish nausea, virtuously went so far as to read 'the thing' 'with care', to make sure that his contempt for it 'was not unjustified'. (One would have thought he would have read 'with care' so celebrated a book before deciding to exclude it from a voluminous and comprehensive survey of the French novel. And observe that he does not say 're-read'. One suspects that he really had never read the masterpiece at all before arriving at his donkeyish decision.) But the care was all to no avail (a foregone conclusion to anyone knowing the real Saintsbury and his terrible limitations: his want of vision, his radical incompetence, once he moved into certain territory). There follows a page or so of inept rigmarole, **of** which the upshot is that Saintsbury 'cannot see how any interest can be taken in the book'! There were so many things he could not see, poor man . . . Those who do not suffer from Saintsbury's inhibitions and prepossessions, and know a masterpiece when they meet one, will agree with Swinburne, Arnold Bennett and the other admirers of Laclos, and adjudge that here as in certain other matters Saintsbury has acquired eminence as an ass. (It will no doubt be inferred that I have little or no esteem for him. That is not true. I admire and enjoy him, but for qualities (literary) other than those for which he has won a reputation.)

It would be easy to trace the influence of Laclos on Swinburne's novelistic work. Joseph Knight, writing to him about *Love's Cross Currents* in 1866, remarked on the filiation, and compared him to the French writer alone: 'I think the letters are fuller of character than those in the work which first suggested to you the idea, and the characters are every whit as life-like as those of Choderlos de Laclos.' I have given pointers to the influence here and there in my Commentary.

[160] PAUL ET VIRGINIE: Innocent and edifying, the book *par excellence* for schoolgirls who study French.

[161] HIS TELEMAQUE: Of course the author of Télémaque is Fénelon and not Bernardin de Saint-Pierre, who wrote *Paul et Virginie*. The deliberate confusing error is Lady Midhurst's way of showing her contempt for this representative of the 'educated' classes of the British race. Things are no better to-day—if anything, they are worse—than in mid-Victorian times.

[162] Deleted after TELEMAQUE: *ou les malheurs de la vertu*. See Note [129].

[163] ANYONE QUI NE POUVAIT SE CONSOLER: A reference to the first sentence of the book: 'Calypso ne pouvoit se consoler du départ d'Ulysse'. There is probably also a reference to the fact that Telemachus left, more or less inconsolable, three women who set their caps at him.

[164] LATTER-DAY PAMPHLETS: Swinburne's feelings about Carlyle were very mixed. He detested many of the Scottish sage's opinions and especially of his appreciations—or rather depreciations—of men whom he himself reverenced. Cf. his published sonnets against Carlyle, and also the following from a letter to Norman MacColl (Feb. 3, 1877):

'. . . Mr. Carlyle's political predications—in which that great and maleficent old man has insulted every principle that I cherish and well-nigh every man whom I revere.' But he liked certain things even in his philosophy (e.g. traits in his portrait of Frederick the Great), and he was strongly attracted by much in his style.

[165] SCOTCH ALE WITH LAFFITTE: Lafourcade, with his usual stupidity, takes all this phrase as being a description of *Latter-day Pamphlets*. Of course Laffitte is Balzac; Mr. Linley's thought is: Can one have a taste for two authors as dissimilar as the best claret and Scotch ale?

[166] Deleted after DELICIOUSLY AS THUNDER: *rolling thunderclaps of humour: : growling clouds of eloquence broken by sharp thunder-claps of humour.*

[167] HE FLOUNDERS VIOLENTLY IN DETAILS, etc.: Mr. Linley is right against Lady Midhurst's unqualified enthusiasm. Swinburne no doubt was thinking particularly of Balzac's not infrequent collapse into grotesque crudity of metaphor. Cf. 'César tomba de toute la hauteur de son espoir dans les marais fangeux de l'incertitude'. (*César Birotteau*); 'Madame Vanquer se coucha en rôtissant comme une perdrix dans sa barde, au feu du desir qui la saisit de quitter le suaire de Vauquer pour renaître en Goriot. (*Le Père Goriot.*) Cf. also, in another direction, the terrible comic pathos of 'N'aigrissez pas le lait d'une mère', said by Mme. de Mortsauf to the young man who was trying to overcome her virtue.

[168] HIS CHIEF IMITATOR, etc.: Much of what follows concerning this somewhat cryptic person applies to the work of Dickens.

But Dickens could not be called an imitator of Balzac; and at the date of the dinner-party (1850) he was definitively established, and there could be no question of his having to wait ten years before being given rank as a master; besides, Swinburne from the first had a great and almost thoroughgoing admiration for him, and would not be likely to make Lady Midhurst, a mouthpiece of his own dearest opinions, impugn him in such an unsparing manner. Charles Reade appears to be the only alternative. He wrote *The Autobiography of a Thief* (1858), originally a part of *It is Never too Late to Mend* (1856). ('Blackleg' at the time Swinburne wrote *Lesbia Brandon* did not have its present-day sense, but meant a turf-swindler or a sharper generally, and might be taken as a generic word covering 'thief'.) The date does not fit, as Lady Midhurst is speaking in 1850, but such an anachronism is admissible in a novel, and is the opposite of surprising in one by Swinburne, and cannot be taken as proving anything except his weakness where figures are concerned. Reade might loosely be called an imitator of Balzac in so far as he strove to be a realist, and made much use of the 'document', in the exploitation of which however he rather is to be compared with Zola. And his frequent theatricality and sensationalism give ground for much that is here urged against him. 'He will never do it but once' etc. may be taken as a prophetic reference to his masterpiece *The Cloister and the Hearth*, which had appeared when Swinburne wrote this chapter. If, as is very probable, Lady Midhurst's criticism of Reade is Swinburne's own, it was considerably qualified towards laudation in later years: see the essay on him published in *Miscellanies*. Here, while several reserves are maintained, he is proclaimed as 'by far the greatest master of narrative whom our country has produced since the death of Scott'; as superior not only to Defoe but also to Balzac in this same respect. Reade is also spoken of here as 'a writer of conscientious and pertinacious industry, combined with genuine self-respect': which corrects another of the adverse

543

judgments passed upon him (among contemporary English writers in general) by Lady Midhurst in her keenness to place Balzac above all comers.

The asinine Lafourcade—*mirabilissimum* (if the indispensable superlative may be allowed) *dictu*—suggests that the author here in question may be Champfleury or Flaubert! Of course, however he is, he could not be either of these (Flaubert would be excluded in any case), for he is English, as is quite clear from the context. ('All your men here,' says Lady Midhurst; and, further on, 'this English uncleanness.')

[169] SHAKESPEARE CONDEMNING . . . BALZAC DEPLORING: Cf. A remark in Swinburne's essay on Charles Reade on 'the preacher's or the lecturer's aim', à propos of George Eliot's Tito and similar didactic characters in the work of Reade: 'Tito is presented—after the fashion of Richardson or George Sand—as a warning or fearful example, rather than simply represented—after the fashion of Shakespeare or of Balzac—as a natural and necessary figure.'

[170] PERVERSITY: *degradation and perversity.* 'Degredation' would have denoted the very type of moral judgment which Swinburne says the greatest masters of creative fiction never descend to.

[171] MADAME DE SAN-REAL: The lesbian lover of Paquita Valdès in *La Fille aux yeux d'or.* When she discovers that Paquita, during her absence, has become the lover of her (Madame de Real's) half-brother, de Marsay, she daggers her to death in the course of a long and terrible struggle.

[172] THERE'S NAE MAIR LANDS TO TYNE, MY DEAR, etc.: Published under the title of *A Jacobite's Farewell* in *The Magazine of Art,* January 1889, and later in the same year in *Poems and Ballads* III.

[173] LOST ALL IN THE '15 . . . IN THE '45: Swinburne had in mind his own family, 'which in every Catholic rebellion from the

day of my own Queen Mary to those of Charles Edward
had given their blood like water and their lands like dust
for the Stuarts.' (Letter to E. C. Stedman, Feb. 20th, 1875.)

[174] THE DEFENCE OF ROME AGAINST THESE FRENCH: In April
1849 the Republicans under Garibaldi successfully defended Rome against the French army sent by Louis-
Napoleon to restore the Pope; in June Swinburne's hero
Mazzini fought in person along with Garibaldi against
further French attacks; in July the French took the city,
and Mazzini and Garibaldi had to flee into exile.

[175] DERWENTWATER: One of the leaders of the Northumberland Jacobites in the '15.

[176] BRED UP . . . IN BORDER AIR . . . STRONG MEAT OF BALLADS:
This largely applies to Swinburne himself. 'Swinburne
being a Northumbrian to the very marrow, was steeped in
the border ballads to such an extent that it was almost
impossible to quote any verse of any border ballad that was
unfamiliar to him . . . Rossetti used to say that if the knowledge of all the specialists in this line were put together,
they would not equal that of his "little Northumbrian
friend".' (T. Watts-Dunton, Prefatory Note to Lord Soulis,
1909.) William Morris, another expert, paid the same tribute in terms of further reach. 'With regard to Swinburne's
unequalled skill in reproducing the texture of style [of the
old ballad poetry] . . . Mr. Sydney C. Cockerell tells me that
William Morris, when he was dying, started making a selection of border ballads, which he declared were the finest
poems in the English language, to be printed at the Kelms-
cott Press. The difficulties of gaps and various readings
were too great for Morris in his enfeebled condition, and
Mr. Cockerell suggested that the editing should be handed
over to Swinburne. "Oh, no!" answered Morris, "that
would never do. He would be writing-in verses that no one
would be able to tell from the original stuff!"' (Gosse,
Preface to Posthumous Poems by Algernon Charles Swin-

burne, 1917.) One of the numerous asinine things in Lafourcade's doctoral thesis *La Jeunesse de Swinburne* (1928) is the statement that Swinburne's ballads, with the exception of a few lines, have no qualities of soul in them. ('. . . les ballades de Swinburne manquent d'âme.')

[177] GOD SEND THE SEA SORROW, etc.: Published by Gosse and Wise in *Posthumous Poems* (1917), and again by the same two miscreants in the Bonchurch mendaciously called 'complete' edition (1925), in both cases with errors of transcription and one couplet missing, and under the absurd title *A Song for Margaret Midhurst*: there is no person of this name in *Lesbia Brandon* nor in any of Swinburne's works: Herbert's sister was Margaret Seyton before marriage made her Lady Wariston. This is one typical instance out of hundreds or thousands of the shocking incompetence of these two interlopers into the field of Swinburne's work and all that concerns him. Swinburne himself named the poem *The Watcher*: see the account of Mr. Meyerstein's galley in the third chapter of the Commentary.

[178] TWINED: put asunder, disjointed, parted.

[179] BUT NO MAN'S SAIL BETWEEN: *But no man's white sail between.* A good example of an alteration made to secure the effect of 'dropped syllable and rough edges' mentioned in the preceding paragraph as characteristic of ballads of the English border.

[180] INHALED THE HOT FRAGRANCE: *drew in with great dim delight the sweet odour.*

[181] ITS SOFT COVERING: *the thin soft stocking*: : *the thin soft silk.*

[182] PRESSED DOWN UPON HIS NECK . . . TREAD ME TO DEATH: See Note [52] of this chapter.

[183] HAIR: *close curls of rebellious hair.*

[184] A TEMPEST . . . RADIANT: *in a heavy and tawny torrent,* [*darker*] *duskier in the mass and glittering in the light and* [*rustling*] *rioting.*

[185] Deleted after PASSION: *of gratitude and delight.* 'Passion' alone is more suggestive of incestuous feeling.

[186] LOSE: misprinted as 'love' in the galley-proof.

[187] FERVOUR AND SPIRIT: *singleness.*

CHAPTER IV

[1] SUPERB: In the root sense of 'proud', 'lordly'.

[2] IN SCHOOL . . . IT WAS NO LIFE FOR HIM etc.: Much if not all of this may be taken as part of the history of Swinburne's life at Eton. It modifies considerably the current and more or less canonical account (given by Gosse, Lafourcade and others) of this important period of his formative years.

[3] A DEAR AND CLOSE FRIEND OR TWO . . . RAMBLED AND READ VERSE . . . WINDSOR, etc.: Swinburne had two particular friends at Eton, his cousin Algernon Bertram Mitford (late Lord Redesdale) and Sir George Young. The latter has recorded that 'he was not at home among Eton boys'. 'We used', the former wrote in a letter to Gosse, 'to take long walks together in Windsor Forest and in the Home Park . . . As he walked along with that peculiar dancing step of his, his eyes gleaming with enthusiasm, and his hair, like the zazzera of the old Florentines, tossed about by the wind, he would pour out in his unforgettable voice the treasures which he had gathered at his last sitting.'

[4] THE SEAGULL: Cf. 'no seagull likes to have his wings clipt' (p.13); and 'Denham, though not such a seagull' (i.e. as Herbert) (p.19). This is another proof that this section, like many others concerning Herbert, is autobiographical; for Mrs. Disney Leith, a cousin of Swinburne, records that 'sea-

gull' was 'one of his home nicknames.' (*The Boyhood of Algernon Charles Swinburne,* 1917.)

⁵ LORD ALTHORP: Courtesy title of the third Earl Spencer (1782–1845); Chancellor of the Exchequer and leader of the House of Commons in Lord Grey's administration (1830–1834); one of those chiefly instrumental in carrying the Reform Bill. He was called to the Upper House in 1834, and thereafter gave himself up to what for him were the delights of country life.

⁶ EMBITTER: *weary.*

⁷ BROUGHT FORTH: the galley (28) gives 'brought first', which is evidently a misprint (the sheet on which this paragraph was written is not among those of the extant manuscript, and was probably lost before the latter was purchased by Wise).

CHAPTER V

¹ THE COUNTRY SEASON . . . CHARADES AND PROVERBS, etc.: Probably biographical reminiscences. Mrs. Disney Leith (*op. cit.*), speaking of her and Swinburne's childhood, says: 'I remember one occasion on which he made us all into a kind of *tableau* out of "Dombey and Son"—himself taking the part of Mrs. Skewton in her Bath chair!' And again, refering to life in their youth: 'Some of our happiest days together were spent at his grandfather's (my great uncle) Sir John Swinburne's house at Capheaton . . . A large cousin-hood gathered there in those bright autumn days, where everything seemed to combine for the delight of youth . . .' 'Passengers' here seems to have the obsolete meaning of 'birds of passage' used metaphorically.

² DID NOT ENJOY THE CHANGE: *did not enjoy the social differences* : : *did not enjoy the change as other boys might.*

548

[3] THE WORTHY JOCKEY: *Lord Charles.*

[4] A CERTAIN FIRE AND MUSIC . . . WHICH STUNG AND SOOTHED ALTERNATELY . . . THE RELAXATION OF NERVES OVERSTRUNG . . . A PULSE AND PLAY OF BLOOD: This might be a general description of Swinburne's own verse in the 60s.

[5] EVENING'S SHOW: *night's charade.* The manuscript has 'evening's show-proverb', but Swinburne deleted '-proverb' in one set of the galleys.

[6] A CAVALIER: *Gubetta* : : *a bravo.* Gubetta, in Hugo's *Lucrèce Borgia,* an agent of Lucrezia, who poisoned or otherwise got rid of people she desired to have suppressed.

[7] HIS TWO BROTHERS: In Chapter I we are told that Walter Lunsford was the only male of the children of that family, and that his mother was an invalid; Swinburne was not above discrepancies of this sort; it is just possible, however, that two boys had been added to the family in the interval, but they would be very young at the date of this chapter.

[8] QUEM SI PUELLARUM INSERERES CHORO: Horace, *Carm.* II, 5.

[9] SOLUTIS CRINIBUS AMBIGUOQUE VULTU: Id., ib.

[10] LUCREZIA: Of Hugo's *Lucrèce Borgia.*

[11] GENNARO: *Gubetta.* Cf. Note [6]. Gennaro, a purely imaginary character, is represented by Hugo as the incestuous offspring of Lucrezia and her brother the Duke of Gandia; Lucrezia loves him deeply, with perhaps more than a maternal love, and he kills her for having poisoned five of his friends, not knowing who she is till she tells him just as she dies. Is there any significance in Swinburne's having changed Lunsford's rôle from that of a bravo to that of an attractive young man who is the object of a passionate interest on the part of the character which Margaret plays?

[12] LOOKED . . . EXCITEMENT: *was excited and luminous with life after the fashion of a girl.*

549

[13] MME. DE ROCHELAURIER: A character in *Loves' Cross Currents*.

[14] Deleted after EYELASHES: *All the other features as well were soft, warm.*

[15] SHOULDERS: *bust.*

[16] SAID: *said softly.*

[17] OF A SCENE . . . THEIR CHARADE: *of the great cut down for private acting into three or four scenes.*

[18] THE PRINCESS NEGRONI: Another character in *Lucrèce Borgia*.

[19] Deleted after LET IN UPON BERTIE: *who had hitherto suffered enough—too much—in his opinion—for incompetence and idleness in the matter of his studies, classic or arithmetic.*

[20] THIS QUARTER: *a poetess who had long lived far off before his eyes : : a poetess whose image had long floated and pressed upon his eyes, and was now visibly in the flesh before him.*

[21] GUANHUMARA . . . REGINA . . . OTBERT: Characters in Hugo's *Les Burgraves*.

CHAPTER VI

[1] GIRL: *fellow who.* The deleted noun indicates that the girl was not anyone of importance in the story. 'Girl' was un-undoubtedly substituted for 'fellow' simply in order to make the situation more dramatic or appealing.

CHAPTER VII

[1] TOUT LE MONDE: In modern French (including that of Swinburne's day) this phrase almost always means 'every-

body' and not 'the whole world', of which *le monde entier*
is the regular or at least usual equivalent. One cannot accuse
Swinburne of having made a mistake here; all that one can
say is that the sense in which he used the expression is rare.
In the next stanza, the construction 'Veux-tu *de* la mer?'
is odd, especially in view of the preceding 'Si tu veux mon
cœur' etc., and the following 'Si tu veux . . . cette mer
profonde', and if one assumes that what is meant is 'Do you
want (or Would you like) the sea?' The most natural sense
of 'Veux-tu de la mer?', occurring in such a context as this,
is a partitive one: 'Would you like some sea?' (just as, in
similar circumstances, 'Veux-tu du vin?' would normally be
taken as meaning 'Would you like some wine?'), but this
of course cannot have been the sense Swinburne wished to
convey. It looks as though he made a slip here, and introduced into a positive sentence containing *vouloir* followed
by a non-partitive object the construction required by a
negatived *vouloir* governing a partitive object. 'Je veux
cette chose'; 'Je ne veux pas de vin' are examples of the two
kinds of sentence in question. (It is true that *de* may be
used with the positive of *vouloir,* but then the combination
vouloir de is equivalent to another verb, less strong than
vouloir, and having a shade of significance that does not
essentially belong to the latter. The nearest English equivalent, I should say, is not 'to have a desire for', but 'to find
acceptable', and, in the negative, 'to have no use for' etc.—
It is just possible, but it is not at all probable, that Swinburne meant to use *vouloir de* in its proper sense.)

For the quality of Swinburne's French, see Note [15] on
Chapter XV.

[2] SING . . . RIDE: For Swinburne's throwing off of poetry as
he was riding, cf. Mrs. Disney Leith, *op. cit.*: 'I had my
first impressions of Macaulay's "Lays of Ancient Rome"
from him. I was always fond of Roman history as a child.
And the spirited, sounding periods of the "Lays" repeated
to me by Algernon—often when we were riding together—

took a lively hold of my imagination'; and again, of another period: '. . . many a masterpiece of the Victorian poets was recited—as only Algernon could recite—during a spiri ed canter . . .' Cf. also: 'I am bound to confess that if a fearless he was also a reckless rider, and more than once I remember his start ending in disaster.' Cf. also Swinburne himself:

> . . . When ever in August holiday times
> I rode or swam through a rapture of rhymes,
> Over heather and crag, and by scaur and by stream,
> Clothed with delight by the might of a dream,
> With the sweet sharp wind blown hard through my hair;
> On eyes enkindled and head made bare,
> Reining my rhymes into royal order
> Through honied leagues of the northland border . . .
>> (Verses published under title (not Swinburne's)
>> of 'Recollections' in *Posthumous Poems*, 1917.)

In this chapter, as in many other parts of the book, there is a good deal that is autobiographical.

[3] AN ATTACHÉ: There is an Arthur Lunsford who is an attaché in *Love's Cross Currents*.

[4] I WISH YOU'D HORSEWHIP ME: I'M SO AWFULLY HAPPY: This shows another of the sources of Swinburne's masochism. Cf. Notes [52] and [180] on Chapter III. Unpublished letters to more than one of his familiars indicate that this wish was not a mere *façon de parler* and that it sometimes did receive satisfaction. But Walter Lunsford was not an initiate.

[5] NOT UP IN FALSTAFF: *King Henry the Fourth, Part II, Act* 2, *sc. iv.*

[6] O WHATTEN A THING HAD YE THERE TO DRINK, etc.: These two quatrains are also the first two (but in the reverse order) of an unpublished poem of four stanzas of which the manuscript is in the British Museum. They are written on a sheet of white notepaper; only the figures 18 of the watermark date appear on this sheet, which was torn from one

that was twofold. The only variant in this copy is that 'And' in 'And wine was never sae red' is corrected to 'Nor'.

[7] THERE'S NAE MAN BY YON BURN-SIDE, etc.: There is also a separate manuscript (with a couple of minor variants) of these two quatrains in the British Museum. They are written on a sheet of white notepaper, with the printed address Ashburnham Place, Battle, Sussex (the seat of the poet's maternal uncle, the Earl of Ashburnham) and the watermark date 1864.

[8] OR YOU'LL LICK ME, WE'RE NOT IT ETON: The same 'wish' of Note [4] struggling into an ineffectual hint. Cf. *Love's Cross Currents,* letter XX, Reginald Harewood to Lady Cheyne: 'They want to diplomatise me: I am to have some secretaryship or other under Lord Fotherington . . . I shall have Arthur Lunsford for a colleague . . . A.L. was a great swell in our schooldays, and used to ride over the heads of us lower boys with spurs on . . . To have him over one again will be very comic; he never *could* get on without fags. Do you think the service admits of his licking them? I suspect he might thrash me still if he tried: you know what a splendid big fellow he is.'

In the present instance, of course, it is as an expression of extreme devotion to an absent woman that suffering of pain is desired; it is not mere flagellation in the void, so to speak, as is usually the case with flagellomaniacs, that is here required. And one is pretty safe in assuming that in all his flagellantic appetitions or sufferings Swinburne's imagination was active, set towards something in the way of an ideal.

[9] POSSESSED—WITH THE WIND; IMPREGNATED LIKE THE MARES IN THESSALY: '. . . vento gravidae . . .' (Virgil, *Georgics,* Book 3.) But Thessaly is not mentioned in this passage.

[10] A STRANGE DREAM . . . STAR . . . FLOWERLIKE , , , WHITE ROSE . . . REDDENING CENTRE . . . A LIVING MOUTH: One of the most impressive, most poetically powerful dreams in the whole

553

extent of literature. 'A red rose, the old symbol of passion' is the most obvious commentary, and most people would doubtless be content, or would prefer, to leave it at that; but modern psychology has more to say, and it cannot be ignored altogether. According to Freud, *Introductory Lectures on Pyscho-Analysis*, 'Blossoms and flowers [in dreams] represent the female sexual organs, more particularly, in virginity'. And in *The Interpretation of Dreams* he analyses a 'flower-dream' in which the following occurs: '. . . she is carrying a big branch . . . which is thickly studded with red flowers': 'red flowers' is one of the elements of the dream which he says should be interpreted sexually. Jung, in his masterly and intensely interesting *Wandlungen und Symbole der Libido*, speaks to the same effect. Discussing a poem of Hölderlin's addressed to the rose ('Little rose, the storm's fierce power/Strips our leaves and alters us' etc.) he says 'The rose is the symbol of the beloved woman . . . The rose blooms in the "rose garden" of the maiden; therefore it is also a direct symbol of the libido'; and elsewhere he recalls that stars figure in the ancient Mithraic liturgy as an 'ecstatic symbol of the libido': '. . . you will see many five-pointed stars coming down from the sun and filling the whole lower air.' As for the 'reddening centre that grew as it descended liker and liker a living mouth', it is enough to mention that for Freud the mouth in dreams is one of the symbols of 'the female genital orifice'. (*The Interpretation of Dreams.*)

It is almost as though Swinburne had had the advantage of reading Freud and Jung: it appears that he has here, by the sheer force of creative intuition,† composed an erotic dream which in its esoteric symbolism is a well-nigh perfect specimen of its class according to the teaching of the most advanced psychology of the present day!—But it is not so surprising as it seems at first sight; as Freud himself says,

† Unless—which is almost improbable—he was recording an actual dream of his own or of someone else.

'the dream makes use of such symbolisations as are to be found ready-made in unconscious thinking'; and again, 'symbolism does not appertain especially to dreams, but rather to the unconscious imagination'. And, of course, it is from the unconscious imagination in large part that what is greatest in art derives. (Cf. Dr. Ernest Jones, *Papers on Psycho-Analysis*: 'A number of Freud's individual conclusions had been anticipated by previous writers, particularly by artists.')

[11] THE SEA . . . THE SALT FROTH: According to Freud, Jung, etc., water in dreams has esoteric significance. Cf., e.g. Jung, *op. cit.* 'All that is living rises . . . from water. Born from the springs, the rivers, the seas, at death man arrives at the waters of the Styx in order to enter upon the "night journey on the sea". The wish is that the black water of death might be the water of life; that death . . . might be the mother's womb . . .' The second last sentence seems particularly applicable to the passage to which this note refers. Swinburne ('I will go back to the great sweet mother' etc., etc.) would have provided these psychologists with many effective illustrations on this and other of their pet themes, but they appear to be quite ignorant of him. When I called Freud's attention (shortly before his death) to passages in Swinburne's work that in part confirmed and in part invalidated one of his most recondite essays in psychological exegesis, he seemed no less surprised than interested.

For Herbert's dream cf. the following from Balzac's *La Fille aux yeux d'or*, one of the inspirational sources of *Lesbia Brandon*: 'Il rêva de la *Fille aux yeux d'or*, comme rêvent les jeunes gens passionnés. Ce fut des images monstrueuses, des bizarreries insaisissables, pleines de lumière, et qui révèlent les mondes invisibles, mais d'une manière toujours incomplète, car un voile interposé change les conditions de l'optique.'

CHAPTER VIII

[1] GO RIGHT OVER THE CLIFF: Cf. Notes [52] and [180] on Chapter III.

[2] THINKING . . . MAKE YOU: *thinking it would please you and make you.*

[3] TO BE YOUR HUSBAND'S BRIDESMAN: The extreme of moral masochism. Cf. Reginald Harewood in *Love's Cross Currents* speaking of his love for Clara: 'It gives one the wish to be hurt for her. I think I should let him [her husband] insult me and strike me if she wanted it.'

[4] WERE NOT LESS THAN BROTHER AND SISTER: *were brother and sister.*

CHAPTER IX

[1] ILLA RUDEM CURSA PRIMA IMBUIT AMPHITRITEN: Catullus LXIV.

[2] DO NOT MAKE DEAD METAL: *is not dead metal.*

CHAPTER X

[1] WHICH SEEMS IMPROBABLE: On this and related questions of religious belief, cf. the following definitive expression of Swinburne's attitude from the *Dedicatory Epistle* prefixed to the first collected edition of his poetical works (1904):

'I never pretended to see eye to eye with my illustrious friends and masters, Victor Hugo and Guseppe Mazzini, in regard to the positive and passionate confidence of their sublime and purified theology.'

[2] SPERONI . . . CANACE: Sperone Speroni was a member of a

sort of committee to which the MS of Tasso's *Gerusalemme* was submitted for criticism. They all found fault; plagiarism was one of the most wounding of Speroni's charges. He also helped to launch the notion that Tasso was mad. Speroni's play *Canace* deals with a subject that had been handled by Euripides in his *Aeolus*. Canace and Macareo, brother and sister, and twins, have incestuous intercouse, from which a child results; the latter is murdered at birth; Aeolus, the father of the twins, is shocked into angry action, the affair becomes public, and the guilty pair commit suicide one after the other. This story, it may be noted, is, in an extreme form, one of the themes of *Lesbia Brandon* and of the cycle generally to which the latter belongs. It is therefore not altogether out of place that Swinburne should refer to it here. In an indirect or distant way it adds to the suggestion of incest that runs through the book.

[3] In 1849: See Note [173] on Chapter III.

[4] TITULAR: *fictitious*.

[5] BECAME IN TIME IMMEASURABLE: As did that of Mazzini over Swinburne. Cf. Note [6] on Chapter XI.

[6] UNITY: *freedom*.

[7] NOT ON ANY TERMS . . . A KING: Cf. Note [4] on Chapter XI.

CHAPTER XI

[1] 1861: *1862*. Another instance of Swinburne's weakness in the matter of dates.

[2] THE GENERAL HAS CAPRERA: Garibaldi, for some years a fugitive after his flight from Rome (see Note [173] on Chapter III), had been allowed to retire to the islet of Caprera in 1854. He was in the field again in 1859; and in 1860, after conquering Naples and Sicily, and acquiescing in the rule of King Victor Emmanuel, he retired once more to his island

home, refusing all awards, bittering disappointed that he had been restrained from attempting to capture Rome (which would have led to a war with France).

[5] ALL: Swinburne wrote both 'all' and 'aught', one above the other, and cancelled neither.

[4] HE HAS FAITH IN THIS KINGDOM: Garibaldi, on laying down his dictatorship, had urged all Italians to 'join in consummating the great work of Italian unity under the *re galantuomo*, who is the symbol of our regeneration'. But Mazzini and the Republican extremists (of whom Swinburne's Mariani was one) never had any faith in monarchy in general and in particular in the Italian kings. 'Better Italy enslaved than handed over to the son of the traitor Carlo Alberto' expressed the deepest feeling of Mazzini and those on his side. Swinburne echoes this in *Songs before Sunrise* (to which this chapter of *Lesbia Brandon* is a sort of annexe):

> How shall the spirit be loyal
> To the shell of a spiritless thing?
> :: :: ::
> Calling a crowned man royal
> That was no more than a king.

[5] FA, FA . . . L'ANGEL DI DIO: *Purgatorio*, Canto II.

[6] FOR VERY LOVE AND REVERENCE NEITHER WOULD NAME THE GREAT NAME OF MAZZINI: One of the few enthusiasms of Swinburne that seem wildly beyond the worth of the object (and this is true of the whole Italian theme to which he devoted so much magnificent poetry). Cf. '. . . what I . . . still hold as the very highest honour, privilege, and happiness of my whole life—that of being presented to the man who was to me, I should think, what Christ himself must have seemed to his very first disciples—and to whom and for whom I would very gladly have given all the blood of my body and all the powers of my heart and mind and soul and spirit, as gladly and thankfully as if I had still been in the

first fever of a boy's loving worship and passionate reverence.' (Letter to Watts-Dunton, Feb. 14th, 1877.) For the reticence conveyed in the words which are the subject of this note, cf. the following sentence in a letter from Swinburne to W. M. Rossetti in the course of which he refers to 'long interviews' he had recently had 'with the Chief': 'He said things to me and told me stories that honestly I can't write about'. Lecky said of the Italian *Risorgimento* that it was 'the one moment of nineteenth-century history when politics assumed something of the character of poetry'. It certainly did for Swinburne's idealising self! Lady Midhurst's corrective (Chapter III), à propos of this movement, 'Mind, I don't say the men are not mad, or not fools', is very much in place here.

[7] HAYNAU: Cf. *Love's Cross Currents*, Letter XXV: '. . . she couldn't expect any fellow to stand and look on while such things were—and I would as soon have looked on at Haynau any day.' Haynau (1786–1853), 'the Hyaena of Brescia', was an Austrian general noted for his ferocity; so evil was his reputation that when he came to England in 1850 he was thrown into a horse-trough by a party of draymen; Palmerston met the resulting diplomatic protest with the declaration that he was ' a great moral criminal'. He figures among the villains in *Les Châtiments* of Hugo.

[8] IF YOU OR I WERE TO BE SHOT . . . WOULD IT HELP ITALY AT ALL: Mazzini may have spoken thus to Swinburne, who perhaps, like Herbert, had wished to give physical service to Italy; he certainly urged the poet to serve her (and the Mazzinian doctrine) with his poetry, and to give over the less austere themes that had hitherto engaged his attention: '. . . the poet ought to be the apostle of a Crusade, his word the watchword of the fighting nations and the dirge of the oppressors . . . shake up, reproach, encourage, insult, brand the cowards, hail the martyrs, tell us all that we have a great Duty to fulfil [sic]' etc. (Letter in the British Museum. Lafourcade cites it, and gives 1867 as the year; but this is no

more than conjectural, as March 10 is all that Mazzini gave of the date.)

[9] READY TO GIVE YOUR HONOUR: The logical extreme of mere patriotism. It would cover all political crimes, including aggrandisement at the expense of another power, and so would justify the very Austrian oppression against which it was directed. But such apostles of nationalism cannot think straight.

[10] IN OCTOBER 1866: This somewhat awkward obtrusion of a date about five and a half years later than that of what takes place in the chapter fixes a time after which the latter must have been written.

[11] I SEE HUMANITY AND TIME: It was judicious of Swinburne to give this sentiment, which makes the nationalism of the mere patriot look small, to a Frenchman, for it is a part of the better French tradition, that of which Montesquieu and Voltaire are two of the representative creators. Cf.: 'Si je savais quelque chose qui me fût utile et qui fût préjudici-able à ma famille, je le rejetterais de mon esprit. Si je savais quelque chose qui fût utile à ma famille et qui ne le fût pas à ma patrie, je chercherais à l'oublier. Si je savais quelque chose utile à ma patrie et qui fût préjudiciable à l'Europe et au genre humain, je la regarderais comme un crime.' (Montesquieu, *Pensées diverses*.)

CHAPTER XII

[1] UP TO A CERTAIN POINT . . . A LADY'S: *passable*.

[2] HEIN? WAS A DELICATE AND PARISIAN SOUND IN HIS EARS: Cf. '. . . she [Lady Midhurst] had a way of saying "Hein?" and glancing up or sideways with an eye at once bird-like and feline.' (*Love's Cross Currents*, Prologue) Swinburne, prob-ably took his *Hein?* from Balzac, where it is fairly common. Faguet pours scorn on Balzac for making a duchess say

Hein?, and affirms that it shows he was very ill-acquainted with the upper classes; but this judgment has rightly in its turn been made fun of by Brunetière and other critics with a better knowledge of the period.

[3] TO BACCHUS: *from Theseus to Bacchus.*

[4] SHE SAID COLDLY: For the peevishness of the demi-semi-mondaine (and the scene in general) cf. Chapter XXXV of *La Cousine Bette*, where a party of gentlemen dine with a set of women of the vocation for which Mr. Linley has trained this unpromising material: 'Le Brésilien resta grave comme un homme de bronze. Ce sang-froid irrita Carabine. Elle savait parfaitement que Montès aimait madame Marneffe; mais elle ne s'attendait pas à cette foi brutale, à ce silence obstiné de l'homme convaincu.'

[5] A FACE UNLIKE HERS: Lesbia's, of course. Cf. the close similarity of details here with those given in Chapter V: a fine and close mouth'; 'her eyes . . . sombre and mobile'; 'a certain trouble perceptible in the face'.

CHAPTER XIII

[1] THAT RIVER: The Thames at Eton, called the Isis at Oxford. Swinburne may have had in mind here the death (1862) by drowning in the Isis of G. R. Luke, one of his contemporaries and best friends at Balliol.

[2] 'make that demand of his Maker': The exact words are 'Make that demand to the Creator' (*Troilus and Cressida*, II, 3).

[3] TAIL TRASH: More than probably a misprint (this section exists only in galley-proofs: the manuscript of it is not extant). The phrase would be odd in any context: its pejorative meaning seems out of place here.

[4] NATURE IS A DEMOCRAT . . . THE FORCE THAT FIGHTS HER:

The philosophy of aristocracy of all sorts. This dualistic conception of a Life Force of some kind fighting *against* Nature is much likelier and much more attractive than the unitary one of the evolutionists or vitalists expressed, for example, by Mr. Bernard Shaw in *Back to Methuselah* and elsewhere in his works.

[5] AND GENIUS: the galley-proof gives 'a genius'. Swinburne's shortened 'and' (he hardly ever writes the word in full) was obviously misread as the indefinite article.

[6] SOCIETY . . . IN A SOMEWHAT INTOLERANT WAY: Cf. her 'quiet intolerance of people in general', Chapter V, first paragraph.

CHAPTER XIV

[1] QUORSUM HAEC TAM PUTIDA?: Horace, *Sat* 2, VII. The citation is peculiarly apt coming from Mr. Linley, as there follow, after a short interval, some twenty-five lines on the vices of slaves and masters, which the prim editor of the Oxford Clarendon Press edition omits as being too 'coarse' for modern readers.

[2] ELLE L'A VOULU. GEORGETTE DANDIN: 'Vous l'avez voulu, vous l'avez voulu, George Dandin, vous l'avez voulu.' (Molière, *George Dandin*, I, VII.)

[3] PRETTY: *handsome.*

[4] CAME OFF: Apparently means 'come to an end' here. The more ordinary meaning (which occurs a few lines down) would not suit the general context. Cf. *Love's Cross Currents*, Letter VI: '. . . an attachment more or less was not much to him—he was off with her in no time. But. . . . at one time he had been on with her . . .'

[5] BOTH . . . BLOWN UPON: Why both of them? Probably because Swinburne had originally thought of them as twins (see Note [76] on Chapter III), and this idea remained at the

back of his mind, although he had abandoned it and made their ages different (at least he appears to have done so; he refers to them as 'the elder' and 'the younger'; it is true, of course, that these terms might be applied to twins, to distinguish the first-born from the other; but had he continued to think of them as twins he would probably have mentioned them as such—unless he forgot that he had cancelled the passage where he does so in a previous chapter, and thought of it as still holding good. If they were twins, of course, one would easily be mistaken for the other, and any opprobrium incurred by one would attach to the other too; and this might even happen if, although not twins, they resembled each other to a marked degree.

[6] FRED NEVER KNEW YOU WERE IN THIS WORLD: But it appears from what he said on his death-bed that he did: '. . . I should have taken the little thing and kept it . . .' (Chapter I).

[7] AND TOOK UP IN TIME WITH: (*without a penny I needn't tell you*) *and caught up some*.

[8] YOU KNOW AT LEAST WHAT THAT IS: *it was fatal*.

[9] THE YOUNGER MARRIED LORD CHARLES BRANDON: But Mr. Linley has already said that he himself married the younger. The meaning no doubt is 'what people mistakenly thought was the younger' because the names had 'got mixed up'. Cf. also what is said of their possible twinship in Note [5].

[10] YOUR COMMON GRANDMOTHER: The galley gives the misprint 'your cousin's grandmother'.

[11] SUNDON: Wariston. See Note [128] on Chapter III.

[12] OVER TENDER: *virtuous* : : *virtuous or tender*.

[13] FLOGGED AT HOME ONCE A WEEK: The sadistic father appears now and again in the unpublished flogging-pieces. In one place he is fiendish in the extent to which he inflicts pain.

CHAPTER XV

[1] Deleted after TO SET HER FREE: *like men in stories.*

[2] FLUTTERING: *vibrating.*

[3] GREW: *wept.*

[4] MY LIFE PLEASANT FOR A YEAR: *my life for a year full of divine pleasure.*

[5] Deleted after WHAT WILL HAPPEN: *or what has to happen.*

[6] Deleted after THINK: *it will not be face to face again any more, I wonder* : : *it will not be what it is now again any more, I wonder.*

[7] Deleted after PITIFUL NOTE OF PAIN: *like the prisoner's cry upon God after the question extraordinary by water.*

[8] CRUSHED: *devoured.*

[9] SELF-KNOWLEDGE: *thought*

[10] Deleted after THE TORN FEET PAUSED: *upon the burning shores.*

[11] MIGHT: *was to.*

[12] TU ME DIS: SOIS BONNE; *L'amour m'a fait bonne* : : *La vie est si bonne,*
JE TE DIS: SOIS BEAU. *Puisqu'il t'a fait beau* : : *Et le temps si beau!* These variants are written in the margin; nothing in the three couples of lines is deleted.

[13] ECOUTE: TU M'AIMES: *Alors, si tu m'aimes.*
This variant is writen in the margin; neither line is deleted.

[14] QUAND MAI LE VEUT BIEN: *Au temps qui fait bien* : : *Que je l'amais.*
These variants were written in the margin and cancelled.

[15] TU FUS BIEN AIMÉ: Much could be said as to the quality,

grammatical and other, of the French of these verses. I will limit myself here to the following observations:

(*i*) The change from plural to singular in 'Tressez ma couronne . . . Tu me dis': The change sometimes corresponds to a heightening of sentiment; this does not seem to be the case here. The plural might be addressed to companions of the two lovers. But it remains awkward after one has done one's best for it.

(*ii*) 'Des fleurs de roseau' is at least questionable. 'De fleurs du roseau' would be better.

(*iii*) 'Allons par nous-mêmes': 'Let us go off *all by ourselves*' in the sense of '*all alone*' is apparently what the poet means. '*Tout seuls*' is the French for this. ('Faire quelque chose *par soi-même*' = 'To do something *by oneself*' in the sense of '*unaided*').

(*iv*) 'DIEUX À DEUX': If this is intended to mean 'two by two' it should be 'deux par deux'. Gosse, in a note on this verse in *Posthumous Poems* and in the Bonchurch edition, says 'This line must be a slip. "Allons deux à deux" suggests a procession of couples, not a single pair.' But it is just possible that 'two by two' is not at variance with 'all alone', and that Swinburne meant 'Let all lovers present pair off and let each pair go off alone'. Gosse was not aware of the mistake in French. Here as elsewhere Gosse was a fraud; although his main professional occupation before becoming Librarian to the House of Lords was that of translator to the Board of Trade, his knowledge of French, presumably the language he would be expected to know best, was grotesquely imperfect (as one could show with devastating ease if this point were questioned). Gosse of course noticed none of the other errors to which attention is drawn here.

(*v*) 'Nous vivons une heure; Nous mourrons un jour.' The adverbial 'un jour', indicating a point of time, is awkward coming immediately after the adverbial 'une heure', indicating duration.

(*vi*) 'Qu'on rehausse en tour': 'rehausse' is at least questionable; 'exhausse' would be more idiomatic.

(*vii*) 'Quand mai le veut bien . . . Les jours où l'on cueille . . . quand l'hirondelle Chante': The tenses here should be future. This is the biggest of all the howlers in these French poems. (One might by very special pleading make out a questionable case for 'cueille': taking the verb not as applying to a point of time in the future but as forming part of an adjectival phrase: 'the flower-gathering days'; but it is more than doubtful if this is what Swinburne meant.)

(*viii*) 'chèvrefeuille': Swinburne made this feminine. There is in the British Museum a separate extra portion of galley-proof containing these two French poems and the one following: although Swinburne made a number of corrections here, he did not alter this gender. (Nor did he correct any of the other errors mentioned in this note.)

(*ix*) In the following poem '*Pour* une nuit', '*pour* un jour' are wrong. The answer to 'Combien de temps me serez-vous fidèle?' is 'Une nuit', and not 'Pour une nuit'.

For other mistakes in Swinburne's French see Note [1] of Chapter VII. It may be noted here that there is extant a French composition he did at Eton (presumably), which contains errors that are really shameful.

These mistakes, and the fact that in his third year at school he was awarded the second Prince Consort's prize for French and Italian, show that the standard of French at Eton was very low. In fact, apart from Latin and Greek, education at Eton until long after Swinburne left was in a deplorable condition, and the appointment of a Royal Commission in 1861 'ostensibly to inquire into the working of the nine chief public schools, but with the obvious intention of subjecting Eton to the most assiduous and searching criticism' (Lionel Cust, *Eton College*) was very much called for. Until the governance of Dr. Hawtry, the Headmaster in Swinburne's time, 'French had been taught . . . only as an extra out of play hours' (Cust, ib.). And even under Dr. Hawtry things were hardly better. 'French, German, and Italian were, however, . . . treated for many years to come almost as *objets de luxe*.' (Id., ib.). But, it appears from the case of such an exceptionally gifted pupil as Swinburne, even as an object (or subject) of this category French as taught at Eton was a very poor article.

In the next decade or so (after writing these verses), however, Swinburne made a considerable advance in his command of this language; in 1876 Mallarmé expressed admiring astonishment at the quality of his French, and saluted him as a master poet in the tongue which he himself knew as a master. Cf. especially 'aucune expression (je le dis en critique incorruptible et farouche) ne détonne ni quant au sens ni quant au son' [this in reference to a French poem which Swinburne had sent the chief of the Symbolists]; and 'votre génie si mystéricusement parent de nos plus chères gloires . . . vous avez dans l'âme un vaste coin français . . .' This disposes of the inept remarks of the unqualified George Moore on the worth of Swinburne's French.

[16] ET S'ENFUIT: These two stanzas were written by Swinburne in an album belonging to his mistress Adah Menken; from there (apparently) they were taken and, without Swinburne's permission, published in *Walnuts and Wine: A Christmas Annual*, in 1883; and the same year they were published by R. H. Shepherd in a brochure entitled *In the Album of Adah Menken*. The only difference in the poem as it appears in the Album is that the dash before 'Pour' in the third line follows 'fidèle' in the second.

[17] THE WEARY WEDDING: Published in *Poems and Ballads III* (1889), with six additional stanzas at the beginning, and a few variations in those of the *Lesbia Brandon* text. In a marginal note in the Brotherton galley Swinburne says that the refrains ' "One with another" and "Mother, my mother" should be printed throughout in Italics'; but he did not

567

observe this injunction when he published the poem in the volume just named.

[18] THEY WERE LIKE RIVER-FLOWERS DEAD: *The lids of her eyes were like cold lead.*

[19] SILLY: *a lie.*

[20] ARTHUR: *Arden.*

[21] AND MY BODY WERE DEAD: This and the two preceding stanzas were published, with slight variations, in *Poems and Ballads III*, as part of *The Witch Mother.*

[22] ELAINE: the cat.

[23] A GRAND WISE WORD: Swinburne deleted 'grand' in the Brotherton galley.

[24] AND PAIN TO DRINK AND MEAT: These four stanzas and the two following were also published, with variations, as part of *The Witch Mother* in *Poems and Ballads* III. In the margin of the Brotherton galley, opposite the first line of them, Swinburne wrote the title *The Black Bridal.*

[25] Deleted after THE FIRST LINES: *There was another funereal wedding song rather like it.* Presumably the following two stanzas were originally thought of as part of another poem; and so too no doubt were the three referred to in Note [21]; otherwise Lady Wariston's remark, 'I never knew the rest of that' would be odd, as the latter, as well as the two following her remark, are part of 'the rest' published as *The Witch Mother.*

[26] THE WIND WAKES NA ME: Wise in his Bonchurch *Bibliography of Swinburne* says that these three stanzas 'conclude' *The Witch Mother* 'in *Lesbia Brandon*', and MacInnes (*Ballads of the English Border*) repeats this. But nothing shows that these stanzas belong to *The Witch Mother*, or are in any way connected with those that precede them; on the contrary, it is certain that they are not; for one thing,

the published conclusion of *The Witch Mother* is really conclusive, and even a less incongruous addition than the one in question would be most inartistic.

[27] TO HEAR: *be vexed by.*

[28] THAT NURSERY JINGLE: Published, with a few variations, under the title of *A Lyke-Wake Song* in *Poems and Ballads* III. 'Sit down at night in the worm's way', 'Now the worm is a sweet thing', and 'Fine gold and fair face' appear in the published version as 'Sit down at night in the red worm's way', 'Now the worm is a saft sweet thing', and 'Fine gold and blithe fair face' respectively. Here, in the filling out of the line to more normal rhythm by the addition of a syllable, we have the opposite of the process referred to in Note [179] on Chapter III.

[29] PROUD YE WERE A' DAY LONG;: This is one example of many that might be cited of Swinburne's variation as regards punctuation. He wrote a semi-colon in the manuscript, and finding this misprinted as a comma in the (Brotherton) galley corrected this comma to a semi-colon; but in the published verson a colon replaces the semi-colon, and this was doubtless passed by him as correct.

[30] ETHELBERT . . . ROSAMOND . . . THE TWO ELDER: In this chapter there is an eldest boy Arthur (Atty); a next eldest, Cecil; then, younger still, a girl, Rosamond; and, youngest of all, Ethelbert, also called Bertie and (confusingly) Ethel. Swinburne has forgotten that in Chapter II the birth of the eldest was followed by that of twins, a boy and a girl; and, finally, by that of another boy. Had he kept to this table, he could not have paired Cecil with Arthur to make 'the two elder', and Rosamond with Ethelbert to make 'the little ones'.

[31] THE TYNESIDE WIDOW: It was under this title that the verses were published, with slight alterations, in *The Fortnightly Review*, April 1888, and in *Poems and Ballads* III.

[32] WILLIE'S NECK-SONG: The following poem, with variations

and an additional stanza, was published under the title of *A Riever's Neck-Verse* in *Poems and Ballads* III.

[33] BULMER: Mrs. Bulmer, Chapter II, p. 64.

[34] Deleted after SHINING EYES: *Mamma, I'm sure you're ill said the girl, for.*

[35] PAUSED BETWEEN HIM AND THE CHILDREN: *paused and faced him.*

CHAPTER XVI

[1] LEUCADIA: The entitling this chapter 'Leucadia' underlines the sapphic or lesbian element in the character and fate of the heroine. Sappho is fabled to have committed suicide, because of frustrate love, by throwing herself into the sea from a rock on the shore of the island of Leucadia. But there is a notable difference between her suicide and that of Lesbia Brandon: in the case of the Greek poetess a man (this time) was the object of her love: Lesbia Brandon remained lesbian to the end.

[2] A HOPELESS HOPE: *a love buried alive.*

[3] AS THE SCRAWL OF A CHILD WITH SHUT EYES: *as the light scrawl of a child's writing.*

[4] CORBACCIA: Feminine (coined—apparently—by Swinburne) of 'corbaccio', a pejorative of 'corbo', a variant of 'corvo', a crow or raven. 'Cornacchia' is the regular feminine word in the sense intended by Swinburne. Cf. in *Love's Cross Currents* what Frank Cheyne says of Lady Midhurst: 'she is rather of the vulturine order as to beak and diet'.

[5] WATER-FLOWERS: *full-blown waterlilies.*

[6] WANSDALE: In the neighbourhood of Ensdon. Cf. in Chapter VII the reference to 'the bay under Wansdale Point'.

[7] KNEES: *waist* : : *ankles.*

[8] AND I BEGAN TO WONDER IF SHE WOULD MELT ENTIRELY INTO THAT LIKENESS: *till like hers they seemed of live and molten gold.*

[9] TO SEE YOU AS YOU WERE THAT FIRST TIME . . . GO AND DRESS UP: Cf. in *La Fille aux yeux d'or* Paquita's desire—fulfilled in this case—to have de Marsay dressed as a woman before they get down to amorous business:

> —Tiens, mon amour, dit-elle, . . . veux-tu me plaire?
> —Je ferai tout ce que tu voudras . . ., répondit en riant de Marsay . . .
> —Eh bien, lui dit-elle, laisse-moi t'arranger à mon goût.
> —Mets-moi donc à ton goût, dit Henri.
> Paquita joyeuse alla prendre . . . une robe de velours rouge, dont elle habilla de Marsay, puis elle le coiffa d'un bonnet de femme et l'entortilla d'un châle . . .

[10] THE REALITY OF FATE: INEVITABLE, NOT TO BE CAJOLED BY RESIGNATION . . . NOT LIABLE TO REPENTANCE, etc.: A constant article of Swinburne's creed, so superior to the Christian with its repentance, resignation, and dependence on something outside oneself. There is a fuller expression of it in a letter of Lady Midhurst's in *Love's Cross Currents*: '. . . I do not profess to keep moral medicines on hand against a time of sickness . . . I prefer things of the cold sharp taste to the faint tepid mixtures of decocted sentiment which religious or verbose people serve out so largely and cheaply . . . I for one cannot write or talk about hopes of reunion, better life, expiation, faith, and such other things. I believe that those who cannot support themselves cannot be supported . . . Stoicism is not an exploded system of faith. It may be available still when resignation in the modern sense breaks down. Resign yourself by all means to the unavoidable; take patiently what will come; refuse yourself the relaxation of complaint. Have as little as you can to do with fear, or repentance, or retrospection of any kind.

Fear is unprofitable; to look back will weaken your head.
As to repentence, it never did any good or undid harm . . .
It would not be rebellion, but pure idiocy or lunacy, for us
to begin spluttering and kicking against the pricks; but, on
the other hand, there is no reason why we should grovel and
blubber . . . Courage, taking the word how you will, I have
always put at the head of the virtues. Any sort of faith or
humility that interferes with it, or impairs its working
power, I have no belief in.' etc.

CHAPTER XVII

[1] RATAZZI: Head of various ministries under Victor
Emmanuel; Premier March–December 1862 and April–
October 1867; an ambitious and intriguing man, one of the
'trained statesmen' mentioned in the third paragraph.

[2] PALLA FERRANTE: A character in Stendhal's *La Chartreuse
de Parme*. Balzac sums him up thus in his admirable and
all too little known essay on this work:

'Palla Ferrante est un grand poëte . . . il est républicain
radical . . . Il a la foi, il est le saint Paul de la République,
un martyre de *la Jeune Italie*, il est sublime dans l'art,
comme le *Saint-Barthélemy* de Milan, comme le *Spartacus*
de Foyatier, comme Marius sur les ruines de Carthage.
Tout ce qu'il fait, tout ce qu'il dit est sublime. Il a la
conviction, la grandeur, la passion du croyant . . . Plus
grand que sa misère, prêchant L'Italie du fond de ses
cavernes, sans pain pour sa maîtresse et ses cinq enfants;
volant sur la grande route pour les nourrir et tenant note
de ses vols et des volés pour leur restituer cet emprunt
forcé de la République *au jour où il aura le pouvoir* . . .
Palla Ferrante est le type d'une famille d'esprits qui vit
en Italie, sincères mais abusés, pleins de talent mais
ignorant les funestes effets de leur doctrine.'

(*Revue Parisienne*, 25 septembre, 1840).

[3] I AM TOLD . . . IMPERFECT: *it is evident, was unskilled in the art of politics.*

REGINALD HAREWOOD

(*KIRKLOWES* fragment)

[1] ON THE S.W. FRONTIER OF NORTHUMBERLAND: *north-west frontier of Westmoreland.*

[2] The house etc.: For details of the Kirklowes home cf. *Lesbia Brandon*, Chapter II, pp.5-6, Chapter III p.41; and *Love's Cross Currents*, p.21.

[3] After GOOD-NATURED the following passage is deleted with a wavy vertical line: *Thus, when his son grew to be ten years old, Mr. Harewood took a great liking to him; and the main way in which this goodwill showed itself was in reading him Latin by five minute doses at a time, and flogging him about four times a week till he was too tired to strike hard enough. It was his earnest good faith, that by these singular rites some infinite inward good was wrought upon the boy; and it may be noted that in all other matters he was as indulgent as need be. Reginald generally got all he asked for, except the remission of a penalty, that had fallen due; but not one cut of the birch less. As it happened, bodily pain was the only thing which the boy really minded in the least; a fact which assured his father of the virtues of his method.*

[4] FLOGGED HIM FOUR TIMES A WEEK TILL THE BLOOD RAN: Cf. Note [12] on Chapter XIV of *Lesbia Brandon*.

[5] A SPECIAL AND RELIGIOUS OBJECTION . . . HIS DEEPEST MORAL FEELING IN THE WORLD: Cf. Gautier, *Mademoiselle de Maupin*, passim; e.g. 'Voilà où se réduisent toutes mes notions morales. Ce que est beau physiquement est bien, tout ce qui est laid est mal.'

⁶ After CHARACTER the following passage is deleted: *He was very fond of reading the first division of the Bible, and would broach most original heresies with a grave zest. Not religious heresies; at least he believed every letter in the book literally; but would draw the most wonderful conclusions as to people mentioned therein. For instance, Jezebel excited in him a sincere admiration: he used to dilate on her excellence and greatness with fervour when her name occurred in reading to his children. There was a story that once, when he came to the last scene of that lady's life, he was impelled to commit an interpolation in the text and read forth with extreme vigour of accent the apostrophe to Jehu as follows: Had Zimri peace who slew his master? eh, ma man? and at the account of her murder threw his book across the room with a strong expression regarding Jehu.* The last sentence (from 'and at the account') is cancelled with the whole deleted passage.

⁷ THE SEAT OF INTELLECT . . . IN THE HEAD: *whose conscience and mind could be affected only through the physical appeal to his skin and muscles.* There are other deleted attempts towards a satisfactory effect.

⁸ Cancelled portions between HEAD and HE HAD: *He had the love and hatred of an animal, and moved about like a sort of cat.* [Margaret] *Annie the daughter was.* There are several other deletions in this interval.

⁹ Deleted before SHE IN RETURN. *Eleanor had no*; and there is a deleted *Eleanor* after 'affection' (the last word of this sentence). This, and the 'Annie' and 'Margaret' of the last Note, show that within the space of a line or two Swinburne changed his mind twice as to the name the daughter should bear. He finally decided on Helen (but in one place after beginning to use Helen he inadvertently wrote 'Eleanor' and omitted to make the necessary change).

¹⁰ FOND OF HIM: *fonder of him than of anyone else.* Perhaps a toning down of a vague suggestion of incestuous feeling.

574

[11] Deleted between OTHERS and BEYOND: *desired only that they would further her own enjoyment* : : *wished no man ill, did no man good, but was probably incapable of seeing any sin in the removal.*

[12] Lavater: Swinburne was probably put on the track of this physiognomist by Balzac and Baudelaire, who frequently mention him. Cf. Baudelaire, *Salon de 1846*: 'Que Lavater se soit trompé dans le détail, c'est possible; mais il avait l'idée du principe.'

[13] AS TYPICAL OF FACES NOT TO BE TRUSTED: *to distinguish faces of people without moral feeling.*

[14] polished: See Note [114] on Chapter III of *Lesbia Brandon.*

[15] A NERVOUS PLEASURE: Cf. *Love's Cross Currents*: '. . . She [Lady Midhurst] had not an atom of doubt he [Captain Harewood] had some nervous physical pleasure in the idea of others' sufferings . . .' Thus the manuscript; but when the book came out in volume form 'nervous' was omitted.

[16] COMFORT . . . NEVER . . . INTERCEDE FOR HIM: Cf. *Lesbia Brandon*, Chapter II: 'she [Margaret] gave him [her brother] all condolence but no intercession.'

[17] MORE THAN ONCE: *at least once.* Swinburne was not so self-suppressive in this earlier work as he was in *Lesbia Brandon.*

[18] Deleted after WAS MARRIED,: *and her brother sent to the nearest school that could be pitched upon, Mr. H. remaining alone for the most part of the year.* Swinburne changed his mind, and decided to allow the boy's education to remain in his father's hands.

[19] Deleted after CONTEMPLATING HIM: *with as perfect calm as if he had been in full dress.*

[20] SPOKE TO HER: *addressed her with a bland dullness.*

[21] RAN AWAY: Cf., in *Love's Cross Currents*, Lady Midhurst on Captain Harewood: 'his treatment of the poor boy . . .

was horrible, disgraceful for its stupidity and cruelty; and '. . . . when he [the boy] was fourteen, and ran away from home . . .'

[22] four dozen cuts: See Note [66] on Chapter II of *Lesbia Brandon*.

[23] Deleted after HELEN: *laughed more than ever at his condition.*

[24] After LAY THE ROD the following passage is deleted: *Soon after her brother's visit Helen carried off her husband to London. Before the end of the year Mr. Harewood received a letter from her complaining angrily of her husband, and begging him to come to London. He set out at once and arrived in two days from the receipt of her letter.*

[25] Deleted after UNHAPPY ENOUGH: *and chafed at the sense of their sorrow, for hitherto they had gone on lightly and easily enough, with plenty of rough work and enjoyment and affection on both sides.*

[26] Deleted before AND THE FIRST VISIT: *at last Helen sent a letter inviting them over for a.*

[27] WANTED . . . THE KIRKLOWES LIFE BACK AGAIN: Cf. Margaret's nostalgic memories of Kirklowes in *Lesbia Brandon*, p.41.

[28] MANAGING THE LAND . . . POLITICS: Cf. Lord Wariston: 'It was already enough for him to ride and read and legislate' (*Lesbia Brandon*, Chapter IV); and '. . . content to farm, to shoot, to vote in the House where he never speaks . . .' (*Ib.*, Chapter XVII.)

[29] Deleted after GAMEKEEPER: *Mr. Ashurst accepted his existence as a necessary part of his marriage.*

[30] Faublas: See Note [75] on Chapter III of *Lesbia Brandon*.

[31] Deleted after FOR EXAMPLE: *with those great men disputing about her and for her.*

[32] PASSED FOR: *dispensed with.*

[33] Deleted after LIKING TOWARDS HIM: *the boy too was grown handsome and helpful in many ways.*

[34] RELIEF: Cf. *Lesbia Brandon*, Chapter III, p.32: 'it was such an absurd relief this' [that Denham found in flogging Herbert].

[35] THREE: *six*: Note [17]. Here Swinburne did check the tendency of his imagination to run to dreadful extremes of punishment.

[36] TO BE: Apparently: the writing is very illegible. What I have tentatively transcribed as 'to be' may be 'and too'.

[37] The portion after 'waited, and went' (which is on sheet 7), down to and including 'if he went' is written on the back of the sixth sheet; it occupies two and half lines of the page; no concluding stroke follows it, and the rest of the page is blank. The section is obviously unfinished. What follows begins at the top of a fresh sheet of a different colour (blue: the seven preceding sheets are white).

HERBERT WINWOOD

USES OF PROSODY

[1] FEELING AFTER DOUBTFUL FLOWERS: *stretching doubtful hands after the places where.*

[2] PRESENT AS GUESTS: *Herbert, his mother.*

[3] MARGARET: Not Lady Waristoun, who 'never rode now', we are told below. Apparently Margaret Lunsford.

[4] ANNE: *Helen.*

[5] CIS: Lady Waristoun's son Cecil.

[6] BERTIE: Not Herbert, but Lady Waristoun's son Ethelbert, also called Ethel.

[7] STING: *pungency.*

[8] ETHEL: *Bertie.*

[9] ELAINE: The cat, as in Chapter XV of *Lesbia Brandon.*

[10] NOVELS . . . OF THE BICIPITAL OR MUSCULAR TYPE: Cf. 'that muscular morality and sinewy sanctity preached and extolled by performers in the writing-school of Christian gymnastics', *Lesbia Brandon*, Chapter III. Kingsley's *Two Years Ago* (1857) belongs to this type, which had a large vogue in the '50s. The agnostic central character of this work is the ideal muscular hero; but Swinburne was probably not thinking so much of Kingsley (whom he admired) as of G. A. Lawrence, the chief of this school, whose *Guy Livingstone, or Thorough* appeared in the same year as the less extravagant production of Kingsley. Guy Livingstone is a berserk personage, a Nordic superman, an embodiment of what Lawrence himself refers to as 'the Physical Force Doctrine'; he dies a hero's death in the hunting-field. The first syllable of Swinburne's 'Horseleigh', a few lines down, is probably a hit at the hunting-field scenes in these novels (Cf. 'the fence-jumping feats') ('-leigh' may perhaps be meant to suggest the second syllable of 'Kingsley'); and the 'stone' of the other imaginary name is undoubtedly intended to suggest 'Livingstone', while the 'Hurl-' suggests the precipitate energy of these vikings of the Victorian upper classes. (Cf. Bret Harte's later 'Guy Heavystone' in his parody (1870) of the archetype of Lawrence's strong (but not silent) man novels, of which there were nine all told.)

Tom Brown's Schooldays, which appeared a year earlier than the two above-mentioned books, is a representative of 'the Christian-muscular section of this stimulant class of higher literature'. It was followed by a large number of imitations. Kingsley's *Westward Ho!* (1855) might also be ranged in this class, but it is immeasurably superior to the class as a whole.

Swinburne here anticipated well-known reactions against

this type of literature and the spirit producing and resultant from it; e.g. Wilkie Collins' *Man and Wife* (1870), where Collins inveighs against 'the present mania for athletic sports'. But the reaction had already begun before Swinburne wrote this passage; Lawrence himself had spoken of it in *Sword and Gown* (1859): 'There is', he said, 'a heavy run just now against the Physical Force Doctrine . . . "Muscular Christianity" is the stock sarcasm of the opposite party . . .'

The Crimean War was the chief force that set going the 'bicipital' movement. It fired Swinburne himself, who was later to deride the movement; 'The Balaklava Charge', he says, referring to himself in the third person in a letter cited by Mrs. Disney Leith in *The Boyhood of A. C. Swinburne*, 'eclipsed all other visions. To be prepared for such a chance as that, instead of being prepared for Oxford, was the dream of his life'. Cf. Kingsley, writing to F. D. Maurice in 1854: 'This war would have made me half mad, if I had let it. It seemed so dreadful to hear of those Alma heights being taken and not to be there . . .'

[11] ROOGE: A term of Eton football, more commonly spelt 'rouge'. It means either a score or (as here) a scrimmage. (Cf., in the letter of Swinburne mentioned in the last Note, '. . . it came upon me that it was all very well to fancy or dream of "deadly danger" and forlorn hopes and cavalry charges when I had never run any greater risk than a football "rooge" . . .'

Lafourcade, in *La Jeunesse de Swinburne*, makes the extraordinary statement that 'le cricket était le seul jeu reconnu' at Eton. 'Reconnu' by whom? In any case, football is listed in *Nugae Etonenses* (c.1770) as one of the games played at the school; it is even mentioned by Horman, a master at the school in 1487, in his *Vulgaria Puerorum*; Cust (*Eton College*, 1899) says it 'has been played at Eton for generations'.

[12] HIC, Herbert; ILLA, Rosamund; ILLE, Ethelbert; HAEC, Margaret.

[13] BURNS: *reddens.*

[14] ENDED BY . . . TO THINK OF: *ended by murdering the girl in a way.*

[15] LA TÊTE RENVERSÉE, etc.: Lafourcade says: "Quant aux extraits du roman imaginaire *La Chimère*, ils sont une parodie évidente de la manière "forte" de Balzac. On doit aussi y reconnaître une imitation de *Madame Bovary* ou peut-être des romans de Champfleury . . .' There are many passages of French Romantic or ultra-Romantic erotic literature of the period 1830–1860 which Swinburne might have had in mind when writing this parody. Pétrus Borel, Süe, the early work of Gautier (especially *Albertus*), Baudelaire, and even certain things of Balzac—but not Champfleury and certainly not *Madame Bovary*—are among the possibilities that occur to one. I should say, however, that Swinburne was here thinking particularly, and almost exclusively, of Feydeau, as represented by such passages as the following:

> "Parlant bas, de nous seuls, en nous tenant les mains, avec des paroles incohérentes, nous nous contemplions d'abord éperdument, absorbés dans une émotion délicieuse et profonde qui nous serrait doucement le cœur et nous amenait des pleurs dans les yeux. Nos épanchements étaient infinis comme notre amour . . . Et comme nous nous dévorions de caresses! Quelle suave énergie dans nos étreintes! quelle avidité dans nos baisers! quel tremblement fébrile dans nos gestes pendant que je lui disputais en silence les vêtements épars qu'elle retenait sur elle, à toutes mains, pâle d'un vague affroi! A deux genoux, désespéré, je me jetais devant elle, j'enlaçais sa taille souple de mes bras, et elle, se cambrant sous mon étreinte, m'appuyait la paume des mains sur le front, me tenait

doucement en arrière et détournait la tête comme si elle avait eu peur de mes yeux."

"Et, comme pour m'anéantir devant elle, je me prosternais et je baisais longuement ses pieds nus. J'aurais voulu mourir là, les lèvres collées sur ses pieds d'enfant blancs et roses . . ." (*Fanny* 1858).

"Il y avait deux âmes bien différentes qui s'exhalaient de ses lèvres et de ses regards. La première était celle d'une Phryné absorbée et sérieuse, nourrie des plus fines primeurs comme des épices les plus corrosives de la passion . . ." (*Ib.*)

". . . de ses mains tremblantes, elle essuyait sur mon front l'âcre sueur du désespoir . . ." (*Ib.*)

Swinburne was well acquainted with Feydeau's work; and in *Love's Cross Currents* he (or rather Lady Midhurst) speaks of him as a writer who would give good sport to a parodist.

As regards the title of Swinburne's imaginary novel, Lafourcade, with laborious ineptitude, notes that 'Un roman intitulé "La Chimère" fut publié en 1851 par un certain Paulin Niboyet'—of which and of whom Swinburne probably knew nothing at all. It was no doubt Feydeau again of whom he was thinking particularly here: cf. the following, from a passage in the same work relative to the heroine with her excessive erotic idealism:

"Tant qu'elle vivra, elle poursuivra fatalement sa chimère. L'idéal de l'amour que l'entraîne ne s'effacera même pas dans les neiges de l'âge . . . Il lui manquera toujours un vice pour être heureuse . . ."

And one could cite several other passages from writers well known to Swinburne where the word *chimère* is similarly used.

[16] CÉCILE: *Bathilde.*

[17] Deleted after SIFFLER: *dans l'oreille de son am* ['am' presumably being the first two letters of 'amant'].

[18] À TIRE-D'AILES: The normal French is *à tire-d'aile*; but Voltaire wrote *à tire d'ailes* at least once.

[19] BEFORE A PENTAMETER: Evidently the boy intended the vowel of the enclitic *que* to be elided before another vowel at the beginning of the pentameter. But this is forbidden (by schoolmasters' rules) in Latin verse, although it occurs in Greek poetry, and is possible in Latin as well as in Greek verse from one hexameter to another.

[20] SENSE: This word, which occurs in two previous paragraphs of the chapter, is an Etonian term that has apparently become obsolete. It means provision in English of material or subject-matter (beyond the mere theme or title) on which to write verses in Latin or Greek. 'Full sense' would be very detailed help.

[21] Deleted after SHAKY: *A quivered chaplet is enough to bring half the.*

ARDEN MAJOR TO LADY WARISTOUN

[1] ARDEN: *Ethel.* It is rather confusing that Arden should be both the Christian and the family name of the second-oldest of the three brothers.

[2] IT'S SOMETHING OUT OF THE WAY: *It's some Windsor nuisance* : : *it's something out of the way, not yesterday's work.*

[3] AFTER TWELVE: See Note [96] on Chapter III of *Lesbia Brandon*.

[4] I HAVE GOT MY REMOVE: This simply means 'I have been promoted'. Each form consisted of three removes, lower, middle and upper.

[5] HERBERT: *Uncle Herbert* : : *the cousin.*

[6] ETHEL: *Bertie No. 2.*

[7] IN LOWER REMOVE: In the lower remove of Remove, a form intermediary between the fourth and the fifth forms.

[8] SURLEY: 'Surly' appears to be the more usual spelling. 'In the following year [1862] Dr. Goodford put a stop to the 'Oppidan dinner', which had been given annually by the Captain of the Boats, to the popular leaders of the School, at the White Hart Hotel, Windsor [cf. the first deletion in Note [2]], and at the same time he abolished 'check-nights'. Hitherto it had been the custom for the crews of the three Upper Boats to row up to Surly Hall, in their 4th of June dresses, on certain specified evenings, to sup there on ducks, green peas and champagne, meeting the Lower Boats on their way home, and returning with them in regular procession; but these 'check-night' suppers, as they were called, were condemned by the authorities as affording great temptations to idleness and self-indulgence.'—(H. C. Maxwell Lyte, *A History of Eton College*, 1875).

[9] AFTER NINE: At that time there was a free period after nine as well as after twelve.

[10] CAN'T SIT DOWN: Cf. Note [39] on Chapter II of *Lesbia Brandon*.

[11] COMPLAINED OF: A technical term, meaning reported to the Headmaster for idleness, bad work, etc.